By Connie Willis

A Lot Like Christmas

Crosstalk

All About Emily

All Clear

Blackout

All Seated on the Ground

D.A.

Inside Job

Passage

To Say Nothing of the Dog

Bellwether

Uncharted Territory

Remake

Doomsday Book

Lincoln's Dreams

A Lot Like Christmas

A Lot Like Christmas

An expanded, updated edition of Connie Willis's

beloved Miracle and Other Christmas Stories

CONNIE WILLIS

Del Rey Books
New York

2017 Del Rey Trade Paperback Edition

Copyright © 2017 by Connie Willis

All rights reserved.

Published in the United States by Del Rey, an imprint of Random House, a division of Penguin Random House LLC, New York.

DEL REY and the HOUSE colophon are registered trademarks of Penguin Random House LLC.

This is an expanded edition of *Miracle and Other Christmas Stories* by Connie Willis (New York: Bantam Spectra, 1999), copyright © 1999 by Connie Willis.

The stories that appear in this work have been previously published and are reprinted here by permission of the author: "Miracle" in *Asimov's*, December 1991, copyright © 1991 by Doubleday Dell Magazines; "All About Emily" (Burton, MI: Subterranean Press, 2011), copyright © 2011 by Connie Willis; "Inn" in *Asimov's*, December 1993, copyright © 1993 by Doubleday Dell Magazines; "All Seated on the Ground" in *Asimov's*, December 2007, copyright © 2007 by Dell Magazines, a division of Crosstown Publishing; "In Coppelius's Toyshop" in *Asimov's*, December 1996, copyright © 1996 by Dell Magazines, a division of Crosstown Publishing; "Adaptation" in *Asimov's*, December 1994, copyright © 1994 by Doubleday Dell Magazines; "deck.halls@boughs/holly" in *Asimov's*, December 2001, copyright © 2001 by Dell Magazines, a division of Crosstown Publishing; "Cat's Paw" in *Miracle and Other Christmas Stories* (New York: Bantam Spectra, 1999), copyright © 1999 by Connie Willis; "Now Showing" in *Rogues*, edited by George R. R. Martin and Gardner Dozois (New York: Bantam Books, 2014), copyright © 2014 by Connie Willis; "Newsletter" in *Asimov's*, December 1997, copyright © 1997 by Dell Magazines, a division of Crosstown Publishing; "Epiphany" in *Miracle and Other Christmas Stories* (New York: Bantam Spectra, 1999), copyright © 1999 by Connie Willis; "Just Like the Ones We Used to Know" in *Asimov's*, 2003, copyright © 2003 by Dell Magazines, a division of Crosstown Publishing.

ISBN 978-0-399-18234-1
Ebook ISBN 978-0-399-18235-8

Printed in the United States of America on acid-free paper

randomhousebooks.com

9 8 7 6 5 4 3 2 1

Book design by Virginia Norey

TO CHARLES DICKENS AND GEORGE SEATON,
who knew how to keep Christmas

Contents

Introduction

I love Christmas. All of it—decorating the tree and singing in the choir and baking cookies and wrapping presents. I even like the parts most people hate—shopping in crowded malls and reading Christmas newsletters and seeing relatives and standing in baggage check-in lines at the airport.

Okay, I lied. Nobody likes standing in baggage check-in lines. I love seeing people get off the plane, though, and holly and candles and egg-nog and carols.

But most of all, I love Christmas stories and movies. Okay, I lied again. I don't love *all* Christmas stories and movies. *It's a Wonderful Life,* for instance. And Hans Christian Andersen's "The Fir Tree."

But I love *Miracle on 34th Street* and Christopher Morley's "The Tree That Didn't Get Trimmed" and Christina Rossetti's poem "In the Bleak Midwinter." My family watches *The Sure Thing* and *A Christmas Story* each year, and we read George V. Higgins's "The Impossible Snowsuit of Christmas Past" out loud every Christmas Eve, and eagerly look for new classics to add to our traditions.

There aren't a lot. This is because Christmas stories are much harder to write than they look, partly because the subject matter is fairly limited, and people have been writing it for nearly two thousand years, so they've just about rung all the changes possible on snowmen, Santas, and shepherds.

Stories have been told from the point of view of the fourth wise man (who got waylaid on the way to Bethlehem), the innkeeper, the innkeeper's wife, the donkey, and the star. There've been stories about department-store Santas, phony Santas, burned-out Santas, substitute Santas, reluctant Santas, and dieting Santas, to say nothing of Santa's wife, his elves, his reindeer, and Rudolph. We've had births at Christmas (natch!), deaths, partings, meetings, mayhem, attempted suicides, and sanity hearings. And Christmas in Hawaii, in China, in the past, the future, and outer space. We've heard from the littlest shepherd, the littlest wise man, the littlest angel, and the mouse who wasn't stirring. There's not a lot out there that hasn't already been done.

In addition, the Christmas-story writer has to walk a narrow tightrope between sentiment and skepticism, and most writers end up falling off into either cynicism or mawkish sappiness.

And, yes, I am talking about Hans Christian Andersen. He invented the whole three-hanky sob story, whose plot Maxim Gorky, in a fit of pique, described as taking a poor girl or boy and letting them "freeze somewhere under a window, behind which there is usually a Christmas tree that throws its radiant splendor upon them." Match girls, steadfast tin soldiers, even snowmen (melted, not frozen) all met with a fate they (and we) didn't deserve, especially at Christmas.

Nobody, before Andersen came along, had thought of writing such depressing Christmas stories. Even Dickens, who had killed a fair number of children in his books, didn't kill Tiny Tim. But Andersen, apparently hell-bent on ruining everybody's holidays, froze innocent children, melted loyal toys into lumps of lead, and chopped harmless fir trees who were just standing there in the forest, minding their own business, into kindling.

Worse, he inspired dozens of imitators, who killed off saintly children (some of whom, I'll admit, were pretty insufferable and deserved to die) and poor people for the rest of the Victorian era.

In the twentieth century, the Andersen-style tearjerker moved into the movies, which starred Margaret O'Brien (who definitely deserved to die) and other child stars, chosen for their pallor and their ability to cough. They had titles like *All Mine to Give* and *The Christmas Tree*, which tricked hapless moviegoers into thinking they were going to see a cheery Christmas movie, when really they were about little boys who succumbed to radiation poisoning on Christmas Eve.

When television came along, this type of story turned into the "Very

Special Christmas Episode" of various TV shows, the worst of which was *Little House on the Prairie,* which killed off huge numbers of children in blizzards and other pioneer-type disasters every Christmas for years. Hadn't any of these authors ever heard that Christmas stories are supposed to have happy endings?

Well, unfortunately, they had, and it resulted in improbably sentimental and saccharine stories too numerous to mention.

So are there any good Christmas stories out there? You bet, starting with the original. The recounting of the first Christmas (you know, the baby in the manger) has all the elements of great storytelling: drama, danger, special effects, dreams and warnings, betrayals, narrow escapes, and—combined with the Easter story—the happiest ending of all.

And it's got great characters—Joseph, who's in over his head but doing the best he can; the wise men, expecting a palace and getting a stable; slimy Herod, telling them, "When you find this king, tell me where he is so I can come and worship him," and then sending out his thugs to try to murder the baby; the ambivalent innkeeper. And Mary, fourteen years old, pondering all of the above in her heart. It's a great story. No wonder it's lasted two thousand years.

Modern Christmas stories I love (for a more complete list, see the end of this book) include O. Henry's "The Gift of the Magi," T. S. Eliot's "Journey of the Magi," and Barbara Robinson's *The Best Christmas Pageant Ever,* about a church Nativity pageant overrun by a gang of hooligans called the Herdmans. The Herdmans bully everybody and smoke and cuss and come only because they'd heard there were refreshments afterward. And they transform what was a sedate and boring Christmas pageant into something extraordinary.

Since I'm a science-fiction writer, I'm of course partial to science-fiction Christmas stories. Science fiction has always had the ability to make us look at the world from a different angle, and Christmas is no exception. Science fiction has looked at the first Christmas from a new perspective (Michael Moorcock's classic *Behold the Man*) and in a new guise (Joe L. Hensley and Alexei Panshin's "Dark Conception").

It's shown us Christmas in the future (Cynthia Felice's "Track of a Legend") and Christmas in space (Ray Bradbury's wonderful "The Gift"). And it's looked at the dark side of Christmas (Mildred Clingerman's disturbing "The Wild Wood").

My favorite science-fiction Christmas stories are Arthur C. Clarke's "The Star," which tells the story of the Christmas star that guided the wise men to Bethlehem, and Thomas Disch's hilarious story "The Santa Claus Compromise," in which two intrepid six-year-old investigative reporters expose the shocking scandal behind Santa Claus.

I also love mysteries. You'd think murder and Christmas wouldn't mesh, but the setting and the possibility of mistletoe/plum pudding/Santa Claus–connected murders has inspired any number of mystery writers, starting with Arthur Conan Doyle and his "The Adventure of the Blue Carbuncle," which involves a Christmas goose. Some of my favorite mysteries are Dorothy Sayers's "The Necklace of Pearls," Agatha Christie's *Murder for Christmas*, and Jane Langton's *The Shortest Day: Murder at the Revels*. My absolute favorite is John Mortimer's comic "Rumpole and the Spirit of Christmas," which stars the grumpy old Scrooge of a barrister, Horace Rumpole, and his wonderful wife, She Who Must Be Obeyed.

Comedies are probably my favorite kind of Christmas story. I love Damon Runyon's "Dancing Dan's Christmas." (Actually, I love everything Damon Runyon ever wrote, and if you've never read him, you need to go get *Guys and Dolls* immediately. Ditto P. G. Wodehouse, whose "Jeeves and the Yule-tide Spirit" and "Another Christmas Carol" are vintage Wodehouse, which means they're indescribable. If you've never read Wodehouse either, what a treat you're in for! He wrote over a hundred books. Start anywhere.) Both Runyon and Wodehouse balance sentiment and cynicism, irony and the Christmas spirit, human nature and happy endings, without a single misstep.

And then there's Christopher Morley's "The Tree That Didn't Get Trimmed," which was clearly written in reaction to Hans Christian Andersen's "The Fir Tree." Unlike Andersen, however, Morley understands that the purpose of Christmas is to remind us not only of suffering but of salvation. His story makes you ache, and then despair. And then rejoice.

Almost all great stories (Christmas or otherwise) have that one terrible moment when all seems lost, when you're sure things won't work out, the bad guys will win, the cavalry won't arrive in time, and they (and we) won't be saved. John Ford's Christmas Western, *3 Godfathers*, has a moment like that. So does *The Miracle of Morgan's Creek*, and

Miracle on 34th Street, which I consider to be The Best Christmas Movie Ever.

I know, I know, *It's a Wonderful Life* is supposed to be The Best Christmas Movie Ever, with ten million showings and accompanying merchandising. (I saw an *It's a Wonderful Life* mouse pad this last Christmas.) And I'm not denying that there are some great scenes in it (see my story "Miracle" on this subject), but the movie has real problems. For one thing, the villainous Mr. Potter is still loose and unpunished at the end of the movie, something no good fairy tale ever permits. The dreadful little psychologist in *Miracle on 34th Street* is summarily, and very appropriately, fired, and the DA, who after all was only doing his job, repents.

But in *It's a Wonderful Life,* Mr. Potter is free, with his villainy undetected, though he's already proved to be a vindictive and malicious villain. Since this didn't work, he'll obviously try something else. And poor George is still faced with embezzlement charges, which the last time I looked don't disappear just because you pay back the money, even if the cop is smiling in the last scene.

But the worst problem seems to me to be that the ending depends on the goodness of the people of Bedford Falls, something that (especially in light of previous events) seems like a dicey proposition.

Miracle on 34th Street, on the other hand, relies on no such thing. The irony of the miracle (and let's face it, maybe what really galls my soul is that *It's a Wonderful Life* is a work *completely* without irony) is that the miracle happens not because of people's behavior, but in spite of it.

Christmas is supposed to be based on selflessness and innocence, but until the very end of *Miracle on 34th Street,* virtually no one except Kris Kringle exhibits these qualities. Quite the opposite. Everyone, even the hero and heroine, acts from a cynical, very modern self-interest. Macy's Santa goes on a binge right before Macy's Thanksgiving Day Parade, Doris hires Kris to get herself out of a jam and save her job, John Payne invites the little girl Susan to watch the parade as a way to meet the mother.

And in spite of Kris Kringle's determined efforts to restore the true spirit of Christmas to the city, it continues. Macy's and then Gimbel's go along with the gag of recommending other stores, not because they believe in it, but because it means more money. The judge in Kris's sanity case makes favorable rulings only because he wants to get reelected. Even the postal workers who provide the denouement just want to get rid of stuff piling up in the dead-letter office.

But in spite of this (actually, in a delicious irony, *because* of it) and with only very faint glimmerings of humanity from the principals, and in spite of how hopeless it all seems, the miracle of Christmas occurs, right on schedule. Just as it does every year.

It's this layer of symbolism that makes *Miracle on 34th Street* such a satisfying movie. Also its script (by George Seaton) and perfect casting (especially Natalie Wood and Thelma Ritter) and any number of delight-ful moments (Santa's singing a Dutch carol to the little Dutch orphan and the disastrous bubble-gum episode and Natalie Wood's disgusted expression when she's told she has to have faith even when things don't work out). Plus, of course, the fact that Edmund Gwenn could make any-one believe in Santa Claus. All combine to make it The Best Christmas Movie Ever Made.

Not, however, the best story. That honor belongs to Dickens and his deathless *A Christmas Carol.* The rumor that Dickens invented Christ-mas is not true, and neither, probably, is the story that when he died, a poor costermonger's little girl sobbed, "Dickens dead? Why, then, is Christmas dead, too?" But they should be.

Because Dickens did the impossible—he wrote not only a master-piece that captures the essence of Christmas, but one that was good enough to survive its own fame. There have been a million mostly awful TV, movie, and musical versions and variations, with Scrooge played by everybody from Basil Rathbone to the Fonz, but even the worst of them haven't managed to damage the wonderful story of Scrooge and Tiny Tim.

One reason it's such a great story is that Dickens loved Christmas. (And no wonder. His childhood was Oliver Twist's and Little Dorrit's combined, and no kindly grandfather or Arthur Clennam in sight. His whole adult life must have seemed like Christmas.) I think you have to love Christmas to write about it.

For another, he knew a lot about human nature. Remembering the past, truly seeing the present, imagining the consequences of our actions, are the ways we actually grow and change. Dickens knew this years be-fore Freud.

He also knew a lot about writing. The plot's terrific, the dialogue's great, and the opening line—"Marley was dead: to begin with"—is second only to "Call me Ishmael" as one of the great opening lines of literature. He knew how to end stories, too, and that Christmas stories were supposed to have happy endings.

Finally, the story touches us because we want to believe people can change. They don't. We've all learned from bitter experience (though probably not as bitter as Dickens's) that the world is full of money-grubbers and curtain-ring stealers, that Scrooge stays Scrooge to the bitter end, and nobody will lift a finger to help Tiny Tim.

But Christmas is about someone who believed, in spite of overwhelming evidence, that humanity is capable of change and worth redeeming. And Dickens's Christmas story is in fact *The* Christmas Story. And the hardened heart that cracks open at the end of it is our own.

If I sound passionate (and sometimes curmudgeonly) about Christmas stories, I am. I *love* Christmas, in all its complexity and irony, and I *love* Christmas stories.

So much so that I've been writing them for years. Here they are—an assortment of stories about church choirs and Christmas presents and pod people from outer space, about wishes that come true in ways you don't expect and wishes that don't come true and wishes you didn't know you had, about stars and shepherds, wise men and Santa Claus, mistletoe and *It's a Wonderful Life* and Christmas cards on recycled paper. There's even a murder. And a story about Christmas Yet to Come.

I hope you like them. And I hope you have a very merry Christmas!

—Connie Willis

A Lot Like Christmas

Miracle

There was a Christmas tree in the lobby when Lauren got to work, and the receptionist was sitting with her chin in her hand, watching the security monitor. Lauren set her shopping bag down and looked curiously at the screen. On it, Jimmy Stewart was dancing the Charleston with Donna Reed.

"The Personnel Morale Special Committee had cable piped in for Christmas," the receptionist explained, handing Lauren her messages. "I love *It's a Wonderful Life,* don't you?"

Lauren stuck her messages in the top of her shopping bag and went up to her department. Red and green crepe paper hung in streamers from the ceiling, and there was a big red crepe-paper bow tied around Lauren's desk.

"The Personnel Morale Special Committee did it," Evie said, coming over with the catalog she'd been reading. "They're decorating the whole building, and they want us and Document Control to go caroling this afternoon. Don't you think PMS is getting out of hand with this Christmas spirit thing? I mean, who wants to spend Christmas Eve at an office party?"

"I do," Lauren said. She set her shopping bag down on the desk, sat down, and began taking off her boots.

"Can I borrow your stapler?" Evie asked. "I've lost mine again. I'm ordering my mother the Water of the Month, and I need to staple my check to the order form."

"The Water of the Month?" Lauren said, opening her desk drawer and taking out her stapler.

"You know, they send you bottles of a different one every month. Perrier, Evian, Calistoga." She peered into Lauren's shopping bag. "Do you have Christmas presents in there? I hate people who have their shopping done four weeks before Christmas."

"It's four *days* till Christmas," Lauren said, "and I don't have it all done. I still don't have anything for my sister. But I've got all my friends, including you, done." She reached into the shopping bag and pulled out her pumps. "And I found a dress for the office party."

"Did you buy it?"

"No." She put on one of her shoes. "I'm going to try it on during my lunch hour."

"If it's still there," Evie said gloomily. "I had this echidna toothpick holder all picked out for my brother, and when I went back to buy it, they were all gone."

"I asked them to hold the dress for me," Lauren said. She put on her other shoe. "It's gorgeous. Black, off-the-shoulder. Sequined."

"Still trying to get Scott Buckley to notice you, huh? I don't do things like that anymore. Nineties women don't use sexist tricks to attract men. Besides, I decided he was too cute to ever notice somebody like me." She sat down on the edge of Lauren's desk and started leafing through the catalog. "Here's something your sister might like. The Vegetable of the Month. February's okra."

"She lives in southern California," Lauren said, shoving her boots under the desk.

"Oh. How about the Sunscreen of the Month?"

"No," Lauren said. "She's into New Age stuff. Channeling. Aromatherapy. Last year she sent me a crystal pyramid mate selector for Christmas."

"The Eastern Philosophy of the Month," Evie said. "Zen, Sufism, tai chi—"

"I'd like to get her something she'd really like," Lauren mused. "I always have a terrible time figuring out what to get people for Christmas. So this year, I decided things were going to be different. I wasn't going to be tearing around the mall the day before Christmas, buying things no one would want and wondering what on earth I was going to wear to the office party. I started doing my shopping in September, I wrapped my presents as soon as I bought them, I have all my Christmas cards done and ready to mail—"

"You're disgusting," Evie said. "Oh, here, I almost forgot." She pulled a folded slip of paper out of her catalog and handed it to Lauren. "It's your name for the Secret Santa gift exchange. PMS says you're supposed to bring your present for it by Friday so it won't interfere with the presents Santa Claus hands out at the office party."

Lauren unfolded the paper, and Evie leaned over to read it. "Who'd you get? Wait, don't tell me. Scott Buckley."

"No. Fred Hatch. And I know just what to get him."

"Fred? The fat guy in Documentation? What is it, the Diet of the Month?"

"This is supposed to be the season of love and charity, not the season when you make mean remarks about someone just because he's overweight," Lauren said sternly. "I'm going to get him a videotape of *Miracle on 34th Street*."

Evie looked uncomprehending.

"It's Fred's favorite movie. We had a wonderful talk about it at the office party last year."

"I never heard of it."

"It's about Macy's Santa Claus. He starts telling people they can get their kids' toys cheaper at Gimbel's, and then the store psychiatrist decides he's crazy—"

"Why don't you get him *It's a Wonderful Life*? That's *my* favorite Christmas movie."

"Yours and everybody else's. I think Fred and I are the only two people in the world who like *Miracle on 34th Street* better. See, Edmund Gwenn, he's Santa Claus, gets committed to Bellevue because he thinks he's Santa Claus, and since there isn't any Santa Claus, he has to be crazy, but he *is* Santa Claus, and Fred Gailey, that's John Payne, he's a lawyer in the movie, he decides to have a court hearing to prove it, and—"

"I watch *It's a Wonderful Life* every Christmas. I love the part where Jimmy Stewart and Donna Reed fall into the swimming pool," Evie said. "What happened to the stapler?"

They had the dress and it fit, but there was an enormous jam-up at the cash register, and then they couldn't find a hanging bag for it.

"Just put it in a shopping bag," Lauren said, looking anxiously at her watch.

"It'll wrinkle," the clerk said ominously and continued to search for a hanging bag. By the time Lauren convinced her a shopping bag would work, it was already 12:15. She had hoped she'd have a chance to look for a present for her sister, but there wasn't going to be time. She still had to run the dress home and mail the Christmas cards.

I can pick up Fred's video, she thought, fighting her way onto the escalator. That wouldn't take much time, since she knew what she wanted, and maybe they'd have something with Shirley MacLaine in it she could get her sister. *Ten minutes to buy the video,* she thought, *tops.*

It took her nearly half an hour. There was only one copy, which the clerk couldn't find.

"Are you sure you wouldn't rather have *It's a Wonderful Life*?" she asked Lauren. "It's my favorite movie."

"I want *Miracle on 34th Street,*" Lauren said patiently. "With Edmund Gwenn and Natalie Wood."

The clerk picked up a copy of *It's a Wonderful Life* from a huge display. "See, Jimmy Stewart's in trouble and he wishes he'd never been born, and this angel grants him his wish—"

"I know," Lauren said. "I don't care. I want *Miracle on 34th Street.*"

"Okay!" the clerk said, and wandered off to look for it, muttering, "Some people don't have any Christmas spirit."

She finally found it, in the M's, of all places, and then insisted on gift wrapping it.

By the time Lauren made it back to her apartment, it was a quarter to one. She would have to forget lunch and mailing the Christmas cards, but she could at least take them with her, buy the stamps, and put the stamps on at work.

She took the video out of the shopping bag and set it on the coffee table next to her purse, picked up the bag, and started for the bedroom.

Someone knocked on the door.

"I don't have time for this," she muttered, and opened the door, still holding the shopping bag.

It was a young man wearing a "Save the Whales" T-shirt and khaki pants. He had shoulder-length blond hair and a vague expression that made her think of southern California.

"Yes? What is it?" she asked.

"I'm here to give you a Christmas present," he said.

"Thank you, I'm not interested in whatever you're selling," she said, and shut the door.

He knocked again immediately. "I'm not selling anything," he said through the door. "Really."

I don't have time *for this,* she thought, but she opened the door again.

"I'm not a salesguy," he said. "Have you ever heard of the Maharishi Ram Dass?" A religious nut.

"I don't have time to talk to you." She started to say, "I'm late for work," and then remembered you weren't supposed to tell strangers your apartment was going to be empty. "I'm very busy," she said and shut the door, more firmly this time.

The knocking commenced again, but she ignored it. She started into the bedroom with the shopping bag, came back and pushed the deadbolt across and put the chain on, and then went in to hang up her dress. By the time she'd extricated it from the tissue paper and found a hanger, the knocking had stopped. She hung up the dress, which looked just as deadly now that she had it home, and went back into the living room.

The young man was sitting on the couch, messing with her TV remote. "So, what do you want for Christmas? A yacht? A pony?" He punched buttons on the remote, frowning. "A new TV?"

"How did you get in here?" Lauren said squeakily. She looked at the door. The deadbolt and chain were both still on.

"I'm a spirit," he said, putting the remote down. The TV suddenly blared on. "The Spirit of Christmas Present."

"Oh," Lauren said, edging toward the phone. "Like in *A Christmas Carol.*"

"No," he said, flipping through the channels. She looked at the remote. It was still on the coffee table. "Not Christmas Present. Christmas *Present.* You *know,* Barbie dolls, ugly ties, cheese logs, the stuff people give you for Christmas."

"Oh, Christmas *Present.* I see," Lauren said, carefully picking up the phone.

"People *always* get me confused with him, which is really insulting. I mean, the guy obviously has a really high cholesterol level. Anyway, I'm the Spirit of Christmas Present, and your sister sent me to—"

Lauren had dialed 9-1. She stopped, her finger poised over the second 1. "My sister?"

"Yeah," he said, staring at the TV. Jimmy Stewart was sitting in the guard's room, wrapped in a blanket. "Oh, wow! *It's a Wonderful Life.*"

My sister sent you, Lauren thought. It explained everything. He was not a Moonie or a serial killer. He was this year's version of the crystal pyramid mate selector. "How do you know my sister?"

"She channeled me," he said, leaning back against the sofa. "The Maharishi Ram Dass was instructing her in trance-meditation, and she accidentally channeled my spirit out of the astral plane." He pointed at the screen. "I love this part where the angel is trying to convince Jimmy Stewart he's dead."

"I'm not dead, am I?"

"No. I'm not an angel. I'm a spirit. The Spirit of Christmas Present. You can call me Chris for short. Your sister sent me to give you what you really want for Christmas. You know, your heart's desire. So what is it?"

For my sister not to send me any more presents, she thought. "Look, I'm really in a hurry right now. Why don't you come back tomorrow and we can talk about it then?"

"I hope it's not a fur coat," he said as if he hadn't heard her. "I'm opposed to the killing of endangered species." He picked up Fred's present. "What's this?"

"It's a videotape of *Miracle on 34th Street.* I really have to go."

"Who's it for?"

"Fred Hatch. I'm his Secret Santa."

"Fred Hatch." He turned the package over. "You had it gift wrapped at the store, didn't you?"

"Yes. If we could just talk about this later—"

"This is a great part, too," he said, leaning forward to watch the TV. The angel was explaining to Jimmy Stewart how he hadn't gotten his wings yet.

"I *have* to go. I'm on my lunch hour, and I need to mail my Christmas cards, and I have to be back at work by"—she glanced at her watch—"oh, my God, fifteen minutes ago."

He put down the package and stood up. "Gift-wrapped presents," he said, making a "tsk"-ing noise. "Everybody rushing around spending money, rushing to parties, never stopping to have some eggnog or watch a movie. Christmas is an endangered species." He looked longingly back at the screen, where the angel was trying to convince Jimmy Stewart he'd never been alive, and then wandered into the kitchen. "You got any Evian water?"

"No," Lauren said desperately. She hurried after him. "Look, I really have to get to work."

He had stopped at the kitchen table and was holding one of the Christmas cards. "Computer-addressed," he said reprovingly. He tore it open.

"Don't—" Lauren said.

"Printed Christmas cards," he said. "No letter, no quick note, not even a handwritten signature. That's exactly what I'm talking about. An endangered species."

"I didn't have time," Lauren said defensively. "And I don't have time to discuss this or anything else with you. I have to get to work."

"No time to write a few words on a card, no time to think about what you want for Christmas." He slid the card back into the envelope. "Not even on recycled paper," he said sadly. "Do you know how many trees are chopped down every year to send Christmas cards?"

"I am *late* for—" Lauren said, and he wasn't there anymore.

He didn't vanish like in the movies, or fade out slowly. He simply wasn't there.

"—work," Lauren said. She went and looked in the living room. The TV was still on, but he wasn't there, or in the bedroom. She went into the bathroom and pulled the shower curtain back, but he wasn't there, either.

"It was a hallucination," she said out loud, "brought on by stress." She looked at her watch, hoping it had been part of the hallucination, but it still read 1:15. "I will figure this out later," she said. "I *have* to get back to work."

She went back in the living room. The TV was off. She went into the kitchen. He wasn't there. Neither were her Christmas cards, exactly.

"You! Spirit!" she shouted. "You come back here this minute!"

"You're late," Evie said, filling out a catalog form. "You will not believe who was just here. Scott Buckley. God, he is so cute." She looked up. "What happened?" she said. "Didn't they hold the dress?"

"Do you know anything about magic?" Lauren said.

"What *happened*?"

"My sister sent me her Christmas present," Lauren said grimly. "I need to talk to someone who knows something about magic."

"Fat Fred . . . I mean, Fred Hatch is a magician. What did your sister send you?"

Lauren started down the hall to Documentation at a half run.

"I told Scott you'd be back any minute," Evie said. "He said he wanted to talk to you."

Lauren opened the door to Documentation and started looking over partitions into the maze of cubicles. They were all empty.

"Anybody here?" Lauren called. "Hello?"

A middle-aged woman emerged from the maze, carrying five rolls of wrapping paper and a large pair of scissors. "You don't have any Scotch tape, do you?" she asked Lauren.

"Do you know where Fred Hatch is?" Lauren asked.

The woman pointed toward the interior of the maze with a roll of reindeer-covered paper. "Over there. Doesn't *anyone* have any tape? I'm going to have to staple my Christmas presents."

Lauren worked her way toward where the woman had pointed, looking over partitions as she went. Fred was in the center one, leaning back in a chair, his hands folded over his ample stomach, staring at a screen covered with yellow numbers.

"Excuse me," Lauren said, and Fred immediately sat forward and stood up.

"I need to talk to you," she said. "Is there somewhere we can talk privately?"

"Right here," Fred said. "My assistant's on the 800 line in my office, placing a catalog order, and everyone else is next door in Graphic Design at a Tupperware party." He pushed a key, and the computer screen went blank. "What did you want to talk to me about?"

"Evie said you're a magician," she said.

He looked embarrassed. "Not really. The PMS Committee put me in charge of the magic show for the office party last year, and I came up with an act. This year, luckily, they assigned me to play Santa Claus." He smiled and patted his stomach. "I'm the right shape for the part, and I don't have to worry about the tricks not working."

"Oh, dear," Lauren said. "I hoped . . . do you know any magicians?"

"The guy at the novelty shop," he said, looking worried. "What's the matter? Did PMS assign you the magic show this year?"

"No." She sat down on the edge of his desk. "My sister is into New Age stuff, and she sent me this spirit—"

"Spirit," he said. "A ghost, you mean?"

"No. A person. I mean he looks like a person. He says he's the Spirit of Christmas Present, as in Gift, not Here and Now."

"And you're sure he's not a person? I mean, tricks can sometimes really look like magic."

"There's a Christmas tree in my kitchen," she said.

"Christmas tree?" he said warily.

"Yes. The spirit was upset because my Christmas cards weren't on recycled paper. He asked me if I knew how many trees were chopped down to send Christmas cards, then he disappeared, and when I went back in the kitchen there was this Christmas tree in my kitchen."

"And there's no way he could have gotten into your apartment earlier and put it there?"

"It's *growing* out of the floor. Besides, it wasn't there when we were in the kitchen five minutes before. See, he was watching *It's a Wonderful Life* on TV, which, by the way, he turned on without using the remote, and he asked me if I had any Evian water, and he went into the kitchen and . . . this is ridiculous. You have to think I'm crazy. *I* think I'm crazy just listening to myself tell this ridiculous story. Evian water!" She folded her arms. "People have a lot of nervous breakdowns around Christmastime. Do you think I could be having one?"

The woman with the wrapping-paper rolls peered over the cubicle. "Have you got a tape dispenser?"

Fred shook his head.

"How about a stapler?"

Fred handed her his stapler, and she left.

"Well," Lauren said when she was sure the woman was gone, "do you think I'm having a nervous breakdown?"

"That depends," he said.

"On what?"

"On whether there's really a tree growing out of your kitchen floor. You said he got angry because your Christmas cards weren't on recycled paper. Do you think he's dangerous?"

"I don't know. He says he's here to give me whatever I want for Christmas. Except a fur coat. He's opposed to the killing of endangered species."

"A spirit who's an animal-rights activist!" Fred said delightedly. "Where did your sister get him from?"

"The astral plane," Lauren said. "She was trance-channeling or something. I don't care where he came from. I just want to get rid of him before he decides my Christmas presents aren't recyclable, too."

"Okay," he said, hitting a key on the computer. The screen lit up. "The first thing we need to do is find out what he is and how he got here. I want you to call your sister. Maybe she knows some New Age spell for getting rid of the spirit." He began to type rapidly. "I'll get on the Net and see if I can find someone who knows something about magic." He swiveled around to face her. "You're sure you want to get rid of him?"

"I have a *tree* growing out of my kitchen floor!"

"But what if he's telling the truth? What if he really can get you what you want for Christmas?"

"What I *wanted* was to mail my Christmas cards, which are now shedding needles on the kitchen tile. Who knows what he'll do next?"

"Yeah," he said. "Listen, whether he's dangerous or not, I think I should go home with you after work, in case he shows up again, but I've got a PMS meeting for the office party—"

"That's okay. He's an animal-rights activist. He's not dangerous."

"That doesn't necessarily follow," Fred said. "I'll come over as soon as my meeting's over, and meanwhile I'll check the Net. Okay?"

"Okay," she said. She started out of the cubicle and then stopped. "I really appreciate your believing me, or at least not saying you don't believe me."

He smiled at her. "I don't have any choice. You're the only other person in the world who likes *Miracle on 34th Street* better than *It's a Wonderful Life.* And Fred Gailey believed Macy's Santa Claus was really Santa Claus, didn't he?"

"Yeah," she said. "I don't think this guy is Santa Claus. He was wearing Birkenstocks."

"I'll meet you at your front door," he said. He sat down at the computer and began typing.

Lauren went out through the maze of cubicles and into the hall.

"*There* you are!" Scott said. "I've been looking for you all over." He smiled meltingly. "I'm in charge of buying gifts for the office party, and I need your help."

"My help?"

"Yeah. Picking them out. I hoped maybe I could talk you into going shopping with me after work tonight."

"Tonight?" she said. "I can't. I've got—" *A Christmas tree growing in my kitchen.* "Could we do it tomorrow after work?"

He shook his head. "I've got a date. What about later on tonight? The stores are open till nine. It shouldn't take more than a couple of hours to do the shopping, and then we could go have a late supper somewhere. What say I pick you up at your apartment at six-thirty?"

And have the spirit lying on the couch, drinking Evian water and watching TV? "I can't," she said regretfully.

Even his frown was cute. "Oh, well," he said, and shrugged. "Too bad. I guess I'll have to get somebody else." He gave her another adorable smile and went off down the hall to ask somebody else.

I hate you, Spirit of Christmas Present, Lauren thought, standing there watching Scott's handsome back recede. *You'd better not be there when I get home.*

A woman came down the hall, carrying a basket of candy canes. "Compliments of the Personnel Morale Special Committee," she said, offering one to Lauren. "You look like you could use a little Christmas spirit."

"No, thanks, I've already got one," Lauren said.

The door to her apartment was locked, which didn't mean much, since the chain and the deadbolt had both been on when he got in before. But he wasn't in the living room, and the TV was off.

He had been there, though. There was an empty Evian water bottle on the coffee table. She picked it up and took it into the kitchen. The tree was still there, too. She pushed one of the branches aside so she could get to the wastebasket and threw the bottle away.

"Don't you know plastic bottles are nonbiodegradable?" the spirit said. He was standing on the other side of the tree, hanging things on it. He was dressed in khaki shorts and a "Save the Rain Forest" T-shirt, and had a red bandanna tied around his head. "You should recycle your bottles."

"It's your bottle," Lauren said. "What are you doing here, Spirit?"

"Chris," he corrected her. "These are organic ornaments," he said. He held one of the brown things out to her. "Handmade by the Yanomamo Indians. Each one is made of natural by-products found in the Brazilian rain forest." He hung the brown thing on the tree. "Have you decided what you want for Christmas?"

"Yes," she said. "I want you to go away."

He looked surprised. "I can't do that. Not until I give you your heart's desire."

"That is my heart's desire. I want you to go away and take this tree and your Yanomamo ornaments with you."

"You know the biggest problem I have as the Spirit of Christmas Present?" he said. He reached into the back pocket of his shorts and pulled out a brown garland of what looked like coffee beans. "My biggest problem is that people don't know what they want."

"I know what I want," Lauren said. "I don't want to have to write my Christmas cards all over again—"

"You didn't write them," he said, draping the garland over the branches. "They were printed. Do you know that the inks used on those cards contain harmful chemicals?"

"I don't want to be lectured on environmental issues, I don't want to have to fight my way through a forest to get to the refrigerator, and I don't want to have to turn down dates because I have a spirit in my apartment. I want a nice, quiet Christmas with no hassles. I want to exchange a few presents with my friends and go to the office Christmas party and..." *And dazzle Scott Buckley in my off-the-shoulder black dress,* she thought, but she decided she'd better not say that. The spirit might decide Scott's clothes weren't made of natural fibers or something and turn him into a Yanomamo Indian.

"... and have a nice, quiet Christmas," she finished lamely.

"Take *It's a Wonderful Life,*" the spirit said, squinting at the tree. "I watched it this afternoon while you were at work. Jimmy Stewart didn't know what he wanted."

He reached into his pocket again and pulled out a crooked star made of Brazil nuts and twine. "He thought he wanted to go to college and travel and get rich, but what he *really* wanted was right there in front of him the whole time."

He did something, and the top of the tree lopped over in front of him. He tied the star on with the twine, and did something else. The tree straightened up. "You only think you want me to leave," he said.

Someone knocked on the door.

"You're right," Lauren said. "I don't want you to leave. I want you to stay right there." She ran into the living room.

The spirit followed her into the living room. "Luckily, being a spirit, I know what you really want," he said, and disappeared.

She opened the door to Fred. "He was just here," she said. "He disappeared when I opened the door, which is what all the crazies say, isn't it?"

"Yeah," Fred said. "Or else, 'He's right there. Can't you see him?'" He looked curiously around the room. "Where was he?"

"In the kitchen," she said, shutting the door. "Decorating a tree which probably isn't there, either." She led him into the kitchen.

The tree was still there, and there were large brownish cards stuck all over it.

"You really do have a tree growing in your kitchen," Fred said, squatting down to look at the roots. "I wonder if the people downstairs have roots sticking out of their ceiling." He stood up. "What are these?" he said, pointing at the brownish cards.

"Christmas cards." She pulled one off. "I told him I wanted mine back." She read the card aloud. "'In the time it takes you to read this Christmas card, eighty-two harp seals will have been clubbed to death for their fur.'" She opened it up. "'Happy Holidays.'"

"Cheery," Fred said. He took the card from her and turned it over. "'This card is printed on recycled paper with vegetable inks and can be safely used as compost.'"

"Did anyone on the Net know how to club a spirit to death?" she asked.

"No. Didn't your sister have any ideas?"

"She didn't know how she got him in the first place. She and her Maharishi were channeling an Egyptian nobleman and he suddenly appeared, wearing a 'Save the Dolphins' T-shirt. I got the idea the Maharishi was as surprised as she was." She sat down at the kitchen table. "I tried to get him to go away this afternoon, but he said he has to give me my heart's desire first." She looked up at Fred, who was cautiously sniffing one of the organic ornaments. "Didn't you find out anything on the Net?"

"I found out there are a lot of loonies with computers. What *are* these?"

"By-products of the Brazilian rain forest." She stood up. "I told him my heart's desire was for him to leave, and he said I didn't know what I really wanted."

"Which is what?"

"I don't know," she said. "I went into the living room to answer the door, and he said that luckily he knew what I wanted because he was a spirit, and I told him to stay right where he was, and he disappeared."

"Show me," he said.

She took him into the living room and pointed at where he'd been standing, and Fred squatted down again and peered at the carpet.

"How does he disappear?"

"I don't know. He just . . . isn't there."

Fred stood up. "Has he changed anything else? Besides the tree?"

"Not that I know of. He turned the TV on without the remote," she said, looking around the room. The shopping bags were still on the coffee table. She looked through them and pulled out the video. "Here. I'm your Secret Santa. I'm not supposed to give it to you till Christmas Eve, but maybe you'd better take it before he turns it into a snowy owl or something."

She handed it to him. "Go ahead. Open it."

He unwrapped it. "Oh," he said without enthusiasm. "Thanks."

"I remember last year at the party we talked about it, and I was afraid you might already have a copy. You don't, do you?"

"No," he said, still in that flat voice.

"Oh, good. I had a hard time finding it. You were right when you said we were the only two people in the world who liked *Miracle on 34th Street*. Everybody else I know thinks *It's a Wonderful Life* is—"

"You bought me *Miracle on 34th Street*?" he said, frowning.

"It's the original black-and-white version. I hate those colorized things, don't you? Everyone has gray teeth."

"Lauren." He held the box out to her so she could read the front. "I think your friend's been fixing things again."

She took the box from him. On the cover was a picture of Jimmy Stewart and Donna Reed dancing the Charleston.

"Oh, no! That little rat!" she said. "He must have changed it when he was looking at it. He told me *It's a Wonderful Life* was his favorite movie."

"*Et tu, Brute?*" Fred said, shaking his head.

"Do you suppose he changed all my other Christmas presents?"

"We'd better check."

"If he has . . ." she said, darting into the kitchen. She dropped to her knees and started rummaging through them.

"Do you think they look the same?" Fred asked, squatting down beside her.

"*Your* present looked the same." She grabbed a package wrapped in red-and-gold paper and began feeling it. "Evie's present is okay, I think."

"What is it?"

"A stapler. She's always losing hers. I put her name on it in Magic Marker." She handed it to him to feel.

"It feels like a stapler, all right," he said.

"I think we'd better open it and make sure."

Fred tore off the paper. "It's still a stapler," he said, looking at it. "What a great idea for a Christmas present! Everybody in Documentation's always losing their staplers. I think PMS steals them to use on their Christmas memos." He handed it back to her. "Now you'll have to wrap it again."

"That's okay," Lauren said. "At least it wasn't a Yanomamo ornament."

"But it might be any minute," Fred said, straightening up. "There's no telling what he might take a notion to transform next. I think you'd better call your sister again, and ask her to ask the Maharishi if *he* knows how to send spirits back to the astral plane, and I'll go see what I can find out about exorcism."

"Okay," Lauren said, following him to the door. "Don't take the videotape with you. Maybe I can get him to change it back."

"Maybe," Fred said, frowning. "You're sure he said he was here to give you your heart's desire?"

"I'm sure."

"Then why would he change my videotape?" he said thoughtfully. "It's too bad your sister couldn't have conjured up a nice, straightforward spirit."

"Like Santa Claus," Lauren said.

Her sister wasn't home. Lauren tried her off and on all evening, and when she finally got her, she couldn't talk. "The Maharishi and I are going to Barbados—they're having a harmonic divergence there on Christmas Eve. So you need to send my Christmas present to Barbados," she said, and hung up.

"I don't even have her Christmas present bought yet," Lauren said to the couch, "and it's all your fault."

She went into the kitchen and glared at the tree. "I don't even dare go shopping because you might turn the couch into a humpback whale while I'm gone," she said, and then clapped her hand over her mouth.

She peered cautiously into the living room and then made a careful circuit of the whole apartment, looking for endangered species. There were no signs of any, and no sign of the spirit. She went back into the living room and turned on the TV. Jimmy Stewart was dancing the Charleston with Donna Reed. She picked up the remote and hit the channel button. Now Jimmy Stewart was singing "Buffalo Gals, Won't You Come Out Tonight?"

She hit the automatic channel changer. Jimmy Stewart was on every channel except one. The Ghost of Christmas Present was on that one, telling Scrooge to change his ways. She watched the rest of *A Christmas Carol.* When it reached the part where the Cratchits were sitting down to their Christmas dinner, she remembered she hadn't had any supper and went into the kitchen.

The tree was completely blocking the cupboards, but by mightily pushing several branches aside she was able to get to the refrigerator. The eggnog was gone. So were the Stouffer's frozen entrées. The only thing in the refrigerator was a half-empty bottle of Evian water.

She shoved her way out of the kitchen and sat back down on the couch. Fred had told her to call if anything happened, but it was after eleven o'clock, and she had a feeling the eggnog had been gone for some time.

A Christmas Carol was over, and the opening credits of the next movie were starting. "Frank Capra's *It's a Wonderful Life.* Starring Jimmy Stewart and Donna Reed."

She must have fallen asleep. When she woke up, *Miracle on 34th Street* was on, and the store manager was giving Edmund Gwenn as Macy's Santa Claus a list of toys he was supposed to push if Macy's didn't have what the children asked Santa for.

"Finally," Lauren said, watching Edmund Gwenn tear the list into pieces, "something good to watch," and promptly fell asleep. When she woke up again, John Payne as Fred Gailey was kissing Doris, a.k.a. Maureen O'Hara, and someone was knocking on the door.

I don't remember anyone knocking on the door, she thought groggily. Fred told Doris how he'd convinced the State of New York that Edmund Gwenn was Santa Claus, and then they both stared disbelievingly at a cane standing in the corner. "The End" came on the screen.

The knocking continued.

"Oh," Lauren said, and answered the door.

It was Fred, carrying a McDonald's sack.

"What time is it?" Lauren said, blinking at him.

"Seven o'clock. I brought you an Egg McMuffin and some orange juice."

"Oh, you wonderful person!" she said. She grabbed the sack and took it over to the coffee table. "You don't know what he did." She reached into the sack and pulled out the sandwich. "He transformed the food in my refrigerator into Evian water."

He was looking curiously at her. "Didn't you go to bed last night? He didn't come back, did he?"

"No. I waited for him, and I guess I fell asleep." She took a huge bite of the sandwich.

Fred sat down beside her. "What's that?" He pointed to a pile of dollar bills on the coffee table.

"I don't know," Lauren said.

Fred picked up the bills. Under them was a handful of change and a piece of pink paper. "'Returned three boxes Christmas cards for refund,'" Lauren said, reading it. "'$38.18.'"

"That's what's here," Fred said, counting the money. "He didn't turn your Christmas cards into a Douglas fir after all. He took them back and got a refund."

"Then that means the tree isn't in the kitchen!" she said, jumping up and running to look. "No, it doesn't."

She came back and sat down on the couch.

"But at least you got your money back," Fred said. "And it fits in with what I learned on the Net last night. They think he's a friendly presence, probably some sort of manifestation of the seasonal spirit. Apparently these are fairly common, variations of Santa Claus being the most familiar, but there are other ones, too. All benign. They think he's probably telling the truth about wanting to give you your heart's desire."

"Do they know how to get rid of him?" she asked, and took a bite.

"No. Apparently no one's ever wanted to exorcise one." He pulled a piece of paper out of his pocket. "I got a list of exorcism books to try, though, and this one guy, Clarence, said the most important thing in an exorcism is to know exactly what kind of spirit it is."

"How do we do that?" Lauren asked with her mouth full.

"By its actions," Fred said. "He said appearance doesn't mean anything because seasonal spirits are frequently in disguise. He said we need to write down everything the spirit's said and done, so I want you to tell me exactly what he did." He took a pen and a notebook out of his jacket pocket. "Everything from the first time you saw him."

"Just a minute." She finished the last bite of sandwich and took a drink of the orange juice. "Okay. He knocked on the door, and when I answered it, he told me he was here to give me a Christmas present, and I told him I wasn't interested, and I shut the door and started into the bedroom to hang up my dress and—my dress!" she gasped, and went tearing into the bedroom.

"What's the matter?" Fred said, following her.

She flung the closet door open and began pushing clothes madly along the bar. "If he's transformed this—" She stopped pushing hangers. "I'll kill him," she said, and lifted out a brownish collection of feathers and dried leaves. "Benign??" she said. "Do you call that benign??"

Fred gingerly touched a brown feather. "What was it?"

"A dress," she said. "My beautiful black, off-the-shoulder, drop-dead dress."

"Really?" he said doubtfully. He lifted up some of the brownish leaves. "I think it still is a dress," he said. "Sort of."

She crumpled the leaves and feathers against her and sank down on the bed. "All I wanted was to go to the office party!"

"Don't you have anything else you can wear to the office party? What about that pretty red thing you wore last year?"

She shook her head emphatically. "Scott didn't even notice it!"

"And that's your heart's desire?" Fred said after a moment. "To have Scott Buckley notice you at the office party?"

"Yes, and he would have, too! It had sequins on it, and it fit perfectly!" She held out what might have been a sleeve. Greenish-brown lumps dangled from brownish strips of bamboo. "And now he's ruined it!"

She flung the dress on the floor and stood up. "I don't care what this Clarence person says. He is not benign! And he is not trying to get me what I want for Christmas. He is trying to ruin my life!"

She saw the expression on Fred's face and stopped. "I'm sorry," she said. "None of this is your fault. You've been trying to help me."

"And I've been doing about as well as your spirit," he said. "Look, there has to be some way to get rid of him. Or at least get the dress back. Clarence said he knew some transformation spells. I'll go on to work and see what I can find out."

He went out into the living room and over to the door. "Maybe you can go back to the store and see if they have another dress like it." He opened the door.

"Okay." Lauren nodded. "I'm sorry I yelled at you. And you have been a lot of help."

"Right," he said glumly, and went out.

"Where'd you get that dress?" Jimmy Stewart said to Donna Reed.

Lauren whirled around. The TV was on. Donna Reed was showing Jimmy Stewart her new dress.

"Where are you?" Lauren demanded, looking at the couch. "I want you to change that dress back right now!"

"Don't you like it?" the spirit said from the bedroom. "It's completely biodegradable."

She stomped into the bedroom. He was putting the dress on the hanger and making little "tsk"-ing noises. "You have to be careful with natural fibers," he said reprovingly.

"Change it back the way it was. This instant."

"It was handmade by the Yanomamo Indians," he said, smoothing down what might be the skirt. "Do you realize that their natural habitat is being destroyed at the rate of 750 acres a day?"

"I don't care. I want my dress back."

He carried the dress on its hanger over to the chest. "It's so interesting. Donna Reed knew right away she was in love with Jimmy Stewart, but he was so busy thinking about college and his new suitcase, he didn't even know she existed." He hung up the dress. "He practically had to be hit over the head."

"I'll hit you over the head if you don't change that dress back this instant, Spirit," she said, looking around for something hard.

"Call me Chris," he said. "Did you know sequins are made from non-renewable resources?" and disappeared as she swung the lamp.

"And good riddance," she shouted to the air.

🎄

They had the dress in a size three. Lauren put herself through the indignity of trying to get into it and then went to work. The receptionist was watching Jimmy Stewart standing on the bridge in the snow and weeping into a Kleenex. She handed Lauren her messages.

There were two memos from the PMS Committee—they were having a sleigh ride after work, and she was supposed to bring cheese puffs to the office party. There wasn't a message from Fred.

"Oh!" the receptionist wailed. "This part is so sad!"

"I hate *It's a Wonderful Life*," Lauren said, and went up to her desk. "I hate Christmas," she said to Evie.

"It's normal to hate Christmas," Evie said, looking up from the book she was reading. "This book, it's called *Let's Forget Christmas,* says it's because everyone has these unrealistic expectations. When they get presents, they—"

"Oh, that reminds me," Lauren said. She rummaged in her bag and brought out Evie's present, fingering it quickly to make sure it was still a stapler. It seemed to be. She held it out to Evie. "Merry Christmas."

"I don't have yours wrapped yet," Evie said. "I don't even have my wrapping paper bought yet. The book says I'm suffering from an avoidance complex." She picked up the package. "Do I have to open it now? I know it will be something I love, and you won't like what I got you half as well, and I'll feel incredibly guilty and inadequate."

"You don't have to open it now," Lauren said. "I just thought I'd better give it to you before—" She picked her messages up off her desk and started looking through them. "Before I forgot. There haven't been any messages from Fred, have there?"

"Yeah. He was here about fifteen minutes ago looking for you. He said to tell you the Net hadn't been any help, and he was going to try the library." She looked sadly at the present. "It's even wrapped great," she said gloomily. "I went shopping for a dress for the office party last night, and do you think I could find anything off-the-shoulder or with sequins? I couldn't even find anything I'd be caught dead in. Did you know the rate of stress-related illnesses at Christmas is seven times higher than the rest of the year?"

"I can relate to that," Lauren said.

"No, you can't. You didn't end up buying some awful gray thing with gold chains hanging all over it. At least Scott will notice me. He'll say, 'Hi, Evie, are you dressed as Marley's ghost?' And there you'll be, looking fabulous in black sequins—"

"No, I won't," Lauren said.

"Why? Didn't they hold it for you?"

"It was . . . defective. Did Fred want to talk to me?"

"I don't know. He was on his way out. He had to go pick up his Santa Claus suit. Oh, my God." Her voice dropped to a whisper. "It's Scott Buckley."

"Hi," Scott said to Lauren. "I was wondering if you could go shopping with me tonight."

Lauren stared at him, so taken aback she couldn't speak.

"When you couldn't go last night, I decided to cancel my date."

"Uh . . . I . . ." she said.

"I thought we could buy the presents and then have some dinner."

She nodded.

"Great," Scott said. "I'll come over to your apartment around six-thirty."

"No!" Lauren said. "I mean, why don't we go straight from work?"

"Good idea. I'll come up here and get you." He smiled meltingly and left.

"I think I'll kill myself," Evie said. "Did you know the rate of suicides at Christmas is four times higher than the rest of the year? He is so cute," she said, looking longingly down the hall after him. "There's Fred."

Lauren looked up. Fred was coming toward her desk with a Santa Claus costume and a stack of books. Lauren hurried across to him.

"This is everything the library had on exorcisms and the occult," Fred said, transferring half of the books to her arms. "I thought we could both go through them today, and then get together tonight and compare notes."

"Oh, I can't," Lauren said. "I promised Scott I'd help him pick out the presents for the office party tonight. I'm sorry. I could tell him I can't."

"Your heart's desire? Are you kidding?" He started awkwardly piling the books back on his load. "You go shopping. I'll go through the books and let you know if I come up with anything."

"Are you sure?" she said guiltily. "I mean, you shouldn't have to do all the work."

"It's my pleasure," he said. He started to walk away and then stopped. "You didn't tell the spirit Scott was your heart's desire, did you?"

"Of course not. Why?"

"I was just wondering . . . nothing. Never mind." He walked off down the hall. Lauren went back to her desk.

"Did you know the rate of depression at Christmas is sixteen times higher than the rest of the year?" Evie said. She handed Lauren a package.

"What's this?"

"It's from your Secret Santa."

Lauren opened it. It was a large book entitled *It's a Wonderful Life: The Photo Album.* On the cover, Jimmy Stewart was looking depressed.

"**I figure it'll** take a half hour or so to pick out the presents," Scott said, leading her past two inflatable palm trees into The Upscale Oasis. "And then we can have some supper and get acquainted." He lay down on a massage couch. "What do you think about this?"

"How many presents do we have to buy?" Lauren asked, looking around the store. There were a lot of inflatable palm trees, and a jukebox, and several life-size cardboard cutouts of Malcolm Forbes and Leona Helmsley. Against the far wall were two high-rise aquariums and a bank of televisions with neon-outlined screens.

"Seventy-two." He got up off the massage couch, handed her the list of employees, and went over to a display of brown boxes tied with twine. "What about these? They're handmade Yanomamo Christmas orna-ments."

"No," Lauren said. "How much money do we have to spend?"

"The PMS Committee budgeted six thousand, and there was five hun-dred left in the Sunshine fund. We can spend . . ." He picked up a pocket calculator in the shape of Donald Trump and punched several buttons. "Ninety dollars per person, including tax. How about this?" He held up an automatic cat feeder.

"We got those last year," Lauren said. She picked up a digital umbrella and put it back down.

"How about a car fax?" Scott said. "No, wait. This, this is it!"

Lauren turned around. Scott was holding up what looked like a gold cordless phone. "It's an investment pager," he said, punching keys. "See, it gives you the Dow Jones, treasury bonds, interest rates. Isn't it per-fect?"

"Well," Lauren said.

"See, this is the hostile takeover alarm, and every time the Federal Reserve adjusts the interest rate it beeps."

Lauren read the tag. "'Portable Plutocrat, $74.99.'"

"Great," Scott said. "We'll have money left over."

"To invest," Lauren said.

He went off to see if they had seventy-two of them, and Lauren wan-dered over to the bank of televisions.

There was a videotape of *Miracle on 34th Street* lying on top of the VCR/shower massage. Lauren looked around to see if anyone was watching and then popped the *Wonderful Life* tape out and stuck in *Miracle.*

A dozen Edmund Gwenns dressed as Macy's Santa Claus appeared on the screens, listening to twelve store managers tell them which over-stocked toys to push.

Scott came over, lugging four shopping bags. "They come gift wrapped," he said happily, showing her a Portable Plutocrat wrapped in green paper with gold dollar signs. "Which gives us a free evening."

"That's what I've been fighting against for years," a dozen Edmund Gwenns said, tearing a dozen lists to bits, "the way they commercialize Christmas."

🌲

"**What I thought,**" Scott said when they got in the car, "was that instead of going out for supper, we'd take these over to your apartment and order in."

"Order in?" Lauren said, clutching a bag of Portable Plutocrats on her lap.

"I know a great Italian place that delivers. Angel-hair pasta, wine, everything. Or, if you'd rather, we could run by a grocery store and pick up some stuff to cook."

"Actually, my kitchen's kind of a mess," she said. *There is a Christmas tree in it,* she thought, *with organic by-products hanging on it.*

He pulled up outside her apartment building. "Then Italian it is." He got out of the car and began unloading shopping bags. "You like pro-sciutto? They have a great melon and prosciutto."

"Actually, the whole apartment's kind of a disaster," Lauren said, following him up the stairs. "You know, wrapping presents and everything. There are ribbons and tags and paper all over the floor and—"

"Great," he said, stopping in front of her door. "We have to put tags on the presents, anyway."

"They don't need tags, do they?" Lauren said desperately. "I mean, they're all exactly alike."

"It personalizes them," he said. "It shows the gift was chosen especially for them." He looked expectantly at the key in her hand and then at the door.

She couldn't hear the TV, which was a good sign. And every time Fred had come over, the spirit had disappeared. *So all I have to do is keep him out of the kitchen,* she thought.

She opened the door and Scott pushed past her and dumped the shopping bags onto the coffee table. "Sorry," he said. "Those were really heavy." He straightened up and looked around the living room. There was no sign of the spirit, but there were three Evian water bottles on the coffee table. "This doesn't look too messy. You should see my apartment. I'll bet your kitchen's neater than mine, too."

Lauren walked swiftly over to the kitchen and pulled the door shut. "I wouldn't bet on it. Aren't there still some more presents to bring up?"

"Yeah. I'll go get them. Shall I call the Italian place first?"

"No," Lauren said, standing with her back against the kitchen door. "Why don't you bring the bags up first?"

"Okay," he said, smiling meltingly, and went out.

Lauren leaped to the door, put the deadbolt and the chain on, and then ran back to the kitchen and opened the door. The tree was still there. She pulled the door hastily to and walked rapidly into the bedroom. He wasn't there, or in the bathroom. "Thank you," she breathed, looking heavenward, and went back in the living room.

The TV was on. Edmund Gwenn was shouting at the store psychologist.

"You know, you were right," the spirit said. He was stretched out on the couch, wearing a "Save the Black-Footed Ferret" T-shirt and jeans. "It's not a bad movie. Of course, it's not as good as *It's a Wonderful Life,* but I like the way everything works out at the end."

"What are you doing here?" she demanded, glancing anxiously at the door.

"Watching *Miracle on 34th Street,*" he said, pointing at the screen. Edmund Gwenn was brandishing his cane at the store psychiatrist. "I like the part where Edmund Gwenn asks Natalie Wood what she wants for Christmas, and she shows him the picture of the house."

Lauren picked up Fred's video and brandished it at him. "Fine. Then you can change Fred's video back."

"Okay," he said, and did something. She looked at Fred's video. It showed Edmund Gwenn hugging Natalie Wood in front of a yellow moon with Santa Claus's sleigh and reindeer flying across it. Lauren put the video hastily down on the coffee table.

"Thank you," she said. "And my dress."

"Natalie Wood doesn't really want a house, of course. What she really wants is for Maureen O'Hara to marry John Payne. The house is just a symbol for what she really wants."

On the TV Edmund Gwenn rapped the store psychologist smartly on the forehead with his cane.

There was a knock on the door. "It's me," Scott said.

"I also like the part where Edmund Gwenn yells at the store manager for pushing merchandise nobody wants. Christmas presents should be something the person wants. Aren't you going to answer the door?"

"Aren't you going to disappear?" she whispered.

"Disappear?" he said incredulously. "The movie isn't over. And besides, I still haven't gotten you what you want for Christmas." He did something, and a bowl of trail mix appeared on his stomach.

Scott knocked again.

Lauren went over to the door and opened it two inches.

"It's me," Scott said. "Why do you have the chain on?"

"I . . ." She looked hopefully at Chris. He was eating trail mix and watching Maureen O'Hara bending over the store psychologist, trying to wake him up.

"Scott, I'm sorry, but I think I'd better take a rain check on supper."

He looked bewildered. And cute. "But I thought . . ." he said.

So did I, she thought. *But I have a spirit on my couch who's perfectly capable of turning you into a Brazilian rain forest by-product.*

"The Italian takeout sounds great," she said, "but it's kind of late, and we've both got to go to work tomorrow."

"Tomorrow's Saturday."

"Uh . . . I meant go to work on wrapping presents. Tomorrow's Christmas Eve, and I haven't even started my wrapping. And I have to make cheese puffs for the office party and wash my hair and . . ."

"Okay, okay, I get the message," he said. "I'll just bring in the presents and then leave."

She thought of telling him to leave them in the hall, and then closed the door a little and took the chain off the door.

Go away*! s*he thought at the spirit, who was eating trail mix.

She opened the door far enough so she could slide out, and pulled it to behind her. "Thanks for a great evening," she said, taking the shopping bags from Scott. "Good night."

"Good night," he said, still looking bewildered. He started down the hall. At the stairs he turned and smiled.

I'm going to kill him, Lauren thought, waving back, and took the shopping bags inside.

The spirit wasn't there. The trail mix was still on the couch, and the TV was still on.

"Come back here!" she shouted. "You little rat! You have ruined my dress and my date, and you're not going to ruin anything else! You're going to change back my dress and my Christmas cards, and you're going to get that tree out of my kitchen right *now*!"

Her voice hung in the air. She sat down on the couch, still holding the shopping bags. On the TV, Edmund Gwenn was sitting in Bellevue, staring at the wall.

"At least Scott finally noticed me," she said, and set the shopping bags down on the coffee table. They rattled.

"Oh, no!" she said. "Not the Plutocrats!"

"The problem is," Fred said, closing the last of the books on the occult, "that we can't exorcise him if we don't know which seasonal spirit he is, and he doesn't fit the profiles of any of these. He must be in disguise."

"I don't want to exorcise him," Lauren said. "I want to kill him."

"Even if we did manage to exorcise him, there'd be no guarantee that the things he's changed would go back to their original state."

"And I'd be stuck with explaining what happened to six thousand dollars' worth of Christmas presents."

"Those Portable Plutocrats cost six thousand dollars?"

"$5895.36."

Fred gave a low whistle. "Did your spirit say why he didn't like them? Other than the obvious, I mean. That they were nonbiodegradable or something?"

"No. He didn't even notice them. He was watching *Miracle on 34th Street,* and he was talking about how he liked the way things worked out at the end and the part about the house."

"Nothing about Christmas presents?"

"I don't remember." She sank down on the couch. "Yes, I do. He said he liked the part where Edmund Gwenn yelled at the store manager for talking people into buying things they didn't want. He said Christmas presents should be something the person wanted."

"Well, that explains why he transformed the Plutocrats then," Fred said. "It probably also means there's no way you can talk him into changing them back. And I've got to have something to pass out at the office party, or you'll be in trouble. So we'll just have to come up with replacement presents."

"Replacement presents?" Lauren said. "How? It's ten o'clock, the office party's tomorrow night, and how do we know he won't transform the replacement presents once we've got them?"

"We'll buy people what they want. Was six thousand all the money you and Scott had?"

"No," Lauren said, rummaging through one of the shopping bags. "PMS budgeted sixty-five hundred."

"How much have you got left?"

She pulled out a sheaf of papers. "He didn't transform the purchase orders or the receipt," she said, looking at them. "The investment pagers cost $5895.36. We have $604.64 left." She handed him the papers. "That's $8.39 apiece."

He looked at the receipt speculatively and then into the shopping bag. "I don't suppose we could take these back and get a refund from The Upscale Oasis?"

"They're not going to give us $5895.36 for seventy-two 'Save the Ozone Layer' buttons," Lauren said. "And there's nothing we can buy for eight dollars that will convince PMS it cost sixty-five hundred. And where am I going to get the money to pay back the difference?"

"I don't think you'll have to. Remember when Chris changed your Christmas cards into the tree? He didn't really. He returned them somehow to the store and got a refund. Maybe he's done the same thing with the Plutocrats and the money will turn up on your coffee table tomorrow morning."

"And if it doesn't?"

"We'll worry about that tomorrow. Right now we've got to come up with presents to pass out at the party."

"Like what?"

"Staplers."

"Staplers?"

"Like the one you got Evie. Everybody in my department's always losing their staplers, too. And their tape dispensers. It's an office party. We'll buy everybody something they want for the office."

"But how will we know what that is? There are seventy-two people on this list."

"We'll call the department heads and ask them, and then we'll go shopping." He stood up. "Where's your phone book?"

"Next to the tree." She followed him into the kitchen. "How are we going to go shopping? It's ten o'clock at night."

"Bizmart's open till eleven," he said, opening the phone book, "and the grocery store's open all night. We'll get as many of the presents as we can tonight and the rest tomorrow morning, and that still gives us all afternoon to get them wrapped. How much wrapping paper do you have?"

"Lots. I bought it half price last year when I decided this Christmas was going to be different. A stapler doesn't seem like much of a present."

"It does if it's what you wanted." He reached for the phone.

It rang. Fred picked up the receiver and handed it to Lauren.

"Oh, Lauren," Evie's voice said. "I just opened your present, and I *love* it! It's exactly what I wanted!"

"Really?" Lauren said.

"It's perfect! I was so depressed about Christmas and the office party and still not having my shopping done. I wasn't even going to open it, but in *Let's Forget Christmas* it said you should open your presents early so they won't ruin Christmas morning, and I did, and it's wonderful! I don't even care whether Scott notices me or not! Thank you!"

"You're welcome," Lauren said, but Evie had already hung up. She looked at Fred. "That was Evie. You were right about people liking staplers." She handed him the phone. "You call the department heads. I'll get my coat."

He took the phone and began to punch in numbers, and then put it down. "What exactly did the spirit say about the ending of *Miracle on 34th Street*?"

"He said he liked the way everything worked out at the end. Why?"

He looked thoughtful. "Maybe we're going about this all wrong."

"What do you mean?"

"What if the spirit really does want to give you your heart's desire, and all this transforming stuff is some roundabout way of doing it? Like the angel in *It's a Wonderful Life.* He's supposed to save Jimmy Stewart from committing suicide, and instead of doing something logical, like talking him out of it or grabbing him, he jumps in the river so Jimmy Stewart has to save *him*."

"You're saying he turned seventy-two Portable Plutocrats into 'Save the Ozone Layer' buttons to help me?"

"I don't know. All I'm saying is that maybe you should tell him you want to go to the office party in a black sequined dress with Scott Buckley, and see what happens."

"See what happens? After what he did to my dress? If he knew I wanted Scott, he'd probably turn him into a harp seal." She put on her coat. "Well, are we going to call the department heads or not?"

🎄

The Graphic Design department wanted staplers, and so did Accounts Payable. Accounts Receivable, which was having an outbreak of stress-related Christmas colds, wanted Puffs Plus and cough drops. Document Control wanted scissors.

Scott looked at the list, checking off Systems and the other departments they'd called. "All we've got left is the PMS Committee," he said.

"I know what to get them," Lauren said. "Copies of *Let's Forget Christmas.*"

They got some of the things before Bizmart closed, and Fred was back at nine Saturday morning to do the rest of it. At the bookstore they ran into the woman who had been stapling presents together the day Lauren enlisted Fred's help.

"I completely forgot my husband's first wife," she said, looking desperate, "and I don't have any idea of what to get her."

Fred handed her the videotape of *It's a Wonderful Life* they were giving the receptionist. "How about one of these?" he said.

"Do you think she'll like it?"

"*Everybody* likes it," Fred said.

"Especially the part where the bad guy steals the money, and Jimmy
Stewart races around town, trying to replace it," Lauren said.

It took them most of the morning to get the rest of the presents and
forever to wrap them. By four they weren't even half done.

"What's next?" Fred asked, tying the bow on the last of the staplers.
He stood up and stretched.

"Cough drops," Lauren said, cutting a length of red paper with Santa
Clauses on it.

He sat back down. "Ah, yes. Accounts Receivable's heart's desire."

"What's your heart's desire?" Lauren asked, folding the paper over the
top of the cough drops and taping it. "What would you ask for if the
spirit inflicted himself on you?"

Fred unreeled a length of ribbon. "Well, not to go to an office party,
that's for sure. The only year I had an even remotely good time was last
year, talking to you."

"I'm serious," Lauren said. She taped the sides and handed the package to Fred. "What do you really want for Christmas?"

"When I was eight," he said thoughtfully, "I asked for a computer for
Christmas. Home computers were new then and they were pretty expensive, and I wasn't sure I'd get it. I was a lot like Natalie Wood in *Miracle
on 34th Street.* I didn't believe in Santa Claus, and I didn't believe in
miracles, but I really wanted it."

He cut off the length of ribbon, wrapped it around the package, and
tied it in a knot.

"Did you get the computer?"

"No," he said, cutting off shorter lengths of ribbon. "Christmas morning I came downstairs, and there was a note telling me to look in the
garage." He opened the scissors and pulled the ribbon across the blade,
making it curl. "It was a puppy." He smiled, remembering. "The thing

was, a computer was too expensive, but there was an outside chance I'd get it, or I wouldn't have asked for it. Kids don't ask for stuff they *know* is impossible."

"And you hadn't asked for a puppy because you knew you couldn't have one?"

"No, you don't understand. There are things you don't ask for because you know you can't have them, and then there are things so far outside the realm of possibility, it would never even occur to you to want them." He made the curled ribbon into a bow and fastened it to the package.

"So what you're saying is your heart's desire is something so far outside the realm of possibility, you don't even know what it is?"

"I didn't say that," he said. He stood up again. "Do you want some eggnog?"

"Yes, thanks. If it's still there."

He went into the kitchen. She could hear forest-thrashing noises and the refrigerator opening. "It's still here," he said.

"It's funny Chris hasn't been back," she called to Fred. "I keep worrying he must be up to something."

"Chris?" Fred said. He came back into the living room with two glasses of eggnog.

"The spirit. He told me to call him that," she said. "It's short for Spirit of Christmas Present." Fred was frowning. "What's wrong?" Lauren asked.

"I wonder . . . nothing. Never mind." He went over to the TV. "I don't suppose *Miracle on 34th Street*'s on TV this afternoon?"

"No, but I made him change your video back." She pointed. "It's there, on top of the TV."

He turned on the TV, inserted the video in the VCR, and hit play. He came and sat down beside Lauren. She handed him the wrapped cough drops, but he didn't take them. He was watching the TV. Lauren looked up. On the screen, Jimmy Stewart was walking past Donna Reed's house, racketing a stick along the picket fence.

"That isn't *Miracle*," Lauren said. "He told me he changed it back." She snatched up the box. It still showed Edmund Gwenn hugging Natalie Wood. "That little sneak! He only changed the box!"

She glared at the TV. On the screen Jimmy Stewart was glaring at Donna Reed.

"It's all right," Fred said, taking the package and reaching for the ribbon. "It's not a bad movie. The ending's too sentimental, and it doesn't really make sense. I mean, one minute everything's hopeless, and Jimmy Stewart's ready to kill himself, and then the angel convinces him he had a wonderful life, and suddenly everything's okay." He looked around the table, patting the spread-out wrapping paper. "But it has its moments. Have you seen the scissors?"

Lauren handed him one of the pairs they'd bought. "We'll wrap them last."

On the TV Jimmy Stewart was sitting in Donna Reed's living room, looking awkward. "What I have trouble with is Jimmy Stewart's being so self-sacrificing," she said, cutting another length of red paper with Santa Clauses on it. "I mean, he gives up college so his brother can go, and then when his brother has a chance at a good job, he gives up college *again*. He even gives up committing suicide to save Clarence. There's such a thing as being too self-sacrificing, you know."

"Maybe he gives up things because he thinks he doesn't deserve them."

"Why wouldn't he?"

"He's never gone to college, he's poor, he's deaf in one ear. Sometimes when people are handicapped or overweight they just assume they can't have the things other people have."

The telephone rang. Lauren reached for it and then realized it was on TV.

"Oh, hello, Sam," Donna Reed said, looking at Jimmy Stewart.

"Can you help me with this ribbon?" Fred said.

"Sure," Lauren said. She scooted closer to him and put her finger on the crossed ribbon to hold it taut.

Jimmy Stewart and Donna Reed were standing very close together, listening to the telephone. The voice on the phone was saying something about soybeans.

Fred still hadn't tied the knot. Lauren glanced up at him. He was looking at the TV, too.

Jimmy Stewart was looking at Donna Reed, his face nearly touching her hair. Donna Reed looked at him and then away. The voice from the phone was saying something about the chance of a lifetime, but it was obvious neither of them was hearing a word. Donna Reed looked up at him. His lips almost touched her forehead. They didn't seem to be breathing.

Lauren realized she wasn't, either. She looked at Fred. He was holding the two ends of ribbon, one in each hand, and looking down at her.

"The knot," she said. "You haven't tied it."

"Oh," he said. "Sorry."

Jimmy Stewart dropped the phone with a clatter and grabbed Donna Reed by both arms. He began shaking her, yelling at her, and then suddenly she was wrapped in his arms, and he was smothering her with kisses.

"The knot," Fred said. "You have to pull your finger out."

She looked uncomprehendingly at him and then down at the package. He had tied the knot over her finger, which was still pressing against the wrapping paper.

"Oh. Sorry," she said, and pulled her finger free. "You were right. It does have its moments."

He yanked the knot tight. "Yeah," he said. He reached for the spool of ribbon and began chopping off lengths for the bow. On the screen Donna Reed and Jimmy Stewart were being pelted with rice.

"No. You were right," he said. "He is too self-sacrificing." He waved the scissors at the screen. "In a minute he's going to give up his honeymoon to save the building and loan. It's a wonder he ever asked Donna Reed to marry him. It's a wonder he didn't try to fix her up with that guy on the phone."

The phone rang. Lauren looked at the screen, thinking it must be in the movie, but Jimmy Stewart was kissing Donna Reed in a taxicab.

"It's the phone," Fred said.

Lauren scrambled up and reached for it.

"Hi," Scott said.

"Oh, hello, Scott," Lauren said, looking at Fred.

"I was wondering about the office party tonight," Scott said. "Would you like to go with me? I could come get you and we could take the presents over together."

"Uh . . . I . . ." Lauren said. She put her hand over the receiver. "It's Scott. What am I going to tell him about the presents?"

Fred motioned her to give him the phone. "Scott," he said. "Hi. It's Fred Hatch. Yeah, Santa Claus. Listen, we ran into a problem with the presents."

Lauren closed her eyes.

"We got a call from The Upscale Oasis that investment pagers were being recalled by the Federal Safety Commission."

Lauren opened her eyes. Fred smiled at her. "Yeah. For excessive cupidity," he said.

Lauren grinned.

"But there's nothing to worry about," Fred said. "We replaced them. We're wrapping them right now. No, it was no trouble. I was happy to help. Yeah, I'll tell her." He hung up. "Scott will be here to take you to the office party at seven-thirty," he said. "It looks like you're going to get your heart's desire after all."

"Yeah," Lauren said, looking at the TV. On the screen, the building and loan was going under.

🎄

They finished wrapping the last pair of scissors at six-thirty, and Fred went back to his apartment to change clothes and get his Santa Claus costume. Lauren packed the presents in three of the Upscale Oasis shopping bags, said sternly, "Don't you dare touch these," to the empty couch, and went to get ready.

She showered and did her hair, and then went into the bedroom to see if the spirit had biodegraded her red dress, or, by some miracle, brought the black off-the-shoulder one back. He hadn't.

She put on her red dress and went back into the living room. It was only a little after seven. She turned on the TV and put Fred's video into the VCR. She hit play. Edmund Gwenn was giving the doctor the X-ray machine he'd always wanted.

Lauren picked up one of the shopping bags and felt the top pair of scissors to make sure they hadn't been turned into bottles of Evian water. There was an envelope stuck between two of the packages. Inside was a check for $5895.36. It was made out to the Children's Hospital fund.

She shook her head, smiling, and put the check back into the envelope.

On TV, Maureen O'Hara and John Payne were watching Natalie Wood run through an empty house and out the back door to look for her swing.

They looked seriously at each other. Lauren held her breath. John Payne moved forward and kissed Maureen O'Hara.

Someone knocked on the door. "That's Scott," Lauren said to John Payne, and waited till Maureen O'Hara had finished telling him she loved him before she went to open the door.

It was Fred, carrying a foil-covered plate. He was wearing the same sweater and pants he'd worn to wrap the presents. "Cheese puffs," he said. "I figured you couldn't get to your stove." He looked seriously at her. "I wouldn't worry about not having your black dress to dazzle Scott with."

He went over and set the cheese puffs on the coffee table. "You need to take the foil off and heat them in a microwave for two minutes on high. Tell PMS to put the presents in Santa's bag, and I'll be there at eleven-thirty."

"Aren't you going to the party?"

"Office parties are your idea of fun, not mine," he said. "Besides, *Miracle on 34th Street*'s on at eight. It may be the only chance I have to watch it."

"But I wanted you—"

There was a knock on the door. "That's Scott," Lauren said.

"Well," Fred said, "if the spirit doesn't do something in the next fifteen seconds, you'll have your heart's desire in spite of him." He opened the door. "Come on in," he said. "Lauren and the presents are all ready." He handed two of the shopping bags to Scott.

"I really appreciate your helping Lauren and me with all this," Scott said.

Fred handed the other shopping bag to Lauren. "It was my pleasure."

"I wish you were coming with us," she said.

"And give up a chance of seeing the real Santa Claus?" He held the door open. "You two had better get going before something happens."

"What do you mean?" Scott said, alarmed. "Do you think these presents might be recalled, too?"

Lauren looked hopefully at the couch and then the TV. On the screen Jimmy Stewart was standing on a bridge in the snow, getting ready to kill himself.

"Afraid not," Fred said.

It was snowing by the time they pulled into the parking lot at work. "It was really selfless of Fred to help you wrap all those presents," Scott said, holding the lobby door open for Lauren. "He's a nice guy."

"Yes," Lauren said. "He is."

"Hey, look at that!" Scott said. He pointed at the security monitor. "*It's a Wonderful Life.* My favorite movie!" On the monitor Jimmy Stewart was running through the snow, shouting, "Merry Christmas!"

"Scott," Lauren said, "I can't go to the party with you."

"Just a minute, okay?" Scott said, staring at the screen. "This is my favorite part." He set the shopping bags down on the receptionist's desk and leaned his elbows on it. "This is the part where Jimmy Stewart finds out what a wonderful life he's had."

"You have to take me home," Lauren said.

There was a gust of cold air and snow. Lauren turned around.

"You forgot your cheese puffs," Fred said, holding out the foil-covered plate to Lauren.

"There's such a thing as being too self-sacrificing, you know," Lauren said.

He held the plate out to her. "That's what the spirit said."

"He came back?" She shot a glance at the shopping bags.

"Yeah. Right after you left. Don't worry about the presents. He said he thought the staplers were a great idea. He also said not to worry about getting a Christmas present for your sister."

"My sister!" Lauren said, clapping her hand to her mouth. "I completely forgot about her."

"He said since you didn't like it, he sent her the Yanomamo dress."

"She'll love it," Lauren said.

"He also said it was a wonder Jimmy Stewart ever got Donna Reed, he was so busy giving everybody else what they wanted," he said, looking seriously at her.

"He's right," Lauren said. "Did he also tell you Jimmy Stewart was incredibly stupid for wanting to go off to college when Donna Reed was right there in front of him?"

"He mentioned it."

"What a great movie!" Scott said, turning to Lauren. "Ready to go up?"

"No," Lauren said. "I'm going with Fred to see a movie." She took the cheese puffs from Fred and handed them to Scott.

"What am I supposed to do with these?"

"Take the foil off," Fred said, "and put them in a microwave for two minutes."

"But you're my date," Scott said. "Who am I supposed to go with?"

There was a gust of cold air and snow. Everyone turned around.

"How do I look?" Evie said, taking off her coat.

"Wow!" Scott said. "You look terrific!"

Evie spun around, her shoulders bare, the sequins glittering on her black dress. "Lauren gave it to me for Christmas," she said happily. "I love Christmas, don't you?"

"I *love* that dress," Scott said.

"He also told me," Fred said, "that his favorite thing in *Miracle on 34th Street* was Santa Claus's being in disguise—"

"He wasn't in disguise," Lauren said. "Edmund Gwenn told everybody he was Santa Claus."

Fred held up a correcting finger. "He told everyone his name was Kris Kringle."

"Chris," Lauren said.

"Oh, I love this part," Evie said.

Lauren looked at her. She was standing next to Scott, watching Jimmy Stewart standing next to Donna Reed and singing "Auld Lang Syne."

"He makes all sorts of trouble for everyone," Fred said. "He turns Christmas upside down—"

"Completely disrupts Maureen O'Hara's life," Lauren said.

"But by the end, everything's worked out, the doctor has his X-ray machine, Natalie Wood has her house—"

"Maureen O'Hara has Fred—"

"And no one's quite sure how he did it, or if he did anything."

"Or if he had the whole thing planned from the beginning." She looked seriously at Fred. "He told me I only thought I knew what I wanted for Christmas."

Fred moved toward her. "He told me just because something seems impossible doesn't mean a miracle can't happen."

"What a great ending!" Evie said, sniffling. "*It's a Wonderful Life* is my favorite movie."

"Mine, too," Scott said. "Do you know how to heat up cheese puffs?" He turned to Lauren and Fred. "Cut that out, you two, we'll be late for the party."

"We're not going," Fred said, putting his arm around Lauren. They started for the door. "*Miracle*'s on at eight."

"But you can't leave," Scott said. "What about all these presents? Who's going to pass them out?"

There was a gust of cold air and snow. "Ho ho ho," Santa Claus said.

"Isn't that your costume, Fred?" Lauren said.

"Yes. It has to be back at the rental place by Monday morning," he said to Santa Claus. "And no changing it into rain forest by-products."

"*Merry* Christmas!" Santa Claus said.

"I like the way things worked out at the end," Lauren said.

"All we need is a cane standing in the corner," Fred said.

"I have no idea what you're talking about," Santa Claus said. "Where are all these presents I'm supposed to pass out?"

"Right here," Scott said. He handed one of the shopping bags to Santa Claus.

"Plastic shopping bags," Santa Claus said, making a "tsk"-ing sound. "You should be using recycled paper."

"Sorry," Scott said. He handed the cheese puffs to Evie and picked up the other two shopping bags. "Ready, Evie?"

"We can't go yet," Evie said, gazing at the security monitor. "Look, *It's a Wonderful Life* is just starting." On the screen Jimmy Stewart's brother was falling through the ice. "This is my favorite part," she said.

"Mine, too," Scott said, and went over to stand next to her.

Santa Claus squinted curiously at the monitor for a moment and then shook his head. "*Miracle on 34th Street*'s a much better movie, you know," he said reprovingly. "More realistic."

All About Emily

"Fuck The Red Shoes.
I wanted to be a Rockette."
—*A Chorus Line*

All right, so you're probably wondering how I, Claire Havilland—three-time Tony winner, Broadway legend, and star of *Only Human*—ended up here, standing outside Radio City Music Hall in a freezing rain two days before Christmas, soaked to the skin and on the verge of pneumonia, accosting harmless passersby.

Well, it's all my wretched manager Torrance's fault. And Macy's. And the movie *All About Eve*'s.

You've never heard of *All About Eve*? Of course you haven't. Neither has anyone else. Except Emily.

It starred Anne Baxter and Bette Davis, and was the first movie Marilyn Monroe appeared in. She played Miss Caswell, a producer's girlfriend, but the movie's not about her. It's about an aging Broadway actress, Margo Channing, and the young aspiring actress, Eve Harrington, who insinuates herself into Margo's life and makes off with her starring role, her career, and, very nearly, her husband.

All About Eve was made into a musical called *Applause* and then into a straight dramatic play which was then made into *another* musical. (Broadway has never been terribly creative.) The second musical, which was called *Bumpy Night* and starred Kristen Stewart as Eve and me as

Margo, only ran for three months, but it won me my second Tony and got me the lead in *Feathers,* which won me my third.

Macy's is a New York department store, in case you don't know that, either. Except for Emily, no one today seems to know anything that happened longer than five minutes ago. Macy's sponsors a parade on Thanksgiving Day every year, featuring large balloons representing various cartoon characters, the stars of various Broadway shows waving frozenly from floats, and the Rockettes.

And my manager Torrance is a lying, sneaky, conniving snake. As you shall see.

❦

The Wednesday night before Thanksgiving he knocked on my dressing room door during intermission and said, "Do you have a minute, dear one? I've got *fabulous* news!"

I should have known right then he was up to something. Torrance only comes backstage when: one, he has bad news to deliver, or two, he wants something. And he never knocks.

"The show's closing," I said.

"*Closing!* Of course not. The house is sold out every night through Christmas. And it's no wonder! You get more dazzling with every performance!" He clutched his chest dramatically. "When you sang that Act I finale, the audience was eating out of your hand!"

"If you're still trying to talk me into having lunch with Nusbaum, the answer is no," I said, unzipping my garden party costume. "I am *not* doing the revival of *Chicago.*"

"But you were the best Roxie Hart the show ever had—"

"That was twelve years ago," I said, shimmying out of it. "I have no intention of wearing a leotard at my age. I am too old—"

"Don't even *say* that word, dear one," he said, looking anxiously out into the hall and pulling the door to behind him. "You don't know who might hear you."

"They won't have to hear me. One look at me in fishnet stockings, and the audience will be able to figure it out for themselves."

"Nonsense," he said, looking appraisingly at me. "Your legs aren't that bad."

Aren't that bad. "Dance ten, looks three?" I said wryly.

He stared blankly at me.

"It's a line from *A Chorus Line,* a show I was in which you apparently never bothered to see. It's a line which proves my point about the fishnet stockings. I am *not* doing *Chicago.*"

"All Nusbaum's asking is that you meet him for lunch. What harm could that do? He didn't even say what role he wanted you for. It may not be Roxie at all. He may want you for the part of—"

"Who? The warden?" I said, scooping up my garden party costume into a wad. "I told you I was too old for fishnet stockings, not old enough to be playing Mama Morton." I threw it at him. "Or Mama Rose. Or *I Remember Mama.*"

"I only meant he might want you to play Velma," he said, fighting his way out of the yards of crinoline.

"No," I said. "Absolutely not. I need a role where I keep my clothes on. I hear Austerman's doing a musical version of *Desk Set.*"

"*Desk Set*?" he asked. "What's it about?"

Apparently he never watched movies, either. "Computers replacing office workers," I said. "It was a Julia Roberts–Richard Gere movie several years ago, and there are no fishnet stockings in it anywhere." I wriggled into my ball gown. "Was that all you wanted?"

I knew perfectly well it wasn't. Torrance has been my manager for over fifteen years, and one thing I've learned during that time is that he never gets around to what he really wants till Act Two of a conversation, apparently in the belief that he can soften me up by asking for some other thing first. Or for two other things, if what he wants is particularly unpleasant, though how it could be worse than doing *Chicago,* I didn't know.

"What did you come in here for, Torrance?" I asked. "There are only five minutes to curtain."

"I've got a little publicity thing I need you to do. Tomorrow's Thanksgiving, and the Macy's parade—"

"No, I am not riding on the *Only Human* float, or standing out in a freezing rain again saying, 'Look! Here comes the *Wall-E* balloon!'"

There was a distinct pause, and then Torrance said, "How did you know there's a *Wall-E* balloon in the parade? I thought you only read *Variety.*"

"There was a picture of it on the home page of the *Times* yesterday."

"Did you click to the article?"

"No. Why? As you say, I never read the news. You didn't already tell them I'd do it, did you?" I said, my eyes narrowing.

"No, of course not. You don't have to go anywhere near the parade."

"Then why did you bring it up?"

"Because the parade's Grand Marshal is coming to the show Friday night, and I'd like you to let him come backstage after the performance to meet you."

"Who is it this year?" I asked. It was always a politician, or whatever talentless tween idol was going to be starring on Broadway next. "If it's any of Britney Spears's offspring, the answer is no."

"It's not," Torrance said. "It's Dr. Edwin Oakes."

"*Doctor?*"

"Of physics. Nobel Prize for his work on artificial neurotransmitters. He founded AIS."

"Why on earth is a physicist the Grand Marshal of the Macy's Thanksgiving Day Parade?" I said. "Oh, wait, is he the robot scientist?"

There was another pause. "I thought you said you didn't read the article."

"I didn't. My driver Jorge told me about him."

"Where'd *he* hear about Dr. Oakes?"

"On the radio. He listens to it in the limo while he's waiting."

"Oh. What did Jorge tell you about him?"

"Just that he'd invented some new sort of robot that was supposed to replace ATMs and subway-ticket dispensers, and that I shouldn't believe it, they were going to steal all our jobs—oh, my God, you're bringing some great, clanking Robby the Robot backstage to meet me!"

"No, of course not. Don't be ridiculous. Would I do that?"

"Yes. And you didn't answer my question. *Is* this the same Dr. Oakes? The robot scientist?"

"Yes, only they're not robots, they're 'artificials.'"

"I don't care what they're called. I'm not granting a backstage interview to C-3PO."

"You're dating yourself, dear one," he said. "C-3PO was *eons* ago. The reason Dr. Oakes was asked to be the Grand Marshal is because this year's parade theme is robots, in honor of—"

"Don't tell me—*Forbidden Planet,* right? I should have known."

Forbidden Planet. The second-worst show to ever have been on Broadway, but that hasn't stopped it from packing them in down the street at the Majestic, thanks to Robby the Robot and a never-ending procession of tween idols (at this point it's Shiloh Jolie-Pitt and Justin Bieber, Jr.) in the starring roles. "And I suppose that's where this Dr. Oakes is tonight?"

"No, they didn't want to see *Forbidden Planet*—"

"They?" I said suspiciously.

"Dr. Oakes and his niece. They didn't want to meet Shiloh and Justin. They want to see *Only Human.* And to meet you."

I'll bet, I thought, waiting for Torrance to get to the real reason he'd come backstage to see me, because meeting a couple of fans couldn't be it. He dragged a ragtag assortment of people backstage every week. He wasn't still trying to talk me into doing the latest revival of *Cats,* was he? It was not only *the* worst musical ever produced on Broadway, but it required tights *and* whiskers.

"Dr. Oakes's niece is really eager to meet you," Torrance was saying. "She's a huge fan of yours. It will only take five minutes," he pleaded. "And it would really help with ticket sales."

"Why do the ticket sales need help? I thought you said we had full houses through Christmas."

"We do, but the weather's supposed to turn bad next week, and sales for after New Year's have been positively *limp.* Management's worried we won't last through January. And the word is Disney's scouting for a theater where they can put a new production of *Tangled.* If they get nervous about our closing—"

"I don't see how meeting them will help us get publicity. Physicists are hardly front-page news."

"I can guarantee it'll get us publicity. WNET's already said they'll be here to live-stream it. And Sirius. And when Emily said she wanted to meet you on *Good Morning, America* yesterday, ticket sales for this weekend went through the roof."

"I thought you said we were already sold out through Christmas."

"I said *Only Human* was playing to full houses."

Which meant half the tickets were going for half price at the TKTS booth in Times Square and the back five rows of the balcony were roped off for "repairs."

"And you know what the management's like when they think they're going to lose their investment. They'll jump at anything—"

"All right," I said. "I'll meet with Dr. Nobel Prize and his niece, if she *is* his niece. Which I seriously doubt."

"Why do you say that?" Torrance said sharply.

"Because all middle-aged men are alike, even scientists. Her name wouldn't be Miss Caswell, would it?"

"Who?"

"The producer's girlfriend," I said. I pantomimed a pair of enormous breasts. "Ring a bell?" He looked blank. "Really, Torrance, you should at least *pretend* to have watched the plays I'm starring in."

"I do. I have. I just don't remember any Miss Caswell in *Only Human.*"

"That's because she wasn't in *Only Human.* She was in *Bumpy Night.* Lindsay Lohan played her, remember?" and when he still looked blank, "Marilyn Monroe played her in the original movie. And please don't tell me you don't know who that is, or you'll make me feel even more ancient than I am."

"You're not ancient, dear one," he said, "and I wish you'd stop being so hard on yourself. You're a legend."

Which is a word even more deadly to one's career than "old" or "cellulite." And only slightly less career-ending than "First Lady of the Theater." I said, "Yes, well, this 'legend' just changed her mind. No backstage interview."

"Okay," he said. "I'll tell them no dice. But don't be surprised if they decide to go to *Forbidden Planet* instead. Their entire cast has agreed to a backstage interview, including Justin."

"All right, fine. I'll do it," I said. "If you get me out of the lunch with Nusbaum and talk to Austerman about *Desk Set.*"

"I will. This interview will help on the *Desk Set* thing," he said, though I couldn't see how. "Star Meets Fans" is hardly home-page news. "You'll be glad you did this. You're going to like Emily."

There was only one thing to like about having been blackmailed into doing the interview: our discussion of it had taken up the entire intermission, and Torrance hadn't had time to ask me the thing he'd actually come backstage to.

I expected him to try again after the show, but he didn't. He left a message saying, "WABC will be there to film meeting. Wear something suitable for Broadway legend. *Sunset Boulevard?*" Which was proof either that he saw me much as I was beginning to see myself, as a fading (and deranged) star, or that he hadn't seen the musical *Sunset Boulevard,* either.

I had the wardrobe mistress hunt me up the magenta hostess gown from *Mame* and a pair of *Evita* earrings, signed autographs for the fans waiting outside the stage door, turned my phone off, and went home to bed.

I kept my phone off through Thanksgiving Day so Torrance couldn't call me and insist I watch Dr. Oakes in the parade, but I didn't want to miss a possible call from Austerman about *Desk Set,* so Friday I turned my phone back on, assuming (incorrectly) that Torrance would immediately call and make another attempt at broaching the subject of whatever it was he'd really come to my dressing room about.

Because it couldn't possibly be the scruffy-looking professor and his all-dressed-up niece who Torrance brought to my dressing room Friday night after the show. I could see why Torrance had rejected the idea of her being the producer's mistress. This petite, fresh-scrubbed teenager with her light brown hair and upturned nose and pink cheeks was nothing like Marilyn Monroe. She was nothing like the gangly, tattooed, tipped, and tattered girls who clustered outside *Forbidden Planet* every night either, waiting for Justin Jr. to autograph their *Playbill*s.

This girl, who couldn't be more than five foot two, looked more like the character of Peggy in the first act of *42nd Street,* wide-eyed and giddy at being in New York City for the first time. Or a sixteen-year-old Julie Andrews. The sort of dewy-eyed innocent ingénue that every established actress hates on sight. And that the New York press can't wait to get its claws into.

But they were being oddly deferential. And they were all here. Not just *Good Morning America,* but the other networks, the cable channels, the *Times,* the *Post–Daily News,* and at least a dozen bloggers and streamers.

"How'd you manage to pull this off?" I whispered to Torrance as they squeezed into my dressing room. Apart from the Tonys, *Spiderman III* accidents, and Hollywood stars, it's impossible to get the media to cover anything theatrical. "Lady Gaga's not replacing me in the role, is she?"

He ignored that. "Claire, dear one," he said, as if he were in a production of Noël Coward's *Private Lives,* "allow me to introduce Dr. Edwin Oakes. And this," he said, presenting the niece to me with a flourish, "is Emily."

"Oh, Miss Havilland," she said eagerly. "It's so exciting to meet you. You were just wonderful."

Well, at least she hadn't said it was an honor to meet me, or called me a legend.

"I loved *Only Human,*" she said. "It's the best play I've ever seen."

It was probably the *only* play she'd ever seen, but Torrance had been right, this meeting would be good publicity. The media were recording every word and obviously responding to Emily's smile, which even I had to admit was rather sweet.

"You sing and dance so beautifully, Miss Havilland," she said. "And you make the audience believe that what they're seeing is real—"

"You're Emily's favorite actress," Torrance cut in. "Isn't that right, Emily?"

"Oh, yes. I've seen all your plays—*Feathers* and *Play On!* and *The Drowsy Chaperone* and *Fender Strat* and *Anything Goes* and *Love, Etc.*"

"But I thought Torrance said this was your first time in New York," I said. And she was much too young to have seen *Play On!* She'd have been five years old.

"It *is* my first time," she said earnestly. "I haven't seen the plays onstage, but I've seen all your filmed performances and the numbers you've done at the Tony Awards—'When They Kill Your Dream' and 'The Leading Lady's Lament.' And I've watched your interviews on YouTube and read all your online interviews and listened to the soundtracks of *A Chorus Line* and *Tie Dye* and *In Between the Lines.*"

"My, you are a fan!" I said. "Are you sure your name's Emily and not Eve?"

"Eve?" Dr. Oakes said sharply.

Torrance shot me a warning glance, and the reporters all looked up alertly from the Androids they were taking notes on. "Why would you think her name was Eve, Miss Havilland?" one of them asked.

"I was making a joke," I said, taken aback at all this reaction. And if I said it was a reference to Eve Harrington, none of them would have ever heard of her, and if I said she was a character in *Bumpy Night,* none of them would have heard of that, either. "I . . ."

"She called me Eve because I was doing what Eve Harrington did," Emily said. "That's who you meant, isn't it, Miss Havilland? The character in the musical *Bumpy Night*?"

"I . . . y-yes," I stammered, trying to recover from the shock that she'd recognized the allusion. The younger generation's knowledge usually doesn't extend further back than *High School Musical: The Musical.*

"When Eve meets the actress Margo Channing," Emily was cheerfully telling the reporters, "she gushes to her about what a wonderful actress she is."

"*Bumpy Night*?" one of the reporters said, looking as lost as Torrance usually does.

"Yes," Emily said. "The musical was based on the movie *All About Eve,* which starred Bette Davis and Anne Baxter."

"And Marilyn Monroe," I said.

"Right," Emily said, dimpling. "As Miss Caswell, the producer's girlfriend. It was her screen debut."

I was beginning to like this girl, in spite of her perfect skin and perfect hair and the way she could hold an audience. The media were hanging on her every word. Although that might be because they were as astonished as I was at a teenager's knowledge of the movie.

"Marilyn Monroe—she was in *Gentlemen Prefer Blondes* and *How to Marry a Millionaire,*" she said, "which Lauren Bacall was in, too. She starred in the first musical they made of *All About Eve*: *Applause*. It wasn't nearly as good as *Bumpy Night,* or as faithful to the movie."

And since she knew so much about movies, maybe this was a good time to put in a pitch for my doing Austerman's play. "Have you ever seen *Desk Set,* Emily?" I asked her.

"Which one? The Julia Roberts–Richard Gere remake or the original with Katharine Hepburn and Spencer Tracy?"

Good God. "The original."

"Yes, I've seen it. I *love* that movie."

"So do I," I said. "Did you know they're thinking of making a musical of it?"

"Oh, you'd be wonderful in the Katharine Hepburn part!"

I definitely liked this girl.

"What about *Cats*?" Torrance asked.

I glared at him, but he ignored me.

"Have you ever seen the musical *Cats*?" he persisted.

"Yes," she said, and wrinkled her nose in distaste. "I didn't like it. There's no plot at all, and 'Memory' is a terrible song. *Cats* isn't nearly as good as *Only Human*."

"You see, Torrance?" I said, and turned my widest smile on Emily. "I'm so glad you came to the show tonight."

"So am I," she said. "I'm sorry I sounded like Eve Harrington before. I wouldn't want to be her. She wasn't a nice person," she explained to the reporters. "She tried to steal Margo's part in the play from her."

"You're right, she wasn't very nice," I said. "But I suppose one can't blame her for wanting to be an actress. After all, acting's the most rewarding profession in the world. What about you, Emily? Do you want to be an actress?"

It should have been a perfectly safe question. Every teenage girl who's ever come backstage to meet me has been seriously stagestruck, especially after seeing her first Broadway musical, and Emily *had* to be, given her obsessive interest in the movies and my plays.

But she didn't breathe "Oh, yes," like every other girl I'd asked. She said, "No, I don't."

You're lying, I thought.

"I could never do what you do, Miss Havilland," Emily went on in that matter-of-fact voice.

"Then what *do* you want to do? Paint? Write?"

She glanced uncertainly at her uncle and then back at me.

"Or does your uncle want you to be a neurophysicist like him?" I asked.

"Oh, no, I couldn't do that, either. Any of those things."

"Of course you could, an intelligent girl like you. You can do anything you want to do."

"But I—" Emily glanced at her uncle again, as if for guidance.

"Come, you must want to be something," I said. "An astronaut. A ballerina. A real boy."

"Claire, dear one, stop badgering the poor child," Torrance said with an artificial-sounding laugh. "She's in New York for the very first time. It's scarcely the time for career counseling."

"You're right. I'm sorry, Emily," I said. "How are you liking New York?"

"Oh, it's wonderful!" she said.

The eagerness was back in her voice, and Dr. Oakes had relaxed. Did she want to go on the stage and her uncle didn't approve? Or was something else going on? "How are you liking New York?" was hardly riveting stuff, but there wasn't a peep out of the media. They were watching us raptly, as if they expected something to happen at any second.

I should have read the article in the Times, I thought, and asked Emily if she'd been to the Empire State Building yet.

"No," she said, "we do that tomorrow morning after we do *NBC Weekend,* and then at ten I'm going ice-skating at Rockefeller Center. It would be wonderful if you could come, too."

"At ten in the morning?" I said, horrified. "I'm not even up by then," and the reporters laughed. "Thank you for asking me, though. What are you doing tomorrow night?" I asked, and then realized she was likely to say, "We're seeing *Forbidden Planet,*" but I needn't have worried.

"We're going to see the Christmas show at Radio City Music Hall," she said.

"Oh, good. You'll love the Rockettes. Or have you seen them already? They were in the parade, weren't they?"

"No," Emily said. "What are—?"

"They don't ride in the parade," Torrance said, cutting in. "They dance outside Macy's on Thirty-fourth Street. What else are you and your uncle doing tomorrow, Emily?"

"We're going to Times Square, and then Macy's and Bloomingdale's to see the Christmas windows, and then the Disney store—"

"Good God," I said. "All in one day? It sounds exhausting!"

"But I don't—" Emily began.

This time it was Dr. Oakes who cut in. "She's too excited at being here to be tired," he said. "There's so much to see and do. Emily's really looking forward to seeing the Rockettes, aren't you?" He nodded at her, as if giving her a cue, and the reporters leaned forward expectantly. But they weren't looking at her, they were looking at me.

And suddenly it all clicked into place—their wanting to avoid the subject of her being tired, and Torrance's wanting to know what I'd read about the parade, and Emily's encyclopedic knowledge of plays, and the Wall-E balloon.

The parade's robot theme wasn't in honor of *Forbidden Planet*. It was in honor of Dr. Oakes and his "artificials," one of which was standing right in front of me. And those cheeks were produced by sensors; that wide-eyed look and dimpled smile were programmed in.

Torrance, the little rat, had set me up. He'd *counted* on the fact that I only read *Variety* and wouldn't know who Emily was.

And no wonder the media was all here. They were waiting with bated breath for the moment when I realized what was going on. It would make a great YouTube video—my shocked disbelief, Dr. Oakes's self-satisfied smirk, Torrance's laughter.

And if I hadn't tumbled to it, and she'd managed to fool me all the way to the end of the interview with me none the wiser, so much the better. It would be evidence of what Dr. Oakes was obviously here to prove—that his artificials were indistinguishable from humans.

Emily really is Eve Harrington, I thought. *Innocent and sweet and vulnerable-looking. And not at all what she appears to be.*

But if I said that, if I suddenly pointed an accusing finger at her and shouted, "Impostor!" it would blow the image Dr. Oakes and AIS were trying to promote and make Torrance furious. And, from what I'd seen so far, Emily might be capable of bursting into authentic-looking tears, and I'd end up looking like a bully, just like Margo Channing had at the party at the end of Act One of *Bumpy Night,* and there would go any chance I had of getting the lead in *Desk Set.*

But if I went on pretending I hadn't caught on and continued playing the part Torrance had cast me in in this little one-act farce, I'd look like a prize fool. I could see the headline crawl on the *Times* building in Times Square now: "Bumpy Night for Broadway Legend." And "Robot Fools First Lady of the Theater." Not exactly the sort of publicity that gets an actress considered for a Tony.

Plus, the entire point of *Desk Set* was that humans are smarter than technology. *What would Katharine Hepburn do in this situation?* I wondered. *Or Margo Channing?*

"You'll love the Christmas show," Torrance was saying. "Especially the Nativity scene. They have real donkeys and sheep. And camels."

"I'm sure it will be wonderful," Emily said, smiling winsomely over at me, "but I don't see how it can be any better than *Only Human.*"

Only human. Of course. That was why they'd wanted to see the play and come backstage to trick me. *Fasten your seat belts,* I said silently. *It's going to be a bumpy night.*

"And you'll love Radio City Music Hall itself," Torrance said. "It's this beautiful Art Deco building."

Dr. Oakes nodded. "They've offered to give us a tour before the show, haven't they, Emily?"

This was my cue. "Emily," I repeated musingly. "That's such a pretty name. You never hear it anymore. Were you named after someone?"

The reporters looked up as one from their corders and Androids, and Dr. Oakes tensed visibly. Which meant I was right.

"Yes," Emily said. "I was named after Emily Webb from—"

"*Our Town,*" I said, thinking, *Of course.* It was perfect. Except for Little Eva in *Uncle Tom's Cabin,* Emily Webb was the most sickeningly sweet ingénue to ever grace the American stage, tripping girlishly around in a white dress with a big bow in her hair and prattling about how much she loves sunflowers and birthdays and "sleeping and waking up," and then dying tragically at the beginning of Act Three.

"It was her mother's favorite play," Dr. Oakes said. "And Emily was her favorite character."

"Oh," I said, and added casually, "I hadn't realized she was named after someone. I'd just assumed it was an acronym."

"An acronym?" Dr. Oakes said sharply.

"Yes, you know. MLE. For 'Manufactured Lifelike Entity' or something."

There was a dead silence, like the one that follows the revelation that I'm Hope's daughter in the third act of *Only Human,* and the reporters began to thumb their Androids furiously.

I ignored them. "And then I thought it might be your model number," I said to Emily. "Was your face modeled on Martha Scott's? She—"

"Played Emily Webb in the original production, which starred Frank Craven as the Stage Manager," Emily said. "No, actually, it was modeled on Jo Ann Sayers, who played Eileen in—"

"The original Broadway production of *My Sister Eileen,*" I said.

"Yes," she said happily. "I wanted to be named Eileen, but Uncle—

I mean, Dr. Oakes—was worried that the name might suggest the wrong things. Eileen was much sexier than Emily Webb."

And Eileen had caused an uproar everywhere she went, ending up with half of New York and the entire Brazilian navy following her in a wild conga line, something I was sure Dr. Oakes didn't want to have happen with his artificial.

"Women sometimes find sexiness in other women intimidating," Emily said. "I'm designed to be nonthreatening."

"So of course the name Eve was out, too?"

"Yes," she said earnestly. "But we couldn't have used it anyway. It tested badly among religious people. And there was the Wall-E problem. Dr. Oakes didn't want a name that made people immediately think of robots."

"So I suppose the Terminator was out, as well," I said dryly. "And HAL."

The media couldn't restrain themselves any longer. "When did you realize Emily was an artificial?" the *Times* reporter asked.

"From the moment I saw her, of course. After all, acting is my specialty. I knew at once she wasn't the real thing."

"What tipped you off exactly?" the YouTube reporter said.

"Everything," I lied. "Her inflection, her facial expressions, her timing—"

Emily looked stricken.

"But the flaws were all *very* minor," I said reassuringly. "Only someone—"

I'd started to say "Only someone who's been on the stage as long as I have," but caught myself in time.

"Only a pro could have spotted it," I said instead. "Professional actors can spot someone acting when the audience can't."

And that had better be true, or they'd realize I was lying through my teeth. "You're very, very good, Emily," I said, and smiled at her.

She still looked upset, and even though I knew it wasn't real, that there was no actual emotion behind her troubled expression, her bitten lip, I said, "I'm not even certain *I* would have spotted it except that you were so much more knowledgeable about the theater than the young women who usually come backstage. Most of them think *A Little Night Music* is a song from *Twilight: The Musical.*"

All but two of the reporters laughed. They—and Torrance—looked blank.

"You're simply too intelligent for your own good, darling," I said, smiling at her. "You should take a lesson from Carol Channing when she played—"

"Lorelei Lee in *Gentlemen Prefer Blondes*," she said, and then clapped her hand to her mouth.

The reporters laughed.

"But what really tipped me off," I said, squeezing her lifelike-feeling shoulder affectionately, "was that you were the only person your age I've ever met who wasn't stagestruck."

"Oh, dear." Emily looked over at Dr. Oakes. "I *knew* I should have said I wanted to be an actress." She turned back to me. "But I was afraid that might give the impression that I wanted your job, and of course I don't. Artificials don't want to take *anyone's* job away from them."

"Our artificials are designed solely to help humans," Dr. Oakes said, "and to do only tasks that make humans' jobs easier and more pleasant," and this was obviously the company spiel. "They're here to bring an end to those machines everyone hates—the self-service gas pump, the grocery store checkout machine, electronic devices no one can figure out how to program. Wouldn't you rather have a nice young man fixing the bug in your computer than a repair program? Or have a friendly, intelligent operator connect you to the person you need to talk to instead of trying to choose from a dozen options, none of which apply to your situation? Or"—he nodded at me—"tell you who starred in the original production of a musical rather than having to waste time looking it up on Google?"

"And you can do all that?" I asked Emily. "Pump gas and fix computers and spit out twenties?"

"Oh, no," she said, her eyes wide. "I'm not programmed to do any of those things. I was designed to introduce artificials to the public."

And to convince them they weren't a threat, to stand there and look young and decorative. Just like Miss Caswell.

"Emily's merely a prototype," Dr. Oakes said. "The actual artificials will be programmed to do a variety of different jobs. They'll be your maid, your tech support, your personal assistant."

"Just like Eve Harrington," I said.

"What?" Dr. Oakes said, frowning.

"Margo Channing hired Eve Harrington as her personal assistant," Emily explained, "and then she stole Margo's career."

"But that can't happen with artificials," Dr. Oakes said. "They're programmed to assist humans, not supplant them." He beamed at me. "You won't ever have to worry about an Eve Harrington again."

"Dr. Oakes, you said they're forbidden to take our jobs," one of the reporters called out, "but if they're as intelligent as we've just seen Emily is, how do we know they won't figure out a way to get around those rules?"

"Because it's not a question of rules," Dr. Oakes said. "It's a question of programming. A human could 'want' someone else's job. An artificial can't. 'Wanting' is not in their programming."

"But when I asked Emily about her name," I reminded him, "she said she originally wanted to be called Eileen."

"She was speaking metaphorically," Dr. Oakes said. "She didn't 'want' the name in the human sense. She was expressing the fact that she'd made a choice among options and then altered that choice based on additional information. She was simply using the word 'want' as a shortcut for the process."

And to persuade us she thinks just like we do, I thought. In other words, she was acting. "And what about when she said she loved the play?" I asked him.

"I *did* love it," Emily said, and it might all be programming and sophisticated sensors, but she looked genuinely distressed. "Our preferences are just like humans'."

"Then what's to keep them from 'preferring' they had our jobs?" the same reporter asked.

"Yeah," another one chimed in. "Wouldn't it be safer to program them not to have preferences at all?"

"That's not possible," Emily said. "Simulating human behavior requires higher-level thinking, and higher-level thinking requires choosing between options—"

"And often those options are equally valid," Dr. Oakes said, "the choice of which word or facial expression to use, of which information to give or withhold—"

Like the fact that you're an artificial, I thought, wondering if Dr. Oakes would include in his lecture the fact that higher-level thinking involved the ability to lie.

"Or the option of which action to take," he was saying. "Without the ability to choose one thing over another, action, speech—even thought— would be impossible."

"But then what keeps them from 'choosing' to take over?" a third reporter asked.

"They've been programmed to take into consideration the skills and attributes humans have which make them better qualified for the vast majority of jobs. But the qualities which cause humans to *desire* jobs and careers are not programmed in—initiative, drive, and the need to stand out individually."

"Which means your job's safe, Claire," Torrance said.

"Exactly," Dr. Oakes said without irony. "In addition, since artificials' preferences are not emotion-based, they lack the lust for power, sex, and money, the other factors driving job motivation. *And,* as a final safeguard, we've programmed in the impulse to please humans. Isn't that right, Emily?"

"Yes," she said. "I wouldn't want to steal anybody's job. Especially yours, Miss Havilland."

Which is exactly what Eve Harrington said, I thought.

But this was supposed to be a photo op, not a confrontation, and it was clear the reporters—and Torrance—had bought her act hook, line, and sinker, and that if I said anything, I'd come off just like Margo Channing at the party—as a complete bitch.

So I smiled and posed for photos with Emily and when she asked me if I'd go with them to the Radio City Music Hall Christmas Show ("I'm sure the mayor can get us an extra ticket") I didn't say, "Over my dead body."

I said regretfully, "I have a show to do, remember?" And to make Torrance happy, "All of you out there watching, come see *Only Human* at the Nathan Lane Theater on West Forty-fourth Street. Eight o'clock."

🎄

"You were absolutely marvelous!" Torrance said after everyone had gone. "Your best performance ever! We'll be sold out through Easter. I don't suppose you'd be willing to reconsider doing the ice-skating-at-Rockefeller-Center thing? It would make a great photo op. All you'd have to do is put on a cute little skating skirt and spend half an hour gliding around—"

"No skating skirts," I said, stripping off my earrings. "No tights. No—"

"No leotards. Sorry, I forgot. Maybe we can get her back here for a tour of the theater. If we can, we'll be sold out all the way through summer. Or you could invite her to your apartment for luncheon tomorrow."

"No luncheon," I said, wiping off my makeup. "No tours. And no robots."

"Artificials," he corrected automatically, and then frowned. "I thought you liked Emily."

"That's called acting, darling."

"But why don't you like her?"

"Because she's dangerous."

"Dangerous? That sweet little thing?"

"Exactly. That sweet little innocent, adorable, utterly harmless Trojan horse."

"But you heard Dr. Oakes. His artificials are programmed to help people, not steal their jobs."

"And they said movies wouldn't kill vaudeville, the synthesizer wouldn't eliminate the theater orchestra, and CGI sets wouldn't replace the stage crew."

"But you heard him, they've put in safeguards to prevent that. And even if they hadn't, Emily couldn't replace you. She can't act."

"Of course she can act. What do you think she was doing in here for the last hour? Mimicking emotions one doesn't have—I believe that's the definition of acting."

"I can't believe you're worried about this. No one could replace you, Claire. You're one of a kind. You're a—"

"Don't you dare say 'legend.'"

"I was going to say 'a star.' Besides, you heard Emily. She doesn't want to be an actress."

"I heard her, but that doesn't mean she won't be waiting outside that stage door when I leave, asking if she can be my assistant. And the next thing you know, I'll be stuck in the middle of Vermont, out of gas and out of a job."

"Vermont?" Torrance said blankly. "Why are you going to Vermont? You're not thinking of doing summer stock this year, are you?"

Which made me wonder if I should hire her as my personal assistant after all, just to have *someone* around who'd actually seen *Bumpy Night*. And knew what "Dance ten, looks three" meant.

But she wasn't in the crowd of autograph seekers—a crowd considerably smaller than that outside the Majestic, where *Forbidden Planet* was playing, I couldn't help noticing. Nor was she waiting by the limo, nor at my apartment, already making herself at home, like Eve had done in Scene Three.

And she wasn't outside my door when I got up the next morning. The *Post–Daily News* was, no doubt left there by Torrance, with a very nice write-up—a photo and two entire columns about the backstage visit, which I was happy to see did not refer to me as a legend, and half an hour later Torrance called to tell me *Only Human* was sold out through February. "And it's all thanks to you, darling."

"Flattery will get you nowhere," I said. "I'm still not going ice-skating."

"Neither is Emily," he said. "It's pouring rain outside."

Good, I thought. Emily would have to go convince the public she wasn't a threat to them at the Chrysler Building or MOMA or something. *Or if she's such a huge fan of mine, maybe she'll come see* Only Human *again.* But she wasn't in the audience at the matinee.

I was relieved. In spite of Dr. Oakes's assurances that AIS's artificials weren't here to steal our jobs, and Emily's earnest protestations that she didn't want to be an actress, the parallels to *All About Eve* were a bit too close for comfort. I mean, who were we kidding? If artificials weren't a threat, Dr. Oakes and AIS wouldn't be expending so much time and effort convincing us they weren't.

So I wasn't at all unhappy when the rain turned into a sleety downpour just before the evening performance, even though it meant there were cancellations and the audience that did come out smelled like wet wool. They coughed and sneezed their way through both acts and dropped their umbrellas noisily on every important line, but at least Emily wouldn't be waiting for me outside the stage door afterward like Eve Harrington in Scene Two.

In fact, no one was at the stage door or out front, though the sleet apparently hadn't stopped the *Forbidden Planet* fans down the street. A huge crowd of them huddled under umbrellas, clutching their sodden *Playbill*s, waiting for Shiloh and Justin Jr. And so much for Torrance's saying my meeting with Emily would bring in the younger demographic.

My driver Jorge splashed toward me with an open umbrella. I ducked gratefully under its shelter and let him shepherd me toward the waiting limo and into the backseat.

I sat down and shook out the tails of my coat while he went around to the driver's side, and then I bent to see how much damage had been done to my shoes.

A girl was banging on my window with the flat of her hand. I could see the hand but not who it was through the fogged-up window. But whoever it was knew my name. "Miss Havilland!" she called, her voice muffled by the closed window and the traffic going by. "Wait!"

Justin's not the only one with fans who are willing to freeze to death to get an autograph, I thought, and fumbled with the buttons in the door, attempting to roll down the window. "Which button is it?" I asked Jorge as he eased his bulk into the driver's seat.

"The one on the left," he said, slamming his door and starting the car. "If you want, I can drive off."

"And leave a fan?" I said. "Heaven forbid," even though with the week I'd had it would probably only turn out to be a *Forbidden Planet* fan who'd gotten tired of waiting and decided to get my autograph instead of Justin's so she could get in out of the sleety rain. "Signing autographs is a Broadway legend's duty," I said, and pushed the button.

"Oh, *thank* you, Miss Havilland," the girl said, clutching the top of the window as it began to roll down. "I was afraid you were going to drive away."

It was Emily, looking like a drowned rat, her light brown hair plastered to her forehead and cheeks, rain dripping off her eyelashes and nose.

"What are you doing here?" I demanded, though it was obvious. This was exactly like the scene in *Bumpy Night* when Eve told Margo Channing she hadn't eaten for days because she'd spent all her money on tickets to Margo's play.

"I have to talk to you," she said urgently, and I had to admire Dr. Oakes's engineering genius. Emily's cheeks and nose were the vivid red of freezing cold, her lips looked pale under her demure pink lipstick, and the knuckles of her hands, clutching the rolled-down window, were white.

She's not really cold, I told myself. *That's all done with sensors. They're programmed responses.* But it was difficult not to feel sorry for her standing there, the illusion was so perfect.

And it had obviously convinced Jorge. He leaned over the backseat to ask, "Shouldn't you ask her to get in the car?"

No, I thought. *If I do, she'll tell me some sob story, and the next thing you know I'll be hiring her on as my understudy. And I have no intention of being the next Margo Channing, even if she does look pathetic.*

I didn't say that. I said, "Where's Dr. Oakes? I thought you two were supposed to go see the Christmas show at Radio City Music Hall tonight."

"We were . . . we . . . I did," she stammered. "But something happened—"

"To Dr. Oakes?" I said, and had a sudden image of her killing him like Frankenstein's monster and rampaging off into the night.

"No," she said. "He doesn't know I'm gone. I sneaked away so I could talk to you about what happened. Something . . . I . . . something happened to me while I was watching the show."

Of course. "And you decided you want to be an actress after all," I said dryly, or rather, with as much dryness as it was possible to muster with gusts of icy rain blowing on me.

Her eyes widened in a perfect imitation of astonishment. "No. Please, Miss Havilland," she pleaded. "I *have* to talk to you."

"You can't just let her stand out there like that," Jorge said reproachfully. "She'll catch pneumonia."

No, she won't, I thought, but he was right. I couldn't just let her stand out there. The water might short out her electronics or rust her gears or something. And if anyone happened to see her standing there, begging to be let in, I'd look like a monster.

And even if I told them she was a robot, they'd never believe it, seeing her standing there with her red nose and blue lips. And now her teeth were chattering, for God's sake. "Get in the car," I said.

Jorge hurried around to open the door for Emily, and she scrambled in, getting water everywhere. "Thank you *so* much, Miss Havilland," she said, grabbing my hand, and her sensors were even better than I'd thought they were. Her hands felt exactly as icy as a fan's would have, standing out in that sleety rain.

"Turn on the heat," I ordered Jorge. "Emily, where were you when you sneaked away from Dr. Oakes? At Radio City Music Hall?"

"Yes. I told him I needed to go to the ladies' room off the Grand Lounge."

The ladies' room? Just how authentic was she?

"To see the murals," she said. "They were done by Witold Gordon, and they show the history of cosmetics through the ages—Cleopatra and the Greeks and Marie Antoinette and—"

"And something happened to you in the ladies' room?"

"No," she said, frowning. "I told him I was going to the ladies' room so I could sneak out the side door."

Definitely able to lie, I thought. "How long ago was this?" I asked her.

"Eighteen minutes. I ran all the way."

Less than twenty minutes, which hopefully meant Dr. Oakes hadn't panicked yet and filed a "Missing Robot" report. "Jorge, give me your phone," I said.

He did.

"Emily, what's Dr. Oakes's cell phone number?"

"Oh, don't send me back!"

"I won't," I promised. "Tell me his number."

She did.

"This is Claire Havilland," I told him when he answered. "I called to tell you not to worry—Emily's with me. I'm giving her a tour of the theater and then we're going out for some authentic New York cheesecake."

"She can't eat cheesecake. She's an artifi—"

"Yes, I know, but *I* can eat it, and I thought she'd enjoy seeing a genuine theater-district deli. I'll bring her home afterwards. Are you at your hotel?"

He wasn't; he was still at Radio City Music Hall. "The staff and I have been looking for her everywhere. I was about to call the police. Why didn't she tell me you were giving her a tour?"

"It was a simple case of miscommunication," I said. "She thought I'd told you, and I thought you were there when we discussed it," I said, hoping he wouldn't remember we hadn't had any opportunity to talk alone, that he'd been there the entire time. "I am *so* sorry about the mixup, Dr. Oakes."

"She still should have told me she was leaving," he said. "She should have known I'd be worried."

"How could she?" I said. "As you said, she doesn't have human emotions."

"But I specifically programmed her to—"

He wasn't going to let go of it. "You sound hoarse," I said to distract him. "Are you catching a cold?"

"I probably am. I got drenched standing out front waiting for her. If I catch pneumonia because of this—"

"You poor thing," I said, summoning every bit of acting ability I'd acquired over the last twenty-five years in order to sound sympathetic. "Go straight home and get into bed. And have room service send you up a hot toddy. I'll take care of Emily and see she gets home safely," and after a few more disgruntled-parent sounds, he hung up.

"There," I said. "That's taken care of—"

"Are we really going to a deli?" Emily asked unhappily.

"No, not unless you want to. I just told him that to keep him from coming here to the theater. Where would you like to go? Back into the theater? I think Benny's still here. He could let us in."

"Could we just stay here in the car?"

"Certainly," I said, and told Jorge to pull in closer to the curb.

He did, and then got a plaid blanket out of the trunk and put it over Emily's knees. "Oh, but I don't—" she began.

I shook my head at her.

She nodded and let him cover her knees with the blanket and drape his jacket around her shoulders. "Thank you," she said, smiling enchantingly up at him.

"Would you like something hot to drink?" he asked her as if he'd forgotten I was even in the car. "Coffee or—?"

"Oh, no," she said. "I'm afraid I can't—"

"She'll have cocoa," I interrupted, thinking how much I would give to be able to look as young and helplessly appealing as she did, "and bring me a coffee with a shot of rum in it. Not that mud they make at Dark Brew," I added. "Go to Finelli's." Which was six blocks away.

He trotted off obediently. "Good," I said. "Now we can talk. Tell me what's happened. You went to see the Christmas show at Radio City Music Hall. . . ."

"Yes, and it's beautiful. It's *huge,* with gold curtains and chandeliers and statues and this enormous stage—"

"I know. I've been there. You said something happened?"

"Yes, the show started and there was all this singing and dancing, and then the Rockettes came out. They're this group of eighty dancers, though only forty dance in each performance. There were originally sixteen of them, called the Roxyettes, who danced at the Roxy Theater, but when Radio City Music Hall opened in 1932, they were a big hit because of the way they looked on the stage—it's 144 feet wide—and they added twenty more dancers, and then four more, and they've been there ever since. They're all the same height, and they're all dressed alike—"

"I know what the Rockettes do," I said, but there was no stopping her. She was in full spate.

"They've done over a hundred thousand shows, and in the 1970s they *rescued* Radio City Music Hall! It was going to be torn down, and they went out in their Rockette costumes and stood all around the building, asking people to sign petitions to save the building. All eighty of them stood out there. In the middle of winter, when it was snowing and everything—"

I waited for her to pause for breath and then realized that wasn't going to happen. I was going to have to break in and stop her. "The Rockettes came out, and then what happened?" I asked.

"They formed this long, perfectly straight line. They were wearing these red leotards with white fur trim and hats and gold tap shoes. That's one of their traditional Christmas show costumes. They've been doing a Christmas show since 1933—"

At this rate, we could be here all night. I broke in again. "They formed a straight line, and then what?"

"They linked arms and kicked their legs in the air at the same time," she said, her eyes bright with excitement as she described it, "as high as their heads. And all the kicks were to exactly the same height."

I nodded. "That's what the Rockettes are known for. Their precision eye-high kicks."

"And then these skaters came out and skated on a pond—right on the stage—to the song 'A Simple Little Weekend'—"

From *Bumpy Night.*

"And then the Rockettes came out again in pale blue leotards with sequins on the top and silver tap shoes and kicked some more and then—"

Was I going to have to listen to a blow-by-blow of the entire show? "Emily," I said. "What exactly hap—?"

"And then they opened the curtain, and there was a toyshop, and the Rockettes came out dressed as toy soldiers, and they all fell down—"

The Rockettes were famous for that, too, the long line of ramrod-stiff soldiers collapsing like dominoes, one against the other, till they were all in a carefully lined-up pile on the stage.

"And *then*," Emily said, "they came out dressed all in silver with these square boxes on their heads and flashing lights—"

Robots, I thought. *Of course. In keeping with the theme of the Macy's parade and the department stores' Christmas windows.*

"And they all tap-danced," she said breathlessly, "and turned and kicked, all exactly alike. And that was when I realized . . . when you asked me the other night what I wanted to be, I didn't know what you meant. By wanting to be something, I mean. But now I do." She looked up at me with shining eyes. "I want to be a Rockette!"

My first thought was, *Thank God it's the Rockettes and not musical comedy!* I wouldn't have to compete with that youthful innocence, that disarming enthusiasm.

My second thought was, *How ironic!* Dr. Oakes had brought her here specifically to convince people artificials weren't after their jobs, and now here she was announcing she wanted one of the most sought-after jobs in New York. She was now a threat to thousands of aspiring Rockettes, and tens of thousands of little girls in dance classes all over America.

It's his own fault, I thought. *He should have known better than to have let her see them.* Even when they weren't dressed up like robots, they looked like them, with their identical costumes and long legs and smiling faces. And performed like them, their synchronized tap steps, their uniformly executed turns and time steps and kicks. Dr. Oakes should have known it was bound to dazzle her.

Add to that her youth (and I wasn't talking about her sixteen-year-old packaging, I was talking about her lack of experience—and who has less knowledge of the world than a robot?) and the fact that every little girl who'd ever gone to see them had come out of the show wanting to be a Rockette, and what had happened was inevitable.

And impossible. In the first place, she was designed to do photo ops and interviews with unsuspecting dupes, not dance. And in the second place, Dr. Oakes would never let her.

"You can't be a Rockette," I said. "You told me yourself artificials aren't allowed to take humans' jobs."

"But it's *not* a job!" she said passionately. "It's ... jobs are tasks humans *have* to do to keep society functioning and to earn money to pay their living expenses. Being a Rockette is something totally different! It doesn't have anything to do with money. It's like a ... a dream or a ... a quest or ... it's—"

"What I did for love."

"*Yes,*" she said, and now I knew for certain she was stagestruck: she hadn't even noticed that was a line from a Broadway musical.

"But it's still a job," I said. "The Rockettes are paid—"

"They wouldn't have to pay *me*. I'd do it for nothing!"

"And even if artificials were allowed to take humans' jobs, there's still the problem of your height."

"My height?"

"Yes, you're too short. The Rockettes have a height restriction."

"I know. They're all the same height. What is it?"

"They're not actually all one height," I said. "That's an optical illusion. They put the tallest girls in the middle and then go downward to either end."

"Well, then, I could be one of the ends."

I shook my head. "No, you couldn't. You have to be between five foot six and five foot ten, or at any rate that's what it was when I auditioned to be a Rockette. It may have gone up since th—"

"*You* were a Rockette?" she squealed, and it was clear I'd just gone up several notches in her estimation. "Why didn't ... ? It didn't say that in your bio."

"That's because I wasn't one. While the auditions were still going on, I got offered a part in the chorus of *The Drowsy Chaperone,* and I took it. It turned out to be my big break."

"But how could you give up being a *Rockette*? I wouldn't ever want to be anything else!"

It didn't seem like a good idea to tell her I hadn't actually wanted to be a Rockette, that I'd only auditioned because I'd hoped it might get me noticed, or to tell her that when I'd heard I'd made the chorus of *Chaperone,* I'd walked out of the Radio City rehearsal hall without a backward glance.

"You have to tell me what I need to do to become a Rockette," she said, clutching my arm. "I know you have to learn tap dancing—"

"And jazz dancing and ballet. *En pointe.*"

She nodded as if she'd expected that. "I can have those programs installed."

"A program of dance steps isn't the same as actually learning the steps," I said. "It takes *years* of training and hard work to become a dancer."

She nodded. "Like in *A Chorus Line.*"

"Yes, exactly," I said. "But even if you had that experience, it wouldn't matter. You're only—what? Five foot two, at the most?"

"One."

"And the height requirement's five foot six," I said, hoping the appeal to logic would convince her what she wanted wasn't a good idea, as had happened when she'd wanted to be named Eileen. "You're simply too short."

She nodded thoughtfully.

"I'm sorry. I know it's disappointing, but it's all part of being in the theater. I didn't get the part of Fantine in the revival of *Les Mis* because I was too tall. And Bernadette Peters lost the part of—"

She wasn't listening. "What about bingo-bongos?" she asked.

"What?"

"Bingo-bongos. Should I have them done?" and when I still looked blank, "In *A Chorus Line.* The 'Dance Ten, Looks Three' number. Val said she had the bingo-bongos done."

Indeed, she had. She'd been talking about having her breasts enlarged and her derriere lifted, or as she referred to it, having her "tits and ass" done, which I refused to explain to a dewy-eyed innocent. Or a robot.

"It wouldn't do any good," I told her. "As I said, you're not tall enough to meet the height requirement."

"What did you do in the audition?"

She was too stagestruck to hear a word I was saying. "I'm trying to explain, you won't make the first *cut* for the aud—"

"What did you have to do?"

"They taught us a series of combinations, which we did in groups of three. And then if we made callbacks, we had to learn a full routine, with time steps and kicks, and do a tap solo."

"What did you do for your solo?"

"'Anything Goes.' But you won't *get* to do a solo. You won't even make the initial cut. You're too short. And even if you met all the requirements, you'd only have a miniscule chance of getting in. Hundreds of dancers audition every year, and only one or two make it. I'm not trying to discourage you, Emily," I said, even though that was exactly what I was trying to do. "I'm just trying to be realistic."

She nodded and was silent for a moment. "Thank you for all the advice, Miss Havilland. You've been most awfully kind," she said, and was out of the car and splashing down the street through the rain, which was coming down harder than ever.

"Emily!" I shouted, "Wait!" but by the time I got the window down, she was half a block away.

"Come back!" I called after her. "I know you're disappointed, but you can't walk home in this. Jorge will be back in a few minutes. He'll drive you home. It's late, and your hotel is *miles* from here."

She shook her head, flinging raindrops everywhere. "It's only forty-five blocks," she said cheerfully, and vanished around the corner.

Jorge, arriving moments later with two cardboard cups, was furious. "You let her walk home in the rain?" he said disapprovingly. "She'll catch pneumonia."

"She can't," I said, but he wasn't listening to me, either.

"Poor kid," he muttered, pulling away from the curb with a jerk that spilled coffee all over me. "Poor little thing!"

"Poor little thing" was right. Because even if she could charm the choreographer into waiving the height requirement (which wasn't entirely out of the realm of possibility, given her programmed-in charm), there was no chance at all of Dr. Oakes's allowing her to be a Rockette. It would undermine the image he and AIS were trying to convince the public of. Even her raising the possibility of being a Rockette would be too dangerous. *He'll cut short their tour, and they'll be out of here on the next plane,* I thought. *If they haven't left already.*

But the next morning, there she was on TV, smiling and waving from

the foot of the Statue of Liberty and later from a horse-drawn carriage in
Central Park, and on Monday night there was coverage of her charming
the pants off reporters and the TSA as she and Dr. Oakes went through
security at LaGuardia on their way home, with no sign that she'd had her
hopes dashed.

"Will you be coming back to the Big Apple soon, Emily?" one of the
dozens of reporters asked her.

"No, I'm afraid not," she said, and there wasn't even a hint of regret in
her voice. "I had a wonderful time here in New York! The Empire State
Building and everything! I especially loved seeing *Only Human*."

Well, at least Torrance will be happy about her mentioning the play, I
thought, waiting to hear what she'd say about the Rockettes.

"What did you think of the Radio City Christmas show?" the reporter
asked.

She smiled winsomely. "I loved the Nativity scene. They had real camels and everything!"

"Where do you go next, Emily?" another reporter asked. "Back to San
Jose?"

"Yes, and then we'll be in Williamsburg for Christmas."

"And then L.A. for the Rose Bowl parade," Dr. Oakes said. "You're
really looking forward to that, aren't you, Emily?"

"Oh, yes," she said, dimpling. "I *love* flowers! And football!"

"One last question," the reporter said. "What was your favorite part of
your visit?"

Here it comes, I thought.

"Meeting Claire Havilland. She's *such* an amazing actress!"

I suppose I should have been grateful to her, especially when Torrance
called the next day to tell me *Only Human* was sold out through Easter
and three days later to say Austerman wanted to have lunch with me to
talk about *Desk Set.*

But I wasn't. I was suspicious. That touching little scene in my car
had obviously been just that—a scene, performed by a very skilled
actress—and she hadn't fallen in love with the Rockettes at all. But then
what had its purpose been? To soften me up like Eve Harrington's made-

up story about seeing Margo Channing in a play and falling in love with
the theater, so that she could worm her way into my life?

I half expected her to be in the audience on Tuesday night, in spite of
the LaGuardia scene, but she wasn't, and on the way home after the
show, Jorge told me there'd been a story on the radio about their arrival
in California.

"Did she say anything about the Rockettes?" I asked him.

"No. She didn't say anything about your making her walk halfway
across Manhattan in a rainstorm, either." He glared at me in the rearview
mirror. "You're lucky she didn't catch her death of cold."

She wasn't in the Saturday matinee audience either, or backstage after
the show, and by the middle of December I had more important things to
worry about, like Austerman's insistence on a dream-sequence number in
Desk Set with me in, you guessed it, a leotard and fishnet stockings.

Add to that the management's decision to put an additional matinee
on the schedule because of increased ticket demand, Austerman's wanting me to help audition the Spencer Tracy role, and every reporter in
town wanting to do an interview on *Only Human*'s Tony nomination
prospects. By mid-December I was exhausted.

Which was why I was taking a nap in my dressing room before the
show when Benny the stage manager knocked and said there was someone to see me. "A Cassie Ferguson," he said. "She says she knows you."

"Cassie what?" I said blurrily, wondering if that was the name of Austerman's assistant. "What does she look like?"

"Blond, tall, hot."

All of Austerman's assistants were tall, blond, and hot. He was as bad
as Miss Caswell's producer boyfriend. And if she was from Austerman, I
couldn't afford to let her see me like this. The nap had added ten years
to my face. "Tell her I'm doing an interview with *Tiger Beat* and I'll meet
with her during intermission."

He looked unhappy. "She said she needed to see you right away."

"Oh, all right," I said. "Give me five minutes and then send her in," and
frantically started to repair my makeup, but almost immediately there
was a second knock on the door.

Benny was right. She was a knockout: tall and leggy, with gorgeous
long blond hair, and, even though she was wearing a belted raincoat, it
was obvious she had a great figure.

"Well?" she said. "What do you think?"

"Emily!" I said, staring. "My God! What—?"

"I had the bingo-bongos done," she said happily.

"I can see that."

"I was just going to get longer legs, but the proportions didn't look right, so, since I had to get a new torso anyway, I thought I might as well get a new ass, like in the song, and new—"

"But why?" I said.

"To meet the height requirement," she said, as if it were self-evident.

Oh, my God, I thought. *She was serious. She's going to try to become a Rockette.*

"The upper limit's five ten and a half," she said, "but the median of the current Rockettes is five nine, so I went with that and with thirty-six for my chest. I did a C so I could be sure I'd fit in a size six—that's the most common costume size. And people tend to be less intimidated by flatter-chested girls."

She untied the belt and opened her raincoat wide to reveal a spaghetti-strap black leotard and sheer tights.

"Hot" was an understatement. She had definitely had the bingo-bongos done.

It was too bad Torrance wasn't here. "*This*," I would have told him, "is what one is supposed to look like in a leotard. Which is why I have no intention of wearing one in *Desk Set* or anywhere else."

"Do you think I should have gone with a D instead?" Emily asked.

"No," I said.

"What about my outfit? Is it all right for the audition? I analyzed audition videos and photos from the past ten years, and this was the most common, but some of the dancers wore colored leotards or leggings, and I was wondering if I should do that to make them notice me."

"Trust me, they'll notice you," I said.

"What about my shoes?" she said, sticking out her foot and pointing a toe in a T-strap black tap shoe. "The audition brochure said character heels, but I didn't know if I should wear black or beige."

"Black," I said. "But auditions aren't till summer."

"I know, but they have a vacancy they need to fill."

Good God, I thought. *She's killed a Rockette,* and she must have guessed what I was thinking because she said, "A Rockette on one of the tours quit to get married, and they had to replace her with one of the New York troupe, so they're holding a special audition."

"But you have to know how to tap dance—"

"I do," she said. "And I've learned jazz, modern, and ballet. Here, I brought an audition tape." She pulled out an Android, swiped through several screens, and handed it to me.

And there she was, tap-dancing, executing flawless time steps and cramp rolls and Maxie Fords—and the eye-high kicks the Rockettes were famous for.

"I've had all the choreography terms programmed in, and I've memorized three different routines for my audition solo—'Anything Goes' and 'One' from *A Chorus Line* and '42nd Street.' Which one do you think I should do?"

"Emily—"

"I learned all the routines from the Christmas show, too, but I wasn't sure I should do one of those," she said. "Oh, and what about my hair? Is blond okay? Sixty-two percent of the Rockettes are blondes."

"Blond is more than okay," I said.

"And you think I look like a Rockette?"

Like the perfect Rockette. "Yes," I said.

"What about my face? The age requirement's eighteen, so I had it altered to look older—"

She had. Her cheekbones were more defined, and her face thinner, though it was still recognizably Emily's and had retained the wide, innocent eyes and the disarming smile.

"—but I was wondering if I should change it to look more like the other Rockettes. I made a composite of the current troupe's faces, and it has a straighter nose and fuller lips."

And much less vulnerability, I thought. A modern-woman-in-Manhattan-who's-had-lots-of-bad-experiences-and-worse-boyfriends face. The idea of Emily with that face was unthinkable.

And besides, if she was actually going to try and become a Rockette, she would need all the help she could get. And her face was her biggest weapon. *Well, not her biggest,* I thought. But definitely a weapon, as witness the reporters' behavior at that backstage interview. And Jorge's.

"What do you think?" Emily asked. "Should I change my face?"

"No," I said. "Absolutely not," and posed the question I should have asked in the first place, especially since he was liable to come bursting in here any minute. "What does Dr. Oakes say about all this? Did he authorize these changes?"

"No, of course not," she said. "He'd never let me do this. I got some of the engineers to help me."

"How did you talk them into it?" I was about to ask, and then realized I already knew. She'd charmed them just like she'd charmed Jorge and the TSA. "And Dr. Oakes didn't object?"

"No. He doesn't know about it. He's in Japan with Aiko."

Of course, I thought. *He's off introducing his artificials to other countries.* And different cultures would have different ideas of what was threatening about artificials. They'd require different models, all with faces and names carefully chosen to make them seem harmless: an Aiko even shorter than the original Emily for Japan, and a Rashmika for India, a Mei-Li for China.

And meanwhile his American model had turned into a combination of Eliza Doolittle and Frankenstein's monster.

"I'm not sure you're right about my keeping the face," she said. "What if one of the Rockettes recognizes me? I met some of them that night at Radio City Music Hall."

And they'd have seen her on the news or in that interview with me. "So you were planning to audition as Cassie somebody?"

"Ferguson. Yes, because the rules say you have to be at least eighteen years old, and I'm only one."

One. But what a one! "Definitely a singular sensation," I murmured under my breath.

"You don't think I should do that?" she asked anxiously. "I know it's lying, but if they know I'm an artificial—"

They'll never let you audition, I thought. They'd have exactly the same reaction I'd had, and Emily was even more of a threat to them than she had been to me. As Torrance had said, actresses get where they are by being one of a kind, but with the Rockettes, sameness was the whole point.

And the Rockettes weren't stupid. They'd see instantly that if one of them could be replaced, all of them could, and that once the management realized they could have Rockettes who didn't want health benefits or time-and-a-half for overtime, it would be all over.

So she was going to have to lie and tell them she was a human. But she'd never get away with it. Even if she managed to fool them at the audition, she wouldn't make it through her first rehearsal. She didn't sweat, she didn't get out of breath, she didn't make mistakes. And she could learn an entire tap routine by watching it once. They'd spot her instantly.

Emily was watching me with a worried expression. "You don't think I should tell them I'm human?"

"I don't know. Let me think," I said, wishing I had Emily's computer brain to help me figure out what to tell her. I knew what I should tell her: the cold hard truth. That there was no way she could ever be a Rockette and she should go back home to San Jose and do what she'd been designed to do.

It would be much kinder than letting her batter herself to death trying, like a moth against a porch light. But I also knew she wouldn't listen, any more than I had when I was eighteen.

"What do you think?" Emily was asking me. "Should I put 'artificial' on my audition form?"

"No," I said. "You're not going to audition."

"But you can't become a Rockette if you don't audition."

"Only if you're an ordinary human," I said. "When does Dr. Oakes get back from Japan?"

"Not till the twenty-second. That's when we were supposed to go to Williamsburg for Christmas."

The twenty-second was a week away, but we didn't actually have that much time. AIS would already be looking for Emily. Multinational corporations don't just let a valuable piece of equipment walk away, especially one who was ruining any hope they had of selling the idea of artificials to the public.

On the other hand, they could hardly let it get out that one of their "perfectly harmless" robots had gone rogue. They'd have to look for her through private channels, which would slow them down. And even if they did decide to go public and had the police put out an APB on her, they'd be looking for a five-foot-one sixteen-year-old with light brown hair, which gave us a little time.

But the minute Emily went public, they'd come after her and Dr. Oakes would be on the first plane home from Japan. So we'd have to make sure that by the time he got here he wouldn't be able to do anything.

"All right, Emily," I said. "Here's what we're going to do. You're going to go on every news and talk and late-night show we can find and tell them how much you want to be a Rockette. You're going to tell them all those things you told me that night in the limo, how the Rockettes started and what they've done over the years—dancing in the Macy's Parade and saving Radio City Music Hall. And you're going to tell them all the things *you've* done so that you could become a Rockette—how you learned to dance and memorized the routines and studied their history. We're going to convince them you deserve to be one of them."

That wasn't quite true. What we were going to do was convince the *public* she deserved to be a Rockette and hope the resulting pressure would force the Rockettes to let her in. "Do you remember the names of the talk show hosts who interviewed you when you were here for the Macy's parade?" I asked her.

"Of course."

Of course. "Good. I want you to make a list of them and how we can contact them."

"Do you want me to call them and set up interviews?"

"No, we don't want anyone to know where you are till you show up for the interviews. I'm going to send you to my apartment—Jorge will take you—and I want you to use my computer to find some photographs of Rockette costumes. Preferably one of their Christmas costumes—if we can tie this in with Christmas, it will help. People love Christmas stories with happy endings. Find a photograph, and then call Jorge and have him come and get it and bring it back here to our wardrobe mistress—"

"Why?"

"So you can wear it to these interviews. We're going to arrange for you to dance as part of your appearances. You can do one of the routines you learned."

"But—"

"I know, it won't be the same as doing the routine with the Rockettes, but it's a way to show them what you can do. Think of it as your audition. You can do that, can't you?"

"Of course," she said. "It's just that a photo's not necessary. I've already made all the costumes."

"All the . . . you made all the costumes in the Christmas show?"

"No. I made all the costumes the Rockettes have ever worn."

🎄

The plan worked even better than I'd envisioned. Emily went on all the shows and tapped and talked her way into their audiences' hearts, modeling an array of costumes, from the costume of the original Roxyettes to Bob Mackie's "Shine," with its three thousand Swarovski crystals, to the merry-go-round horse costume the Rockettes had worn at the "last" performance, when it had looked like Radio City Music Hall would be torn down, and regaling her enraptured hosts with little-known facts about the Rockettes: that before coming to New York, they had danced in St. Louis as the Missouri Rockets; that in the days when they danced between movie showings, they had practically lived at Radio City Music Hall, sleeping on cots and eating at a special canteen set up for them; that in the open competition at the Paris Exposition, they had defeated the Russians and the *corps de ballet* of the Paris Opera.

"Lucille Bremer was a Rockette," she told them. "You know, Judy Garland's older sister in *Meet Me in St. Louis.* And Vera Ellen, from *White Christmas,* but she kept showing off. A good Rockette never tries to stand out. She tries to dance just like every other Rockette."

And on every show and podcast she told the story of how the Rockettes had saved Radio City Music Hall, standing outside and asking passersby to sign a petition to make the building a national landmark. "They went on TV and radio shows just like this one to plead their cause," she said, "and they all testified at the Landmarks Commission hearing. They did a kick line with the mayor on the steps outside."

The audiences ate it—and her own eye-high kicks—up, and her appearances became instant YouTube hits. One, in which she talked reverently about why being a Rockette meant so much to her, went viral.

The only hitch was Torrance, who thought I was taking a huge risk by helping her. "It's dangerous," he said. "There's a lot of hostility to artificials out there. Some of it could spill over to you, and then there goes your Tony nomination."

"I thought you were the one who was convinced Emily was harmless," I said.

"That was before she decided she wanted to be a Rockette," he said disgustedly. "And why are you so set on helping her? I thought you hated her."

"I just didn't want her trying to steal my career. And if she gets to be a Rockette, she won't be, and Jeannette will be safe."

"Jeannette? Who's Jeannette?"

"The role I have been playing eight times a week for the past year," I said. "A fact which Emily would know."

"And that's why you're helping her? Because she knows what parts you've played?"

"Yes. And because if I get that Tony nomination you're so worried about me losing, it will be thanks to all the publicity Emily gave me. I'm just repaying the favor."

"Ha!" he said. "You know what I think? *I* think you orchestrated this whole PR thing to set her up."

Like Eve Harrington had set up Margo Channing, siphoning gas from her car and stranding her in Vermont so she could take her place.

"Are you sure you didn't put her on all those TV shows so Dr. Oakes would find out where she is and take her home?" Torrance asked.

And if I did, wouldn't that be a good thing? And not only for me, for everybody else who happens to be "only human"? I mean, she could rattle off the names of every play and musical and movie ever done and their cast lists *and* their song lyrics and librettos and dance routines and scripts. And when she was asking all those questions about what to wear to the audition, she'd said, "Should I wear my hair in a topknot?"

"No, a ponytail," I'd told her. "With a rose scarf to bring out the color in your cheeks."

"Should I make them pinker?" she asked, and she wasn't talking about makeup.

How can anyone compete against that? Or the fact that she'd never miss a step. Or forget her lines. Or get old.

Torrance was right. She *was* dangerous.

But I didn't say that. I said, "I'm just trying to help her. And me. If she's a Rockette, she can't steal Bunny out from under me."

"Bunny?" he said, looking confused. "Is that Margo Channing's husband? The one Eve tries to steal?"

"No. It's the lead in *Desk Set*. The musical Austerman's doing," I said wryly. "Ring a bell?"

If they turn her down for the Rockettes, I thought, *I'm firing Torrance and making* her *my manager.*

But it didn't look like they'd turn her down. After only two days of appearances, the public and press response to Emily was overwhelmingly positive, and the Rockettes who were questioned by reporters as to what they thought of her chances said things like, "She knows more about the Rockettes than we Rockettes do," and "I don't know. I mean, I'm worried about artificials taking over and everything, but she wants it so *bad!*" and I thought, *Good God, she's actually going to pull it off.*

So it was a shock when she showed up after the Wednesday matinee. "I thought you were doing *The View*," I said.

She shook her head, looking so pale I thought her sensors must have malfunctioned. "They just changed the rules for being a Rockette so I don't qualify," she said.

"Then you'll have to do what you did before," I said firmly. "Change yourself so you do meet them."

"I can't," she said, and showed me the new rule.

"No artificials," it read. *Only humans need apply,* I thought.

"Then we have to make them change the rule," I said.

"How?"

"We're going to make them look like monsters for picking on a sweet, harmless child like you. Do you remember the party scene from *Bumpy Night*? Where Margo Channing tries to expose Eve and says all those terrible things to her?"

She nodded.

"And do you remember how it backfired? How it made Margo look like a bully and Eve look like a victim? Well, that's what we're going to do. Can you cry?"

"No, but I can look really sad."

"Good. You're going to do that. And you're going to look helpless and victimized. I want you to go watch *All About Eve* and memorize Eve's tone of voice and mannerisms while I write the script you're going to follow. You never wanted to hurt anyone or cause any trouble. You just admire the Rockettes so much!"

"But—" Emily said, looking up at me with those wide, innocent eyes. "I don't want to be Eve Harrington. She's not a nice person."

"Let me tell you a little secret, Emily," I said. "Nearly every actress is Eve Harrington at some point or other and has lied about her age or used her feminine wiles or taken unfair advantage to get a part. How do you think Margo Channing knew what Eve was up to?" I asked her. "Because when she looked at her, she reminded her of herself."

"Did you ever do anything like—?"

"Of course. I lied about my age and my Off-Broadway experience when I tried out for *Love, Etc.* And when I found out they'd moved the audition time I didn't tell anybody." And I had slept with the director.

"But I got what I wanted," I said. I looked at her. "How badly do you want to be a Rockette?"

And Dr. Oakes was wrong. He'd said his artificials had been designed to lack initiative, drive, preference. But once you wire in preference, even if it's only the ability to choose one word, one gesture over another, everything else comes with it. And when he'd put in safeguards against all those driving forces—lust and greed and ambition—he'd forgotten the most dangerous one of all, the one that overrides all the others.

Torrance wasn't the only one who could have benefited from watching a few musicals. If Dr. Oakes had seen *A Chorus Line,* this never would have happened. And he'd have known what was going to happen when I asked Emily what she was willing to do to be a Rockette.

"Well?" I said, repeating the question. "How much do you want to be a Rockette?"

She raised her artificial chin and looked steadily at me. "More than anything else in the world."

She wanted to know how we planned to make the Rockettes management look like bullies.

"Do you remember how the Rockettes saved Radio City Music Hall?" I said. "Well, you're going to make them make you a Rockette the same way. What's the weather like this week?"

"A high of twenty degrees Fahrenheit with a rain-snow mix."

"Good," I said, remembering her standing outside my car in the rain, shivering and bedraggled. "I want you to wear the skimpiest Rockette costume there is, preferably something with a feathered headdress. And mascara that runs. And I know you don't wear mascara," I said before she could interrupt me. "But you're going to wear it for this. You're going to stand out there twenty-four hours a day looking half frozen, asking people to sign a petition to make them change the rules so you can be a Rockette, and I'm going to see to it the media's there to film it."

I picked up the phone to call Torrance and have him arrange for the camera crews.

"But they know artificials can't feel cold or heat—"

"It doesn't matter, trust me," I said, thinking of Jorge, who still wasn't speaking to me. "I want you to shiver and do the teeth-chattering thing, and when passersby ask you if you're all right, you need to say, 'Yes, I'm just so *cold*!' and ask them to sign your petition."

"But won't the rain-snow mix run the signatures?"

"Yes, which is even better. It'll look like tears."

"But—"

"This isn't about getting signatures. It's about making the Rockettes management look like bullies."

"But I don't see how . . . Margo said mean things to Eve. . . ."

"And they're making you stand outside," I said. "At Christmas. In the rain. Trust me, they'll look like bullies. And people don't like to look like bullies—or like the kind of people who'd let a historic landmark be torn down. They like to see themselves as the hero who rescues the building— or damsel—in distress. You stand out there in the rain in a skimpy strap-less costume, and by Friday the Rockettes will be begging you to join them. And if it starts snowing, we'll have action by Thursday."

It didn't take even that long. When I called Torrance the next morning to ask him when the film crews were going to be there, he said, "There's no point in sending them. It's all over."

"You mean, they got rid of the 'no artificials' rule? That's wonderful!"

"No," he said. "I mean she's over wanting to be a Rockette."

"Over?"

"Oakes reprogrammed her."

"Reprogrammed her," I repeated dully. "When?"

"This morning. I thought you'd be pleased. It means you won't have to worry about her poaching your career anymore. Oh, and speaking of your career, Austerman called and said this'll be great publicity for *Desk Set*. You know, '*Only Human* Actress Sends Artificial Packing.' He said it'll make you a shoo-in for the Tony nomination. So it's just like the ending of *Bumpy Night,* only this time Margo wins the Tony, not Eve."

"It wasn't a Tony," I said. "It was the Sarah Siddons Award, which you'd know if you ever watched the play." *Like Emily did,* I thought.

"I don't know what you're so upset about," Torrance said. "She changed her height and her measurements and her hair color. This is no different."

Yes, it is. "Did they erase her entire memory?" I asked. "When they reprogrammed her?" All those plays and cast lists and lines, all that Rockette history.

"No, no, nothing like that," Torrance said. "According to Dr. Oakes, they just made a couple of adjustments to her software. They tamped down the preference thing so she wouldn't have such a strong response to the Rockette stimulus and adjusted her obstacle-to-action ratio. But she's still the same Emily."

No, she's not, I thought. *The real Emily wanted to be a Rockette.*

🦌

So here I am, standing in a freezing snow-rain mix in the leotard and fishnet stockings I swore I'd never be seen in, plus the trademark maroon-and-gold Rockette cap, which is doing nothing at all to keep the rain from dripping down the back of my neck.

I am clutching a clipboard for warmth and trying not to shiver convulsively as I accost passersby and attempt to get them to sign a petition to get Emily's software put back the way they found it and the Rockettes' rules changed so she can have a shot at her heart's desire.

And yes, I know artificials don't have hearts, and what about all the human girls out there between five foot six and five ten and a half with tap, jazz, and ballet experience whose job she'll be stealing?

And yes, I know I'm probably also opening the floodgates to a horde of robots whose dream it is to be ballerinas and neurophysicists and traffic controllers, and that I'll go back to my dressing room some night in the near future to find some disarming young woman who's the spitting image of Anne Baxter and wants to be my assistant, and I'll be really sorry I did this.

But I didn't have any choice. When I announced I wanted to be on Broadway, my mother told me I'd be mugged and raped and pushed onto the subway tracks, my father told me I'd end up broke and waiting tables, and the first three agents and five directors I auditioned for told me to "go back to Kansas and get married, sweetheart." Everybody had done everything they could think of to talk me out of it.

But they hadn't had me lobotomized. They hadn't cut out my stage-struck heart and replaced it with one that would have been willing to settle down in Topeka and have babies. Or adjusted my obstacle-to-action ratio so I'd give up and go home.

So here I stand, trying to blow some warmth into my frozen fingers and wishing I'd worn a warmer costume and that my skin turned rosy like Emily's when it gets cold.

It doesn't. When cellulite gets cold, it turns a mottled purple and ash gray. The rain's washed away every bit of my age-defying makeup; I've completely lost my voice from calling to passersby to come sign my petition, so heaven knows how I'm going to get through tonight's performance; and Torrance dropped by a few minutes ago to tell me I was making a fool of myself and jeopardizing the *Desk Set* lead *and* the Tony.

And in three days out here I've collected signatures from exactly eighteen people, including Torrance (I told him if he didn't sign it, I was getting a new manager), Jorge (who said sternly, "Now you know how it feels to be made to stand out in the freezing cold"), and a couple of teenagers who didn't care what they were signing so long as it got them on TV.

But the camera crews left an hour ago, driven inside by the icy rain and the fact that nothing was happening, and now it looks like it's going to snow, so the only thing that will bring them back is the discovery of my huddled, frozen body in a snowdrift. Even the tourists are giving up and going home. In a few minutes the only people left on the premises will be the Rockettes, and I haven't seen hide nor hair of them since I started this. They must be going in and out a door on the other side of the building to avoid me.

No, wait, here comes one out of the same side door Emily used that night she ran away to talk to me. The young woman's definitely a Rockette. Her coffee-colored legs are even longer than Emily's, and she's dressed like a Christmas present, with a wide candy-cane-striped red and green sash slanting over one dark shoulder and tied in a Christmas bow at her hip.

She looks cautiously around, and I think, disappointed, *She just sneaked out for a cigarette,* but no, after a second look around, she shuts the door silently behind her and hurries over to me, her character heels tap-tap-tapping on the sidewalk.

"Hi, my name's Leonda," she says, hugging her arms to her chest. "Brr, it's *cold* out here!"

"Did you come out to sign my petition?" I ask hopefully. The Rockettes resisted hiring minorities for a long time. They claimed audiences would be distracted if the Rockettes didn't all look exactly alike, including the color of their skin, and (according to Emily when she did the *Today* show) they'd resisted doing the right thing till 1982, when they'd finally hired the first African American, and three years after that, the first Asian American. Maybe Leonda heard Emily say that and decided she had to do the right thing, too, even if it *did* mean risking her job.

Or not. "Oh, no, I can't sign it," she says, glancing anxiously back at the side door. "I just wanted to tell you what a wonderful actress I think you are, Miss Havilland. I saw you in *The Drowsy Chaperone* when I was a little girl, and you were amazing!" She looks at me with starry eyes. "Seeing you was why I decided to be a dancer, and I was wondering if I could have your autogr—?"

"Leonda!" someone shouts from the door.

Another Rockette, dressed as a toy soldier, is leaning out, frowning. "What are you doing out here?" she says. "You've got to get changed! It's almost time!"

"I was just . . . Sorry," she says to me, and runs back to the door, her taps echoing on the wet pavement.

"I'll give you my autograph if you'll sign my petition," I call after her, but she's already gone back inside, and it's clear they aren't going to rise to the occasion like they did when Radio City Music Hall was about to be torn down. Or maybe Emily was wrong about them, and they weren't wonderful. Maybe they hadn't been trying to do something noble after all. They'd just been trying to hang on to their jobs.

And of course now that the two Rockettes are gone, a *TMZ* reporter and a cameraman with his videocam wrapped in plastic to protect it from the rain show up, looking annoyed. "Where are the Rockettes?" the reporter demands. "We were told to get over here because something was going on. So where are they?"

"There was one here just a minute ago," I say, but that's clearly not good enough, and to add insult to injury, a cab driver rolls down his window and leans out into the rain to shout, "Traitor! What the hell are ya doin' standin' out there trying to get a robot a job? Why don't you stick up for your own kind, lady?" and of course the cameraman's getting it all.

"That's First Lady of the Theater to you!" I shout back at the cabbie, and he waves a hand dismissively and drives off.

"How do you answer that question?" the reporter asks, sticking a microphone in my face. "Why *aren't* you sticking up for your own kind?"

"I am," I say. "I'm sticking up for the Rockettes and for the theater. They've always stood courageously for doing what's right," a speech which would have been more impressive if I thought it was true. And if my teeth weren't chattering. "I'm also, in spite of what he thinks, standing up for the human race. If we're going to make humanity such a hard show to get into, then we'd better make sure it's worth auditioning for by acting the way humans are supposed to."

"Which is?"

"Humane."

"And that's why you're doing this," he says skeptically.

"Yes," I tell him, but I'm lying. I'm not doing this to defend a noble cause, or because Emily looked like Peggy in *42nd Street* or the poor, doomed heroine of *Our Town*.

I'm out here ruining my voice and my chance at ever getting a decent role again because that night in my limo, sitting there in her drenched coat, pouring out her nonexistent heart about tap steps and precision kicks, she had looked like me.

And I realize for the first time that that's why Margo Channing helped Eve Harrington. Not because Eve manipulated her into it, but because when she looked at her, she saw her younger, stagestruck self, that girl who'd fallen in love, who just wanted a shot at doing what she'd been born to do.

If they ever do a revival of *Bumpy Night* and I get to play Margo again, I'll have to remember that. It could add a whole new dimension to the character.

But at this point, getting the part—or any part, even Mama Morton—looks extremely doubtful. The reporter wasn't at all impressed with my "proud tradition of the theater and humanity" speech. For the entire length of it, he was looking past me, scanning for possible Rockettes.

But they're not going to show, and the reporter's apparently reached the same conclusion. "I told you they were getting us over here for nothing," he says to the cameraman.

The cameraman nods and lowers the plastic-covered camera from his shoulder.

"Let's go," the reporter says. "I'm freezing my balls off out here."

"Wait," I say, grabbing his arm. "Won't you at least sign my petition before you go?" But they're not listening. They're looking over at the side door, which is opening again.

It's only Leonda, I think, back for a second try at an autograph—which she is *not* going to get—but it's not. It's the Rockette who yelled at her before. She's changed out of her toy soldier getup into the Rockettes' signature red and white fur Christmas costume, and, as we watch, she pushes the door wide, braces it open with her gold-shod foot, and makes a beckoning motion to whoever's inside.

And out comes a Rockette dressed just like her who's . . . oh, my God! holding a clipboard. And on her heels is another Rockette. And another. And Leonda, who as she passes me turns her clipboard so I can see the petition and whispers, "I'd already signed mine. That's why I couldn't sign yours," and smiles a smile almost as sweet and disarming as Emily's.

"Are you getting this?" I ask the cameraman, but of course he is. Because what a glorious sight! They march out, heads up, chests out, as oblivious to the frigid wind as if they were Emily, even though I know it's cutting right through those tights, right through the toes of those gold tap shoes.

Here they come in a gorgeous, unending line that is going to go all the way around the building, every one of them in a red leotard and white fur hat. And TMZ isn't the only one getting this. Other camera crews are arriving every minute, and so are tourists, holding up their cell phones and Androids to record this. Taxi drivers are slowing down to whistle and cheer, Jorge shows up with a cup of hot brandy-laced coffee for me, and even though the Rockettes aren't even all out the door yet, people are flocking around them, wanting to sign their petitions. And mine.

The only thing that could make this a better finale is if it would start snowing, which it does just as the last of the Rockettes step smartly out the door. Starry white flakes fall on their white fur hats and their eyelashes as they move into position, and their cheeks are almost as pink as Emily's.

They take up their places, eighty Rockettes and—I find out later—thirty-two former Rockettes and every female dancer from *A Chorus Line, Forbidden Planet,* and *Almost Human.* And the chorus line from *La Cage aux Folles.* And they all stand there, backs straight, heads held high, facing into the bitter wind that seems always to be whipping around Radio City Music Hall, with their petitions and their fabulous legs and their knock-'em-dead smiles. And right now even I want to be a Rockette.

They're all in place now, every last one of them dressed in golden tap shoes and a red and white fur costume. Except for me. And the last eight out the door, who station themselves on either side of me, right beneath Radio City Music Hall's chrome-and-neon marquee.

They're dressed as robots.

Inn

Christmas Eve. *The organ played the last notes of "O Come, O Come, Emmanuel," and the choir sat down. Reverend Wall hobbled slowly to the pulpit, clutching his sheaf of yellowed typewritten sheets.*

In the choir, Dee leaned over to Sharon and whispered, "Here we go. Twenty-four minutes and counting."

On Sharon's other side, Virginia murmured, "'And all went to be taxed, every one into his own city.'"

Reverend Wall set the papers on the pulpit, looked rheumily out over the congregation, and said, "'And all went to be taxed, every one into his own city. And Joseph also went up from Galilee, out of the city of Nazareth, into Judea, unto the city of David, which is called Bethlehem, because he was of the house and lineage of David. To be taxed with Mary, his espoused wife, being great with child.'" He paused.

"We know nothing of that journey up from Nazareth," Virginia whispered.

"We know nothing of that journey up from Nazareth," Reverend Wall said, in a wavering voice, "what adventures befell the young couple, what inns they stopped at along the way. All we know is that on a Christmas Eve like this one they arrived in Bethlehem, and there was no room for them at the inn."

Virginia was scribbling something on the margin of her bulletin. Dee started to cough. "Do you have any cough drops?" she whispered to Sharon.

"What happened to the ones I gave you last night?" Sharon whispered back.

"Though we know nothing of their journey," Reverend Wall said, his voice growing stronger, "we know much of the world they lived in. It was a world of censuses and soldiers, of bureaucrats and politicians, a world busy with property and rules and its own affairs."

Dee started to cough again. She rummaged in the pocket of her music folder and came up with a paper-wrapped cough drop. She unwrapped it and popped it into her mouth.

"... a world too busy with its own business to even notice an insignificant couple from far away," Reverend Wall intoned.

Virginia passed her bulletin to Sharon. Dee leaned over to read it, too. It read, "What happened here last night after the rehearsal? When I came home from the mall, there were police cars outside."

Dee grabbed the bulletin and rummaged in her folder again. She found a pencil, scribbled "Somebody broke into the church," and passed it across Sharon to Virginia.

"You're kidding," Virginia whispered. "Were they caught?"

"No," Sharon said.

🎄

The rehearsal on the twenty-third was supposed to start at seven. By a quarter to eight the choir was still standing at the back of the sanctuary waiting to sing the processional, the shepherds and angels were bouncing off the walls, and Reverend Wall, in his chair behind the pulpit, had nodded off. The assistant minister, Reverend Lisa Farrison, was moving poinsettias onto the chancel steps to make room for the manger, and the choir director, Rose Henderson, was on her knees, hammering wooden bases onto the cardboard palm trees. They had fallen down twice already.

"What do you think are the chances we'll still be here when it's time for the Christmas Eve service to start tomorrow night?" Sharon said, leaning against the sanctuary door.

"I can't be," Virginia said, looking at her watch. "I've got to be out at the mall before nine. Megan suddenly announced she wants Senior Prom Barbie."

"My throat feels terrible," Dee said, feeling her glands. "Is it hot in here, or am I getting a fever?"

"It's hot in these *robes*," Sharon said. "Why *are* we wearing them? This is a rehearsal."

"Rose wanted everything to be exactly like it's going to be tomorrow night."

"If I'm exactly like this tomorrow night, I'll be dead," Dee said, trying to clear her throat. "I *can't* get sick. I don't have any of the presents wrapped, and I haven't even *thought* about what we're having for Christmas dinner."

"At least you *have* presents," Virginia said. "I have eight people left to buy for. Not counting Senior Prom Barbie."

"I don't have anything done. Christmas cards, shopping, wrapping, baking, nothing, and Bill's parents are coming," Sharon said. "Come *on*, let's get this show on the road."

Rose and one of the junior choir angels hoisted the palm trees to standing. They listed badly to the right, as if Bethlehem were experiencing a hurricane. "Is that straight?" Rose called to the back of the church.

"Yes," Sharon said.

"Lying in church," Dee said. "Tsk, tsk."

"All right," Rose said, picking up a bulletin. "Listen up, everybody. Here's the order of worship. Introit by the brass quartet, processional, opening prayer, announcements—Reverend Farrison, is that where you want to talk about the 'Least of These' Project?"

"Yes," Reverend Farrison said. She walked to the front of the sanctuary. "And can I make a quick announcement right now?" She turned and faced the choir. "If anybody has anything else to donate, you need to bring it to the church by tomorrow morning at nine," she said briskly. "That's when we're going to deliver the donations to the homeless. We still need blankets and canned goods. Bring them to the Fellowship Hall."

She walked back down the aisle, and Rose started in on her list again. "Announcements, 'O Come, O Come, Emmanuel,' Reverend Wall's sermon—"

Reverend Wall nodded awake at his name. "Ah," he said, and hobbled toward the pulpit, clutching a sheaf of yellowed typewritten papers.

"Oh, no," Sharon said. "Not a Christmas pageant *and* a sermon. We'll be here forever."

"Not *a* sermon," Virginia said. "*The* sermon. All twenty-four minutes of it. I've got it memorized. He's given it every year since he came."

"Longer than that," Dee said. "I swear last year I heard him say something in it about World War I."

"'And all went to be taxed, every one into his own city,'" Reverend Wall said. "'And Joseph also went up from Galilee, out of the city of Nazareth.'"

"Oh, *no*," Sharon said. "He's going to give the whole sermon right now."

"We know nothing of that journey up from Bethlehem," he said.

"Thank you, Reverend Wall," Rose said. "After the sermon, the choir sings 'O Little Town of Bethlehem' and Mary and Joseph—"

"What message does the story of their journey hold for us?" Reverend Wall said, picking up steam.

Rose was hurrying up the aisle and up the chancel steps. "Reverend Wall, you don't need to run through your sermon right now."

"What does it say to us," he asked, "struggling to recover from a world war?"

Dee nudged Sharon.

"Reverend *Wall*," Rose said, reaching the pulpit. "I'm afraid we don't have time to go through your whole sermon right now. We need to run through the pageant now."

"Ah," he said, and gathered up his papers.

"All right," Rose said. "The choir sings 'O Little Town of Bethlehem' and Mary and Joseph, you come down the aisle."

Mary and Joseph, wearing bathrobes and Birkenstocks, assembled themselves at the back of the sanctuary and started down the center aisle.

"No, no, Mary and Joseph, not that way," Rose said. "The wise men from the East have to come down the center aisle, and you're coming up from Nazareth. You two come down the side aisle."

Mary and Joseph obliged, taking the aisle at a trot.

"No, no, slow *down*," Rose said. "You're tired. You've walked all the way from Nazareth. Try it again."

They raced each other to the back of the church and started again, slower at first and then picking up speed.

"The congregation won't be able to see them," Rose said, shaking her head. "What about lighting the side aisle? Can we do that, Reverend Farrison?"

"She's not here," Dee said. "She went to get something."

"I'll go get her," Sharon said, and went down the hall.

Miriam Hoskins was just going into the adult Sunday school room with a paper plate of frosted cookies. "Do you know where Reverend Farrison is?" Sharon asked her.

"She was in the office a minute ago," Miriam said, pointing with the plate.

Sharon went down to the office. Reverend Farrison was standing at the desk, talking on the phone. "How soon can the van be here?" She motioned to Sharon she'd be a minute. "Well, can you find out?"

Sharon waited, looking at the desk. There was a glass dish of paper-wrapped cough drops next to the phone, and beside it a can of smoked oysters and three cans of water chestnuts. *Probably for the 'Least of These' Project,* she thought ruefully.

"Fifteen minutes? All right. Thank you," Reverend Farrison said, and hung up. "Just a minute," she told Sharon, and went to the outside door. She opened it and leaned out. Sharon could feel the icy air as she stood there. She wondered if it had started snowing.

"The van will be here in a few minutes," Reverend Farrison said to someone outside.

Sharon looked out the stained-glass panels on either side of the door, trying to see who was out there.

"It'll take you to the shelter," Reverend Farrison said. "No, you'll have to wait outside." She shut the door. "Now," she said, turning to Sharon, "what did *you* want, Mrs. Englert?"

Sharon said, still looking out the window, "They need you in the sanctuary." It *was* starting to snow. The flakes looked blue through the glass.

"I'll be right there," Reverend Farrison said. "I was just taking care of some homeless. That's the second couple we've had tonight. We always get them at Christmas. What's the problem? The palm trees?"

"What?" Sharon said, still looking at the snow.

Reverend Farrison followed her gaze. "The shelter van's coming for them in a few minutes," she said. "We can't let them stay in here unsupervised. First Methodist's had their collection stolen twice in the last month, and we've got all the donations for the 'Least of These' Project in there." She gestured toward the Fellowship Hall.

I thought they were for the homeless, Sharon thought. "Couldn't they just wait in the sanctuary or something?" she said.

Reverend Farrison sighed. "Letting them in isn't doing them a kindness. They come here instead of the shelter because the shelter confiscates their liquor." She started down the hall. "What did they need me for?"

"Oh," Sharon said, "the lights. They wanted to know if they could get lights over the side aisle for Mary and Joseph."

"I don't know," she said. "The lights in this church are such a mess." She stopped at the bank of switches next to the stairs that led down to the choir room and the Sunday school rooms. "Tell me what this turns on."

She flicked a switch. The hall light went off. She switched it back on and tried another one.

"That's the light in the office," Sharon said, "and the downstairs hall, and that one's the adult Sunday school room."

"What's this one?" Reverend Farrison said. There was a yelp from the choir members. Kids screamed.

"The sanctuary," Sharon said. "Okay, that's the side aisle lights." She called down to the sanctuary. "How's that?"

"Fine," Rose called. "No, wait, the organ's off."

Reverend Farrison flicked another switch, and the organ came on with a groan.

"Now the side lights are off," Sharon said, "and so's the pulpit light."

"I told you they were a mess," Reverend Farrison said. She flicked another switch. "What did that do?"

"It turned the porch light off."

"Good. We'll leave it off. Maybe it will discourage any more homeless from coming," she said. "Reverend Wall let a homeless man wait inside last week, and he relieved himself on the carpet in the adult Sunday school room. We had to have it cleaned." She looked reprovingly at Sharon. "With these people, you can't let your compassion get the better of you."

No, Sharon thought. *Jesus did, and look what happened to him.*

"The innkeeper could have turned them away," Reverend Wall intoned. "He was a busy man, and his inn was full of travelers. He could have shut the door on Mary and Joseph."

Virginia leaned across Sharon to Dee. "Did whoever broke in take anything?"

"No," Sharon said.

"Whoever it was urinated on the floor in the nursery," Dee whispered, and Reverend Wall trailed off confusedly and looked over at the choir.

Dee began coughing loudly, trying to smother it with her hand. He smiled vaguely at her and started again. "The innkeeper could have turned them away."

Dee waited a minute, and then opened her hymnal to her bulletin and began writing on it. She passed it to Virginia, who read it and then passed it back to Sharon.

"Reverend Farrison thinks some of the homeless got in," it read. "They tore up the palm trees, too. Ripped the bases right off. Can you imagine anybody doing something like that?"

"As the innkeeper found room for Mary and Joseph that Christmas Eve long ago," Reverend Wall said, building to a finish, "let us find room in our hearts for Christ. Amen."

The organ began the intro to "O Little Town of Bethlehem," and Mary and Joseph appeared at the back with Miriam Hoskins. She adjusted Mary's white veil and whispered something to them. Joseph pulled at his glued-on beard.

"What route did they finally decide on?" Virginia whispered. "In from the side or straight down the middle?"

"Side aisle," Sharon whispered.

The choir stood up. "'O little town of Bethlehem, how still we see thee lie,'" they sang. "'Above thy deep and dreamless sleep, the silent stars go by.'"

Mary and Joseph started up the side aisle, taking the slow, measured steps Rose had coached them in, side by side. No, *Sharon thought.* That's not right. They didn't look like that. Joseph should be a little ahead of Mary, protecting her, and her hand should be on her stomach, protecting the baby.

They eventually decided to wait on the decision of how Mary and Joseph would come, and started through the pageant. Mary and Joseph knocked on the door of the inn, and the innkeeper, grinning broadly, told them there wasn't any room.

"Patrick, don't look so happy," Rose said. "You're supposed to be in a bad mood. You're busy and tired, and you don't have any rooms left."

Patrick attempted a scowl. "I have no rooms left," he said, "but you can stay in the stable." He led them over to the manger, and Mary knelt down behind it.

"Where's the baby Jesus?" Rose said.

"He's not due till tomorrow night," Virginia whispered.

"Does anybody have a baby doll they can bring?" Rose asked.

One of the angels raised her hand, and Rose said, "Fine. Mary, use the blanket for now, and, choir, you sing the first verse of 'Away in a Manger.' Shepherds," she called to the back of the sanctuary, "as *soon* as 'Away in a Manger' is over, come up and stand on *this* side." She pointed.

The shepherds picked up an assortment of hockey sticks, broom handles, and canes taped to one-by-twos and adjusted their headcloths.

"All right, let's run through it," Rose said. "Organ?"

The organ played the opening chord, and the choir stood up.

"A-way," Dee sang and started to cough, choking into her hand. "Do—cough—drop?" she managed to gasp out between spasms.

"I saw some in the office," Sharon said, and ran down the chancel steps, down the aisle, and out into the hall.

It was dark, but she didn't want to take the time to try to find the right switch. She could more or less see her way by the lights from the sanctuary, and she thought she knew right where the cough drops were.

The office lights were off, too, and the porch light Reverend Farrison had turned off to discourage the homeless. She opened the office door, felt her way over to the desk, and patted around till she found the glass dish. She grabbed a handful of cough drops and felt her way back out into the hall.

The choir was singing "It Came Upon a Midnight Clear," but after two measures they stopped, and in the sudden silence Sharon heard knocking.

She started for the door and then hesitated, wondering if this was the same couple Reverend Farrison had turned away earlier, coming back to make trouble, but the knocking was soft, almost diffident, and through the stained-glass panels she could see it was snowing hard.

She switched the cough drops to her left hand, opened the door a little, and looked out. There were two people standing on the porch, one in front of the other. It was too dark to do more than make out their outlines, and at first glance it looked like two women, but then the one in front said in a young man's voice, *"Erkas."*

"I'm sorry," Sharon said. "I don't speak Spanish. Are you looking for a place to stay?" The snow was turning to sleet, and the wind was picking up.

"Kumrah," the young man said, making a sound like he was clearing his throat, and then a whole string of words she didn't recognize.

"Just a minute," she said, and shut the door. She went back into the office, felt for the phone, and, squinting at the buttons in the near-darkness, punched in the shelter number.

It was busy. She held down the receiver, waited a minute, and tried again. Still busy. She went back to the door, hoping they'd given up and gone away.

"Erkas," the man said as soon as she opened it.

"I'm sorry," she said. "I'm trying to call the homeless shelter," and he began talking rapidly, excitedly.

He stepped forward and put his hand on the door. He had a blanket draped over him, which was why she'd mistaken him for a woman. *"Erkas,"* he said, and he sounded upset, desperate, and yet somehow still diffident, timid.

"Bott lom," he said, gesturing toward the woman, who was standing back almost to the edge of the porch, but Sharon wasn't looking at her. She was looking at their feet.

They were wearing sandals. At first she thought they were barefoot and she squinted through the darkness, horrified. Barefoot in the snow! Then she glimpsed the dark line of a strap, but they still might as well be. And it was snowing hard.

She couldn't leave them outside, but she didn't dare bring them into the hall to wait for the van either, not with Reverend Farrison around.

The office was out—the phone might ring—and she couldn't put them in the Fellowship Hall with all the stuff for the homeless in there.

"Just a minute," she said, shutting the door, and went to see if Miriam was still in the adult Sunday school room. It was dark, so she obviously wasn't, but there was a lamp on the table by the door. She switched it on. No, this wouldn't work either, not with the communion silver in a display case against the wall, and anyway, there was a stack of paper cups on the table, and the plates of Christmas cookies Miriam had been carrying, which meant there'd be refreshments in here after the rehearsal. She switched off the light, and went out into the hall.

Not Reverend Wall's office—it was locked anyway—and certainly not Reverend Farrison's, and if she took them downstairs to one of the Sunday school rooms, she'd just have to sneak them back up again.

The furnace room? It was between the adult Sunday school room and the Fellowship Hall. She tried the doorknob. It opened, and she looked in. The furnace filled practically the whole room, and what it didn't was taken up by a stack of folding chairs. There wasn't a light switch she could find, but the pilot light gave off enough light to maneuver by. And it was warmer than the porch.

She went back to the door, looked down the hall to make sure nobody was coming, and let them in. "You can wait in here," she said, even though it was obvious they couldn't understand her.

They followed her through the dark hall to the furnace room, and she opened out two of the folding chairs so they could sit down, and motioned them in.

"It Came Upon a Midnight Clear" ground to a halt, and Rose's voice came drifting out of the sanctuary. "Shepherd's crooks are not weapons. All right. Angel?"

"I'll call the shelter," Sharon said hastily, and shut the door on them.

She crossed to the office and tried the shelter again. "Please, please answer," she said, and when they did, she was so surprised, she forgot to tell them the couple would be inside.

"It'll be at least half an hour," the man said. "Or forty-five minutes."

"Forty-five minutes?"

"It's like this whenever it gets below zero," the man said. "We'll try to make it sooner."

At least she'd done the right thing—they couldn't possibly stand out in that snow for forty-five minutes. The right thing, she thought ruefully, sticking them in the furnace room. But at least it was warm in there and out of the snow. And they were safe, as long as nobody came out to see what had happened to her.

"Dee," she said suddenly. Sharon was supposed to have come out to get her some cough drops.

They were lying on the desk where she'd laid them while she phoned. She snatched them up and took off down the hall and into the sanctuary.

The angel was on the chancel steps, exhorting the shepherds not to be afraid. Sharon threaded her way through them up to the chancel and sat down between Dee and Virginia.

She handed the cough drops to Dee, who said, "What took you so long?"

"I had to make a phone call. What did I miss?"

"Not a thing. We're still on the shepherds. One of the palm trees fell over and had to be fixed, and then Reverend Farrison stopped the rehearsal to tell everybody not to let homeless people into the church, that Holy Trinity had had its sanctuary vandalized."

"Oh," she said. She gazed out over the sanctuary, looking for Reverend Farrison.

"All right, now, after the angel makes her speech," Rose said, "she's joined by a multitude of angels. That's *you,* junior choir. No. Line up on the steps. Organ?"

The organ struck up "Hark, the Herald Angels Sing," and the junior choir began singing in piping, nearly inaudible voices.

Sharon couldn't see Reverend Farrison anywhere. "Do you know where Reverend Farrison went?" she whispered to Dee.

"She went out just as you came in. She had to get something from the office."

The office. What if she heard them in the furnace room and opened the door and found them in there? She half stood.

"Choir," Rose said, glaring directly at Sharon. "Will you help the junior choir by humming along with them?"

Sharon sat back down, and after a minute Reverend Farrison came in from the back, carrying a pair of scissors.

"'Late in time, behold Him come,'" the junior choir sang, and Miriam stood up and went out.

"Where's Miriam going?" Sharon whispered.

"How would I know?" Dee said, looking curiously at her. "To get the refreshments ready, probably. Is something the matter?"

"No," she said.

Rose was glaring at Sharon again. Sharon hummed, "'Light and life to all He brings,'" willing the song to be over so she could go out, but as soon as it was over, Rose said, "All right, wise men," and a sixth-grader carrying a jewelry box started down the center aisle. "Choir, 'We Three Kings.' Organ?"

There were four long verses to "We Three Kings of Orient Are." Sharon couldn't wait.

"I have to go to the bathroom," she said. She set her folder on her chair and ducked down the stairs behind the chancel and through the narrow room that led to the side aisle. The choir called it the flower room because that was where they stored the out-of-season altar arrangements. They used it for sneaking out when they needed to leave church early, but right now there was barely room to squeeze through. The floor was covered with music stands and pots of silk Easter lilies, and a huge spray of red roses stood in front of the door to the sanctuary.

Sharon shoved it into the corner, stepping gingerly among the lilies, and opened the door.

"Balthazar, lay the gold in front of the manger, don't drop it. Mary, you're the Mother of God. Try not to look so scared," Rose said.

Sharon hurried down the side aisle and out into the hall, where the other two kings were waiting, holding perfume bottles.

"'Westward leading, still proceeding, guide us to thy perfect light,'" the choir sang.

The hall and office lights were still off, but light was spilling out of the adult Sunday school room all the way to the end of the hall. She could see that the furnace room door was still shut.

I'll call the shelter again, she thought, *and see if I can hurry them up, and if I can't, I'll take them downstairs till everybody's gone, and then take them to the shelter myself.*

She tiptoed past the open door of the adult Sunday school room so Miriam wouldn't see her, and then half sprinted down to the office and opened the door.

"Hi," Miriam said, looking up from the desk. She had an aluminum pitcher in one hand and was rummaging in the top drawer with the other. "Do you know where the secretary keeps the key to the kitchen? It's locked, and I can't get in."

"No," Sharon said, her heart still pounding.

"I need a spoon to stir the Kool-Aid," Miriam said, opening and shutting the side drawers of the desk. "She must have taken them home with her. I don't blame her. First Baptist had theirs stolen last month. They had to change all the locks."

Sharon glanced uneasily at the furnace room door.

"Oh, well," Miriam said, opening the top drawer again. "I'll have to make do with this." She pulled out a plastic ruler. "The kids won't care."

She started out and then stopped. "They're not done in there yet, are they?"

"No," Sharon said. "They're still on the wise men. I needed to call my husband to tell him to take the turkey out of the freezer."

"I've got to do that when I get home," Miriam said. She went across the hall and into the library, leaving the door open. Sharon waited a minute and then called the shelter. It was busy. She held her watch to the light from the hall. They'd said half an hour to forty-five minutes. By that time the rehearsal would be over and the hall would be full of people.

Less than half an hour. They were already singing "Myrrh is mine, its bitter perfume." All that was left was "Silent Night" and then "Joy to the World," and the angels would come streaming out for cookies and Kool-Aid.

She went over to the front door and peered out. Below zero, the woman at the shelter had said, and now there was sleet, slanting sharply across the parking lot.

She couldn't send them out in that without any shoes. And she couldn't keep them up here, not with the kids right next door. She was going to have to move them downstairs.

But where? Not the choir room. The choir would be taking their folders and robes back down there, and the pageant kids would be getting their coats out of the Sunday school rooms. And the kitchen was locked.

The nursery? That might work. It was at the other end of the hall from the choir room, but she would have to take them past the adult Sunday school room to the stairs, and the door was open.

"'Si-i-lent night, ho-oh-ly night,'" came drifting out of the sanctuary, and then was cut off, and she could hear Reverend Farrison's voice lecturing, probably about the dangers of letting the homeless into the church.

She glanced again at the furnace room door and then went into the adult Sunday school room. Miriam was setting out the paper cups on the table. She looked up. "Did you get through to your husband?"

"Yes," Sharon said. Miriam looked expectant.

"Can I have a cookie?" Sharon said at random.

"Take one of the stars. The kids like the Santas and the Christmas trees the best."

She grabbed up a bright yellow-frosted star. "Thanks," she said, and went out, pulling the door shut behind her.

"Leave it open," Miriam said. "I want to be able to hear when they're done."

Sharon opened the door back up half as far as she'd shut it, afraid any less would bring Miriam to the door to open it herself, and walked quietly to the furnace room.

The choir was on the last verse of "Silent Night." After that there was only "Joy to the World" and then the benediction. Open door or no open door, she was going to have to move them now. She opened the furnace room door.

They were standing where she had left them between the folding chairs, and she knew, without any proof, that they had stood there like that the whole time she had been gone.

The young man was standing slightly in front of the woman, the way he had at the door, only he wasn't a man, he was a boy, his beard as thin and wispy as an adolescent's, and the woman was even younger, a child of ten maybe, only she had to be older, because now that there was light from the half-open door of the adult Sunday school room Sharon could see that she was pregnant.

She regarded all this—the girl's awkward bulkiness and the boy's beard, the fact that they had not sat down, the fact that it was the light from the adult Sunday school room that was making her see now what she hadn't before—with some part of her mind that was still functioning, that was still thinking how long the van from the shelter would take, how to get them past Reverend Farrison, some part of her mind that was taking in the details that proved what she had already known the moment she opened the door.

"What are you *doing* here?" she whispered, and the boy opened his hands in a gesture of helplessness. *"Erkas,"* he said.

And that still-functioning part of her mind put her fingers to her lips in a gesture he obviously understood because they both looked instantly frightened. "You have to come with me," she whispered.

But then it stopped functioning altogether, and she was half running them past the open door and onto the stairs, not even hearing the organ blaring out "Joy to the world, the Lord is come," whispering, "Hurry! Hurry!" and they didn't know how to get down the steps, the girl turned around and came down backwards, her hands flat on the steps above, and the boy helped her down, step by step, as if they were clambering down rocks, and she tried to pull the girl along faster and nearly made her stumble, and even that didn't bring her to her senses.

She hissed, "Like this," and showed them how to walk down the steps, facing forward, one hand on the rail, and they paid no attention, they came down backwards like toddlers, and it took forever, the hymn she wasn't hearing was already at the end of the third verse and they were only halfway down, all of them panting hard, and Sharon scurrying back up above them as if that would hurry them, past wondering how she would ever get them up the stairs again, past thinking she would have to call the van and tell them not to come, thinking only, *Hurry, hurry,* and *How did they* get *here?*

She did not come to herself until she had herded them somehow down the hall and into the nursery, thinking, *It can't be locked, please don't let it be locked,* and it wasn't, and gotten them inside and pulled the door shut and tried to lock it, and it didn't have a lock, and she thought, *That must be why it wasn't locked,* an actual coherent thought, her first one since that moment when she opened the furnace room door, and seemed to come to herself.

She stared at them, breathing hard, and it *was* them, their never having seen stairs before was proof of that, if she needed any proof, but she didn't, she had known it the instant she saw them, there was no question.

She wondered if this was some sort of vision, the kind people were always getting where they saw Jesus's face on a refrigerator, or the Virgin Mary dressed in blue and white, surrounded by roses. But their rough brown cloaks were dripping melted snow on the nursery carpet, their feet in the useless sandals were bright red with cold, and they looked too frightened.

And they didn't look at all like they did in religious pictures. They were too short, his hair was greasy and his face was tough-looking, like a young punk's, and her veil looked like a grubby dishtowel and it didn't hang loose, it was tied around her neck and knotted in the back, and they were too young, almost as young as the children upstairs dressed like them.

They were looking around the room frightenedly, at the white crib and the rocking chair and the light fixture overhead. The boy fumbled in his sash and brought out a leather sack. He held it out to Sharon.

"How did you *get* here?" she said wonderingly. "You're supposed to be on your way to Bethlehem."

He thrust the bag at her, and when she didn't take it, untied the leather string and took out a crude-looking coin and held it out.

"You don't have to pay me," she said, which was ridiculous. He couldn't understand her. She held a flat hand up, pushing the coin away and shaking her head. That was a universal sign, wasn't it? And what was the sign for welcome? She spread her arms out, smiling at the youngsters. "You are welcome to stay here," she said, trying to put the meaning of the words into her voice. "Sit down. Rest."

They remained standing. Sharon pulled the rocking chair. "Sit, please."

Mary looked frightened, and Sharon put her hands on the arms of the chair and sat down to show her how. Joseph immediately knelt, and Mary tried awkwardly to.

"No, no!" Sharon said, and stood up so fast she set the rocking chair swinging. "Don't kneel. I'm nobody." She looked hopelessly at them. "How did you *get* here? You're not supposed to be here."

Joseph stood up. *"Erkas,"* he said, and went over to the bulletin board.

It was covered with colored pictures from Jesus's life: Jesus healing the lame boy, Jesus in the temple, Jesus in the Garden of Gethsemane.

He pointed to the picture of the Nativity scene. *"Kumrah,"* he said.

Does he recognize himself? she wondered, but he was pointing at the donkey standing by the manger. *"Erkas,"* he said. *"Erkas."*

Did that mean "donkey," or something else? Was he demanding to know what she had done with theirs, or trying to ask her if she had one? In all the pictures, all the versions of the story, Mary was riding a donkey, but she had thought they'd gotten that part of the story wrong, as they had gotten everything else wrong, their faces, their clothes, and above all their youth, their helplessness.

"Kumrah erkas," he said. *"Kumrah erkas. Bott lom?"*

"I don't know," she said. "I don't know where Bethlehem is."

Or what to do with you, she thought. Her first instinct was to hide them here until the rehearsal was over and everybody had gone home. She couldn't let Reverend Farrison find them.

But surely as soon as she saw who they were, she would—what? Fall to her knees? Or call for the shelter's van? "That's the second couple to-night," she'd said when she shut the door. Sharon wondered suddenly if it was them she'd turned away, if they'd wandered around the parking lot, lost and frightened, and then knocked on the door again.

She couldn't let Reverend Farrison find them, but there was no reason for her to come into the nursery. All the children were upstairs, and the refreshments were in the adult Sunday school room. But what if she checked the rooms before she locked up?

I'll take them home with me, Sharon thought. *They'll be safe there.* If she could get them up the stairs and out of the parking lot before the rehearsal ended.

I got them down here without anybody seeing them, she thought. But even if she could manage it, which she doubted, if they didn't die of fright when she started the car and the seat belts closed down over them, home was no better than the shelter.

They had gotten lost through some accident of time and space, and ended up at the church. The way back—if there was a way back, there had to be a way back, they had to be at Bethlehem by tomorrow night— was here.

It occurred to her suddenly that maybe she shouldn't have let them in, that the way back was outside the north door. *But I couldn't not let them in,* she protested, *it was snowing, and they didn't have any shoes.*

But maybe if she'd turned them away, they would have walked off the porch and back into their own time. Maybe they still could.

She said, "Stay here," putting her hand up to show them what she meant, and went out of the nursery into the hall, shutting the door tightly behind her.

The choir was still singing "Joy to the World." They must have had to stop again. Sharon ran silently up the stairs and past the adult Sunday school room. Its door was still half open, and she could see the plates of cookies on the table. She opened the north door, hesitating a moment as if she expected to see sand and camels, and leaned out. It was still sleeting, and the cars had an inch of snow on them.

She looked around for something to wedge the door open with, pushed one of the potted palms over, and went out on the porch. It was slick, and she had to take hold of the wall to keep her footing. She stepped carefully to the edge of the porch and peered into the sleet, already shivering, looking for what? A lessening of the sleet, a spot where the darkness was darker, or not so dark? A light?

Nothing. After a minute she stepped off the porch, moving as cautiously as Mary and Joseph had going down the stairs, and made a circuit of the parking lot.

Nothing. If the way back had been out here, it wasn't now, and she was going to freeze if she stayed out here. She went back inside, and then stood there, staring at the door, trying to think what to do. *I've got to get help,* she thought, hugging her arms to herself for warmth. *I've got to tell somebody.* She started down the hall to the sanctuary.

The organ had stopped. "Mary and Joseph, I need to talk to you for a minute," Rose's voice said. "Shepherds, leave your crooks on the front pew. The rest of you, there are refreshments in the adult Sunday school room. Choir, don't leave. I need to go over some things with you."

There was a clatter of sticks and then a stampede, and Sharon was overwhelmed by shepherds elbowing their way to the refreshments. One of the wise men caught his Air Jordan in his robe and nearly fell down, and two of the angels lost their tinsel halos in their eagerness to reach the cookies.

Sharon fought through them and into the back of the sanctuary. Rose was in the side aisle, showing Mary and Joseph how to walk, and the choir was gathering up their music. Sharon couldn't see Dee.

Virginia came down the center aisle, stripping off her robe as she walked. Sharon went to meet her. "Do you know where Dee is?" she asked her.

"She went home," Virginia said, handing Sharon a folder. "You left this on your chair. Dee's voice was giving out completely, and I said, 'This is silly. Go home and go to bed.'"

"Virginia . . ." Sharon said.

"Can you put my robe away for me?" Virginia said, pulling her stole off her head. "I've got exactly ten minutes to get to the mall."

Sharon nodded absently, and Virginia draped it over her arm and hurried out. Sharon scanned the choir, wondering who else she could confide in.

Rose dismissed Mary and Joseph, who went off at a run, and crossed to the center aisle. "Rehearsal tomorrow night at 6:15," she said. "I need you in your robes and up here right on time, because I've got to practice with the brass quartet at 6:40. Any questions?"

Yes, Sharon thought, looking around the sanctuary. *Who can I get to help me?*

"What are we singing for the processional?" one of the tenors asked.

"'*Adeste Fideles,*'" Rose said. "Before you leave, let's line up so you can see who your partner is."

Reverend Wall was sitting in one of the back pews, looking at the notes to his sermon. Sharon sidled along the pew and sat down next to him.

"Reverend Wall," she said, and then had no idea how to start. "Do you know what *erkas* means? I think it's Hebrew."

He raised his head from his notes and peered at her. "It's Aramaic. It means 'lost.'"

"Lost." He'd been trying to tell her at the door, in the furnace room, downstairs. "We're lost."

"'Forgotten,'" Reverend Wall said. "'Misplaced.'"

Misplaced, all right. By two thousand years, an ocean, and how many miles?

"When Mary and Joseph journeyed up to Bethlehem from Nazareth, how did they go?" she asked, hoping he would say, "Why are you asking all these questions?" so she could tell him, but he said, "Ah. You weren't listening to my sermon. We know nothing of that journey, only that they arrived in Bethlehem."

Not at this rate, she thought.

"Pass in the anthem," Rose said from the chancel. "I've only got thirty copies, and I don't want to come up short tomorrow night."

Sharon looked up. The choir was leaving. "On this journey, was there anyplace where they might have gotten lost?" she said hurriedly.

"*Erkas* can also mean 'hidden, passed out of sight,'" he said. "Aramaic is very similar to Hebrew. In Hebrew, the word—"

"Reverend Wall," Reverend Farrison said from the center aisle. "I need to talk to you about the benediction."

"Ah. Do you want me to give it now?" he said, and stood up, clutching his papers.

Sharon took the opportunity to grab her folder and duck out. She ran downstairs after the choir.

There was no reason for any of the choir to go into the nursery, but she stationed herself in the hall, sorting through the music in her folder as if she were putting it in order, and trying to think what to do.

Maybe, if everyone went into the choir room, she could duck into the nursery or one of the Sunday school rooms and hide until everybody was gone. But she didn't know whether Reverend Farrison checked each of the rooms before leaving. Or worse, locked them.

She could tell her she needed to stay late, to practice the anthem, but she didn't think Reverend Farrison would trust her to lock up, and she didn't want to call attention to herself, to make Reverend Farrison think, "Where's Sharon Englert? I didn't see her leave." Maybe she could hide in the chancel, or the flower room, but that meant leaving the nursery unguarded.

She had to decide. The crowd was thinning out, the choir handing Rose their music and putting on their coats and boots. She had to do something. Reverend Farrison could come down the stairs any minute to search the nursery. But she continued to stand there, sorting blindly through her music, and Reverend Farrison came down the steps, carrying a ring of keys.

Sharon stepped back protectively, the way Joseph had, but Reverend Farrison didn't even see her. She went up to Rose and said, "Can you lock up for me? I've got to be at Emmanuel Lutheran at 9:30 to collect their 'Least of These' contributions."

"I was supposed to go meet with the brass quartet—" Rose said reluctantly.

Don't let Rose talk you out of it, Sharon thought.

"Be sure to lock *all* the doors, including the Fellowship Hall," Reverend Farrison said, handing her the keys.

"No, I've got mine," Rose said. "But—"

"And check the parking lot. There were some homeless hanging around earlier. Thanks."

She ran upstairs, and Sharon immediately went over to Rose. "Rose," she said.

Rose held out her hand for Sharon's anthem.

Sharon shuffled through her music and handed it to her. "I was wondering," she said, trying to keep her voice casual, "I need to stay and practice the music for tomorrow. I'd be glad to lock up for you. I could drop the keys by your house tomorrow morning."

"Oh, you're a godsend," Rose said. She handed Sharon the stack of music and got her keys out of her purse. "These are the keys to the outside doors, north door, east door, Fellowship Hall," she said, ticking them off so fast, Sharon couldn't see which was which, but it didn't matter. She could figure them out after everybody left.

"This is the choir room door," Rose said. She handed them to Sharon. "I *really* appreciate this. The brass quartet couldn't come to the rehearsal, they had a concert tonight, and I really need to go over the introit with them. They're having a terrible time with the middle part."

So am I, Sharon thought.

Rose yanked on her coat. "And after I meet with them, I've got to go over to Sara Berg's and pick up the baby Jesus." She stopped, her arm half in her coat sleeve. "Did you need me to stay and go over the music with you?"

"No!" Sharon said, alarmed. "No, I'll be fine. I just need to run through it a couple of times."

"Okay. Great. Thanks again," she said, patting her pockets for her keys. She took the key ring away from Sharon and unhooked her car keys. "You're a godsend, I mean it," she said, and took off up the stairs at a trot.

Two of the altos came out, pulling on their gloves. "Do you know what I've got to face when I get home?" Julia said. "Putting up the tree."

They handed their music to Sharon.

"I hate Christmas," Karen said. "By the time it's over, I'm worn to a frazzle."

They hurried up the stairs, still talking, and Sharon leaned into the choir room to make sure it was empty, dumped the music and Rose's robe on a chair, took off her robe, and went upstairs.

Miriam was coming out of the adult Sunday school room, carrying a pitcher of Kool-Aid. "Come on, Elizabeth," she called into the room. "We've got to get to Buymore before it closes. She managed to completely destroy her halo," she said to Sharon, "so now I've got to go buy some more tinsel. Elizabeth, we're the last ones *here*."

Elizabeth strolled out, holding a Christmas tree cookie in her mittened hand. She stopped halfway to the door to lick the cookie's frosting.

"Elizabeth," Miriam said. "Come on."

Sharon held the door for them, and Miriam went out, ducking her head against the driving sleet. Elizabeth dawdled after her, looking up at the sky.

Miriam waved. "See you tomorrow night."

"I'll be here," Sharon said, and shut the door. *I'll* still *be here,* she thought. *And what if they are? What happens then? Does the Christmas pageant disappear, and all the rest of it? The cookies and the shopping and the Senior Prom Barbies? And the church?*

She watched Miriam and Elizabeth through the stained-glass panel till she saw the car's taillights, purple through the blue glass, pull out of the parking lot, and then tried the keys one after the other, till she found the right one, and locked the door.

She checked quickly in the sanctuary and the bathrooms, in case somebody was still there, and then ran down the stairs to the nursery to make sure *they* were still there, that they hadn't disappeared.

They were there, sitting on the floor next to the rocking chair and sharing what looked like dried dates from an unfolded cloth. Joseph started to stand up as soon as he saw her poke her head in the door, but she motioned him back down. "Stay here," she said softly, and realized she didn't need to whisper. "I'll be back in a few minutes. I'm just going to lock the doors."

She pulled the door shut, and went back upstairs. It hadn't occurred to her they'd be hungry, and she had no idea what they were used to eating—unleavened bread? Lamb? Whatever it was, there probably wasn't any in the kitchen, but the deacons had had an Advent supper last week. With luck, there might be some chili in the refrigerator. Or, better yet, some crackers.

The kitchen was locked. She'd forgotten Miriam had said that, and anyway, one of the keys must open it. None of them did, and after she'd tried all of them twice she remembered they were Rose's keys, not Reverend Farrison's, and turned the lights on in the Fellowship Hall. There was tons of food in there, stacked on tables alongside the blankets and used clothes and toys. And all of it was in cans, just the way Reverend Farrison had specified in the bulletin.

Miriam had taken the Kool-Aid home, but Sharon hadn't seen her carrying any cookies. *The kids probably ate them all,* she thought, but she went into the adult Sunday school room and looked. There was half a paper plateful left, and Miriam had been right—the kids liked the Christmas trees and Santas the best—the only ones left were yellow stars. There was a stack of paper cups, too. She picked them both up and took them downstairs.

"I brought you some food," she said, and set the plate on the floor between them.

They were staring in alarm at her, and Joseph was scrambling to his feet.

"It's food," she said, bringing her hand to her mouth and pretending to chew. "Cakes."

Joseph was pulling on Mary's arm, trying to yank her up, and they were both staring, horrified, at her jeans and sweatshirt. She realized \ suddenly they must not have recognized her without her choir robe. Worse, the robe looked at least a little like their clothes, but this getup must have looked totally alien.

"I'll bring you something to drink," she said hastily, showing them the paper cups, and went out. She ran down to the choir room. Her robe was still draped over the chair where she'd dumped it, along with Rose's and the music. She put the robe on and then filled the paper cups at the water fountain and carried them back to the nursery.

They were standing, but when they saw her in the robe, they sat back down. She handed Mary one of the paper cups, but she only looked at her fearfully. Sharon held it out to Joseph. He took it, too firmly, and it crumpled, water spurting onto the carpet.

"That's okay, it doesn't matter," Sharon said, cursing herself for being an idiot. "I'll get you a real cup."

She ran upstairs, trying to think where there would be one. The coffee cups were in the kitchen, and so were the glasses, and she hadn't seen anything in the Fellowship Hall or the adult Sunday school room.

She smiled suddenly. "I'll get you a real cup," she repeated, and went into the adult Sunday school room and took the silver Communion chalice out of the display case. There were silver plates, too. She wished she'd thought of it sooner.

She went into the Fellowship Hall and got a blanket and took the things downstairs. She filled the chalice with water and took it in to them, and handed Mary the chalice, and this time Mary took it without hesitation and drank deeply from it.

Sharon gave Joseph the blanket. "I'll leave you alone so you can eat and rest," she said, and went out into the hall, pulling the door nearly shut again.

She went down to the choir room and hung up Rose's robe and stacked the music neatly on the table. Then she went up to the furnace room and folded up the folding chairs and stacked them against the wall. She checked the east door and the one in the Fellowship Hall. They were both locked.

She turned off the lights in the Fellowship Hall and the office, and then thought, *I should call the shelter,* and turned them back on. It had been an hour since she'd called. They had probably already come and not found anyone, but in case they were running really late, she'd better call.

The line was busy. She tried it twice and then called home. Bill's parents were there. "I'm going to be late," she told him. "The rehearsal's running long," and hung up, wondering how many lies she'd told so far tonight.

Well, it went with the territory, didn't it? Joseph lying about the baby being his, and the wise men sneaking out the back way, the Holy Family hightailing it to Egypt and the innkeeper lying to Herod's soldiers about where they'd gone.

And in the meantime, more hiding. She went back downstairs and opened the door gently, trying not to startle them, and then just stood there, watching.

They had eaten the cookies. The empty paper plate stood on the floor next to the chalice, not a crumb on it. Mary lay curled up like the child she was under the blanket, and Joseph sat with his back to the rocking chair, guarding her.

Poor things, she thought, leaning her cheek against the door. *Poor things. So young, and so far away from home.* She wondered what they made of it all. Did they think they had wandered into a palace in some strange kingdom? *There's stranger yet to come,* she thought, *shepherds and angels and old men from the east, bearing jewelry boxes and perfume bottles. And then Cana. And Jerusalem. And Golgotha.*

But for the moment, a place to sleep, out of the weather, and something to eat, and a few minutes of peace. How still we see thee lie. She stood there a long time, her cheek resting against the door, watching Mary sleep and Joseph trying to stay awake.

His head nodded forward, and he jerked it back, waking himself up, and saw Sharon. He stood up immediately, careful not to wake Mary, and came over to her, looking worried. *"Erkas kumrah,"* he said. *"Bott lom?"*

"I'll go find it," she said.

She went upstairs and turned the lights on again and went into the Fellowship Hall. The way back wasn't out the north door, but maybe they had knocked at one of the other doors first and then come around to it when no one answered. The Fellowship Hall door was on the northwest corner. She unlocked it, trying key after key, and opened it. The sleet was slashing down harder than ever. It had already covered up the tire tracks in the parking lot.

She shut the door and tried the east door, which nobody used except for the Sunday service, and then the north door again. Nothing. Sleet and wind and icy air.

Now what? They had been on their way to Bethlehem from Nazareth, and somewhere along the way they had taken a wrong turn. But how? And where? She didn't even know what direction they'd been heading in. Up. Joseph had gone *up* from Nazareth, which meant north, and in "The First Nowell" it said the star was in the northwest.

She needed a map. The ministers' offices were locked, but there were books on the bottom shelf of the display case in the adult Sunday school room. Maybe one was an atlas.

It wasn't. They were all self-help books, about coping with grief and codependency and teenage pregnancy, except for an ancient-looking concordance and a Bible dictionary.

The Bible dictionary had a set of maps at the back. Early Israelite Settlements in Canaan, The Assyrian Empire, The Wanderings of the

Israelites in the Wilderness. She flipped forward. The Journeys of Paul. She turned back a page. Palestine in New Testament Times.

She found Jerusalem easily, and Bethlehem should be northwest of it. There was Nazareth, where Mary and Joseph had started from, so Bethlehem had to be farther north.

It wasn't there. She traced her finger over the towns, reading the tiny print. Cana, Kedesh, Jericho, but no Bethlehem. Which was ridiculous. It had to be there. She started down from the north, marking each of the towns with her finger.

When she finally found it, it wasn't at all where it was supposed to be. Like them, she thought. It was south and a little west of Jerusalem, so close it couldn't be more than a few miles from the city.

She looked down at the bottom of the page for the map scale, and there was an inset labeled "Mary and Joseph's Journey to Bethlehem," with their route marked in broken red.

Nazareth was almost due north of Bethlehem, but they had gone east to the Jordan River, and then south along its banks. At Jericho they'd turned back west toward Jerusalem through an empty brown space marked Judean Desert.

She wondered if that was where they had gotten lost, the donkey wandering off to find water and them going after it and losing the path. If it was, then the way back lay southwest, but the church didn't have any doors that opened in that direction, and even if it did, they would open on a twentieth-century parking lot and snow, not on first-century Palestine.

How had they gotten here? There was nothing in the map to tell her what might have happened on their journey to cause this.

She put the dictionary back and pulled out the concordance.

There was a sound. A key, and somebody opening the door. She slapped the book shut, shoved it back into the bookcase, and went out into the hall. Reverend Farrison was standing at the door, looking scared. "Oh, Mrs. Englert," she said, putting her hand to her chest. "What are you still doing here? You scared me half to death."

That makes two of us, Sharon thought, her heart thumping. "I had to stay and practice," she said. "I told Rose I'd lock up. What are you doing here?"

"I got a call from the shelter," she said, opening the office door. "They got a call from us to pick up a homeless couple, but when they got here there was nobody outside."

She went in the office and looked behind the desk, in the corner next to the filing cabinets. "I was worried they got into the church," she said, coming out. "The last thing we need is someone vandalizing the church two days before Christmas." She shut the office door behind her. "Did you check all the doors?"

Yes, she thought, *and none of them led anywhere.* "Yes," she said. "They were all locked. And anyway, I would have heard anybody trying to get in. I heard you."

Reverend Farrison opened the door to the furnace room. "They could have sneaked in and hidden when everyone was leaving." She looked in at the stacked folding chairs and then shut the door. She started down the hall toward the stairs.

"I checked the whole church," Sharon said, following her.

She stopped at the stairs, looking speculatively down the steps.

"I was nervous about being alone," Sharon said desperately, "so I turned on all the lights and checked all the Sunday school rooms and the choir room and the bathrooms. There isn't anybody here."

She looked up from the stairs and toward the end of the hall. "What about the sanctuary?"

"The sanctuary?" Sharon said blankly.

She had already started down the hall toward it, and Sharon followed her, relieved, and then, suddenly, hopeful. Maybe there was a door she'd missed. A sanctuary door that faced southwest. "Is there a door in the sanctuary?"

Reverend Farrison looked irritated. "If someone went out the east door, they could have gotten in and hidden in the sanctuary. Did you check the pews?" She went into the sanctuary. "We've had a lot of trouble lately with homeless people sleeping in the pews. You take that side, and I'll take this one," she said, going over to the side aisle. She started along the rows of padded pews, bending down to look under each one. "Our Lady of Sorrows had their Communion silver stolen right off the altar."

The Communion silver, Sharon thought, working her way along the rows. She'd forgotten about the chalice.

Reverend Farrison had reached the front. She opened the flower room door, glanced in, closed it, and went up into the chancel. "Did you check the adult Sunday school room?" she said, bending down to look under the chairs.

"Nobody could have hidden in there. The junior choir was in there, having refreshments," Sharon said, and knew it wouldn't do any good. Reverend Farrison was going to insist on checking it anyway, and once she'd found the display case open, the chalice missing, she would go through all the other rooms, one after the other. Till she came to the nursery.

"Do you think it's a good idea us doing this?" Sharon said. "I mean, if there is somebody in the church, they might be dangerous. I think we should wait. I'll call my husband, and when he gets here, the three of us can check—"

"I called the police," Reverend Farrison said, coming down the steps from the chancel and down the center aisle. "They'll be here any minute."

The police. And there they were, hiding in the nursery, a bearded punk and a pregnant teenager, caught red-handed with the Communion silver.

Reverend Farrison started out into the hall.

"I didn't check the Fellowship Hall," Sharon said rapidly. "I mean, I checked the door, but I didn't turn on the lights, and with all those presents for the homeless in there . . ."

She led Reverend Farrison down the hall, past the stairs. "They could have gotten in the north door during the rehearsal and hidden under one of the tables."

Reverend Farrison stopped at the bank of lights and began flicking them. The sanctuary lights went off, and the light over the stairs came on.

Third from the top, Sharon thought, watching Reverend Farrison hit the switch. *Please. Don't let the adult Sunday school room come on.*

The office lights came on, and the hall light went out. "This church's top priority after Christmas is labeling these lights," Reverend Farrison said, and the Fellowship Hall light came on.

Sharon followed her right to the door and then, as Reverend Farrison went in, Sharon said, "You check in here. I'll check the adult Sunday school room," and shut the door on her.

She went to the adult Sunday school room door, opened it, waited a full minute, and then shut it silently. She crept down the hall to the light bank, switched the stairs light off and shot down the darkened stairs, along the hall, and into the nursery.

They were already scrambling to their feet. Mary had put her hand on the seat of the rocking chair to pull herself up and had set it rocking, but she didn't let go of it.

"Come with me," Sharon whispered, grabbing up the chalice. It was half full of water, and Sharon looked around hurriedly, and then poured it out on the carpet and tucked it under her arm.

"Hurry!" Sharon whispered, opening the door, and there was no need to motion them forward, to put her fingers to her lips. They followed her swiftly, silently, down the hall, Mary's head ducked, and Joseph's arms held at his sides, ready to come up defensively, ready to protect her.

Sharon walked to the stairs, dreading the thought of trying to get them up them. She thought for a moment of putting them in the choir room and locking them in. She had the key, and she could tell Reverend Farrison she'd checked it and then locked it to make sure no one got in. But if it didn't work, they'd be trapped, with no way out. She had to get them upstairs.

She halted at the foot of the stairs, looking up around the landing and listening. "We have to hurry," she said, taking hold of the railing to show them how to climb, and started up the stairs.

This time they did much better, still putting their hands on the steps in front of them instead of the rail, but climbing up quickly. Three-fourths of the way up, Joseph even took hold of the rail.

Sharon did better, too, her mind steadily now on how to escape Reverend Farrison, what to say to the police, where to take them.

Not the furnace room, even though Reverend Farrison had already looked in there. It was too close to the door, and the police would start with the hall. And not the sanctuary. It was too open.

She stopped just below the top of the stairs, motioning them to keep down, and they instantly pressed themselves back into the shadows. Why was it those signals were universal—danger, silence, run? *Because it's a dangerous world,* she thought, *then and now, and there's worse to come. Herod, and the flight into Egypt. And Judas. And the police.*

She crept to the top of the stairs and looked toward the sanctuary and then the door. Reverend Farrison must still be in the Fellowship Hall. She wasn't in the hall, and if she'd gone in the adult Sunday school room, she'd have seen the chalice was missing and sent up a hue and cry.

Sharon bit her lip, wondering if there was time to put it back, if she dared leave them here on the stairs while she sneaked in and put it in the display case, but it was too late. The police were here. She could see their red and blue lights flashing purply through the stained-glass door panels. In another minute they'd be at the door, knocking, and Reverend Farrison would come out of the Fellowship Hall, and there'd be no time for anything.

She'd have to hide them in the sanctuary until Reverend Farrison took the police downstairs, and then move them—where? The furnace room? It was still too close to the door. The Fellowship Hall?

She waved them upward, like John Wayne in one of his war movies, along the hall and into the sanctuary. Reverend Farrison had turned off the lights, but there was still enough light from the chancel cross to see by. She laid the chalice in the back pew and led them along the back row to the shadowed side aisle, and then pushed them ahead of her to the front, listening intently for the sound of knocking.

Joseph went ahead with his eyes on the ground, as if he expected more sudden stairs, but Mary had her head up, looking toward the chancel, toward the cross.

Don't look at it, Sharon thought. *Don't look at it.* She hurried ahead to the flower room.

There was a muffled sound like thunder, and the bang of a door shutting.

"In here," she whispered, and opened the flower room door.

She'd been on the other side of the sanctuary when Reverend Farrison checked the flower room. Sharon understood now why she had given it only the most cursory of glances. It had been full before. Now it was crammed with the palm trees and the manger. They'd heaped the rest of the props in it—the innkeeper's lantern and the baby blanket. She pushed the manger back, and one of its crossed legs caught on a music stand and tipped it over. She lunged for it, steadied it, and then stopped, listening.

Knocking out in the hall. And the sound of a door shutting. Voices.

She let go of the music stand and pushed them into the flower room, shoving Mary into the corner against the spray of roses and nearly knocking over another music stand.

She motioned to Joseph to stand on the other side and flattened herself against a palm tree, shut the door, and realized the moment she did that it was a mistake.

They couldn't stand here in the dark like this—the slightest movement by any of them would bring everything clattering down, and Mary couldn't stay squashed uncomfortably into the corner like that for long.

She should have left the door slightly open, so there was enough light from the cross to see by, so she could hear where the police were. She couldn't hear anything with the door shut except the sound of their own light breathing and the clank of the lantern when she tried to shift her weight, and she couldn't risk opening the door again, not when they might already be in the sanctuary, looking for her. She should have shut Mary and Joseph in here and gone back into the hall to head the police off. Reverend Farrison would be looking for her, and if she didn't find her, she'd take it as one more proof that there was a dangerous homeless person in the church and insist on the police searching every nook and cranny.

Maybe she could go out through the choir loft, Sharon thought, if she could move the music stands out of the way, or at least shift things around so they could hide behind them, but she couldn't do either in the dark.

She knelt carefully, slowly, keeping her back perfectly straight, and put her hand out behind her, feeling for the top of the manger. She patted spiky straw till she found the baby blanket and pulled it out. They must have put the wise men's perfume bottles in the manger, too. They clinked wildly as she pulled the blanket out.

She knelt farther, feeling for the narrow space under the door, and jammed the blanket into it. It didn't quite reach the whole length of the door, but it was the best she could do. She straightened, still slowly, and patted the wall for the light switch.

Her hand brushed it. *Please,* she prayed, *don't let this turn on some other light,* and flicked it on.

Neither of them had moved, not even to shift their hands. Mary, pressed against the roses, took a caught breath, and then released it slowly, as if she had been holding it the whole time.

They watched Sharon as she knelt again to tuck in a corner of the blanket and then turned slowly around so she was facing into the room. She reached across the manger for one of the music stands and stacked it against the one behind it, working as gingerly, as slowly, as if she were defusing a bomb. She reached across the manger again, lifted one of the music stands, and set it on the straw so she could push the manger back far enough to give her space to move. The stand tipped, and Joseph steadied it.

Sharon picked up one of the cardboard palm trees. She worked the plywood base free, set it in the manger, and slid the palm tree flat along the wall next to Mary, and then did the other one.

That gave them some space. There was nothing Sharon could do about the rest of the music stands. Their metal frames were tangled together, and against the outside wall was a tall metal cabinet, with pots of Easter lilies in front of it. She could move the lilies to the top of the cabinet at least.

She listened carefully with her ear to the door for a minute, and then stepped carefully over the manger between two lilies. She bent and picked up one of them and set it on top of the cabinet and then stopped, frowning at the wall. She bent down again, moving her hand along the floor in a slow semicircle.

Cold air, and it was coming from behind the cabinet. She stood on tiptoe and looked behind it. "There's a door," she whispered. "To the outside."

"Sharon!" a muffled voice called from the sanctuary.

Mary froze, and Joseph moved so he was between her and the door. Sharon put her hand on the light switch and waited, listening.

"Mrs. Englert?" a man's voice called. Another one, farther off, "Her car's still here," and then Reverend Farrison's voice again, "Maybe she went downstairs."

Silence. Sharon put her ear against the door and listened, and then edged past Joseph to the side of the cabinet and peered behind it. The door opened outward. They wouldn't have to move the cabinet out very far, just enough for her to squeeze through and open the door, and then there'd be enough space for all of them to get through, even Mary. There were bushes on this side of the church. They could hide underneath them until after the police left.

She motioned Joseph to help her, and together they pushed the cabinet a few inches out from the wall. It knocked one of the Easter lilies over, and Mary stooped awkwardly and picked it up, cradling it in her arms.

They pushed again. This time it made a jangling noise, as if there were coat hangers inside, and Sharon thought she heard voices again, but there was no help for it. She squeezed into the narrow space, thinking, *What if it's locked?* and opened the door.

Onto warmth. Onto a clear sky, black and pebbled with stars.

"How—" she said stupidly, looking down at the ground in front of the door. It was rocky, with bare dirt in between. There was a faint breeze, and she could smell dust and something sweet. Oranges?

She turned to say, "I found it. I found the door," but Joseph was already leading Mary through it, pushing at the cabinet to make the space wider. Mary was still carrying the Easter lily, and Sharon took it from her and set it against the base of the door to prop it open and went out into the darkness.

The light from the open door lit the ground in front of them and at its edge was a stretch of pale dirt. The path, she thought, but when she got closer, she saw it was the dried bed of a narrow stream. Beyond it the rocky ground rose up steeply. They must be at the bottom of a draw, and she wondered if this was where they had gotten lost.

"Bott lom?" Joseph said behind her.

She turned around. *"Bott lom?"* he said again, gesturing in front and to the sides, the way he'd done in the nursery. Which way?

She had no idea. The door faced west, and if the direction held true, and if this was the Judean Desert, it should lie to the southwest. "That direction," she said, and pointed up the steepest part of the slope. "You go that way, I think."

They didn't move. They stood watching her, Joseph standing slightly in front of Mary, waiting for her to lead them.

"I'm not—" she said, and stopped. Leaving them here was no better than leaving them in the furnace room. Or out in the snow. She looked back at the door, almost wishing for Reverend Farrison and the police, and then set off toward what she hoped was the southwest, clambering awkwardly up the slope, her shoes slipping on the rocks.

How did they do this, she thought, grabbing at a dry clump of weed for a handhold, *even with a donkey?* There was no way Mary could make it up this slope. She looked back, worried.

They were following easily, sturdily, as certain of themselves as she had been on the stairs.

But what if at the top of this draw there was another one, or a dropoff? And no path. She dug in her toes and scrambled up.

There was a sudden sound, and Sharon whirled around and looked back at the door, but it still stood half open, with the lily at its foot and the manger behind.

The sound scraped again, closer, and she caught the crunch of footsteps and then a sharp wheeze.

"It's the donkey," she said, and it plodded up to her as if it were glad to see her.

She reached under it for its reins, which were nothing but a ragged rope, and it took a step toward her and blared in her ear, "Haw!" and then a wheeze that was practically a laugh.

She laughed, too, and patted his neck. "Don't wander off again," she said, leading him over to Joseph, who was waiting where she'd left them. "Stay on the path." She scrambled on up to the top of the slope, suddenly certain the path would be there, too.

It wasn't, but it didn't matter. Because there to the southwest was Jerusalem, distant and white in the starlight, lit by a hundred hearthfires, a thousand oil lamps, and beyond it, slightly to the west, three stars low in the sky, so close they were almost touching.

They came up beside her, leading the donkey. *"Bott lom,"* she said, pointing. "There, where the star is."

Joseph was fumbling in his sash again, holding out the little leather bag.

"No," she said, pushing it back to him. "You'll need it for the inn in Bethlehem."

He put the bag back reluctantly, and she wished suddenly she had something to give them. Frankincense. Or myrrh.

"Hunh-haw," the donkey brayed, and started down the hill. Joseph lunged after him, grabbing for the rope, and Mary followed them, her head ducked.

"Be careful," Sharon said. "Watch out for King Herod." She raised her hand in a wave, the sleeve of her choir robe billowing out in the warm breeze like a wing, but they didn't see her. They went on down the hill, Mary with her hand on the donkey for steadiness, Joseph a little ahead. When they were nearly at the bottom, Joseph stopped and pointed at the ground and led the donkey off at an angle out of her sight, and Sharon knew they'd found the path.

She stood there for a minute, enjoying the scented breeze, looking at the almost-star, and then went back down the slope, skidding on the rocks and loose dirt, and took the Easter lily out of the door and shut it. She pushed the cabinet back into position, took the blanket out from under the door, switched off the light, and went out into the darkened sanctuary.

There was no one there. She went and got the chalice, stuck it into the wide sleeve of her robe, and looked out into the hall. There was no one there, either. She went into the adult Sunday school room and put the chalice back into the display case and then went downstairs.

"*Where* have you been?" Reverend Farrison said. Two uniformed policemen came out of the nursery, carrying flashlights.

Sharon unzipped her choir robe and took it off. "I checked the Communion silver," she said. "None of it's missing." She went into the choir room and hung up her robe.

"We looked in there," Reverend Farrison said, following her in. "You weren't there."

"I thought I heard somebody at the door," she said.

⁂

By the end of the second verse of "O Little Town of Bethlehem," Mary and Joseph were only three-fourths of the way to the front of the sanctuary.

"At this rate, they won't make it to Bethlehem by Easter," Dee whispered. "Can't they get a move on?"

"They'll get there," Sharon whispered, watching them. They paced slowly, unperturbedly, up the aisle, their eyes on the chancel. "'How silently, how silently,'" Sharon sang, "'the wondrous gift is given.'"

They went past the second pew from the front and out of the choir's sight. The innkeeper came to the top of the chancel steps with his lantern, determinedly solemn.

"'So God imparts to human hearts,
  The blessings of his heaven.'"

"Where did they go?" Virginia whispered, craning her neck to try and see them. "Did they sneak out the back way or something?"

Mary and Joseph reappeared, walking slowly, sedately, toward the palm trees and the manger. The innkeeper came down the steps, trying hard to look like he wasn't waiting for them, like he wasn't overjoyed to see them.

"'No ear may hear his coming,
  But in this world of sin . . .'"

At the back of the sanctuary, the shepherds assembled, clanking their staffs, and Miriam handed the wise men their jewelry box and perfume bottles. Elizabeth adjusted her tinsel halo.

"'Where meek souls will receive him still,
  The dear Christ enters in.'"

Joseph and Mary came to the center and stopped. Joseph stepped in front of Mary and knocked on an imaginary door, and the innkeeper came forward, grinning from ear to ear, to open it.

All Seated on the Ground

I'd always said that if and when the aliens actually landed, it would be a letdown. I mean, after *War of the Worlds, Close Encounters,* and *E.T.,* there was no way they could live up to the image in the public's mind, good or bad.

I'd also said that they would look nothing like the aliens of the movies, and that they would *not* have come to A) kill us, B) take over our planet and enslave us, C) save us from ourselves à la *The Day the Earth Stood Still,* or D) have sex with Earthwomen. I mean, I realize it's hard to find someone nice, but would aliens really come thousands of light-years just to get a date? Plus, it seemed just as likely they'd be attracted to warthogs. Or yucca. Or air-conditioning units.

I've also always thought A) and B) were highly unlikely, since imperialist invader types would probably be too busy invading their next-door neighbors and being invaded by other invader types to have time to go after an out-of-the-way place like Earth, although you never know. I mean, look at Iraq. And as to C), I'm wary of people *or* aliens who say they've come to save you, as witness Reverend Thresher. And it seemed to me that aliens who were capable of building the spaceships necessary to cross all those light-years would necessarily have complex civilizations and therefore more complicated motives for coming than merely incinerating Washington or phoning home.

What had *never* occurred to me was that the aliens would arrive and we still wouldn't know what those motives were after almost nine months of talking to them.

Now, I'm not talking about an arrival where the UFO swoops down in the Southwest in the middle of nowhere, mutilates a few cows, makes a crop circle or two, abducts an *extremely* unreliable and unintelligent-sounding person, probes them in embarrassing places, and takes off again. I'd never believed the aliens would do that, either, and they didn't, although they did land in the Southwest, sort of.

They landed their spaceship in Denver, in the middle of the DU campus, and marched—well, actually "marched" is the wrong word; the Altairi's method of locomotion is somewhere between a glide and a waddle—straight up to the front door of University Hall in classic "Take me to your leader" fashion.

And that was it. They (there were six of them) didn't say, "Take us to your leader!" or "One small step for aliens, one giant leap for alienkind," or even "Earthmen, hand over your females." Or your planet. They just stood there.

And stood there. Police cars surrounded them, lights flashing. TV news crews and reporters pointed cameras at them. F-16s roared overhead, snapping pictures of their spaceship and trying to determine whether A) it had a force field or B) weaponry or C) they could blow it up (they couldn't). Half the city fled to the mountains in terror, creating an enormous traffic jam on I-70, and the other half drove by the campus to see what was going on, creating an enormous traffic jam on Evans.

The aliens, who by now had been dubbed the Altairi because an astronomy professor at DU had announced they were from the star Altair in the constellation Aquila (they weren't), didn't react to any of this, which apparently convinced the president of DU they weren't going to blow up the place à la *Independence Day*. He came out and welcomed them to Earth and to DU.

They continued to stand there. The mayor came and welcomed them to Earth and to Denver. The governor came and welcomed them to Earth and to Colorado, assured everyone it was perfectly safe to visit the state, and implied the Altairi were just the latest in a long line of tourists who had come from all over to see the magnificent Rockies, though that seemed unlikely since they were facing the other way, and they didn't turn around, even when the governor walked past them to point at Pikes Peak. They just stood there, facing University Hall.

They continued to stand there for the next three weeks, through an endless series of welcoming speeches by scientists, State Department officials, foreign dignitaries, and church and business leaders, and an assortment of weather, including a late April snowstorm that broke branches and power lines. If it hadn't been for the expressions on their faces, everybody would have assumed the Altairi were plants.

But no plant ever glared like that. It was a look of utter, withering disapproval. The first time I saw it in person, I thought, *Oh, my God, it's Aunt Judith.*

She was actually my father's aunt, and she used to come over once a month or so, dressed in a suit, a hat, and white gloves, and sit on the edge of a chair and glare at us, a glare which drove my mother into paroxysms of cleaning and baking whenever she found out Aunt Judith was coming. Not that Aunt Judith criticized Mom's housekeeping or her cooking. She didn't. She didn't even make a face when she sipped the coffee Mom served her or draw a white-gloved finger along the mantelpiece, looking for dust. She didn't have to. Sitting there in stony silence while my mother desperately tried to make conversation, her entire manner indicated disapproval. It was perfectly clear from that glare of hers that she considered us untidy, ill-mannered, ignorant, and utterly beneath contempt.

Since she never said what it was that displeased her (except for the occasional "Properly brought-up children do not speak unless spoken to"), my mother frantically polished silverware, baked petits fours, wrestled my sister Tracy and me into starched pinafores and patent-leather shoes and ordered us to thank Aunt Judith nicely for our birthday presents—a card with a dollar bill in it—and scrubbed and dusted the entire house to within an inch of its life. She even redecorated the entire living room, but nothing did any good. Aunt Judith still radiated disdain.

It would wilt even the strongest person. My mother frequently had to lie down with a cold cloth on her forehead after a visit from Aunt Judith, and the Altairi had the same effect on the dignitaries and scientists and politicians who came to see them. After the first time, the governor refused to meet with them again, and the President, whose polls were already in the low twenties and who couldn't afford any more pictures of irate citizens, refused to meet with them at all.

Instead he appointed a bipartisan commission, consisting of representatives from the Pentagon, the State Department, Homeland Security, the House, the Senate, and FEMA, to study them and find a way to communicate with them, and then, after that was a bust, a second commission consisting of experts in astronomy, anthropology, exobiology, and communications, and then a third, consisting of whoever they were able to recruit and who had anything resembling a theory about the Altairi or how to communicate with them, which is where I come in. I'd written a series of newspaper columns on aliens both before and after the Altairi arrived. (I'd also written columns on tourists, texting while driving, the traffic on I-70, the difficulty of finding any nice men to date, and Aunt Judith.)

I was recruited in late November to replace one of the language experts, who quit "to spend more time with his wife and family." I was picked by the chair of the commission, Dr. Morthman, who clearly didn't realize that my columns were humorous, but it didn't matter, since he had no intention of listening to me, or to anyone else on the commission, which at that point consisted of three linguists, two anthropologists, a cosmologist, a meteorologist, a botanist (in case they were plants after all), experts in primate, avian, and insect behavior (in case they were one of the above), an Egyptologist (in case they turned out to have built the Pyramids), an animal psychic, an Air Force colonel, a JAG lawyer, an expert in foreign customs, an expert in nonverbal communications, a weapons expert, Dr. Morthman (who, as far as I could see, wasn't an expert in anything), and, because of our proximity to Colorado Springs, the head of the One True Way Maxichurch, Reverend Thresher, who was convinced the Altairi were a herald of the End Times. "There is a reason God had them land here," he said. I wanted to ask him why, if that was the case, they hadn't landed in Colorado Springs instead, but he wasn't a good listener, either.

The only progress these people and their predecessors had made by the time I joined the commission was to get the Altairi to follow them various places, like in out of the weather and into the various labs that had been set up in University Hall for studying them, although when I saw the videotapes, it wasn't at all clear they were responding to anything the commission said or did. It looked to me like following Dr. Morthman and the others was their own idea, particularly since at nine o'clock every night they turned and glided/waddled back outside and disappeared into their ship.

The first time they did that, everyone panicked, thinking they were leaving. "Aliens Depart. Are They Fed Up?" the evening news logo read, a conclusion which I felt was due to their effect on people rather than any solid evidence. I mean, they could have gone home to watch Jon Stewart on *The Daily Show,* but even after they reemerged the next morning, the theory persisted that there was some sort of deadline, that if we didn't succeed in communicating with them within a fixed amount of time, the planet would be reduced to ash. Aunt Judith had always made me feel exactly the same way, that if I didn't measure up, I was toast.

But I never did measure up, and nothing in particular happened, except she stopped sending me birthday cards with a dollar in them, and I figured if the Altairi hadn't obliterated us after a few conversations with Reverend Thresher (he was constantly reading them passages from Scripture and trying to convert them), they weren't going to.

But it didn't look like they were going to tell us what they were doing here, either. The commission had tried speaking to them in nearly every language, including Farsi, Navajo code-talk, and Cockney slang. They had played them music, drummed, written out greetings, given them several PowerPoint presentations, text-messaged them, and shown them the Rosetta Stone. They'd also tried Ameslan and pantomime, though it was obvious the Altairi could hear. Whenever someone spoke to them or offered them a gift (or prayed over them), their expression of disapproval deepened to one of utter contempt. Just like Aunt Judith.

By the time I joined the commission, it had reached the same state of desperation my mother had when she redecorated the living room, and had decided to try to impress the Altairi by taking them to see the sights of Denver and Colorado, in the hope they'd react favorably.

"It won't work," I said. "My mother put up new drapes *and* wallpaper, and it didn't have any effect at all," but Dr. Morthman didn't listen.

We took them to the Denver Museum of Art and Rocky Mountain National Park and the Garden of the Gods and a Broncos game. They just stood there, sending out waves of disapproval.

Dr. Morthman was undeterred. "Tomorrow we'll take them to the Denver Zoo."

"Is that a good idea?" I asked. "I mean, I'd hate to give them ideas," but Dr. Morthman didn't listen.

Luckily, the Altairi didn't react to anything at the zoo, or to the Christmas lights at Civic Center, or to the *Nutcracker* ballet. And then we went to the mall.

🌲

By that point, the commission had dwindled down to seventeen people (two of the linguists and the animal psychic had quit), but it was still a large enough group of observers that the Altairi ran the risk of being trampled in the crowd. Most of the members, however, had stopped going on the field trips, saying they were "pursuing alternate lines of research" that didn't require direct observation, which meant they couldn't stand to be glared at the whole way there and back in the van. So the day we went to the mall, there were only Dr. Morthman, the aroma expert Dr. Wakamura, Reverend Thresher, and me. We didn't even have any press with us. When the Altairi'd first arrived, they were all over the TV networks and CNN, but after a few weeks of the aliens doing nothing, the networks had shifted to showing more exciting scenes from *Alien, Invasion of the Body Snatchers,* and *Men in Black II,* and then completely lost interest and gone back to Paris Hilton and stranded whales. The only photographer with us was Leo, the teenager Dr. Morthman had hired to videotape our outings, and as soon as we got inside the mall, he said, "Do you think it'd be okay if I ducked out to buy my girlfriend's Christmas present before we start filming? I mean, face it, they're just going to stand there."

He was right. The Altairi glide-waddled the length of several stores and then stopped, glaring impartially at the Sharper Image and Gap window displays and the crowds who stopped to gawk at the six of them and who then, intimidated by their expressions, averted their eyes and hurried on.

The mall was jammed with couples loaded down with shopping bags, parents pushing strollers, children, and a mob of middle-school girls in green choir robes apparently waiting to sing. The malls invited school and church choirs to come and perform this time of year in the food court. The girls were giggling and chattering; a toddler was shrieking, "I don't *want* to!"; Julie Andrews was singing "Joy to the World" on the piped-in Muzak; and Reverend Thresher was pointing at the panty-, bra-,

and wing-clad mannequins in the window of Victoria's Secret and saying, "Look at that! Sinful!"

"This way," Dr. Morthman, ahead of the Altairi, said, waving his arm
like the leader of a wagon train, "I want them to see Santa Claus," and I
stepped to the side to get around a trio of teenage boys walking side by
side who'd cut me off from the Altairi.

There was a sudden gasp, and the mall went quiet except for the
Muzak. "What—?" Dr. Morthman said sharply, and I pushed past the
teenage boys to see what had happened.

The Altairi were sitting calmly in the middle of the space between the
stores, glaring. A circle of fascinated shoppers had formed a circle
around them, and a man in a suit who looked like the manager of the
mall was hurrying up, demanding, "What's going on here?"

"This is wonderful," Dr. Morthman said. "I knew they'd respond if we
just took them enough places." He turned to me. "You were behind them,
Miss Yates. What made them sit down?"

"I don't know," I said. "I couldn't see them from where I was. Did—?"

"Go find Leo," he ordered. "He'll have it on tape."

I wasn't so sure of that, but I went to look for him. He was just coming out of Victoria's Secret, carrying a small bright pink bag. "Meg, what
happened?" he asked.

"The Altairi sat down," I said.

"Why?"

"That's what we're trying to find out. I take it you weren't filming
them?"

"No, I told you, I had to buy my girlfriend— Jeez, Dr. Morthman will
kill me." He jammed the pink bag into his jeans pocket. "I didn't think—"

"Well, start filming now," I said, "and I'll go see if I can find somebody
who caught it on their cell phone camera." With all these people taking
their kids to see Santa, there was bound to be someone with a camera. I
started working my way around the circle of staring spectators, keeping
away from Dr. Morthman, who was telling the mall manager he needed
to cordon off this end of the mall and everyone in it.

"Everyone in it?" the manager gulped.

"Yes, it's essential. The Altairi are obviously responding to something
they saw or heard—"

"Or smelled," Dr. Wakamura put in.

"And until we know what it was, we can't allow anyone to leave," Dr. Morthman said. "It's the key to our being able to communicate with them."

"But it's only two weeks till Christmas," the mall manager said. "I can't just shut off—"

"You obviously don't realize that the fate of the planet may be at stake," Dr. Morthman said.

I hoped not, especially since no one seemed to have caught the event on film, though they all had their cell phones out and pointed at the Altairi now, in spite of their glares. I looked across the circle, searching for a likely parent or grandparent who might have—

The choir. One of the girls' parents was bound to have brought a video camera along. I hurried over to the troop of green-robed girls. "Excuse me," I said to them, "I'm with the Altairi—"

Mistake. The girls instantly began bombarding me with questions.

"Why are they sitting down?"

"Why don't they talk?"

"Why are they always so mad?"

"Are we going to get to sing? We didn't get to sing yet."

"They said we had to stay here. How long? We're supposed to sing over at Flatirons Mall at six o'clock."

"Are they going to get inside us and pop out of our stomachs?"

"Did any of your parents bring a video camera?" I tried to shout over their questions, and when that failed, "I need to talk to your choir director."

"Mr. Ledbetter?"

"Are you his girlfriend?"

"No," I said, trying to spot someone who looked like a choir director type. "Where is he?"

"Over there," one of them said, pointing at a tall, skinny man in slacks and a blazer. "Are you going out with Mr. Ledbetter?"

"No," I said, trying to work my way over to him.

"Why not? He's really nice."

"Do you have a boyfriend?"

"No," I said as I reached him. "Mr. Ledbetter? I'm Meg Yates. I'm with the commission studying the Altairi—"

"You're just the person I want to talk to, Meg," he said.

"I'm afraid I can't tell you how long it's going to be," I said. "The girls told me you have another singing engagement at six o'clock."

"We do, and I've got a rehearsal tonight, but that isn't what I wanted to talk to you about."

"She doesn't have a boyfriend, Mr. Ledbetter," one of the girls said. I took advantage of the interruption to say, "I was wondering if anyone with your choir happened to record what just happened on a video camera or a—"

"Probably. Belinda," he said to the one who'd told him I didn't have a boyfriend, "go get your mother." She took off through the crowd. "Her mom started recording when we left the church. And if she didn't happen to catch it, Kaneesha's mom probably did. Or Chelsea's dad."

"Oh, thank goodness," I said. "Our cameraman didn't get it on film, and we need it to see what triggered their action."

"What made them sit down, you mean?" he said. "You don't need a video. I know what it was. The song."

"What song?" I said. "A choir wasn't singing when we came in, and anyway, the Altairi have already been exposed to music. They didn't react to it at all."

"What kind of music? Those notes from *Close Encounters*?"

"Yes," I said defensively, "and Beethoven and Debussy and Charles Ives. A whole assortment of composers."

"But instrumental music, not vocals, right? I'm talking about a song. One of the Christmas carols on the piped-in Muzak. I saw them sit down. They were definitely—"

"Mr. Ledbetter, you wanted my mom?" Belinda said, dragging over a large woman with a videocam.

"Yes," he said. "Mrs. Carlson, I need to see the video you shot of the choir today. From when we got to the mall."

She obligingly found the place and handed it to him. He fast-forwarded a minute. "Oh, good, you got it," he said, rewound, and held the camera so I could see the little screen. "Watch."

The screen showed the bus with *First Presbyterian Church* on its side, the girls getting off, the girls filing into the mall, the girls gathering in front of Crate and Barrel, giggling and chattering, though the sound was too low to hear what they were saying. "Can you turn the volume up?" Mr. Ledbetter said to Mrs. Carlson, and she pushed a button.

The voices of the girls came on: "Mr. Ledbetter, can we go to the food court afterward for a pretzel?"

"Mr. Ledbetter, I don't want to stand next to Heidi."

"Mr. Ledbetter, I left my lip gloss on the bus."

"Mr. Ledbetter—"

The Altairi aren't going to be on this, I thought. Wait—there, past the green-robed girls, were Dr. Morthman and Leo with his video camera, and then the Altairi. They were just glimpses, though, not a clear view. "I'm afraid—" I said.

"Shh," Mr. Ledbetter said, pushing down on the volume button again. "Listen."

He had cranked the volume all the way up. I could hear Reverend Thresher saying, "Look at that! It's absolutely disgusting!"

"Can you hear the Muzak on the tape, Meg?" Mr. Ledbetter asked. "Sort of," I said. "What is that?"

"'Joy to the World,'" he said, holding it so I could see. Mrs. Carlson must have moved to get a better shot of the Altairi, because there was no one blocking the view of them as they followed Dr. Morthman. I tried to see if they were glaring at anything in particular—the strollers or the Christmas decorations or the Victoria's Secret mannequins or the sign for the restrooms—but if they were, I couldn't tell.

"This way," Dr. Morthman said on the tape, "I want them to see Santa Claus."

"Okay, it's right about here," Mr. Ledbetter said. "Listen."

"'While shepherds watched . . .'" the Muzak choir sang tinnily.

I could hear Reverend Thresher saying, "Blasphemous!" and one of the girls asking, "Mr. Ledbetter, after we sing can we go to McDonald's?" and the Altairi abruptly collapsed onto the floor with a floomphing motion, like a crinolined Scarlett O'Hara sitting down suddenly. "Did you hear what they were singing?" Mr. Ledbetter said.

"No—"

"'All seated on the ground.' Here," he said, rewinding. "Listen."

He played it again. I watched the Altairi, focusing on picking out the sound of the Muzak through the rest of the noise. "'While shepherds watched their flocks by night,'" the choir sang, "'all seated on the ground.'"

He was right. The Altairi sat down the instant the word "seated" ended. I looked at him.

"See?" he said happily. "The song said to sit down and they sat. I happened to notice it because I was singing along with the Muzak. It's a bad habit of mine. The girls tease me about it."

But why would the Altairi respond to the words in a Christmas carol when they hadn't responded to anything else we'd said to them over the last nine months? "Can I borrow this videotape?" I asked. "I need to show it to the rest of the commission."

"Sure," he said, and asked Mrs. Carlson.

"I don't know," she said reluctantly. "I have tapes of every single one of Belinda's performances."

"She'll make a copy and get the original back to you," Mr. Ledbetter told her. "Isn't that right, Meg?"

"Yes," I said.

"Great," he said. "You can send the tape to me, and I'll see to it Belinda gets it. Will that work?" he asked Mrs. Carlson.

She nodded, popped the tape out, and handed it to me. "Thank you," I said, and hurried back over to Dr. Morthman, who was still arguing with the mall manager.

"You can't just close the entire mall," the manager was saying. "This is the biggest profit period of the year—"

"Dr. Morthman," I said, "I have a tape here of the Altairi sitting down. It was taken—"

"Not now," he said. "I need you to go tell Leo to film everything the Altairi might have seen."

"But he's taping the Altairi," I said. "What if they do something else?" but he wasn't listening.

"Tell him we need a video record of everything they might have responded to, the stores, the shoppers, the Christmas decorations, everything. And then call the police department and tell them to cordon off the parking lot. Tell them no one's to leave."

"Cordon off—!" the mall manager said. "You can't hold all these people here!"

"All these people need to be moved out of this end of the mall and into an area where they can be questioned," Dr. Morthman said.

"Questioned?" the mall manager, almost apoplectic, said.

"Yes, one of them may have seen what triggered their action—"

"Someone did," I said. "I was just talking to—"

He wasn't listening. "We'll need names, contact information, and depositions from all of them," he said to the mall manager. "And they'll need to be tested for infectious diseases. The Altairi may be sitting down because they don't feel well."

"Dr. Morthman, they aren't sick," I said. "They—"

"Not *now*," he said. "Did you tell Leo?"

I gave up. "I'll do it now," I said, and went over to where Leo was filming the Altairi and told him what Dr. Morthman wanted him to do.

"What if the Altairi do something?" he said, looking at them sitting there glaring. He sighed. "I suppose he's right. They don't look like they're going to move anytime soon." He swung his camera around and started filming the Victoria's Secret window. "How long do you think we'll be stuck here?"

I told him what Dr. Morthman had said.

"Jeez, he's going to question all these people?" he said, moving to the Williams-Sonoma window. "I had somewhere to go tonight."

All *these people have somewhere to go tonight,* I thought, looking at the crowd—mothers with babies in strollers, little kids, elderly couples, teenagers. Including fifty middle-school girls who were supposed to be at another performance an hour from now. And it wasn't the choir director's fault Dr. Morthman wouldn't listen.

"We'll need a room large enough to hold everyone," Dr. Morthman was saying, "and adjoining rooms for interrogating them," and the mall manager was shouting, "This is a *mall,* not Guantanamo!"

I backed carefully away from Dr. Morthman and the mall manager and then worked my way through the crowd to where the choir director was standing, surrounded by his students. "But, Mr. Ledbetter," one of them was saying, "we'd come right back, and the pretzel place is right over there."

"Mr. Ledbetter, could I speak to you for a moment?" I said.

"Sure. Shoo," he said to the girls.

"But, Mr. Ledbetter—"

He ignored them. "What did the commission think of the Christmas carol theory?" he asked me.

"I haven't had a chance to ask them. Listen, in another five minutes they're going to lock down this entire mall."

"But I—"

"I know, you've got another performance and if you're going to leave, do it right now. I'd go that way," I said, pointing to the east door.

"*Thank* you," he said earnestly, "but won't you get into trouble—?"

"If I need your choir's depositions, I'll call you," I said. "What's your number?"

"Belinda, give me a pen and something to write on," he said. She handed him a pen and began rummaging in her backpack.

"Never mind," he said, "there isn't time." He grabbed my hand and wrote the number on my palm.

"You said we aren't allowed to write on ourselves," Belinda said.

"You're not," he said. "I really appreciate this, Meg."

"Go," I said, looking anxiously over at Dr. Morthman. If they didn't go in the next thirty seconds, they'd never make it, and there was no way he could round up fifty middle-school girls in that short a time. Or even make himself heard . . .

"Ladies," he said, and raised his hands as if he were going to direct a choir. "Line up." And to my astonishment, they instantly obeyed him, forming themselves silently into a line and walking quickly toward the east door with no giggling, no "Mr. Ledbetter—?" My opinion of him went up sharply.

I pushed quickly back through the crowd to where Dr. Morthman and the mall manager were still arguing. Leo had moved farther down the mall to film the Verizon Wireless store, away from the east door. Good. I rejoined Dr. Morthman, moving to his right side so if he turned to look at me, he couldn't see the door.

"But what about *bathrooms*?" the manager was yelling. "The mall doesn't have nearly enough bathrooms for all these people."

The choir was nearly out the door. I watched till the last one disappeared, followed by Mr. Ledbetter.

"We'll get in portable toilets. Miss Yates, arrange for porta-potties to be brought in," Dr. Morthman said, turning to me, and it was obvious he had no idea I'd ever been gone. "And get Homeland Security on the phone."

"Homeland Security!" the manager wailed. "Do you know what it'll do to business when the media gets hold—" He stopped and looked over at the crowd around the Altairi.

There was a collective gasp from them and then a hush. Someone must have turned the Muzak off at some point because there was no sound at all in the mall. "What—? Let me through," Dr. Morthman said, breaking the silence. He pushed his way through the circle of shoppers to see what was happening.

I followed in his wake. The Altairi were slowly standing up, a motion somewhat like a string being pulled taut.

"Thank goodness," the mall manager said, sounding infinitely relieved. "Now that that's over, I assume I can reopen the mall."

Dr. Morthman shook his head. "This may be the prelude to another action, or the response to a second stimulus. Leo, I want to see the video of what was happening right before they began to stand up."

"I didn't get it," Leo said.

"Didn't *get* it?"

"You told me to tape the stuff in the mall," he said, but Dr. Morthman wasn't listening. He was watching the Altairi, who had turned around and were slowly glide-waddling back toward the east door.

"Go after them," he ordered Leo. "Don't let them out of your sight, and get it on tape this time." He turned to me. "You stay here and see if the mall has surveillance tapes. And get all these people's names and contact information in case we need to question them."

"Before you go, you need to know—"

"Not *now*. The Altairi are leaving. And there's no telling where they'll go next," he said, and took off after them. "See if anyone caught the incident on a video camera."

As it turned out, the Altairi went only as far as the van we'd brought them to the mall in, where they waited, glaring, to be transported back to DU. When I got back, they were in the main lab with Dr. Wakamura. I'd been at the mall nearly four hours, taking down names and phone numbers from Christmas shoppers who said things like, "I've been here six hours with two toddlers. Six hours!" and "I'll have you know I missed my grandson's Christmas concert." I was glad I'd helped Mr. Ledbetter and his seventh-grade girls sneak out. They'd never have made it to the other mall in time.

When I was finished taking names and abuse, I went to ask the mall manager about surveillance tapes, expecting more abuse, but he was so glad to have his mall open again, he turned them over immediately. "Do these tapes have audio?" I asked him, and when he said no, "You wouldn't also have a tape of the Christmas music you play, would you?"

I was almost certain he wouldn't—Muzak is usually piped in—but to my surprise he said yes and handed over a CD. I stuck it and the tapes in my bag, drove back to DU, and went to the main lab to find Dr. Morthman. I found Dr. Wakamura instead, squirting assorted food court smells—corn dog, popcorn, sushi—at the Altairi to see if any of them made them sit down. "I'm convinced they were responding to one of the mall's aromas," he said.

"Actually, I think they may have—"

"It's just a question of finding the right one," he said, squirting pizza at them. They glared.

"Where's Dr. Morthman?"

"Next door," he said, squirting essence of funnel cake. "He's meeting with the rest of the commission."

I winced and went next door. "We need to look at the floor coverings in the mall," Dr. Short was saying. "The Altairi may well have been responding to the difference between wood and stone."

"And we need to take air samples," Dr. Jarvis said. "They may have been responding to something poisonous to them in our atmosphere."

"Something poisonous?" Reverend Thresher said. "Something blasphemous, you mean! Angels in filthy underwear! The Altairi obviously refused to go any farther into that den of iniquity, and they sat down in protest. Even aliens know sin when they see it."

"I don't agree, Dr. Jarvis," Dr. Short said, ignoring Reverend Thresher. "Why would the air in the mall have a different composition from the air in a museum or a sports arena? We're looking for variables here. What about sounds? Could they be a factor?"

"Yes," I said. "The Altairi were—"

"Did you get the surveillance tapes, Miss Yates?" Dr. Morthman cut in. "Go through and cue them up to the point just before the Altairi sat down. I want to see what they were looking at."

"It wasn't what they were looking at," I said. "It was—"

"And call the mall and get samples of their floor coverings," he said. "You were saying, Dr. Short?"

I left the surveillance tapes and the lists of shoppers on Dr. Morthman's desk, and then went to the audio lab, found a CD player, and listened to the songs: "Here Comes Santa Claus," "White Christmas," "Joy to the World"—

Here it was. "'While shepherds watched their flocks by night, all seated on the ground, the angel of the Lord came down, and glory shone around.'" Could the Altairi have thought the song was talking about the descent of their spaceship? Or were they responding to something else entirely, and the timing was simply coincidental?

There was only one way to find out. I went back to the main lab, where Dr. Wakamura was sticking lighted candles under the Altairi's noses. "Good grief, what is that?" I asked, wrinkling my nose.

"Bayberry magnolia," he said.

"It's awful."

"You should smell sandalwood violet," he said. "They were right next to Candle in the Wind when they sat down. They may have been responding to a scent from the store."

"Any response?" I said, thinking their expressions, for once, looked entirely appropriate.

"No, not even to spruce watermelon, which smelled *very* alien. Did Dr. Morthman find any clues on the security tapes?" he asked hopefully.

"He hasn't looked at them yet," I said. "When you're done here, I'll be glad to escort the Altairi back to their ship."

"Would you?" he said gratefully. "I'd really appreciate it. They look exactly like my mother-in-law. Can you take them now?"

"Yes," I said, and went over to the Altairi and motioned them to follow me, hoping they wouldn't veer off and go back to their ship since it was nearly nine o'clock. They didn't. They followed me down the hall and into the audio lab. "I just want to try something," I said, and played them "While Shepherds Watched."

"'While shepherds watched their flocks,'" the choir sang. I watched the Altairi's unchanging faces. *Mr. Ledbetter was wrong,* I thought. *They must have been responding to something else. They're not even listening.* "'. . . by night, all seated . . .'"

The Altairi sat down.

I've got to call Mr. Ledbetter, I thought. I switched off the CD and punched in the number he'd written on my hand. "Hi, this is Calvin Ledbetter," his recorded voice said. "Sorry I can't come to the phone right now," and I remembered too late that he'd said he had a rehearsal. "If you're calling about a rehearsal, the schedule is as follows: Thursday, Mile-High Women's Chorus, eight P.M., Montview Methodist; Friday, chancel choir, eleven A.M., Trinity Episcopal; Denver Symphony, three P.M.—" It was obvious he wasn't home. And that he was far too busy to worry about the Altairi.

I hung up and looked over at them. They were still sitting down, and it occurred to me that playing them the song might have been a bad idea, since I had no idea what had made them stand back up. It hadn't been the Muzak because it had been turned off, and if the stimulus had been something in the mall, we could be here all night. After a few minutes, though, they stood up, doing that odd pulled-string thing, and glared at me. "'While shepherds watched their flocks by night,'" I said to them, "'all seated on the ground.'"

They continued to stand.

"'*Seated* on the ground,'" I repeated. "*Seated.* Sit!" No response at all.

I played the song again. They sat down right on cue. Which still didn't prove they were doing what the words told them to do. They could be responding to the mere sound of singing. The mall had been noisy when they first walked in. "While Shepherds Watched" might have been the first song they'd been able to hear, and they'd sit down whenever they heard singing. I waited till they stood up again and then played the two preceding tracks. They didn't respond to Bing Crosby singing "White Christmas" or to Julie Andrews singing "Joy to the World." (Or to the breaks between songs.) There wasn't even any indication they were aware anyone was singing.

"'While shepherds watched their flocks by-y night...'" the choir began. I tried to stay still and keep my face impassive, in case they were responding to nonverbal cues I was giving them. "'... ah-all seated—'"

They sat down at exactly the same place, so it was definitely those particular words. Or the voices singing them. Or the particular configuration of notes. Or the rhythm. Or the frequencies of the notes.

Whatever it was, I couldn't figure it out tonight. It was nearly ten o'clock. I needed to get the Altairi back to their spaceship. I waited for them to stand up and then led them, glaring, out to their ship, and went back to my apartment.

The message light on my answering machine was flashing. It was probably Dr. Morthman, wanting me to go back to the mall and take air samples. I hit play. "Hi, this is Mr. Ledbetter," the choir director's voice said. "From the mall, remember? I need to talk to you about something." He gave me his cell phone number and repeated his home phone, "In case it washed off. I should be home by eleven. Till then, whatever you do, *don't* let your alien guys listen to any more Christmas carols."

There was no answer at either of the numbers. *He turns his cell phone off during rehearsals,* I thought. I looked at my watch. It was ten-fifteen. I grabbed the yellow pages, looked up the address of Montview Methodist, and took off for the church, detouring past the Altairi's ship to make sure it was still there and hadn't begun sprouting guns from its ports or flashing ominous lights. It hadn't. It was its usual Sphinx-like self, which reassured me. A little.

It took me twenty minutes to reach the church. *I hope rehearsal isn't over and I've missed him,* I thought, but there were lots of cars in the parking lot, and light still shone through the stained-glass windows. The front doors, however, were locked.

I went around to the side door. It was unlocked, and I could hear singing from somewhere inside. I followed the sound down a darkened hall.

The song abruptly stopped, in the middle of a word. I waited a minute, listening, and when it didn't start up again, began trying doors. The first three were locked, but the fourth opened onto the sanctuary. The women's choir was up at the very front, facing Mr. Ledbetter, whose back was to me. "Top of page ten," he was saying.

Thank goodness he's still here, I thought, slipping in the back.

"From 'O hear the angel voices,'" he said, nodded to the organist, and raised his baton.

"Wait, where do we take a breath?" one of the women asked. "After 'voices'?"

"No, after 'divine,'" he said, consulting the music in front of him on the music stand, "and then at the bottom of page thirteen."

Another woman said, "Can you play the alto line for us? From 'Fall on your knees'?"

This was obviously going to take a while, and I couldn't afford to wait. I started up the aisle toward them, and the entire choir looked up from their music and glared at me.

Mr. Ledbetter turned around, and his face lit up. He turned to the women again, said, "I'll be right back," and sprinted down the aisle to me. "Meg," he said, reaching me. "Hi. What—?"

"I'm sorry to interrupt, but I got your message, and—"

"You're not interrupting. Really. We were almost done anyway."

"What did you mean, don't play them any more Christmas carols? I didn't get your message till after I'd played them some of the other songs from the mall—"

"And what happened?"

"Nothing, but on your message you said—"

"Which songs?"

"'Joy to the World' and—"

"All four verses?"

"No, only two. That's all that were on the CD. The first one and the one about 'wonders of his love.'"

"One and four," he said, staring past me, his lips moving rapidly as if he were running through the lyrics. "Those should be okay—"

"What do you mean? Why did you leave that message?"

"Because if the Altairi were responding literally to the words in 'While Shepherds Watched,' Christmas carols are full of dangerous—"

"Dangerous—?"

"Yes. Look at 'We Three Kings of Orient Are.' You didn't play them that, did you?"

"No, just 'Joy to the World' and 'White Christmas.'"

"Mr. Ledbetter," one of the women called from the front of the church. "How long are you going to be?"

"I'll be right there," he said. He turned back to me. "How much of 'While Shepherds Watched' did you play them?"

"Just the part up to 'all seated on the ground.'"

"Not the other verses?"

"No. What—?"

"Mr. Ledbetter," the same woman said impatiently, "some of us have to leave."

"I'll be right there," he called to her, and to me, "Give me five minutes," and sprinted back up the aisle.

I sat down in a back pew, picked up a hymnal, and tried to find "We Three Kings." That was easier said than done. The hymns were numbered, but they didn't seem to be in any particular order. I turned to the back, looking for an index.

"But we still haven't gone over 'Saviour of the Heathen, Come,'" a young, pretty redhead said.

"We'll go over it Saturday night," Mr. Ledbetter said.

The index didn't tell me where "We Three Kings" was, either. It had rows of numbers—5.6.6.5. and 8.8.7.D.—with a column of strange words below them—Laban, Hursley, Olive's Brow, Arizona—like some sort of code. Could the Altairi be responding to some sort of cipher embedded in the carol like in *The Da Vinci Code*? I hoped not.

"When are we supposed to be there?" the women were asking.

"Seven," Mr. Ledbetter said.

"But that won't give us enough time to run over 'Saviour of the Heathen, Come,' will it?"

"And what about 'Santa Claus Is Coming to Town'?" the redhead asked. "We don't have the second soprano part at all."

I abandoned the index and began looking through the hymns. If I couldn't figure out a simple hymnal, how could I hope to figure out a completely alien race's communications? *If* they were trying to communicate. They might have been sitting down to listen to the music, like you'd stop to look at a flower. Or maybe their feet just hurt.

"What kind of shoes are we supposed to wear?" the choir was asking.

"Comfortable," Mr. Ledbetter said. "You're going to be on your feet a long time."

I continued to search through the hymnal. Here was "What Child Is This?" I had to be on the right track. "Bring a Torch, Jeanette, Isabella." It had to be here somewhere. "On Christmas Night, All People Sing—"

They were finally gathering up their things and leaving. "See you Saturday," he said, herding them out the door, all except for the pretty redhead, who buttonholed him at the door to say, "I was wondering if you could stay and go over the second soprano part with me again. It'll only take a few minutes."

"I can't tonight," he said. She turned and glared at me, and I knew *exactly* what that glare meant.

"Remind me and we'll run through it Saturday night," he said, shut the door on her, and sat down next to me. "Sorry, big performance Saturday. Now, about the aliens. Where were we?"

"'We Three Kings.' You said the words were dangerous."

"Oh, right." He took the hymnal from me, flipped expertly to the right page, pointed. "Verse four. 'Sorrowing, sighing, bleeding, dying'—I assume you don't want the Altairi locking themselves in a stone-cold tomb."

"No," I said fervently. "You said 'Joy to the World' was bad, too. What does it have in it?"

"'Sorrow, sins, thorns infesting the ground.'"

"You think they're doing whatever the hymns tell them? That they're treating them like orders to be followed?"

"I don't know, but if they are, there are all kinds of things in Christmas carols you don't want them doing: running around on rooftops, bringing torches, killing babies—"

"Killing *babies*?" I said. "What carol is that in?"

"'The Coventry Carol,'" he said, flipping to another page. "The verse about Herod. See?" He pointed to the words. "'Charged he hath this day . . . all children young to slay.'"

"Oh, my gosh, that carol was one of the ones from the mall. It was on the CD," I said. "I'm so glad I came to see you."

"So am I," he said, and grinned at me.

"You asked me how much of 'While Shepherds Watched' I'd played them," I said. "Is there child-slaying in that, too?"

"No, but verse two has got 'fear' and 'mighty dread' in it, and 'seized their troubled minds.'"

"I definitely don't want the Altairi to do that," I said, "but now I don't know *what* to do. We've been trying to establish communications with the Altairi for nine months, and that song was the first thing they've ever responded to. If I can't play them Christmas carols—"

"I didn't say that. We just need to make sure the ones you play them don't have any murder and mayhem in them. You said you had a CD of the music they were playing in the mall?"

"Yes. That's what I played them."

"Mr. Ledbetter?" a voice said tentatively, and a balding man in a clerical collar leaned in the door. "How much longer will you be? I need to lock up."

"Oh, sorry, Reverend McIntyre," he said, and stood up. "We'll get out of your way."

He ran up the aisle, grabbed his music, and came back. "You'll be at the aches, right?" he said to Reverend McIntyre.

The *aches*? *You must have misunderstood what he said,* I thought.

"I'm not sure," Reverend McIntyre said. "My handle's pretty rusty."

Handle? What *were* they talking about?

"Especially the 'Hallelujah Chorus.' It's been years since I last sang it."

Oh, Handel, not handle.

"I'm rehearsing it with Trinity Episcopal's choir at eleven tomorrow if you want to come and run through it with us."

"I just may do that."

"Great," Mr. Ledbetter said. "Good night." He led me out of the sanctuary. "Where's your car parked?"

"Out in front."

"Good. Mine, too." He opened the side door. "You can follow me to my apartment."

I had a sudden blinding vision of Aunt Judith glaring disapprovingly at me and saying, "A nice young lady *never* goes to a gentleman's apartment alone."

"You did say you brought the music from the mall with you, didn't you?" he asked.

Which is what you get for jumping to conclusions, I thought, following him to his apartment and wondering if he was going out with the redheaded second soprano.

"On the way over I was thinking about all this," he said when we got to his apartment building, "and I think the first thing we need to do is figure out exactly which element or elements of 'all seated on the ground' they're responding to, the notes—I know you said they'd been exposed to music before, but it could be this particular configuration of notes—or words."

I told him about reciting the lyrics to them.

"Okay, then, the next thing we do is see if it's the accompaniment," he said, unlocking the door. "Or the tempo. Or the key."

"The key?" I said, looking down at the keys in his hand.

"Yeah, have you ever seen *Jumpin' Jack Flash*?"

"No."

"Great movie. Whoopi Goldberg. In it, the key to the spy's code is the key. Literally. B flat. 'While Shepherds Watched' is in the key of C, but 'Joy to the World' is in D. That may be why they didn't respond to it. Or they may only respond to the sound of certain instruments. What Beethoven did they listen to?"

"The Ninth Symphony."

He frowned. "Then that's unlikely, but there might be a guitar or a marimba or something in the 'While Shepherds Watched' accompaniment. We'll see. Come on in," he said, opening the door and immediately vanishing into the bedroom. "There's soda in the fridge," he called back out to me. "Go ahead and sit down."

That was easier said than done. The couch, chair, and coffee table were all covered with CDs, music, and clothes. "Sorry," he said, coming back in with a laptop. He set it down on top of a stack of books and moved a pile of laundry from the chair so I could sit down. "December's a bad month. And this year, in addition to my usual five thousand concerts and church services and cantata performances, I'm directing aches."

Then I hadn't misheard him before. "Aches?" I said.

"Yeah. A-C-H-E-S. The All-City Holiday Ecumenical Sing. ACHES. Or, as my seventh-grade girls call it, Aches and Pains. It's a giant concert—well, not actually a concert because everybody sings, even the audience. But all the city singing groups and church choirs participate." He moved a stack of LPs off the couch and onto the floor and sat down across from me. "Denver has it every year. At the convention center. Have you ever been to a Sing?" he said, and when I shook my head, "It's pretty impressive. Last year three thousand people and forty-four choirs participated."

"And you're directing?"

"Yeah. Actually, it's a much easier job than directing my church choirs. Or my seventh-grade girls' glee. And it's kind of fun. It used to be the All-City *Messiah,* you know, a whole bunch of people getting together to sing Handel's *Messiah,* but then they had a request from the Unitarians to include some Solstice songs, and it kind of snowballed from there. Now we do Hanukkah songs and 'Have Yourself a Merry Little Christmas' and 'The Seven Nights of Kwanzaa,' along with Christmas carols and selections from the *Messiah*. Which, by the way, we can't let the Altairi listen to, either."

"Is there children-slaying in that, too?"

"Head-breaking. 'Thou shalt break them with a rod of iron' and 'dash them in pieces.' There's also wounding, bruising, cutting, deriding, and laughing to scorn."

"Actually, the Altairi already know all about scorn," I said.

"But hopefully not about shaking nations. And covering the earth with darkness," he said. "Okay"—he opened his laptop—"the first thing I'm going to do is scan in the song. Then I'll remove the accompaniment so we can play them just the vocals."

"What can I do?"

"You," he said, disappearing into the other room again and returning with a foot-high stack of sheet music and music books, which he dumped in my lap, "can make a list of all the songs we don't want the Altairi to hear."

I nodded and started through *The Holly Jolly Book of Christmas Songs*. It was amazing how many carols, which I'd always thought were about peace and good will, had really violent lyrics. "The Coventry Carol" wasn't the only one with child-slaying in it. "Christmas Day Is Come" did, too, along with references to sin, strife, and militants. "O Come, O Come, Emmanuel" had strife, too, and envy and quarrels. "The Holly and the Ivy" had thorns, blood, and bears, and "Good King Wenceslas" talked about cruelty, bringing people flesh, freezing their blood, and heart failure.

"I had no idea Christmas carols were so grim," I said.

"You should hear Easter," Mr. Ledbetter said. "While you're looking, see if you can find any songs with the word 'seated' in it so we can see if it's that particular word they're responding to."

I nodded and went back to reading lyrics. In "Let All Mortal Flesh Keep Silence" everyone was standing, not seated, plus it had "fear," "trembling," and a line about giving oneself for heavenly food. "The First Noel" had "blood," and the shepherds were lying, not sitting.

What Christmas song has "seated" in it? I thought, trying to remember. *Isn't there something in "Jingle Bells" about Miss Somebody or Other being seated by someone's side?*

There was, and in "Wassail, Wassail," there was a line about "a-sitting" by the fire, but not the word "seated."

I kept looking. The nonreligious Christmas songs were almost as bad as the carols. Even a children's song like "I'm Getting' Nuttin' for Christmas" gaily discussed smashing bats over people's heads, and there seemed to be an entire genre of "Grandma Got Run Over by a Reindeer"–type songs: "Grandma's Killer Fruitcake," "I Came Upon a Roadkill Deer," and "Grandpa's Gonna Sue the Pants Off Santa."

And even when the lyrics weren't violent, they had phrases in them like "rule o'er all the earth" and "over us all to reign," which the Altairi might take as an invitation to global conquest.

There have to be some carols that are harmless, I thought, and looked up "Away in a Manger" in the index (which *The Holly Jolly Book,* unlike the hymnal, did have): ". . . lay down his sweet head . . . the stars in the sky . . ." *No mayhem here,* I thought. *I can definitely add this to the list.* "Love . . . blessings . . ."

"And take us to heaven to live with thee there." A harmless enough line, but it might mean something entirely different to the Altairi. I didn't want to find myself on a spaceship heading back to Aquila or wherever it was they came from.

We worked till almost three in the morning, by which time we had separate recordings of the vocals, accompaniment, and notes (played by Mr. Ledbetter on the piano, guitar, and flute and recorded by me) of "all seated on the ground," a list, albeit rather short, of songs the Altairi could safely hear, and another, even shorter list of ones with "seated," "sit," or "sitting" in them.

"Thank you so much, Mr. Ledbetter," I said, putting on my coat.

"Calvin," he said.

"Calvin. Anyway, thank you. I really appreciate this. I'll let you know the results of my playing the songs for them."

"Are you kidding, Meg?" he said. "I want to be there when you do this."

"But I thought— Don't you have to rehearse with the choirs for your ACHES thing?" I said, remembering the heavy schedule he'd left on his answering machine.

"Yes, and I have to rehearse with the symphony, and with the chancel choir and the kindergarten choir and the handbell choir for the Christmas Eve service—"

"Oh, and I've kept you up so late," I said. "I'm really sorry."

"Choir directors never sleep in December," he said cheerfully, "and what I was going to say was that I'm free in between rehearsals and till eleven tomorrow morning. How early can you get the Altairi?"

"They usually come out of their ship around seven, but some of the other commission members may want to work with them."

"And face those bright shiny faces before they've had their coffee? My bet is you'll have the Altairi all to yourself."

He was probably right. I remembered Dr. Jarvis saying he had to work himself up to seeing the Altairi over the course of the day: "They look just like my fifth-grade teacher."

"Are you sure *you* want to face them first thing in the morning?" I asked him. "The Altairi's glares—"

"Are nothing compared to the glare of a first soprano who didn't get the solo she wanted. Don't worry, I can handle the Altairi," he said. "I can't wait to find out what it is they're responding to."

☙

What we found out was nothing.

Calvin had been right. There was no one else waiting outside University Hall when the Altairi appeared. I hustled them into the audio lab, locked the door, and called Calvin, and he came right over, bearing Starbucks coffee and an armload of CDs.

"Yikes!" he said when he saw the Altairi standing over by the speakers. "I was wrong about the first soprano. This is more a seventh-grader's 'No, you can't text-message during the choir concert—or wear face glitter' glare."

I shook my head. "It's an Aunt Judith glare."

"I'm very glad we decided not to play them the part about dashing people's heads into pieces," he said. "Are you sure they didn't come to Earth to kill everybody?"

"No," I said. "That's why we have to establish communications with them."

"Right," he said, and proceeded to play the accompaniment we'd recorded the night before. Nothing, and nothing when he played the notes with piano, guitar, and flute, but when he played the vocal part by itself, the Altairi promptly sat down.

"Definitely the words," he said, and when we played them "Jingle Bells," they sat down again at "seated by my side," which seemed to confirm it. But when he played them the first part of "Sit Down, You're Rocking the Boat" from *Guys and Dolls* and "Sittin' on the Dock of the Bay," they didn't sit down for either one.

"Which means it's the word 'seated,'" I said.

"Or they only respond to Christmas songs," he said. "Do you have some other carol we can play them?"

"Not with 'seated,'" I said. "'All I Want for Christmas Is My Two Front Teeth' has 'sitting' in it."

We played it for them. No response, but when he played "We Need a Little Christmas," from the musical *Mame,* the Altairi sat down the moment the recording reached the word "sitting."

Calvin cut off the rest of the phrase, since we didn't want the Altairi sitting on our shoulders, and looked at me. "So why did they respond to this 'sitting' and not the one in 'All I Want for Christmas Is My Two Front Teeth'?" he mused.

I was tempted to say, "Because 'All I Want for Christmas' is an absolutely terrible song," but I didn't. "The voices?" I suggested.

"Maybe," he said, and shuffled through the CDs till he found a recording of the same song by the Statler Brothers. The Altairi sat down at exactly the same place.

So not the voices. And not just Christmas. When Calvin played them the opening song from *1776,* they sat down again as the Continental Congress sang orders to John Adams to sit down. And it wasn't the verb "to sit." When we played them "The Hanukkah Song," they spun solemnly in place.

"Okay, so we've established it's ecumenical," Calvin said.

"Thank goodness," I said, thinking of Reverend Thresher and what he'd say if he found out they'd responded to a Christmas carol, but when we played them a Solstice song with the phrase "the earth turns round again," they just stood there and glared.

"Words beginning with *s*?" I said.

"Maybe." He played them, in rapid succession, "The Snow Lay on the Ground," "Santa Claus Is Coming to Town," and "Suzy Snowflake." Nothing.

At ten forty-five Calvin left to go to his choir rehearsal. "It's at Trinity

Episcopal, if you want to meet me there at noon," he said, "and we can go over to my apartment from there. I want to run an analysis on the frequency patterns of the phrases they responded to."

"Okay," I said, and delivered the Altairi to Dr. Wakamura, who wanted to squirt them with perfumes from the Crabtree and Evelyn store. I left them glaring at him and went up to Dr. Morthman's office. He wasn't there. "He went to the mall to collect paint samples," Dr. Jarvis said.

I called him on his cell phone. "Dr. Morthman, I've run some tests," I said, "and the Altairi are—"

"Not now. I'm waiting for an important call from ACS," he said, and hung up.

I went back to the audio lab and listened to the Cambridge Boys' Choir, Barbra Streisand, and Barenaked Ladies Christmas albums, trying to find songs with variations of "sit" and "spin" in them and no bloodshed. I also looked up instances of "turn." They hadn't responded to "turns" in the Solstice song, but I wasn't sure that proved anything. They hadn't responded to "sitting" in "All I Want for Christmas," either.

At noon I went to meet Calvin at Trinity Episcopal. They weren't done rehearsing yet, and it didn't sound like they would be for some time. Calvin kept starting and stopping the choir and saying, "Basses, you're coming in two beats early, and altos, on 'singing,' that's an A flat. Let's take it again, from the top of page eight."

They went over the section four more times, with no discernible improvement, before Calvin said, "Okay, that's it. I'll see you all Saturday night."

"We are *never* going to get that entrance right," several of the choir members muttered as they gathered up their music, and the balding minister from last night, Reverend McIntyre, looked totally discouraged.

"Maybe I shouldn't sing after all," he told Calvin.

"Yes, you should," Calvin said, and put his hand on Reverend McIntyre's shoulder. "Don't worry. It'll all come together. You'll see."

"Do you really believe that?" I asked Calvin after Reverend McIntyre had gone out.

He laughed. "I know it's hard to believe listening to them now. I never think they're going to be able to do it, but somehow, no matter how awful they sound in rehearsal, they always manage to pull it off. It's enough to restore your faith in humanity." He frowned. "I thought you were going to come over, and we were going to look at frequency patterns."

"We are," I said. "Why?"

He pointed behind me. The Altairi were standing there with Reverend McIntyre. "I found them outside," he said, smiling. "I was afraid they might be lost."

"Oh, dear, they must have followed me. I'm so sorry," I said, though Reverend McIntyre didn't seem particularly intimidated by them. I said as much.

"I'm not," he said. "They don't look nearly as annoyed as my congregation does when they don't approve of my sermon."

"I'd better take them back," I said to Calvin.

"No, as long as they're here, we might as well take them over to my apartment and try some more songs on them. We need more data."

I somehow squeezed all six of them into my car and took them over to Calvin's apartment, and he analyzed frequency patterns while I played some more songs for them. It definitely wasn't the quality of the songs or the singers they were responding to. They wouldn't sit down for Willie Nelson's "Pretty Paper" and then did for a hideous falsetto children's recording of "Little Miss Muffet" from the 1940s.

It wasn't the words' meaning, either. When I played them "Adeste Fideles" in Latin, they sat down when the choir sang, *"tibi sit gloria."*

"Which proves they're taking what they hear literally," Calvin said when I took him into the kitchen out of earshot of the Altairi to tell me.

"Yes, which means we've got to make sure they don't hear any words that have double meanings," I said. "We can't even play them 'Deck the Halls,' for fear they might deck someone."

"And we definitely can't play them 'laid in a manger,'" he said, grinning.

"It's not funny," I said. "At this rate, we aren't going to be able to play them *anything.*"

"There must be some songs—"

"*What* songs?" I said in frustration. "'I've Got My Love to Keep Me Warm' talks about hearts that are on fire, 'Christmastide' might bring on a tsunami, and 'be born in us today' sounds like a scene out of *Alien.*"

"I know," he said. "Don't worry, we'll find something. Here, I'll help you." He cleared off the kitchen table, brought in the stacks of sheet music, albums, and CDs, and sat me down across from him. "I'll find songs and you check the lyrics."

We started through them. "No . . . no . . . what about 'I Heard the Bells on Christmas Day'?"

"No," I said, looking up the lyrics. "It's got 'hate,' 'wrong,' 'dead,' and 'despair.'"

"Cheery," he said. There was a pause while we looked through more music. "John Lennon's 'Happy Xmas'?"

I shook my head. "'War.' Also 'fights' and 'fear.'"

Another pause, and then he said, "All I want for Christmas is you."

I looked up at him, startled. "What did you say?"

"'All I Want for Christmas Is You,'" he repeated. "Song title. Mariah Carey."

"Oh." I looked up the lyrics. "I think it might be okay. I don't see any murder or mayhem." But he was shaking his head.

"On second thought, I don't think we'd better. Love can be even more dangerous than war."

I looked into the living room, where the Altairi stood glaring through the door at me. "I seriously doubt they're here to steal Earthwomen."

"Yeah, but we wouldn't want to give anybody any ideas."

"No," I said. "We definitely wouldn't want to do that."

We went back to searching for songs. "How about 'I'll Be Home for Christmas'?" he said, holding up a Patti Page album.

"I'll Be Home" passed muster, but the Altairi didn't respond to it, or to Ed Ames singing "Ballad of the Christmas Donkey" or Miss Piggy singing "Santa Baby."

There didn't seem to be any rhyme or reason to their responses. The keys weren't the same, or the notes, or the accompaniment. They responded to the Andrews Sisters but not to Randy Travis, and it wasn't the voices, either, because they responded to Julie Andrews's "Awake, Awake Ye Drowsy Souls." We played them her "Silver Bells." They didn't laugh (which didn't really surprise me) or bustle, but when the song got to the part about the traffic lights blinking red and green, all six of them blinked their eyes. We played them her "Rise Up, Shepherd, and Follow." They just sat there.

"Try the 'Christmas Waltz,'" I said, looking at the album cover.

He shook his head. "It's got love in it, too. You *did* say you didn't have a boyfriend, didn't you?"

"That's right," I said, "and I have no intention of dating the Altairi."

"Good," he said. "Can you think of any other songs with 'blink' in them?"

By the time he left to rehearse with the symphony, we didn't know any more than when we'd started. I took the Altairi back to Dr. Wakamura, who didn't seem all that happy to see them, tried to find a song with "blink" in it, to no avail, had dinner, and went back over to Calvin's apartment.

He was already there, working. I started through the sheet music. "What about 'Good Christian Men, Rejoice'?" I said. "It's got 'bow' in it," and the phone rang.

Calvin answered it. "What is it, Belinda?" he said, listened a moment, and then said, "Meg, turn on the TV," and handed me the remote.

I switched on the television. Marvin the Martian was telling Bugs Bunny he planned to incinerate the earth. "CNN," Calvin said. "It's on forty."

I punched in the channel and then was sorry. Reverend Thresher was standing in the audio lab in front of a mob of reporters, saying, "—happy to announce that we have found the answer to the Altairi's actions in the mall yesterday. Christmas carols were playing over the sound system in the mall—"

"Oh, no," I said.

"I thought the surveillance tapes didn't have any sound," Calvin said.

"They don't. Someone else in the mall must have had a videocam."

"—and when the Altairi heard those holy songs," Reverend Thresher was saying, "they were overcome by the truth of their message, by the power of God's blessed word—"

"Oh, no," Calvin said.

"—and they sank to the ground in repentance for their sins."

"They did not," I said. "They sat down."

"For the past nine months, scientists have been seeking to discover the reason why the Altairi came to our planet. They should have turned to our Blessed Savior instead, for it is in Him that all answers lie. Why have the Altairi come here? To be saved! They've come to be born again, as we shall demonstrate." He held up a CD of Christmas carols.

"Oh, *no!*" we both said. I grabbed for my cell phone.

"Like the wise men of old," Reverend Thresher was saying, "they have come seeking Christ, which proves that Christianity is the only true religion."

Dr. Morthman took forever to answer his phone. When he did, I said, "Dr. Morthman, you mustn't let the Altairi listen to any Christmas carols—"

"I can't talk now," he said. "We're in the middle of a press conference," and hung up.

"Dr. Morthman—" I hit redial.

"There's no time for that." Calvin, who'd snatched up his keys and my coat, said, "Come on, we'll take my car," and as we racketed downstairs, "There were a lot of reporters there, and he just said something that will make every Jew, Muslim, Buddhist, Wiccan, and nonevangelical Christian on the planet go ballistic. If we're lucky, he'll still be answering questions when we get there."

"And if we're not?"

"The Altairi will be out seizing troubled minds, and we'll have a holy war on our hands."

We almost made it. There were, as Calvin had predicted, a *lot* of questions, particularly after Reverend Thresher stated that the Altairi agreed with him on abortion, gay marriage, and the necessity of electing Republicans to all political offices in the next election.

But the clamoring reporters clogging the steps, the door, and the hall made it nearly impossible to get through, and by the time we reached the audio lab, Reverend Thresher was pointing proudly to the Altairi kneeling on the other side of the one-way mirror and telling the reporters, "As you can see, their hearing the Christmas message has made them kneel in reverence—"

"Oh, no, they must be listening to 'O Holy Night,'" I said, "or 'As with Gladness Men of Old.'"

"What did you play them?" Calvin demanded. He pointed at the kneeling Altairi.

"The One True Way Maxichurch Christmas CD," Reverend Thresher said proudly, holding up the case, which the reporters obligingly snapped, filmed, and downloaded to their iPods. *Christmas Carols for True Christians.*"

"No, no, what *song*?"

"Do the individual carols hold a special significance for them?" the reporters were shouting, and "What carol were they listening to in the mall?" and "Have they been baptized, Reverend Thresher?" while I tried to tell Dr. Morthman, "You've got to turn the music off."

"Off?" Dr. Morthman said incredulously, yelling to be heard over the reporters. "Just when we're finally making progress communicating with the Altairi?"

"You *have* to tell us which songs you've played!" Calvin shouted.

"Who are *you*?" Reverend Thresher demanded.

"He's with me," I said, and to Dr. Morthman, "You have to turn it off right now. Some of the carols are dangerous."

"Dangerous?" he bellowed, and the reporters' attention swiveled to us.

"What do you mean, dangerous?" they asked.

"I mean dangerous," Calvin said. "The Altairi aren't repenting of anything. They're—"

"How dare you accuse the Altairi of not being born again?" Reverend Thresher said. "I saw them respond to the hymnwriter's inspiring words with my own eyes, saw them fall on their knees—"

"They responded to 'Silver Bells,' too," I said, "and to 'The Hanukkah Song.'"

"'The Hanukkah Song'?" the reporters said, and began pelting us with questions again. "Does that mean they're Jewish?" "Orthodox or Reform?" "What's their response to Hindu chants?" "What about the Mormon Tabernacle Choir? Do they respond to that?"

"This doesn't have anything to do with religion," Calvin said. "The Altairi are responding to the literal meaning of certain words in the songs. Some of the words they're listening to right now could be dangerous for them to—"

"Blasphemy!" Reverend Thresher bellowed. "How could the blessed Christmas message be dangerous?"

"'Christmas Day Is Come' tells them to slay young children," I said, "and the lyrics of other carols have blood and war and stars raining fire. That's why you've got to turn off the music right now."

"Too late," Calvin said, and pointed through the one-way mirror.

The Altairi weren't there. "Where are they?" the reporters began shouting. "Where did they go?" and Reverend Thresher and Dr. Morthman both turned to me and demanded to know what I'd done with them.

"Leave her alone. She doesn't know where they are any more than you do," Calvin said, in his choir director voice.

The effect on the room was the same as it had been on his seventh-graders. Dr. Morthman let go of me, and the reporters shut up. "Now, what song were you playing?" Calvin said to Reverend Thresher.

"'God Rest Ye Merry, Gentlemen,'" Reverend Thresher said, "but it's one of the oldest and most beloved Christmas carols. It's ridiculous to think hearing it could endanger anyone—"

"Is 'God Rest Ye' why they left?" the reporters were shouting, and "What are the words? Is there any war in it? Or children-slaying?"

"'God rest ye merry, gentlemen,'" I muttered under my breath, trying to remember the lyrics. "'Let nothing you dismay...'"

"Where did they go?" the reporters clamored.

"'... O, tidings of comfort and joy,'" I murmured. I glanced over at Calvin. He was doing the same thing I was. "'... To save us all... when we were gone...'"

"Where do you think they've gone?" a reporter called out. Calvin looked at me. "Astray," he said grimly.

The Altairi weren't in the other labs, in any of the other buildings on campus, or in their ship. Or at least no one had seen the ramp to it come down and them go inside. No one had seen them crossing the campus, either, or on the surrounding streets.

"I hold you entirely responsible for this, Miss Yates," Dr. Morthman said. "Send out an APB," he told the police. "And put out an Amber Alert."

"That's for when a child's been kidnapped," I said. "The Altairi haven't—"

"We don't know that," he snapped. He turned back to the police officer. "And call the FBI."

The police officer turned to Calvin. "Dr. Morthman said you said the aliens were responding to the words 'gone astray.' Were there any other words in the song that are dangerous?"

"Sa—" I began.

"No," Calvin said, and, while Dr. Morthman was telling the officer to call Homeland Security and tell them to declare a Code Red, hustled me down the sidewalk and behind the Altairi's ship.

"Why did you tell them that?" I demanded. "What about 'scorn'? What about 'Satan's power'?"

"Shh," he whispered. "He's already calling Homeland Security. We don't want him to call out the Air Force. And the nukes," he said. "And there's no time to explain things to them. We've got to find the Altairi."

"Do you have any idea where they could have gone?"

"No. At least their ship's still here," he said, looking over at it.

I wasn't sure that meant anything, considering the Altairi had been able to get out of a lab with a locked door. I said as much, and Calvin agreed. "'Gone astray' may not even be what they were responding to. They may be off looking for a manger or shepherds. And there are different versions. *Christmas Carols for True Christians* may have used an older one."

"In which case we need to go back to the lab and find out exactly what it was they heard," I said, my heart sinking. Dr. Morthman was likely to have me arrested.

Apparently Calvin had reached the same conclusion, because he said, "We can't go back in there. It's too risky, and we've got to find the Altairi before Reverend Thresher does. There's no telling what he'll play them next."

"But how—?"

"If they did go astray, then they may still be in the area. You go get your car and check the streets north of the campus, and I'll do south. Do you have your cell phone?"

"Yes, but I don't have a car. Mine's at your apartment. We came over in yours, remember?"

"What about the van you use to take the Altairi places in?"

"But won't that be awfully noticeable?"

"They're looking for six aliens on foot, not in a van," he said, "and besides, if you find them, you'll need something to put them in."

"You're right," I said, and took off for the faculty parking lot, hoping Dr. Morthman hadn't had the same idea.

He hadn't. The parking lot was deserted. I slid the van's back door open, half hoping this was the Altairi's idea of astray, but they weren't inside, or on any of the streets for an area two miles north of DU. I drove up University Boulevard and then slowly up and down the side streets, terrified I'd find them squished on the pavement.

It was already dark. I called Calvin. "No sign of them," I told him. "Maybe they went back to the mall. I'm going to go over there and—"

"No, don't do that," he said. "Dr. Morthman and the FBI are there. I'm watching it on CNN. They're searching Victoria's Secret. Besides, the Altairi aren't there."

"How do you know?"

"Because they're here at my apartment."

"They are?" I said, weak with relief. "Where did you find them?"

He didn't answer me. "Don't take any major streets on your way over here," he said. "And park in the alley."

"Why? What have they done?" I asked, but he'd already hung up.

🌲

The Altairi were standing in the middle of Calvin's living room when I got there. "I came back here to check on alternate lyrics for 'God Rest Ye' and found them waiting for me," Calvin explained. "Did you park in the alley?"

"Yes, at the other end of the block. What have they done?" I repeated, almost afraid to ask.

"Nothing. At least nothing that's been on CNN," he said, gesturing at the TV, which was showing the police searching the candle store. He had the sound turned down, but across the bottom of the screen was the logo "Aliens AWOL."

"Then why all the secrecy?"

"Because we can't afford to let them find the Altairi till we've figured out why they're doing what they're doing. Next time it might not be as harmless as going astray. And we can't go to your apartment. They know where you live. We're going to have to hole up here. Did you tell any-body you were working with me?"

I tried to think. I'd attempted to tell Dr. Morthman about Calvin when I got back from the mall, but I hadn't gotten far enough to tell him Cal-vin's name, and when Reverend Thresher had demanded, "Who are you?" all I'd said was "He's with me."

"I didn't tell anybody your name," I said.

"Good," he said. "And I'm pretty sure nobody saw the Altairi coming here."

"But how can you be sure? Your neighbors—"

"Because the Altairi were waiting for me inside," he said. "Right where they are now. So they can either pick locks, walk through walls, or tele-port. My money's on teleportation. And it's obvious the commission doesn't have any idea where they are," he said, pointing at the TV, where a mugshot-like photo of the Altairi was displayed, with "Have you seen these aliens?" and a phone number to call across their midsections. "And luckily, I went to the grocery store and stocked up the other day so I wouldn't have to go shopping in between all my concerts."

"Your concerts! And the All-City Sing! I forgot all about them," I said, stricken with guilt. "Weren't you supposed to have a rehearsal tonight?"

"I canceled it," he said, "and I can cancel the one tomorrow morning if I have to. The Sing's not till tomorrow night. We've got plenty of time to figure this out."

If they don't find us first, I thought, looking at the TV, where they were searching the food court. Eventually, when they couldn't find the Altairi anywhere, they'd realize I was missing, too, and start looking for us. And the reporters today, unlike Leo, had all been videotaping. If they put Calvin's picture on TV with a number to call, one of his church choir members or his seventh-graders would be certain to call in and identify him.

Which meant we'd better work fast. I picked up the list of songs and actions we'd compiled. "Where do you want to start?" I asked Calvin, who was starting through a stack of LPs.

"*Not* with 'Frosty the Snowman,'" he said. "I don't think I can stand any chasing here and there."

"How about, 'I Wonder as I Wander'?"

"Very funny," he said. "Since we know they respond to 'kneeling,' why don't we start with that?"

"Okay." We played them "fall on your knees" and "come adore on bended knee" and "whose forms are bending low," some of which they responded to and some of which they didn't, for no reason we could see.

"'The First Noel' has 'full reverently upon their knee' in it," I said, and Calvin started toward the bedroom to look for it.

He stopped as he passed in front of the TV. "I think you'd better come look at this," he said, and turned it up.

"The Altairi were not at the mall, as we had hoped," Dr. Morthman was saying, "and it has just come to our attention that a member of our commission is also missing, Margaret Yates." Video of the scene at the lab came on behind Dr. Morthman and the reporter, with me shouting for him to shut the music off. Any second a picture of Calvin would appear, demanding to know which carol they were playing.

I grabbed up my phone and called Dr. Morthman, hoping against hope they couldn't trace cell phone calls and that he'd answer even though he was on TV.

He did, and the camera blessedly zoomed in on him so only a tiny piece of the video remained visible. "Where are you calling from?" he demanded. "Did you find the Altairi?"

"No," I said, "but I think I have an idea where they might be."

"Where?" Dr. Morthman said.

"I don't think they've gone astray. I think they may be responding to one of the other words in the song. 'Rest' or possibly—"

"I knew it," Reverend Thresher said, shoving in front of Dr. Morthman. "They were responding to the words 'Remember Christ our Savior was born on Christmas Day.' They've gone to church. They're at the One True Way right this minute."

It wasn't what I had in mind, but at least a photo of the One True Way Maxichurch was better than one of Calvin. "That should give us at least two hours. His church is way down in Colorado Springs," I said, turning the TV back down, and went back to playing songs to the Altairi and logging their responses and nonresponses, but half an hour later, when Calvin went into the bedroom to try to find a Louis Armstrong CD, he stopped in front of the TV again and frowned.

"What happened?" I said, dumping the pile of sheet music on my lap on the couch beside me and sidling past the Altairi to get to him. "Didn't they take the bait?"

"Oh, they took it, all right," he said, and turned up the TV.

"We believe the Altairi are in Bethlehem," Dr. Morthman was saying. He was standing in front of a departures board at DIA.

"*Bethlehem*?" I said.

"It's mentioned in the lyrics twice," Calvin said. "At least if they're off in Israel it gives us more time."

"It also gives us an international incident," I said. "In the Middle East, no less. I've got to call Dr. Morthman." But he must have turned his cell phone off, and I couldn't get through to the lab.

"You could call Reverend Thresher," Calvin said, pointing to the TV screen.

Reverend Thresher was surrounded by reporters as he got into his Lexus. "I'm on my way to the Altairi right now, and tonight we will hold a Praise Worship Service, and you'll be able to hear their Christian witness, and the Christmas carols that first brought them to the Lord—"

Calvin switched the TV off. "It's a sixteen-hour flight to Bethlehem," he said encouragingly. "It surely won't take us that long to figure this out."

The phone rang. Calvin shot me a glance and then picked it up. "Hello, Mr. Steinberg," he said. "Didn't you get my message? I canceled tonight's rehearsal." He listened awhile. "If you're worried about your entrance on page twelve, we'll run over it before the Sing." He listened some more. "It'll all come together. It always does."

I hoped that would be true of our solving the puzzle of the Altairi. If it wasn't, we'd be charged with kidnapping. Or starting a religious war. But both were better than letting Reverend Thresher play them "slowly dying" and "thorns infest the ground." Which meant we'd better figure out what the Altairi were responding to, and fast. We played them Dolly Parton and Manhattan Transfer and the Barbershop Choir of Toledo and Dean Martin.

Which was a bad idea. I'd had almost no sleep the last two days, and I found myself nodding off after the first few bars. I sat up straight and tried to concentrate on the Altairi, but it was no use. The next thing I knew, my head was on Calvin's shoulder, and he was saying, "Meg? Meg? Do the Altairi sleep?"

"Sleep?" I said, sitting up and rubbing my eyes. "I'm sorry, I must have dozed off. What time is it?"

"A little after four."

"In the *morning*?"

"Yes. Do the Altairi sleep?"

"Yes, at least we think so. Their brain patterns alter, and they don't respond to stimuli, but then again, they *never* respond."

"Are there visible signs that they're asleep? Do they close their eyes or lie down?"

"No, they sort of droop over, like flowers that haven't been watered. And their glares diminish a little. Why?"

"I have something I want to try. Go back to sleep."

"No, that's okay," I said, suppressing a yawn. "If anybody needs to sleep, it's you. I've kept you up the last two nights, and you've got to direct your Sing thing tonight. I'll take over and you go—"

He shook his head. "I'm fine. I told you, I never get any sleep this time of year."

"So what's this idea you want to try?"

"I want to play them the first verse of 'Silent Night.'"

"'Sleep in heavenly peace,'" I said.

"Right, and no other action verbs *and* I've got at least fifty versions of it. Johnny Cash, Kate Smith, Britney Spears—"

"Do we have time to play them fifty different versions?" I asked, looking over at the TV. A split screen showed a map of Israel and the outside of the One True Way Maxichurch. When I turned the volume up, a reporter's voice said, "Inside, thousands of members are awaiting the appearance of the Altairi, whom Reverend Thresher expects at any minute. A twenty-four-hour High-Powered Prayer Vigil—"

I turned it back down. "I guess we do. You were saying?"

"'Silent Night' is a song everybody—Gene Autry, Madonna, Burl Ives—has recorded. Different voices, different accompaniments, different keys. We can see which versions they respond to—"

"And which ones they don't," I said, "and that may give us a clue to what they're responding to."

"Exactly," he said, opening a CD case. He stuck it in the player and hit Track 4. "Here goes."

The voice of Elvis Presley singing "'Silent night, holy night'" filled the room. Calvin came back over to the couch and sat down next to me. When Elvis got to "'tender and mild,'" we both leaned forward expectantly, watching the Altairi. "'Sleep in heavenly peace,'" Elvis crooned, but the Altairi were still stiffly upright, and they remained that way through the repeated "'sleep in heavenly peace.'" And through Alvin the Chipmunk's solo of it. And Celine Dion's.

"Their glares don't appear to be diminishing," Calvin said. "If anything, they seem to be getting worse."

They were. "You'd better play them Judy Garland," I said.

He did, and Dolly Parton and Harry Belafonte. "What if they don't respond to any of them?" I asked.

"Then we try something else. I've also got twenty-six versions of 'Grandma Got Run Over by a Reindeer.'" He grinned at me. "I'm kidding. I do, however, have nine different versions of 'Baby, It's Cold Outside.'"

"For use on redheaded second sopranos?"

"No," he said. "Shh, I love this version. Nat King Cole."

I shh-ed and listened, wondering how the Altairi could resist falling asleep. Nat King Cole's voice was even more relaxing than Dean Martin's. I leaned back against the couch. "'All is calm . . .'"

I must have fallen asleep again, because the next thing I knew, the music had stopped and it was daylight outside. I looked at my watch. It said two P.M. The Altairi were standing in the exact same spot they'd been in before, glaring, and Calvin was sitting hunched forward on a kitchen chair, his chin in his hand, watching them and looking worried.

"Did something happen?" I glanced over at the TV. Reverend Thresher was talking. The logo read "Thresher Launches Galaxywide Christian Crusade." At least it didn't say "Air Strikes in Middle East."

Calvin was slowly shaking his head.

"Wasn't there any response to 'Silent Night'?" I asked.

"No, there was," he said. "You responded to the version by Nat King Cole."

"I know," I said. "I'm sorry. I meant the Altairi. They didn't respond to any of the 'Silent Night's?"

"No, they responded," he said, "but just to one version."

"But that's good, isn't it?" I asked. "Now we can analyze what it was that was different about it that they were responding to. Which version was it?"

Instead of answering, he walked over to the CD player and hit play. A loud chorus of nasal female voices began belting out, "'Silent night, holy night,'" shouting to be heard over a cacophony of clinks and clacks. "What *is* that?" I asked.

"The Broadway chorus of the musical *42nd Street* singing and tap-dancing to 'Silent Night.' They recorded it for a special Broadway Christmas charity project."

I looked over at the Altairi, thinking maybe Calvin was wrong and they hadn't really fallen asleep, but in spite of the din, they had sagged limply over, their heads nearly touching the ground, looking almost peaceful. Their glares had faded from full-bore Aunt Judith to only mildly disapproving.

I listened to the *42nd Street* chorines tapping and belting out "Silent Night" at the top of their lungs some more. "It is kind of appealing," I said, "especially the part where they shout out 'Mother and child!'"

"I know," he said. "I'd like it played at our wedding. And obviously the Altairi share our good taste. But aside from that, I'm not sure *what* it tells us."

"That the Altairi like show tunes?" I suggested.

"God forbid. Think what Reverend Thresher would do with that," he said. "Besides, they didn't respond to 'Sit Down, You're Rocking the Boat.'"

"No, but they did to that song from *Mame*."

"And to the one from *1776* but not to *The Music Man* or *Rent*," he said frustratedly. "Which puts us right back where we started. I have no clue what they're responding to!"

"I know," I said. "I'm so sorry. I should never have gotten you involved in this. You have your ACHES thing to direct."

"It doesn't start till seven," he said, rummaging through a stack of LPs, "which means we've got another four hours to work. If we could just find another 'Silent Night' they'll respond to, we might be able to figure out what in God's name they're doing. What the hell happened to that *Star Wars Christmas* album?"

"Stop," I said. "This is ridiculous." I took the albums out of his hands.

"You're exhausted, and you've got a big job to do. You can't direct all those people on no sleep. This can wait."

"But—"

"People think better after a nap," I said firmly. "You'll wake up, and the solution will be perfectly obvious."

"And if it isn't?"

"Then you'll go direct your choirs, and—"

"Choirs," he said thoughtfully.

"Or All-City Sing or Aches and Pains or whatever you call it, and I'll stay here and play the Altairi some more 'Silent Night's till you get back and—"

"'Sit Down, John' was sung by the chorus," he said, looking past me at the drooping Altairi. "And so was 'While Shepherds Watched.' And the *42nd Street* 'Silent Night' was the only one that wasn't a solo." He grabbed my shoulders. "They're all choruses. That's why they didn't respond to Julie Andrews singing 'Rise Up, Shepherd, and Follow,' or to Stubby Kaye singing 'Sit Down, You're Rocking the Boat.' They only respond to groups of voices."

I shook my head. "You forgot 'Awake, Awake, Ye Drowsy Souls.'"

"Oh," he said, his face falling, "you're right. Wait!" He lunged for the Julie Andrews CD and stuck it in the recorder. "I think Julie Andrews sings the verse and then a chorus comes in. Listen."

He was right. The chorus had sung "Awake, awake."

"Who sang the 'Joy to the World' you played them on the CD from the mall?" Calvin asked.

"Just Julie Andrews," I said. "And Brenda Lee sang 'Rockin' Around the Christmas Tree.'"

"And Johnny Mathis sang 'Angels from the Realms of Glory,'" he said happily. "But the Hanukkah song, which they *did* respond to, was sung by the . . ." he read it off the CD case, "the Shalom Singers. That's got to be it." He began looking through the LPs again.

"What are you looking for?" I asked.

"The Mormon Tabernacle Choir," he said. "They've *got* to have recorded 'Silent Night.' We'll play it for the Altairi, and if they fall asleep, we'll know we're on the right track."

"But they're already asleep," I pointed out, gesturing to where they stood looking like a week-old flower arrangement. "How—?"

He was already digging again. He brought up a Cambridge Boys' Choir album, pulled the LP out, and read the label, muttering, "I know it's on here . . . Here it is." He put it on, and a chorus of sweet boys' voices sang, "'Christians awake, salute the happy morn.'"

The Altairi straightened immediately and glared at us. "You were right," I said softly, but he wasn't listening. He had the LP off the turntable and was reading the label again, muttering, "Come on, you have to have done 'Silent Night.' Everyone does 'Silent Night.'" He flipped the LP over, said, "I *knew* it," popped it back on the turntable, and dropped the needle expertly.

"'. . . and mild,'" the boys' angelic voices sang, "'sleep . . .'"

The Altairi drooped over before the word was even out. "That's definitely it!" I said. "That's the common denominator."

He shook his head. "We need more data. It could just be a coincidence. We need to find a choral version of 'Rise Up, Shepherd, and Follow.' And 'Sit Down, You're Rocking the Boat.' Where did you put *Guys and Dolls*?"

"But that was a solo."

"The first part, the part *we* played them was a solo. Later on all the gamblers come in. We should have played them the whole song."

"We couldn't, remember?" I said, handing it to him. "Remember the parts about dragging you under and drowning, not to mention gambling and drinking?"

"Oh, right," he said. He put headphones on, listened, and then unplugged them. "'Sit down . . .'" a chorus of men's voices sang lustily, and the Altairi sat down.

We played choir versions of "All I Want for Christmas Is My Two Front Teeth" and "Rise Up, Shepherds, and Follow." The Altairi sat down and stood up. "You're right," he said after the Altairi knelt to the Platters singing "The First Noel." "It's the common denominator, all right. But why?"

"I don't know," I admitted. "Maybe they can't understand things said to them by fewer voices than a choir. That would explain why there are six of them. Maybe each one only hears certain frequencies, which singly are meaningless, but with six of them—"

He shook his head. "You're forgetting the Andrews Sisters. And Barenaked Ladies. And even if it is the choir aspect they're responding to, it still doesn't tell us what they're doing here."

"But now we know how to get them to tell us," I said, grabbing up *The Holly Jolly Book of Christmas Songs*. "Can you find a choir version of 'Adeste Fideles' in English?"

"I think so," he said. "Why?"

"Because it's got 'we greet thee' in it," I said, running my fingers down the lyrics of "Good Christian Men, Rejoice."

"And there's 'Watchmen, Tell Us of the Night,'" he said. "And 'great glad tidings tell.' They're bound to respond to one of them."

But they didn't. Peter, Paul, and Mary ordered the Altairi to go tell (we blanked out the "on the mountain" part), but either the Altairi didn't like folk music, or the Andrews Sisters had been a fluke.

Or we had jumped to conclusions. When we tried the same song again, this time by the Boston Commons Choir, there was still no response. And none to choral versions of "Deck the Halls" ("while I tell"), "Jolly Old St. Nicholas" ("don't you tell a single soul" minus "don't" and "a single soul"). Or to "The Friendly Beasts," even though all six verses had "tell" in them.

Calvin thought the tense might be the problem and played parts of "Little St. Nick" ("tale" and "told") and "The Carol of the Bells" ("telling"), but to no avail. "Maybe the word's the problem," I said. "Maybe they just don't know the word 'tell.'" But they didn't respond to "say" or "saying" or "said," to "messages" or to "proclaim."

"We must have been wrong about the choir thing," Calvin said, but that wasn't it, either. While he was in the bedroom putting his tux on for the Sing, I played them snatches of "The First Noel" and "Up on the Rooftop" from the Barenaked Ladies CD, and they knelt and jumped right on cue.

"Maybe they think Earth's a gym and this is an exercise class," Calvin said, coming in as they were leaping to the St. Paul's Cathedral Choir singing "The Twelve Days of Christmas." "I don't suppose the word 'calling' had any effect on them."

"No," I said, tying his bow tie, "and 'I'm bringing you this simple phrase' didn't, either. Has it occurred to you that the music might not be having any effect at all, and they just happen to be sitting and leaping and kneeling at the same time as the words are being sung?"

"No," he said. "There's a connection. If there wasn't, they wouldn't look so irritated that we haven't been able to figure it out yet."

He was right. Their glares had, if anything, intensified, and their very posture radiated disapproval.

"We need more data, that's all," he said, going to get his black shoes. "As soon as I get back, we'll—" He stopped.

"What is it?"

"You'd better look at this," he said, pointing at the TV. The screen was showing a photo of the ship. All the lights were on, and exhaust was coming out of assorted side vents. Calvin grabbed the remote and turned it up.

"It is now believed that the Altairi have returned to their ship and are preparing to depart," the newscaster said. I glanced over at the Altairi. They were still standing there. "Analysis of the ignition cycle indicates that takeoff will be in less than six hours."

"What do we do now?" I asked Calvin.

"We figure this out. You heard them. We've got six hours till blastoff."

"But the Sing—"

He handed me my coat. "We know it's got *something* to do with choirs, and I've got every kind you could want. We'll take the Altairi to the convention center and hope we think of something on the way."

We didn't think of anything on the way. "Maybe I should take them back to their ship," I said, pulling into the parking lot. "What if I cause them to get left behind?"

"They are *not* E.T.," he said.

I parked at the service entrance, got out, and started to slide the back door of the van open. "No, leave them there," Calvin said. "We've got to find a place to put them before we take them in. Lock the car."

I did, even though I doubted if it would do any good, and followed Calvin through a side door marked "Choirs Only" and through a maze of corridors lined with rooms marked "St. Peter's Boys' Choir," "Red Hat Glee Club," "Denver Gay Men's Chorus," "Sweet Adelines Show Chorus," "Mile High Jazz Singers." There was a hubbub in the front of the building, and when we crossed the main corridor, we could see people in gold and green and black robes milling around talking.

Calvin opened several doors one after the other, ducked inside the rooms, shutting the doors after him, and then reemerged, shaking his head. "We can't let the Altairi hear the *Messiah,* and you can still hear the noise from the auditorium," he said. "We need someplace soundproof."

"Or farther away," I said, leading the way down the corridor and turning down a side hall. And running smack into his seventh-graders coming out of one of the meeting rooms. Mrs. Carlson was videotaping them, and another mother was attempting to line them up to go in, but as soon as they saw Calvin, they clustered around him saying, "Mr. Ledbetter, where have you been? We thought you weren't coming," and "Mr. Ledbetter, Mrs. Carlson says we have to turn our cell phones off, but can't we just have them on vibrate?" and "Mr. Ledbetter, Shelby and I were supposed to go in together, but she says she wants to be partners with Danika."

Calvin ignored them. "Kaneesha, could you hear any of the groups rehearsing when you were in getting dressed?"

"Why?" Belinda asked. "Did we miss the call to go in?"

"Could you, Kaneesha?" he persisted.

"A little bit," she said.

"That won't work, then," he said to me. "I'll go check the room at the end. Wait here." He sprinted along the hall.

"You were at the mall that day," Belinda said accusingly to me. "Are you and Mr. Ledbetter going out?"

We may all be going out together—with a bang—if we don't figure out what the Altairi are doing, I thought. "No," I said.

"Are you hooking up?" Chelsea asked.

"Chelsea!" Mrs. Carlson said, horrified.

"Well, are you?"

"Aren't you supposed to be lining up?" I asked.

Calvin came back at a dead run. "It should work," he said to me. "It seems fairly soundproof."

"Why does it have to be soundproof?" Chelsea asked.

"I bet it's so nobody can hear them making out," Belinda said, and Chelsea began making smooching noises.

"Time to go in, ladies," he said in his choir director's voice, "line up," and he really was amazing. They immediately formed pairs and began making a line.

"Wait till everybody's gone into the auditorium," he said, pulling me aside, "and then go get them and bring them in. I'll do a few minutes' intro of the orchestra and the organizing committee so the Altairi won't hear any songs while you're getting them to the room. There's a table you can use to barricade the door so nobody can get in."

"And what if the Altairi try to leave?" I asked. "A barricade won't stop them, you know."

"Call me on my cell phone, and I'll tell the audience there's a fire drill or something. Okay? I'll make this as short as I can." He grinned. "No 'Twelve Days of Christmas.' Don't worry, Meg. We'll figure this out."

"I *told* you she was his girlfriend."

"*Is* she, Mr. Ledbetter?"

"Let's go, ladies," he said, and led them down the hall and into the auditorium. Just as the auditorium doors shut on the last stragglers, my cell phone rang. It was Dr. Morthman, calling to say, "You can stop looking. The Altairi are in their ship."

"How do you know? Have you seen them?" I asked, thinking, *I knew I shouldn't have left them in the car.*

"No, but the ship's begun the ignition process, and it's going faster than NASA previously estimated. They're now saying it's no more than four hours to takeoff. Where are you?"

"On my way back," I said, trying not to sound like I was running out to the parking lot and unlocking the van, which, thank goodness, was at least still there and intact.

"Well, hurry it up," Dr. Morthman snapped. "The press is here. You're going to have to explain to them exactly how you let the Altairi get away." I pulled open the van's door.

The Altairi weren't inside.

Oh, no. "I blame this entire debacle on you," Dr. Morthman said. "If there are international repercussions—"

"I'll be there as soon as I can," I said, hung up, and turned to run around to the driver's side.

And collided with the Altairi, who had apparently been standing behind me the entire time. "Don't scare me like that," I said. "Now come on," and led them rapidly into the convention center, past the shut doors of the auditorium, where I could hear talking but not singing, thank goodness, and along the long hall to the room Calvin had indicated.

It was empty except for the table Calvin had mentioned. I herded the

Altairi inside and then tipped the table on its side, pushed it in front of the door, wedging it under the doorknob, and leaned my ear against it to see if I could hear any sound from the auditorium, but Calvin had been right. I couldn't hear anything, and they should have started by now.

And now what? With takeoff only four hours away, I needed to take advantage of every second, but there was nothing in the room I could use—no piano or CD player or LPs. *We should have used his seventh-graders' dressing room,* I thought. *They'd at least have had iPods or something.*

But even if I played the Altairi hundreds of Christmas carols being sung by a choir, and they responded to them all—bowing, decking halls, dashing through snow in one-horse open sleighs, following yonder stars—I'd still be no closer to figuring out why they were here or why they'd decided to leave. Or why they'd taken the very loud tap-dancing chorus of *42nd Street* singing "Sleep in heavenly peace" as a direct order. If they even knew what the word "sleep"—or "seated" or "spin" or "blink"—meant.

Calvin had surmised they could only hear words sung to them with more than one voice, but that couldn't be it. Someone hearing a word for the first time would have no idea what it meant, and they'd never heard "all seated on the ground" till that day in the mall. They had to have heard the word before to have known what it meant, and they'd only have heard it spoken. Which meant they could hear spoken words as well as sung ones.

They could have read the words, I thought, remembering the Rosetta Stone and the dictionaries Dr. Short had given them. But even if they'd somehow taught themselves to read English, they wouldn't know how it was pronounced. They wouldn't have recognized it when they heard it spoken. The only way they could do that was by hearing the spoken word. Which meant they'd been listening to and understanding every word we'd said for the past nine months. Including Calvin's and my conversations about them slaying babies and destroying the planet. No wonder they were leaving.

But if they understood us, then that meant one of two things—they were either unwilling to talk to us or were incapable of speaking. Had their sitting down and their other responses been an attempt at sign language?

No, that couldn't be it, either. They could have responded just as easily to a spoken "sit" and done it months earlier. And if they were trying to communicate, wouldn't they have given Calvin and me some hint we were on the right—or the wrong—track instead of just standing there with that we-are-not-amused glare? And I didn't believe for a moment those expressions were an accident of nature. I knew disapproval when I saw it. I'd watched Aunt Judith too many years not to—

Aunt Judith. I took my cell phone out of my pocket and called my sister Tracy. "Tell me everything you can remember about Aunt Judith," I said when she answered.

"Has something happened to her?" she said, sounding alarmed. "When I talked to her last week she—"

"Last week?" I said. "You mean Aunt Judith's still *alive*?"

"Well, she was last week when we had lunch."

"*Lunch?* With Aunt Judith? Are we talking about the same person? Dad's Aunt Judith? The Gorgon?"

"Yes, only she's not a Gorgon. She's actually very nice when you get to know her."

"Aunt Judith," I said, "the one who always glared disapprovingly at everybody?"

"Yes, only she hasn't glared at me in years. As I say, when you get to know her—"

"And exactly how did you do that?"

"I thanked her for my birthday present."

"And—?" I said. "That can't have been all. Mom always made both of us thank her nicely for our presents."

"I know, but they weren't proper thank-yous. 'A prompt handwritten note expressing gratitude is the only proper form of thanks,'" Tracy said, obviously quoting. "I was in high school, and we had to write a thank-you letter to someone for class. She'd just sent me my birthday card with the dollar in it, so I wrote her, and the next day she called and gave me this long lecture about the importance of good manners and how shocking it was that no one followed the most basic rules of etiquette anymore and how she was delighted to see that at least one young person knew how to behave, and then she asked me if I'd like to go see *Les Mis* with her, and I bought a copy of Emily Post, and we've gotten along great ever since. She sent Evan and me a sterling silver fish slice when we got married."

"For which you sent her a handwritten thank-you note," I said absently. Aunt Judith had been glaring because we were boorish and unmannered. Was that why the Altairi looked so disapproving, because they were waiting for the equivalent of a handwritten thank-you note from us?

If that was the case, we were doomed. Rules of etiquette are notoriously illogical and culture-specific, and there was no intergalactic Emily Post for me to consult. And I had, oh, God, less than two hours till liftoff.

"Tell me exactly what she said that day she called you," I said, unwilling to give up the idea that she was somehow the key.

"It was eight years ago—"

"I know. Try to remember."

"Okay . . . there was a lot of stuff about gloves and how I shouldn't wear white shoes after Labor Day and how I shouldn't cross my legs. 'Well-bred young ladies sit with their ankles crossed.'"

Had the Altairi's sitting down in the mall been an etiquette lesson in the proper way to sit? It seemed unlikely, but so did Aunt Judith's refusal to speak to people because of the color of their shoes on certain calendar dates.

". . . and she said if I got married, I needed to send out engraved invitations," Tracy said. "Which I did. I think that's why she gave us the fish slice."

"I don't care about the fish slice. What did she say about your thank-you note?"

"She said, 'Well, it's about time, Tracy. I'd nearly given up hope of anyone in your family showing any signs of civilized behavior.'"

Civilized behavior. That was it. The Altairi, like Aunt Judith sitting in our living room glaring, had been waiting for a sign that we were civilized. And singing—correction, *group* singing—was that sign. But was it an arbitrary rule of etiquette, like white shoes and engraved invitations, or was it a symbol of something else? I thought of Calvin telling his chattering seventh-graders to line up, and the milling, giggling, chaotic muddle of girls coming together in an organized, beautifully behaved, *civilized* line.

Coming together. That was the civilized behavior the Altairi had been waiting for a sign of. And they'd seen precious little of it in the nine months they'd been here: the disorganized commission with members quitting and those who were left not listening to anyone; that awful rehearsal where the basses couldn't get the entrance right to save them; the harried shoppers in the mall, dragging their screaming children after them. The piped-in choir singing "While Shepherds Watched" might have been the first indication they'd seen—correction, *heard*—that we were capable of getting along with each other at all.

No wonder they'd sat down right there in the middle of the mall. They must have thought, like Aunt Judith, "Well, it's about time!" But then why hadn't they done the equivalent of calling us and asking us to go see *Les Mis?*

Maybe they hadn't been sure that what they'd seen—correction, heard—was what they thought it was. They'd never *seen* people sing, except for Calvin and those pathetic basses. They'd seen no signs we were capable of singing beautifully in harmony.

But "While Shepherds Watched" had convinced them it might be possible, which was why they'd followed us around and why they'd sat and slept and gone astray whenever they heard more than one voice, hoping we'd get the hint, waiting for further proof.

In which case we should be in the auditorium, listening to the Sing, instead of in this soundproof room. Especially since the fact that their ship was getting ready to take off indicated they'd given up and decided they were mistaken after all. "Come on," I said to the Altairi, and stood up. "I need to show you something." I shoved the table away from the door, and opened it.

On Calvin. "Oh, good, you're here," I said. "I— Why aren't you in directing?"

"I announced an intermission so I could tell you something. I think I've got it, the thing the Altairi have been responding to," he said, grabbing me by the arms, "the reason they reacted to Christmas songs. I thought of it while I was directing 'Chestnuts Roasting on an Open Fire.' What do nearly all Christmas songs have in them?"

"I don't know," I said. "Chestnuts? Santa Claus? Bells?"

"Close," he said. "Choirs."

Choirs? "We already knew they responded to songs sung by choirs," I said, confused.

"Not just to songs sung by choirs. Songs *about* choirs. Christmas carols being sung by the choir, angel choirs, children's choirs, wassailers, carolers, 'strike the harp and join the *chorus*,'" he said. "The angels in 'Angels We Have Heard on High' are 'sweetly singing o'er the plains.' In 'It Came Upon the Midnight Clear,' all the world gives back the song they sing. They're all about singing," he said excitedly. "'That glorious song of old,' 'whom angels greet with anthems sweet.' Look," he flipped through the pages of his music, pointing out phrases, "'oh, hear the angel voices,' 'as men of old have sung,' 'whom shepherds guard and angels sing,' 'let men their songs employ.' There are references to singing in songs by Randy Travis, the Peanuts kids, Paul McCartney, *How the Grinch Stole Christmas*. It wasn't just that 'While Shepherds Watched' was sung by a choir. It was that it was a song *about* choirs singing. And not just singing, but what they're singing." He thrust the song in front of me, pointing to the last verse. "'Good will, henceforth from heaven to men.' That's what they've been trying to communicate to us."

I shook my head. "It's what they've been waiting for us to communicate to them. Just like Aunt Judith."

"Aunt Judith?"

"I'll explain later. Right now we've got to prove we're civilized before the Altairi leave."

"And how do we do that?"

"We sing to them, or rather, the All-City Holiday Ecumenical Sing does."

"What do we sing?"

I wasn't sure it mattered. I was pretty certain what they were looking for was proof we could cooperate and work together in harmony, and in that case, "Mele Kalikimaka" would work as well as "The Peace Carol." But it wouldn't hurt to make things as clear to them as we could. And it would be nice if it was also something that Reverend Thresher couldn't use as ammunition for his Galaxywide Christian Crusade.

"We need to sing something that will convince the Altairi we're a civilized species," I said, "something that conveys good will and peace. Especially peace. And not religion, if that's possible."

"How much time have we got to write it?" Calvin asked. "And we'll have to get copies made—"

My cell phone rang. The screen showed it was Dr. Morthman. "Hang on," I said, hitting talk. "I should be able to tell you in a second. Hello?"

"Where *are* you?" Dr. Morthman shouted. "The ship's beginning its final ignition cycle."

I whirled around to make sure the Altairi were still there. They were, thank goodness, and still glaring. "How long does the final cycle take?" I asked.

"They don't know," Dr. Morthman said, "ten minutes at the outside. If you don't get here immediately—"

I hung up.

"Well?" Calvin said. "How much time have we got?"

"None," I said.

"Then we'll have to use something we've already got," he said, and began riffling through his sheaf of music, "and something people know the harmony to. Civilized . . . civilized . . . I think . . ." He found what he was looking for and scanned it. ". . . Yeah, if I change a couple of words, this should do the trick. Do you think the Altairi understand Latin?"

"I wouldn't put it past them."

"Then we'll just do the first two lines. Wait five minutes—"

"Five minutes?"

"—so I can brief everybody on the changes, and then bring the Altairi in."

"Okay," I said, and he took off at a run for the auditorium.

🌲

There was an expectant buzz in the audience when we came through the double doors, and the ranks of choirs arrayed around the stage, a sea of maroon and gold and green and purple robes, began whispering to each other behind their music.

Calvin had apparently just finished his briefing. Some of the choirs and the audience were busily scribbling notes on their music, and passing pencils, and asking each other questions. The orchestra, on one side of the stage, was warming up in a jumbled cacophony of screeches and hoots and blats.

On the other side, the sopranos of the Mile-High Women's Chorus were apparently filling the altos in on my interrupting rehearsal the other night, because they all turned to glare at me. "I think it's ridiculous that we can't sing the words we know," an elderly woman wearing gloves and a hat with a veil said to her companion.

Her companion nodded. "If you ask me, they're carrying this entire ecumenical thing too far. I mean, humans are one thing, but *aliens!*"

There's no way this is going to work, I thought, looking over at Calvin's seventh-graders, who were leaning over the backs of each other's chairs, giggling and chewing gum. Belinda was text-messaging someone on her cell phone, and Kaneesha was listening to her iPod. Chelsea had her hand up and was calling, "Mr. Ledbetter! Mr. Ledbetter, Shelby took my music."

Over in the orchestra, the percussionist was practicing crashing his cymbals. *It's hopeless,* I thought, looking over at the glaring Altairi. *There's no way we can convince them we're sentient, let alone civilized.*

My cell phone rang. *And that's it, the straw that's going to break the camel's back,* I thought, fumbling for it. Now everyone, even the musician with the cymbals, was glaring at me. "How rude!" the elderly woman in the white gloves said.

"The ship's started its countdown!" Dr. Morthman bellowed in my ear.

I hit "end" and turned the phone off. "Hurry," I mouthed to Calvin, and he nodded and stepped up on the dais.

He tapped the music stand with his baton, and the entire auditorium fell silent. "Adeste Fideles," he said, and everyone opened their music.

"Adeste Fideles?" What's he doing? I thought. *"O come, all ye faithful" isn't what we need.* I ran mentally through the lyrics: "Come ye to Bethlehem . . . come let us adore him . . ." *No, no, not religious!*

But it was too late. Calvin had already spread his hands out, palms up, and lifted them, and everyone was getting to their feet. He nodded to the orchestra, and they began playing the introduction to "Adeste Fideles."

I turned to look at the Altairi. They were glaring even more condemningly than usual. I moved between them and the doors.

The symphony was reaching the end of the introduction. Calvin glanced at me. I smiled, I hoped encouragingly, and held up crossed fingers. He nodded and then raised his baton again and brought it down.

"Have you ever been to a Sing?" Calvin had said. "It's pretty impressive." There had to be nearly four thousand people in that auditorium, all of them singing in perfect harmony, and if they'd been singing "The

Chipmunks Song," it would still have been awe-inspiring. But the words they were singing couldn't have been more perfect if Calvin and I had written them to order. "'Sing, earthly choirs,'" they trilled, "'sing in exultation. Sing, all ye citizens of heaven above,'" and the Altairi glide-waddled up the aisle to the stage and sat down at Calvin's feet.

I ducked outside to the hall and called Dr. Morthman. "What's happening with the ship?" I asked him.

"Where *are* you?" he demanded. "I thought you said you were on your way over here."

"There's a lot of traffic," I said. "What's the ship doing?"

"It's aborted its ignition sequence and shut down its lights," he said.

Good, I thought. *That means what we're doing is working.*

"It's just sitting there on the ground."

"How appropriate," I murmured.

"What do you mean by that?" he said accusingly. "Spectrum analysis shows the Altairi aren't in their ship. You've got them, haven't you? Where are you and what have you done to them? If—"

I hung up, switched off my phone, and went back inside. They'd finished "Adeste Fideles" and were singing "Hark, the Herald Angels Sing." The Altairi were still sitting at Calvin's feet. "'. . . Reconciled,'" the assemblage sang, "'Joyful, all ye nations rise,'" and the Altairi rose.

And rose, till they were a good two feet above the aisle. There was a collective gasp, and everyone stopped singing and stared at them floating there.

No, don't stop, I thought, and hurried forward, but Calvin had it under control. He turned a glare worthy of Aunt Judith on his seventh-grade girls, and they swallowed hard and started singing again, and after a moment everyone else recovered themselves and joined in to finish the verse.

When the song ended, Calvin turned and mouthed at me, "What do I do next?"

"Keep singing," I mouthed back.

"Singing what?"

I shrugged him an "I don't know," and mouthed, "What about this?" and pointed at the fourth song on the program.

He grinned, turned back to his choirs, and announced, "We will now sing, 'There's a Song in the Air.'"

There was a rustle of pages, and they began singing. I eyed the Altairi warily, looking for a lessening in elevation, but they continued to hover, and when the choir reached, "'and the beautiful sing,'" it seemed to me their glares became slightly less fierce.

"'And that song from afar has swept over the earth,'" the assemblage sang, and the auditorium doors burst open and Dr. Morthman, Reverend Thresher, and dozens of FBI agents and police and reporters and cameramen came rushing in. "Stay where you are," one of the FBI agents shouted.

"Blasphemous!" Reverend Thresher roared. "Look at this! Witches, homosexuals, liberals—!"

"Arrest that young woman," Dr. Morthman said, pointing at me, "and the young man directing—" He stopped and gaped at the Altairi hovering above the stage. Flashes began to go off, reporters started talking into microphones, and Reverend Thresher positioned himself squarely in front of one of the cameras and clasped his hands. "Oh, Lord," he shouted, "drive Satan's demons out of the Altairi!"

"No!" I shouted to Calvin's seventh-graders, "don't stop singing," but they already had. I looked desperately at Calvin. "Keep directing!" I said, but the police were already moving forward to handcuff him, stepping cautiously around the Altairi, who were drifting earthward like slowly leaking balloons.

"And teach these sinners here the error of their ways," Reverend Thresher was intoning.

"You can't do this, Dr. Morthman," I said desperately. "The Altairi—"

He grabbed my arm and dragged me to one of the police officers. "I want both of them charged with kidnapping," he said, "and I want her charged with conspiracy. She's responsible for this entire—" He stopped and stared past me.

I turned around. The Altairi were standing directly behind me, glaring. The police officer, who'd been about to clamp a pair of handcuffs on me, let go of my wrist and backed away, and so did the reporters and the FBI.

"Your excellencies," Dr. Morthman said, taking several steps back, "I want you to know the commission had nothing to do with this. We knew nothing about it. It's entirely this young woman's fault. She . . ."

"We acknowledge your greetings," the Altairus in the center said, bowing to me, "and greet you in return."

A murmur of surprise rumbled through the auditorium, and Dr. Morthman stammered, "Y-you speak English?"

"Of course," I said, and bowed to the Altairi. "It's nice to finally be able to communicate with you."

"We welcome you into the company of citizens of the heavens," the one on the end said, "and reciprocate your offers of good will, peace on earth, and chestnuts."

"We assure you that we come bearing gifts as well," the Altairus on the other end said.

"It's a miracle!" Reverend Thresher shouted. "The Lord has healed them! He has unlocked their lips!" He dropped to his knees and began to pray. "Oh, Lord, we know it is our prayers which have brought this miracle about—"

Dr. Morthman bounded forward. "Your excellencies, allow me to be the first to welcome you to our humble planet," he said, extending his hand. "On behalf of the government of the—"

The Altairi ignored him. "We had begun to think we had erred in our assessment of your world," the one who'd spoken before said to me, and the one next to her? him? said, "We doubted your species was fully sentient."

"I know," I said. "I doubt it myself sometimes."

"We also doubted you understood the concept of accord," the one on the other end said, and turned and glared pointedly at Calvin's wrists.

"I think you'd better unhandcuff Mr. Ledbetter," I said to Dr. Morthman.

"Of course, of course," he said, motioning to the police officer. "Explain to them it was all a little misunderstanding," he whispered to me, and the Altairi turned to glare at him and then at the police officer.

When Calvin was out of the handcuffs, the one on the end said, "As the men of old, we are with gladness to be proved wrong."

So are we, I thought. "We're delighted to welcome you to our planet," I said.

"Now if you'll accompany me back to DU," Dr. Morthman cut in, "we'll arrange for you to go to Washington to meet with the President and—"

The Altairi began to glare again. *Oh, no,* I thought, and looked frantically at Calvin. "We have not yet finished greeting the delegation, Dr. Morthman," Calvin said. He turned to the Altairi. "We would like to sing you the rest of our greeting songs."

"We wish to hear them," the Altairus in the center said, and the six of them immediately turned, walked back up the aisle, and sat down.

"I think it would be a good idea if you sat down, too," I said to Dr. Morthman and the FBI agents.

"Can some of you share your music with them?" Calvin said to the people in the last row. "And help them find the right place?"

"I have no intention of singing with witches and homo—" Reverend Thresher began indignantly, and the Altairi all turned to glare at him. He sat down, and an elderly man in a yarmulke handed him his music.

"What do we do about the words to the 'Hallelujah Chorus'?" Calvin whispered to me, and the Altairi stood up and walked back down the aisle to us.

"There is no need to alter your joyful songs. We wish to hear them with the native words," the one in the center said.

"We have a great interest in your planet's myths and superstitions," the one on the end said, "the child in the manger, the lighting of the Kwanzaa menorah, the bringing of toys and teeth to children. We are eager to learn more."

"We have many questions," the next one in line said. "If the child was born in a desert land, then how can King Herod have taken the children on a sleigh ride?"

"Sleigh ride?" Dr. Morthman said, and Calvin looked inquiringly at me.

"'All children young to sleigh,'" I whispered.

"Also, if holly is jolly, then why does it bark?" the one on the other end said. "And, Mr. Ledbetter, *is* Ms. Yates your girlfriend?"

"There will be time for questions, negotiations, and gifts when the greetings have been completed," the second Altairus on the left, the one who hadn't said anything up till then, said, and I realized he must be the leader. *Or the choir director,* I thought. When he spoke, the Altairi instantly formed themselves into pairs, walked back up the aisle, and sat down.

I picked up Calvin's baton and handed it to him. "What do you think we should sing first?" he asked me.

"All I want for Christmas is you," I said.

"Really? I was thinking maybe we should start with 'Angels We Have Heard on High,' or—"

"That wasn't a song title," I said.

"Oh," he said, and turned to the Altairi. "The answer to your question is yes."

"These are tidings of great joy," the one in the center said.

"There shall be many mistletoeings," the one on the end added.

The second Altairus on the left glared at them. "I think we'd better sing," I said, and squeezed into the first row, between Reverend McIntyre and an African American woman in a turban and dashiki.

Calvin stepped onto the podium. "The Hallelujah Chorus," Calvin said, and there was a shuffling of pages as people found their music. The woman next to me held out her music so we could share and whispered, "It's considered proper etiquette to stand for this. In honor of King George the Third. He's supposed to have stood up the first time he heard it."

"Actually," Reverend McIntyre whispered to me, "he may merely have been startled out of a sound sleep, but rising out of respect and admiration is still an appropriate response."

I nodded. Calvin raised his baton, and the entire auditorium, except for the Altairi, rose as one and began to sing. And if I'd thought "Adeste Fideles" sounded wonderful, "The Hallelujah Chorus" was absolutely breathtaking, and suddenly all those lyrics about glorious songs of old and anthems sweet and repeating the sounding joy made sense. *And the whole world give back the song,* I thought, *which now the angels sing.*

And apparently the Altairi were as overwhelmed by the music as I was. After the fifth "Hal-leh-eh-lu-jah!" they rose into the air like they'd done before. And rose. And rose, till they floated giddily just below the high domed ceiling.

I knew just how they felt.

It was definitely a communications breakthrough. The Altairi haven't stopped talking since the All-City Sing, though we're not actually much further along than we were before. They're much better at asking questions than answering them. They did finally tell us where they came from—the star Alsafi in the constellation Draco. But since the meaning of Altair is "the flying one" (and Alsafi means "cooking tripod"), everyone still calls them the Altairi.

They also told us why they'd turned up at Calvin's apartment and kept following me ("We glimpsed interesting possibilities of accord between you and Mr. Ledbetter") and explained, more or less, how their spaceship works, which the Air Force has found extremely interesting. But we still don't know why they came here. Or what they want. The only thing they've told us specifically was that they wanted to have Dr. Morthman and Reverend Thresher removed from the commission and to have Dr. Wakamura put in charge. It turns out they like being squirted, at least as much as they like anything we do. They still glare.

So does Aunt Judith. She called me the day after the All-City Sing to tell me she'd seen me on CNN and thought I'd done a nice job saving the planet, but what on earth was I wearing? Didn't I know one was supposed to dress up for a concert? I told her everything that had happened was all thanks to her, and she glared at me (I could feel it, even over the phone) and hung up.

But she must not be too mad. When she heard I was engaged, she called my sister Tracy and told her she expected to be invited to the wedding shower. My mother is cleaning like mad.

I wonder if the Altairi will give us a fish slice. Or a birthday card with a dollar in it. Or faster-than-light travel.

In Coppelius's Toyshop

So here I am, stuck in Coppelius's Toyshop, the last place I wanted to be. Especially at Christmas.

The place is jammed with bawling babies and women with shopping bags and people dressed up like teddy bears and Tinkerbell. The line for Santa Claus is so long, it goes clear out the door and all the way over to Madison Avenue, and the lines at the cash registers are even longer.

There are kids everywhere, running up and down the aisles and up and down the escalators, screaming their heads off, and crowding around Rapunzel's tower, gawking up at the row of little windows. One of the windows opens, and inside it there's a ballerina. She twirls around, and the little window closes, and another one opens. This one has a mouse in it. A black cat rears up behind it with its mouth open and the mouse leans out the window and squeaks, "Help, help!" The kids point and laugh.

And over the whole thing the Coppelius's Toyshop theme song plays, for the thousandth time:

> *"Come to Dr. Coppelius's*
> *Where all is bright and warm,*
> *And there's no fear*
> *For I am here*
> *To keep you safe from harm."*

I am not supposed to be here. I am supposed to be at a Knicks game. I had a date to take Janine to see them play the Celtics this afternoon, and instead, here I am, stuck in a stupid toy store, because of a kid I didn't even know she had when I asked her out.

Women always make this big deal about men being liars and not telling them you're married, but what about them? They talk about honesty being the most important thing in a "relationship," which is their favorite word, and they let you take them out and spend a lot of money on them and when they finally let you talk them into going up to their apartment, they trot out these three little brats in pajamas and expect you to take them to the zoo.

This has happened to me about ten times, so before I asked Janine out, I asked Beverly, who works in Accounting with her, whether she lived alone. Beverly, who didn't tell me about *her* kid till we'd been going out over a month and who was really bent out of shape when I dumped her, said, yeah, Janine lived alone and she'd only been divorced about a year and was very "vulnerable" and the last thing she needed in her life was a jerk like me.

She must've given Janine the same line because I had to really turn on the old charm to get her to even talk to me and had to ask her out about fifteen times before she finally said yes.

So, anyway, the Knicks game is our third date. Bernard King is playing and I figure after the game I'm gonna get lucky, so I'm feeling pretty good, and I knock on her door, and this little kid answers it and says, "My mom's not ready."

I should've turned around right then and walked out. I could've scalped Janine's ticket for fifty bucks, but she's already coming to the door, and she's wiping her eyes with a Kleenex and telling me to come in, this is Billy, she's so sorry she can't go to the game, this isn't her weekend to have the kid, but her ex-husband made her switch, and she's been trying to call me, but I'd already left.

I'm still standing in the hall. "You can't get tickets to Knicks games at the last minute," I say. "Do you know what scalpers charge?" She says, no, no, she doesn't expect me to get an extra ticket, and I breathe a sigh of relief, which I shouldn't have, because then she says she just got a call, her mom's in the hospital, she's had a heart attack, and she's got to go to Queens right away and see her, and she tried to get her ex on the phone but he's not there.

"You better not expect me to take the *kid* to the Knicks game," I say, and she says, no, she doesn't, she's already called Beverly to watch him, and all she wants me to do is take the kid to meet her on the corner of Fifth Avenue and Fifty-eighth.

"I wouldn't ask you to do this if I had anybody else I could ask, but they said I needed to come"—she starts to cry again—"right . . . away."

The whole time she's telling me this, she's been putting on her coat and putting the kid's coat on him and locking the door. "I'll say hi to Grandma for you," she says to the kid. She looks at me, her eyes all teary. "Beverly said she'll be there at noon. Be a good boy," she says to the kid, and is down the stairs and out the door before I can tell her no way.

So I'm stuck with taking this kid up to Fifth Avenue and Fifty-eighth, which is the corner Coppelius's Toyshop is on. Coppelius's is the biggest toy store in New York. It's got fancy red-and-gold doors, and two guys dressed up like toy soldiers standing on both sides of them, saluting people when they walk in, and a chick dressed like Little Red Riding Hood with a red cape and a basket, passing out candy canes to every-body who walks by.

There's a whole mob of people and kids looking at the windows, which they decorate every Christmas with scenes from fairy tales. You know the kind, with Goldilocks eating a bowl of porridge, lifting a spoon to her mouth over and over, and stuffed bears that turn their heads and blink their eyes. It looks like half of New York is there, looking in the windows. Except for Beverly.

I look at my watch. It's noon, and Beverly better get here soon or the kid can wait by himself. The kid sees the windows and runs over to them. "Come back here!" I yell, and grab him by the arm and yank him away from the windows. "Get over here!" I drag him over to the curb. "Now stand there."

The kid is crying and wiping his nose, just like Janine. "Aunt Beverly said she was going to take me to look at the windows," he says.

"Well, then, *Aunt Beverly* can," I say, "when she finally gets here. Which better be pretty damn soon. I don't have all day to wait around."

"I'm cold," he says.

"Then zip up your coat," I say, and I zip up mine and stick my hands in my pockets. There's one of these real cold New York winds whipping around the corner, and it's starting to snow. I look at my watch. It's a quarter past twelve.

"I hafta go to the bathroom," he says.

I tell him to shut up, that he's not going anywhere, and he starts in crying again.

"And quit crying or I'll give you something to cry about," I say.

Right then Red Riding Hood comes over and hands the kid a candy cane. "What's the matter, honey?" she says.

The kid wipes his nose on his sleeve. "I'm cold and I hafta go to the bathroom," he says, and she says, "You just come with me to Coppelius's," and takes hold of his hand and takes him into the store before I can stop her.

"Hey!" I say, and go after them, but the toy-soldier guys are already shutting the doors behind them, and they go through their whole stiff-armed saluting routine before they open them again and I can get in.

When I finally do, I wish I hadn't. The place is a nightmare. There are about a million kids hollering and running around this huge room full of toys and people in costumes demonstrating things. A magician is juggling glow-in-the-dark balls and Raggedy Ann is passing out licorice sticks and a green-faced witch is buzzing the customers with a plane on a string. Around the edges of the room, trains are running on tracks built into the walls, hooting and whistling and blowing steam.

In the middle of this mess is a round purple tower, at least two stories high. There's a window at the very top and a mechanical Rapunzel is leaning out of it, combing her blond hair, which hangs all the way down to the bottom of the tower. Underneath Rapunzel's window there's a row of little windows that open and close, one after the other, and different things poke out, a baby doll and a white rabbit and a spaceship. All of them do something when their window opens. The doll says "Ma-ma," the rabbit pulls out a pocket watch and looks at it, shaking his head, the spaceship blasts off.

A whole bunch of kids are standing around the tower, but Janine's kid isn't one of them, and I don't see him or Red Riding Hood anywhere. Along the back wall there's a bunch of escalators leading up and down to the other floors, but I don't see the kid on any of them and I don't see any signs that say "Bathrooms," and the lines for the cash registers are too long to ask one of the clerks.

A chick dressed up like Cinderella is standing in the middle of the aisle, winding up green toy frogs and setting them down on the floor to hop all over and get in everybody's way.

"Where are your toilets?" I say, but she doesn't hear me, and no wonder. Screaming kids and hooting trains and toy guns that go rat-a-tat-tat, and over the whole thing a singsongy tune is playing full blast:

> "I am Dr. Coppelius.
> Welcome to my shop.
> Where we have toys
> For girls and boys,
> And the fun times never stop."

It's sung in a croaky old man's voice and after the second verse finishes, the first one starts in again, over and over and over.

"How do you stand that godawful noise?" I shout to Cinderella, but she's talking to a little kid in a snowsuit and ignores me.

I look around for somebody else I can ask and just then I catch sight of a red cape at the top of one of the escalators and take off after it.

I'm about to step on, when an old guy dressed in a long red coat and a gray ponytail wig moves in front of me and blocks my way. "Welcome to Coppelius's Toyshop," he says in a phony accent. "I am Dr. Coppelius, the children's friend." He does this stupid bow. "Here in Coppelius's, children are our first concern. How may I assist you?"

"You can get the hell out of my way," I say, and shove past him and get on the escalator.

The red cape has disappeared by now, and the escalator's jammed with kids. Half of them are hanging over the moving handrail, looking at the stuffed animals along the sides, teddy bears and giraffes and a life-size black velvet panther. It's got a pink silk tongue and real-looking teeth with a price tag hanging from one of its fangs. "One of a kind," the price tag says. Four thousand bucks.

When I get to the top of the escalator, I can't see Janine's kid or Red Riding Hood anywhere, but there's a red-and-gold signpost with arrows pointing off in all directions that say "To Hot Wheels Country" and "To Babyland" and "To the Teddy Bears' Picnic." One of them says "To the Restrooms" and points off to the left.

I go in the direction the sign says, but the place is a maze, with aisles leading off in all directions and kids jamming every aisle. I go through fire engines and chemistry sets and end up in a big room full of *Star Wars* stuff, blasters and swords that light up and space fighters. But no signposts.

I ask a gold-colored robot for directions, feeling like an idiot, and he says, "Go down this aisle and turn left. That will bring you to Building Blocks. Turn left at the Tinker Toys and left again. The restrooms are right next to the Lego display."

I go down the aisle and turn left, but it doesn't bring me to Building Blocks. It brings me to the doll department and then the stuffed animals, more giraffes and bunnies and elephants, and every size teddy bear you've ever seen.

Holding on to one of them is a toddler bawling its head off. The kid's been eating candy, and the tears are running down into the chocolate for a nice sticky mess.

It's wailing, "I'm lost," and as soon as it sees me, it lets go of the teddy bear and heads straight for me with its sticky hands. "I can't find my mommy," it says.

The last thing I need is chocolate all over my pants. "You shoulda stayed with your mommy, then," I say, "instead of running off," and head back into the doll department, and old Coppelius must've been lying about the panther, because there, right in the middle of the Barbie dolls, is another one, staring at me with its yellow glass eyes.

I head back through the dollhouses and end up in Tricycles, and this is getting me nowhere. I could wander around this place forever and never find Janine's kid. And it's already one o'clock. If I don't leave by one-thirty, I'll miss the start of the game. I'd leave right now, but Janine would be steamed and I'd lose any chance I had of getting her in the sack on one of those weekends when her ex has the kid.

But I'm not going to find him by wandering around like this. I need to go back down to the main room and wait for Red Riding Hood to bring him back.

I find a down escalator in the sled department and get on it, but when I get off, it's not the main floor. I'm in Babyland with the baby buggies and yellow rubber ducks and more teddy bears.

I must not have gone down far enough. "Where's the escalator?" I say to a chick dressed like Little Bo Peep. She's kootchy-cooing a baby, and I have to ask her again. "Where's the down escalator?"

Bo Peep looks up and frowns. "Down?"

"Yeah," I say, getting mad. "Down. An escalator."

Still nothing.

"I want to get the hell out of this place!"

She makes a move toward the baby, like she's going to cover its ears or something, and says, "Go down past the playpens and turn left. It's at the end of Riding Toys."

I do what she says, but when I get there, it goes up, not down. I decide to take it anyway and go back up to the tricycles and find the right escalator myself, but Babyland must be in the basement because at the top is the main room.

The place is even crazier and more crowded than it was before. A clown's demonstrating bright orange yo-yos, Humpty Dumpty's winding up toy dinosaurs, and there are so many kids and baby buggies and shopping bags, it takes me fifteen minutes to make it over to Rapunzel's tower.

There's no sign of Red Riding Hood and the kid or Beverly, but I can see the door from here and all the escalators. Dr. Coppelius is standing over at the foot of them, bowing to people and passing out big red suckers.

The kids around the tower shout and point, and I look up. A puppet with a hooked nose and a pointy hat is leaning out of one of the windows. He's holding a stick between his puppet hands, and he waves it around. The kids laugh.

The window shuts and another one opens. The ballerina twirls. The black cat, with teeth as sharp as a panther's, rears up behind the mouse, and the mouse squeaks, "Help, help!" Rapunzel combs her hair. And over it all, in time to the squeaking and the twirling and the combing, the song plays over and over:

> "... *For girls and boys,*
> *And the fun times never stop.*"

And after I've been standing there five minutes, the whole thing is stuck in my head.

I look at my watch. It's one-fifteen. How the hell long does it take to take a kid to the bathroom?

The first verse finishes and the second one starts in:

> *"Come to Dr. Coppelius's*
> *Where all is bright and warm . . ."*

I'm going to go crazy if I have to stand here and listen to this gas much longer, and where the hell is Beverly?

I look at my watch again. It's one-thirty. I'm going to give it five more minutes and then take one more look around, and then I'm going to the game, kid or no kid.

Somebody yanks on my coat. "Well, it's about time," I say. "Where the hell have you been?" I look down.

It's a kid with dishwater-blond hair and glasses. "When will he come and get her?" she says.

"Get who?" I say.

She pushes the glasses up on her nose. "Rapunzel in her tower. When will the prince come and get her down?"

I stoop down and get real close. "Never," I say.

The kid blinks at me through her glasses. "Never?" she says.

"He got sick of waiting around for her," I say. "He waited and waited, and finally he got fed up and went off and left her there."

"All alone?" she squeaks, just like the mouse.

"All alone. Forever and ever."

"Doesn't she ever get out of the tower?"

"She's not going anywhere, and it serves her right. It's her own fault."

The kid backs away and looks like she's going to bawl, but she doesn't. She just stares at me through her glasses and then looks back up at the tower.

The rabbit checks his watch. A dragon breathes orange tinfoil flames. The baby doll goes, "Ma-ma." The singsongy tune bellows, *"To keep you safe from harm,"* and starts over, *"I am Dr. Coppelius,"* and I shove my way over to where he's standing at the foot of the escalators.

"How do I find a lost kid?" I say to Dr. Coppelius.

"Up this escalator to Painter's Corner," he says in his phony accent. "Turn right at the modeling-clay display and go all the way to the end."

He puts his hand on my arm. "And don't worry. He's perfectly safe. No child ever comes to harm in Coppelius's Toyshop."

"Yeah, well, I know one who's going to when I finally find him," I say, and get on the escalator.

I thought it was the same one I went up before, but it's not. There's no panther, and no signpost at the top, but I can see paints and crayons down one of the halls, and I head that way. Halfway there, the aisle's blocked with kids and mothers pushing strollers.

"What the hell's this?" I say to a guy dressed up like an elf.

"It's the line for Santa Claus," he says. "You'll have to go around. Halfway down that aisle to the basketballs and turn left."

So I go down, but there aren't any basketballs, there's a big Atari sign and a bunch of kids playing Pac-Man, and when I turn left, I run into a room full of toy tanks and bazookas. I go back and turn left and run smack into the Santa Claus line again.

I look at my watch. It's a quarter past two. The hell with this. I've already missed the start of the game, and I'm not going to miss the rest of it. Beverly can try and find the kid, if and when she ever gets here. I'm leaving.

I squeeze through the line to the nearest escalator and take it down, but I must have gotten up on the third floor somehow, because here's the *Star Wars* stuff. I find an escalator and go down it, but when I get to the bottom, I'm back in Babyland and now I have to take the escalator up. But at least I know where it is. I go down past the playpens and over to Riding Toys, and sure enough, there's the escalator. I start to get on it.

The panther is standing at the bottom of the escalator, the price tag dangling from his sharp teeth.

I change my mind and go back through the riding toys and turn left, and now I'm back in Dolls, which can't be right. I backtrack to the playpens, but now I can't find them, either. I'm in Puzzles and Games.

I look around for somebody to ask, but there aren't any clerks or Mother Gooses around, and no kids, either. They must all be in line to see Santa Claus. I decide to go back to the doll department and get my bearings, and I go up the jigsaw puzzle aisle, but I can't seem to find a way out, and I am getting kind of worried when I see Dr. Coppelius.

He walks past the Candyland display and into a door in the wall between Jeopardy! and Sorry! and I catch a glimpse of gray walls and metal stairs. I figure it must be an employee stairway.

I wait a few minutes so the clown won't see me and then open the door. It's an employee stairway, all right. There are stacks of boxes and wooden crates piled against the wall, and on the stairs there's a big sign headed "Store Policy." I look up the metal stairway, and it has to lead up to the main floor because I can hear the sound of the song jangling far above:

> "... For girls and boys,
>   And the fun times never stop."

I shut the door behind me, and start up the stairs. It's dark with the door shut, and it gets darker as I climb, and narrower, but the song is getting steadily louder. I keep climbing, wondering what kind of stairway this is. It can't be for bringing up stock because it keeps making all these turns and when I decide I'd better turn around and go back down, somebody's locked the door at the bottom, so I have to keep climbing up, and it keeps getting narrower and narrower and darker and darker, till I can feel the walls on both sides and the last few steps I practically have to squeeze through, but I can see the door up ahead, there's light all around the edges, and the song is getting really loud.

> "Come to Dr. Coppelius's
>   Where all is bright and warm ..."

I squeeze up the last few steps and open the door, only it isn't a door. It's one of the little windows the mouse and the ballerina and the white rabbit come out of, and I have somehow gotten inside of Rapunzel's tower. This must be the stairs they use to come fix the mechanical toys when they break down.

Kids are looking up, and when I open the window, they point and laugh like I was one of the toys. I shut the window and squeeze back down the stairs. I break a piece of wood off one of the crates on the stairs to use to pry the door open, but I must have made a wrong turn somewhere, because I end up back in the same place. I open the door and yell, "Hey! Get me out of here!" but nobody pays any attention.

I look around, trying to spot Red Riding Hood or the robot or Dr. Coppelius to signal them to come help me, and I see Beverly walking to the front door. She's got Janine's kid, and he is wiping his nose on his sleeve and clutching a red sucker. Beverly squats down and wipes his eyes with a Kleenex. She zips up his coat, and they start out the door, which a toy soldier is holding open for them.

"Wait!" I shout, waving the piece of wood to get their attention, and the kids point and laugh.

I am going to have to climb out the window and down the side of the tower, hanging on to Rapunzel's hair. I put my foot up over the windowsill. It's a tight squeeze to get my leg up onto the sill, but I manage to do it, and when I get out of here, I know a little boy with a sucker who's going to be really sorry. I hitch my leg over and start to hoist my other foot up over the sill.

I look down. The panther is sitting at the foot of the tower, crouched and waiting. He licks his velvet chops with his pink silk tongue. His sharp teeth glitter.

So here I am, stuck in Coppelius's Toyshop, for what seems like forever, with kids screaming and running around and trains whistling and that stupid song playing over and over and over,

> "*I am Dr. Coppelius.*
> *Welcome to my shop . . .*"

I take out my watch and look at it. It says five to twelve. I've kind of lost track of how long I've been stuck here. It can't be more than two days, because on Monday Janine or Beverly or one of the chicks at work will notice I'm not there, and they'll figure out this is the last place anybody saw me. But it seems longer, and I am getting kind of worried.

Every time the window opens there seem to be different toys, fancy games you play on computers and cars that run by remote control and funny-looking roller skates with only one row of wheels. And the people demonstrating them and handing out candy canes are different, too, mermaids and turtles wearing headbands and a hunchback in a jester's hat and a purple cape.

And the last time I looked out, a woman with dishwater-blond hair and glasses was standing under the tower, looking up at me. "When I was little," she said to the guy she was with, "I hated this place. I was so worried about Rapunzel."

She pushed her glasses up on her nose. "I didn't know she was a toy. I thought she was real, and I thought the prince had just gone off and abandoned her. I thought he'd gotten fed up and gone off and left her there. All alone."

She said it to the guy, but she was looking straight at me. "Forever and ever. And it served her right. It was her own fault."

But there are lots of people who wear glasses, and even if Janine's mother died and she had to go to the funeral, she'd still be back at work by Wednesday.

I look over at the exit. The toy soldiers are still there, saluting, on either side of the door, and in between them Dr. Coppelius smiles and bows. Overhead the song screeches:

> *"And there's no fear*
> *For I am here*
> *To keep you safe from harm."*

And starts in on the first verse again.

I take out my watch and look at it, and then I shut the window and go look for a way out, but I get confused on the stairs and make a wrong turn and end up in the same place. The little window opens, and I lean out. "Help! Help!" I shout.

The kids point and laugh.

Adaptation

"Heap on more wood!—the wind is chill;
But, let it whistle as it will,
We'll keep our Christmas merry still."
—Sir Walter Scott

Marley was dead: to begin with.

Dickens's story *A Christmas Carol,* however, of which the aforementioned is the first sentence, is alive and well and available in any number of versions. In the books department of Harridge's, where I work, we have nineteen, including *Mickey's Christmas Carol, The Muppet Christmas Carol,* the CuddlyWuddlys' *Christmas Carol,* and one with photographs of dogs dressed as Scrooge and Mrs. Cratchit.

We also have an assortment of *Christmas Carol* cookbooks, Advent calendars, jigsaw puzzles, and an audiotape on which Captain Picard of the American television series *Star Trek: The Next Generation* takes all the parts.

All of these are, of course, adaptations, shortened and altered and otherwise bowdlerized. No one reads the original, though we carry it, in paperback. In the two years I've worked here, we've only sold a single copy, and that to myself. I bought it last year to read to my daughter, Gemma, when I had her for Christmas, but then I did not have time to do so. My ex-wife, Margaret, came to pick her up early for a pantomime she and Robert were taking her to, and we only got as far as Marley's ghost.

Gemma knows the story, though, in spite of never having read it, and the names of all the characters, as does everyone. They are so well-known, in fact, that at the beginning of the season this year Harridge's management had suggested the staff dress in costume as Scrooge and Tiny Tim, to increase profits and "provide a seasonal atmosphere."

There was a general outcry at this, and the idea had been dropped. But on the morning of the twenty-second when I arrived at work, there was a figure in a floor-dragging black robe and a hood standing by the order desk with Mr. Voskins, who was smiling smugly.

"Good morning, Mr. Grey," Mr. Voskins said to me. "This is your new assistant," and I half expected him to say, "Mr. Black," but instead he said pleasedly, "the Spirit of Christmas Future."

It is actually Christmas Yet to Come, but Mr. Voskins has not read the original, either.

"How do you do?" I said, wondering if Mr. Voskins was going to demand that I wear a costume as well, and why he had hired someone just now. The books department had been shorthanded all of December.

"Mr. Grey will explain things to you," Mr. Voskins said to the spirit. "Harridge's has been able to arrange for an author autographing," he said to me, which explained this hiring three days before Christmas. No doubt the book being autographed was yet another version of *A Christmas Carol.* "We will be holding it the day after tomorrow."

"On Christmas Eve?" I said. "At what time? I'd arranged to leave early on Christmas Eve."

"It will depend on the author's schedule," Mr. Voskins said. "He's an extremely busy man."

"My daughter's spending the evening with me," I explained. "It's the only time I'll have her." They would be at Robert's parents' in Surrey for the rest of Christmas week.

"I'm discussing the details with the author this morning," he said. "Oh, and your wife telephoned. She wants you to ring her back."

"Ex-wife," I corrected him, but he had already hurried off, leaving me with my new assistant.

"I'm Mr. Grey," I said, extending my hand.

The spirit silently extended a skinny hand for me to shake, and I remembered that the Spirit of Christmas Yet to Come was mute, communicating solely by pointing.

"Have you worked in a books department before?" I asked.

He shook his hooded head. I hoped he didn't plan to stay in character while waiting on the customers, or perhaps that was the idea, and he was here for "seasonal atmosphere" only.

"What am I supposed to call you?" I said.

He extended a bony finger and pointed at the *Wild West Christmas Carol,* on the cover of which a black-hatted spirit stood, pointing at a tombstone with Scrooge's name on it.

"Spirit? Christmas? Yet to Come?" I said, thinking that an "atmospheric" assistant was worse than none at all.

But I was wrong. He proved to be very efficient, learning the cash register and the credit-card procedure with ease, and waiting on customers promptly. They seemed delighted when he extended his bony finger from his black sleeve and pointed at the books they'd asked for. By ten o'clock I felt confident enough to leave him in charge of the department while I went to the employee lounge to telephone Margaret.

The line was engaged. I intended to ring her up again at a quarter past, but we had a surge of shoppers, and although Christmas Yet to Come was extremely helpful, I couldn't get away again till nearly eleven. When I dialed Margaret's flat, there was no answer.

I was almost glad. I wanted to know the time of the autographing before I spoke to her. We had already had two fights over the "visitation schedule," as Margaret calls it. I was originally to have had Gemma on Boxing Day as well as Christmas Eve, but Robert's parents had invited them up to Surrey for the entire week. We had compromised by my having Gemma on Christmas Eve and part of Christmas Day. Then last week Margaret had rung up to say Robert's parents especially wanted them there for church on Christmas morning as it was a family tradition that Robert read the Scripture. "You can have her all Christmas Eve day," Margaret had said.

"I have to work."

"You could insist on having the day off," she'd said, letting her voice die away.

It is a trick she has of leaving a sentence unfinished but her meaning perfectly clear. She used it to excellent account during the divorce, claiming she had not said any of the things I accused her of, as in fact she had not, and though I only see her now when she brings Gemma, I still understand her perfectly.

"You could insist on having the day off," she meant now, "if you really cared about Gemma." And there is no answer to that, no way to make her understand that Christmas Eve is not a day a shopclerk can insist on taking off, to explain to her that it is different from being an accountant. No way to explain why I gave up being an accountant.

And no way to explain to her that I might need to change the schedule because of an autographing. I decided to wait to try again till I had spoken to Mr. Voskins.

He did not come back till after noon. "The autographing will take place from eleven to one," he said, handing us a stack of red-and-green flyers. "Hand these out to the customers," he said.

I read the top flyer, relieved that the autographing wouldn't cause a problem with Gemma. "A Special Signing of Sir Spencer Siddon's latest book," it read. "*Making Money Hand Over Fist.*"

"It's on the bestseller list," Mr. Voskins said happily. "We were very lucky to get him. His secretary will be here at half past one to discuss the arrangements."

"We'll need more staff," I said. "The two of us can't possibly run an autographing and wait on customers at the same time."

"I'll try to hire someone," he said vaguely. "We'll discuss everything when Sir Spencer's secretary arrives."

"Shall I go to lunch now, then?" I said, "and let Mr. . . ." I pointed at the spirit, "go second so I'll be back in time for the meeting?"

"No," he said. "I want you both here. Go now." He waved vaguely in our direction.

"Which?"

"Both of you. I'll get someone from the housewares department to cover your department. Be back by 1:00."

When our replacement came, I told the spirit, "You can go to lunch," stuck *A Christmas Carol,* which I'd been reading on my lunch and tea breaks, in my coat pocket, and went to telephone Margaret. The line was engaged again.

When I came out of the lounge, the spirit was standing there, waiting for me, and I realized he wouldn't know where to go for lunch. Since Harridge's had closed its employee dining room to increase profits, employees had half an hour to get to, partake of, and return from lunch. "I know of a place that's quick," I told him.

He nodded, and I led off through the crowded aisles, hoping he would keep up. I need not have had any fear—he kept pace with me easily, in spite of not saying, as I did, "Sorry," to dozens of shoppers blocking the way. By the time we'd reached the south door, he was even with me, and, before I could turn toward Cavendish Square, he'd moved ahead, his arm extended and his long, bony finger pointing toward Regent Street.

All the luncheon places in Regent Street are expensive and invariably crammed with shoppers resting their feet, and are a good ten minutes' walk away. We would have just enough time to walk there, not get waited on, and return empty-handed.

"I usually go to Wilson's," I said, "it's closer," but he continued to point commandingly and we had no time for arguing, either. I followed him down the street, down a lane I hadn't known was there, and into a dismal-looking lunch counter called Mama Montoni's.

It wasn't crowded, at any rate, and the small tables looked comparatively clean, though the made sandwiches on top of the counter looked several days old.

At one of the tables was an enormous man with a full brown beard, and I saw why the spirit had brought me here. The man was dressed as the Spirit of Christmas Present, in a green robe edged with white fur, and a crown of holly.

"Come in! Come in!" he said, even though we were already in, and my companion glided over to him.

The enormous man shook his head and said, "No, he can't make it for lunch today," as if Christmas Yet to Come had spoken.

I wondered who the "he" they referred to was. The Spirit of Christmas Past, perhaps?

"Neither of us got anything, I'm afraid," the enormous man said to Yet to Come, sounding discouraged. "Most of the bank executives are on holiday. But the teller said the Adelphi is holding pantomime auditions this afternoon."

I wondered if the pantomime was *A Christmas Carol,* or if they had previously been in a production and were now trying to find employment that fit the costumes. It was a good costume. The holly crown had the requisite icicles, and the green robe was belted with a rusted scabbard, just as in the original. His chest was not bare, though, and neither were his feet. He had compromised with the weather by wearing sandals with thick socks and had fastened the open robe across his massive chest with a large green button.

I was still standing just inside the door. My companion turned and pointed at me, and the enormous man boomed out, "Come in! and know me better, man!" and beckoned me to the table.

I was going to say that I needed to order first, but the old woman behind the counter—Mama Montoni?—had disappeared into the back. I went over to the table. "How do you do?" I said. "I'm Edwin Grey."

"Delighted to meet you," the enormous man said heartily. "Sit down, sit down. My friend tells me you work together."

"Yes." I sat down. "At Harridge's."

"He tells me you are hiring additional staff in your department. Is that right?"

"Possibly," I said, wondering how Sir Spencer Siddon would feel at being confronted with half the characters from *A Christmas Carol.* Would he think he was meant to be Scrooge? "It would be only temporary, though. Just the three days till Christmas."

"Till Christmas," he said, and the old woman emerged from the back with a fistful of silverware and two plates of congealed-looking spaghetti.

"I'll have what they're having," I said, "and a paper cup of tea to take with me."

The old woman, who was clearly related to Yet to Come, didn't answer or even acknowledge that I'd spoken to her, but she disappeared into the back again.

"I didn't know this café was here," I said, so he wouldn't bring up the topic of job openings again.

"Excellent choice of book," he said, pointing at my *Christmas Carol,* which was protruding from my coat pocket.

"I should imagine it's your favorite," I said, laying it on the table, smiling.

He shook his shaggy brown head. "I prefer Mr. Dickens's *Little Dorrit,* so patient and cheerful in her imprisonment, and Trollope's *Barchester Towers.*"

"Do you read a good deal?" I asked. It's rare to find anyone who reads the older authors, let alone Trollope.

He nodded. "I find it helps to pass the time," he said. "Especially at this time of year, 'When dark December glooms the day / And takes our autumn joys away / When short and scant the sunbeam throws / Upon the weary waste of snows / A cold and profitless regard . . .' 'Marmion.' Sir Walter Scott."

"Introduction to the fifth canto," I said, and he beamed at me.

"You are a reader, too?" he said eagerly.

"I find books a great comfort," I said, and he nodded.

"Tell me what you think of *A Christmas Carol*," he said.

"I think it has lasted all these years because people want to believe it could happen," I said.

"But you don't believe it?" he said. "You don't believe a man might hear the truth and be changed by it?"

"I think Scrooge seems quite easily reformed," I said, "compared with the Scrooges I have known."

Mama Montoni emerged from the back again, glaring, and slapped down a plate of lukewarm spaghetti and a crockery cup half full of tea.

"So you have read 'Marmion'?" the Spirit of Christmas Present said. "Tell me, what did you think of the tale of Sir David Lindesay?" and we launched into an eager discussion that lasted far too long. I would be late getting back for the meeting with Scrooge's secretary.

I stood up, and my assistant did, too. "We must be getting back," I said, pulling on my coat. "It was a pleasure meeting you, Mr. . . . ?"

He extended his huge hand. "I am the Spirit of Christmas Present."

I laughed. "Then you're missing your third. Where's Christmas Past?"

"In America," he said quite seriously, "where he has been much corrupted by nostalgia and commercial interests."

He saw me looking skeptically at his socks and sandals. "You do not see us at our best," he said. "I fear we have fallen on hard times."

Apparently. "I should think these would be good times, with any number of Scrooges you could reform."

"And so there are," he said, "but they are praised and much rewarded for their greed, and much admired. And"—he looked sternly at me— "they do not believe in spirits. They lay their visions to Freud and hormonal imbalance, and their therapists tell them they should feel no guilt, and advise them to focus further on themselves."

"Yes, well," I said, "I must be getting back." I pointed at my assistant, not knowing whether Present would expect me to address him as the

Spirit of Christmas Yet to Come. "You can stay and talk to your friend if you wish," and made my escape, glad that at least I hadn't suggested he come speak to Mr. Voskins about being taken on, and wondering what Mr. Voskins would do when he found out he had hired a lunatic.

Mr. Voskins wasn't on the floor, and neither was the secretary. I looked at my watch, expecting it to be well past one, but it was only a quarter till. I rang up Margaret. The line was engaged.

My assistant was there when I got back, waiting on a customer, but there was still no sign of Mr. Voskins. He finally came up at two to tell us the secretary had phoned to change the schedule.

"Of the autographing?" I said anxiously.

"No, of the meeting with us. His secretary won't be here till half past."

I took advantage of the delay to try Margaret again. And got Gemma.

"Mummy's downstairs talking to the doorman about our being gone," she told me.

"Do you know what she wanted to speak to me about?" I asked her.

"No . . . o," she said, thinking, and added, with a child's irrelevance, "I went to the dentist. She'll be back up in a minute."

"I'll talk to you in the meantime, then," I said. "What shall we have to eat for Christmas Eve?"

"Figs," she said promptly.

"Figs?"

"Yes, and frosted cakes. Like the little princess and Ermengarde and Becky had at the feast. Well, actually, they didn't have it. Horrid Miss Minchin found out and took it all away from them. And red-currant wine. Only I suppose you won't let me have wine. But red-currant drink or red-currant juice. Red-currant *something*."

"And figs," I said distastefully.

"Yes, and a red shawl for a tablecloth. I want it *just* like in the book."

"What book?" I said, teasing.

"*A Little Princess.*"

"Which one is that?"

"You *know*. The one where the little princess is rich and then she loses her father and Miss Minchin makes her live in the garret and be a servant and the Indian gentleman feels sorry for her and sends her things. You *know*. It's my favorite book."

I do know, of course. It has been her favorite for two years now, displacing both *Anne of Green Gables* and *Little Women* in her affections. "It's because we're just alike," she'd told me when I asked her why she liked it so much.

"You both live in a garret," I'd said.

"No. But we're both tall for our age, and we both have black hair."

"Of course," I said now. "I forgot. What do you want for Christmas?"

"Not a doll. I'm too old for dolls," she said promptly, and then hesitated. "The little princess's father always gave her books for Christmas."

"Did he?"

Mr. Voskins appeared at my elbow, looking agitated. "I'll be right there," I said, cupping my hand over the mouthpiece.

"It's nearly half past," he said.

"I'll be right there." I promised Gemma I'd purchase figs and redcurrant *something,* and told her to tell her mother I'd phoned, and went to meet the secretary, wondering if he'd look like Bob Cratchit. That would make the cast complete, except for the Spirit of Christmas Past, of course, who was in America.

The secretary wasn't there yet. At a quarter to three, Mr. Voskins informed us that the secretary had phoned to change the meeting time to four. I used the extra time to purchase Gemma's present, a copy of *A Little Princess.* She owns a paperback, which she has read a dozen times, but this was a reproduction of the original, with a dark blue cloth cover and colored plates. Gemma looked at it longingly every time she came to see me, and had given all sorts of not-very-veiled hints, like her "The little princess's father bought her books," just now.

I had Yet to Come ring the book up for me, and I put it with my coat and went back into the stockroom to get another copy so Gemma wouldn't see it was gone when she came to the store the day after tomorrow, and guess.

When I came out with the copy, Mr. Voskins was there with Sir Spencer's secretary. I was wrong about the secretary's looking like Bob Cratchit. She was a smartly dressed young woman, with a short, sleek haircut and a gold Rolex watch.

"Sir Spencer requires a straight-backed chair without arms, with a wood table seventy centimeters high, and two fountain pens with viridian ink. Where did you plan to have him sit?"

I showed her the table in the literature section. "Oh, this won't do at all," she said, looking at the books. "A photographer will be coming. These shelves will all have to be filled with copies of *Making Money Hand Over Fist.* Facing out. And the rest of them *here*," she said, pointing at the history shelves, "so that they're easily accessible from the queue. Who will be in charge of that?"

"He will," I said, pointing at Yet to Come.

"Single file," she said, looking at her notes. "Two books per person. New hardbacks only, no paperbacks, and nothing previously owned."

"Do you want them to write the name they wish inscribed on a slip of paper," I said, "so they won't have to spell their names for him?"

She stared at me coldly. "Sir Spencer does not personalize books, he signs them. Sir Spencer prefers Armentières water, *not* Perrier, and some light refreshments—water biscuits and dietetic cheese." She checked off items in her notebook. "We'll need an exit through which he can depart without being seen."

"A trapdoor?" I said, looking at Yet to Come, who seemed positively friendly by comparison.

She turned to Mr. Voskins. "How many staff do you have?"

"I'm hiring additional help," he said, "and we're getting in additional books from the publishers."

She snapped the notebook shut. "Sir Spencer will be here from eleven to one. You were very lucky to get him. Sir Spencer is very much in demand."

We spent the rest of the day bringing up books and scouring the basement and the furniture department for a table that would meet specifications. I had intended to shop for the ingredients for Gemma's feast after work, but instead I went from shop to shop looking for Armentières water, which I found on the sixth try, and for red-currant juice, which I did not find. I bought a box of black-currant tea and hoped that would do.

It was nearly ten when I got home, but I phoned Margaret twice more. Both times the line was engaged.

Next morning I left Yet to Come in charge of the department and went down to the food hall to arrange for the dietetic cheese and water biscuits. When I got back, Margaret was there, asking Yet to Come where I was.

"I suppose it was *your* idea to have a shopclerk that's mute," Margaret said.

"What are you doing here?" I said. "Is Gemma here, too?"

"Yes," Gemma said, coming up, smiling.

"I needed to speak to you," Margaret said. "Gemma, go over to the children's department and see if you can find a hair bow to match your Christmas dress."

Gemma was looking at Yet to Come, who was pointing at the travel section. "Is that the Spirit of Christmas Yet to Come?" she said. "From *A Christmas Carol*?"

"Yes," I said. "The genuine article."

"Gemma," Margaret said. "Go find a hair bow. Burgundy, to match the dress Robert gave you." She sent her off, watching her till she was a good distance down the aisle, and then turned back to me. "It was obvious you weren't going to return my call."

"I did," I said. "Didn't Gemma tell you I'd phoned?"

"She *told* me you couldn't wait even a few moments till I returned, that you were too *busy*."

Gemma told her no such thing, of course. "What did you want to speak to me about?" I said.

"Your daughter's welfare." She looked pointedly at the boxes of books. "Or are you too busy for that, as well?"

There are times when it is hard for me to imagine that I ever loved Margaret. I know rationally that I did, that when she told me she wanted a divorce it was like a blade going through me, but I cannot call up the feeling, or remember what it was about her that I loved.

I said ploddingly, "What about her welfare?"

"She needs a brace. The dentist says she has an overbite and that it needs to be corrected. It will be expensive," she said, and let her voice die away.

Too expensive for a shopclerk, she means. An accountant could have afforded it.

There is no answer to that, even if she had actually said it. She believes I quit my job as an accountant out of spite, to keep her from collecting a large amount of child support, and there is nothing I could say that would convince her otherwise. Certainly not the truth, which is that having lost her, having lost Gemma, I could not bear to do without books as well.

"Robert has offered to pay for the brace," she said, "which I think is very generous of him, but he was afraid you might object. Do you?"

"No," I said, wishing I could say, "I want to pay for the brace," but, as she had not said, a shopclerk doesn't earn enough to pay for it. "I don't have any objections."

"I told him you wouldn't care," she said. "It's become increasingly clear over the past two years that you don't care about Gemma at all."

"And it's becoming increasingly clear," I said, raising my voice, "that you are systematically attempting to take my daughter away from me. You can't even stand to let me see her on Christmas!" I shouted, and saw Gemma.

She was over in the literature section, standing with her back to the shelves. She was holding the copy of *A Little Princess,* and she had obviously come back to see if it was still there, to see if I'd bought it yet.

And heard her parents trying to tear her in two. She huddled back against the shelves, looking small and hunted, clutching the book.

"Gemma," I said, and Margaret turned and saw her.

"Did you find a burgundy hair bow?" she said.

"No," Gemma said.

"Well, come along. We have shopping to do."

Gemma put the book back carefully, and started toward us.

"I'll see you tomorrow night," I said, trying to smile. "I found some black-currant tea for our feast."

She said solemnly, "Did you get the figs?"

"Come along, Gemma," Margaret said. "Tell your father goodbye."

"Goodbye," she said, and smiled tentatively at me.

"I'll get the figs," I promised.

Which was easier said than done. Harridge's food hall didn't have them, either canned or fresh, and neither did the grocer's down the street. There wasn't time to walk to the market and back on my lunch break. I would have to go after work.

And I didn't want to go to Mama Montoni's. I didn't want Christmas Present making more inquiries about whether we were hiring additional staff. And I didn't feel like talking to anyone, sane or not. I ducked down the alley to Wilson's, intending to get a bacon sandwich to take.

The Spirit of Christmas Present was there, sitting at one of the tiny tables, reading *Making Money Hand Over Fist.* He looked up when I came in and motioned me eagerly over to the table.

"I am supposed to meet Jacob Marley here," he said, waving me over. "Come, we'll discuss *Ivanhoe* and *The Mystery of Edwin Drood.*" He pulled a chair out for me. "I have always wondered if Edwin were truly dead, or if he could be brought to life again."

I sat down and picked up *Making Money Hand Over Fist.* "I thought you kept to the older authors."

"Research," he said, taking the book back. "Jacob has high hopes of a job for us. He went to the Old Bailey this morning to speak with a barrister."

"Who specializes in divorce, no doubt," I said. "Or did he go to speak to the barrister about getting his sentence reduced?"

"About repentance," he said.

I laughed humorlessly. "You really believe you're the incarnation of Dickens's spirits."

"Not Dickens's," he said.

"That you're really Christmas Present and my assistant is Christmas Yet to Come? Is that why he never speaks? Because the Spirit of Christmas Yet to Come in Dickens's story is mute?"

"He can speak," he said, quite seriously. "But he does not like to. Many find the sound of his voice distressing."

"And you believe your job is to reform misers and spread Christmas cheer?" I swung my arm wide. "Then why don't you do something?" I said bitterly. "Use your magic powers. Help the needy. House the homeless. Reunite fathers with their children."

"We have no such powers. A little skill with locks, some minor dexterity with time. We cannot change what is, or was. Our power is only to rebuke and to remind, to instruct and to forewarn."

"Like books," I said. "Which no one reads anymore."

"Your daughter."

"My daughter," I said, and brightened. "Do you know where I can find figs?"

"Tinned or fresh?"

"Either," I said.

"Fortnum and Mason's," he said, and as soon as I stood up, went back to reading Sir Spencer's book. There was not time to go to Fortnum's, though when I got back to Harridge's and looked at my watch, I had nearly ten minutes of my lunch break left.

Mr. Voskins was waiting for me.

"Sir Spencer's secretary phoned. Sir Spencer can't be here till half past one." He handed me a stack of revised flyers. "The autographing will be from half past one to half past three."

I looked at the flyers, dismayed.

"It was the only free time in his schedule," he said defensively. "We're lucky he can fit us in at all."

I thought of the cleaning up afterward. "I'll need to leave by four," I said. "My daughter's coming for Christmas Eve."

It was a long afternoon. Yet to Come took the books down from the literature shelves and put up Sir Spencer's books, facing out, bright green volumes with a hundred-pound note design and gold lettering. I taped up flyers and dealt with customers who had gotten a gift they had not expected and who now had, grudgingly, to return the favor, "And nothing over two pounds." I gave them credit-card receipts and flyers, thinking, *Only one more day till I have Gemma.*

After work I went to Fortnum's, which had both fresh and tinned figs. I bought them both, and frosted cakes, and chocolates, which I intended to tell her the Indian gentleman had sent.

When I got home I rooted out an old red wool scarf to use as a table-cloth, and tidied up the flat. Only one more day.

Which day came at last, and with it a new flyer (half past one to half past three) and the Spirit of Christmas Present. "What are you doing here?" I said.

"We have found employment," he said, beaming.

"We?" I said, looking around for Marley. I didn't see anyone who looked the part, and Present was already piling copies of Sir Spencer's book on the display tables.

"What sort of employment?" I said suspiciously. "You're not planning some sort of demonstration against Sir Spencer, are you?"

"I'm your new assistant," he said, stacking books on the floor by the order desk. "I'm supposed to pass out numbers for queueing up."

"I can't imagine that many people will come," I said, but by ten o'clock there were twenty people clutching their numbered chits.

I sold them copies of *Making Money Hand Over Fist* and explained why Sir Spencer wouldn't be there at eleven as advertised. "He's a very busy man," I said. "We're lucky he was able to fit us in at all."

Mr. Voskins came up at eleven to tell us we would have to forgo lunch, which was patently obvious. The department was filled with milling people, Yet to Come had had to go down to the basement for more books, and Present was writing numbers on more chits.

By noon the queue had begun to form according to the numbers and was halfway down the aisle.

"You'd best go get more books," I told Yet to Come, and turned round to find Margaret standing there.

"What are you doing here?" I said blankly. "Where's Gemma?"

"She's up on fifth, looking at dolls," she said.

"I thought she didn't want a doll."

"She said she just wanted to look at them," she said. *Yes,* I thought, *and hide a safe two floors away from her parents' fighting.*

"Christmas Eve won't work," Margaret said.

"What?" I said blankly, though I knew already what she meant, felt it like a blade going in.

"We need to take an earlier train. Robert's parents are having a friend of theirs down who's an orthodontist, and he's agreed to look at Gemma's overbite, but he's only going to be there for Christmas Eve."

"I'm to have Gemma Christmas Eve," I said stupidly.

"I *know.* That's why I came, so we can rework the schedule. We're coming back the day after New Year's. You can have her then."

"Why can't she see the orthodontist after New Year's?"

"He's a very busy man. Ordinarily Gemma would have to be put on a waiting list, but he's agreed to see her as a special favor. I think we should be very grateful he was able to fit us in at all."

"I have to work inventory the day after New Year's," I said.

"Of course," she said, and let her voice die away. "The next weekend, then. Whenever you like."

And the next weekend she will have to be fitted for the brace, I thought, *and the following one it will have to be tightened or she will have to have bands put on.* "I was counting on Gemma's being with me Christmas Eve. Can't you take a later train?" I said, though I already knew it was hopeless, knew I was standing against the bookcase the way Gemma had, looking hunted.

"The only trains are at four and half past ten. The late one doesn't get in till one o'clock. You can hardly expect Robert to ask his parents and the orthodontist to wait up for us. I really do think you could be a bit more accommodating. . . ."

"Mr. Grey, we're out of chits," Mr. Voskins said. "And I need to speak to you about the queue."

"We'll come back a day early, and you can have Gemma for New Year's," she said.

"It's nearly to the end of the aisle," Mr. Voskins said. "Should we loop it round?"

Margaret started toward the jammed aisle. "Wait," I said, "I have Gemma's present at home. Just a moment."

I hurried over to the literature shelves and then remembered those books had been moved over under Travel. I knelt and looked for the other copy of *A Little Princess.* It wasn't wrapped, but she would at least have it for Christmas.

It wasn't there. I looked through the B's twice, and then ran a finger along the backs, looking for the dark blue cover. It wasn't there. I checked Children's, thinking Yet to Come might have put it there, but it wasn't, and when I stood up from checking Literature again, Margaret was gone.

"I've made it a double queue," Mr. Voskins said. "This is going to be a great success, isn't it? Mr. Grey?"

"A great success," I said, and went to write more numbers on slips of paper.

Sir Spencer arrived at a quarter till two in a Savile Row suit. He settled himself in the straight-backed chair, looked disdainfully at the table and the queue, and uncapped one of the fountain pens.

He began to sign the books that were placed before him, and to dispense wisdom to the admiring queue.

"Christmas is an excellent time to think about your future," he said, scrawling a squiggle that might have been an S followed by a long, uneven line. "And an excellent time to plan your financial strategy for the new year."

Four persons back in the queue was someone who could only be meant to be Marley, an old-fashioned coat and trousers draped with heavy chains and a good deal of gray-green greasepaint. He had a kerchief tied round his head and jaw and was clutching a copy of *Making Money Hand Over Fist.*

"They're actually going to try to reform him," I thought, and wondered what Sir Spencer would say.

Marley moved to the front of the queue and laid his open book down on the table. "In life . . ." he said, and it was a curious voice, brittle, dry, a voice that sounded as if it had died away once and for all.

"In life I was Jacob Marley," he said, in that faint dead voice, and shook his chain with a gray-green hand, but Sir Spencer was already handing his book back to him and was reaching for the next.

"There are those who say that money isn't everything," Sir Spencer said to the crowd. "It isn't. Money is the *only* thing."

The queue applauded.

At half past two, Sir Spencer stopped to flex the fingers of his writing hand and drink his Armentières water. He consulted, whispering, with his secretary, looked at his watch, and took another sip.

I went over to the order desk to get another bottle, and when I came back I nearly collided with the Spirit of Christmas Present. He was carrying a huge plum pudding with a sprig of holly on top.

"What are you doing?" I said.

"Christmas is an excellent time to think about your future," he said, winking, and started toward the table, but the sleek secretary interposed herself between him and Sir Spencer.

He tried to give the plum pudding to her, still laughing, but she handed it back. "I specifically requested *light* refreshments," she said sharply, and went back over to Sir Spencer, looking at her watch.

Present followed her. "Come, know me better," he said to her, but she was consulting with Sir Spencer again, and they were both looking at their watches.

She came over to me. "The queue needs to move along more quickly," she said. "Tell them to have their books open to the title page."

I did, working my way back along the queue. There was a sudden silence, and I looked back at the table. Yet to Come had glided in front of a middle-aged woman at the front of the queue, and she had stepped back, clutching her book to her wide bosom.

He's going to do it, I thought, and almost wished he could. It would be nice to see something good happen.

Sir Spencer reached his hand out for the book, and Yet to Come drew himself up and pointed his finger at him, and it was not a finger, but the bones of a skeleton.

I thought, *He's going to speak,* and knew what the voice would sound like. It was the voice of Margaret, telling me she wanted a divorce, telling me they had to take an earlier train. The voice of doom.

I drew in my breath, afraid to hear it, and the secretary leaned forward. "Sir Spencer does not sign body parts," she said sternly. "If you do not have a book, please step aside."

And that was that. Sir Spencer signed newly purchased hardbacks until a quarter of three and then stood up in midscrawl and went out the previously arranged back way.

"He didn't finish," the young girl whose book he had been in the midst of signing said plaintively, and I took the book and the pen and started after him, though without much hope.

I caught him at the door. "There are still people in the queue who haven't had their books signed," I said, holding out the book and pen, but the secretary had interposed herself between us.

"Sir Spencer will be signing on the second at Hatchard's," she said. "Tell them they can try again there."

"It's Christmas," I said, and took hold of his sleeve.

He looked pointedly at it.

"You'll miss your plane to Majorca," the secretary said, and he pulled his sleeve free and swept away, looking at his watch. "Late," I heard the secretary say.

I was still holding the pen and the open book, with its half-finished S. I took it back to the girl. "If you'd like to leave it, I'll try to get it signed for you. Was it a Christmas present?"

"Yes, for my father," she said, "but I won't see him till after Christmas, so that's all right."

I took her name and telephone number, set the books on the order desk, and began taking down the posters.

I had thought perhaps Yet to Come would have disappeared after his failure with Sir Spencer like the others had, but he was still there, putting books into boxes.

He seemed somehow more silent—which was impossible, he had never spoken a word—and downcast, which was ridiculous, as well. The

Spirit of Christmas Yet to Come was supposed to be dreadful, terrifying, but he seemed to have shrunk into himself. Like Gemma, shrinking against the shelves.

It's Sir Spencer that's terrifying, I thought, *and his secretary. And her gold Rolex watch.* "Scrooges are praised and much rewarded for their greed," Present had said, and so they were, with Savile Row suits and knighthoods and Majorca. No wonder the spirits had fallen on hard times.

"At least you tried," I said. "There are some battles that are lost before they're begun."

Children's came over to buy a gift. "For Housewares. I told her I didn't believe in exchanging with colleagues," she said irritably, "but she's bought me something anyway. And I'd planned on leaving early. I suppose you are, too, so you can spend the evening with your little girl."

I looked at my watch. It was after three. They would be leaving for the station soon, and Robert's parents, and the orthodontist.

I cleared away the refreshments. I put foil over the plum pudding and set it next to the girl's book, which I had no hope of getting signed, and went back to help Yet to Come take *Making Money Hand Over Fist* down from the shelves, trying not to think about Gemma and Christmas Eve.

The spirit stopped suddenly and drew himself up and pointed, the robe falling away from his bony hand. I turned, afraid of more bad news, and there was Gemma in the aisle, working her way toward us.

She was pushing steadily upstream through shoppers who all seemed to be going in the opposite direction, ducking between shopping bags with a determined expression on her narrow face.

"Gemma!" I said, and pulled her safely out of the aisle. "What are you doing here?"

"I wanted to tell you goodbye and that I'm sorry I can't come for Christmas Eve."

I raised my head and tried to see down the aisle. "Where's your mother? You didn't come here alone, did you?"

"Mummy's up on fifth," she said. "With the dolls. I told her I'd changed my mind about wanting one. A bride doll. With green eyes." She looked pleased with herself, as well she might. It was no small accomplishment to have gotten Margaret back here half an hour before they were to meet Robert at the station, and she would never have agreed if she'd known why Gemma wanted to come. I could imagine her arguments—there isn't time, you'll see him the day after New Year's, we can't inconvenience Robert, who after all is paying for your brace—and so could Gemma, apparently, and had sidestepped them neatly.

"Did you tell her you were coming down to third?" I said, trying to look disapproving.

"She told me to go look at games so I wouldn't see her buying the doll," she said. "I wanted to tell you I'd rather be with you Christmas Eve."

I love you, I thought.

"I think when I *do* come," she said seriously, "that we should pretend that it *is* Christmas Eve, like the little princess and Becky."

"They pretended it was Christmas Eve?"

"No. When the little princess was cold or hungry or sad she pretended her garret was the Bastille."

"The Bastille," I said thoughtfully. "I don't think they had figs in the Bastille."

"No." She laughed. "The little princess pretended all sorts of things. When she couldn't have what she wanted. So *I* think we should pretend it's Christmas Eve, and wear paper hats and light the tree and say things like, 'It's nearly Christmas,' and 'Oh, listen, the Christmas bells are chiming.'"

"And 'Pass the figs, please,'" I said.

"This is *serious,*" she said. "We'll be together next Christmas, but till then we'll have to *pretend.*" She paused, and looked solemn. "I'm going to have a good time in Surrey," she said, and her voice died away uncertainly.

"Of *course* you'll have a good time," I said heartily. "You'll get huge heaps of presents, and eat lots of goose. And figs. I hear in Surrey they use figs for stuffing." I hugged her to me.

A thin gray woman with rather the look of Miss Minchin came up. "Pardon me, do you work here?" she said disapprovingly.

"I'll be with you in just a moment," I said.

Yet to Come hurried up, but the woman waved him away. "I'm looking for a book," she said.

I said to Gemma, "You'd best get back before your mother finishes buying the doll and misses you."

"She won't. The bride dolls are all sold. I asked when I was here before." She smiled, her eyes crinkling. "She'll have to send them to check the stockroom," she said airily, looking just like her mother, and I remembered suddenly what I had loved about Margaret—her cleverness and the innocent pleasure she took in it, her resourcefulness. Her smile. And it was like being given a boon, a Christmas gift I hadn't known I wanted.

"I'm looking for a book," Miss Minchin repeated. "I saw it in here several weeks ago."

"I'd better go," Gemma said.

"Yes," I said, "and tell your mother you don't want the doll before she turns the stockroom inside out."

"I do want it, though," she said. "The little princess had a doll," and again that trailing away, as if she had left something unsaid.

"I thought you said all of them had been sold."

"They have," she said, "but there's one in the window display, and you know Mummy. She'll *make* them give it to her."

"*Pardon* me," Miss Minchin said insistently. "It was a green book, green and gold."

"I'd better go," Gemma said again.

"Yes," I said regretfully.

"Goodbye," she said, and plunged into the crush of shoppers, which now was going the other way.

"Hardback," Miss Minchin said. "It was *right* here on this shelf."

Gemma stopped halfway down the aisle, shoppers milling about her, and looked back at me. "You'd better eat the frosted cakes so they won't grow stale. I'm going to have a good time," she said, more firmly, and was swallowed by the crowd.

"It had gold lettering," Miss Minchin said. "It was by an earl, I think."

The book Miss Minchin wanted, after a protracted search, was Sir Spencer's *Making Money Hand Over Fist.* Of course.

"What a sweet little girl you have," she said as I rang up the sale, all friendliness now that she had gotten what she wanted. "You're very lucky."

"Yes," I said, though I did not feel lucky.

I looked at my watch. Five past four. Gemma had already taken the train to Surrey, and I would not see her sweet face again this year, and even if I stayed after closing and put everything back as it had been, there were still all the hours of Christmas Eve to be gotten through. And the day after. And all the days after.

And the rest of the afternoon, and all the shoppers who had left their shopping till too late, who were cross and tired and angry that we had no more copies of *The Outer Space Christmas Carol,* and who had *counted* on our gift wrapping their purchases.

And Mr. Voskins, who came up to say disapprovingly that he had been very disappointed in the sales from the autographing, and that he wanted the shelves back in order.

In between, Yet to Come and I folded chairs and carried boxes of Sir S's books to the basement.

It grew dark outside, and the crush of shoppers subsided to a trickle. When Yet to Come came over to me with his bony hands full of a box of books, I said, "You needn't come back up again," and didn't even have the heart to wish him a happy Christmas.

The trickle of shoppers subsided to two desperate-looking young men. I sold them scented journals and started taking Sir S's books off the literature shelves and putting them in boxes.

On the second shelf from the top, wedged in behind *Making Money Hand Over Fist,* I found the other copy of *A Little Princess.*

And that seemed somehow the final blow. Not that it had been here all along—there was no real difference between its not being there and my not being able to find it, and Gemma would love it as much when I gave it to her next week as she would have Christmas morning—but that Sir Spencer Siddon, Sir Scrawl of the new hardbacks only and the Armentières water, Sir Scrooge and his damnable secretary who had not even recognized the Spirits of Christmas, let alone heeded them, who had no desire to keep Christmas, had cost Gemma hers.

"Hard times," I said, and sank down in the wing chair. "I have fallen on hard times." After a while I opened the book and turned the pages, looking at the colored plates. The little princess and her father in her carriage. The little princess and her father at the school. The little princess and her father.

The birthday party. The little princess huddled against a wall, her doll clutched to her, looking hunted.

"The little princess had a doll," she'd said, and meant, "to help her through hard times."

The way the little princess's doll had helped her when she lost her father. The way the book had helped Gemma.

"I find books a great comfort," I had told the Spirit of Christmas Present. And so had Gemma, who had lost her father.

"I'm going to have a good time in Surrey," she had said, her voice trailing off, and I could finish that sentence, too. "In spite of everything."

Not a hope, but a determination to try to be happy in spite of circumstance, as the little princess had tried to be happy in her chilly garret. "I'm going to have a good time," she'd said again, turning at the last minute, and it was rebuke and reminder and instruction, all at once. And comfort.

I stood a moment, looking at the book, and then closed it and put it carefully back on the shelf, the way Gemma had.

I went over to the order desk and picked up the plum pudding. The book the girl had left for Sir Spencer to finish signing was under it. I opened it and took out the paper with her name and address on it.

Martha. I found the fountain pen, with its viridian ink, uncapped it, and drew a scrawl that looked a little like Sir Spencer's. "To Martha's father," I wrote above it. "Money isn't everything!" And I went to find the spirits.

If they could be found. If they had not, after all, found other employment with the barrister or the banker, or taken a plane to Majorca, or gone up to Surrey.

Mama Montoni's had a large Closed sign hanging inside the door, and the light above the counter was switched off, but when I tried the door it wasn't locked. I opened it, carefully, so the buzzer wouldn't sound, and leaned in. Mama Montoni must have switched off the heat as well. It was icy inside.

They were sitting at the table in the corner, hunched forward over it as if they were cold. Yet to Come had his hands up inside his sleeves, and Present kept tugging at his button as if to pull the green robe closer. He was reading to them from *A Christmas Carol*.

"''You will be haunted,' resumed the Ghost of Marley, 'by three spirits,'''" Present read. "''Is this the chance and hope you mentioned, Jacob?' he demanded in a faltering voice. 'It is.' 'I—I think I'd rather not,' said Scrooge. 'Without their visits,' said the Ghost, 'you cannot hope to shun the path I tread.'''"

I banged the door open and strode in. "'Come, dine with me, uncle,'" I said.

They all turned to look at me.

"We are past that place," Marley said. "Scrooge's nephew has already gone home, and so has Scrooge."

"We are at the place where Scrooge is being visited by Marley," Present said, pulling out a chair. "Will you join us?"

"No," I said. "You are at the place where you must visit me."

Mama Montoni came rushing out from the back. "I'm closed!" she growled. "It's Christmas Eve."

"It's Christmas Eve," I said, "and Mama Montoni's is closed, so you must dine with me."

They looked at each other. Mama Montoni snatched the Closed sign from the door and brandished it in my face. "I'm *closed*!"

"I can't offer much. Figs. I have figs. And frosted cakes. And Sir Walter Scott. ''Twas Christmas broach'd the mightiest ale, / 'Twas Christmas told the merriest tale.'"

"'A Christmas gambol oft could cheer / The poorest man's heart through half the year,'" Present murmured, but none of them moved. Mama Montoni started for the phone, to dial 999, no doubt.

"No one should be alone on Christmas Eve," I said.

They looked at each other again, and then Yet to Come stood up and glided over to me.

"The time grows short," I said, and Yet to Come extended his finger and pointed at them. Marley stood up, and then Present, closing his book gently.

Mama Montoni herded us out the door, looking daggers. I pulled *A Christmas Carol* out of my pocket and handed it to her. "Excellent book," I said. "Instructive."

She banged the door shut behind us and locked it. "Merry Christmas," I said to her through the door, and led the way home, though before we had reached the tube station, Yet to Come was ahead, his finger pointing the way to the train, and my street, and my flat.

"We've black-currant tea," I said, going into the kitchen to put on the kettle. "And figs. Please, make yourselves at home. Present, the Dickens is in that bookcase, top shelf, and the Scott's just under it."

I set out sugar and milk and the frosted cakes I'd bought for Gemma. I took the foil off the plum pudding. "Courtesy of Sir Spencer Siddon, who, unfortunately, remains a miser," I said, setting it on the table. "I'm sorry you failed to find someone to reform."

"We have had some small success," Present said from the bookcase, and Marley smiled slyly.

"Who?" I said. "Not Mama Montoni?"

The kettle whistled. I poured the boiling water over the tea and brought the teapot in. "Come, come, sit down. Present, bring your book with you. You can read to us while the tea steeps." I pulled out a chair for him. "But first you must tell me about this person you reformed."

Marley and Yet to Come looked at each other as if they shared a secret, and both of them looked at Christmas Present.

"You have read Scott's 'Marmion,' have you not?" he said, and I knew that, whoever it was, they weren't going to tell me. One of the people in the queue, perhaps? Or Harridge?

"I always think 'Marmion' an excellent poem for Christmas," Present said, and opened the book.

"'And well our Christian sires of old,'" he read, "'loved when the year its course had roll'd, / and brought blithe Christmas back again, / with all his hospitable train.'"

I poured out the tea.

"'The wassail round, in good brown bowls,'" he read, "'garnished with ribbons, blithely trowls.'" He put down the book and raised his teacup in a toast. "To Sir Walter Scott, who knew how to keep Christmas!"

"And to Mr. Dickens," Marley said, "the founder of the feast."

"To books!" I said, thinking of Gemma and *A Little Princess*, "which instruct and sustain us through hard times."

"'Heap on more wood!'" Present said, taking up his book again, "'the wind is chill; / But let it whistle as it will, / We'll keep our Christmas merry still.'"

I poured out more tea, and we ate the frosted cakes and Gemma's figs and half a meat pie I found in the back of the refrigerator, and Present read us "Lochinvar," with sound effects.

As I was bringing in the second pot of tea, the clock began to strike, and outside, church bells began to ring. I looked at the clock. It was, impossibly, midnight.

"Christmas already!" Present said jovially. "Here's to evenings with friends that fly too fast."

"And the friends who make it fly," I said.

"To small successes," Marley said, and raised his cup to me.

I looked at Christmas Present, and then at Yet to Come, whose face I still could not see, and then back at Marley. He smiled slyly.

"Come, come," Present said into the silence. "We have not had a toast from Christmas Yet to Come."

"Yes, yes," Marley said, clanking his chains excitedly. "Speak, Spirit."

Yet to Come took hold of his teacup handle with his bony fingers and raised his cup.

I held my breath.

"To Christmas," he said, and why had I ever feared that voice? It was clear and childlike. Like Gemma's voice, saying, "We'll be together next Christmas."

"To Christmas," the Spirit of Christmas Yet to Come said, his voice growing stronger with each word. "God bless us, every one!"

deck.halls@boughs/holly

As soon as the nearly empty maglev pulled out of the station, Linny uplinked to Inge. "I need a netcheck on a Mrs. Shields," she said. "3404 Aspen Lane, Greater Denver."

"Today?" Inge said. "It's Thanksgiving."

I didn't think they celebrated Thanksgiving in Norway, Linny thought, but Inge was obviously going somewhere. She was wearing a velvet slash top and sequined makeup. "I know, sorry, but I'm on my way to see a new client," Linny said. "You can wait on the financial, I just need some background so I have an idea of what she might like—occupation, hobbies, interests—"

"Right now?" Inge said plaintively. "I was hoping . . . see, the thing is, I told Carlo I'd have Thanksgiving dinner with him, and it's only a few minutes from now."

"Can't you be a little late?" Linny asked. "A background check should only take half an hour or so."

"*No.* Remember, he's at Tombaugh Station, and there's only a four-hour window, and personal calls don't have priority. I promised him I'd talk to him while they were having their dinner. They're on Canaveral time."

Linny'd forgotten Carlo was on the Moon. "Go have dinner," she said. "And tell Carlo happy Thanksgiving. I'll run a preliminary myself, and you can do a full netcheck later."

"Really? Thanks! I was afraid I wasn't going to make it," she said, though now that Linny'd given her permission, she didn't seem to be in all that much of a hurry. "Is Norwall taking you out for Thanksgiving dinner?" she asked.

"He has an installation," Linny said.

"So you aren't having Thanksgiving dinner with anybody?"

"I already had it with Mom."

"I thought she was in Riyadh."

"She is. We did it online earlier." In the middle of the night, actually, with Linny sitting half asleep in front of the screen in her nightshift and the vidcam carefully focused so her mother couldn't see that all she was eating was a bowl of soyflakes.

Inge sniffed. "I still think Norwall could have taken you out. Carlo and I have more dates than you two, and he's 240,000 miles away. I know it's your busy season, but—"

"Are there any messages for me?" Linny cut in.

"Yes. Soothethesavagebeast.com are out of Beethovens. They wanted to know if Bachs would work. And the Standishes want you to do their e-cards after all."

Wonderful, Linny thought, but at least there weren't any messages from Pandora Freeh, which meant she was still happy with High School Memories. Now, if it just stayed that way till she could get there with the contract. Last year Pandora had changed her mind nine times, the last one the day before her installation, and this year they had already gone through Christmas in the Sahara, Board Games, and nine others before Linny had come up with a Christmas theme Pandora would actually stick with for more than two days. Now if she could just stick with it a couple more hours while Linny interviewed Mrs. Shields—

"I'd better go," she told Inge. "I need to run that netcheck."

"And I—yipes! Look what time it is! I don't even have my eyes inked yet—" Inge said, and abruptly downlinked.

Linny linked to soothethesavagebeast. It had a "Closed for Thanksgiving" banner on it. She connected to the netcheck site, typed in "Mrs. Shields," and requested a general background check and a marketing profile.

Nothing happened. *What did I forget to do?* she wondered. She hadn't done a netcheck in ages. Inge did all of them. She must have—

The screen buzzed an override. It was Norwall, looking irritated.

"Where have you been?" he snapped. "I've been trying both you and Inge for forty-five minutes."

"I gave her the afternoon off. It's Thanksgiving, and—"

"Wonderful," he said. "Like everything else about this day. Teddy Lopez just called. They want to switch themes."

"Why? I thought he and Emil loved their jazz theme."

"They did, but they got *engaged*," he said disgustedly.

"How nice—" Linny began.

"I'm glad *you* think so. Because now they want a whole new love design, hearts and Cupids and orange blossoms, and they want their installation moved up to the twelfth so they can have it for their engagement party."

"Goin'tothechapel.com has some darling diamond ring ornaments," Linny said, "and a glitteroptic tree would be the perfect—"

"Legally, I don't have to let them switch. They've already signed a contract. I have every right to hold them to it."

"But, Norwall, they just got engaged," Linny protested, "and it's Christmas."

"Don't remind me. I've got four installations to do in the next six days." His image leaned forward as if trying to see what was behind her. "I see movement. Where are you?"

"On the maglev. I'm on my way out to Aspen Lane."

"Aspen Lane? Don't tell me Pandora Freeh still hasn't signed her contract. You let your clients walk all over you, Linny. You have to be firm with them. This is a business, not some sentimental—"

She'd heard this lecture before. "Pandora Freeh's signing her contract today."

"How long will it take? I could use you here at the installation to string lights for the outdoor tableau."

"I can't," she said. "I have to interview a client."

"Interview? Don't tell me you're taking on a new client? It's the twenty-eighth of November! Did you tell her the deadline for new clients is June?"

"She's never had a professional Christmas. She's always done her own, so she didn't know how it works."

"And you felt sorry for her?"

Linny nodded. "She was really desperate." And very insistent. Linny hadn't really had a chance to say no, but she couldn't tell that to Norwall. "It's a chance to broaden our client base. And I'm in good shape. Three of my installations are already done, and she doesn't need hers till after the fifteenth. I'll have no trouble fitting her in."

"Unless she keeps changing her mind like Pandora Freeh."

"She won't. She was terribly grateful I could take her on—"

"Yes, and she'll probably tell all her friends that you're willing to take new clients in December. Who is she anyway? Have you run a financial check on her?"

"Yes," Linny said, even though she hadn't. But the fact that Mrs. Shields lived in the same exclusive community as Pandora Freeh meant she was at least moderately rich, and this was her client, after all, not his, and if Mrs. Shields turned out to be a lot of extra work, it was her problem.

"Well, don't leave without getting a signed contract. And why do you have to go all the way out there? Why couldn't you do it from your office?"

"She doesn't like talking to people online. She's not very knowledgeable about computers—"

"So you have to waste a whole day going out there, and I don't have anybody to string lights for me. If I'd known you were so far ahead you were in a position to take on new clients, you could have taken over some of my installations for me," he said, and downlinked before she could wish him a happy Thanksgiving, which, under the circumstances, was probably just as well.

She called up the netcheck again. The screen buzzed an override immediately. It was Pandora Freeh. "Are you still coming out with the contract this afternoon?"

"Yes. At four."

"Oh, dear."

Oh, no. "Is there a problem?" Linny asked fearfully.

"I just got to thinking, there's no point in doing High School Memories if we can't get a bust of Shakespeare. English was my favorite class, and—"

"We have a bust," Linny said. "I've already ordered it."

"But what if it's different from the one in Mr. Spoonmaker's class? I just don't think I should sign until I've seen it."

So you want me to lug it all the way out to your house so you can look at it, Linny thought. "I don't know if the supplier's open today—" she said.

"Oh, there's no hurry. I can sign the contract next week."

By which time she would have come up with a dozen more objections. "Let me try them," she said.

She linked to Rock and a Hard Place, which was, thankfully, open till five, and then linked back to Pandora and changed their appointment to seven, which was still cutting it close. Her interview with Mrs. Shields couldn't last more than two hours, and then she'd have to go all the way back into town to get the bust, which the guy at Rock had said was too heavy for one person to carry. She'd have to call Norwall.

She relinked to him. "I know you're busy, but if you could just help me get it to the station, I could handle it from there." How she would manage the ten blocks to Pandora's house she wasn't sure, but maybe she could get a taxi.

"It's out of the question," he said. "I'll be here till midnight. If you'd had Pandora Freeh sign her contract right after the interview like I told you to, you wouldn't be in this mess. You're going to have to call this new client of yours and tell her you can't—"

"We're coming into the station. I've got to go," Linny said.

And I still don't have a netcheck, she thought, setting out on the walk to Mrs. Shields's house. Well, she'd just have to do without. Maybe she could pick up some hints from the house. She already knew Mrs. Shields was a technophobe, and, from her image on the screen when they talked, that she was in her late fifties and didn't dye her hair. That, and her use of the old-fashioned "Mrs." indicated she was pre-retro, so one of their traditional themes. Maybe #23 A Little House on the Prairie Christmas, or #119 Over the River and Through the Woods.

Here it was, 3404 Aspen Lane. The house wasn't as expensive-looking as she'd expected. She'd assumed that anything in Pandora Freeh's neighborhood would be in the hideous mansion category, but 3404 was a long, low-roofed house set well back from the street. Maybe she should have done a financial netcheck after all.

But the wide lawn looked professionally groomed, and what furniture she could see through the large front window looked like mission-style Arts and Crafts.

The door didn't have any sensors or identity screen, just an old-fashioned doorbell. Linny rang it, and after a minute a tall young man in a wool pullover with a napkin stuck in the neck opened it. "Can I help you?" he asked, frowning.

"I'm Linny Chiang," she said. "I have an appointment with—"

"Come in, come in! Brian, don't make her stand outside like that!" Mrs. Shields pushed in front of the young man and practically dragged Linny into the house. "It's freezing out!"

She had a napkin, too, in her hand. "Am I interrupting your Thanksgiving dinner?" Linny asked anxiously.

"Oh, no, not at all, we'd finished," she said with a pointed look at Brian, who was still frowning. "Brian, take her coat," she said, wrestling Linny out of it and handing it to him, "and go turn on the fire in the study."

Brian left, bearing the coat. "The handsome young man is my nephew, Brian West," Mrs. Shields said. "We're both so grateful you agreed to give up your Thanksgiving to come do this. Have you had dinner? Would you like some turkey and dressing? My nephew makes wonderful oyster dressing."

"No, thank you. I had dinner earlier."

"With your family?" she said, leading Linny through the living room to the study.

"My mother and I had dinner online. She's in Riyadh."

"But you must have had to eat in the middle of the night."

Linny was surprised Mrs. Shields knew what time zone Riyadh was in. Even her mother hadn't had it straight. "It must be late there for you, darling," she'd kept saying. "What is it? Nine o'clock?"

"Have you had anything to eat since then?" Mrs. Shields was asking anxiously. "There's cranberry sauce and candied yams and—"

"No, thanks, really, I had something to eat on the maglev," she lied.

"Some chai then, or what is it you young people drink nowadays? Maxpresso? Red tea?"

Linny could see the onslaught wasn't going to stop until she'd agreed to eat or drink something. "Chai would be nice," she said, and Mrs. Shields bustled out of the room.

Linny looked around. Mission-style furniture in here, too, and from the looks of it, genuine Stickley, and the carpet, though worn, was an antique Navajo. She revised her financial estimate considerably upward.

No knickknacks, though, to give a clue as to a possible theme—no stuffed unicorns or tribal masks or model biplanes. And no signs of a pet, which was too bad. Pets were so easy. All you had to do was link to notacreaturewasstirring.com, type in the breed, and they supplied everything: audio ornaments, needlepoint stockings, beribboned Milk-Bones, even a rom of dog or cat carols.

There weren't any holos either, just an oil painting of a bridge above the fireplace. Bridges of the World? Golden Gate ornaments and a covered bridge diorama for the outdoor tableau? Or maybe Mrs. Shields was interested in painting, or a particular artist. Linny leaned forward to look at the signature.

"My nephew Brian does bridges," Mrs. Shields said, bustling back in. "He's an engineer. I'll bet you two are the same age." She handed Linny a mug of chai. "He's twenty-eight." She waited expectantly.

"I'm twenty-seven," Linny said. "Did you want to do the interview in here?"

"Yes. Do you need to hook anything up or plug anything in? I'm afraid I'm a complete ignoramus when it comes to computers, and Brian isn't much better."

"No, I'm all set," Linny said, opening her notebook and switching it on, but Mrs. Shields was already calling, "Brian! Brian!"

He came in, minus the napkin. "This is Miss Chiang, our new Christmas designer," she said.

"Christmas designer?" he said, with a puzzled look at his aunt.

"Yes." Mrs. Shields smiled at him and then looked back at Linny. "I've always done my own Christmases, but this year I decided it was all too much for me, and I was going to have a professional Christmas."

"You did," he said.

He clearly disapproved. Linny had seen this kind of resistance before, the men in the family wanting to keep Christmas the way it had been, which meant the women doing all the work.

"Christmas requires much more planning and work than it used to," Linny said. "Shopping, decorating, cleaning, baking, wrapping gifts, sending e-cards. It's impossible for one person to do it all, and even if they somehow manage to, they're far too stressed and exhausted to enjoy the holidays."

"Exactly," Mrs. Shields said, looking at Brian. "I want to *enjoy* my Christmas, and this young woman is going to help me do that, so it's no use your trying to talk me out of it, Brian. I've made up my mind. Why don't you show us what you have in mind, Ms. Chiang?"

"It's what *you* have in mind that's important," Linny said, setting up the portable holo projector. "Deck.halls custom-tailors Christmas to your wishes. We have over nine hundred holiday themes to choose from, and if you don't see the theme you want, we can custom-design one for you. Did you have anything in mind?"

"Oh, yes, I'd say she definitely has something in mind," Brian said.

Linny looked inquiringly at Mrs. Shields.

"I really don't know," Mrs. Shields said. "Our Christmases have always been very simple, just a tree and stockings hung by the fireplace."

"Right, nothing fancy," the nephew said.

"Well, then let me show you something simple."

"Oh, no, I want to see *all* of your ideas. If I'm going to do a professional Christmas, I might as well go all the way."

"All right, let me begin by outlining the services we offer," Linny said, giving Mrs. Shields a handheld. "So you can jot down the numbers of themes that you like. We offer a full range of services. Decorating, lighting, gift wrapping, shopping—"

"Shopping?" Brian said, sounding shocked.

"Yes, by client list or using marketing profiles. We can also do your Christmas cards, e- or vmail with full graphics, or handwritten, and party invitations. We can also arrange for caroling. You pick the services you want."

She printed out two price lists and handed the pages to them. Neither one did more than glance at them. She revised her financial estimate upward again.

"Now let me show you some possibilities. This is Number 68 Winter Wonderland," she said, typing in the code.

A full-color hologram of a stairway entwined with darting white and silver lights filled an all-white room. The diamond-flocked tree at the foot of the stairs was hung with white velvet angel knots, and crystal snowflakes filled the air. "The snowflakes are Waterford, and the diamonds are each an eighth of a carat.

"Or if you prefer something less formal, we have Number 241 Christmas at Loch Ness." The white room changed to one done in red-and-green Scotch plaid. A large bush of purple heather stood between the plaid couch and the plaid chair, hung with tam o'shanters, thistles, and sea serpents. "The furniture, draperies, and carpet are available in the full slate of clan tartans," Linny said.

"Some people plan their Christmases around a hobby—" She clicked to #110 A Crossword Puzzle Christmas, done all in black-and-white squares, "or a political affiliation. This one is called Elephants Never Forget," she said, showing them a holo of a room draped in red-white-and-blue bunting punctuated with elephants. The red tree was covered in U.S. flags and models of the White House, and on its top was a replica of Mount Rushmore with Reagan's face, Newt Gingrich's, and those of all three Bushes.

"You have to be kidding," the nephew said.

"There's of course a Democratic version," she said, and when Mrs. Shields didn't look enthusiastic, "and our Globalization Christmas: It's a Small World After All." Mrs. Shields still didn't look impressed.

"Most clients choose a Christmas that reflects their occupation," Linny said, wishing she had a bridge theme to show them, "or some personal interest. Their favorite flower"—she called up #309 Tiptoe Through the Tulips—"or a favorite color." The room turned purple. "This is our Mauve Melody." The room went yellow-green. "And this is Number 116, Cantata in Chartreuse. Or you could plan it around a family memory or an upcoming event. Two of my partner's clients just got engaged, so their theme is the engagement, with hearts and Cupids."

"How nice," Mrs. Shields said, and to her nephew, "How does something like that sound?"

"We have several love-related themes—Moonlight and Roses," Linny said, clicking them into the center of the room, "Romeo and Juliet, Harlequin Romance—"

"Which one did you have when you got engaged?" Mrs. Shields asked.

"Me?" Linny said. "Oh, I'm not engaged."

"Oh, when you said your partner, I assumed—"

"Oh, no, I was referring to my business partner, Norwall Hirsch."

"And he's not your boyfriend?" Mrs. Shields persisted.

Boyfriend, Linny thought. *Definitely pre-retro.* "No, I mean, yes, I mean, we date . . ."

"But you're not engaged," Mrs. Shields said. "Brian's not engaged, either. He says he just doesn't meet anyone. Will he be working with you on the Christmas?"

"Brian?"

"No, your partner."

"No, we each have our own clients."

"But you share office space."

Definitely *pre-retro.* "We don't have an office, per se. Everything's done by wireless or Internet except for installations. Our secretary, Inge, lives in Oslo."

"And your partner?"

"He lives here," she said, "though we hardly ever see each other," and added silently, not even on Thanksgiving.

"Oslo," Mrs. Shields said. "I've always wanted to go to Scandinavia. Do you have some sort of Scandinavian theme?"

"Oh, yes," Linny said, clicking back to the main menu. "We have several: Santa Lucia's Day; Christmas in Norway; Christmas in Sweden; Wonderful, Wonderful Copenhagen. Or we can do any city you like, with holos of the local sights, and regional foods: lutefisk, pancakes with lingonberries, blood pudding."

"Oh, you do food, too," Mrs. Shields said, and Brian shook his head, as if in disgust.

"The standard package includes a thematic Christmas dinner," Linny said, printing out a list of caterers and sample menus, "but we also do Christmas Eve suppers, parties, buffets. Would you like to see our Christmas on the Fjords?"

Mrs. Shields shook her head. "I've never liked herring. What other places do you have?"

"Anywhere on-planet or off. We have a complete line of outer space themes—both Moonbases, Mars, the solar system, with or without Pluto—as well as every country and all major cities: London, New Delhi, Paris," she said, clicking onto one after the other, "Las Vegas—"

The Eiffel Tower changed to a wedding chapel with flashing neon signs, slot machines, and an Elvis impersonator conducting a wedding between Santa Claus and a showgirl with a pink ostrich feather tail. "We also do fictional places," she said.

"As if Las Vegas wasn't fictional enough," the nephew said.

Linny ignored him. "Neverland," she said, clicking, "Middle Earth, Atlantis, Hogwarts. And historical sites: Gettysburg, Waterloo, Saigon. Deck.halls has a full line of historical themes, both events and people: Cleopatra, General Patton, Bill Gates—"

"Dolly Levi," Brian said.

"From *Hello, Dolly?*" Linny said, glad she recognized the allusion. She pulled up the theater menu. "We have a complete line of Broadway, movie, and TV themes. *Les Mis, Star Wars: Episode Nine, The Iceman Cometh, Cats.*" She clicked to *Hello, Dolly.* "As you can see, the tree is decorated with hats from Irene Molloy's millinery shop, the dining room is done as Harmonia Gardens, and in front of the house," she clicked on Lawn Decorations, "are a greater-than-life-size full-action Barbra Streisand and Louis Armstrong performing the title song."

Mrs. Shields was shaking her head at Brian.

"We also have Carol Channing, if you don't like Barbra Streisand," Linny said. "Or Britney Spears and the rest of the cast from the revival."

"It's not the cast. It's just that *Hello, Dolly* doesn't—"

"Have anything at all to do with Christmas?" Brian put in.

"Well, yes," Mrs. Shields said reluctantly. "I know people don't want the same old themes every year, that they want something new and different, but—"

"We also have a large assortment of traditional Christmas packages: A Nutcracker Christmas, The Twelve Days of Christmas, Silver Bells, How the Grinch Stole Christmas," she said, looking at Brian, "or if you prefer a religious theme," she clicked to a new menu, "we have No Room at the Inn, We Three Kings, Angels We Have Heard on High, and, of course, a full range of Hanukkah, Ramadan, Winter Solstice, and Kwanzaa themes. Or there's our historical line: A Renaissance Christmas, A Victorian Christmas, A Naughty Nineties Christmas—"

"Oh, that's nice," Mrs. Shields said, looking at the tree hung with cell phones and PalmPilots. "Young people had so many opportunities to meet someone back in the nineties—chat rooms, personal ads, online dating services. They had all sorts of ways of getting to know each other. Nowadays they don't even work together. They sit in tiny little cubicles staring at an image on a screen and talking into a headset. It's just like that story by—you know who I mean, Brian, he wrote it years and years ago—that author you like, not H. G. Wells, the other one."

"Isaac Asimov?" Brian ventured.

"No, the *other* one. About the future where everyone stays inside and communicates by computer, only they didn't have computers back then, and no one goes *any*where or meets *any*one face-to-face. Oh, what is it called?"

"'The Machine Stops,'" Linny said, and they both looked at her in surprise. "By E. M. Forster."

"That's the one," Mrs. Shields said delightedly. "You're an E. M. Forster fan?"

"I did an E. M. Forster Christmas for the Ledbetters two years ago."

"An E. M. Forster Christmas. Oh, I can see it now," Brian said sarcastically. "In the living room, a holo of the bookcase falling on Leonard Bast, and out on the front lawn," he spread his arms to illustrate, "a tableau of the *Where Angels Fear to Tread* carriage tipping over and killing the baby."

"No, of course not," Linny said indignantly. "It was the kissing scene from *A Room with a View.*"

"Where George kisses Lucy in the barley field?" Mrs. Shields said. "Oh, I love that scene, the way he strides through the barley toward her, and then, without so much as a word, takes her in his arms and kisses her. How did you manage a barley field at Christmastime?"

"Magicarpet does wonderful grain field mats," Linny said. "Their corn is especially nice. I used that for An Oklahoma Christmas last year. They also do very nice poppies."

"For An Opium Addict's Christmas," Brian said.

"I remember there were poppies in the barley field," Mrs. Shields said. "I love the way she just stands there waiting while he strides toward her."

"An E. M. Forster Christmas would be just the thing for your house," Linny said, thinking, *If I could do the E. M. Forster again, it would be perfect. I know exactly where to get the costumes and the holo of Florence.* "Your living room window provides an excellent view," she said.

But Mrs. Shields was shaking her head again. "It sounds lovely, but this first time I think I'd like to have something more . . . Christmassy. Do you have any just Christmas Christmases?"

"Certainly," Linny said, thinking, *I am going to have to show her every single design I have.* "Here's a very nice Currier and Ives Christmas. Or Christmas in Toyland, A Child's Christmas in Wales," she said, clicking rapidly through the holos, "Christmas with the Waltons, Christmas with the Cleavers, Christmas in Manhattan—that one's really fun. Empire State Building and Statue of Liberty ornaments, and a yard display of the Rockettes *and* a full-size balloon from the Macy's parade."

"Oh, my," Mrs. Shields said. "Don't you have something more . . . traditional?"

"Of course," Linny said, clicking to the Christmas Past menu. "We have A Dickens Christmas, A Williamsburg Christmas," she said, showing holos of them in quick succession, "A Regency Christmas, Gone with the Wind Christmas. Did you have any particular historical period in mind? Your house would be ideal for our Roaring Twenties Christmas. Bathtub gin, raccoon coats—"

"Zelda and Scott Fitzgerald passed out on the front lawn," the nephew put in.

Linny glared at him. "We can do a specific year if you like, or a specific date. I did a really fun 2001 Christmas three years ago—Millennium fireworks, Stanley Kubrick ornaments—"

The nephew grinned and started to make another smart remark.

"Or a favorite decade," Linny said quickly. "Here's one you might like." She clicked to A Retro Christmas. "The tree's aluminum with an authentic rotating colored light."

"Oh, my grandmother had one of those," Mrs. Shields said, and Linny began to get her hopes up again, but she didn't want that, either.

"Maybe something more modern," she said questioningly, so Linny went through Christmas by Laserlight, Christmas on the Space Station, A Cloned Christmas, Christmas in Cyberspace, all to no avail.

"I just don't know . . . they all seem so fancy . . . and as you can see, I like to keep it simple. Maybe something to do with nature?"

Linny sneaked a look at the time. Nearly four. She was going to have to leave if she wanted to get to the statuary warehouse before it closed.

"I'm keeping you, aren't I?" Mrs. Shields said, and looked at her own watch. "Oh, my goodness, it's nearly suppertime. You'll stay for supper, won't you?"

"I'm afraid I can't. I have an appointment—"

"And you need me to make up my mind," Mrs. Shields said, flustered. "Do I have to do it today? I just can't seem . . ."

"No, of course not," Linny said, thinking, *Norwall will have a fit.* "Why don't I leave a rom with you? You can look through the themes at your leisure, and when you decide, or if you have any questions, you can get in touch with me." She called up her card, added her address, and printed one out. "This is my office at home, but I'm hardly ever there. I spend most of my time on-site, supervising installations. Vmail is your best bet. I recommend the Retro Christmas. It's very classic." She turned to Brian. "If I could just get my coat."

"Oh, surely you can stay for a quick supper," Mrs. Shields said. "It will only take a moment. Turkey skin sandwiches and pie."

"No, really, I have to catch the maglev—"

"Brian can take you," she said. "He'd be delighted."

He didn't look delighted.

"No, really, I have several errands to run on the way home. I have to pick up something and then—"

"All the more reason, then. You can't carry a bunch of packages on the maglev—"

"I don't want to put Mr. West out," Linny said uncomfortably. "One of the places I need to go is clear on the east side of Greater Denver—"

"Then you can't possibly take the maglev. Brian can take you right to the door, can't you, Brian?" Mrs. Shields said, not giving him a chance to answer. She produced a set of car keys, their coats, and, in spite of Linny's protests, a turkey skin sandwich, and bundled them into the car, which was Ferrari's new fusion-cell Incite. Linny revised her financial estimate upward again.

"Just tell him where you need to go," Mrs. Shields said, pushing down the door.

"I still don't think I should impose on—"

"You're not imposing. Brian's *happy* to do it for you, and this will give the two of you a chance to talk," she said, and waved them out of the driveway.

"Where to?" he asked.

"Look, I know your aunt meant well, but I don't want to ruin your Thanksgiving. Why don't you just take me to the station?"

"You're not ruining my Thanksgiving," he said. "Where to?"

She gave him the directions to the statuary warehouse.

He made no move to enter the directions into the Incite's computer or even to put the controls on drive-assist, which was a clear sign he didn't want to talk, so Linny didn't say anything either till they got to Bowles. "You take a left here. Rock and a Hard Place is six blocks down on the right. There's a sign out front that says 'Statuary and Stone-work.'"

"So what are you picking up? Tombstones for Number 257 Christmas in the Cemetery?"

"You don't approve of what I do, do you?" she asked.

"I just don't see what crossword puzzles and tombstones have to do with Christmas."

"It's not a tombstone. It's a bust of Shakespeare."

"For A Classics Christmas? Silas Marner ornaments and a Jude the Obscure lawn display? Why can't you do something *connected* to Christmas?"

"Like mistletoe?" she asked. "Which was co-opted from the Druids? Nearly everything we associate with Christmas was tacked on after the fact. The Yule log was lifted from the Druids, too, Christmas trees *and* presents were co-opted from the Roman Saturnalia. Even Santa's sleigh and flying reindeer were stolen from Norse mythology."

"But there's still a connection, no matter how tenuous. Unlike Atlantis. And Coca-Cola ornaments."

"Like Christmas cards, you mean?" she said. "They were invented in 1843 to advertise a publishing company. People have been complaining about the commercialization of Christmas since back in E. M. Forster's day."

They were in front of Rock and a Hard Place. Brian and Linny got out and went into the warehouse. Statues and busts stood everywhere: Ben Franklin and Winnie-the-Pooh and Patsy Ramsey. Linny stepped among a flock of stone sheep to the counter and typed her name and order into the computer.

"I just think the celebration of Christmas should retain some connection to the original meaning," he said, draping his arm over a statue of a very young Angelina Jolie.

"Which is?"

"Good will toward men. Kindness, sharing, forgiveness, love."

A robo-dolly brought the bust of Shakespeare up. "Follow me," Linny said, and led it out to the car. The dolly loaded it into the backseat, and Brian strapped the bust in.

"Things like good will and family and being together can't be captured in Number 194 Ferns of the Mesozoic," he said.

"They can't be captured in stockings hung by the chimney with care, either. The tree, the candles—"

"The Elvis impersonator—"

"Are all just trappings," she said. "They don't affect the spirit of Christmas. Most of the people I do installations for hire me so they can spend more time with their loved ones, so they're not run so ragged by shopping and cooking and decorating that they're screaming at everyone."

"That does not explain Christmas Number 265 Keeping Up with the Joneses."

Like Pandora Freeh, she thought. "People have always wanted to impress their neighbors. And they've always made things bigger and fancier than they needed to be, from their clothes to their houses. To their cars," she added pointedly.

He grinned. "Where would you like my *car* to go next?"

"Back to Aspen Lane."

"What for?" he said sharply.

"Not to your aunt's. To Ms. Freeh's." She gave the address. "I'm sorry you had to come all this way in and back—"

"I told you, it's no imposition." He started the car. "I suppose you're right about people overdoing things," he said when they were back on the highway. "Look at the Tower of Babel. It wasn't enough to build a skyscraper, they had to build a tower right up to heaven— No, don't tell me," he said at her expression. "You have a Tower of Babel Christmas."

"Number 605. It's part of our Evangelical line," she admitted. "We also have Noah's Ark, Daniel in the Lion's Den, and the Battle of Armageddon."

"Which is Number 666, no doubt."

She laughed. "I know a lot of them are silly, but they're what people want. My job is to try to make Christmas as happy and stress-free as I can for my clients. Surely that's in the Christmas spirit."

It seemed to take no time at all to get to Pandora's, which was good because it was nearly seven. She would never have made it on the mag-lev.

"What's her theme?" Brian asked when they pulled up in front of Pandora's mansion. "A Forbes 500 Christmas?"

"No, High School Memories. If this bust is the right one." She pressed the door sensor.

"Who shall I say is calling?" it asked.

"Linny Chiang," she said, pressing her hand to the ID pad.

"And her delivery boy," Brian said.

The door opened, and they went in. Linny began looking around for a place for Brian to set the bust down, but before they could, Pandora Freeh was upon them, crying out, "Oh, what a pity you brought it all this way!"

"It's not the same Shakespeare?" Linny asked.

"No, it *is*! It looks exactly like the one in Mr. Spoonmaker's class, right down to the nick in his beard. Oh, I can't even look at it!" she said, waving Brian away.

"Should I take it back out to the car?" he whispered to Linny.

She shook her head. "But if it's perfect, Pandora, why—?"

Ms. Freeh ignored her. "I knew it was such a good theme someone was bound to steal it, and now we're going to have to come up with a completely new theme!"

Linny's heart sank. "Someone else is doing a high school memories theme?"

"They might as well be," Pandora said, flouncing down on the couch. "Joan and Claudette Proudell are doing Rah! Rah! Sis Boom Bah!"

Linny didn't dare look at Brian. "Rah, rah, sis boom bah?"

"Yes, their entire house," she flung her arm out, "is being decorated in pom-poms, megaphones, and holos of girls in pleated skirts doing the splits—"

"Oh," Linny said, finally understanding. "And you think that will take away from the basketball holo you intended to have in the living room. But we can change that to something else. A holo of typing class, or the lunchroom."

"Lunchroom?" Pandora shuddered. "Nobody has happy memories of their high school lunchroom. I was going to have the league championship game right before the final buzzer, with the crowd roaring and the cheerleaders leaping into the air," she explained to Brian, who was still holding the bust of Shakespeare.

"This is Brian, by the way," Linny said, leading him over to an end table where he could set it down. "His aunt is having her Christmas done for the first time. She lives near you."

"Really, what's her name?"

"Shields," Brian said reluctantly, and who could blame him?

Pandora waved her hand in a dismissive gesture that meant she didn't know her, which was surprising. From the number of friends and relatives Pandora cited when she was changing her mind, Linny assumed she knew everybody in a thousand-mile radius.

"Well, tell her to make *sure* no one else is doing the same theme before she signs her contract," Pandora said, "so she doesn't have to change it and start all over again a month from Christmas the way I am."

"Oh, I'm sure that won't be necessary," Linny said, trying not to sound as desperate as she felt. She had already ordered all the glassware and the black rubber aprons for the chemistry lab and the prom ornaments and disco ball for the tree.

"What if we changed it from a memories theme to a modern high school?" she said. "They don't have cheerleaders, and we could add girls' bocce ball and KI and virtual learning labs, and your bust of Shakespeare could—"

"They don't even *teach* Shakespeare in today's high schools," Pandora sniffed. "And I won't do a Christmas theme without it. No, it's going to have to be something completely different. Joan and Claudette have ruined it. I don't even want to think about high schools anymore. So," she said brightly, "what do you suggest?" She clasped her hands and looked up expectantly at Linny.

"I . . ." Oh, my God. Something with a bust of Shakespeare. Christmas in Stratford-on-Avon? No, she knew of at least two other Christmas designers who'd done it. Famous People Who've Been Cut Off Just Below the Shoulders?

"You know," Brian said, "this bust of Shakespeare just gave me an idea. Your theme could be a Shakespearean play."

"Grimshaw Powell's ex already did *Macbeth* two years ago," Pandora said.

"No, I was thinking a Christmas play. We were just talking," he said, nodding at Linny, "about how so many Christmas themes aren't really related to Christmas at all."

Like High School Memories, Linny thought, but Pandora didn't look at all offended. "I didn't know Shakespeare wrote a Christmas play," she said.

I didn't either, Linny thought.

"Oh, yes," Brian said. "It's called *Twelfth Night,* and it was meant to be performed during the Christmas season, on Epiphany. It would be a perfect theme—it's got a shipwreck, and . . ."

"A palace," Linny said, coming to his aid, "and gorgeous velvet and satin costumes—"

"And cross-gartering," Brian said.

"Cross-gartering?" Pandora said doubtfully.

"'I will be strange, stout, in yellow stockings, and cross-gartered,'" he quoted, "and there are rings and love notes and disguises and romance. 'If music be the food of love, play on—'"

"And your bust of Shakespeare will fit right in," Linny put in.

"And I'm sure no one's ever done it before," Brian said.

"I don't doubt that," Pandora said, frowning. "But do you think it's well-known enough? I've never even heard of it. What if people don't recognize it?"

"That is a consideration," Brian said, and Linny wondered whether he was deliberately trying to undermine what he'd just suggested. "It certainly has more substance than Rah! Rah! Sis Boom Bah!"

Pandora looked delighted. "I hate frivolous themes," she said, "and, as you say, it's directly related to Christmas. Cheerleading has *nothing* at all to do with Christmas."

"Exactly," they both said.

"And I wouldn't have to give up my bust of Shakespeare."

"It could be right in the entry hall," Linny said, and Brian promptly picked it up and carried it in, "where it would be the first thing your guests would see."

"I *love* it!" Pandora said, clasping her hands under her chin. "*Twelfth Night* it is."

"You're a genius," Linny said on their way out to the car. "Have you ever considered being a Christmas designer?"

"God forbid," he said, popping the doors. "I just didn't want to carry that thing back to the tombstone store. I hope I didn't let you in for too much work."

"Are you kidding?" Linny said, getting in. "The other theme she was considering before she decided on High School Memories was whaling."

He laughed. "All right, where to next?"

"Just the maglev station, thanks," she said. "That was my last errand, and there's no point in your driving me all the way back into town. You're only a few blocks from your aunt's."

"I like to show off my overly big and fancy car," he said, and pulled out into the street.

"No, really," she protested, "you've already done enough by suggesting *Twelfth Night*. It's an inspired theme. I can do the dining room as Maria's kitchen and the living room as Olivia's garden, and for an outdoor tableau . . . Sorry," she said when she saw he was looking at her. "I get a little carried away."

"You really like doing this stuff, don't you?"

"It's fun," she said, "doing research—I get to find out about so many different things—"

"Like E. M. Forster."

She nodded. "Most jobs are so narrowly focused these days. And I love taking an idea and thinking how it can be adapted to lights and tree decorations. You do the same thing, I suppose, with your bridges?"

"Bridges?" he said blankly.

"Your aunt told me you were an engineer, and I assumed you built bridges."

"Oh. No," he said, frowning. "Dams. I build dams."

"Oh, but I mean, seeing where the water needs to go and then translating that into blueprints and then concrete. It must be the same kind of thing."

"What's the hardest Christmas you've ever had to design?" he asked.

"Gum Disease," she said promptly. "It was for this oral surgeon. The most fun one was the one I did for an ex-stripper named Bubbles O'Halloran. Her theme was—"

"Let me guess. Bubbles?"

She nodded. "I had bubble lights and a bubble machine and bubble gum and bubble wrap and those bubble dresses from the 1960s—"

"What, no champagne?"

"No, but for the outdoor tableau I had an animated Don Ho singing 'Tiny Bubbles.'"

They chatted the rest of the way home, him asking her about the best Christmas she'd ever designed and the easiest and the craziest. He was still driving the Incite on his own, only occasionally glancing sideways at her, and she was grateful it wasn't on comp-drive because it was already awfully cozy in the darkened car.

She was hardly ever this close to anyone in person—she couldn't remember the last time she and Norwall had sat side by side—and looking at someone's image on a screen just wasn't the same thing. For one thing, there was the scent. Brian smelled faintly of soap and aftershave and sweat. And video images, even high-definition, didn't pick up details like the fine hairs on the backs of his hands as he gripped the steering wheel.

Mrs. Shields had a point about people spending too much time alone staring at a screen. She was proof of it. The mere presence of another person was turning her into one of Pandora's cheerleaders.

He had pulled onto her block. "The corner's fine," she said.

"I don't suppose you'd have time to grab a pita or a cone of red tea—"

"You're kidding, right?" she said.

"No, I—too busy, huh?"

"Busy isn't even the word. Hysterical. The busy season's from January through April, when we do our prelim plans and put in orders. From then on it's chaos. And now I have to completely redo Pandora's financial estimate and décor plan.

"I don't have time to breathe, let alone sit down and have a—" She realized suddenly how ungracious she sounded. "But thank you for asking me. And *thank* you for talking Pandora into *Twelfth Night*. If it were any other time—"

"Except January through December," he said. "I could take you back to Rock and a Hard Place so you can order Patience on a monument."

"That's okay, I'll order it online," she said, laughing. She got out of the car and leaned in. "I really wish I could."

"It's okay. You need to go order fake mustaches, and I need to go talk to my aunt. I have a few things I want to discuss with her," he said grimly.

"You're not still trying to talk her out of a professional Christmas, are you?"

"No, definitely not. I was thinking of Number 941 A Dam Christmas. What do you think?" he said, and smelled so good as he said it that she almost said yes, she'd go for a cone of tea.

It was a good thing she didn't, though, because she had 226 incomings, nineteen of them emergency override messages. The Ledbetters needed their installation moved up to the fourteenth, Jack and Jill Halsey needed theirs moved back to the eighth, The Hanging Tree was out of otter candles and wanted to know if wolverines would work. Stitch in Time wanted to know whether she wanted walnut brown, espresso, or sludge.

There was an animated emessage from cyberfloral wishing her a happy Thanksgiving and another one from Online Medical Supplies. "For That Unique Christmas Theme."

Careen Everett wanted to change from a vegetarian Christmas Eve buffet to a sit-down vegan dinner. Oppie Harper-Groves wanted to change from Rottweilers to Skye terriers. The Throckmortons wanted to change from twenty-four-caliber to nine-millimeter.

Surprisingly, there were no messages from Pandora Freeh. It usually took her about ten minutes to find something wrong with Linny's proposals. She must have really been impressed with Brian's idea.

Linny had been, too. It wasn't often you met somebody who read Shakespeare's comedies *and* E. M. Forster novels. It wasn't often you met anyone, period. Mrs. Shields was right. There were very few romantic opportunities these days. The only other people besides Norwall she ever saw were the guys from FedXUPS and deliveries.com, and the only thing they ever said was, stolidly, "I don't know anything about that. All I got is these two boxes," and even if she, inconceivably, had wanted to go out with one of them, when exactly would she find the time to do that? Before she'd even finished reading through her messages, seventeen more had come in.

Linny read through the other two hundred and twenty and then moved the Emory installation and vmailed the Taylors to see if she could shift theirs to the thirteenth so the Ledbetters could have the fourteenth. She vmailed alfalfa.com for possible vegan menus, decided on a brown (soy sauce), did a global otter candle search, and ordered Skye terrier ornaments from Dog Depot, critturama.com, and the Spot Spot, and then called Norwall.

He didn't answer (a bad sign) but when she checked her vmail, there weren't any messages from him (a good sign), and none from Mrs. Shields, deciding on a theme. There was, however, one from Pandora. She had known it was too good to be true.

"*Twelfth Night* isn't an R, is it?" a message so incomprehensible that even though it was after eleven, she called Pandora back.

"I remembered your young man said something about garters, and Charmaine Kagasaki's ex's children are going to be here," she said. "You aren't planning anything with lingerie, are you?"

"Cross-gartering doesn't have anything to do with lingerie," Linny said firmly. "They're ribbons. Yellow ribbons."

"Erna Bunrath's designer is doing a wonderful Iran hostage crisis," Pandora said. "Maybe a political theme—"

"It wouldn't have your bust of Shakespeare," Linny pointed out, "which I assure you is the centerpiece of your theme."

"Really?" Pandora said, pleased.

"Absolutely. I've been thinking, maybe instead of the entry hall, it should be in the living room, in a sort of specially built niche—"

They spent the next hour and a half discussing the optimal location for the bust of Shakespeare, but at least at the end of it, Pandora sounded definitely committed to *Twelfth Night*. Even better, after Linny vmailed her her proposal three days later, there were only two overrides from her, and they were both about the buffet: "I like your 'If music be the food of love, play on' idea, but I think trumpets would make a nicer centerpiece than a violin," and "Primula Outridge's new live-in is allergic to strawberries."

The thirteenth, however, would not work for the Niedmores. They could do either the tenth or the eighteenth, both of which were booked. Soy sauce was unavailable, and sludge was back-ordered till March eighth. Linny mentally rolled up her sleeves and got to work. She called Wang Ho to see if *he'd* be willing to have his installation on the thirteenth and then checked for messages from Mrs. Shields.

Still nothing. She was going to have to help her. She vmailed Inge and asked her if she'd finished the netcheck yet.

"Sorry, no," Inge said. "I forgot all about it, I was so swamped after Thanksgiving. By the way, *thank* you for letting me take it off. Carlo was really homesick. The food they have up there is *terrible*. I'll get right on that netcheck."

"Great," Linny said, and then, curiously, "How did you meet Carlo?"

"My sister fixed us up," she said. "Did you decide which cookies you wanted for the Tornado Christmas afternoon tea?"

Linny hadn't. She picked them (chocolate swirls and mincemeat bars), checked the measurements of the Fanworthys' dining room for their rodeo holo, and then got busy on the Mannings' installation, which was on the eighth and which took every waking moment till then to get ready. She didn't even have time to answer her incomings, except for Brian's. He had called her twice, once to tell her his aunt had decided against the catering package, and again to tell her she'd narrowed it down to six themes. "None of which, I am happy to say, is Number 332 A Harley-Davidson Christmas."

Inge still hadn't gotten the netcheck to her, but it was just as well. She wouldn't have had time to read it. She was too busy locating three tons of granite boulders.

The Manning installation took two days. Linny was standing on a ladder on the second, stringing up largemouth bass, when Brian appeared. "Don't tell me," he said. "Number 54 A Carp Christmas."

"Wrong," she said, coming down off the ladder. "Number 152 Fisherman's Paradise. What are you doing here? How did you know where I was?"

"My aunt had something she wanted me to ask you," he said, "but your incoming box was full, so I thought I'd come over here. She was wondering if she could move the date of her installation."

"To when?" Linny asked, getting out her handheld, thinking, *Not to the fourteenth. Please not to the fourteenth.*

"To the morning of the twenty-third," he said. "She has a big dinner party that night. I know it's awfully close to Christmas—"

"No, that's great. People always want their installations early, so they can have them up for the whole season."

"I can see why," he said, looking at the tree. It was hung with fishhooks, sinkers, and feathered lures, and topping it was a gold-plated casting reel.

"You ain't seen nothing yet," she said, and led the way into the family room where a stream trickled between artificial mossy banks.

"A River Runs Through It," he said.

"Exactly. And it's stocked, so the Mannings' guests can fish."

He picked up a sign that said "Gone Fishing." "How about you put this on the front door and go out for chai with me. You could say it's research for a new theme. Number 928 Chai and Chit-Chat."

"I can't," she said regretfully. "The nets aren't here yet, and I've still got the master bedroom to do."

"What's going to be in there, a reservoir?" he said, and insisted on looking at all the other rooms before he left.

"I thought you didn't approve of professional Christmases," she said.

"I don't," he said, pointing to the waders hanging in front of the fire-place and the Styrofoam cooler filled with beer on the mantel, "but it's fascinating, in a horrible sort of way. Speaking of which, how's our friend Ms. Freeh? Is she still *Twelfth Night*ing it?"

Amazingly, she was, though she vmailed Linny twice a day with questions: "Could we have the shipwreck for the lawn decoration instead of as a holo?" "Do you think widows' weeds are really a good idea? I look so fat in black." And "Illyria's not in the Middle East, is it?"

Linny answered them as best she could, did three Hanukkah installations and the Immerguts' Christmas Down Under, and tried to track down a set of Masai drums FedXUPS had lost. They were in Honolulu. Linny got them rerouted and was trying to calculate how long it would take for them to get there when there was a buzz.

Linny reached for the delete button and then realized it was the door. *It can't be the Masai drums already*, she thought, and opened the door.

It was Brian, carrying two cardboard cones. "I knew you'd be too busy to go out for red tea, so I brought it here," he said. He handed her a cone and walked past her. "So this is your apartment?" he said, walking into the kitchen, her bedroom, her barely-room-for-one-person-and-a-computer office. "Definitely 'The Machine Stops,'" he said, looking at her flatscreen, streamer, rom files. "No Christmas tree? No largemouth bass?"

"I can't afford a Christmas designer," she said. "What are you doing here? Please tell me your aunt's picked a theme."

"No, but"—he set his cone down and pulled a sheaf of papers from his jacket with a flourish and presented it to her—"I have the contract, signed, sealed, and delivered."

"But if she hasn't picked a theme—" Linny said.

He took the contract back from her and flipped to the second page. "Here," he said, showing her. "'Theme to be chosen by Christmas designer,'" he read aloud. "She thinks you should pick the theme since you're the expert."

"That's wonderful," Linny said. If she got to choose the theme, she could base it on what was available and pretty. There was that gorgeous beaten-copper angel at ohheavens.com. It would go perfectly with Mrs. Shields's Arts and Crafts furniture—

"All she asks is that it be something related to Christmas, not Las Vegas. Or whaling."

Linny nodded happily. "Of course. Thank you for bringing it. You didn't have to drive all the way over here, you know," she said. "You could have just emailed it."

"Aunt Darby doesn't trust computers, especially where contracts are concerned. She likes having an actual piece of paper in front of her. Your computer's buzzing."

She went into the office. It was Pandora. "*Twelfth Night* is *not* going to work," she said icily. "I just talked to Cecelia Towstrapp. Why didn't you tell me it was about transvestites? I *knew* cross-gartering was an R—"

"It's not about transvestites," Linny said. "I mean, Viola does dress up like a man, but it isn't because of a sexual—"

"Put it on speaker," Brian, who'd followed her in, said, and pulled up a stool to sit next to her. "Ms. Freeh, do you remember me? I met you on Thanksgiving?"

"Yes, you were the one who talked me into doing *Twelfth Night,*" she said, but considerably less icily. "You should have told me it had cross-dressing in it. Lulu Pazanetta's already doing *Rocky Horror Picture Show,* so I can't—"

"Viola dresses up like a man because she's afraid for her safety as a woman alone in a strange country," Brian said. "She doesn't intentionally mean to fool the duke." He leaned in to look directly into the screen. "She wants to tell him, but she can't. Telling the duke the truth means admitting she's tricked him, that she's lied to him."

Linny wished there was a little more room in here. He was sitting even closer than he had in the car, and the smell of his skin, his breath, as he spoke earnestly to Pandora—

"She can't risk telling him. She's in love with him," he said. "But she also knows he's bound to find out sooner or later, and when he does, he's bound to feel betrayed and never want to speak to her again. So she's trapped."

There was a long, silent pause, and then Pandora said, "Oh, that's so romantic! You're right. It's a wonderful theme. Cecelia's a moron. You've convinced me. Transmit the contract."

You're kidding, Linny almost said, but she quickly typed in the contract details and sent it through. "*Thank* you," she whispered as soon as the contract replaced Pandora on the screen. "I cannot tell you how much work you've saved me."

"Good," he said, still much too close. "Then you've got time to go out to dinner with me."

"I can't," she said regretfully. "I have to do a long-distance installation in Aruba starting at five, and I still haven't found a decontamination suit."

"I won't even ask what *their* Christmas theme is," he said. "Look, I know this is your busy season, and probably you're already lining up clients for next year, but you can't tell me you can't take at least one day off a year. I know it won't be till after Christmas," he said when she started to protest, "I just want to put my bid in now."

Pandora's image reappeared on the screen. "The sixteenth won't work. You couldn't do it tomorrow, could you?"

If only she could. She'd be free of Pandora for the rest of the season. "I'm afraid not."

"Oh, dear, it's the only day I've got free. I'll have to see what I can juggle in my calendar and get back to you."

And probably tell me Twelfth Night *won't work,* Linny thought, waiting for her override, but she didn't send a single vmessage. She didn't send the contract either, but at least she hadn't changed her mind. A week later they were still with *Twelfth Night.*

"It's a miracle," she told Norwall and Inge during their mid-December three-way conference. "I think she's actually ready to sign a contract. And that will only leave Mrs. Shields."

"I wanted to talk to you about that," Inge said. "When I tried to run the netcheck on her, I couldn't find anything."

"What do you mean?" Linny asked. "There was a block on the information?"

"I thought you said the financial check had already been done," Norwall said.

"It wasn't blocked," Inge said. "There wasn't a firewall, but when I put her name in, it gave me information on the house, but nothing else. When I ask for personal data, financial records, medical history, there's nothing, just a blank. And when I tried the address, I got the same thing. Her name as owner and nothing else."

"Sounds like some kind of sophisticated privacy baffle system," Norwall said, "but why—? What did you say her name was?"

"Shields," Inge said. "I didn't have a first name."

But a last name and an address should have been enough to get the rest of the information, Linny thought. "Are you sure you spelled Shields right?" she asked.

"Do you know her first name?" Norwall said.

"Yes," Linny said. "Darby."

"Darby?" he said, and then sharply, "What about the nephew, the engineer?"

"Brian West."

"Do you want me to try his name?" Inge asked.

"No, I'll take care of this," Norwall said, and downlinked, even though they still had several things to discuss.

It was just as well. The Masai drums had gotten lost again, and it took her the better part of two days she didn't have to track them down in Nashville. She did the Kwanzaa installations and an Extreme Sports Christmas and then, emboldened by the fact that Pandora hadn't messaged her, sent her a *Twelfth Night* contract.

She got an override from her immediately. And she should never have said that about it being a miracle because the first words out of Pandora's mouth were "It isn't going to work."

"Why not?" Linny asked. She refused to believe anyone else was doing *Twelfth Night.*

"It's the jester, Festus. Charlton Lebrock's ex is doing Christmas in Dodge City, and there's a Festus in that. He's a drunk."

"The jester's name is Feste," Linny protested, but to no avail. Pandora's mind, such as it was, was made up.

"We'll have to do a different play. One that no one else has done."

"*Coriolanus*," Linny suggested, wishing Brian was here and wondering if she could send him an override. "*The Tempest*."

"That people have *heard* of," Pandora said.

Othello, Linny thought, *with an outdoor tableau of you being smothered with a pillow.* "As You Like It. Richard the Third."

But all the plays people had heard of had already been done by Pandora's friends, or Pandora's friends' exes, or their exes. *Brian's right,* Linny thought, *this whole theme thing has gotten out of hand. Why can't people have a Christmas they like? Why do they have to have something completely unique?*

They finally settled on *A Midsummer's Night Dream,* which should at least be comparatively easy—flowers, fairies, a woodland holo. She started a search for a donkey's head.

Costumes.com didn't have one. She tried Don We Now Our Gay Apparel.

The screen buzzed, and Norwall's image appeared. "She's Sara Darbingdon," he said.

"Who is?" Linny said blankly.

"Your client. Darby Shields. She's the head of Galatek International."

"Galatek International?" Linny said. "The software company?"

"The software *conglomerate.* Your client's the computer genius who started it."

"But that's impossible," Linny said. "Mrs. Shields doesn't know anything about computers. She doesn't even like sending emails."

"That's what she *told* you. Trust me, I ran a complete profile of her. Dr. Sara Darbingdon, 3404 Aspen Lane—"

Norwall's image disappeared and a news photo of Sara Darbingdon appeared. "Galatek CEO Announces Intel Merger." It was Mrs. Shields.

"But why would she pretend—?"

"Because she didn't want you to know who you were talking to. She's obviously after deck.halls."

"After deck.halls? What do you mean?"

"I mean, they're researching a takeover. Or else starting their own Christmas company. With your ideas. How many themes did you show her?"

"Quite a few," Linny said, thinking of that first interview and the num-

ber of holos she'd clicked through. "But why—she's never even had a
professional Christmas."

"Wrong again," he said, and a list came up on the screen. "Home and
office Christmases for the last ten years, all done by Galatek's in-house
designers: Christmas in the Country, O Holy Night, A Norman Rockwell
Christmas, Christmas in Connecticut . . ."

At least she was telling the truth about liking traditional Christmases,
Linny thought irrelevantly. "But I still don't understand. If they already
have Christmas designers—"

"Because we're successful, and conglomerates like Galatek are always
looking for ways to co-opt successes. Look what Time-Warner-Microsoft
did to graduation planning. They put every private planner out of business. You didn't give her a rom, did you?"

"She couldn't make up her mind which package—"

Norwall groaned. "Goodbye, deck.halls. Hello, Galatek Christmases,
Inc."

She was shaking her head. "But she seemed so nice," she said, but she
was thinking of how she'd kept asking to see different themes, how she'd
asked her about her office, how she'd insisted Brian take her to Rock and
a . . . Brian.

"You're wrong," she said. "She can't be Sara Darbingdon. There has to
be some mistake. Her nephew helped me come up with a theme for
Pandora Freeh. He wouldn't be a party to—"

"He's not her nephew."

After several seconds she managed to say, "What?"

"He works at Galatek. He's no relation to Dr. Darbingdon."

"I don't believe you," she said. "He hates the whole idea of professional Christmases."

"That's something he obviously said so you wouldn't catch on."

So she wouldn't catch on. She thought of Brian showing up at the
Manning installation, at her apartment, of his walking into her office,
looking at her equipment. And all the while pretending that he—

"They were obviously after your designs," Norwall said, "pumping
you for the names of clients and suppliers."

"Who do you get a largemouth bass from anyway?" Brian had said,
and he'd asked her all about her best Christmas and her most difficult.

"What's his name?" she said.

"Who? Oh, the so-called nephew? He actually used his own name, I suppose because it isn't one you'd recognize, but he's not an engineer. He's a marketing designer."

"I have to go," Linny said.

"The house is hers, too. I was surprised. When I saw your proposal layouts, I assumed it had to be a rental for the occasion, but no, she actually lives in it when she's not in San Francisco. Or Stockholm. She's got houses there, too, plus apartments in Manhattan, Sydney, São Paulo, Addis Ababa, and Beijing. And a villa in Iceland."

"I like to keep things simple," she'd said.

"I've got an override from Pandora Freeh," Linny lied. "I've got to go."

"Pandora will have to wait," Norwall said. "We have to talk about what you're going to do about this."

"I'll call you back," she said, and downlinked before he could protest.

And then sat there, thinking, *I don't believe it.* But she did. After all, it was the oldest trick in the book—#145 Romantic Con Men. Sweet-talk the mark into revealing her secrets. Buy her red tea, help her carry something heavy, sit too close to her in her office, and for good measure, pretend he liked E. M. Forster, which he had no doubt found out about from one of those netchecks.

And she had fallen for it, hook, line, and sinker—#182 Fisherman's Paradise.

The screen buzzed an override. She reached for the delete key, but it wasn't Norwall. It was Pandora.

"*A Midsummer Night's Dream* won't work, after all," she said. "Fashad Tweedlowe did Christmas at the Grand Canyon last year."

"The Grand Canyon?" Linny said, unable to see the connection.

"Riding down to the bottom of the *Grand Canyon*," Pandora said.

Oh, she can't mean—

"*Burros,*" Pandora said. "They ride burros."

"Bottom's an ass."

"Ass, burro, it's the same thing. Maybe your young man was right. I should do *Twelfth Night*."

He's not my young man, Linny thought. *He's a marketing designer for Galatek.*

"But it's just so obscure. Didn't Shakespeare write any other plays?"

"Just the thirty-nine," Linny said. "And 154 sonnets."

"The sonnets," Pandora said thoughtfully. "That's an idea. Let me think about that." Her image blinked off. The screen immediately buzzed again.

It was Brian. She hit "record answer," and Brian said, "Look, I know you're wildly busy and my chances of taking you out for a red tea are nonexistent till after Christmas, but if you'll tell me where you're going to be stringing up hot dogs or synchronized swimmers, I'll bring you a cone. I'll even hold it for you so you can keep both hands free for plucking chickens or whatever it is you'll be doing."

Fighting off intellectual property thieves, she thought. Norwall was right. They had to talk about what she was going to do.

She uplinked to him.

"You don't do anything. If she gets demanding, you tell her you know what she's up to and you have no intention of helping her steal deck .halls out from under you."

But she has all those people coming for dinner, Linny thought, and then realized that was probably a lie, too.

"I know this is Galatek you're dealing with," Norwall was saying, "but there's no contract, and she's on very shaky legal ground herself: fraud, criminal misrepresentation—"

"I'm afraid there is a contract," Linny said ruefully. "She signed it yesterday."

"Online?"

"No, an actual signature."

Norwall nodded. "So there wouldn't be a corneal ID."

Of course. "Aunt Darby doesn't trust online contracts," my foot. She hadn't wanted electronic identification of her signature.

"What name did she use?" Norwall said. "If she used Shields, the contract's invalid."

Linny went and got the contract, hoping that was the case, but it was an illegible scrawl. She scanned it in for Norwall.

"No, that's definitely Sara Darbingdon's signature," he said. "And it's the address of the house that's listed on the contract, not the owner. This changes things."

"How?"

"If you've got a legally binding contract—she didn't snail-mail this to you, did she?"

"No, her—Bri—the marketing designer brought it over."

"Too bad," he said. "We might have been able to prove mail fraud. But under the circumstances, unless you can prove fraudulent signing conditions—"

"I thought I was signing a contract with someone else," Linny said. "Doesn't that count as fraudulent?"

He shook his head. "It's your word against hers, or, rather, against Galatek's legal department, which is like going up against—"

"Are you telling me that even though she's trying to steal my ideas, I might have to do her *Christmas*?" she said, feeling sick at the thought of it. What if Brian showed up?

"Calm down," Norwall said. "Let me uplink to lawyer.com and see where we stand, and then we'll decide what to do. Don't worry. They're not going to get away with this."

They've already gotten away with it, Linny thought numbly. She called up her messages and tried to get some work done, but she couldn't concentrate. She ended up going through Shakespeare's sonnets, looking for one she could use for Pandora, but there wasn't much to work with. "Bare ruined choirs"? The "barren rage of death's eternal cold"?

The screen buzzed. "It's what I was afraid of. The contract's legally binding, and the payment-on-signing's already been deposited in your online account. You're legally obligated to do the Christmas."

"I can't—" Linny said.

"The object is to minimize the damage and not reveal any more trade secrets than you already have. What theme is it? How detailed was your proposal?"

"I haven't done it yet. Mrs. Shie—she left the theme to my discretion."

"And that's in the contract?" he said excitedly.

"Yes. No. I mean, that line was left blank, to be filled in by me."

"This changes everything. Let me—" he said, and his image disappeared.

She went back to dissecting sonnets: "Roses have thorns, and silver fountains mud." "My grief lies onward, and my joy behind."

She gave up and sat there waiting for Norwall to override. "I checked with lawyer.com," he said when he came on, "and it's perfectly legal. Thank God she didn't pick a theme. There isn't a thing Dr. Darbingdon or Galatek will be able to do about it."

"About what?" Linny asked.

"About the elegant revenge you're going to work on them."

"Revenge?"

"Yes," he said eagerly. "You get to pick the theme. All right. You pick Death and Destruction or Nightmares or Strip Mining. You do the installation—when is it, by the way?"

"A week from now. The twenty-third. But—"

"You decorate her house totally as per the contract, only with Disgusting Things in Caves or Revenge Is Sweet, and when she sees it, you've not only ruined her Christmas, but she knows she can't go around stealing people's concepts. And you have your revenge."

"What does that have to do with Christmas?" Linny murmured.

"What?" Norwall said.

"Nothing. Isn't it enough to tell them we know what they're up to and refuse to do the installation?"

"She'll just get Galatek's designers to do it. This way, she's publicly humiliated. She's having a dinner party for Galatek's board of directors the night of the day you're scheduled to do the installation."

She wasn't lying about that, either, Linny thought.

"I think Hell Hath No Fury would be perfect," Norwall said.

"But it's Christmas. It's not supposed to be a time for revenge. It's supposed to be the season of forgiveness and good will."

"After what they've done to you? All right, no revenge themes. But you have to do *something,* unless you just want to hand your clients over to them."

"I'll go talk to them," she said, but her heart quailed at the thought.

"Have it your way, no revenge," Norwall said, throwing up his hands. "But let me handle it. I don't trust you to be tough enough. Let me be the one to confront them."

"All right," Linny said gratefully.

"Good," Norwall said. "Don't worry, I'll take care of everything."

But she did worry. She tried to take her mind off it by focusing on the sonnet problem, but it wasn't much help.

"Poems, you mean?" Pandora said vaguely when Linny called her with her proposal. "Oh, I don't want *poems.* They're so—don't you have any other ideas?"

"Stock car racing?" Linny said at random. "Herbs and spices? Duck decoys? Media bias?"

"It has to have the bust in it."

Pikes Peak or Bust? she thought wildly. *Or Great Busts of History, with Madonna and Diana Dors and the Great Crash of 2006.* "How about Famous Dramatists?"

"Mitzi Poulakakos did that five years ago."

I wonder if I could talk her into "Fire" as a theme, Linny wondered. *That way I could just burn down her house.* "Or Christmas at the Globe Theater?"

"I don't know . . . maybe . . . why don't you work up a proposal?"

Linny did, and installed the Goldfarbs' Christmas and the Marcianos' Hanukkah, trying to reach Norwall at intervals and finally succeeding around noon on the twenty-third.

"All taken care of," he said. "You don't have to worry about anything."

"You talked to them?"

"I did, and told her in no uncertain terms to leave you alone or you'd sue."

"What did she say?" she said, wanting to ask if Brian had been there.

"They . . . oh, my God, the Pyramids just fell down," he said. "Don't give it another thought. All taken care of. If you get any messages from them, delete them."

Linny did, putting them on "automatic delete" so she didn't even have to hear Brian's voice, and moving on to messages about the Carmodys' flamingos, a delivery of wrapping paper that had butterflies instead of caterpillars on it, and the ever-present problem of Pandora, who had decided Christmas at the Globe was too confusing.

"People might be expecting to see an actual globe," she said, and Linny thought, *Why did I get angry when I found out Brian and Dr. Darbingdon were trying to steal my business? Why didn't I jump at the chance?*

"How about Christmas in Westminster Abbey?" she suggested. "Candles, a holo of the nave, busts of Byron and Shakespeare and Keats. All the famous poets are buried there."

Shakespeare wasn't, but Pandora and her friends wouldn't know that. "I can see it all now—Poet's Corner, Queen Elizabeth's tomb, the Crown Jewels—"

"The Crown Jewels," Pandora said, pleased. "I don't suppose you could work King Harry's coronation in somehow?"

"Why not?" Linny said. *I have nothing else to do between now and the twenty-fifth.* She uplinked to Fergie's Fripperies and reserved an ermine cape and then called Rock and a Hard Place and asked what they had left in literary busts.

"Not a thing. I've got some statues—rappers, mostly, and a Sammy Sosa. I don't have a Judas, either."

A Judas?

"The closest thing I've got is an Adonis," he went on. "You could maybe put a tunic on him and thirty pieces of silver in his hand. Do you want me to send it over?"

"Send it over where?" Linny asked with a sinking feeling.

"Mrs. Shields, 3404 Aspen Lane," he said. "Do you want the Adonis or not?"

"Not," Linny said, hit "end," and called a taxi.

She worried the whole way out on the maglev and in the taxi from the station about what she might find, but when it pulled up in front of the house she saw a row of life-size tin soldiers standing stiffly in red and blue uniforms.

"Oh, good, Norwall thought better of getting revenge," she murmured, sliding her card through the taxi's reader. He'd decided to fulfill their contract with a standard treatment instead, and one Galatek couldn't learn anything from. Babes in Toyland was one of the most common Christmas themes.

She hurried across the street and up the path to the door, and then stopped short. The soldiers had their toy rifles raised and pointed at a life-size doll in a pink dress and a blindfold. "Oh, no," Linny murmured, and hurried inside.

The tree in the hall was swathed in crime scene tape and flashing red-white-and-blue police lights, and there was a painting of Benedict Arnold on the wall behind it.

She went into the living room, where a holo of Julius Caesar being stabbed was playing on a continuous loop. She walked through Brutus and into the dining room.

The walls and table were draped in black and in the center of the table was a horse's head with a sign pinned to the mane. "This is what happens to people who try to steal our design concepts," it read. "Merry Christmas from deck.halls."

Linny pulled the sign off, wadded it up, and walked warily into the study. Statues filled the room, cups of wassail in their hands as if this was a Christmas party. Nero, and Hitler, who was *Sieg Heil*ing with his other hand, and Simon Legree, and someone who was probably supposed to be Iago from the handkerchief in his hand.

Oh, no. I can't let Mrs. Shields see this, Linny thought, and then remembered she wasn't Mrs. Shields.

I still can't let her see it, she thought, sick at the thought of what Brian would say when he saw this, of what he'd think if he believed she'd done this. Even though he'd—

"Revenge doesn't have anything to do with Christmas," she said firmly, and began pulling down the black garlands looped all around the room.

There was a tree here, too, hidden behind Billy the Kid. It was lying under a guillotine, its tip, with the star still on it, chopped off, and ornaments in the shape of instruments of torture. Linny finished pulling down the garlands, stuffed them into a trash bag, and began unhooking the ornaments.

There was a sound. *Oh, God, what if it's Brian?* she thought, leaping for the door, but it was only a workman, wearing the red-white-blue-and-brown coveralls of FedXUPS and carrying a toga'd and gold-laurel-wreathed mannequin.

"What's this?" she asked.

The workman righted the mannequin and set it down. "Nero," he said, though she had already figured that out from the plaster violin under the statue's chin. "Where do you want it?"

"Back where you got it," she said. "Put it back in the truck."

"I've got a delivery order for this address," he said, pulling out his handheld.

"I'm rescinding the order." She reached for the handheld and clicked "cancel." "I want all of these returned," she said, indicating Hitler et al.

"Those aren't ours," he said. "We don't do statues. Or fictionals. The fictionals are from Eveningprimrose. The only ones that are ours are the toy soldiers and the doll." He checked his manifest. "And the Pontius Pilate in the bathroom."

Oh, Norwall. "Well, take it back, too."

"I'll have to charge you extra for an unscheduled pickup."

"Fine," Linny said, and then, as he picked up Nero, "What would you charge to take the rest of these back to—" she tipped Stalin forward to take a look at the bottom of his foot, "Rock and a Hard Place and Eveningprimrose?"

"Two days before Christmas? Are you kidding?" He picked up Nero and started out. "You're lucky I've got room on the truck for the toy soldiers. Otherwise, you'd have had to wait till January. There's no way you're going to get anybody to do unscheduled pickups this close to Christmas."

He was right, but she tried anyway, calling Rock and a Hard Place and Eveningprimrose, and then Nowheretoturn Trucking, which had helped her one time on the twenty-fourth with an emergency delivery to Pandora's, but she got voice mail on all three, and her overrides didn't work. She would have to talk the FedXUPS guy into taking at least some of the statues, but he and his truck were already gone.

At least he took the firing squad, she thought, looking at the trampled snow, and went back inside. She would have to do it herself. Dr. Darbingdon couldn't walk in here and see the house like this. She went out to the dining room and scooped up the tablecloth by the corners, the centerpiece and dishes and all, into a clanking bundle, tied the ends, and carried it out back to the trash recycle, and then went back into the study and began wrestling Nixon through the dining room toward the back door.

She made it as far as the door to the kitchen, which apparently wasn't as wide as the study's, because his arms, raised in his trademark V's for victory, got wedged in the door and wouldn't budge. She tried to turn him sideways, but his arms were jammed tight.

They'll have to come off, she thought, and began unbuttoning his jacket so she could unscrew the arms. The front door opened. *Oh, good,* she thought, *he came back for the Pilate in the bathroom.* "Can you give me a hand? I'm in the dining room," she called, struggling with the sleeve.

"What the hell's the idea?" Brian said.

She looked up. He was standing in the door to the living room, his fists full of police car lights and crime scene tape. The lights were still flashing blindingly.

"You found out," he said.

"I found out," she said.

"And you did this," he said, looking at Brutus.

"No, though it would have been an appropriate reaction. What did you expect me to do, be overjoyed?"

"No," he said. "I thought maybe . . . no, I suppose not."

It wasn't at all the reaction she'd expected. She'd expected slick explanations, but he just stood there, his hands full of flashing red and blue, staring at the holo and looking like he'd been kicked in the stomach. After a long minute, he said bitterly, "I suppose you ran a background check and found out who she really was."

Linny nodded. "They're routine for all new clients, even with a little-nobody Christmas company like deck.halls."

"I told her you were bound to find out," he said. "I told her lying to you was terminally stupid, that we should just tell you—"

"And that would somehow make it more acceptable to me?"

He waited a minute before answering. "I thought it might be a possibility."

A possibility. The arrogance of the man. "Well, it's not," she snapped.

"Apparently not," he said, looking at John Wilkes Booth pouring himself a cup of wassail. "And so you—"

"I told you, I didn't do this. In fact, I was trying to get it taken down before anybody saw it. I don't believe in an eye for an eye, especially at Christmas." She reached forward and took the lights and tape from him and stuffed them in a garbage bag. "Dr. Darbingdon's going to be here in a few minutes," she said, "and some of this is too heavy for me to move, so if you don't want her to see this, you're going to have to help me. And, no, you don't have to remind me that I'm under contract. I am painfully aware of that."

"I definitely don't want her to see this," he said, and seemed to come to himself. He hoisted Nixon up. "Where do you want me to put this?"

"Out back behind the spruces for now," she said, and went ahead into the kitchen to open the back door for him. A grim-looking automated store mannequin in a navy dress stood at the stove, stirring a pot.

"Who's that supposed to be?" Brian asked, grunting as he maneuvered Nixon through the door. "Lucrezia Borgia?"

"Linda Tripp," she said, and as soon as Brian and Nixon went out, switched it off, unplugged the control box, and began winding up the cord. "I can get this one," she said when he came back in. "You get the ones in the study."

She dismantled Linda and then the guillotine in the living room and put them out back while he carried out Haldeman and Ehrlichman, and then linked to hollyandivy.com to order a Number One. It wasn't much, but there wasn't time for anything but standard decorations, if that.

Hollyandivy was sold out. She linked to Everything Christmas. "Site closed," it said. She punched in their emergency number. "We've been completely cleaned out since the nineteenth," Nadia told her. "Did you try Holiday Heaven?"

She tried Holiday Heaven, and Christmas"R"Us and Partyplus. "Everyone's completely sold out," she told Brian when he reappeared with O. J. Simpson. "The only supplier who has anything in stock is thegooseisgettingfat.com, and all they've got is a Mayan snake god and two dozen yellow polka-dot bikinis, no candles, no lights. Dr. Darbingdon wouldn't have her old decorations in the basement, would she?"

He shook his head. "She gave them all to charity after she started having Galatek do her Christmases. Nobody's got anything?"

"No," she said, scrolling through a list of electronics suppliers. Maybe one of them would have some colored LEDs that could pass for Christmas tree lights—

Her screen buzzed. "The Westminster Abbey theme won't work," Pandora Freeh said.

"Who is it?" Brian said.

"I just found out Sashine Nackerty's new live-in's old live-in's theme last year was A Double-Decker Tour of London—the Tower, Madame Tussauds, mad cow disease, Big Ben—"

"*Who* is it?"

"I can't talk right now," Linny said desperately. "I've got an emergency."

"An emergency!" Pandora said, waving it aside. "The Abbey's in London! If Jane sees it, she'll think I'm trying to remind him of his old live-in, and—"

"Who *is* it?" Brian said. "Is it my aunt?"

"No," Linny hissed, and hit "speaker" so he could hear for himself.

"Besides which, Westminster Abbey's only one tiny stop on this elaborate tour!" Pandora said. "The theme just won't work. You'll have to come up with something else."

"Westminster Abbey?" Brian whispered. "What happened to *Twelfth Night*?"

"Too intellectual," she whispered back. "And she insisted it had to be something that involved Shakespeare's bust. Poet's Corner was the only thing I could think of."

"—and it needs to be done by tomorrow because that's when Griselda and Carlos are coming. I invited them to lunch, having no idea—"

"Shakespeare wasn't buried in Westminster Abbey," Brian whispered.

"I am aware of that, but I had to come up with something, and since when are you such a stickler for the truth?"

"Touché," he said.

"I sympathize with your situation," Linny said into the phone, "but I have a client arriving any minute to no Christmas at all, so if I could call you back—"

"What happened?" Pandora said, instantly interested. "Didn't FedX-UPS arrive? That happened to me one time before I hired you—it was *why* I hired you, as a matter of fact. The truck was one of those un-manned robot things, which they assured me was perfectly reliable—"

"No, it wasn't the truck. It—" Linny glanced at Brian. "It's too complicated to explain right now. I have to try and find some Christmas decorations—"

"What do you need?" Pandora said. "Maybe I can help."

"No, you don't understand, none of the suppliers—"

"Have you got decorations?" Brian cut in.

"Yes, a whole attic full. Grisham says I never throw anything away, but I always say, you never know when things might come in handy. They're the ones I used before I started hiring it done. It's mostly non-themed stuff. Santas and snowmen and jingle bells."

"I'll be right over," Brian said, grabbing his coat.

"Oh, and I've got several antelope from this darling Home on the Range Christmas I did. If you have some antlers, they'd look just like reindeer."

"You're a godsend," Brian said, starting for the door.

"Well, after all, that's what Christmas is all about, isn't it, helping each other? Oh, dear, I just thought of something. I don't have a tree. I do have a crane, from Christmas on a Construction Site. You could—"

"We're set for trees. Brian will be right over," Linny said, and hung up. "Don't let her give you a crane," she called after Brian, "or a bulldozer. And no roaming buffaloes."

She wrestled O.J. out the back door and then took down the rack and Iron Maiden ornaments, trying to gauge how long it would take Brian to get there and back if he floored the Incite.

The answer was: over half an hour. "I had a terrible time getting away from her," he said, coming in carrying a dusty plastic wise man, a bouquet of even dustier poinsettias, and a Styrofoam snowman.

"She wanted to tell me all about what she wants for her new Christmas theme."

"Pandora can have whatever her little heart desires," Linny said, putting the wise man where the guillotine had stood. She took the poinsettias from Brian.

"Everything's pretty grubby," Brian said, wiping the snowman against his sleeve. "It'll need to be washed off."

"We don't have time," Linny said, hurrying into the kitchen for a vase for the poinsettias. "They'll be here—oh, gosh, in five minutes. We'll call it An Attic Christmas. Go get the rest of the decorations."

He returned with a second wise man, two ceramic elves, and an armful of cobwebby bubble lights. "The good news is the Christmas spirit is alive and well in spite of professional Christmases," he said, handing her the lights. "The bad news is, Pandora's decided her new theme should be Godsends of History. People who've given aid and assistance through the centuries: the Good Samaritan, Florence Nightingale, the inventor of laserliposuction."

"What about the all-essential bust of Shakespeare?" Linny asked, draping the lights haphazardly around the tree.

"He's in the car," Brian said. "Pandora could only find two of the wise men. She sent Shakespeare as a third. And a bathrobe to drape him in. Where do you want the elves?"

"Coffee table," she said, plugging in the lights. Two of them were burnt out. "Did she send any replacement bulbs?"

"I'll check," he said, rummaging in an enormous box he'd brought in of ornaments, burned-down candles, plastic mistletoe, and bedraggled tinsel.

Linny set him to decorating the tree while she finished placing the candles, five swans-a-swimming with several feathers missing, and a Victorian angel with a bent wing, looking anxiously at her watch. Dr. Darbingdon was already late.

"Where do you want this?" Brian asked, and held up a chicken-wire sleigh and eight tiny reindeer.

"Good Lord," she said.

"I know. I apologize for ever criticizing Christmas designers. It's obvious you're saving people from themselves. Bathroom?"

Linny nodded. "Bathroom." She began arranging the snow village houses on the sideboard.

"Linny!" Brian called.

"What?" she said, hurrying into the bathroom. A six-foot, solid-looking, toga'd statue stood over the sink, its marble hands extended. "Oh, I forgot all about Pilate."

"Pilate? What's he doing in the bathroom?"

"Washing his hands."

"Of course," he said. "Don't tell me he's marble."

"No, plaster, I think," she said.

He took hold of Pilate's waist and tried to lift him. "Definitely marble. Any chance of getting the robo-dolly back?"

She shook her head. "He had six more deliveries."

"When's my aunt due here?"

She looked at her watch. "Fifteen minutes ago."

"Then we'll just have to manhandle him out of here. Wait," he said as she moved to take hold of one of Pilate's hands, "let me get around behind him first. Then you pull and I'll . . . what's this?"

"What's what?" Linny asked, leaning around Pilate to see. Brian had untaped a sign from the statue's back and was reading it.

"What is it?" she asked, though it was obvious it was another of Norwall's signs, and when he didn't answer, "What does it say?"

"It says, 'This is what you get for trying to steal my concepts and my clients,'" Brian read. He looked up. "You thought that's what we were trying to do—take over your clientele?"

"Isn't that what you *were* trying to do?"

"Of *course* not. How could you even *think* that? No wonder you put up all this," he said, gesturing to include Pilate and the rest of the house.

"I told you, I didn't put it up. But if you weren't spying on me," she said, bewildered, "what *were* you doing?"

"It's a long story," he said. "Aunt Darby—"

"She's not your aunt," Linny said coldly.

"Not my . . . ?" he said, and now he was the one who looked bewildered. "No, she's not genetically related to me but . . . she's my parents' best friend. I lived with her while they were at Tombaugh Station when I was a kid, and again in high school when they were out in the Asteroid Belt."

And Norwall knew that, Linny thought. Inge had said she'd run complete personal histories. *He knew it and didn't tell me.*

"I wasn't lying when I called her Aunt Darby," he said. "I've always called her that."

"And I suppose her name really is Mrs. Shields and you really are an engineer and you build dams? What about her telling me she didn't understand computers? And that she'd never had a professionally done Christmas before, that she's always put up her decorations with her own two little hands?"

"She was afraid if you knew who she was, you'd wonder why she wasn't using Galatek's decorators and would assume she had plenty of other options, so you'd refuse to take her on, especially at such a late date. Plus, she knew you did your interviews online and she needed to get you out to the house, so she came up with that whole ridiculous technophobic Mrs. Shields thing, and by the time I realized what she was up to, it was too late to stop her. She'd already told you so many lies about who and what we were—"

"Stop her from what?"

"You did a Christmas display for Howard Greenfeld in October."

"Hanukkah," she said. "Hanukkah in Lapland. He needed the installation early because he was leaving for New Palestine."

"Hanukkah in Lapland?" Brian said. "Do they even *have* Hanukkah in Lapland? What did you do?"

"Reindeer and menorahs. And a holo of the aurora borealis. What about Howard Greenfeld?"

"He's a friend of Aunt Darby's. She was talking to him online when she apparently spotted you among the caribou and decided you were just what I needed."

"Needed?"

"Aunt Darby's one of the world's great fixers. Galatek doesn't take over businesses—it fixes them. Unfortunately, Aunt Darby doesn't confine herself to fixing companies' problems. She also fixes people's problems. Or what she perceives to be their problems. When I was ten, she decided I needed work on coordination skills and insisted I take tuba lessons. And learn to bowl. Two years ago she decided my work wasn't challenging enough and got me a job at Galatek. This year she decided my problem was that I was spending too much time at said job and not seeing anybody."

She was trying to fix us up, Linny thought. *That was why he was so rude that first day. That was why she kept talking about "The Machine Stops" and how hard it is for young people to meet.* "Your aunt was matchmaking?" she said.

He nodded grimly. "She was matchmaking. Her first plan was to invite you to a party at Galatek, but after she ran a netcheck on you and found out how busy you are this time of year, she came up with the bright idea of hiring you to do her house."

"And of sending you to my apartment and the Manning installation."

"No," Brian said. "After that first day, she didn't have to send me. It was all my own idea. The contract was just an excuse." He smiled crookedly at her. "I loved playing the tuba."

"What?" she said, bewildered again.

"I even ended up loving bowling. Aunt Darby's always right. My old job wasn't challenging enough. I love working for Galatek. She always knows exactly what I need, even if I don't. Only her way of going about it—"

He reached up and smacked the back of Pilate's head with his open palm. "I *told* her you'd find out and feel betrayed and—I told her it would end up like this," he said, gesturing to include the whole house, "with you—"

"I told you, I didn't do this."

He stopped in mid-gesture, his hand still out. "You thought I was spying on you," he said slowly, "that we were trying to steal your business, but even though you thought that, you were still trying to take the decorations down before we arrived. Why?"

"I told you, I didn't want her to see them," she said. "I knew she had the board of directors coming for dinner and . . ."

"Even though you thought she had lied to you," he said, coming around from behind Pilate toward her. "Even though you thought I'd romanced you to get information out of you . . ."

"I . . . revenge didn't seem to have anything to do with Christmas. I . . . it," she stammered, trying not to be so aware of his scent, "it's supposed to be about forgiveness and . . . and . . . good will . . . and . . ."

"Love?"

She backed into the sink. "Charity," she said, and the doorbell rang.

"Oh, my God, it's Aunt Darby," Brian said.

It was the caterers. Brian recruited them and their robo-dolly to help lug Pilate out back behind the spruces, and Linny ran through the house, making sure they hadn't missed anything else.

They hadn't, except for the chicken-wire sleigh and reindeer, which had gotten bent when Brian was removing Pilate. She unbent it, more or less.

"The decorations look awful," she told Brian, setting it on the sink. "This won't fool anybody."

"I think there's been enough fooling of people," he said. "Aunt Darby will love it. This is just what she wanted. As you said, Christmas is the season of charity."

"I hope so."

"And forgiveness?" he said, backing her into the sink again.

"Oh, I just *love* it," a woman's voice, not Aunt Darby's, said. "How perfectly pre-retro!"

"Even some of the lights are burnt out," a man's delighted voice said.

"And look at the dust! You were right, Darby, this young woman is a genius!"

"I wonder where she and Brian are," Aunt Darby said.

"Oh, my God, will you look at that!" a third voice exclaimed. "Our neighbors had light-up wise men just like that on their front lawn when I was a kid!"

Linny clapped her hand to her mouth. "Oh, no! I forgot all about the lawn decorations!"

"I have just the thing," Brian said, grabbing her by the hand and leading her through the living room, past the dinner guests and Aunt Darby, out the front door, onto the lawn.

"Room," he said, gesturing toward the window where Aunt Darby and the Galatek board of directors stood watching. "View."

"But this is supposed to be An Attic Christmas, not E. M. Forster," she protested.

"Aunt Darby will love it," he said, walking back to the sidewalk. "Ready?"

"No," she said, but she didn't move. "There's no barley. Or poppies."

"Next Christmas," he said, and strode purposefully toward her.

Cat's Paw

"Come, Bridlings," Touffét said impatiently as soon as I arrived. "Go home and pack your bags. We're going to Suffolk for a jolly country Christmas."

"I thought you hated country Christmases," I said. I had invited him only the week before down to my sister's and gotten a violent rejection of the idea. "Country Christmases! Dreadful occasions!" he had said. "Holly and mistletoe and vile games—blindman's bluff and that ridiculous game where people grab at burning raisins, and even viler food. Plum pudding!" he shuddered. "And wassail!"

I protested that my sister was an excellent cook and that she never made wassail, she made eggnog. "I think you'd have an excellent time," I said. "Everyone's very pleasant."

"I can imagine," he said. "No one drinks, everyone is faithful to his wife, the inheritance is equally and fairly divided, and none of your relatives would ever think of murdering anyone."

"Of course not!" I said, bristling.

"Then I would rather spend Christmas here alone," Touffét said. "At least then I shall not be subjected to roast goose and Dumb Crambo."

"We do not play Dumb Crambo," I replied with dignity. "We play charades."

And now, scarcely a week later, Touffét was eagerly proposing going to the country.

"I have just received a letter from Lady Charlotte Valladay," he said, brandishing a sheet of pale pink notepaper, "asking me to come to Marwaite Manor. She wishes me to solve a mystery for her." He examined the letter through his monocle. "What could be more delightful than murder in a country house at Christmas?"

Actually, I could think of a number of things. I scanned the letter. "You *must* come," she had written. "This is a mystery only you, the world's greatest detective, can solve." Lady Charlotte Valladay. And Marwaite Manor. Where had I heard those names before? Lady Charlotte.

"It doesn't say there's been a murder," I said. "It says a mystery."

Touffét was not listening. "We must hurry if we are to catch the 3:00 train from Euston. There won't be time for you to go home and pack and come back here. You must meet me at the station. Come, don't stand there looking foolish."

"The letter doesn't say anything about my being invited," I said. "It only mentions you. And I've already told my sister I'm spending Christmas with her."

"She does not mention you because it is of course assumed that I will bring my assistant."

"Hardly your assistant, Touffét. You never let me do anything."

"That is because you have not the mind of a detective. Always you see the facade. Never do you see what lies behind it."

"Then you obviously won't need me," I said.

"But I do, Bridlings," he said. "Who will record my exploits if you are not there? And who will point out the obvious and the incorrect, so that I may reject them and find the true solution?"

"I would rather play charades," I said, and picked up my hat. "I hope Lady Charlotte feeds you wassail *and* plum pudding. And makes you play Dumb Crambo."

🌲

In the end I went. I had been with Touffét on every one of his cases, and although I still could not place Lady Charlotte Valladay, it seemed to me her name had been connected to something interesting.

And I had never experienced Christmas in a country manor, with the ancient hall decked in holly and Gainsboroughs, a huge Yule log on the fire, an old-fashioned Christmas feast—poached salmon, a roast joint, and a resplendent goose, with a different wine for every course. Perhaps they might even have a boar's head.

The bullet trains to Suffolk were all filled, and we could only get seats on an express. It was filled as well, and every passenger had not only luggage but huge shopping bags crammed with gifts, which completely filled all the overhead compartments. I had to hold my bag and Touffét's umbrella on my lap.

I thought longingly of the first-class compartment I had booked on the train to my sister's and hoped Marwaite Manor was at the near end of Suffolk.

Marwaite Manor. Where had I heard that name? And Lady Charlotte's? Not in the tabloids, I decided, though I had a vague idea of something controversial. A protest of some sort. What? Cloning? The revival of fox hunting?

Perhaps she was an actress—they were always getting involved in causes. Or a royal scandal. No, she was too old. I seemed to remember she was in her fifties.

Touffét, across from me, was deep in a book. I leaned forward slightly, trying to read the title. Touffét only reads mystery novels, he says, to study the methods of fictional detectives, but actually to criticize them. And, I suspected, to study their mannerisms. And co-opt them. He had already affected Lord Peter Wimsey's monocle and Hercule Poirot's treatment of his "assistant," and he had met me at the station wearing a Sherlock Holmesian Inverness cape. Thank God he had not adopted Holmes's deerstalker. Or his violin. At least thus far.

The title was in very tiny print. I leaned forward farther, and Touffét looked up irritably. "This Dorothy Sayers, she is ridiculous," he said, "she makes her Lord Peter read timetables of trains, decipher codes, use stopwatches, and it is all, *all* unnecessary. If he would only ask himself, 'Who had a motive to murder Paul Alexis?' he would have no need of all these shirt collar receipts and diagrams."

He flung it down. "It is Sherlock Holmes who has caused this foolish preoccupation with evidence," he said, "with all his tobacco ashes and chemical experiments." He grabbed the carpetbag off my lap and began rummaging through it. "Where have you put my other book, Bridlings?"

I hadn't touched it. I sometimes think he takes me along with him for the same reason that he reads mystery novels—so he can feel superior.

He pulled a book from the bag, Edgar Allan Poe's *The Murders in the Rue Morgue.* No doubt he would find all sorts of things wrong with Inspector Dupin. He would probably think Dupin should have asked himself what motive an orangu—

"Touffét!" I said. "I've remembered who Lady Charlotte Valladay is! She's the ape woman!"

"Ape woman?" Touffét said irritably. "You are saying Lady Charlotte is a carnival attraction? Covered in hair and scratching herself?"

"No, no," I said. "She's a primate-rights activist, claims gorillas and orangutans should be allowed to vote, be given equal standing in the courts, and all that."

"Are you certain this is the same person?" Touffét said.

"Completely. Her father's Lord Alastair Biddle, made his fortune in artificial intelligence. That's how she got interested in primates. They were AI research subjects. She founded the Primate Intelligence Institute. I saw her on television just the other day, soliciting funds for it."

Touffét had taken out Lady Charlotte's pink letter and was peering at it. "She says nothing at all about apes."

"Perhaps one of her orangutans has got loose and committed a murder, just like in *The Murders in the Rue Morgue,*" I said. "Looks like she made a monkey out of you, Touffét."

There was no one at the station to meet us. I suggested taking the single taxi parked at the end of the platform, but Touffét said, "Lady Charlotte will of course send someone to meet us."

After a quarter of an hour, during which it began to rain and I thought fondly of how my sister was always on the platform waiting for me, smiling and waving, I telephoned the manor.

A man with a reedy, refined voice said, "Marwaite Manor," and, when I asked for Lady Valladay, said formally, "One moment, please," and Lady Charlotte came on. "Oh, Colonel Bridlings, I am *so* sorry about there not being anyone to meet you. They've refused to issue D'Artagnan a driver's license, which is perfectly ridiculous, he drives better than I do, and there was no one else to send. If you could take a taxi, D'Artagnan will pay the driver when you get here. I'll see you shortly."

By this time, of course, the taxi had long gone, and I had to telephone for one. As I was hanging up, a sunburned middle-aged man with a full red beard and a black shoulder bag accosted me.

"I couldn't help overhearing," he said in a heavy Australian accent. "You're going to Marwaite Manor, are you, mate?"

"Yes," I said warily. Journalists are always trying for interviews with Touffét, and the shoulder bag looked suspiciously like it could contain a vidcam.

"I was wondering if I could bag a ride with you. I'm going to Marwaite Manor, too." He stuck out his hand. "Mick Rutgers."

"Colonel Bridlings," I said, and turned to Touffét, who had walked over to us and was peering at Mr. Rutgers through his monocle. "Allow me to introduce Inspector Touffét."

"Touffét?" Rutgers said sharply. "The detective?"

"You have heard of me in Australia?" Touffét said.

"Everyone has heard of the world's greatest detective," Rutgers said, recovering himself. "This is an honor. What brings you to Marwaite Manor?"

"Lady Charlotte Valladay has asked me to solve a mystery."

"A mystery?" he said. "What mystery?"

"I do not know," Touffét said. "Ah, the taxi arrives."

I picked up our baggage. "I hope it's not far to the manor."

"Only a coupla miles," Rutgers said.

"Ah, you have been here before?" Touffét said.

"No, mate," Rutgers said, the sharpness back in his voice. "Never set foot in England before, as a matter of fact. No, when she invited me she told me the manor was only a coupla miles from the station. Lady Charlotte. I work for the Australian Broadcasting Network."

I knew he was a journalist, I thought. "Why are you here?" I asked.

"Lady Charlotte said she had a big story, one we'd be interested in covering."

"And she didn't say what the story was?" Touffét asked.

Rutgers shook his head. "But whatever it is, she was paying all expenses, and I'd never seen England. So here I am."

We piled into the taxi and set out. It was, as Mr. Rutgers had said, "a coupla miles," and in no time we'd arrived at Marwaite Manor.

At least that's what the scrolled wrought-iron sign above the granite gates said. But the buildings in the distance looked more like an industrial compound. There were numerous long metal sheds with parking lots between them and a great many ventilators and pipes. They looked grim in the freezing rain.

The taxi driver drove past the compound and up a long hill and stopped in front of a four-story glass-and-chrome affair that looked like a company headquarters. "Are you certain this is Marwaite Manor?" I asked him as he was taking our bags out of the trunk.

He nodded, handing me Touffét's portmanteau and my bag. "Is the monkey paying me or are you?"

"I *beg* your pardon," I said sternly. I glanced toward Touffét, hoping he hadn't heard the rude remark. He and Rutgers had already gone up to the front door. "Lady Charlotte's butler will pay you," I said stiffly, and followed them over to the door.

It opened. A gorilla was standing there, dressed in a butler's cutaway coat and trousers, and white gloves.

"Good Lord," I said.

"We are here to see Lady Charlotte Valladay," Touffét said, peering at him through his monocle.

The gorilla opened the door farther.

"I am Inspector Touffét and this is Mr. Rutgers."

"I think they understand sign language," I whispered. "Rutgers, do you know any?"

"Come please? Take bags?" the gorilla said, and I was so surprised I just stood there, gaping.

"Take bags, sir?" the gorilla said again.

"The taxi's six pounds," the taxi driver said, reaching past me with his hand outstretched. "And that doesn't include the tip."

"Pay moment," the gorilla said, and turned back to me. "Take bags, sir?"

I had recovered myself sufficiently to hand them to him, trying not to flinch away from those huge paws in their incongruous white gloves, and to murmur, "Thank you."

"This way, sir," the gorilla said, dropping to his gloved knuckles, and led us into an enormous entryway.

"Excuse moment," the gorilla said.

It really was too odd, hearing that refined, upper-class voice coming out of that enormous gray-black gorilla.

"Tell Lady Valladay you here." He started out, still on all fours.

"Good Lord, Touffét—" I had started to say, when a middle-aged woman in khaki and pearls bustled in.

"Oh, Inspector Touffét! I'm *so* glad you're here! Tanny, did you pay the taxi driver?"

"Yes, madam," the gorilla said.

"Good. Stand up straight. Inspector Touffét, I'd like you to meet D'Artagnan."

The gorilla straightened, extended a monstrous gloved hand, and Touffét shook it, albeit a bit gingerly.

"D'Artagnan was orphaned by poachers in Uganda when he was only two weeks old," she said.

"Rescued," D'Artagnan said, pointing at Lady Valladay with a white-gloved finger.

"I found him in Hong Kong in a cage the size of a shoebox," she said, looking fondly at him. "He's been here at the Institute twelve years."

"I thought gorillas couldn't speak," I said.

"He's had a laryngeal implant," she said. "When we tour the compound, you'll see our surgical unit."

"How'd he get the name D'Artagnan?" Rutgers asked.

"He chose it himself. I don't believe in picking names for primates as if they were pets. Our research here at the Institute has shown that primates are extremely intelligent. They are capable of high-level thinking, computation skills, and self-awareness. D'Artagnan is a conscious being, fully capable of making personal decisions. He's scored 95 on IQ tests. He named himself after one of the Three Musketeers. It's his favorite book."

"Good Lord, he can read, too?" I said.

She shook her head. "Only a few words. I read it aloud to him."

D'Artagnan nodded his huge head. "Queen," he said.

"Yes, he loves the part about the Three Musketeers coming to the queen's aid." She turned to Rutgers. "And you must be Colonel Bridlings, who chronicles all Inspector Touffét's cases."

"Mick Rutgers," he said, extending his sunburned hand, "of ABN."

She looked confused. "But the press invitations were for the twenty-fifth."

"I'm sure the invitation said the twenty-fourth," he said, fumbling for it in his jacket.

"That's what Ms. Fox said. I really must have Heidi start writing my invitations. Her penmanship is much neater than mine."

"I could come back tomorrow—" Rutgers said.

"No, I'm delighted you're here," she said, and seemed to genuinely mean it. She turned her warm smile on me. "Then *you* must be Colonel Bridlings."

"Yes. How do you do?"

"I'm *so* pleased to meet all of you. Come," she said, taking Touffét's arm, "I want to show you the compound, but first let me introduce you to everyone."

"You spoke of a murder you wished me to solve?" Touffét said.

"A mystery *only* you can solve," she said, smiling that lovely smile. She truly had a gift for making one feel warmly welcome.

I wished I could say the same of Marwaite Manor, but the spacious glass-and-chrome hall she led us into was as welcoming as a dentist's office. And it was cold! The icy rain outside the floor-to-ceiling windows seemed to be falling in the room itself. The only furniture in the room was several uncomfortable-looking chrome-and-canvas chairs and a small glass table with greenery and candles on it.

Two people were huddled in the center of the nearly empty hall, next to the glass table—a stout, balding man and a pretty young woman in a thin dress. The woman had her arms folded across her bosom, as if trying to keep warm, and the stout man's nose was red. A chimpanzee in a maid's apron, a white collar, and a frilly cap was offering them drinks on a tray.

They all looked up expectantly as we entered. Lady Valladay squeezed Touffét's arm. "I have someone I want you to meet, Inspector," she said, and led him over to the chimpanzee.

"Inspector Touffét, I'd like you to meet Heidi," she said. "She came from a medical research lab, and she's one of your most devoted fans."

Now that we were closer to the chimpanzee, I could see that what I had taken for a collar was actually a white bandage round the chimpanzee's shaved neck.

"She just had her laryngeal implant, so she can't speak yet," Lady Valladay said, "but she has the highest IQ of any primate we've ever had here at the Institute, and she's already reading at a primary school level. She's read *The Cat in the Hat* and all the Curious George books, haven't you, Heidi?" and the chimpanzee grinned widely and bobbed her head up and down. "But *your* books are her favorites, Inspector Touffét. She's constantly after me to read them to her, and sometimes she even tries to read them on her own."

Lady Valladay led Touffét over to the table, her arm linked in his. "Our primates have even outperformed A-level students on higher-level-thinking tests, but in spite of all the studies the Institute has done, in spite of the overwhelming evidence of primates' intelligence, people *persist* in thinking of them as animals instead of sentient creatures. They continue to put them in zoos, experiment on them, kill them for trophies. That's why it's so important that the Institute continue to exist."

"Continue to exist?" Touffét asked.

"I'm afraid we're sadly in need of funds," she said. "If we don't find additional donors soon, we'll be forced to close. We—"

"I beg your pardon," the stout man said. "I didn't mean to interrupt. I only wanted to tell you how much I admire your work."

"This is Sergeant Eustis, our local police detective. Perhaps you two can exchange information about your investigations."

"Oh, no," Sergeant Eustis said, fumbling at his tie, "I haven't had any interesting cases, compared to Mr. Touffét."

"What about—" she began, but the sergeant said, "I'd very much like to hear about the Sappina jewel robbery."

"A very satisfying case," Touffét said, and launched into an account of it.

I wandered over to where the pretty young woman stood by the table and introduced myself.

"Leda Fox," she said, and pointed to a press badge. "I'm a reporter with the *Online Times.* And I'm freezing." She leaned forward to warm her hands over one of the candles. "You'd think with all the billions Lord Alastair's got, he could afford to turn up the heat."

"Lord Alastair is a billionaire?"

"Yes. He made his fortune in AI patents."

"I was wondering how the Institute was financed," I said.

"Oh, no, the Institute doesn't get a penny. Lord Alastair never approved of primate research. It's all financed by donations. So, what's this mystery Inspector Touffét's supposed to solve?"

"I'm afraid I have no idea," I said, sipping my drink. "What was the media told?"

"The media?" she said blankly. "Oh. You mean what were we told? Not much. Just that we were all invited to be present at the solving of a mystery by Inspector Touffét. And we were sent a packet of information on primate intelligence." She frowned. "I wonder what the mystery is."

"Something to do with the Institute, perhaps?" I asked. "Lady Charlotte seemed anxious to show us the facilities."

"She dragged me all over them this morning," Leda said.

"You do not like primates?"

She shrugged. "Animals are all right, I suppose, but one tour is enough. She wants me to go again with all of you this afternoon, but there's no way I'm going out in *that*," she said, gesturing at the falling rain. "Tell her I have a headache."

Heidi shambled over with a tray full of silver goblets, one hand under the tray and the other dragging the floor.

"What is it?" I asked Leda, taking one of them.

"Wassail."

Heidi waddled over to Touffét and Sergeant Eustis.

"Poor Touffét," I said.

"Doesn't he like wassail?"

"He doesn't like Christmas."

"Do you think they're really as smart as Lady Charlotte says?" Leda said, watching Heidi offer the tray to the police detective. "She says Heidi can do long division. *I* can't do long division."

"Neither can I," I said, but she wasn't listening. She had turned to look at a tall man in his thirties who had just walked in.

"Who's that?" I asked.

"Lady Charlotte's brother, James," she said. "I met him this morning." She made a face.

"You didn't like him?"

She leaned toward me and whispered, "Drunk."

"Well, well, so this is the Great Detective," James said, walking over to Touffét.

Lady Charlotte looked vexed. "Inspector Touffét, my brother, James."

James ignored her. "Have you solved my sister's mystery yet? I heard you solve them"—he snapped his fingers next to Touffét's nose—"like *that!*"

Touffét stepped back. "Lady Charlotte has not yet informed me of the nature of the mystery."

"Oh, well, then maybe you can solve a mystery for me. Why is it my sister prefers monkeys to her own father and brother?"

"James," Lady Valladay said warningly.

"Heidi!" James said, and snapped his fingers at her. "Bring me a drink."

The chimpanzee hesitated, looking frightened, and then shambled over to him and offered the tray.

James grabbed a drink and turned back to Touffét. "It's a true mystery to me. Why would she rather spend her time with a bunch of dangerous, smelly, stupid—"

"James!" Lady Valladay snapped.

"Oh, that's right. They're not stupid. They can do trigonometry. They can read Shakespeare. Isn't that right, Heidi?" He tweaked her cap. "How much is two plus two, Heidi?"

Heidi looked beseechingly at Lady Charlotte.

"How do you spell 'imbecile,' Heidi?" James persisted.

"That's enough, James," Lady Charlotte said, putting her arm around the chimpanzee. "Heidi, go unpack Inspector Touffét's bags." She took the tray from her. "That's my good girl."

Lady Charlotte set the tray down. "Inspector, you and Colonel Bridlings must both be tired," she said, ignoring James, and he turned on his heel and walked out of the room. "You'll want to get settled in and have a chance to rest before we tour the compound. D'Artagnan will show you to your rooms, and we'll meet in, say, an hour in the entryway."

A door slammed, but she paid no attention. "I do so want you to see our facility." She led us to the door. "D'Artagnan, take them to their rooms."

"Yes, madam," he said. He started to drop to all fours, but then straightened.

"An hour, then," she said, smiling, and went down the corridor and into another room, shutting the door behind her.

D'Artagnan pushed the lift button.

"I don't care"—Lady Charlotte's voice drifted down the hall—"I won't have you ruining this. It's too important."

"It's my house," James's voice said.

"It's Father's house."

"It won't be forever," James said, "and when I inherit it, there won't be any monkeys in it. I'm shipping them back to the jungle the day Father dies."

🎄

So this is your idea of a jolly Christmas?" I asked Touffét, waiting for him to put on his Inverness cape. I had spent the promised half hour attempting to find a telephone. I'd left in such a rush, I hadn't had time to telephone my sister to tell her I couldn't come. I attempted to ask Heidi, who was unpacking my things, but couldn't make her understand, so I went downstairs in search of one myself.

There was one in the study, a small frigid room across from the solarium. My sister was disappointed but optimistic.

"Perhaps your Inspector Touffét will solve the mystery so quickly you can come tonight, or tomorrow. We could wait dinner."

"Better not," I said. "We haven't even been told what the mystery is yet."

I hung up and started back upstairs. As I came into the entryway, I caught a glimpse of Leda, in a hooded raincoat, going out the front door. *She must have changed her mind about touring the compound,* I thought, and wondered if I'd taken so long the others had left without me, but Touffét was in his room, putting on a wool sweater and wrapping a knitted scarf around his neck.

"At least at my sister's house it's warm," I said, "and no one ever threatens to turn anyone else out."

"Exactly," Touffét said. "And there are no mysteries." He put on his cape. "Here already there are several."

"Lady Charlotte's told you why she invited us here?"

He shook his head. "But certain things have struck me. What about you, Bridlings? Have you noticed nothing?"

I thought about it. "I've noticed the brother's a lout. And that Ms. Fox is very pretty."

"Pretty. Alas, Bridlings, once again you see only the facade. You do not look at what lies behind. Do you not think it strange that Sergeant Eustis does not wish me to know of his interesting cases? All detectives wish to brag of their exploits."

Well, that's certainly true, I thought.

"And there is this," he said, handing me Lady Charlotte's letter. "Odd, is it not?"

I read it through. "I don't see anything odd about it. She invites us to come and lists the train times."

"Indeed. Look at the second-to-last train time."

"The 5:48," I said.

"Are you certain?"

"Yes. It says—"

"The five and the four are quite distinct, are they not? And yet both Mr. Rutgers and Ms. Fox say they mistook Lady Charlotte's five for a four and thus came a day early," he said, obviously in his element. "A mystery, yes? Come, we are late."

We went down to the entryway. Lady Charlotte and Mick Rutgers were already there, bundled in coats and scarves. She was telling him about the Institute. "Organizations and ethologists have tried for years to protect primate habitats and regulate the treatment of primates in captivity, but conditions have only gotten worse, and will continue to get worse, so long as people continue to think of them as animals."

She turned to greet us. "Oh, Inspector, Colonel, we're just waiting for D'Artagnan. He's going to drive us down to the compound. I was just telling Mr. Rutgers about the Institute. Some people do not approve of our implanting larynxes and dressing primates in clothing, but the only chance they have of survival is for people to accept them. And to be accepted, unfortunately, they must stand upright, they must have employable skills. They're necessary to make people realize primates are sentient creatures, that they can think and reason and feel as we do. Did you know that humans and pygmy chimpanzees share ninety-nine percent of their genes? Ninety-nine percent. Our genes are their genes. And yet when the University of Oklahoma discontinued their language research project, the apes who had been taught to sign were used in AIDS experiments. Do you remember Lucy?"

"The chimpanzee who was raised as a human and taught to sign?" I asked.

"She was shipped back to Gambia, where she was murdered by poachers." Tears came to Lady Charlotte's eyes. "They cut off her head and hands for trophies. Lucy, who knew three hundred words! Oh, D'Artagnan, there you are," she said.

I turned. D'Artagnan was standing there in the corridor. He was still in his cutaway coat and trousers, but not his white gloves. I wondered how long he'd been there.

"Are you ready to drive us to the compound, Tanny?" Lady Charlotte asked.

"Lord Alastair. Wish meet Inspector," he said in that ridiculously small voice.

"Oh, dear," Lady Charlotte said, as if she'd just heard bad news. She bit her lip, and then, as if she'd realized her response needed some sort of explanation, said, "I'd hoped your arrival hadn't wakened him. My father has so much difficulty sleeping. I'm afraid we'll have to wait until tomorrow morning to tour the compound."

She turned to D'Artagnan. "Tell Nurse Parchtry we'll be up directly," she said, and as he started to leave, "Where are your gloves, Tanny?"

He promptly put his hairy black paws behind his back and hung his head. "Took off. Dishes. Now can't find."

"Well, go and get another pair out of the pantry." She took a bunch of keys out of her pocket and handed them to him.

"D'Artagnan sorry," he said, looking ashamed.

"I'm not angry," she said, putting her arms around his vast back. "You know I love you."

"Love *you*," he said, and flung his huge arms around her.

I looked at Touffét, alarmed after what James had said, but D'Artagnan had already released her and was asking, "Gloves first? Tell first?"

"Tell Nurse Parchtry first, and then go and get a new pair of gloves." She patted his arm.

He nodded and lumbered off, Lady Charlotte smiling affectionately after him. "He's such a dear," she said, and then continued briskly, "Inspector Touffét, if you don't mind, my father's an invalid and gets lonely."

"But of course I should be happy to meet him," he said.

"Can I meet him, too?" Rutgers said. "I've heard so much about his AI work."

"Of course," Lady Valladay said, but she sounded reluctant. "We'll all go up just for a little while. My father tires easily."

She pressed the button for the lift. We stepped inside. "My father's rooms are on the fourth floor," she said, pressing another button. "It used to be the nursery." The lift shot up. "He's been ill for several years."

The lift opened, and Lady Charlotte led the way to a door. "Oh, dear," she said. "I gave my keys to D'Artagnan. Nurse Parchtry will have to let us in."

She knocked. "My father has a wonderful nurse. Marvelously efficient. She's been with us for nearly a year."

The door started to open. I looked curiously at it, wondering if Nurse Parchtry would turn out to be an orangutan in a nurse's cap and stethoscope. But the person who opened the door was a thin, disheveled-looking woman in white trousers and a white smock.

"May we come in, Nurse Parchtry?" Lady Charlotte asked, and the woman nodded and stepped back to let us through into a small room with plastic chairs and a Formica counter along one side.

"You'd best stay here in the anteroom, though," the woman said. "Tapioca for lunch."

If this was Nurse Parchtry, she looked anything but efficient. One pocket of her smock was torn and hanging down, and her fine, gray-brown hair had come out of its bun on one side. There was a huge blob of something yellowish-gray on one trouser leg—the tapioca?

No, the tapioca was splattered across the glass-and-chicken-wire partition that separated the room we were in from the larger one beyond, along with soft brown smears of something. I hoped they weren't what they looked like.

I wondered if I had somehow misunderstood, and Lady Charlotte had taken us to see the primate compound after all instead. The room behind the partition looked almost like a cage, with toys and a large rubber tire in the middle of the floor. No, there was a single bed against the far wall and a rocking chair beside it.

"He heard the taxi," Nurse Parchtry was saying. "I've told that cabbie to drive quietly. I tried to tell him it was just a parcel arriving for Christmas, but he knew it was guests. He always knows, and then there's just no dealing with him till he sees them."

Lady Charlotte nodded sympathetically. "Nurse Parchtry, this is Inspector Touffét."

"I'm *so* pleased to meet you," Nurse Parchtry said, trying to push the straggle of gray-brown hair behind her ear. "I am *such* a fan of your detecting. I adored *The Case of the Clever Cook*. I've always wished I could see you solve one of your murders." She turned to me. "Does he really solve them as quickly as you say, Colonel Bridlings?"

Nurse Parchtry turned to Lady Charlotte. "I was wondering—it *is* Christmas Eve, and I am such a fan of Inspector Touffét's—if I might eat downstairs tonight instead of having a tray."

Lady Charlotte glanced uncertainly at the partition. "I don't know. . . ."

"Lord Alastair always goes to sleep after he's had his cocoa," Nurse Parchtry said, gesturing toward the tray, "and I did so want to hear Inspector Touffét recount some of his celebrated cases. And Lord Alastair's been very good today."

There was a splat, and I looked over at the partition. A large blob of greenish mush was trickling down the center of the glass, and behind it, holding the plastic bowl it had come out of, was Lord Alastair.

If I had been shocked by the sight of a talking gorilla, I was completely overwhelmed by the sight of Lord Alastair, computer genius and billionaire, dressed in wrinkled pajamas, his white hair matted with the greenish stuff he'd just thrown. He was barefoot, and his teeth were bared in a cunning grin.

"Good Lord," I said, and next to me, Rutgers murmured disbelievingly, "Al?"

Lord Alastair stepped back, hunching his shoulders, and I wondered if we had frightened him, but he was still grinning. He reared back and spat at us.

"Oh, *Father*," Lady Charlotte said, and he grinned evilly at her and began smearing the spittle into the tapioca and the brown streaks, as if he were fingerpainting.

"Oh, dear," Nurse Parchtry said, "and you were so good this morning." She pulled a bunch of keys out of her pocket, hastily unlocked a door next to the partition, and disappeared. She reappeared inside a moment later with a wet towel and began wiping Lord Alastair's hands.

I watched, horrified, afraid he was going to spit on her next, but he only struggled to free his hands, slapping weakly at her like a naughty child and shouting a string of garbled obscenities.

Beside me, Rutgers seemed hypnotized. "How long has he been like this?"

"It's gotten gradually worse," Lady Charlotte said. "Ten years."

Nurse Parchtry had Lord Alastair's hands clean and was combing his hair. "You must look nice for your guests," she said, her voice faint but clear through the glass. "Inspector Touffét's here, the famous detective."

She brought him over to the partition, holding his left wrist in a firm grasp. "Lord Alastair, I'd like you to meet Inspector Touffét."

Touffét stepped up to the glass and bowed. "I'm pleased to meet you."

"Inspector Touffét's come to solve a mystery for us, Father," Lady Charlotte said.

"Yes," Touffét said, "I am interested to know more of this mystery."

There was a knock at the door behind us. "Shall I?" I asked Lady Charlotte.

"Please," she said, and I unlocked and opened it. It was Heidi, bearing a tray with a toddler's lidded cup and a plate of graham biscuits on it.

I stepped back so she could enter, and as soon as she did, Lord Alastair exploded. His left arm came up sharply, clipping Nurse Parchtry on the chin, and she reeled back, cradling her jaw. He began pounding on the glass with both hands and hooting wildly. Heidi watched him, clutching the tray, her eyes wide with fright.

"Oh, dear," Lady Charlotte said. "Heidi, set the tray down on the counter."

Heidi did, her eyes still on Lord Alastair, then bobbed a curtsey and ran awkwardly out on all fours. Lord Alastair continued pounding for a moment and then walked over to the plastic bowl, sat down on the floor, and began licking the inside of the bowl.

Rutgers shook his head sadly. "Ten years," he murmured.

Nurse Parchtry disappeared and then reappeared at the door, her jaw and cheek scarlet.

"He doesn't like Heidi," she said unnecessarily. "Or D'Artagnan." She put her hand wincingly up to her cheek. "He threw the rocking chair the last time D'Artagnan brought in his lunch."

"I think you'd best put some ice on that," Lady Charlotte said. "And with Father so upset, I think perhaps you'd better eat up here tonight."

"Oh, no!" Nurse Parchtry said desperately. "He'll quiet down now. He always does after—"

There was a banging on the door, and Touffét moved to open it. James burst in, clutching his thumb. "You will not believe what that monster just did!"

I wheeled and looked at the partition, thinking Lord Alastair must have gotten out somehow, but he was still sitting in the middle of the floor. He'd put the bowl on his head.

"He grabbed my hand and tried to tear it off. Look!" He thrust it at Lady Charlotte. "I think it's broken!"

I couldn't see any telltale redness like that on Nurse Parchtry's jaw.

"The brute tried to kill me!" he said.

"What brute?" Lady Charlotte asked.

"*What brute?* That *ape* of yours! I was walking down the corridor, and he suddenly reached out and grabbed me."

He turned to us. "I've tried to tell my sister her apes are dangerous, but she won't listen!"

"I thought that gorillas had very gentle natures," Rutgers said.

"That's what the so-called scientists at my sister's Institute say, that they're all harmless as kittens, that they wouldn't hurt a fly! Well, what about this?" he said, shaking his hand at us again. "When we're all murdered in our beds some morning, don't say I didn't warn you!"

He stormed out, but his ragings had roused Lord Alastair, who was pounding on the glass again.

"He'll go to sleep as soon as he's had his cocoa," Nurse Parchtry said pleadingly. "He always does, and today he didn't have a nap. And I'd have the monitor with me. I'd be able to hear him if he woke up. And it's Christmas Eve!"

"All right," Lady Charlotte said, relenting. "But if he wakes up, you'll have to come straight back up here."

"I will, I promise," she said, as giddily as if she were Cinderella promising to leave the ball by midnight. "Oh, this will be such fun!"

"It's hardly *my* idea of fun," I told Touffét as we were going down for dinner. "I'd much rather be at my sister's. And I'll wager Lady Charlotte would rather be, too. It's obvious why she prefers apes, with a father and a brother like that."

"The father is a millionaire," Touffét said thoughtfully. "Is that not so?"

"Billionaire," I said.

"Ah. I wonder who is it that inherits his estate when he dies? I wonder also what makes Nurse Parchtry stay with such a disagreeable patient?" He rubbed his hands, obviously enjoying himself. "So many mysteries. And perhaps there will be more at dinner."

There were, the first one being whether Lady Charlotte was even aware it was Christmas. There were no decorations on the table, no holly or pine garlands decking the dining room, and no heat. Leda, who had changed into a fetching little strapless dress, was shivering with cold.

And the dinner was utterly ordinary, no boar's head, no goose, no turkey, only some underseasoned cod and some overdone beef, all served by D'Artagnan, in new gloves, and Heidi. Hardly a festive holiday feast.

Lady Charlotte didn't appear to notice. She was well launched on the subject of primate intelligence, apparently grateful that her brother, James, hadn't come down to dinner. Nurse Parchtry wasn't there, either. Apparently her patient hadn't gone off to sleep as easily as she'd hoped.

"One of the prejudices we're working to overcome is that primate behavior is instinctive," Lady Charlotte said. "We've done research that demonstrates conclusively their behavior is intentional. Primates are capable of conscious thought, of planning, and learning from experience, and of having insights."

Just after the soup course (tinned), Nurse Parchtry hurried in and sat down between Leda and me. She had changed out of her uniform into a gray chiffon thing with floating draperies, and she was all smiles.

"He's finally asleep," she said breathlessly, setting a white plastic box on the table. A series of wheezes and gasping noises came from it. "It's a baby monitor. So I can hear Lord Alastair if he wakes up."

How nice, I thought. *Midway through dinner we shall be treated to a stream of animal screams and obscenities.*

"What is it that Lord Alastair suffers from?" I asked.

"Dementia," she said, "and hatefulness, neither one of which is fatal, unfortunately. He could live for years. Thank you, Heidi," she said, as the chimpanzee set a plate of fish in front of her. "Isn't this exciting, Heidi, having Inspector Touffét here?"

Heidi nodded.

"Heidi and I are both mystery fans. We've been reading *The Case of the Crushed Skull,* haven't we?"

Heidi nodded again and signed something to Nurse Parchtry.

"She says she thinks the vicar did it," she said. She signed rapidly to Heidi. "I think it was the ex-wife. Which of us is right, Colonel Bridlings?"

Neither, as a matter of fact, though I had to give Heidi credit. *I* had thought it was the vicar, too. "I don't want to spoil the ending," I said, and Heidi bobbed her head in approval.

"He was always a dreadful man," Nurse Parchtry said, returning to the topic of Lord Alastair. "And, unfortunately, his son's just like him." She lowered her voice to a whisper. "Which is why he left everything to him in his will, I suppose. A pity. He'll only gamble it away."

"He gambles?" I said.

"He's horribly in debt," she whispered. "I heard him on the phone only this morning, pleading with his tout. You see, Lord Alastair arranged his money so it can't be touched until his death, which I suppose is a good thing. Otherwise there'd be nothing left." She shook her head. "It's Lady Charlotte I feel sorry for."

She leaned closer, her draperies drifting across my arm. "Did you know Lord Alastair stopped her from marrying her true love? She fell in love with one of his AI scientists, Phillip Davidson—Phillip was the one who got her interested in primate intelligence—and when Lord Alastair found out, he trumped up charges of industrial espionage against him, ruined his reputation, forced him to emigrate. Lady Charlotte never married."

Touffét would be interested in knowing that, I thought. I glanced at him, but he was watching Mick Rutgers, who was listening to Lady Charlotte talk of her apes' accomplishments.

"D'Artagnan has learned eight hundred words, and over fifty sentences," she said. "We work for two hours a day on vocabulary." She smiled at D'Artagnan, who was removing the fish course. "And for an hour on serving skills."

Heidi began serving the roast beef. The snores and wheezes from the baby monitor subsided to a heavy, even breathing.

"Heidi and I work on her reading for two hours a day, and she reads on her own for another hour. Heidi," Lady Charlotte said, stopping her as she set a plate of roast beef down in front of Leda. "Tell Inspector Touffét what your favorite case is."

Heidi signed rapidly, grinning widely.

"*The Case of the Cat's Paw,*" Lady Charlotte translated.

Touffét looked pleased. "Ah, yes, a most satisfying case," he said, and launched into an account of it.

"What's a cat's paw?" Leda whispered to me. "It's not like a rabbit's foot, is it?"

"No," I said. "It's when someone uses another person for their own ends. It comes from an old tale about a monkey who used a cat's paw to pull chestnuts out of the fire."

"That's *cruel,*" Nurse Parchtry said.

"No crueler than keeping apes captive and dressing them up in human clothes," Leda hissed.

"You don't approve of Lady Charlotte's work?" Nurse Parchtry said, shocked.

"N-no, of course I didn't mean that," Leda said, looking flustered. She took a forkful of roast beef and then laid it back down on her plate.

"Lady Charlotte has only the primates' best interests at heart in all her work," Nurse Parchtry said firmly. "She's utterly devoted to them, and they'd do anything for her. She saved them, you know, from terrible fates. Heidi was being *experimented* on."

Lady Charlotte had apparently heard the last part of that. "Experiments?" she said, interrupting Touffét in the middle of his case. "Primates are still being experimented on, in spite of our having proved they're conscious creatures and can feel pain just as we do. Our research has shown that they can acquire knowledge, solve complex problems, use tools, and manipulate language. Everything that humans can do."

"Not quite," Sergeant Eustis said. "They can't commit crimes or tell lies. Or cheat at cards."

"As a matter of fact," Mick Rutgers said, "primates can."

"Cheat at cards?" Sergeant Eustis said. "Don't tell me D'Artagnan plays poker, too?"

Everyone laughed.

"Various studies have shown that apes are capable of deception," Rutgers said. "Apes in the wild frequently hide food and then retrieve it when the rest of the troop is asleep, and signing apes who have done something naughty will lie when asked whether they did it. Several times Lucy hid a key in her mouth and waited until her owners were gone, and then let herself out. Their ability to lie and deceive is proof of their capability for higher forms of thinking, since it involves determining what another creature thinks and how it can be fooled."

Lady Charlotte was looking curiously at Rutgers. "You seem to know a great deal about primates, for a reporter," she said.

"It was in the informational packet you sent," he said.

"And you're quite right, they are capable of deception," she said. "But they are also capable of affection, fear, grief, gentleness, and devotion. They are far better creatures than we are."

"Is that why they attack people for no reason?" James said, coming in and sitting down next to his sister. He snapped his fingers, and Heidi hurried to bring him a plate of roast beef, looking frightened. "Is that why the University of Oklahoma had to shut down their research program after one of their apes bit the finger off a visiting surgeon? Because they're better creatures?"

He snatched the plate away from Heidi. "Has my sister told you about Lucy yet? Poor Lucy, who got sent back to the jungle to be killed by poachers? Did she tell you why Lucy got sent back? Because she attacked her owner." He smiled maliciously at Heidi. "That could happen to you, too, you know. And your friend D'Artagnan."

"I'd attack my owner, too, if I were an intelligent creature being treated like a slave," Mick Rutgers said, and Lady Charlotte gave him a grateful look, and then frowned, as if she were trying to place something.

🌲

I'd hoped there would at least be a plum pudding in honor of Christmas, but there was only vanilla custard, which reminded me unpleasantly of Lord Alastair's tapioca, but at least it meant an end to the meal. When Lady Charlotte said, "Shall we adjourn to the solarium?" I practically leaped out of my chair.

"Not yet," Touffét said. "Madam, you still have not informed me of the mystery you wished me to solve."

"All in good time," she said. "We must play a game first. No Christmas Eve is complete without games. Who wants to play Hunt the Slipper?"

"*I* do," Nurse Parchtry piped up, and then looked nervous, as if she should not have called attention to herself.

"I have no intention of hunting all over the house for someone's smelly shoe," James said, and Touffét shot him an approving glance.

"How about Musical Chairs?"

"No. That's as bad as Hunt the Slipper," James said. "*I* think we should play Animal, Vegetable, or Mineral."

"That's because you're so good at it," Lady Charlotte said, but some of the bitterness seemed to have gone out of both their voices, perhaps because it was, after all, Christmas Eve.

Lady Charlotte led the way to the library. "I'm so glad Lord Alastair is still asleep," Nurse Parchtry said to me as we followed Lady Charlotte. She held the monitor up close to my ear. I could barely hear his faint, even breathing. "He won't wake up for hours," she said happily. "I *love* Christmas games."

"You should have come with me to my sister's, Touffét," I whispered to him. "You would only have had to play charades."

"Who shall be first?" Lady Charlotte said after we'd settled ourselves in the canvas chairs. "Sergeant Eustis? You must go and stand out in the corridor while we decide on an object."

Sergeant Eustis obligingly went out of the room and shut the door behind him.

"All right, what shall it be?" Lady Charlotte said brightly.

"Vegetable," Leda said.

"A Christmas tree," Nurse Parchtry said eagerly.

"He'd guess that in a minute," James said. "A literary character. It always takes them at least a dozen questions to determine it's fictional."

"Father Christmas!" Nurse Parchtry said.

Everyone ignored her.

"What do you think it should be, Inspector Touffét?" Lady Charlotte asked.

"The mystery which you asked me here to solve," Touffét said.

"No, that's too complicated," Lady Charlotte said. "I've got it! Fingerprints! It's perfect for a police officer."

A spirited discussion ensued over whether fingerprints were animal, vegetable, or mineral, and, unable to decide, they chose Goldilocks instead.

"She's a fictional character, *and* she committed a crime."

Sergeant Eustis was called in and began guessing. As predicted, he used thirteen of his twenty questions to determine that it was a fictional character, and then astonished everyone by guessing "Goldilocks" immediately.

"How *did* you guess?" Leda asked.

"It's always Goldilocks," he said. "Because I'm a police detective. Breaking and entering, you know."

One by one, everyone except Touffét took their turn at standing in the corridor and attempting to guess—a plum pudding (Nurse Parchtry's suggestion), the slipper in Hunt the Slipper, a map of Borneo, and a pair of embroidery scissors.

When it was James's turn, he demanded to be allowed to take a chair with him out into the corridor. "I don't intend to stand there forever while you all try to pick something that will fool me. I must warn you, I have never failed to guess the answer."

"He's quite right," Lady Charlotte said, smiling. "Last Christmas he guessed it in four."

"Mistletoe," Nurse Parchtry said.

"It's got to be a fictional character," Rutgers said. "He admitted himself it's the hardest to guess."

"No, his is always a fictional character. It needs to be someone real. And someone obscure. Anastasia!"

"I would hardly call Anastasia obscure," I said.

"No, but if he asks 'Is the person living?' we can say we don't know, and he'll think it's a fictional character."

"What if he's already asked if it's a fictional character and we've said no?"

"But it was a fictional character," Leda said. "I saw the Disney film when I was little."

"And when he asks if it's animal, vegetable, or mineral," Sergeant Eustis said. "We can say mineral. Because her body was burned to ashes."

"We don't know that," Lady Charlotte said. "Her bones have never been found."

It was a good thing James had insisted on the chair. It took us nearly fifteen minutes to decide, during which time Touffét looked increasingly as if he were going to explode.

"But, if he knows we know he always guesses fictional characters," Sergeant Eustis said, "then he'll think we won't choose one, so we should."

"King Kong," Nurse Parchtry said.

There was an embarrassed silence.

"I think perhaps we should avoid any references to primates," Lady Charlotte said finally.

We finally decided on R2D2, who was both mineral and animal (the actor inside him) and fictional and real (the actual tin can), and had the advantage of being from an old movie, which Lady Charlotte said her brother never watched.

James guessed it in four questions.

"All right," Lady Charlotte said, looking round the room. "Who hasn't gone yet? Mr. Rutgers?"

"I was a pair of embroidery scissors, remember?"

"Oh, yes. Mr. Touffét, you're the only one left. Come along. I'm sure you'll solve it even more quickly than my brother."

"Madam," Touffét said, and his voice was deadly quiet. "I did not come to Marwaite Manor to play at games. I came in response to your request to solve a mystery. I wish to know what it is."

Either Lady Charlotte was tired of thinking up things, or she sensed the deadliness in Touffét's voice.

"You're quite right," she said. "It is time. What Inspector Touffét said is true. I asked him here to solve a mystery, a mystery so baffling only the greatest detective in the world could solve it."

She stood up, as if to make a speech. "The research my Institute has done has proved that primates are capable of higher-thinking skills and complex planning, that they can think and understand and speak and even write."

"Madam," Touffét said, half rising.

She waved him back to sitting. "The mystery that I wish Inspector Touffét to solve is this: Since it has been proved that primates have thoughts and ideas equivalent to those of humans, that they *are* by every standard human, why are they not treated as human? Why do they not have legal standing in the courts? Why are they not allowed to vote and own property? Why have they not been given their civil rights? Inspector Touffét, only you can solve this mystery. Only you can give us the answer! Why are apes not given equal standing with humans?"

"You've been taken in, Touffét," I said, I must admit with some pleasure. "Lady Charlotte only invited you here as a publicity stunt. She wanted you to be a pitchman for her Institute." I laughed. "This time it's you who's the cat's paw. She's using you to get chimpanzees the vote."

"A cat's paw," he said, offended. "I do not allow myself to be used as a cat's paw." He pulled his bag off the top of the bureau. "What time is the next train to your sister's?"

"You're leaving?" I said.

"*We* are leaving," he said. "Telephone your sister and tell her we will arrive tonight. Inspector Touffét does not allow himself to be used by anyone."

Well, at any rate my sister would be happy, I thought, going downstairs to telephone her. I pulled the train schedule out of my pocket. If we were able to catch the 9:30 train, we could be there before midnight. I wondered whether Lady Charlotte would arrange for us to be driven to the station, and whether the driver would be D'Artagnan. I decided under the circumstances I'd better phone for a taxi as well. D'Artagnan was devoted to her. He might not like the idea of our leaving.

I started to open the door of the study and then stopped at the sound of a woman's voice. "No, it's going fine," she said. "You should have seen me. I was great. I even ate roast beef." There was a pause. "Tomorrow, while they're touring the compound. Listen, I've gotta go."

I backed hastily away, not wishing to be caught eavesdropping, and into the solarium. For a moment I thought there were two people standing by the window, and then I realized it was Heidi and D'Artagnan. Heidi was signing animatedly to the gorilla, and he was nodding.

They stopped as soon as they saw me, and D'Artagnan started toward me. "Help you, sir?"

"I'm looking for a telephone," I said, and he led me out into the corridor and over to the study.

I phoned my sister. "Oh, good," she said. "I'll meet you at the station. Have you had dinner?"

"Only a bite."

"I'll bring you a sandwich."

When I got back upstairs, Touffét was already waiting by the lift with our bags. "Have you telephoned for a taxi?" he asked, pushing the lift button.

"Yes," I'd started to say, when the air was split by a shrill, terrified scream from somewhere above us.

"Good Lord, Touffét!" I said. "It sounds like someone's being murdered."

"No doubt Lady Charlotte has discovered I am leaving," he said dryly, and pushed the button again.

Rutgers came tumbling out of his room, and Leda's blond head appeared. "What was that? It sounded like an animal being tortured."

"I think we should take the stairs," I said, but before I could turn, the lift opened, and Nurse Parchtry fell into my arms.

"It's Lord Alastair!" she sobbed. "He's dead!"

"Dead?" Touffét said.

"Yes!" she said. "You must come!" She stepped back into the lift. "I think he's been murdered!"

We followed her into the lift. "Murdered?" Mick Rutgers said from down the hall, but the door was already shutting.

"See if Sergeant Eustis has gone," Touffét called through the closing door. "Now," he said to Nurse Parchtry as the lift started. "Tell me exactly what happened. Everything. After the games did you return to the nursery?"

"Yes. No, I went to my room to finish wrapping my Christmas presents," she said guiltily. "I had the baby monitor with me."

"And you heard nothing?" Touffét asked.

"No. I thought he was sleeping. He wasn't making any noise at all." She started to sob again. "I didn't know the monitor was broken."

The lift doors parted, and we stepped out. The door to the anteroom stood ajar. "Was this door open when you arrived?"

"Yes," she said, leading the way into the anteroom. "And this one, too."

She pointed at the door to the nursery. "I thought he'd gotten out. But then I saw . . . him. . . ." She buried her head in my jacket.

"Come, madam," Touffét said sternly. "You must pull yourself together. You said you had always wished to see me solve a mystery. Now you shall, but you must help me."

"You're right, I did. I will," she said, but when we went into the nursery, she hung back reluctantly and then grabbed on to my arm for support.

The place was a shambles. Lord Alastair's bed had been overturned and the bedclothes dragged off it. The pillows had been torn up, the stuffing flung in handfuls about the room. The rocking chair, bowls, toys, tire—all looked as if they had been thrown about the room in a violent rage. Lord Alastair lay on his back in the middle of the floor, half on a rumpled blanket, his face swollen and purple.

"Did you touch anything?" Touffét asked, looking around the room.

"No," Nurse Parchtry said. "I knew from your cases not to." She clapped her hand to her mouth. "I did touch him. I took his pulse and listened to his heart. I thought perhaps he wasn't dead."

He looked dead to me. His face was a horrible purplish-blue color, his tongue pushing out of his mouth, his eyes bulging, his neck bruised. And she was a nurse. She should have known at a glance there was no hope of resuscitation.

"Did you touch anything else?" Touffét said, squatting down and holding out his monocle to look closely at Lord Alastair's neck.

"No," she said. "I screamed, and then I ran to find you."

"Where did you scream?"

"Where?" she said blankly. "Right here. By the body."

He stood up and looked at the glass partition and then walked over to the wall. The baby monitor lay against it, its back off and the front of the case broken in two pieces.

"That's why there was no sound from the monitor," I said. "That means he could have been killed anytime after dinner."

"And no one has an alibi," Nurse Parchtry said. "We were all out in the corridor by ourselves for several minutes."

Touffét had picked up the baby monitor and was examining the switch. "Should you be doing that?" I asked. "Won't it smudge the fingerprints?"

"There are no fingerprints," he said, putting the monitor back down, "and none on the neck, either."

"I warned you!" James said, appearing in the doorway. "I told you that ape was dangerous, and now he's killed my father!" He strode over to the body.

"I need to secure this crime scene," Sergeant Eustis said, coming into the room, unreeling yards and yards of yellow "Do Not Cross" tape. "I'll have to ask all of you to leave. *Don't* touch anything," he said sharply to James, who was putting his hand to his father's neck. "This is a murder investigation. I'll want to question everyone downstairs."

"Murder investigation!" James said. "There's no need for any investigation! I'll tell you who murdered my father. It was that ape!"

"The evidence will tell us who killed him," Sergeant Eustis said, walking back over to the body. "Inspector Touffét, come look at this. It's a hair."

He pointed to a long, coarse black hair lying on Lord Alastair's pajama'd chest.

"There! Look at that!" James said. "There's your evidence!"

Sergeant Eustis took out an evidence bag and a pair of tweezers and carefully placed the hair in the bag. While all this was going on, Touffét had walked over to the far wall and was looking at the lidded cup, which had apparently hit the wall and bounced. Cocoa was splattered across the wall in a long arc. Touffét picked up the cup, pried off the lid, sniffed at the contents, and then dipped a finger in and licked it off.

"You mustn't touch that!" Sergeant Eustis said, racing over, trailing long loops of yellow. "The fingerprints!"

"You will not find any fingerprints," Touffét said. "The murderer wore gloves."

"You see!" James shouted. "Even the Great Detective knows D'Artagnan did it. Why aren't you out capturing him? He's liable to kill someone else!"

Touffét ignored him. He handed Sergeant Eustis the cup. "Have the residue analyzed. I think it will yield interesting results."

Sergeant Eustis put the cup into an evidence bag and handed it to the young constable who'd just arrived and was gaping at Lord Alastair. "Have the residue analyzed," Sergeant Eustis said, "and take all these people downstairs. I will want to question everyone in the house."

"Question!" James raged. "This is a waste of time. It's obvious what happened here. I warned you!"

"Yes," Touffét said, looking curiously at James. "You did."

※

I was surprised that Touffét didn't object to being herded out of the nursery and into the lift by the constable, along with everyone else, but he only said, "Has Lady Charlotte been told?"

"I'll tell her," Mick Rutgers volunteered, and Touffét gazed at him for a long moment, as if his mind were elsewhere, and then nodded. He continued to look at Rutgers as he went down the corridor, and then turned to me. "Who do you think committed the murder, Bridlings?"

"It seems perfectly straightforward," I said. "James said the apes were dangerous, and, unfortunately, it appears he was right."

"Appears, yes. That is because you see only the surface."

"Well, what do *you* see?" I demanded. "The old man's been strangled, furniture's been smashed, there's a gorilla hair on the body."

"Exactly. It is like a scene out of a mystery novel. I have something I wish you to do," he said abruptly. "I wish you to find Leda Fox and tell her Sergeant Eustis wishes to speak to her."

"But he didn't say he—"

"He said he wished to question everyone."

"You don't think Leda had anything to do with this?" I said. "She can't have. She's not strong enough. Lord Alastair was strangled. There was a terrific struggle."

"So it would appear," he said. He motioned me out of the room.

I went up to Leda's room and was surprised to find her packing. "I'm not staying in the same house with a killer gorilla," she said. "A *cold* house with a killer gorilla."

"No one's allowed to leave," I said. "Sergeant Eustis wants to question you."

I was surprised at her reaction. She went completely white. "Question me?" she stammered. "What about?"

"Who saw what, where we all were at the time of the murder, and that sort of thing, I suppose," I said, trying to reassure her.

"But I thought they knew who did it," she said. "I thought D'Artagnan did it."

"Knowing who did it and proving it are two different things," I said. "I'm certain it's just routine."

She started up to the nursery, and I went back to the study to find Touffét. He wasn't there, nor was he in his room. Perhaps he'd gone back up to the nursery, too. I went out to the lift, and it opened, revealing Lady Charlotte. She looked pale and drawn. "Oh, Colonel Bridlings," she said, "where is Inspector Touffét?"

"I'm afraid I don't—"

"I am here, madam," Touffét said, and I turned and looked at him in surprise, wondering where he'd come from.

"Oh, Inspector," she said, clutching at his hands. "I know I brought you here under false pretenses, but now you must solve this murder. D'Artagnan could not possibly have killed my father, but my brother is determined to—" She broke down.

"Madam, compose yourself," Touffét said. "I must ask you two questions. First, are any of your household keys missing?"

"I don't know," she said, pulling the bunch of keys out of her pocket and examining them. "The key to the nursery," she said suddenly. "But the keys have been with me all day. No, I didn't have them when we went up to see my father, and Nurse Parchtry had to let us in. Let's see, I had them this morning, and then I gave them to D'Artagnan because he'd misplaced his gloves—" She stopped, as if suddenly aware of what she'd said. "Oh, but you don't think he—"

"My second question is this," Touffét said. "When your father had difficult days, could you hear him on the lower floors of the house?"

"Sometimes," she said. "If only we'd heard him tonight. Poor old . . ." She clutched tearfully at Touffét's sleeve. "Please say you will stay and solve the murder."

"I have already solved it," he said. "I request that you ask everyone to come into the parlor, including Sergeant Eustis, and give them a glass of sherry. Bridlings and I will join you shortly."

As soon as she was gone, Touffét turned to me. "What time is the last train to Sussex?"

"11:14," I said.

"Excellent," he said, consulting his pocket watch. "More than enough time. You shall be at your sister's in time to burn your fingers on the raisins."

"We don't play Snapdragon," I said. "We play charades. And how can you have solved the crime so quickly? Sergeant Eustis's men haven't even had time to gather evidence, let alone run forensics tests."

He waved his hand dismissively. "Forensics, evidence, they tell us only how the murder was done, not why."

They also frequently tell us *who,* I would have said, if Touffét had given me the opportunity, but he was still expounding.

"'Why' is the only question that matters," he said, "for if we know the 'why,' we know both *who* did the murder and *how* it was done. Go and tell your sister we will be on the train without fail."

I went downstairs and telephoned my sister again. "Oh, good," she said, "we're going to play Dumb Crambo this year!"

As I hung up, Touffét said, "Bridlings!"

I turned round, expecting to see him in the door. There was no one there. I went out into the corridor and looked up the stairs.

"Bridlings," Touffét said again, from inside the room. I went back in.

"Bridlings, come here at once. I need you," Touffét said, and laughed.

"Where are you?" I asked, wondering if this was some sort of ventriloquist's joke.

"In the nursery," he said. "Can you hear me?"

Well, of course I could hear him or I wouldn't be answering him. "Yes," I said, looking all round the room and finally spying the baby monitor, half hidden behind a clock on one of the bookshelves. I reached to pick it up. "Don't pick it up," he said. "You will ruin the forensic evidence you consider so important."

"Do you want me to come up to the nursery?"

"That will not be necessary. I have found out what I wished to know. Go into the parlor and make sure that Lady Charlotte has assembled everyone."

She had, though not in the parlor. "We don't have a parlor," she said, meeting me in the corridor as I came out of the library. "I've put everyone in the solarium, where we were last night. I hope that's all right."

"I'm sure it will be fine," I said.

"And I didn't have any sherry." She stopped at the door. "I had Heidi make Singapore slings."

"Probably a very good idea," I said, and opened the door.

Leda was perched on a canvas-covered hassock, with Rutgers behind her. The nurse sat in one of the canvas chairs, and the police sergeant perched next to her on the coffee table. James leaned against one of the bookshelves with a drink in his hand. D'Artagnan stood over by the windows.

As I came in, they all, except James and Heidi, who was offering him a tray of drinks, looked up expectantly and then relaxed.

"Is it true?" Leda asked eagerly. "Has Monsieur Touffét solved the crime? Does he know who murdered Lord Alastair?"

"We *all* know who murdered my father," James said, pointing at D'Artagnan. "That *animal* flew into a rage and strangled him! Isn't that right, Inspector Touffét?" he said to Touffét, who had just come in the door. "My father was killed by that *animal*!"

"So I at first thought," Touffét said, polishing his monocle. "A gorilla goes out of control, kills Lord Alastair in a violent rage, and destroys the nursery as he might his cage, throwing the furniture and the dishes against the wall. The baby monitor, also, was thrown against the wall and broken, which was why the nurse did not hear the murder being committed."

"You see!" James said to his sister. "Even your Great Detective says D'Artagnan did it."

"I said that so it seemed at first," Touffét said, looking irritated at the remark about the Great Detective, "but then I began to notice things— the fact that there were no signs of forcible entry, that the baby monitor had been switched off before it was thrown against the wall, that though it looked like a scene of great violence, none of us had heard anything— things that made me think, perhaps this is not a violent crime at all, but a carefully planned murder."

"Carefully planned!" James shouted. "The gorilla choked the life out of him in a fit of animal rage." He turned to Sergeant Eustis. "Why aren't you upstairs, gathering forensic evidence to prove that was what happened?"

"I do not need the forensic evidence," Touffét said. He took out a meerschaum pipe and filled it. "To solve this murder, I need only the motive."

"The motive?" James shouted. "You don't ask a bear what his motive is for biting off someone's head, do you? It's a *wild* animal!"

Touffét lit his pipe and took several long puffs on it. "So I begin by asking myself," he went on implacably, "who had a motive for killing Lord Alastair? Your father's will left everything to you, Lord James, did it not?"

"Yes," James said. "You're not suggesting *I* put that gorilla up to—"

"I do not suggest anything. I say only that you had a motive." He picked up his monocle and surveyed the crowd. "As does Ms. Fox."

"What?" Leda said, twitching her dress down over her thighs. "I never even met Lord Alastair."

"What you say is the truth," Touffét said, "though it is the only true thing you have said since your arrival, that is. You have even lied about your name, is that not so? You are not Leda Fox, the reporter. You are Genevieve Wrigley."

Lady Charlotte gasped.

"Who's Genevieve Wrigley?" I asked.

"The head of the ARA," Touffét said, looking steadily at her. "The Animal Rescue Army."

Lady Charlotte had jumped up. "You're here to steal D'Artagnan and Heidi from me!" She turned beseechingly to Touffét. "You mustn't let her. The ARA are terrorists."

I looked wonderingly at Leda, or rather Genevieve. Lady Charlotte was right about the ARA, it was a terrorist organization, a sort of IRA for animals. I'd seen them on television, blowing up cosmetics companies and holding zookeepers hostage, but Leda—Genevieve—didn't look like them at all.

Touffét said sternly, "You came here in disguise with the intention of liberating Lady Charlotte's animals, no matter what violent means were necessary."

"That's right," Leda, or rather, Genevieve, said, rearing back dangerously, and I was grateful there wasn't room anywhere for a bomb in that dress. "But I wouldn't have killed animals. I love animals!"

"Releasing pets into a wilderness they can't survive in?" Lady Charlotte said bitterly. "Sending primates back into the jungle to be killed by poachers? You don't love animals. You don't love anyone but yourselves. Well, now you've gone too far. You've murdered my father, and I'll see you convicted."

"Why would I murder your father?" Genevieve sneered. "You're the one I wanted to murder!"

At her words, D'Artagnan and Heidi both moved protectively toward Lady Charlotte.

"Dressing primates up like servants, holding them captive here. You're slaves!" she said to D'Artagnan. "She tells you she loves you, but she just wants to enslave you!"

D'Artagnan took a threatening step toward her, his huge white-gloved fist raised. "It's all right, D'Artagnan," Lady Charlotte said. "Inspector Touffét won't let her hurt me."

Genevieve slumped back in her chair and glared at Touffét. "I can't believe you found me out," she said. "I even ate a piece of that disgusting meat at dinner."

"We were discussing your motive," Touffét said. "Terrorists do not murder secretly. Their crimes are of no use unless they take credit for them. And by killing Lord Alastair, you might have given the Institute bad publicity, but you would not necessarily have succeeded in closing the Institute. Sympathetic donations might have poured in. How much better to blow up the Institute's buildings. It is true, you might have killed primates, but your organization has been known to kill animals before, in the name of saving them."

"You can't prove that!" she said sullenly.

"There are wire and detonating caps in your luggage." He turned to Sergeant Eustis. "Ms. Wrigley was out at the compound this afternoon. When we have concluded our business here, I would suggest searching it for plastic explosives."

Sergeant Eustis nodded and came over to stand behind Genevieve's chair. She rolled her eyes in disgust and crossed her arms over her chest.

"Ms. Wrigley had a motive for murder, but she is not the only one." He took several puffs on his pipe. "Everyone in this room has a motive. Yes, even you, Colonel Bridlings."

"I?" I said.

"You long to spend Christmas at your sister's house, do you not? If

Lord Alastair is murdered, the Christmas celebration at Marwaite Manor will be canceled, and you will be free to attend your sister's celebration instead."

"*If* I'm not detained for questioning," I said. "And I hardly think wanting to spend Christmas with my sister is an adequate motive for murdering a harmless, helpless old man."

Touffét held up an objecting finger. "Helpless, perhaps, but not harmless. But I quite agree with you, Bridlings, your motive is not adequate. People, though, have often murdered for inadequate motives. But you, Bridlings, are incapable of murder, and that is why I do not suspect you of the crime."

"Thank you," I said dryly.

"But. It is a motive," Touffét said. "As for Lady Charlotte, she has told all of us her motive this very evening at dinner. She has no money for her Institute. She is in danger of losing D'Artagnan and Heidi and all her other primates unless she obtains a large sum of money. And she loves them even more than she loves her father."

"But her father's will left all his money to her brother," I blurted out.

"Exactly," Touffét said, "so her brother must be eliminated as well, and what better method than to have him convicted of murder?"

"But Charlotte would never—" Rutgers said, rising involuntarily to his feet.

She looked at him in surprise.

"That is the conclusion to which I came also. Do not excite yourself, Mr. Rutgers," he said, giving the word "Rutgers" a peculiar emphasis. "I do not believe Lady Charlotte committed the murder, even though as the one who invited me here to Marwaite Manor, she was the first person I suspected."

He stopped and lit his pipe again for at least five minutes. "I said, I do not believe Lady Charlotte committed the murder, but not because I do not believe her capable of murder. I believe her desire to protect her primates could easily have driven her to murder. But that same desire would never have allowed her to let her primates be suspected of murder, even with a great detective on hand to uncover the true murderer. She would never have endangered them, even for a few hours." He turned and looked at Mick Rutgers. "You do not need to worry about Lady Charlotte, Mr. Davidson."

Now Lady Charlotte was the one who had risen involuntarily to her feet. "Phillip?" she said. "Is it really you?"

"Yes, it is Phillip Davidson," Touffét said smugly. "Who was ruined by Lord Alastair, who was kept from marrying Lady Charlotte and forced to emigrate to Australia." He paused dramatically. "Who came here determined to murder Lord Alastair for revenge."

"To murder . . ." Lady Charlotte put her hand to her bosom. "Is that true, Phillip?"

"Yes, it's true," Rutgers, or rather Davidson, said. Good Lord, just when I'd learned everyone's names. Now I was going to have to memorize them all over again.

"How did you know?" Rutg—Davidson asked.

"You called Lord Alastair 'Al,' though no one else had called him by that name," Touffét said. "It was also obvious from the way you looked at Lady Charlotte that you were still in love with her."

"It's true. I am," he said, looking at Lady Charlotte.

She was staring at him in horror. "You killed my father?"

"No," he said. "It's true, I came here to. I even brought a pistol with me. But when I saw him, I realized . . . He was a terrible man, but brilliant. To be reduced to that . . . that . . . was a worse revenge than any I could have devised." He looked at Touffét. "You have to believe me. I didn't kill him."

"I know you did not," Touffét said. "This murder required a knowledge of the house and of the people in it which you did not possess. And a revenge killer does not sedate his victim."

"Sedate?" Nurse Parchtry said.

"Yes," Touffét said. "When Sergeant Eustis completes his analysis of the cocoa, he will find the presence of sleeping medication."

I remembered the snoring on the baby monitor, subsiding into heavy, even breathing. Drugged breathing.

"Someone who murders for revenge," Touffét continued, "wishes his victim to know why he is being murdered. And you had worked with primates, Mr. Davidson; it was your interest in their intelligence that had sparked Lady Charlotte's. You would not have attempted to frame them for murder."

"Well, who would have?" Sergeant Eustis blurted.

"An excellent question," Touffét said. "And one which I will address shortly. But first we shall deal with your motive for murder, Sergeant."

"Mine?" Sergeant Eustis said, astonished. "What possible motive could I have had for murdering anyone?"

"Exactly," Touffét said, and everyone looked bewildered. "You had no motive for murdering Lord Alastair in particular, but you *did* have a motive for murdering someone."

"Aren't you forgetting he's a police officer?" James said nastily. "Or are you saying *you* have a motive for murdering my father, too?"

"No," Touffét said calmly. "For I am a great detective, with many solved cases to my credit, and none that I have failed to solve through my own incompetence. That is not, however, true of Sergeant Eustis, is it?"

Leda—Genevieve—gasped. "'Useless' Eustis. I thought you looked familiar."

"Indeed," Touffét said. "Captain Eustis, who had charge of the Tiffany Levinger case."

Tiffany Levinger. Now I remembered. It had been all over the television and the online tabloids. The pretty little girl who had been murdered in her own house, obviously by her own parents, but they had been acquitted because Captain Eustis had bungled the investigation so badly that it was impossible to attain a conviction. Nicknamed Useless Eustis and pilloried in the press, he had been forced to resign. And had apparently ended up here, in this remote area, demoted and disgraced.

"Another murder, the celebrated murder of a billionaire in a country manor, a sensational murder that you solved, could have redeemed your reputation, could it not?" Touffét said. "Especially with the press on the premises to record it all."

"It certainly could have," Sergeant Eustis said. "But even someone as stupid as the press claimed I was wouldn't be stupid enough to commit a murder with Inspector Touffét on the premises, now would he?"

"Exactly the conclusion I came to, Sergeant," Touffét said. "Which leaves Nurse Parchtry and James Valladay."

"Oh," Nurse Parchtry said, distressed, "you don't think I did it, do you? What motive could I have?"

"A cruel and abusive patient."

"But in that case why would I not simply have resigned?"

"That is what I asked myself," Touffét said. "You were obviously sub-jected to daily indignities, yet Lady Charlotte said you had been here nearly a year. Why? I asked myself."

"Because if she left she would forfeit the bonus I had promised her," Lady Charlotte said. She wrung her hands. "Oh, don't tell me I'm respon-sible for her . . . I was desperate. We'd been through seven nurses in less than a month. I thought if I offered her an incentive to stay . . ."

"What was the incentive?" Touffét asked Nurse Parchtry.

"Ten thousand pounds, if I stayed a full year," the nurse said dully. "I didn't think it would be so bad. I'd had difficult patients before, and it was the only way I could ever get out of debt. I didn't think it would be so bad. But I was wrong." She glared at Charlotte. "A million dollars wouldn't have been enough for taking care of that *brute*. I'm *glad* he's dead," she burst out. "I wish I'd killed him myself!"

"But you did not," Touffét said. "You are a nurse. You had at your dis-posal dozens of undetectable drugs, dozens of opportunities. You could have deprived him of his oxygen, given him a lethal dose of lidocaine or insulin, and it would have been assumed that he had died of natural causes. There would not even have been an autopsy. And you liked Heidi. You and she shared a passion for my cases. You would not have committed a murder that implicated her."

"No, I wouldn't have," Nurse Parchtry said tearfully. "She's a dear little thing."

"There is in fact only one person here who had a motive not only to murder Lord Alastair but also to see D'Artagnan charged with it, and that is Lord James Valladay."

"What?" James said, spilling his drink in his surprise.

"You were in considerable debt. Your father's death would mean that you would inherit a fortune. And you hated your sister's primates. You had every reason to murder your father and frame D'Artagnan."

"B-but . . ." he spluttered. "This is ridiculous."

"You put sleeping tablets in your father's cocoa when you were in the nursery, using an attack by D'Artagnan as a distraction. During the game of Animal, Vegetable, or Mineral, you went out into the corridor, having convinced everyone that they must take considerable time in choosing your object, and you took the lift up to the nursery, putting on the gloves you had stolen from D'Artagnan earlier, switched off the baby monitor, and strangled your sleeping father. Then you overturned the bed and placed objects around the room to look as if someone had flung them violently. You hid the key and the gloves, and came back downstairs, where you cold-bloodedly continued playing the game."

"Oh, James, you didn't—" Lady Charlotte cried.

"Of course I didn't. You haven't any proof of any of this, Touffét. You said yourself there weren't any fingerprints."

"Ah," Touffét said, pulling a bottle of sleeping tablets out of his pocket. "This was found in your bureau drawer, and these"—he produced a key and a pair of white gloves—"under your mattress, where you hid them, intending later to put them in the pantry to implicate D'Artagnan." He handed them to Sergeant Eustis. "I think you will find that the sleeping tablets match the residue in the cocoa cup."

"Under my mattress?" James said, doing a very good job of looking bewildered. "I don't understand— How would I have got into the nursery? I don't have a key."

"Ah," Touffét said. "D'Artagnan, come here." The gorilla lumbered forward from where he and Heidi had been watching all this and thinking God knows what. "D'Artagnan, what happened after Lady Charlotte gave you the keys?"

"Unlock," he said. "Get gloves."

"And then what?"

D'Artagnan looked fearfully at James and then back at Touffét.

"I won't let him hurt you," Sergeant Eustis said.

Lady Charlotte nodded at him. "Go ahead, D'Artagnan. Tell the truth. You won't get in trouble."

The gorilla glanced worriedly at James again and then said, "James say. Give me," pantomiming handing over a bunch of keys.

"That's a lie!" James said. "I did no such thing!"

"Then why was this under your mattress inside one of the gloves?" Touffét said, producing a key from his pocket and handing it to Sergeant Eustis.

"But I didn't—!" James said, turning to his sister. "He's lying!"

"How is that possible?" Lady Charlotte said coldly. "He's only an animal."

&

"A satisfying case," Touffét said as we waited for the train.

We had been driven to the station by a hairy orange orangutan named Sven. "He doesn't have a driver's license," Lady Charlotte had said, bidding us goodbye. She smiled up at Phillip Davidson, who had his arm around her. "But every policeman in the county's upstairs collecting evidence," she said, "so you won't have to worry about being ticketed."

It was easy to see why the police refused to issue Sven a driver's license. He was positively wild, and after he had nearly driven us off the road, he slapped the steering wheel with his hairy hands and grinned a teeth-baring smile at me. But he got us there nearly ten minutes before train time.

Touffét was still preoccupied with the case. "It is a pity James would not confess to the murder when I confronted him. Now the police must spend Christmas Day examining evidence."

"I'm sure Sergeant Eustis won't mind," I told him. He had seemed pathetically eager to look for everything Touffét told him to, even writing it all down. "You've redeemed his reputation. And, at any rate, no one confesses these days, even when they've been caught red-handed."

"That is true," he said, checking his pocket watch. "And all has turned out well. Lady Charlotte's Institute is safe, the apes no longer have to fear being homeless, and you shall arrive at your sister's in time to burn your fingers on the raisins."

"Aren't you going with me?"

"I have already endured one evening of Animal, Vegetable, or Mineral. My constitution cannot withstand another. I will disembark in London. You will convey my regrets to your sister, yes?"

I nodded absently, thinking of what he had said about the apes no longer having to fear being homeless. It was true. Until the murder, Lady Charlotte's Institute had been in great financial difficulty. She had said it might have to close. And if it did, the ARA and the other animal rights groups would have insisted on D'Artagnan and Heidi's being sent back to the wilds. Like Lucy.

Touffét had said everyone in the room had a motive, and he was right, but there were two suspects in the room he had overlooked.

James had even accused D'Artagnan of the murder, and D'Artagnan would certainly have done anything to save Lady Valladay's Institute—he was utterly devoted to her. Like D'Artagnan and the other Musketeers, who would have done anything to protect their queen. And he and Heidi were in danger of losing their home.

But killing Lord Alastair would not have saved the Institute. James would have inherited the estate. James, who had threatened to shut down the Institute, who had threatened to sell the apes to the zoo. Killing Lord Alastair would only have made the apes' situation worse.

Unless James could be made to look like the murderer. Because murderers could not inherit.

What if Heidi had put the sleeping pills into Lord Alastair's cocoa before she brought it up to the nursery, and had hidden the bottle in James's bureau? What if D'Artagnan had only pretended to lose his gloves so that Lady Charlotte would give him her keys? What if he and Heidi had gone up to the nursery while everyone was playing Animal, Vegetable, or Mineral, strangled Lord Alastair in his sleep, and then thrown the furniture about?

But that was impossible. They were *animals,* as James said. Animals who were capable of lying, cheating, deceiving. Capable of planning and executing. Executing.

What if D'Artagnan had really twisted James's wrist, so that he would accuse him, so that he'd say the apes were dangerous, and it would look as if he were trying to frame them?

No, it was too complicated. Even if they were capable of higher-level thinking, there was a huge difference between solving maths problems and planning a murder.

Especially a murder that could fool Touffét, I thought, looking across the compartment at him. He was rummaging through his bag, looking for his mystery novel.

They could never have come up with a murder like that on their own. And Touffét's explanation of James's motive made perfect sense. But if James had committed the murder, why hadn't he washed the cocoa out of the cup? Why hadn't he hidden the key and the gloves in the pantry, as Touffét had said he intended to do? He'd had plenty of time after we went to our rooms. Why hadn't he dumped the sleeping tablets down the sink?

"Bridlings," Touffét said, "what have you done with my book?"

I found *The Murders in the Rue Morgue* for him.

"No, no," he said. "Not that one. I do not wish to think any more of primates." He handed it back to me.

I stared at it. What if they hadn't had to plan the murder? What if they had only had to copy someone else's plan? "Monkey see, monkey do," I murmured.

"What?" Touffét said, rummaging irritably through his bag. "What did you say?"

"Touffét," I said earnestly, "do you remember *The Case of the Cat's Paw*?"

"Ah, yes," he said, looking pleased. "The little chimpanzee's favorite book. A most satisfying case."

"The husband did it," I said.

"*And* confessed when I confronted him," he said, looking annoyed. "You, as I recall, thought the village doctor did it."

Yes, I had thought the village doctor did it. Because the husband had made it look as though he had been framed by the doctor, so that suspicion no longer rested on him.

And *The Case of the Cat's Paw* was Heidi's favorite book. What if she and D'Artagnan had simply copied the murder in the book?

But Touffét had solved *The Case of the Cat's Paw*. How could they have been sure he would not solve this one?

"You were particularly obtuse on that case," Touffét said. "That is because you see only the facade."

"In spite of the overwhelming evidence of primates' intelligence," Lady Charlotte had said, "people *persist* in thinking of them as animals."

As animals. Who couldn't possibly have committed a murder.

But Heidi could read. And D'Artagnan had scored 95 on IQ tests. And they would have done anything for Lady Charlotte. Anything.

"Touffét," I said. "I've been thinking—"

"Ah, but that is just the problem. You do not think. You look only at the surface. Never what lies below it."

Or behind it, I thought. To the monkey, putting the cat's paw in the fire.

Unless I told Touffét, James would be convicted of murder. "Useless" Eustis would never discover the truth on his own, and even if he did, he wouldn't dare to contradict Touffét, who had saved his reputation.

"Touffét," I said.

"That is why I am the great detective, and you are only the scribe," Touffét said. "Because you see only the facade. That is why I do not listen to you when you tell me that you think it is the gorilla or the vicar. Well, what is it you wished to say?"

"Nothing," I said. "I was only wondering what we should call this case. *The Case of the Country Christmas*?"

He shook his head. "I do not wish to be reminded of Christmas."

The train began to slow. "Ah, this is where I change for London." He began gathering up his belongings.

If James were allowed to inherit, he would not only shut down the Institute, he would also drink and gamble his way through all the money. And D'Artagnan and Heidi would almost certainly be shipped back to the jungle and the poachers, so it was really a form of self-defense. And even if it was murder, it would be cruel to try them for it when they had no legal standing in the courts.

And the old man had been little more than an animal in need of putting down. Less human than D'Artagnan and Heidi.

The train came to a stop, and Touffét opened the door of the compartment.

"Touffét—" I said.

"Well, what is it?" he said irritably, his hand on the compartment. "I shall miss my stop."

"Merry Christmas," I said.

The conductor called out, and Touffét bustled off toward his train. I watched him from the door of the train, thinking of Lady Charlotte. Finding out the truth, that her beloved primates were far more human than even she had imagined, would kill her. She deserved a little happiness after what her father had done to her. And my sister would be waiting for me at the station. She would have made eggnog.

I stood there in the door, thinking of what Touffét had said about my being incapable of murder. He was wrong. We are all capable of murder. It's in our genes.

Now Showing

"A charming, lighthearted comedy!"
—*Entertainment Daily*

The Saturday before Christmas break, Zara came into my dorm room and asked me if I wanted to go to the movies with her and Kett at the Cinedrome.

"What's playing?" I asked.

"I don't know," she said, shrugging. "Lots of stuff," which meant the point of going wasn't to see a movie at all. Big surprise.

"No, thanks," I said, and went back to typing my econ paper.

"Oh, come on, Lindsay, it'll be fun," she said, flopping down on my bed. "*X-Force* is playing, and *The Twelve Days of Christmas* and the reboot of *Twilight*. The Drome's got a hundred movies. There must be *something* you want to see. How about *Christmas Caper*? Didn't you want to see that?"

Yes, I thought. At least I had eight months ago when I'd seen the preview. But things had changed since then.

"I can't," I said. "I've got to study."

"We've *all* got to study," Zara said. "But it's *Christmas.* The Drome will be all decorated and everybody will be there."

"Exactly, which means the light-rail will be packed and security will take *forever.*"

"Is this about Jack?"

"Jack?" I said, wondering if I could get away with "Jack who?"

Better not. This was Zara. I said instead, "Why would my not going to the Drome with you have anything to do with Jack Weaver?"

"It's . . . I don't know," she stammered, "it's just that you've been so . . . grim since he left, and you two used to watch a lot of movies together."

That was an understatement. Jack was the only guy I'd ever met who liked movies as much as I did, and all kinds, not just comic-book-hero and slasher films. He'd loved everything from Bollywood to romcoms like *French Kiss* to black-and-whites like *The Shop Around the Corner* and *Captain Blood,* and we'd gone to dozens of them at the Drome and streamed hundreds more in the semester we'd been together. Correction, semester minus one week.

Zara was still talking. "And you haven't gone to the Drome once since—"

"Since you talked me into going with you to see *Monsoon Gate,*" I said, "and then when we got there you wanted to eat and talk to guys, and I never did get to see it."

"That won't happen this time. Kett and I promise we'll go to the movie. Come on, it'll be good for you. There'll be tons of guys there. Remember that Sig Tau who said he liked you? Noah? *He* might be there. Come on. *Please* come with us. This is our last chance. We won't be able to go next weekend because of finals, and then we'll be gone on break."

And nobody at home would want to see *Christmas Caper.* If I suggested going to the movies, my sister would insist on us going to *A Despicable Me Noel* with her kids, and we'd end up spending the whole afternoon in the arcade playing Minion Mash and buying *Madagascar* stuffed giraffes and *Ice Age* ICEEs. By the time I got back to school, *Christmas Caper* would be gone. And it wasn't like Jack would magically show up and take me like he'd promised. If I wanted to see it on the big screen, I needed to do it now.

"Okay," I said. "But I'm not going with you to meet guys. I'm going because I really want to see *Christmas Caper.* Understood?"

"Yeah, sure," she said, getting out her phone and punching keys. "I'll just text Kett and—"

"I mean it," I said. "You have to promise me you won't get sidetracked like last time, that we'll actually go to the movie."

"I promise," she said. "No guys and no eating till afterward."

"And no shopping," I said. I had missed *Monsoon Gate* because Zara was trying on Polly Pepper shoes in the *Devil Wears Prada* boutique. "Promise me."

Zara sighed. "Fine. I promise. Cross my heart."

> *"A sweet romantic comedy with lots of action!"*
> —*popcorn.com*

*

Zara's promise meant about as much as the ones Jack had made me. Zara began texting the second we arrived, and we weren't even through the preliminary bag and phone check at the Drome before Kett said, "The NWU guys behind me in line just asked me to ask you if we want to go see the cast of *The Bourne Dynasty.* They're holo-skyping over at the Universal booth."

Zara looked hopefully at me. "We could go to the 12:10 instead of the 10 o'clock."

"Or the 2:20," Kett said.

"No," I said.

"Sorry," Zara said to the guys. "We promised Lindsay we'd go to *Christmas Caper* with her first," and the guys promptly began hitting on the girls behind them.

"I don't see why we couldn't have gone to a later showing," Kett said, pouting, as we went through the explosives check.

"Because after the holo-skyping was over, they'd have wanted to play *Skyfall* or go eat at Harold and Kumar's White Castle, and we'd have missed the 2:20 *and* the 4:30," I said, and as soon as we made it through the body—and retinal—scans and into the Drome, I headed straight for the ticket kiosks, ignoring the barrage of previews and holograms and ads and elves passing out coupons for free cookies and video games and schedules of today's autographing sessions.

"I thought you were going to get the tickets online before we left," Zara said.

"I tried," I said, "but it's playing a special limited engagement, so you have to get them here." I dragged my finger down the list of movies— *Ripper 2, X-Force, The House on Zombie Hill, The Queen's Consort, Switching Gears, Just When You Thought You Were Over Him . . .*

Honestly, you'd think with a hundred movies, they'd put them in alphabetical order. *Lethal Rampage, The Twelve Days of Christmas, Texas Chainsaw Massacre—The Musical, A Star-Crossed Season, Back to Back to the Future, Wicked—*

Here it was. *Christmas Caper.* I tapped the tickets button and "3" and swiped my card.

"Unavailable," the screen said. "Tickets must be purchased at ticket counter," which meant we had to get in line, one of the worst things about going to the Drome.

You'd think as huge as it is and as many people as it has to cope with, they'd have Disneyverse-style back-and-forth lines, but they only use those to line people up for showings. The ticket lines snaked single file all the way back through the Drome's football-field-size lobby, the *Hunger Games* paintball stadium, the *No Reservations* food court, Wetaworks' Last Homely House, the virtual-reality terrace, and half a mile of souvenir shops and boutiques.

It took us twenty minutes just to find the end, and in the process we nearly lost Kett twice, once at Pretty in Pink—"Oh, my God! They have stilettos in fifty shades of gray!"—and again when she saw that Hope Floats, Shakes, and Cones was selling cranberry malts.

Zara and I dragged her out of both and into the end of the line, which was getting longer by the minute. "We're never going to get into the movie," Kett grumbled.

"Yes, we will," I said confidently, though I wasn't sure, there were so many people in line. Most of them were little kids, though, who were obviously going to *The Little Goose Girl* or *The Muppets' It's a Wonderful Life* or *Dora the Explorer Does Duluth.* The adults around us who I asked were all going to *A Tudor Affair* or *Return to the Best Exotic Marigold Hotel,* and everybody else was wearing an *Iron Man 8* T-shirt. "We'll definitely get in."

"We'd better," Kett said. "Why are you so set on seeing this *Christmas Caper,* anyway? I never heard of it. Is it a romcom?"

"No," I said, "more like a romantic spy adventure. Like *Charade.* Or *The Thirty-nine Steps.*"

"I haven't seen previews for either of those," she said, looking up at the schedule board above us. "Are they still playing?"

"No." I should have known better than to mention an old movie. In this day of reboots and remakes nobody watches anything older than last week. Except Jack. He'd even liked silents.

"You know, the kind of movie where the heroine gets accidentally caught up in a crime," I said, "or some kind of conspiracy, and the hero's a spy, like in *Jumpin' Jack Flash,* or a reporter, or a detective who's pretending to be a criminal, like in *How to Steal a Million,* or he's a scoundrel—"

"A scoundrel?" Kett said blankly.

"A rebel," I said, "a rake, a rogue, like Michael Douglas in *Romancing the Stone,* or Errol Flynn—"

"I haven't seen previews for those either," she said. "Is *Arrow Flin* still playing?"

"No," I said. "A scoundrel's a guy who's cocky and doesn't care about rules or laws—"

"Oh, you mean a slimewad," Kett said.

"*No,* a scoundrel's funny and sexy and charming," I said, trying desperately to think of a movie recent enough that she might have seen it. "Like Iron Man. Or Jack Sparrow."

"Or Jack Weaver," Zara said.

"No," I said, "*not* like Jack Weaver. In the first place—"

"Who's Jack Weaver?" Kett asked.

"This guy Lindsay used to be in love with," Zara said.

"I was not in—"

"Wait," Kett said. "Is that the guy who put a whole bunch of ducks in the dean's office last year?"

"Geese," I said.

"Wow!" Kett said, impressed. "You went with him?"

"Briefly," I said. "Before I found out he was—"

"A scoundrel?" Zara put in.

"No," I said. "A slimewad. Who got himself thrown out of Hanover. The week before he was supposed to graduate."

"He didn't actually get thrown out," Zara explained to Kett. "He took off before they could expel him."

"Or press criminal charges," I said.

"That's too bad," Kett said. "He sounds totally *depraved*! I'd have liked to meet him."

"You might get your chance," Zara said in an odd voice. "Look!" She pointed toward the lobby.

And there, leaning against a pillar with his hands in his pockets, looking up at the movie schedule, was Jack Weaver.

"Exciting fun! Sets your pulse racing!"
—*USA Today*

*

"**It *is* him,** isn't it?" Zara asked.

"Yes," I said grimly.

"I wonder what he's doing here."

"As if you didn't know," I said. No wonder she'd been so insistent I come with them. She and Jack had cooked up a—

"Oh, my God!" Kett cried. "Is *that* the guy you were talking about? The—what did you call him?"

"Wanker," I said.

"Scoundrel," Zara said.

"Right, the scoundrel. You didn't tell me he was so hot! I mean, he's positively scorching!"

"*Shh,*" I said, but it was too late. Jack had already looked over and seen us.

"Zara," I said, "if you set this up, I'm never speaking to you again!"

"I didn't, I swear," she said, which didn't mean anything, but two things made me inclined to believe her. One was that even though this looked suspiciously like a movie "meet cute," the expression on Zara's face had been completely stricken, the reason for which became apparent a few seconds later when a trio of Sig Taus, including Noah, sauntered up way too casually.

"Wow!" Noah said. "I had no idea you three were coming to the Drome today, too."

Except for Zara's texting you fifteen times while we were in the security lines, I thought. But at least their being here would keep Jack from coming over to talk to me.

If he even wanted to. Because the other reason I thought Zara didn't have anything to do with Jack's being here had been the look on *his* face.

He'd looked not just surprised to see me here, but dismayed. Which meant I was right—he wasn't a scoundrel, he was a slimewad. And probably here with some other girl.

"I'm especially surprised to see *you* here, Lindsay," Noah, who would never make it as an actor even in the *Twilight* movies, said. "What are you doing at the Drome?"

"The three of us," I said, emphasizing the word "three," "are going to a movie."

"Oh," he said, frowning at Zara, who gave him a "go on" look. "We were just going to get something to eat at the Mos Eisley Cantina, and we wondered if you'd like to come with us."

"Oh, I *love* the Cantina," Kett cooed.

"I'll buy you a Darth Vader daiquiri," Noah said to me.

"Lindsay prefers Pimm's Cups," Zara said. "Don't you?"

I glanced toward the lobby, hoping against hope Jack hadn't heard that.

He wasn't there. He wasn't at the end of the line either, or at the ticket machines. Good, he'd gone off to meet his new girlfriend. I hoped she hated movies.

Noah was saying, "What the hell's a Pimm's Cup?"

"It's a drink from a movie," I said. *My favorite drink,* I added silently. Or at least it used to be. The drink Jack had made me after we'd watched *Ghost Town* and Téa Leoni had said it was *her* favorite drink.

"We could have lunch and *then* go to the movie, couldn't we, Lindsay?" Kett asked, looking adoringly at Noah. "I just got a text coupon for *Breakfast at Tiffany's* breakfast bar."

"No," I said.

Zara gave Noah another nudging look, and he said, "Maybe we could go with you. What are you going to?"

"*Christmas Caper,*" Kett said.

"I never heard of it," Noah said.

"It's a spy adventure," Kett explained. "A *romantic* spy adventure."

Noah made a face. "Are you kidding me? I *hate* romcoms. How about we all go see *Lethal Rampage* instead?"

"No," I said.

"Maybe we could meet you at the Cantina after the movie," Zara suggested.

"Yeah, I don't know," Noah mumbled, looking at the other guys.

"We're pretty hungry. Listen, I'll text you," he said, and the three of them wandered off.

"I can't believe you did that," Zara said. "I was just trying to help you forget about—"

"That Noah guy was scorching," Kett said, looking after him, and sighed. "This better be some movie."

"It is," Jack said at my elbow. "Hi."

"What are you doing here?" I demanded.

"Going to the movies," he said. "What else?" He leaned toward me. "Traitor," he said in my ear. "You promised you'd go to *Christmas Caper* with me."

"You weren't here," I said coldly.

"Yeah, about that," he said. "Sorry. Something came up. I—"

"Is it really a good movie?" Kett asked, sidling over to him. "Lindsay didn't tell us what it was about. All she said was that there was a scoundrel in it."

"Scoundrel," Jack said, raising an eyebrow at me. "I like the sound of that."

"How do you like the sound of 'loser'?" I said. "Or 'slimewad'?"

He ignored me. "Actually," he said to Kett, "he's an undercover agent working on a case, and it's classified, so he can't tell the heroine about it or why he had to leave town—"

"Nice try," I said, and to Kett, "What it's *really* about is this creep who tells the heroine a bunch of lies, does something staggeringly stupid, and then goes off without a *word*—"

"Why don't you come with us, Jack?" Kett interrupted, looking up at him hungrily. "I'm Kett, by the way. I'm friends with Lindsay, but she didn't tell me you were so—"

Zara pushed between them. "Kett and I actually wanted to go play drone tag with these Pi Kappas, Jack," she said. "We—"

"*What* Pi Kappas?" Kett demanded.

Zara ignored her. "We were just going to the movie with Lindsay to keep her company, but now that you're here, you could take her."

"I'd love to," Jack said, frowning, "but unfortunately I can't."

"He has to put a flock of geese a-laying in the theater where *The Twelve Days of Christmas* is showing," I said. "Or is it partridges this time, Jack?"

"Swans a-swimming," he said, grinning. "I've got eight of them in my pocket."

"*Really?*" Kett said, as if it was actually possible to get *anything* through security, let alone a flock of swans.

"That would be so *depraved!*" she purred. "What you did to the dean's office was so amazing! You definitely should come with us to *Christmas Caper!*"

"I have no intention of going anywhere with Jack," I said.

"Then I will." Kett tucked her arm cozily in his. "The two of us can go see it."

"Yeah, well, I'm sure that would be fun," Jack said, disentangling himself from her like she was barbed wire, "but it's not gonna happen. We can't get in. It's sold out."

"It is *not,*" I said, pointing up at the schedule board. "Look."

"Not right now maybe, but trust me, it will be by the time you get to the front of the line."

"You're kidding," Zara said. "After we've stood in line all this time?"

"And told Noah we couldn't go to the Cantina with him," Kett added.

"It's *not* going to be sold out," I said confidently.

"Wrong," Jack said, pointing at the board, where NO TICKETS AVAIL-ABLE had begun flashing next to *Christmas Caper.*

"An engrossing mystery."
—*flickers.com*

*

"Oh, no," Zara said. "What do we do now?"

"We could go see *A Star-Crossed Season,*" Kett said to Jack. "It's supposed to be really good. Or *The Diary.*"

"We're not going to either one," I said. "Just because the 12:10 of *Christmas Caper's* sold out doesn't mean the other showings are. We can still get tickets to the 2:20."

"And wait around for another two *hours?*" Kett wailed.

"Why don't we get lunch first and then get the tickets?" Zara said. "We could go to *Chocolat—*"

"No," I said. "This is not going to turn into another *Monsoon Gate.* We are staying right here till we get our tickets."

"How about you stay in line, Lindsay, and we go and bring you back something?" Kett suggested.

"No," I said. "You promised you'd go with me."

"Yeah, and you promised you'd go with *me*, Lindsay," Jack said.

"You stood me up."

"I did not," he said. "I'm here, aren't I? And anyway, Kevin Kline stood up Meg Ryan in *French Kiss.* Michael Douglas stood up Kathleen Turner in *Romancing the Stone.* Indiana Jones left Marion tied up in the bad guys' tent. Admit it, that's what scoundrels do."

"Yes, well, but they don't throw their entire future away on some stupid prank."

"You mean the geese? That wasn't a prank."

"Oh, really? Then what was it?"

"I can see you two have a lot of stuff to discuss," Zara said. "We don't want to get in the way. We'll catch up with you later. Text me." And before I could protest, she and Kett had vanished into the crowd.

I turned to Jack. "I'm still not going with you to see it."

"True," he said, looking over at the ticket counter. "You're not going to get in to the 2:20 either."

"I suppose now you're going to tell me it'll be sold out, too?"

"No, they usually don't use that one twice," he said. "This time it'll be something more subtle. Free tickets to a Special Christmas Showing of *The Shop Around the Corner* or a personal appearance by the new Hulk. Or, since you like scoundrels, by the new Han Solo." He grinned. "Or me."

"I do *not* like scoundrels," I said. "Not anymore. And what do you mean, 'They don't use that one twice'?"

He shook his head disapprovingly. "*That's* not your line. You're supposed to say, 'I happen to like nice men,' and then I say, '*I'm* a nice man.'" He leaned toward me. "And then *you* say—"

"This is not *The Empire Strikes Back*," I snapped, backing away from him. "And you are not Han Solo."

"True," he said. "I'm more like Peter O'Toole in *How to Steal a Million.* Or Douglas Fairbanks in *The Mask of Zorro.*"

"Or Bradley Cooper in *The World's Biggest Liar*," I said. "Why did you say I'm not going to get in to the 2:20, either? Have you done something to the theater?"

"Nope, not a thing. I swear." He held up his right hand.

"Yes, well, your word isn't exactly trustworthy, is it?"

"Actually, it is. It's just that . . . Never mind. I promise you I didn't have anything to do with the 12:10 being sold out."

"Then why were you so sure it was going to be?"

"Long story. Which I can't tell you here," he said, looking around. "What say we go somewhere quiet and I'll explain everything?"

"Including where you've been for the past eight months? And what possessed you to put those geese in the dean's office?"

"No," he said. "Sorry, I can't until—"

"Until what? Until you've done the same thing here?" I lowered my voice. "Seriously, Jack, you could get in a *lot* of trouble. The Dromes have really heavy security—"

"I *knew* it," he said delightedly. "You're still crazy about me. 'So what say we go discuss this over a nice cozy lunch,' as Peter said to Audrey in *How to Steal a Million.* There's a little place over on Pixar Boulevard called Gusteau's—"

"I am not going anywhere with you," I said. "I am going to the 2:20 showing of *Christmas Caper.* By myself."

"That's what you think," he said.

> *"Watch the sparks fly between these two!"*
> —*The Web Critic*

*

Jack had sauntered off before I could demand to know what "That's what you think" meant, and I couldn't go after him to ask for fear of losing my place in line, so I spent the rest of the wait to get tickets worrying that the 2:20 would be sold out, too, though there were only a couple of dozen people left ahead of me, they were all going to something else, and the schedule boards were still showing tickets were available.

But there were three other lines, and the ticket seller on mine apparently had the brain of a character in *Dumb and Really Really Dumb.* It took him forever to make change and/or swipe people's cards and then shove their tickets at them. It was a good thing I wasn't trying to get a ticket for the 1:10. I'd never have made it.

It was half past before I even got close to the ticket counter, and then the guy three people ahead of me couldn't make up his mind whether to see *Zombie Prom* or *Avatar 4.* He and his girlfriend spent a good ten minutes trying to decide, and then his card wouldn't swipe and they had to use his girlfriend's, and *she* had to search through her entire bag to find it, digging out handfuls of stuff for him to hold while she looked, and standing there to put it all back after they'd finally gotten the tickets.

This is exactly what Jack was talking about, I thought. What if they were doing it purposely to keep me from getting in?

Don't be ridiculous, I told myself. *You're seeing conspiracies where they don't exist.* But I still looked anxiously up at the schedule board as I came up to the counter, afraid the NO TICKETS AVAILABLE would blink on at the last minute.

It didn't, and when I said, "One adult for the 2:20 showing of *Christmas Caper,*" the ticket seller nodded, swiped my card without incident, handed me my ticket, and told me to enjoy the show.

"I will," I said determinedly, and started toward the entrance of the theater complex.

Halfway there, Jack suddenly reappeared and fell in step with me. "Well?" he said.

"They weren't sold out, and I didn't have any trouble getting a ticket. See?" I said, showing it to him.

He wasn't impressed. "Yeah, and in *Romancing the Stone,* they found the diamond," he said, "and Whoopi Goldberg got Jumpin' Jack Flash an exit contact, and look what happened."

"What is that supposed to mean?"

"It means you're not in the theater yet, and if you don't make it by 2:20, they won't let you in."

That was true—it was part of the Drome's security precautions not to let anyone in to a movie after it had started—but it was only 1:30. I told Jack that.

"Yeah, but the line to get in could be really long, or the line to buy popcorn."

"I'm not buying popcorn. And there isn't any line to get in," I said, pointing over at the usher standing all alone in the entrance to the theaters.

"At the moment," he said. "You're not there yet. A horde of middle-aged women could show up for the new *Fifty Shades of Grey* before you get over to the usher. And even if you do make it into the theater, the film could break—"

"The Drome doesn't use film. It's all digital."

"Exactly, which means something could go wrong with the digital feed. It could be contaminated by a virus, or the server could crash. Or something could trigger the TSA's alarms and send the whole Drome into lockdown."

"Like setting geese loose in a theater?" I said. "What are you up to, Jack?"

"I told you, *I'm* not up to anything. I'm just saying you might not get in. In fact, I'm almost certain you won't. And if you don't, I'll be at Gusteau's."

"Nothing is going to happen," I said, and started across the remaining half of the lobby toward the entrance and the usher.

The lobby was getting more crowded by the minute with gaggles of excited children and texting teenagers and families arguing about where to go first. I pushed past and around them, hoping a line wouldn't suddenly collect in front of the usher and prove Jack right, but the usher was still standing there alone, leaning on the ticket stand and looking bored.

I handed him my ticket.

He handed it back. "You can't go in yet. The movie's not over. Excuse me," he said, and reached around me to take the tickets of two eight-year-old boys who'd come up behind me.

He tore their tickets in half and handed them back. "Theater 76. Up the stairs to the third floor and turn right."

The boys went in. I said, "Can't I go in and wait in the hall outside the theater till it lets out?"

He shook his head. "It's against security regulations. I can't let anybody in till the movie gets out."

"Which is when?"

"I'll check," he said, and consulted the schedule. "1:55." Ten minutes from now. "If you don't want to wait—"

"I do." I moved over against the wall, out of the way.

"Sorry, you can't stand there," a manager said, coming up. "That's where the line for *Dr. Who: The Movie* has to go." He began busily cordoning off the space.

I moved to the other wall, but a bunch of little girls and their parents were already lining up there to get in to see *The Little Goose Girl,* and the sole bench near the door was occupied by a mother vainly trying to talk her two daughters into relinquishing their virtual-reality glasses. Shrieking was involved. And kicking.

I was going to have to wait out the ten minutes in the lobby. *Hopefully Jack's gone off to Gusteau's,* I thought, but he hadn't. He was standing just outside the entrance with his hands in his pockets and an "I told you so" smile on his face. "What happened?" he asked.

"Nothing happened," I said, walking past him. "The 12:10's not out yet."

"So you decided to have that talk with me after all. Great," he said, taking hold of my arm and propelling me through the lobby toward Pixar Boulevard. "We can go to Gusteau's and you can tell me what excuse the usher gave you for not letting you in and why they wouldn't let you wait there in the entryway."

"I don't have any intention of telling you *anything,*" I said, wrenching my arm free of him. "Why should I? You didn't tell *me* you were planning to get yourself expelled a week before you were supposed to graduate."

"Yeah, about that," he said, frowning. "I wasn't actually going to graduate—"

"Of course not," I said disgustedly. "Why am I not surprised? Was that why you broke into the dean's office, because you were flunking out and you were trying to change your grades?"

"No," he said. "The fact is, I wasn't actually—"

"You weren't what?"

"I can't tell you," he said. "It's classified."

"Classified!" I said. "That's it. I'm not listening to any more of your paranoid fantasies. I am going to go stand over by the entrance until this movie gets out," I said, pointing, "and then I am going inside, and if you try to follow me, I'll report you to security."

I fought my way back to the entryway through a mob of cloaked and hairy-footed hobbits who were obviously on their way to *The Return of Frodo,* a bunch of old ladies going to see a special Nostalgia Showing of *Sex and the City,* and the mazelike line for *Dr. Who,* which now extended ten yards out into the lobby. By the time I made it to where I intended to wait, there was no longer any reason to. It was already two o'clock.

I went over to the usher and handed him my ticket.

He shook his head. "You can't go in yet."

"But you said the 12:10 got out at 1:55."

"It did, but you can't go in till the crew finishes cleaning."

"Which will be when?"

He shrugged. "I don't know. Some guy threw up all over. It's going to take them at least twenty minutes to clean it up." He handed me back my ticket. "Why don't you go get something to eat? Or do some Christmas shopping? They're having a sale on *Inception* sleep masks over at the *Sleepless in Seattle* shop."

And Jack will be standing right outside of it, smirking, I thought. "No, thanks," I said, and squeezed past the *Dr. Who* and *Little Goose Girl* lines to the bench, hoping the mother and girls had gone.

They had, but the bench was now completely taken up by a passionately kissing and practically horizontal couple. I edged past them to stand by the wall, but by the time I made it, the couple had reached the R-rated stage and was rapidly approaching NC-17. I braced myself for Jack and another round of conspiracy theories and went back out into the lobby again.

"A gift for holiday moviegoers!"
—silverscreen.com

*

Jack wasn't there. But he—and Zara and Kett—were the only ones who weren't in the lobby. It was crammed to bursting with people checking their coats and buying tickets and refreshments and staring up at the previews and schedule boards. I found myself alternately jostled and smushed by the crowds going into and coming out of the theater complex and by kids mobbing the Christmas characters who meandered through, tossing candy canes and distributing Coming Attractions flyers. Alvin the Chipmunk gave me a chit for a free mince pie at Sweeney Todd's snack bar, and a frighteningly friendly Grinch presented me with a coupon for half off a *Twelve Dancing Princesses* T-shirt at the Disney Pavilion.

I'd no sooner handed it off to a NewGoth girl and read a text on my phone, telling me I'd won a free ticket to a special Encore Presentation of *Ghost Town,* than I was nearly run down by an enormous Transformer stomping through the crowd, flailing his huge metal arms and nearly bumping his head against the lobby ceiling. I partly dived and was partly pushed out of its way by the crowd as it scattered and ended up on the opposite side of the lobby.

The crowd surged back toward the Transformer, snapping pictures on their cell phones, jockeying for position to have their photos taken with it, their backs forming an impenetrable wall. There was no way I was getting through that, at least till the Transformer left.

It didn't matter—it was still fifteen minutes till they'd be finished cleaning. I turned to look for a place I could wait without being run down. *Not* Gusteau's—I had no desire to hear Jack say "I told you so." And not Sweeney Todd's. It was too far away.

I needed someplace close so I could start back the second the crowd dwindled or the moment I saw the cleaning crew give the usher the high sign, and someplace with a short line, but finding one was practically impossible. Zombie Juice was even more mobbed than the lobby. *Stargate's* Starbucks, which was advertising Mistletoe Mochas, had a line merging over into Zombie Juice, and the Transformer had apparently been passing out coupons for a Transformer Tea because Tea and Sympathy, usually a safe bet, was jammed, too.

And I was definitely not going to the Cantina, even though at this point I could have used a drink. But Jack had obviously sent that text, which meant he was waiting in the Cantina to get me drunk and tell me more conspiracy theories. I was *not* going there.

That left a hot cocoa at the Polar Express, which was just off the lobby and whose line only had two people in it, but even then it took forever. The guy at the counter wanted a gingerbread clove latte, which the barista didn't know how to make, so he had to give her step-by-step instructions, and then the teenager behind him couldn't get her swipe card to work.

I looked back out at the lobby. The Transformer was gone, but now the zeppelin from *The Steampunk League* was floating above the ticket machines, throwing down gift cards on a converging crowd. If I didn't go soon, the lobby would be even more jammed than it had been with the Transformer.

I decided I'd better bag the cocoa and head back, and I started for the

door. And collided with the gingerbread guy, who was bringing his latte
back for having insufficient whipped cream and who managed to spill
the entire drink down my front.

Customers converged with napkins and commiserations, and the
barista insisted on my waiting while she fetched a wet rag. "That's okay,"
I said. "I'm kind of in a hurry. I have a movie I need to get to."

"It'll just take a sec," she said, running back to the counter. "You can't
go all wet like that."

"I'm fine," I said, and started for the door.

The gingerbread man grabbed my arm. "I insist on buying you a
drink to apologize," he said. "What would you like?"

"Nothing, really," I said. "I need to go—" and the barista came over
with the rag and began swabbing me down.

"That's not necessary. Really," I said, brushing her away.

"You're not going to sue the Polar Express, are you?" she asked tearfully.

Yes, I thought, *if I miss this movie because of you.* "No, of course not,"
I said. "I'm fine. No harm done."

"Oh, good," she said. "If you'll hang on just a minute, I'll get you a
coupon for a free scone the next time you come."

"I don't want—"

"At least let me pay for the cleaners," the guy said, getting out his
phone. "If you'll give me your email address—"

"On second thought," I said, "I think I would like that drink. A peppermint chai," and when he started for the counter, I darted out of the
Polar Express, into the protective cover of the crowd, and into the lobby.

It was even more crowded than it had been with the Transformer. I
pushed into the scrum and started across, and it was a good thing I
hadn't gotten my cocoa. I had to bull my way through with both hands,
prying couples apart and slipping between them, pushing aside excited
kids in bright blue *A Smurf Hanukkah* T-shirts and teenagers staring up
at *House on Zombie Hill* previews.

It was like swimming through molasses, and it seemed to take hours
to get to a place where I could finally see the usher. There was a line in
front of him now, but it wasn't the *Dr. Who* or the *Little Goose Girl* people, who were still waiting in their mazelike lines. I needed to get over to
him before those movies got out, or I'd never get in to *Christmas*—

Someone grabbed me by my arm. *Please don't let it be the Gingerbread Man,* I thought as I was yanked back into the center of the crowd.

It wasn't. It was Santa Claus, with a microphone and a phalanx of reindeer. "What do you want for Christmas, little girl?" he asked, sticking the mike in my face.

"To get over there," I said, pointing.

"Ho ho ho," he said. "How would you like a nice pair of tickets to the 3:25 showing of *The Claus Chronicles*?"

"No, thank you," I said. "I'm going to see *Christmas Caper.*"

"What?" he said. "You don't want to see Santa's own movie?"

He turned to his reindeer. "Did you hear that, Prancer?" he said, loudly enough for the entire lobby to hear. "We have a problem here. I think I need to check my naughty-and-nice list, Blitzen." The list was duly produced, Santa put on a pair of spectacles, and he ran a very slow finger down it while I looked longingly over at the entrance to the theaters, where the line in front of the usher was growing longer by the minute.

"Here she is," Santa finally announced. "Yes, definitely naughty. And what do we give naughty children for Christmas, Vixen?"

"Coal!" the crowd shouted.

Santa reached into his sack and produced a lump of licorice. "Shall I give this to her or shall we give her another chance? After all, it is Christmas."

"Coal!" the crowd bellowed, and Santa had to ask them two more times to persuade them to offer me the tickets again, which this time I had the sense to take.

"And here's a ticket to the 2:30 showing of *The Twelve Days of Christmas* for being such a good sport," he said. "*Merry* Christmas, ho ho ho," and I was finally free.

I shot over to the entrance, where the line in front of the usher had miraculously disappeared, and handed the usher my ticket. "Sorry," he said, handing it back.

"They're *still* cleaning?" I asked incredulously.

"No, but you're late. It's 2:22. The 2:20's already started."

"But they do previews for the first fifteen minutes—"

"Sorry. It's theater policy. No one's allowed in after the start time. I think you can still get tickets to the 4:30."

I don't, I thought, *and I know who's responsible.*

"Do you want me to check and see if there are still tickets available?" he asked.

"No, that's okay. Never mind," I said, and went out, across the lobby, and into the wilds of the Drome to find Jack.

> *"A great movie! Don't miss it!"*
> —*Time Out*

*

I'd expected Gusteau's to be a bar somewhere near the dance clubs and Rick's from *Casablanca,* but it wasn't, and after consulting two maps and a Drome guide dressed as Frosty the Snowman, I found it in the depths of Munchkinland, sandwiched between the *Monsters, Inc.* ball pool and the *Despicable Me* moon drop, both of which were filled with toddlers emitting ear-slashing shrieks of joy and/or terror.

The restaurant was a replica of the French bistro in *Ratatouille,* with rats on the wallpaper and the tables. Jack was seated at a table at the back. "Hi," he shouted over the din from the ball pool. "Didn't get back in, huh?"

"No," I said grimly.

"Sit down. Would you like something to drink? Gusteau's is G-rated, so I can't offer you a Pimm's Cup, but I can get you a mouse mocha."

"No, thank you," I said, ignoring his invitation to sit down. "I want to know what you're up to and why you saw to it I didn't—"

"Hey, what happened to you?" he interrupted, pointing at my still-wet top. "Don't tell me you collided with Hugh Grant carrying an orange juice, like in *Notting Hill*?"

"No," I said through gritted teeth, "a gingerbread latte—"

"And they wouldn't let you in because of the Drome's dress code?"

"*No,* they wouldn't let me in because the movie had already started. Because a guy with a gingerbread latte and Santa Claus kept me from getting back from the Polar Express in time, as you well know. You're the one who put them up to it. This is just another one of your adolescent pranks, isn't it?"

"I told you, that wasn't a prank."

"Then, what was it?"

"It . . . you remember when we watched *Ocean's 17,* and there's a break-in at the casino? Cops, sirens, helicopters, the whole nine yards? But that's just a diversion, and the real crime is taking place over at the bank?"

"You're saying the geese were a diversion?"

"Yeah. Just like Santa Claus. What did he do to delay you?"

"You know perfectly well what he did. You hired him to do it so I wouldn't get in and I'd have to go with you. But it won't work. I have no intention of seeing *Christmas Caper* with you."

"Good," he said, "because you're not going to. Not today, anyway."

"Why not? What did you do?"

"Nothing. I'm not the one responsible for any of this."

"Really?" I said sarcastically. "And who is?"

"If you'll sit down, I'll tell you. I'll also tell you why the 12:10 was sold out, why *The Steampunk League* sent its zeppelin over when it did, and why you couldn't buy tickets to *Christmas Caper* online."

"How did you know that?"

"Lucky guess. The ticket machines wouldn't let you buy them either, would they?"

"No," I said, and sat down. "Why not?"

"I need to know something first. What were you doing at the Polar Express? When I left you, you were handing the usher your ticket."

"He wouldn't let me in. Some guy threw up in the theater."

"Ah, yes, good old vomit. Works every time. But why didn't you just wait there in the entryway?"

I told him about the *Dr. Who* and *Goose Girl* lines and the bench people.

"Did anything else happen while you were waiting? Anybody send you a text telling you you'd won free tickets to something?"

"Yes." I told him about the Encore Presentation of *Ghost Town.* "Which you can't tell me you didn't put them up to. Who else would know *Ghost Town* was one of my favorite movies?"

"Who, indeed?" he said. "When we were in line, you said, 'This isn't going to turn into another *Monsoon Gate.*' I take it you didn't get in to that movie, either. Why not? Did the same thing happen?"

"No," I said. I told him about Zara trying on shoes and us missing the six o'clock showing. "And then she got a tweet saying there was going to be a special preview of *Bachelorette Party—*"

"Which, let me guess, was a movie she really wanted to see?"

"Yes," I said. "So we decided to go to the ten o'clock, but when we checked its running time, it didn't get out till—"

"After the last light-rail back to Hanover," he said, nodding. "Are you sure you don't want something to drink? A rat root beer? A vermin vanilla Coke?"

"No. Why are we here anyway?" I asked, looking around. "Surely there's someplace we could go to that we wouldn't have to shout."

"This and the Tunnel of Love are the only areas not under surveillance. We could go do that."

I had been in the Tunnel of Love with Jack before. "No," I said.

"I heard they've got some new features that are really romantic— Anne Hathaway dying of consumption, Keira Knightley being hit by a train, Edward and Bella catching fire on their wedding night and burning to a crisp—"

"We are *not* going in the Tunnel of Love," I said. "What do you mean, these are the only areas not under surveillance?"

"I mean, there's no need to distract kids from going to see *Ice Age 22*," he said. "Kids *invented* the short attention span. You, on the other hand, have been remarkably single-minded, hence the vomit. And the Gingerbread Man."

"You're saying the *Drome* was the one trying to keep me from seeing *Christmas Caper*?"

"Yup."

"But why?"

"Okay, so you know how this all started, that after the *Batman* and Metrolux and *Hobbit III* massacres, movie attendance totally tanked, and they had to come up with some way to get the public back, so they turned the theaters into fortresses where people felt safe bringing their kids and sending their teenagers. But to do that, they had to introduce all kinds of security—metal detectors, full-body scans, explosives sniffers— and that meant people were standing in line for an hour and forty-five minutes to see a two-hour movie, which only made attendance drop off more. Who wants to stand in a line when you can stay home and stream movies on your ninety-inch screen? They had to come up with something new, something really spectacular—"

"The moviedromes," I said.

"Yup. Turn going to the movies into an all-day full-surround enter-tainment experience—"

"Like Disneyverse."

He nodded. "Or IKEA. Show *lots* of movies. A hundred instead of the multiplexes' twenty. And add lots of razzle-dazzle: 4-D, IMAX, interac-tives, Hollywood-style premieres, celebrity appearances, plus theme res-taurants and shops and rides and dance clubs and Wii arcades. None of which was really new."

"But I thought you said—"

"Movie theaters have never made their money off the movies they showed. They were just a sideline, a way to get the public into the the-ater and buy popcorn and jujubes at outrageous prices. The Dromes just expanded on the concept, to the point that the movies have become less and less important. Did you know fifty-three percent of the people who go to a Drome never see a movie at all?"

"I can believe it," I said, thinking of Kett and Zara.

"And that's not an accident. In the two hours it takes to watch a movie, you could be spending way more than the price of a ticket *and* refresh-ments. And if they can get you to see a later showing, you'll eat lunch *and* dinner here—and stick around to play glittertag afterward. The lon-ger you're at the Drome—"

"The more I spend."

He nodded. "So the Drome does everything it can to see that hap-pens."

"You expect me to believe the Drome orchestrated all that—the tick-ets and the vomit and the text and the sold-out sign—just to get me to buy more souvenirs?"

"No. You know that old movie we watched where the guy's investigat-ing what looks like a simple train accident and then it turns out it *wasn't* an accident?"

"*I Love Trouble,*" I said promptly. "With Nick Nolte and Julia Roberts. She was a reporter—"

"And he was a scoundrel," Jack said, grinning. "Who, as I recall, Julia really liked."

"What's your point?"

"My point is that the train accident was just the tip of the iceberg. And so is *Christmas Caper.* I think there's a whole vast conspiracy—"

"To keep me from seeing a *movie*?"

"Not you. Anyone. And not just *Christmas Caper. The Pimmsleys of Parson's Court,* too, and *Just When You Thought You Were Over Him,* and *Switching Gears,* and possibly a couple of others."

"Why?"

"Because they can't afford to let the public find out what's going on. Remember the things I told you the Dromes used to attract people—lots of razzle-dazzle and merchandise, and lots of movies?"

"Yes."

"Well, that's the problem. The old multiplexes had fifteen screens to fill. The Dromes have a hundred."

"But they show some movies in more than one theater."

"Right, and in 3-D, 4-D, and Wii versions, plus there are tons of sequels and remakes and reboots—"

"And Encore Presentations—"

"And rereleases and film festivals and Harry Potter marathons and sneak previews, but even if you add in foreign films and Bollywood and bad remakes of British romantic comedies and crummy remakes of all three, it's still a hell of a lot of screens to fill. Especially when most people are only interested in seeing *The Return of Frodo.* Do you remember when we went to see *Gaudy Night* and we were the only two people in the theater?"

"Yes—"

"It's like Baskin-Robbins. They advertise thirty-one flavors, but who the hell ever orders raisin or lemon custard? Those could actually be vanilla with a little food coloring added for all anybody knows. And so could half the Dromes' movies."

"So you're saying *Christmas Caper* doesn't exist?"

"I think that's a very real possibility."

"But that's ridiculous. You and I saw a trailer for it. There was a preview on the overheads while we were in line."

"Which was three minutes long and could have been filmed in a day."

"But why would they advertise it if it doesn't exist?"

"Because otherwise somebody—like me, for instance—might get suspicious."

"But there's no way they could get away with—"

"Sure there is. Most people want to see the latest blockbuster, and

with a minor nudge—like a sold-out sign—you can talk ninety-five percent of the rest of them into seeing something else. Or having lunch at
Babette's Feast."

"And the other five percent?"

"You just saw it."

"But movies sell out, especially at Christmastime—"

"And people throw up and accidentally spill drinks and get picked up
by fraternity guys and can't go to the 10:20 showing because it gets out
after the last light-rail train home. But the last showing of every movie I
named gets out after the last scheduled light-rail, and I've tried to get
into *Switching Gears* for the last five days and haven't made it. What
time is it?"

"Four o'clock."

"Come on," he said, grabbing my hand and pulling me up. "We've
gotta get going if we're going to make it to *Christmas Caper.*"

> *"Exciting, suspenseful, and unbelievably romantic!"*
> —Front Row

*

But I thought you said it doesn't exist," I said as he dragged me out of
Gusteau's.

"It doesn't. Come on." He led me through Hogwarts and Neverland
and down an aisle of shops selling *Toy Story* and *The Great Oz* and *Son
of Lion King* souvenirs.

"This isn't the way to the theater complex," I protested.

"We've got some shopping to do first," he said, leading me into the
Disney Princess Boutique.

"Shopping? Why?"

"Because we can't afford to have management notice us, and the sur-
est way to draw attention to yourself in a Drome is by not spending
money," he said, riffling through a rack of *Tangled* T-shirts.

"Besides," he said, moving to another rack, this one full of *Snow White
and the Seven Dwarfs* hoodies, "this is a big date. You should have something special to wear. Something the usher hasn't seen." He flipped
through the entire rack and then one of *Twelve Dancing Princesses* tutus,
pulling them out and then hanging them back up.

"What are you looking for?" I asked.

"I told you. Something special," he said, searching through yet another rack. "And something that doesn't make you smell like Mrs. Claus's kitchen. Ah, here we go," he said, pulling out a yellow *Dora and Diego Do the Himalayas* T-shirt, with Diego pointing his trademark camera at Dora and the monkey, who were standing atop Mount Everest. "Just the ticket."

"I am not wearing—" I began, but he'd already thrust it and a bright pink *Little Goose Girl* baseball cap into my hands.

"Tell the clerk to deactivate the tags so you can wear them now," he said, "and then go in the dressing room, take off your top, and put the shirt on. I'll be in the store next door." He gave me a push in the paydesk's direction. "And no questions."

I did as he said, pulling my top off over my head—he was right, it did reek of gingerbread—and putting the T-shirt on over my singlet.

It was too tight, which I suspected was part of the plan, and looked even worse on me than it had on the hanger. "You could have at least had me get something cute," I told him when I found him in the shop next door, trying on *Risky Business* sunglasses.

"No, I couldn't," he said. "What'd you do with your top?"

"I put it in the bag," I said.

"Good. Come on," he said, taking it from me and steering me out of the shop, back toward Gusteau's, to a recycler. He dropped the bag in.

"I liked that top," I protested.

"Shh, do you want to go to this movie or not?" he said, leading me through a maze of balloon artists and tattoo laser techs and kiddie rides and candy stores to the lobby.

He stopped just short of it. "Okay, I want you to go over to the kiosk and buy a ticket to *Dragonwar*."

"*Dragonwar?* But I thought we were going to—"

"We are. You buy a ticket to *Dragonwar* and then—"

"One ticket? Not two?"

"Definitely not two. We're going in separately."

"What if the machine tells me I have to buy it at the ticket counter?"

"It won't," he said. "Once you're inside—"

"Or what if they say I can't go in yet?"

"They won't do that, either," he said. "Once you're inside, go to the concessions stand and buy a large popcorn and a large 7-Up with two straws, and go down to Theater 17."

"Theater 17? But *Dragonwar's* playing in Theater 24."

"We're not going to *Dragonwar.* Or to *Au Revoir, Mon Fou,* which is what's showing in Theater 17. You're not going into any theater. You're just going to stand in the doorway of 17. I'll meet you there in a couple of minutes."

"And you promise we'll see *Christmas Caper*?"

"I promise I'll *take* you to *Christmas Caper.* Large popcorn," he ordered. "Large 7-Up. *Not* Coke." He jammed the *Goose Girl* cap down over my eyes. "Theater 17," he repeated, and took off through the crowd.

> *"Based on a true story . . . but you won't believe it!"*
> —*At the Movies*
>
> ✳

He was right. No one got in my way or spilled a felony frappe on me or stopped me to give me a free pass to *You're Under Arrest,* and the usher didn't even glance at me as he tore my ticket in half. "Theater 24," he said, and motioned to the right, "End of the hall," and turned his attention to a trio of thirteen-year-olds, and I went down the plush-carpeted hall.

There was no sign of Jack, but he could be hiding in one of the recessed entrances to the theater or past the point halfway down where the hall took a turn to the right.

He wasn't. I stood outside Theater 17 for longer than a couple of minutes and then walked slowly down to 24, where *Dragonwar* was playing, but he wasn't there, either.

He got caught trying to sneak in, and they threw him out, I thought, walking back to Theater 17 and planting myself in the recessed doorway.

I waited some more.

Still no sign of Jack, or of anyone else, except a kid who shot out of Theater 30 and down to the restroom, banging its door loudly behind him. I waited some more. I would have gotten my phone out to see what time it was, but between the giant 7-Up I was cradling in my left arm and the enormous bag of popcorn, there was no way I could manage it.

A door slammed farther down the hall and I looked up eagerly, but it was just the kid, racing back to 30, obviously determined not to miss a second more than necessary of his movie. I wondered what it was that was so riveting. I moved down the hall a little so I could see the marquee above the door.

Lethal Rampage. And next door to it, on the marquee above Theater 28, *Christmas Caper.*

"The cast is terrific!"
—Goin' Hollywood

*

That *rat*! Jack had told me it didn't exist, and yet here it was. And all those problems I'd had, all those people who'd gotten in my way, weren't Drome employees hired to keep me out. They were just moviegoers like me, and the things that had happened were nothing more than coincidences. There *was* no conspiracy.

When are you going to learn you can't trust a word he says? I thought, and if he'd been there, I'd have taken great pleasure in dumping the 7-Up—and the popcorn—over his head and stomping out.

But he'd apparently gotten himself caught and thrown out of the Drome. If he'd ever intended to come. And I was left, quite literally, holding the bag. And now that I thought about it, Nick Nolte had done the same thing to Julia Roberts in *I Love Trouble*—sending her on what else?—a wild-goose chase. With real geese.

I'll kill him when I find him, I thought, and started back toward the entrance, fuming, and then stopped and looked back at Theater 28. I had come to the Drome to see *Christmas Caper,* and it was right here, with the 4:30 showing due to start at any minute. And it would serve Jack right if I saw it without him.

I walked back to the turn and peeked around the corner to make sure no one—especially not somebody on the staff—was coming and would catch me going into a different movie than the one I had the ticket for, and then hurried over to Theater 28 and pulled the door open. That was no mean feat given the popcorn and the 7-Up, but I managed to get it open far enough to hold it with my hip while I sidled through.

It was pitch-dark inside. The door shut behind me, and I stood there in the blackness, waiting for my eyes to adjust. They didn't, even though there should be *some* light from the movie screen, or, if the previews hadn't started yet, from the overhead lights. And weren't these hallways supposed to have strip lighting in case they had to evacuate the theater?

This one obviously didn't, and I couldn't see *anything.* I stood there in the darkness, listening. The previews had definitely started. I could hear crashes and clangs and ominous music. It must be a preview for one of those shot-totally-at-night movies like *The Dark Knight Rises* or the *Alien* reboot, and that was why I couldn't see, and in a minute, when a different preview came on, there'd be enough light to find my way by. But though the sounds changed to laughter and the muffled murmur of voices, the corridor remained coal-mine black.

I was going to have to feel my way along the passage, but I didn't have a free hand to hold on to the wall with. Or to fish out my phone with so I could use its lit screen as a flashlight.

This is all Jack's fault, I thought, stooping to set down the 7-Up so I could get my phone out of my pocket. I flipped it open and held it out in front of me. And no wonder the passage was so dark. It went a few more feet and then turned sharply to the left in a kind of dogleg. If I'd kept going, I'd have run face-first into a wall.

That's a lawsuit waiting to happen, I thought, trying to figure out a way to hold on to my phone and the 7-Up. There wasn't one—the cup was too big around—but if I could just make it past the dogleg, there should be some light from the screen to see by. I put my phone back in my pocket, felt for the cup, picked it up, and started down the passage again, counting the steps to the wall.

"Four . . . five . . ." I whispered. "Six, sev—"

And was grabbed abruptly from behind by a hand around my waist. I yelped, but a second hand was already over my mouth, and Jack's voice was in my ear. "Shh. In here," he whispered, and pulled me, impossibly, right through the wall.

> *"A winner! You'll be glad you came!"*
> —*Variety Online*

*

Amazingly, I hadn't dropped the 7-Up *or* the bag of popcorn. "What do you think you're doing?" I said, wrestling free of him.

"Shh!" he whispered. "These walls aren't soundproof. Did you spill any of the popcorn?"

"Of course I spilled the popcorn," I said. "You scared me half to death!"

"Shh. Look, you can yell at me all you want," he whispered, "but not till the next chase scene. And don't take out your cell phone. I don't want the light to give us away. Stay here," he ordered, and I heard the swish of a door's opening and closing softly, and then nothing but the sounds of pandemonium coming through the left-hand wall.

It sounded similar to what I'd heard before and had thought was from the previews for *Christmas Caper,* but it was clearly coming from the theater next door, which meant it was *Lethal Rampage.*

I couldn't see anything at all, let alone enough to make out my surroundings, but this had to be the corridor leading to *Christmas Caper* because I could hear a voice intoning, "Coming this Valentine's Day!" through the other wall.

Good, the previews were still playing. I hadn't missed the start of the movie. I would have time to tell Jack what I thought of him for grabbing me like that and still make it into the theater in time for the opening credits. If I could find it in the darkness, which was still absolute.

Jack was back. I heard him shut the door. "Luckily, you only spilled a couple of handfuls," he said over the crash of explosions from *Lethal Rampage.* "Which I ate. What took you so long? I was afraid the usher had spotted you, and I was going to have to come back out and rescue you."

"Where *was* I?" I said angrily. "I was standing outside Theater 17 just like you told me to. You *lied* to me—"

"Nobody saw you go in the door to 28, did they?"

"Don't change the subject. You—"

"Did they?" He grabbed my arm, jostling the popcorn.

"No," I said, only half listening. In between deafening explosions, the announcer on the *Christmas Caper* side of the wall was saying muffledly, "And now for our feature presentation."

"Look," I said. "I'd love to stand here in the dark and fight with you, but *I* intend to see *Christmas Caper.* So if you'll please let go of my arm, the movie's about to start."

"No, it's not," he said. He squeezed my arm. "Hang on," he said, let go, and moved away from me, and I could hear him doing something, though I couldn't tell what, and then the wall I was facing lit up with the beam from a penlight.

From what I could see in its dim light, we were in a narrow passage just like the one outside, with carpet on the floor and the walls and no strip lighting, but it was long and straight and ended in a wall, not in the entrance to the theater. There was no sign of the door Jack had just come through, though it had to be in that wall because Jack had taken off his jacket and laid it against the bottom of it.

"To keep any stray light from seeping out," he explained over the racket.

"What *is* this place?" I said. "Where *are* we?"

"Shh," he said, putting a finger to his lips and whispering. "Kissing scene coming up," and he must have been telling the truth because the gunfire and explosions were suddenly replaced by the strains of violins.

He took the popcorn and 7-Up cup from me, tiptoed halfway down the corridor, stooped and set them on the floor, and then stood up again, listening with his finger to his lips. And apparently the lethal rampagers were back, because the romantic violins cut off abruptly, replaced by a blast of trumpets, lots of drumming, and the sound of revving engines and squealing tires.

"Chase scene," Jack said, coming back over to me. "Time to go to work."

"You said you were going to tell me what this place is. Where's the theater?"

"I'll tell you everything, I swear. After we do this. Take off your shirt."

"*What?*"

"Your shirt. Take it off."

"You never change, do you?"

"Wrong line," he said. "You're supposed to say, 'Are you sure we're planning the same sort of crime?' and I say—"

"This is not *How to Steal a Million*," I said.

"You're right," he said. "It's more like *Jumpin' Jack Flash*. Or *I Love Trouble*. Take it off. And hurry. We don't have much time."

"I have no intention of taking off any—"

"Calm down. It's for the photos. Of this passage and the one outside," he said, and when I still stood there, my arms crossed, "The camera the boy on your shirt is holding isn't just a picture. There's a digital-strip camera embedded in it."

And that was why he'd riffled through all those shirts in the Disney Princess boutique. He'd been looking for one with a camera. "Why can't you just use the camera in your phone?"

"When they scan them in the security line, they check your info against the police and FBI databases."

"Which you're in because of the geese," I said. "That's why you wanted me to come with you, so I could smuggle in your camera for you."

"Of course. That's what scoundrels do. They use the girl to smuggle the necklace through customs or to get the news story or to get them out of East Germany—"

"This is *not* a movie!"

"You're right about that. Which is why I've got to get those pictures. So, do you want to give me that shirt or do you want me to take the camera off of it while you're wearing it?"

"Fine," I said, pulled the T-shirt off over my head, handed it to him, and stood there fuming in my singlet while he turned the shirt inside out, peeled off the digital-strip camera, and handed the T-shirt back to me. I pulled it on while he snapped pictures of the passage, motioning me out of the way so he could get a shot of the long wall behind me.

He snapped the end wall he'd dragged me through and the one at the other end, and then came back to me and listened a moment. "I'll be right back," he said, switched off the penlight, plunging us in darkness, and went out into the passage again.

He was gone for what seemed like forever. I put my ear to the door, but all I could hear were detonations and screams from the *Lethal Rampage* side and disgustingly perky music from the other. I listened intently, afraid the din would subside any minute, but it didn't, though on the *Rampage* side I could hear, over the crashing, the sound of muffled voices.

Please don't let that be the usher or Drome security, I thought, *demanding to know what Jack was doing in here,* but it must not have been because the door was opening again, and I had to back away hastily as Jack came in and shut it behind him.

"Can you find my jacket?" he whispered, and I felt around for it in vain, and then pulled my shirt off again and handed it to him to put against the door.

"Thanks," he whispered, and, after a few seconds, switched on the penlight again.

"Did you get the pictures?"

He waved the digital strip at me. "Yeah."

"Good. You *lied* to me."

"No, I didn't. Besides, Jimmy Stewart lied to Margaret Sullavan, Peter O'Toole lied to Audrey Hepburn, Cary Grant lied to Audrey Hepburn. It's what scoundrels do."

"That's no excuse. You promised you'd take me to *Christmas Caper.*"

"And I did," he said. "This is it." He waved his arm to show the passage. "Welcome to Theater 28."

"This isn't a theater," I said.

"You're right," he said. "Come on." He grabbed my hand, led me down to where he'd set the popcorn and 7-Up. "Have a seat, and I'll explain everything. Come on, sit down."

I sat down on the floor, my back against the carpeted wall, my arms folded belligerently across my chest, and he sat down across from me. "That passage outside splits in two and goes into the theaters on either side," he said. "If I hadn't reached out and pulled you in here, you'd have turned and followed that dogleg into Theater 30 and *Lethal Rampage.*

"And if you'd turned the other way, you'd have ended up in Theater 26"—he jerked his thumb toward the wall behind him—"where *Make Way for Ducklings* is now showing, a fact you wouldn't have discovered until you'd sat through fifteen minutes of previews, at which point you'd have thought you'd somehow gotten in the wrong theater, and go tell the usher, who'd tell you he was sorry, but you'd missed the start of *Christmas Caper* and he couldn't let you in, but that there might still be tickets available for the seven o'clock. A neat trick, huh?"

"But why—?"

"They have to have a last line of defense in case a determined fan makes it past all the other firewalls. That hardly ever happens, but occasionally somebody does what you just did—can't get in, buys a ticket for another movie, and then tries to sneak in to what they originally wanted to see."

"Why don't they just *not* put up a marquee for it?"

"They tried that, which is what made us suspicious in the first place, so they had to come up with an alternative plan. Which you see before you."

"Us?" I asked.

"Oops, I almost forgot," he said, scrambling to his feet and going to retrieve his jacket. He put it on, came back, and began searching through its pockets.

"Now what are you doing?" I asked.

"Trying to get this made before *Lethal Rampage* hits another quiet stretch." He frowned at the red Coca-Cola cup. "You *did* get 7-Up, didn't you? Not Coke?"

"I got 7-Up." I handed it over to him. "You're not making a stink bomb out of that, are you?" I asked as he pulled out a flask and poured a brown liquid into the cup.

"No," he said, patting his pockets some more and pulling out a *Terminator 12* commemorative glass and then a baggie full of lemon slices.

He poured half the 7-Up-and-brown-liquid-and-ice mixture into the *Terminator* glass, added a lemon slice and a sprig of mint from his breast pocket, reached inside his jacket, pulled out a stalk of rhubarb with a flourish, stuck it in the glass, stirred the mixture with it, and handed it to me. "Your Pimm's Cup, madam," he said.

"Just like the ones you made the night we watched *Ghost Town*," I said, smiling.

"Well, not just like them. These are made with rum, which was all Tom Cruise's *Cocktail* Bar had. And when I made the *Ghost Town* ones, I was trying to get you into bed."

"And what are you trying to do this time? Get me drunk so I'll agree to help you do something else illegal?"

"No," he said, sitting down next to me. "Not right now, anyway," which wasn't exactly a reassuring answer.

"I got the photos," he went on, "which is what I came for, and, thanks to you and that awful Dora T-shirt"—he raised his Coke cup to me—"I'm a lot less likely to get caught smuggling them out. But it's still too risky to do any more investigating till I've gotten them safely off the premises." He took a leisurely sip of his drink.

"Then, shouldn't we be going?" I asked.

"We can't. Not till *Lethal Rampage* is over and we can blend in with the audience as it leaves. So relax. Drink your Pimm's Cup, have some popcorn. We've got—" He stopped and listened to the din coming through the wall for a moment, "an hour and forty-six minutes to kill. Enough time to—"

"Tell me what's going on, like you promised you would. Or are you going to tell me that's classified, too?"

"As a matter of fact, it is," he said. "And you've already seen what *they're* doing—covering up movies that don't exist."

"But why? Most people don't even *care* about the movies part."

"Oh, but they do. They think they've got a hundred to choose from, and that's what makes them come all the way out here on the light-rail and stand in security lines forever. Do you think they'd do that just to buy a bag of popcorn and an overpriced Avengers mug? How long do you think Baskin-Robbins would stay in business if they only had three flavors, even if they were the most popular ones? Look at your friends. They may have spent today shopping and eating and—"

"Picking up guys."

"And picking up guys, but if somebody asked them tomorrow what they did, they'd say they went to the movies, and they'd believe it. The Drome's not selling popcorn, it's selling an *illusion,* an idea—a giant screen with magical images on it, your girlfriend sitting beside you in the dark, romance, adventure, mystery . . ."

"But I still don't understand. Okay, they have to maintain the illusion, but it's not as if they don't have *any* movies. You said there were only four or five movies here that didn't exist, and they already show some movies on more than one screen. Why not just show *X-Force* and *The Return of Frodo* in one more theater instead of making movies up?"

"Because they're already showing *X-Force* in six theaters as it is, and Starstruck just announced they're building a chain of 250-screen Super-dromes. Besides, I don't think the moviegoing public's the only people they're trying to fool."

"What do you mean?"

"I mean, if you're a film company, this could really work to your advantage. If your movie's behind schedule, nobody gets fined or fired for missing the release date. You release it anyway, and then, when it's finished, you put out the DVD and stream it, and nobody's the wiser. Which, by the way, is what happened to *Monsoon Gate* and what I think probably happened to *Christmas Caper.* You can't release a Christmas movie in February. It's got to come out in December or you'll lose your shirt. Figuratively speaking."

"Which means it might show up on the Net in a few months," I said.

"Yeah, and if it does, I'll watch it with you, I promise."

"Do you think that's what happened to the other movies?"

"No. *The Ripper Files* never came out, and neither did *Mission to Antares* or *By the Skin of Our Teeth.* And why spend millions making a movie when you can do a three-minute trailer instead, pay the Dromes to block people from seeing it, and pocket the difference? The shareholders wouldn't even have to know."

"Which would make it fraud."

"It's already fraud," he said. "And false advertising. There are laws against selling products that don't exist."

"Which is why they don't sell the tickets online," I said. "But if they're criminals, isn't what you're doing dangerous?"

"Not if they don't know I'm doing it. Which is why," he said, his voice dropping to a whisper, "we need to sit here quietly, eat our popcorn"—he scooted closer to me—"and watch the movie."

"What's it about?" I whispered.

"This guy who's investigating a conspiracy when who should turn up but his old girlfriend. It's the last thing he needs. He's trying to stay invisible—"

Which explains why he looked so dismayed when he saw me, I thought, a weight lifting from me.

"And he knows he should probably get out of there before she blows his cover, but she already thinks he's a—"

"Scoundrel?"

"I was going to say 'wanker.'"

"Scoundrel," I said firmly, "and besides, he needs her to help him smuggle something in past the guards, like Kevin Kline in *French Kiss.*"

"Exactly," he said. "Plus, he's got some stuff to tell her, so he recruits her to help him, and in the course of their investigations, he convinces her to forgive him, like Olivia de Havilland forgives Errol Flynn and Julia Roberts forgives Nick Nolte and Whoopi Goldberg forgives—"

"Jack. Because that's what scoundrels' girlfriends do."

"Exactly," he said. "Which is why you should—"

"Shh," I said.

"What is it?" he whispered.

"Kissing scene coming up," I said, and switched off the penlight.

"The most fun you can have at the movies!"
—*moviefone.com*

✳

How long does *Lethal Rampage* run?" I asked him a considerable time later. "That sounds like Final Scene music to me."

He raised himself up on one elbow, said, "It is," and went back to nuzzling my neck.

"But don't we have to be out of here before it ends?"

"Yeah, but you're forgetting, it's a Hollywood Blockbuster. Remember when we saw the reboot of *Speed,* how we kept thinking it was over and it wasn't? Or *The Return of the King*? That had like seven endings. *Lethal Rampage* has got at least three more climaxes to go."

"Oh, good," I murmured, snuggling into his shoulder, but a moment later he sat up, reached for his jacket, pulled a phone out of it, and flipped it open.

"I thought you didn't have a phone," I said, sitting up.

"Not one I wanted to get caught with photos on," he said, looking at its screen. "Change of plans. There's something I've got to go take care of." He began buttoning his shirt. "Wait till the next explosion and then slip out into the passage and wait for *Lethal Rampage* to get out. And don't leave anything behind."

I nodded.

"When you get out to the lobby, go over to one of the cafés, *not* the Polar Express, order a drink, text your friends, and then wait at least a few minutes before you try to leave, and you should be fine."

He pulled me to my feet. "Look, I can't tweet or call you—it might be traced—so it may be a while before I can get in touch. All I've proved so far is that there's a blocked-off passageway between theaters and some suspicious activity. I still have to prove the movies don't exist, which I'll have to do in Hollywood." He hesitated. "I feel bad about leaving you here like this."

"But Peter O'Toole left Audrey Hepburn in a closet and Kevin Kline left Meg Ryan in Paris without a passport," I said, following him down to the far end of the passage. "And now I suppose I'm supposed to say, 'It's okay. Go,' and you kiss me goodbye, and I stand in the doorway like Olivia, looking longingly after you with my tresses blowing in a wind that smells like the sea?"

"Exactly. Except in this case it smells more like rancid popcorn oil," he said, "and we can't afford to leave the door open. It lets in too much light. But I can definitely manage the kiss."

He did. "See?" he said. "You do like scoundrels."

"I happen to like nice men," I said. "How are you going to get out of the Drome without security's catching you?"

"I'll be fine," he said. "Look, if you get in trouble—"

"I won't. Go."

He kissed me again, opened the wall, and went through it, only to appear again almost instantly. "By the way," he said, "about the geese and the graduating thing. Remember in *How to Steal a Million* where Peter O'Toole tells Audrey Hepburn he's not a burglar, that he's actually a security expert 'with advanced degrees in art history and chemistry and a diploma, with distinction, from London University in advanced criminology'?"

"Yes," I said. "I suppose now you're going to tell me you have an advanced degree from London University?"

"No, Yale. In consumer fraud," he said, and was gone, leaving me to hurriedly gather up all the telltale trash by the less-than-helpful light of my cell phone screen, get out into the passage, shutting the door soundlessly behind me, and over to the corridor that led to the theater next door, and wait for the movie to let out.

> "A movie experience that leaves you wanting more!
> An enthusiastic thumbs-up!"
> —*rogerebert.net*

*

He'd been right about *Lethal Rampage.* It went on for another twenty minutes, giving me time to make sure the door was completely shut with no seams showing, check again for stray popcorn, and then lean against the corridor wall, listening to a whole symphony of crashes, bangs, and explosions before the lights came up, people started trickling out, and I had to somehow merge with them without being noticed.

It was easier than I'd thought. They were all too intent on switching their cell phones back on and complaining about the movie to pay any attention to me.

Lethal Rampage had apparently been just as awful as it had sounded through the wall. "I couldn't believe how lame the plot was," a twelve-year-old boy said, and his friend nodded. "I *hated* the ending."

Me, too, I thought wistfully.

I eased in behind them and followed them down the passage, eaves-dropping on their conversation so I could talk about the movie in case anybody asked me about it.

Like the ticket-taker, who I still had to get past. I wondered if he'd remember I'd been going to *Dragonwar,* not *Lethal Rampage.* Maybe I should go back to Theater 17 and go out with the *Dragonwar* audience.

But if it had already let out, I'd have to go out past the ticket-taker alone, ensuring he'd notice me. And what if somebody on staff saw me going back and concluded I was sneaking into a second movie? I'd better stick with this crowd.

I stopped just inside the door, loitering by the trash can till a group of high-school kids came by, and then hastily tossed my popcorn sack and Coke cup and attached myself to them. And it was a good thing because there was a cleaning crew lurking just outside the door with their dust-pans and garbage bags, and for all their slouching against the wall, wait-ing for the theater to empty out, they looked unnaturally alert.

I stuck close to the high-schoolers as we passed them, bending over my phone and pretending to text like they were doing, and stayed with them as we merged with the audience from *Pirates of the Caribbean 9,* which had just gotten out.

From the sound of things, *Pirates* hadn't been any better than *Lethal Rampage,* and it occurred to me that I'd had a better time than any of them, even though I hadn't seen a movie, and—

The conclusion of that thought was swept away by a bunch of people pouring down from the upstairs theaters, and it was all I could do to keep my footing as the whole mass of people surged past the ticket-taker and out into the only-slightly-less-crowded lobby, which I was relieved to see wasn't full of security guards and blaring sirens. Jack must have gotten safely away.

But just in case he was still in the Drome somewhere, I needed to do what I could to keep them from getting suspicious.

Which meant detaching myself from the high-schoolers and getting in line to get tickets for the next showing of *Christmas Caper*. If I were still trying to see it, I obviously didn't know it didn't exist.

The high-schoolers were trying to decide which restaurant to go to. "While you make up your minds, I'm going to go get a funnel cake," I said to the nearest of them, who didn't even look up from her smartphone, and went to check the time of the next showing, which should be at 6:40.

It wasn't. It was at 7:30, and the one after that was at 10:00. I stared at the board for a long minute, contemplating what that meant, and then went to try to find the end of the ticket line.

It was ten times longer than it had been when we'd first arrived, snaking all the way back to the Death Star Diner, and it was barely moving. It was a good thing I wasn't trying to actually get in. I wouldn't make it even halfway to the front before the last light-rail train home.

I wondered how long I needed to stand here. Jack had said it wasn't safe to use his phone, but he might have been able to borrow someone else's and send me a text from it, so I turned on my phone and looked at my messages.

There weren't any from him, but there were four from Zara, all of them asking, "Where r u?" except the last one, which said, "Assume ur not ansring means u finally got in 2 *Xmas Cpr*. How was it?"

I needed to text her back, but not till I was far enough along the line that it wouldn't look like I'd just gotten into it. I didn't want her wondering what I'd been doing all this time—she was way too quick to draw connections to Jack. So I switched off my phone and then stood there, periodically inching forward, thinking about Zara's text. "How was it?" she'd asked.

Great, I thought, and remembered those boys complaining about *Lethal Rampage* and my thinking I'd had a much better time at the movies than they had.

And how did I know that wasn't what *I'd* just experienced—an afternoon at the movies? That I hadn't just been participating in a romantic spy adventure concocted by Jack, who knew how much I wanted to believe he'd had a good reason for going off without saying a word to me and who'd heard me complain countless times about going to a movie with Zara and Kett and ending up not getting to see it?

There could have been lots of reasons that that passage was there. It could've been a shortcut between theaters for the projectionist, or some sort of required evacuation route in case of fire that Jack had appropriated for his own private Tunnel of Love. He could have bribed the usher to tell me I couldn't get in and to put *Christmas Caper* up on Theater 28's marquee after the audience for *Make Way for Ducklings* was inside. And the other stuff—the vomit and the spilled gingerbread latte and Santa— could all have been coincidences, and Jack had simply made them sound like a conspiracy.

Don't be ridiculous, I told myself. *Do you honestly think he'd go to that much trouble just to get you into bed?*

Of course he would. Look how much trouble he went to just to play a practical joke on the dean. And the whole thing had been just like the plot of *How to Steal a Million* or *I Love Trouble,* complete with spies, slapstick, a sparring couple forced together into a small confined space, and a hero who was lying to the heroine.

And believing it was a scam made a lot more sense than believing that some vast Hollywood conspiracy lay behind this decorated-for-Christmas Cinedrome.

There isn't any conspiracy, I thought. *You've been had, that's all. Again.* Christmas Caper *is showing right now in Theater 56 or 79 or 100. And Jack is off plotting some other practical joke—or the seduction of some other gullible girl—while I stand here in this stupid line trying to protect him from a danger that never existed.*

I looked back at the end of the line, which I was only a dozen people away from. I still couldn't text Zara, but for a completely different reason now—she couldn't *ever* find out what an idiot I'd been.

So I continued to stand there, thinking about how easy it would have been for Jack to bribe somebody on the staff to put a NO TICKETS AVAILABLE sign on the schedule board, just like he'd bribed some farmer to lend him those geese. And to pay somebody to block me on my way across the lobby. And thinking how, when I found *Christmas Caper* was sold out, I should just have gone to see *A Star-Crossed Season* instead.

Three Hanover freshmen leaned over the barrier to talk to the girls ahead of me in line. "What are you going to?" one of them asked.

"We haven't decided," one of the girls said. "We were thinking maybe *Saw 7*. Or *A Star-Crossed Season*."

"Don't!" the trio shouted, and the middle one said, "We just saw it. It was beyond boring!"

> *"Well worth the trip!"*
> —*comingsoon.com*
>   *

I waited another ten minutes, during which I moved forward about a foot, and then called Zara.

"Where have you *been*?" she asked. "I've been texting and texting you."

"You have?" I said. "I haven't gotten them. I think there's something wrong with my phone."

"So where are you now?"

"Where do you think? In line."

"In *line*?" she said. "You mean you still haven't seen *Christmas Card*?"

"*Caper*," I corrected her. "No, not yet. All three afternoon showings sold out before I got to the front of the line, so I'm trying to get a ticket to the seven o'clock."

"Where are you exactly?" she asked.

I told her.

"I'll be right there," she said, which I doubted. It would take her at least twenty minutes to disentangle herself and Kett from the guys, and then on the way here they'd be delayed by the dress Zooey Deschanel wore in *Son of Elf* or some other guys, and by that time I'd hopefully be far enough forward in the line to make it look like I'd been in line since the 12:10.

But she showed up almost immediately and alone. "This is all the farther you've gotten?" she said. "What happened to Jack?"

"I have no idea," I said. "Where's Kett?"

Zara rolled her eyes. "She texted Noah and they went off to the *Dirty Dancing* Club. Did he tell you where he's been all these months?"

"Who? Noah?"

"Very funny," Zara said. "No. *Jack.*"

"No. In jail, probably."

"It's too bad," Zara said, shaking her head sadly. "I was hoping you might get back together. I mean, I know he's kind of a . . ."

Scoundrel, I thought.

"Wanker," Zara said. "But he's so scorching!"

That he is, I thought. "What are you going to do now?" I asked her, to change the subject.

"I don't know," she said, sighing. "This trip's been a complete bust. I didn't meet anybody even lukewarm, and I couldn't find anything for my family for Christmas. I suppose I should go over to the *Pretty Woman* store and see if they have anything my mom would like, but I think maybe I'll just go see *Christmas Caper* with you. When did you say the next showing was?"

"Seven."

She checked the time on her phone. "It's already 6:30," she said, looking at her phone and then up at the line ahead of us. "We'll never make it."

"When's the showing after that?" I asked her, but before she could look it up, Kett came up, looking annoyed.

"What happened to Noah?" Zara asked her.

"He's at the first-aid station," she said.

"The first-aid—?"

"He had a bloody nose. He said he wanted to take me dancing, but it turned out it was because he wanted to enter me in the wet T-shirt contest, the slimewad," she said. "So what's going on?"

"Lindsay's still trying to get in to see *Christmas Caper,*" Zara said.

"You mean, you haven't managed to see it *yet*?" Kett asked. "Geez, how long have you been standing in line?"

"Forever," Zara said, studying her phone. "And she's definitely not going to get in to see the 7 o'clock. This is showing it as sold out." She scrolled down. "And the next showing isn't till 10"—she scrolled some more—"which doesn't get out till after the last train to Hanover leaves, so that one won't work, either."

"Geez," Kett said. "You spent all this time standing in line for a movie you don't even get to see. Was it worth it spending the whole day on it?"

Oh, yes, I thought. Because, lies or not, bill of goods or not, it was still the best afternoon at the movies I'd had in a long time. Much better than if I'd gone to see *A Star-Crossed Season.* Or *Lethal Rampage.* And *much* better than wandering around looking at Black Widow boots and *Silver Linings Playbook* leotards like Zara, or dealing with creeps, like Kett had. Unlike theirs, my afternoon had been great. It had had everything—adventure, suspense, romance, explosions, danger, snappy dialogue, kissing scenes. The perfect Saturday afternoon at the movies.

Except for the ending.

But it might not be over yet—Jack had after all promised me he'd watch *Christmas Caper* with me if it ended up being streamed. And right before the end of *Jumpin' Jack Flash,* Jack had left Whoopi Goldberg sitting waiting for him in a restaurant. Michael Douglas had left Kathleen Turner standing abandoned on a parapet. Han Solo had left Princess Leia on the rebel moon. And they'd all showed up again, just like they'd said.

Of course Jack had also told me he'd graduated from Yale and was investigating a huge, far-reaching conspiracy, and that putting those geese in the dean's office hadn't been a prank. But not everything he'd told me was a lie. He'd said he loved movies, and that was true. Nobody who didn't love them could have engineered such a perfect one.

And even if he'd made up everything else, even if he was every bit the scoundrel I was afraid he was and I never saw him again, it had still been a terrific afternoon at the movies.

"Well?" Kett was saying. "*Was* it? I mean, you didn't get to *do* anything."

"Or have anything to eat," I said, getting out of line. "Let's go get some sushi or something. How late is Nemo's open?"

"I'll see," Kett said, getting out her phone. "I think it stays open till—Oh, my God!"

"What?" Zara asked. "That slimewad Noah didn't text you something obscene, did he?"

"No," Kett said, scrolling down through her phone-number list. "You won't believe this." She tapped a number and put the phone up to her ear. "Hi," she said into it. "I got your text. What happened? . . . You're kidding! . . . Oh, my God! . . . Are you sure? Which channel?"

Oh, no, I thought, even though I'd decided he'd concocted the whole thing, *they've arrested Jack. They caught him with the camera strip.*

"Oh, my God, *what?*" Zara said.

"Hang on," Kett said to whoever was on the other end, and pressed the phone to her chest. "We should have stayed home," she said to us. "We missed all the excitement."

Jack went back to the campus to leave me a message, I thought, *and the campus police caught him.*

"What excitement?" Zara asked. "*Tell* us."

"Margo says there are all these TV camera crews and squad cars with flashing lights around the admin building, and a few minutes ago Dr. Baker told her the dean's been arrested."

"The *dean?*" I said.

"For what?" Zara asked.

"I don't know," Kett said. She texted like mad for a minute, and then said, "Margo says it has something to do with taking federal loan money for students who don't exist. It's apparently all over the news," and Zara began swiping through screens to find the coverage.

"The dean says it's all a big mistake," Kett said, "but apparently the FBI's consumer fraud division's been investigating him for months, and they've got all kinds of evidence."

I'll bet they do, I thought, thinking of Jack's saying he had to go, that something had come up, and of what a good idea geese had been. In all the chaos—and mess—nobody would have even thought to check the dean's office to see if anything was missing.

"There are?" Kett was saying. She put her hand over her phone. "Margo says the place has been crawling with scorching FBI agents."

"Here it is," Zara said, holding her phone so I could see the screen, which showed the quad full of police officers and FBI agents, and reporters trying to get a shot of the dean as he was perp-walked down the steps and over to a squad car. There was no sign of Jack.

"Are they still there?" Kett said, and then glumly, "Oh." She turned to us. "She says there's no point in our coming home. It's all over. I can't believe we missed it."

"Especially the FBI agents," Zara said teasingly.

"Right," Kett said. She sighed. "Instead, I got felt up by a slimewad."

"And I still don't have a present for my mother," Zara said. She turned to me. "And you didn't get to see your movie, after I *promised* you would."

"It doesn't matter."

"We could go to the 10:00," Zara said, "and leave before it's over. That way you could at least see part of it."

"And miss the ending?" I said, thinking of *Romancing the Stone,* where Michael Douglas comes back when Kathleen Turner least expects it, and of *French Kiss,* where Meg Ryan's already on the plane, and of *Jumpin' Jack Flash,* where he finally shows up in the very last scene and is every bit as wonderful as she thought he was.

"No, that's okay," I said, trying hard not to smile. "I'll watch it when it comes out on the Net."

Newsletter

Later examination of weather reports and newspapers showed that it may have started as early as October nineteenth, but the first indication I had that something unusual was going on was at Thanksgiving.

I went to Mom's for dinner (as usual), and was feeding cranberries and cut-up oranges and apples into Mom's old-fashioned meat grinder for the cranberry relish and listening to my sister-in-law Allison talk about her Christmas newsletter (also as usual).

"Which of Cheyenne's accomplishments do you think I should write about first, Nan?" she said, spreading cheese on celery sticks. "Her playing lead snowflake in *The Nutcracker* or her hitting a home run in Pee-Wee Soccer?"

"I'd list the Nobel Peace Prize first," I murmured, under cover of the crunch of an apple being put through the grinder.

"There just isn't room to put in all the girls' accomplishments," she said, oblivious. "Mitch *insists* I keep it to one page."

"That's because of Aunt Lydia's newsletters," I said. "Eight pages single-spaced."

"I know," she said. "And in that tiny print you can barely read." She waved a celery stick thoughtfully. "That's an idea."

"Eight pages single-spaced?"

"No. I could get the computer to do a smaller font. That way I'd have room for Dakota's Sunshine Scout merit badges. I got the cutest paper for my newsletters this year. Little angels holding bunches of mistletoe."

Christmas newsletters are *very* big in my family, in case you couldn't tell. Everybody—uncles, grandparents, second cousins, my sister Sueann—sends the Xeroxed monstrosities to family, coworkers, old friends from high school, and people they met on their cruise to the Caribbean (which they wrote about at length in their newsletter the year before). Even my Aunt Irene, who writes a handwritten letter on every one of her Christmas cards, sticks a newsletter in with it.

My second cousin Lucille's are the worst, although there are a lot of contenders. Last year hers started:

> *"Another year has hurried past*
> *And, here I am, asking, 'Where did the time go so fast?'*
> *A trip in February, a bladder operation in July,*
> *Too many activities, not enough time, no matter*
>   *how hard I try."*

At least Allison doesn't put Dakota and Cheyenne's accomplishments into verse.

"I don't think I'm going to send a Christmas newsletter this year," I said.

Allison stopped, cheese-filled knife in hand. "Why not?"

"Because I don't have any news. I don't have a new job, I didn't go on a vacation to the Bahamas, I didn't win any awards. I don't have anything to tell."

"Don't be ridiculous," my mother said, sweeping in carrying a foil-covered casserole dish. "Of course you do, Nan. What about that skydiving class you took?"

"That was last year, Mom," I said. And I had only taken it so I'd have something to write about in my Christmas newsletter.

"Well, then, tell about your social life. Have you met anybody lately at work?"

Mom asks me this every Thanksgiving. Also Christmas, the Fourth of July, and every time I see her.

"There's nobody to meet," I said, grinding cranberries. "Nobody new ever gets hired, because nobody ever quits. Everybody who works there's been there for years. Nobody even gets fired. Bob Hunziger hasn't been to work on time in eight years, and *he's* still there."

"What about . . . what was his name?" Allison said, arranging the celery sticks in a cut-glass dish. "The guy you liked who had just gotten divorced?"

"Gary," I said. "He's still hung up on his ex-wife."

"I thought you said she was a real shrew."

"She is," I said. "Marcie the Menace. She calls him twice a week complaining about how unfair the divorce settlement is, even though she got virtually everything. Last week it was the house. She claimed she'd been too upset by the divorce to get the mortgage refinanced and he owed her twenty thousand dollars because now interest rates have gone up. But it doesn't matter. Gary still keeps hoping they'll get back together. He almost didn't fly to Connecticut to his parents' for Thanksgiving because he thought she might change her mind about a reconciliation."

"You could write about Sueann's new boyfriend," Mom said, sticking marshmallows on the sweet potatoes. "She's bringing him today."

This was as usual, too. Sueann always brings a new boyfriend to Thanksgiving dinner. Last year it was a biker. And no, I don't mean one of those nice guys who wear a beard and black Harley T-shirt on weekends and work as accountants between trips to Sturgis. I mean a Hell's Angel.

My sister Sueann has the worst taste in men of anyone I have ever known. Before the biker, she dated a member of a militia group and, after the ATF arrested him, a bigamist wanted in three states.

"If this boyfriend spits on the floor, I'm leaving," Allison said, counting out silverware. "Have you met him?" she asked Mom.

"No," Mom said, "but Sueann says he used to work where you do, Nan. So *somebody* must quit once in a while."

I racked my brain, trying to think of any criminal types who'd worked in my company. "What's his name?"

"David something," Mom said, and Cheyenne and Dakota raced into the kitchen, screaming, "Aunt Sueann's here, Aunt Sueann's here! Can we eat now?"

Allison leaned over the sink and pulled the curtains back to look out the window.

"What does he look like?" I asked, sprinkling sugar on the cranberry relish.

"Clean-cut," she said, sounding surprised. "Short blond hair, slacks, white shirt, tie."

Oh, no, that meant he was a neo-Nazi. Or married and planning to get a divorce as soon as the kids graduated from college—which would turn out to be in twenty-three years, since he'd just gotten his wife pregnant again.

"Is he handsome?" I asked, sticking a spoon into the cranberry relish.

"No," Allison said, even more surprised. "He's actually kind of ordinary-looking."

I came over to the window to look. He was helping Sueann out of the car. She was dressed up, too, in a dress and a denim slouch hat. "Good heavens," I said. "It's David Carrington. He worked up on fifth in Computing."

"Was he a womanizer?" Allison asked.

"No," I said, bewildered. "He's a very nice guy. He's unmarried, he doesn't drink, and he left to go get a degree in medicine."

"Why didn't *you* ever meet him?" Mom said.

🌲

David shook hands with Mitch, regaled Cheyenne and Dakota with a knock-knock joke, and told Mom his favorite kind of sweet potatoes were the ones with the marshmallows on top.

"He must be a serial killer," I whispered to Allison.

"Come on, everybody, let's sit down," Mom said. "Cheyenne and Dakota, you sit here by Grandma. David, you sit here, next to Sueann. Sueann, take off your hat. You know hats aren't allowed at the table."

"Hats for *men* aren't allowed at the table," Sueann said, patting her denim hat. "Women's hats are." She sat down. "Hats are coming back in style, did you know that? *Cosmopolitan*'s latest issue said this is the Year of the Hat."

"I don't care what it is," Mom said. "Your father would never have allowed hats at the table."

"I'll take it off if you'll turn off the TV," Sueann said, complacently opening out her napkin.

They had reached an impasse. Mom always has the TV on during meals. "I like to have it on in case something happens," she said stubbornly.

"Like what?" Mitch said. "Aliens landing from outer space?"

"For your information, there was a UFO sighting two weeks ago. It was on CNN."

"Everything looks delicious," David said. "Is that homemade cranberry relish? I *love* that. My grandmother used to make it."

He had to be a serial killer.

For half an hour, we concentrated on turkey, stuffing, mashed potatoes, green-bean casserole, scalloped corn casserole, marshmallow-topped sweet potatoes, cranberry relish, pumpkin pie, and the news on CNN.

"Can't you at least turn it down, Mom?" Mitch said. "We can't even hear to talk."

"I want to see the weather in Washington," Mom said. "For your flight."

"You're leaving tonight?" Sueann said. "But you just got here. I haven't even seen Cheyenne and Dakota."

"Mitch has to fly back tonight," Allison said. "But the girls and I are staying till Wednesday."

"I don't see why he can't stay at least until tomorrow," Mom said.

"Don't tell me this is homemade whipped cream on the pumpkin pie," David said. "I haven't had homemade whipped cream in years."

"You used to work in computers, didn't you?" I asked him. "There's a lot of computer crime around these days, isn't there?"

"Computers!" Allison said. "I forgot all the awards Cheyenne won at computer camp." She turned to Mitch. "The newsletter's going to have to be at least two pages. The girls just have too many awards—T-ball, tadpole swimming, Bible school attendance."

"Do you send Christmas newsletters in your family?" my mother asked David.

He nodded. "I love hearing from everybody."

"You see?" Mom said to me. "People *like* getting newsletters at Christmas."

"I don't have anything against Christmas newsletters," I said. "I just don't think they should be deadly dull. Mary had a root canal, Bootsy seems to be getting over her ringworm, we got new gutters on the house. Why doesn't anyone ever write about anything *interesting* in their news-letters?"

"Like what?" Sueann said.

"I don't know. An alligator biting their arm off. A meteor falling on their house. A murder. Something interesting to read."

"Probably because they didn't happen," Sueann said.

"Then they should make something up," I said, "so we don't have to hear about their trip to Nebraska and their gallbladder operation."

"You'd do that?" Allison said, appalled. "You'd make something up?"

"People make things up in their newsletters all the time, and you know it," I said. "Look at the way Aunt Laura and Uncle Phil brag about their vacations and their stock options and their cars. If you're going to lie, they might as well be lies that are interesting for other people to read."

"You have plenty of things to tell without making up lies, Nan," Mom said reprovingly. "Maybe you should do something like your cousin Celia. She writes her newsletter all year long, day by day," she explained to David. "Nan, you might have more news than you think if you kept track of it day by day like Celia. She always has a lot to tell."

Yes, indeed. Her newsletters were nearly as long as Aunt Lydia's. They read like a diary, except she wasn't in junior high, where at least there were pop quizzes and zits and your locker combination to give it a little zing. Celia's newsletters had no zing whatsoever:

"Wed. Jan. 1. Froze to death going out to get the paper. Snow got in the plastic bag thing the paper comes in. Editorial section all wet. Had to dry it out on the radiator. Bran flakes for breakfast. Watched *Good Morning America.*

"Thurs. Jan. 2. Cleaned closets. Cold and cloudy."

"If you'd write a little every day," Mom said, "you'd be surprised at how much you'd have to tell by Christmas."

Sure. With my life, I wouldn't even have to write it every day. I could do Monday's right now. "Mon. Nov. 28. Froze to death on the way to work. Bob Hunziger not in yet. Penny putting up Christmas decorations. Solveig told me she's sure the baby is going to be a boy. Asked me which name I liked, Albuquerque or Dallas. Said hi to Gary, but he was too depressed to talk to me. Thanksgiving reminds him of ex-wife's giblets. Cold and cloudy."

I was wrong. It was snowing, and Solveig's ultrasound had showed the baby was a girl. "What do you think of Trinidad as a name?" she asked me. Penny wasn't putting up Christmas decorations, either. She was passing out slips of paper with our Secret Santas' names on them. "The decorations aren't here yet," she said excitedly. "I'm getting something special from a farmer upstate."

"Does it involve feathers?" I asked her. Last year the decorations had been angels with thousands of chicken feathers glued onto cardboard for their wings. We were still picking them out of our computers.

"No," she said happily. "It's a surprise. I love Christmas, don't you?"

"Is Hunziger in?" I asked her, brushing snow out of my hair. Hats always mash my hair down, so I hadn't worn one.

"Are you kidding?" she said. She handed me a Secret Santa slip. "It's the Monday after Thanksgiving. He probably won't be in till sometime Wednesday."

Gary came in, his ears bright red from the cold and a harried expression on his face. His ex-wife must not have wanted a reconciliation.

"Hi, Gary," I said, and turned to hang up my coat without waiting for him to answer.

And he didn't, but when I turned back around, he was still standing there, staring at me. I put a hand up to my hair, wishing I'd worn a hat.

"Can I talk to you a minute?" he said, looking anxiously at Penny.

"Sure," I said, trying not to get my hopes up. He probably wanted to ask me something about the Secret Santas.

He leaned farther over my desk. "Did anything unusual happen to you over Thanksgiving?"

"My sister didn't bring home a biker to Thanksgiving dinner," I said.

He waved that away dismissively. "No, I mean anything odd, peculiar, out of the ordinary."

"That *is* out of the ordinary."

He leaned even closer. "I flew out to my parents' for Thanksgiving, and on the flight home—you know how people always carry on luggage that won't fit in the overhead compartments and then try to cram it in?"

"Yes," I said, thinking of a bridesmaid's bouquet I had made the mistake of putting in the overhead compartment one time.

"Well, nobody did that on my flight. They didn't carry on hanging bags or enormous shopping bags full of Christmas presents. Some people didn't even have a carry-on. And that isn't all. Our flight was half an hour late, and the flight attendant said, 'Those of you who do not have connecting flights, please remain seated until those with connections have deplaned.' And they did." He looked at me expectantly.

"Maybe everybody was just in the Christmas spirit."

He shook his head. "All four babies on the flight slept the whole way, and the toddler behind me didn't kick the seat."

That *was* unusual.

"Not only that, the guy next to me was reading *The Way of All Flesh* by Samuel Butler. When's the last time you saw anybody on an airplane reading anything but John Grisham or Danielle Steel? I tell you, there's something funny going on."

"What?" I asked curiously.

"I don't know," he said. "You're sure you haven't noticed anything?"

"Nothing except for my sister. She always dates these losers, but the guy she brought to Thanksgiving was really nice. He even helped with the dishes."

"You didn't notice anything else?"

"No," I said, wishing I had. This was the longest he'd ever talked to me about anything besides his ex-wife. "Maybe it's something in the air at DIA. I have to take my sister-in-law and her little girls to the airport Wednesday. I'll keep an eye out."

He nodded. "Don't say anything about this, okay?" he said, and hurried off to Accounting.

"What was that all about?" Penny asked, coming over.

"His ex-wife," I said. "When do we have to exchange Secret Santa gifts?"

"Every Friday, and Christmas Eve."

I opened up my slip. Good, I'd gotten Hunziger. With luck I wouldn't have to buy any Secret Santa gifts at all.

Tuesday I got Aunt Laura and Uncle Phil's Christmas newsletter. It was in gold ink on cream-colored paper, with large gold bells in the corners. *"Joyeux Noël,"* it began. "That's French for Merry Christmas. We're sending our newsletter out early this year because we're spending Christmas in Cannes to celebrate Phil's promotion to assistant CEO and my wonderful new career! Yes, I'm starting my own business—Laura's Floral Creations—and orders are pouring in! It's already been written up in *House Beautiful,* and you will *never* guess who called last week—Martha Stewart!" Et cetera.

I didn't see Gary. Or anything unusual, although the waiter who took my lunch order actually got it right for a change. But he got Tonya's (who works up on third) wrong.

"I *told* him tomato and lettuce only," she said, picking pickles off her sandwich. "I heard Gary talked to you yesterday. Did he ask you out?"

"What's that?" I said, pointing to the folder Tonya'd brought with her, to change the subject. "The Harbrace file?"

"No," she said. "Do you want my pickles? It's our Christmas schedule. *Never* marry anybody who has kids from a previous marriage. Especially when *you* have kids from a previous marriage. Tom's ex-wife, Janine, my ex-husband, John, and four sets of grandparents all want the kids, and they all want them on Christmas morning. It's like trying to schedule the D-day invasion."

"At least your husband isn't still hung up on his ex-wife," I said glumly.

"So Gary didn't ask you out, huh?" She bit into her sandwich, frowned, and extracted another pickle. "I'm sure he will. Okay, if we take the kids to Tom's parents at four on Christmas Eve, Janine could pick them up at eight. . . . No, that won't work." She switched her sandwich to her other hand and began erasing. "Janine's not speaking to Tom's parents."

She sighed. "At least John's being reasonable. He called yesterday and said he'd be willing to wait till New Year's to have the kids. I don't know what got into him."

When I got back to work, there was a folded copy of the morning newspaper on my desk.

I opened it up. The headline read "City Hall Christmas Display to Be Turned On," which wasn't unusual. And neither was tomorrow's headline, which would be "City Hall Christmas Display Protested."

Either the Freedom Against Faith people protest the Nativity scene or the fundamentalists protest the elves or the environmental people protest cutting down Christmas trees or all of them protest the whole thing. It happens every year.

I turned to the inside pages. Several articles were circled in red, and there was a note next to them which read "See what I mean? Gary."

I looked at the circled articles. "Christmas Shoplifting Down," the first one read. "Mall stores report incidences of shoplifting are down for the first week of the Christmas season. Usually prevalent this time of—"

"What are you doing?" Penny said, looking over my shoulder.

I shut the paper with a rustle. "Nothing," I said. I folded it back up and stuck it into a drawer. "Did you need something?"

"Here," she said, handing me a slip of paper.

"I already got my Secret Santa name," I said.

"This is for Holiday Goodies," she said. "Everybody takes turns bringing in coffee cake or tarts or cake."

I opened up my slip. It read "Friday Dec. 20. Four dozen cookies."

"I saw you and Gary talking yesterday," Penny said. "What about?"

"His ex-wife," I said. "What kind of cookies do you want me to bring?"

"Chocolate chip," she said. "Everybody loves chocolate."

As soon as she was gone, I got the newspaper out again and took it into Hunziger's office to read. "Legislature Passes Balanced Budget," the other articles read. "Escaped Convict Turns Self In," "Christmas Food Bank Donations Up."

I read through them and then threw the paper into the wastebasket. Halfway out the door I thought better of it and took it out, folded it up, and took it back to my desk with me.

While I was putting it into my purse, Hunziger wandered in. "If anybody asks where I am, tell them I'm in the men's room," he said, and wandered out again.

🎄

Wednesday afternoon I took the girls and Allison to the airport. She was still fretting over her newsletter.

"Do you think a greeting is absolutely necessary?" she said in the baggage check-in line. "You know, like 'Dear Friends and Family'?"

"Probably not," I said absently. I was watching the people in line ahead of us, trying to spot this unusual behavior Gary had talked about, but so far I hadn't seen any. People were looking at their watches and complaining about the length of the line, the ticket agents were calling, "Next. Next!" to the person at the head of the line, who, after having stood impatiently in line for forty-five minutes waiting for this moment, was now staring blankly into space, and an unattended toddler was methodically pulling the elastic strings off a stack of luggage tags.

"They'll still know it's a Christmas newsletter, won't they?" Allison said. "Even without a greeting at the beginning of it?"

With a border of angels holding bunches of mistletoe, what else could it be? I thought.

"Next!" the ticket agent shouted.

The man in front of us had forgotten his photo ID, the girl in front of us in line for the security check was wearing heavy metal, and on the train out to the concourse a woman stepped on my foot and then glared at me as if it were my fault. Apparently all the nice people had traveled the day Gary came home.

And that was probably what it was—some kind of statistical clump where all the considerate, intelligent people had ended up on the same flight.

I knew they existed. My sister Sueann had had an insurance actuary for a boyfriend once (he was also an embezzler, which is why Sueann was dating him), and he had said events weren't evenly distributed, that there were peaks and valleys. Gary must just have hit a peak.

Which was too bad, I thought, lugging Cheyenne, who had demanded to be carried the minute we got off the train, down the concourse. Because the only reason he had approached me was because he thought there was something strange going on.

"Here's Gate 55," Allison said, setting Dakota down and getting out French language tapes for the girls. "If I left off the 'Dear Friends and Family,' I'd have room to include Dakota's violin recital. She played 'The Gypsy Dance.'"

She settled the girls in adjoining chairs and put on their headphones. "But Mitch says it's a letter, so it has to have a greeting."

"What if you used something short?" I said. "Like 'Greetings' or something. Then you'd have room to start the letter on the same line."

"Not 'Greetings.'" She made a face. "Uncle Frank started his letter that way last year, and it scared me half to death. I thought Mitch had been *drafted*."

I had been alarmed when I'd gotten mine, too, but at least it had given me a temporary rush of adrenaline, which was more than Uncle Frank's letters usually did, concerned as they were with prostate problems and disputes over property taxes.

"I suppose I could use 'Holiday Greetings,'" Allison said. "Or 'Christmas Greetings,' but that's almost as long as 'Dear Friends and Family.' If only there were something shorter."

"How about 'hi'?"

"That might work." She got out paper and a pen and started writing. "How do you spell 'outstanding'?"

"O-u-t-s-t-a-n-d-i-n-g," I said absently. I was watching the moving sidewalks in the middle of the concourse. People were standing on the right, like they were supposed to, and walking on the left. No people were standing four abreast or blocking the entire sidewalk with their luggage. No kids were running in the opposite direction of the sidewalk's movement, screaming and running their hands along the rubber railing.

"How do you spell 'fabulous'?" Allison asked.

"Flight 2216 to Spokane is now ready for boarding," the flight attendant at the desk said. "Those passengers traveling with small children or those who require additional time for boarding may now board."

A single old lady with a walker stood up and got in line. Allison unhooked the girls' headphones, and we began the ritual of hugging and gathering up belongings.

"We'll see you at Christmas," she said.

"Good luck with your newsletter," I said, handing Dakota her teddy bear, "and don't worry about the heading. It doesn't need one."

They started down the passageway. I stood there, waving, till they were out of sight, and then turned to go.

"We are now ready for regular boarding of rows 25 through 33," the flight attendant said, and everybody in the gate area stood up. *Nothing unusual here,* I thought, and started for the concourse.

"What rows did she call?" a woman in a red beret asked a teenaged boy.

"Rows 25 through 33," he said.

"Oh, I'm Row 14," the woman said, and sat back down.

So did I.

"We are now ready to board rows 15 through 24," the flight attendant said, and a dozen people looked carefully at their tickets and then stepped back from the door, patiently waiting their turn. One of them pulled a paperback out of her tote bag and began to read. It was *Kidnapped* by Robert Louis Stevenson. Only when the flight attendant said, "We are now boarding all rows," did the rest of them stand up and get in line.

Which didn't prove anything, and neither did the standing on the right of the moving sidewalk. Maybe people were just being nice because it was Christmas.

Don't be ridiculous, I told myself. *People aren't nicer at Christmas. They're ruder and pushier and crabbier than ever. You've seen them at the mall, and in line for the post office. They act worse at Christmas than any other time.*

"This is your final boarding call for Flight 2216 to Spokane," the flight attendant said to the empty waiting area. She called to me, "Are you flying to Spokane, ma'am?"

"No." I stood up. "I was seeing friends off."

"I just wanted to make sure you didn't miss your flight," she said, and turned to shut the door.

I started for the moving sidewalk, and nearly collided with a young man running for the gate. He raced up to the desk and flung his ticket down.

"I'm sorry, sir," the flight attendant said, leaning slightly away from the young man as if expecting an explosion. "Your flight has already left. I'm really terribly sor—"

"Oh, it's okay," he said. "It serves me right. I didn't allow enough time for parking and everything, that's all. I should have started for the airport earlier."

The flight attendant was tapping busily on the computer. "I'm afraid the only other open flight to Spokane for today isn't until 11:05 this evening."

"Oh, well," he said, smiling. "It'll give me a chance to catch up on my reading." He reached down into his attaché case and pulled out a paperback. It was W. Somerset Maugham's *Of Human Bondage.*

"Well?" Gary said as soon as I got back to work Thursday morning. He was standing by my desk, waiting for me.

"There's definitely something going on," I said, and told him about the moving sidewalks and the guy who'd missed his plane. "But what?"

"Is there somewhere we can talk?" he said, looking anxiously around.

"Hunziger's office," I said, "but I don't know if he's in yet."

"He's not," he said, led me into the office, and shut the door behind him.

"Sit down," he said, indicating Hunziger's chair. "Now, I know this is going to sound crazy, but I think all these people have been possessed by some kind of alien intelligence. Have you ever seen *Invasion of the Body Snatchers?*"

"What?" I said.

"*Invasion of the Body Snatchers,*" he said. "It's about these parasites from outer space who take over people's bodies and—"

"I *know* what it's about," I said, "and it's *science fiction.* You think the man who missed his plane was some kind of pod-person? You're right," I said, reaching for the doorknob. "I do think you're crazy."

"That's what Donald Sutherland said in *Leechmen from Mars.* Nobody ever believes it's happening, until it's too late."

He pulled a folded newspaper out of his back pocket. "Look at this," he said, waving it in front of me. "Holiday credit-card fraud down twenty percent. Holiday suicides down thirty percent. Charitable giving up *sixty* percent."

"They're coincidences." I explained about the statistical peaks and valleys. "Look," I said, taking the paper from him and turning to the front page. "'People Against Cruelty to Our Furry Friends Protests City Hall

Christmas Display.' 'Animal Rights Group Objects to Exploitation of Reindeer.'"

"What about your sister?" he said. "You said she only dates losers. Why would she suddenly start dating a nice guy? Why would an escaped convict suddenly turn himself in? Why would people suddenly start reading the classics? Because they've been taken over."

"By aliens from outer space?" I said incredulously.

"Did he have a hat?"

"Who?" I said, wondering if he really was crazy. Could his being hung up on his horrible ex-wife have finally made him crack?

"The man who missed his plane," he said. "Was he wearing a hat?"

"I don't remember," I said, and felt suddenly cold. Sueann had worn a hat to Thanksgiving dinner. She'd refused to take it off at the table. And the woman whose ticket said Row 14 had been wearing a beret.

"What do hats have to do with it?" I asked.

"The man on the plane next to me was wearing a hat. So were most of the other people on the flight. Did you ever see *The Puppet Masters*? The parasites attached themselves to the spinal cord and took over the nervous system," he said. "This morning here at work I counted nineteen people wearing hats. Les Sawtelle, Rodney Jones, Jim Bridgeman—"

"Jim Bridgeman always wears a hat," I said. "It's to hide his bald spot. Besides, he's a computer programmer. All the computer people wear baseball caps."

"DeeDee Crawford," he said. "Vera McDermott, Janet Hall—"

"Women's hats are supposed to be making a comeback," I said.

"George Frazelli, the entire Documentation section—"

"I'm sure there's a logical explanation," I said. "It's been freezing in here all week. There's probably something wrong with the heating system."

"The thermostat's turned down to fifty," he said, "which is something else peculiar. The thermostat's been turned down on all floors."

"Well, that's probably Management. You know how they're always trying to cut costs—"

"They're giving us a Christmas bonus. And they fired Hunziger."

"They fired Hunziger?" I said. Management never fires anybody.

"This morning. That's how I knew he wouldn't be in his office."

"They actually fired Hunziger?"

"And one of the janitors. The one who drank. How do you explain that?"

"I—I don't know," I stammered. "But there has to be some other explanation than aliens. Maybe they took a management course or got the Christmas spirit or their therapists told them to do good deeds or something. Something besides leechmen. Aliens coming from outer space and taking over our brains is impossible!"

"That's what Dana Wynter said in *Invasion of the Body Snatchers.* But it's not impossible. It's happening right here, and we've got to stop it before they take over everybody and we're the only ones left. They—"

There was a knock on the door. "Sorry to bother you, Gary," Carol Zaliski said, leaning in the door, "but you've got an urgent phone call. It's your ex-wife."

"Coming," he said, looking at me. "Think about what I said, okay?" He went out.

I stood looking after him and frowning.

"What was that all about?" Carol said, coming into the office. She was wearing a white fur hat.

"He wanted to know what to buy his Secret Santa person," I said.

🎄

Friday Gary wasn't there. "He had to go talk to his ex-wife this morning," Tonya told me at lunch, picking pickles off her sandwich. "He'll be back this afternoon. Marcie's demanding he pay for her therapy. She's seeing this psychiatrist, and she claims Gary's the one who made her crazy, so he should pick up the bill for her Prozac. *Why* is he still hung up on her?"

"I don't know," I said, scraping mustard off my burger.

"Carol Zaliski said the two of you were talking in Hunziger's office yesterday. What about? Did he ask you out? Nan?"

"Tonya, has Gary talked to you since Thanksgiving? Did he ask you about whether you'd noticed anything unusual happening?"

"He asked me if I'd noticed anything bizarre or abnormal about my family. I told him, in my family bizarre *is* normal. You won't believe what's happened now. Tom's parents are getting a divorce, which means five sets of parents. Why couldn't they have waited till after Christmas to do this? It's throwing my whole schedule off."

She bit into her sandwich. "I'm sure Gary's going to ask you out. He's probably just working up to it."

If he was, he had the strangest line I'd ever heard. Aliens from outer space. Hiding under hats!

Though, now that he'd mentioned it, there were an awful lot of people wearing hats. Nearly all the men in Data Analysis had baseball caps on, Jerrilyn Wells was wearing a wool stocking cap, and Ms. Jacobson's secretary looked like she was dressed for a wedding in a white thing with a veil. But Sueann had said this was the Year of the Hat.

Sueann, who dated only gigolos and Mafia dons. But she had been bound to hit a nice boyfriend sooner or later, she dated so many guys.

And there weren't any signs of alien possession when I tried to get somebody in the steno pool to make some copies for me. "We're *busy*," Paula Grandy snapped. "It's Christmas, you know!"

I went back to my desk, feeling better. There was an enormous dish made of pine cones, filled with candy canes and red and green foil-wrapped chocolate kisses. "Is this part of the Christmas decorations?" I asked Penny.

"No. They aren't ready yet," she said. "This is just a little something to brighten the holidays. I made one for everyone's desk."

I felt even better. I pushed the dish over to one side and started through my mail. There was a green envelope from Allison and Mitch. She must have mailed her newsletters as soon as she got off the plane. *I wonder if she decided to forgo the heading or Dakota's Most Improved Practicing Piano Award,* I thought, slicing it open with the letter opener.

"Dear Nan," it began, several spaces down from the angels-and-mistletoe border. "Nothing much new this year. We're all okay, though Mitch is worried about downsizing, and I always seem to be running from behind. The girls are growing like weeds and doing okay in school, though Cheyenne's been having some problems with her reading and Dakota's still wetting the bed. Mitch and I decided we've been pushing them too hard, and we're working on trying not to overschedule them for activities and just letting them be normal, average little girls."

I jammed the letter back into the envelope and ran up to fourth to look for Gary.

"All right," I said when I found him. "I believe you. What do we do now?"

⟿

We rented movies. Actually, we rented only some of the movies. *Attack of the Soul Killers* and *Invasion from Betelgeuse* were both checked out.

"Which means somebody else has figured it out, too," Gary said. "If only we knew who."

"We could ask the clerk," I suggested.

He shook his head violently. "We can't do anything to make them suspicious. For all we know, they may have taken them off the shelves themselves, in which case we're on the right track. What else shall we rent?"

"What?" I said blankly.

"So it won't look like we're just renting alien invasion movies."

"Oh," I said, and picked up *Ordinary People* and a black-and-white version of *A Christmas Carol*.

It didn't work. *"The Puppet Masters,"* the kid at the rental desk, wearing a blue-and-yellow Blockbuster hat, said inquiringly. "Is that a good movie?"

"I haven't seen it," Gary said nervously.

"We're renting it because it has Donald Sutherland in it," I said. "We're having a Donald Sutherland film festival. *The Puppet Masters, Ordinary People, Invasion of the Body Snatchers*—"

"Is Donald Sutherland in this?" he asked, holding up *A Christmas Carol*.

"He plays Tiny Tim," I said. "It was his first screen appearance."

🎄

"You were great in there," Gary said, leading me down to the other end of the mall to Suncoast to buy *Attack of the Soul Killers*. "You're a very good liar."

"Thanks," I said, pulling my coat closer and looking around the mall. It was freezing in here, and there were hats everywhere, on people and in window displays, Panamas and porkpies and picture hats.

"We're surrounded. Look at that," he said, nodding in the direction of Santa Claus's North Pole.

"Santa Claus has always worn a hat," I said.

"I meant the line," he said.

He was right. The kids in line were waiting patiently, cheerfully. Not a single one was screaming or announcing she had to go to the bathroom. "I want a Masters of Earth," a little boy in a felt beanie was saying eagerly to his mother.

"Well, we'll ask Santa," the mother said, "but he may not be able to get it for you. All the stores are sold out."

"Okay," he said. "Then I want a wagon."

Suncoast was sold out of *Attack of the Soul Killers,* but we bought *Invasion from Betelgeuse* and *Infiltrators from Space* and went back to Gary's apartment to screen them.

"Well?" he said after we'd watched three of them. "Did you notice how they start slowly and then spread through the population?"

Actually, what I'd noticed was how dumb all the people in these movies were. "The brain-suckers attack when we're asleep," the hero would say, and promptly lie down for a nap. Or the hero's girlfriend would say, "They're on to us. We've got to get out of here. Right now," and then go back to her apartment to pack.

And, just like in every horror movie, they were always splitting up instead of sticking together. And going down dark alleys. They deserved to be turned into pod-people.

"Our first order of business is to pool what we know about the aliens," Gary said. "It's obvious the purpose of the hats is to conceal the parasites' presence from those who haven't been taken over yet," he said, "and that they're attached to the brain."

"Or the spinal column," I said, "like in *The Puppet Masters.*"

He shook his head. "If that were the case, they could attach themselves to the neck or the back, which would be much less conspicuous. Why would they take the risk of hiding under hats, which are so noticeable, if they aren't attached to the top of the head?"

"Maybe the hats serve some other purpose."

The phone rang.

"Yes?" Gary answered it. His face lit up and then fell. *His ex-wife,* I thought, and started watching *Infiltrators from Space.*

"You've got to believe me," the hero's girlfriend said to the psychiatrist. "There are aliens here among us. They look just like you or me. You have to believe me."

"I do believe you," the psychiatrist said, and raised his finger to point at her. "Ahhhggghhh!" he screeched, his eyes glowing bright green.

"Marcie," Gary said. There was a long pause. "A friend." Longer pause. "No."

The hero's girlfriend ran down a dark alley, wearing high heels. Halfway through, she twisted her ankle and fell.

"You know that isn't true," Gary said.

I fast-forwarded. The hero was in his apartment, on the phone. "Hello, Police Department?" he said. "You have to help me. We've been invaded by aliens who take over your body!"

"We'll be right there, Mr. Daly," the voice on the phone said. "Stay there."

"How do you know my name?" the hero shouted. "I didn't tell you my address."

"We're on our way," the voice said.

"We'll talk about it tomorrow," Gary said, and hung up.

"Sorry," he said, coming over to the couch. "Okay, I downloaded a bunch of stuff about parasites and aliens from the Internet," he said, handing me a sheaf of stapled papers. "We need to discover what it is they're doing to the people they take over, what their weaknesses are, and how we can fight them. We need to know when and where it started," Gary went on, "how and where it's spreading, and what it's doing to people. We need to find out as much as we can about the nature of the aliens so we can figure out a way to eliminate them. How do they communicate with each other? Are they telepathic, like in *Village of the Damned,* or do they use some other form of communication? If they're telepathic, can they read our minds as well as each other's?"

"If they could, wouldn't they know we're on to them?" I said.

The phone rang again. "It's probably my ex-wife again," he said. I picked up the remote and flicked on *Infiltrators from Space* again.

Gary answered the phone. "Yes?" he said, and then warily, "How did you get my number?"

The hero slammed down the phone and ran to the window. Dozens of police cars were pulling up, lights flashing.

"Sure," Gary said. He grinned. "No, I won't forget."

He hung up. "That was Penny. She forgot to give me my Holiday Goodies slip. I'm supposed to take in four dozen sugar cookies next Monday." He shook his head wonderingly. "Now, *there's* somebody I'd like to see taken over by the aliens."

He sat down on the couch and started making a list. "Okay, methods of fighting them. Diseases. Poison. Dynamite. Nuclear weapons. What else?"

I didn't answer. I was thinking about what he'd said about wishing Penny would be taken over.

"The problem with all of those solutions is that they kill the people, too," Gary said. "What we need is something like the virus they used in *Invasion*. Or the ultrasonic pulses only the aliens could hear in *War with the Slugmen*. If we're going to stop them, we've got to find something that kills the parasite but not the host."

"Do we have to stop them?"

"What?" he said. "Of course we have to stop them. What do you mean?"

"All the aliens in these movies turn people into zombies or monsters," I said. "They shuffle around, attacking people and killing them and trying to take over the world. Nobody's done anything like that. People are standing on the right and walking on the left, the suicide rate's down, my sister's dating a very nice guy. Everybody who's been taken over is nicer, happier, more polite. Maybe the parasites are a good influence, and we shouldn't interfere."

"And maybe that's what they want us to think. What if they're acting nice to trick us, to keep us from trying to stop them? Remember *Attack of the Soul Killers*? What if it's all an act, and they're only acting nice till the takeover's complete?"

If it was an act, it was a great one. Over the next few days, Solveig, in a red straw hat, announced she was naming her baby Jane, Jim Bridgeman nodded at me in the elevator, my cousin Celia's newsletter/diary was short and funny, and the waiter, sporting a soda-jerk hat, got both Tonya's and my orders right.

"No pickles!" Tonya said delightedly, picking up her sandwich. "Ow! Can you get carpal tunnel syndrome from wrapping Christmas presents? My hand's been hurting all morning."

She opened her file folder. There was a new diagram inside, a rectangle with names written all around the sides.

"Is that your Christmas schedule?" I asked.

"No," she said, showing it to me. "It's a seating arrangement for Christmas dinner. It was crazy, running the kids from house to house like that, so we decided to just have everybody at our house."

I took a startled look at her, but she was still hatless.

"I thought Tom's ex-wife couldn't stand his parents."

"Everybody's agreed we all need to get along for the kids' sake. After all, it's Christmas."

I was still staring at her.

She put her hand up to her hair. "Do you like it? It's a wig. Eric got it for me for Christmas. For being such a great mother to the boys through the divorce. I couldn't believe it." She patted her hair. "Isn't it great?"

🌲

They're hiding their aliens under wigs," I told Gary.

"I know," he said. "Paul Gunden got a new toupee. We can't trust anyone." He handed me a folder full of clippings.

Employment rates were up. Thefts of packages from cars, usually prevalent at this time of year, were down. A woman in Minnesota had brought back a library book that was twenty-two years overdue. "Groups Praise City Hall Christmas Display," one of the clippings read, and the accompanying picture showed the People for a Non-Commercial Christmas, the Holy Spirit Southern Baptists, and the Equal Rights for Ethnics activists holding hands and singing Christmas carols around the crèche.

On the ninth, Mom called. "Have you written your newsletter yet?"

"I've been busy," I said, and waited for her to ask me if I'd met anyone lately at work.

"I got Jackie Peterson's newsletter this morning," she said.

"So did I." The invasion apparently hadn't reached Miami. Jackie's newsletter, which is usually terminally cute, had reached new heights:

"*M is for our trip to Mexico*
E is for Every place else we'd like to go
R is for the RV that takes us there...."

And straight through MERRY CHRISTMAS, A HAPPY NEW YEAR, and both her first and last names.

"I do wish she wouldn't try to put her letters in verse," Mom said. "They never scan."

"Mom," I said. "Are you okay?"

"I'm fine," she said. "My arthritis has been kicking up the last couple of days, but otherwise I've never felt better. I've been thinking, there's no reason for you to send out newsletters if you don't want to."

"Mom," I said, "did Sueann give you a hat for Christmas?"

"Oh, she told you," Mom said. "You know, I don't usually like hats, but I'm going to need one for the wedding, and—"

"Wedding?"

"Oh, didn't she tell you? She and David are getting married right after Christmas. I am so relieved. I thought she was never going to meet anyone decent."

I reported that to Gary. "I know," he said glumly. "I just got a raise."

"I haven't found a single bad effect," I said. "No signs of violence or antisocial behavior. Not even any irritability."

"*There* you are," Penny said crabbily, coming up with a huge poinsettia under each arm. "Can you help me put these on everybody's desks?"

"Are these the Christmas decorations?" I asked.

"No, I'm still waiting on that farmer," she said, handing me one of the poinsettias. "This is just a little something to brighten up everyone's desk." She reached down to move the pine-cone dish on Gary's desk. "You didn't eat your candy canes," she said.

"I don't like peppermint."

"Nobody ate their candy canes," she said disgustedly. "They all ate the chocolate kisses and left the candy canes."

"People like chocolate," Gary said, and whispered to me, "*When* is she going to be taken over?"

"Meet me in Hunziger's office right away," I whispered back, and said to Penny, "Where does this poinsettia go?"

"Jim Bridgeman's desk."

I took the poinsettia up to Computing on fifth. Jim was wearing his baseball cap backward. "A little something to brighten your desk," I said, handing it to him, and started back toward the stairs.

"Can I talk to you a minute?" he said, following me out into the stairwell.

"Sure," I said, trying to sound calm. "What about?"

He leaned toward me. "Have you noticed anything unusual going on?"

"You mean the poinsettia?" I said. "Penny does tend to go a little overboard for Christmas, but—"

"No," he said, putting his hand awkwardly to his cap, "people who are acting funny, people who aren't themselves?"

"No," I said, smiling. "I haven't noticed a thing."

I waited for Gary in Hunziger's office for nearly half an hour. "Sorry I took so long," he said when he finally got there. "My ex-wife called. What were you saying?"

"I was saying that even you have to admit it would be a good thing if Penny was taken over," I said. "What if the parasites aren't evil? What if they're those—what are those parasites that benefit the host called? You know, like the bacteria that help cows produce milk? Or those birds that pick insects off of rhinoceroses?"

"You mean symbiotes?" Gary said.

"Yes," I said eagerly. "What if this is some kind of symbiotic relationship? What if they're raising everyone's IQ or enhancing their emotional maturity, and it's having a good effect on us?"

"Things that sound too good to be true usually are. No," he said, shaking his head. "They're up to something, I know it. And we've got to find out what it is."

On the tenth when I came to work, Penny was putting up the Christmas decorations. They were, as she had promised, something special: wide swags of red velvet ribbons running all around the walls, with red velvet bows and large bunches of mistletoe every few feet. In between were gold-calligraphic scrolls reading "And kiss me 'neath the mistletoe, For Christmas comes but once a year."

"What do you think?" Penny said, climbing down from her stepladder. "Every floor has a different quotation." She reached into a large cardboard box. "Accounting's is 'Sweetest the kiss that's stolen under the mistletoe.'"

I came over and looked into the box. "Where did you get all the mistletoe?" I asked.

"This apple farmer I know," she said, moving the ladder.

I picked up a big branch of the green leaves and white berries. "It must have cost a fortune." I had bought a sprig of it last year that had cost six dollars.

Penny, climbing the ladder, shook her head. "It didn't cost anything. He was glad to get rid of it." She tied the bunch of mistletoe to the red velvet ribbon. "It's a parasite, you know. It kills the trees."

"Kills the trees?" I said blankly, staring at the white berries.

"Or deforms them," she said. "It steals nutrients from the tree's sap, and the tree gets these swellings and galls and things. The farmer told me all about it."

As soon as I had the chance, I took the material Gary had downloaded on parasites into Hunziger's office and read through it.

Mistletoe caused grotesque swellings wherever its rootlets attached themselves to the tree. Anthracnose caused cracks and then spots of dead bark called cankers. Blight wilted trees' leaves. Witches' broom weakened limbs. Bacteria caused tumorlike growths on the trunk, called galls.

We had been focusing on the mental and psychological effects when we should have been looking at the physical ones. The heightened intelligence, the increase in civility and common sense, must simply be side effects of the parasites' stealing nutrients. And damaging the host.

I stuck the papers back into the file folder, went back to my desk, and called Sueann.

"Sueann, hi," I said. "I'm working on my Christmas newsletter, and I wanted to make sure I spelled David's name right. Is Carrington spelled C-A-R-R or C-E-R-R?"

"C-A-R-R. Oh, Nan, he's so wonderful! So different from the losers I usually date! He's considerate and sensitive and—"

"And how are you?" I said. "Everybody at work's been down with the flu."

"Really?" she said. "No, I'm fine."

What did I do now? I couldn't ask "Are you sure?" without making her suspicious. "C-A-R-R," I said, trying to think of another way to approach the subject.

Sueann saved me the trouble. "You won't believe what he did yesterday. Showed up at work to take me home. He knew my ankles had been hurting, and he brought me a tube of Bengay and a dozen pink roses. He is so thoughtful."

"Your ankles have been hurting?" I said, trying not to sound anxious.

"Like crazy. It's this weather or something. I could hardly walk on them this morning."

I jammed the parasite papers back into the file folder, made sure I hadn't left any on the desk like the hero in *Parasite People from Planet X*, and went up to see Gary.

He was on the phone.

"I've got to talk to you," I whispered.

"I'd like that," he said into the phone, an odd look on his face.

"What is it?" I said. "Have they found out we're on to them?"

"Shh," he said. "You know I do," he said into the phone.

"You don't understand," I said. "I've figured out what it's doing to people."

He held up a finger, motioning me to wait. "Can you hang on a minute?" he said into the phone, and put his hand over the receiver. "I'll meet you in Hunziger's office in five minutes," he said.

"No," I said. "It's not safe. Meet me at the post office."

He nodded, and went back to his conversation, still with that odd look on his face.

I ran back down to second for my purse and went to the post office. I had intended to wait on the corner, but it was crowded with people jockeying to drop money into the Salvation Army Santa Claus's kettle.

I looked down the sidewalk. Where was Gary? I went up the steps and scanned the street. There was no sign of him.

"Merry Christmas!" a man said, half tipping a fedora and holding the door for me.

"Oh, no, I'm—" I began, and saw Tonya coming down the street. "Thank you," I said, and ducked through the door.

It was freezing inside, and the line for the postal clerks wound out into the lobby. I got in it. It would take an hour at least to work my way to the front, which meant I could wait for Gary without looking suspicious.

Except that I was the only one not wearing a hat. Every single person in line had one on, and the clerks behind the counter were wearing mail carriers' caps. And broad smiles.

"Packages going overseas should really have been mailed by November fifteenth," the middle clerk was saying, not at all disgruntledly, to a little Japanese woman in a red cap, "but don't worry, we'll figure out a way to get your presents there on time."

"The line's only about forty-five minutes long," the woman in front of me confided cheerfully. She was wearing a small black hat with a feather and carrying four enormous packages. I wondered if they were full of pods. "Which isn't bad at all, considering it's Christmas."

I nodded, looking toward the door. Where was he?

"Why are you here?" the woman said, smiling.

"What?" I said, whirling back around, my heart pounding. "What are you here to mail?" she said. "I see you don't have any packages."

"S-stamps," I stammered.

"You can go ahead of me," she said. "If all you're buying is stamps. I've got all these packages to send. You don't want to wait for that."

I do *want to wait,* I thought. "No, that's all right. I'm buying a *lot* of stamps," I said. "I'm buying several sheets. For my Christmas newsletter."

She shook her head, balancing the packages. "Don't be silly. You don't want to wait while they weigh all these." She tapped the man in front of her. "This young lady's only buying stamps," she said. "Why don't we let her go ahead of us?"

"Certainly," the man, who was wearing a Russian karakul hat, said, and bowed slightly, stepping back.

"No, really," I began, but it was too late. The line had parted like the Red Sea.

"Thank you," I said, and walked up to the counter. "Merry Christmas."

The line closed behind me. *They know,* I thought. *They know I was looking up plant parasites.* I glanced desperately toward the door.

"Holly and ivy?" the clerk said, beaming at me.

"What?" I said.

"Your stamps." He held up two sheets. "Holly and ivy or Madonna and Child?"

"Holly and ivy," I said weakly. "Three sheets, please."

I paid for the sheets, thanked the mob again, and went back out into the freezing-cold lobby. And now what? Pretend I had a box and fiddle with the combination? *Where* was he?

I went over to the bulletin board, trying not to seem suspicious, and looked at the Wanted posters. They had probably all turned themselves in by now and were being model prisoners. And it really was a pity the parasites were going to have to be stopped. *If* they could be stopped.

It had been easy in the movies (in the movies, that is, in which they had managed to defeat them, which wasn't all that many. Over half the movies had ended with the whole world being turned into glowing green eyes). And in the ones where they did defeat them, there had been an awful lot of explosions and hanging precariously from helicopters. I hoped whatever we came up with didn't involve skydiving.

Or a virus or ultrasonic sound, because even if I knew a doctor or scientist to ask, I couldn't confide in them. "We can't trust anybody," Gary had said, and he was right. We couldn't risk it. There was too much at stake. And we couldn't call the police. "It's all in your imagination, Miss Johnson," they would say. "Stay right there. We're on our way."

We would have to do this on our own. And *where* was Gary?

I looked at the Wanted posters some more. I was sure the one in the middle looked like one of Sueann's old boyfriends. He—

"I'm sorry I'm late," Gary said breathlessly. His ears were red from the cold, and his hair was ruffled from running. "I had this phone call and—"

"Come on," I said, and hustled him out of the post office, down the steps, and past the Santa and his mob of donors.

"Keep walking," I said. "You were right about the parasites, but not because they turn people into zombies."

I hurriedly told him about the galls and Tonya's carpal tunnel syndrome. "My sister was infected at Thanksgiving, and now she can hardly walk," I said. "You were right. We've got to stop them."

"But you don't have any proof of this," he said. "It could be arthritis or something, couldn't it?"

I stopped walking. "What?"

"You don't have any proof that it's the aliens that are causing it. It's cold. People's arthritis always acts up when it's cold out. And even if the aliens are causing it, a few aches and pains is a small price to pay for all the benefits. You said yourself—"

I stared at his hair.

"Don't look at me like that," he said. "I haven't been taken over. I've just been thinking about what you said about your sister's engagement and—"

"Who was on the phone?"

He looked uncomfortable. "The thing is—"

"It was your ex-wife," I said. "She's been taken over, and now she's nice, and you want to get back together with her. That's it, isn't it?"

"You know how I've always felt about Marcie," he said guiltily. "She says she never stopped loving me."

When something sounds too good to be true, it probably is, I thought.

"She thinks I should move back in and see if we can't work things out. But that isn't the only reason," he said, grabbing my arm. "I've been looking at all those clippings—dropouts going back to school, escaped convicts turning themselves in—"

"People returning overdue library books," I said.

"Are we willing to be responsible for ruining all that? I think we should think about this before we do anything."

I pulled my arm away from him.

"I just think we should consider all the factors before we decide what to do. Waiting a few days can't hurt."

"You're right," I said, and started walking. "There's a lot we don't know about them."

"I just think we should do a little more research," he said, opening the door of our building.

"You're right," I said, and started up the stairs.

"I'll talk to you tomorrow, okay?" he said when we got to second.

I nodded and went back to my desk and put my head in my hands.

He was willing to let parasites take over the planet so he could get his ex-wife back, but were my motives any better than his? Why had I believed in an alien invasion in the first place, and spent all that time watching science-fiction movies and having huddled conversations? So I could spend time with him.

He was right. A few aches and pains were worth it to have Sueann married to someone nice and postal workers nondisgruntled and passengers remaining seated till those people with connecting flights had deplaned.

"Are you okay?" Tonya said, leaning over my desk.

"I'm fine," I said. "How's your arm?"

"Fine," she said, rotating the elbow to show me. "It must have been a cramp or something."

I didn't *know* these parasites were like mistletoe. They might cause only temporary aches and pains. Gary was right. We needed to do more research. Waiting a few days couldn't hurt.

The phone rang. "I've been trying to get hold of you," Mom said. "Dakota's in the hospital. They don't know what it is. It's something wrong with her legs. You need to call Allison."

"I will," I said, and hung up the phone.

I logged on to my computer, called up the file I'd been working on and scrolled halfway through it so it would look like I was away from my desk for just a minute, took off my high heels and changed into my sneakers, stuck the high heels into my desk drawer, grabbed my purse and coat, and took off.

The best place to look for information on how to get rid of the parasites was the library, but the card file was online, and you had to use your library card to get access. The next best was a bookstore. Not the independent on Sixteenth. Their clerks were far too helpful. And knowledgeable.

I went to the Barnes & Noble on Eighth, taking the back way (but no alleys). It was jammed, and there was some kind of book signing going on up front, but nobody paid any attention to me. Even so, I didn't go straight to the gardening section. I wandered casually through the aisles, looking at T-shirts and mugs and stopping to thumb through a copy of

How Irrational Fears Can Ruin Your Life, gradually working my way back to the gardening section.

They had only two books on parasites: *Common Garden Parasites and Diseases* and *Organic Weed and Pest Control.* I grabbed them both, retreated to the literature section, and began to read.

"Fungicides such as benomyl and ferbam are effective against certain rusts," *Common Garden Parasites* said. "Streptomycin is effective against some viruses."

But which was this, if either? "Spraying with diazinon or malathion can be effective in most cases. Note: These are dangerous chemicals. Avoid all contact with skin. Do not breathe fumes."

That was out. I put down *Common Garden Parasites* and picked up *Organic Weed and Pest Control.* At least it didn't recommend spraying with deadly chemicals, but what it did recommend wasn't much more useful. Prune affected limbs. Remove and destroy berries. Cover branches with black plastic.

Too often it said simply: Destroy all infected plants.

"The main difficulty in the case of parasites is to destroy the parasite without also destroying the host." That sounded more like it. "It is therefore necessary to find a substance that the host can tolerate that is intolerable to the parasite. Some rusts, for instance, cannot tolerate a vinegar and ginger solution, which can be sprayed on the leaves of the host plant. Red mites, which infest honeybees, are allergic to peppermint. Frosting made with oil of peppermint can be fed to the bees. As it permeates the bees' systems, the red mites drop off harmlessly. Other parasites respond variously to spearmint, citrus oil, oil of garlic, and powdered aloe vera."

But which? And how could I find out? Wear a garlic necklace? Stick an orange under Tonya's nose? There was no way to find out without their figuring out what I was doing.

I kept reading. "Some parasites can be destroyed by rendering the environment unfavorable. For moisture-dependent rusts, draining the soil can be beneficial. For temperature-susceptible pests, freezing and/or use of smudge pots can kill the invader. For light-sensitive parasites, exposure to light can kill the parasite."

Temperature-sensitive. I thought about the hats. Were they to hide the parasites or to protect them from the cold? No, that couldn't be it. The temperature in the building had been turned down to freezing for two weeks, and if they needed heat, why hadn't they landed in Florida?

I thought about Jackie Peterson's newsletter. She hadn't been affected. And neither had Uncle Marty, whose newsletter had come this morning. Or, rather, Uncle Marty's dog, who ostensibly dictated them. "Woof, woof!" the newsletter had said. "I'm lying here under a Christmas saguaro out on the desert, chewing on a bone and hoping Santa brings me a nice new flea collar."

So they hadn't landed in Arizona or Miami, and none of the newspaper articles Gary had circled had been from Mexico or California. They had all been datelined Minnesota and Michigan and Illinois. *Places where it was cold. Cold and cloudy,* I thought, thinking of Cousin Celia's Christmas newsletter. Cold and cloudy.

I flipped back through the pages, looking for the reference to light-sensitive parasites.

"It's right back here," a voice said.

I shut the book, jammed it in among Shakespeare's plays, and snatched up a copy of *Hamlet.*

"It's for my daughter," the customer, who was, thankfully, hatless, said, appearing at the end of the aisle. "That's what she said she wanted for Christmas when I called her. I was so surprised. She hardly ever reads."

The clerk was right behind her, wearing a mobcap with red and green ribbons. "Everybody's reading Shakespeare right now," she said, smiling. "We can hardly keep it on the shelves."

I ducked my head and pretended to read the *Hamlet.* "O villain, villain, smiling, damned villain!" Hamlet said. "I set it down that one may smile, and smile, and be a villain."

The clerk started along the shelves, looking for the book. *"King Lear, King Lear . . .* let's see."

"Here it is," I said, handing it to her before she reached *Common Garden Parasites.*

"Thank you," she said, smiling. She handed it to the customer. "Have you been to our book signing yet? Darla Sheridan, the fashion designer, is in the store today, signing her new book, *In Your Easter Bonnet.* Hats are coming back, you know."

"Really?" the customer said.

"She's giving away a free hat with every copy of the book," the clerk said.

"*Really?*" the customer said. "Where did you say?"

"I'll show you," the clerk said, still smiling, and led the customer away like a lamb to the slaughter.

As soon as they were gone, I pulled out *Organic Gardening* and looked up "light-sensitive" in the index. Page 264. "Pruning branches above the infection and cutting away surrounding leaves to expose the source to sunlight or artificial light will usually kill light-sensitive parasites."

I closed the book and hid it behind the Shakespeare plays, laying it on its side so it wouldn't show, and pulled out *Common Garden Pests*.

"Hi," Gary said, and I nearly dropped the book. "What are you doing here?"

"What are *you* doing here?" I said, cautiously closing the book.

He was looking at the title. I stuck it on the shelf between *Othello* and *The Riddle of Shakespeare's Identity*.

"I realized you were right." He looked cautiously around. "We've got to destroy them."

"I thought you said they were symbiotes, that they were beneficial," I said, watching him warily.

"You think I've been taken over by the aliens, don't you?" he said. He ran his hand through his hair. "See? No hat, no toupee."

But in *The Puppet Masters* the parasites had been able to attach themselves anywhere along the spine.

"I thought you said the benefits outweighed a few aches and pains," I said.

"I wanted to believe that," he said ruefully. "I guess what I really wanted to believe was that my ex-wife and I would get back together."

"What changed your mind?" I said, trying not to look at the bookshelf.

"You did," he said. "I realized somewhere along the way what a dope I'd been, mooning over her when you were right there in front of me. I was standing there, listening to her talk about how great it was going to be to get back together, and all of a sudden I realized that I didn't want to, that I'd found somebody nicer, prettier, someone I could trust. And that someone was you, Nan." He smiled at me. "So what have you found out? Something we can use to destroy them?"

I took a long, deep breath, and looked at him, deciding.

"Yes," I said, and pulled out the book. I handed it to him. "The section on bees. It says in here that introducing allergens into the bloodstream of the host can kill the parasite."

"Like in *Infiltrators from Space*."

"Yes." I told him about the red mites and the honeybees. "Oil of wintergreen, citrus oil, garlic, and powdered aloe vera are all used on various pests. So if we can introduce peppermint into the food of the affected people, it—"

"Peppermint?" he said blankly.

"Yes. Remember how Penny said nobody ate any of the candy canes she put out? I think it's because they're allergic to peppermint," I said, watching him.

"Peppermint," he said thoughtfully. "They didn't eat any of the ribbon candy Jan Gundell had on her desk, either. I think you've hit it. So how are you going to get them to ingest it? Put it in the water cooler?"

"No," I said. "In cookies. Chocolate chip cookies. Everybody loves chocolate." I pushed the books into place on the shelf and started for the front. "It's my turn to bring Holiday Goodies tomorrow. I'll go to the grocery store and get the cookie ingredients—"

"I'll go with you," he said.

"No," I said. "I need you to buy the oil of peppermint. They should have it at a drugstore or a health food store. Buy the most concentrated form you can get, and make sure you buy it from somebody who hasn't been taken over. I'll meet you back at my apartment, and we'll make the cookies there."

"Great," he said.

"We'd better leave separately," I said. I handed him the *Othello*. "Here. Go buy this. It'll give you a bag to carry the oil of peppermint in."

He nodded and started for the checkout line. I walked out of Barnes & Noble, went down Eighth to the grocery store, ducked out the side door, and went back to the office. I stopped at my desk for a metal ruler, and ran up to fifth. Jim Bridgeman, in his backward baseball cap, glanced up at me and then back down at his keyboard.

I went over to the thermostat.

And this was the moment when everyone surrounded you, pointing and squawking an unearthly screech at you. Or turned and stared at you with their glowing green eyes. I twisted the thermostat dial as far up as it would go, to ninety-five.

Nothing happened.

Nobody even looked up from their computers. Jim Bridgeman was typing intently.

I pried the dial and casing off with the metal ruler and stuck them into my coat pocket, bent the metal nub back so it couldn't be moved, and walked back out to the stairwell.

And now, please let it warm up fast enough to work before everybody goes home, I thought, clattering down the stairs to fourth. *Let everybody start sweating and take off their hats. Let the aliens be light-sensitive. Let them not be telepathic.*

I jammed the thermostats on fourth and third, and clattered down to second. Our thermostat was on the far side, next to Hunziger's office. I grabbed up a stack of memos from my desk, walked purposefully across the floor, dismantled the thermostat, and started back toward the stairs.

"Where do you think you're going?" Solveig said, planting herself firmly in front of me.

"To a meeting," I said, trying not to look as lame and frightened as the hero's girlfriend in the movies always did. She looked down at my sneakers. "Across town."

"You're not going anywhere," she said.

"Why not?" I said weakly.

"Because I've got to show you what I bought Jane for Christmas."

She reached for a shopping bag under her desk. "I know I'm not due till May, but I couldn't resist this," she said, rummaging in the bag. "It is so cute!"

She pulled out a tiny pink bonnet with white daisies on it. "Isn't it adorable?" she said. "It's newborn size. She can wear it home from the hospital. Oh, and I got her the cutest—"

"I lied," I said, and Solveig looked up alertly. "Don't tell anybody, but I completely forgot to buy a Secret Santa gift. Penny'll kill me if she finds out. If anybody asks where I've gone, tell them the ladies' room," I said, and took off down to first.

The thermostat was right by the door. I disabled it and the one in the basement, got my car (looking in the backseat first, unlike the people in the movies) and drove to the courthouse and the hospital and McDonald's, and then called my mother and invited myself to dinner. "I'll bring dessert," I said. I drove out to the mall, and hit the bakery, the Gap, the video-rental place, and the theater multiplex on the way.

🎄

Mom didn't have the TV on. She did have the hat on that Sueann had given her. "Don't you think it's adorable?" she said.

"I brought cheesecake," I said. "Have you heard from Allison and Mitch? How's Dakota?"

"Worse," she said. "She has these swellings on her knees and ankles. The doctors don't know what's causing them." She took the cheesecake into the kitchen, limping slightly. "I'm so worried."

I turned up the thermostats in the living room and the bedroom and was plugging the space heater in when she brought in the soup. "I got chilled on the way over," I said, turning the space heater up to high. "It's freezing out. I think it's going to snow."

We ate our soup, and Mom told me about Sueann's wedding. "She wants you to be her maid of honor," she said, fanning herself. "Aren't you warm yet?"

"No," I said, rubbing my arms.

"I'll get you a sweater," she said, and went into the bedroom, turning the space heater off as she went.

I turned it back on and went into the living room to build a fire in the fireplace.

"Have you met anyone at work lately?" she called in from the bedroom.

"What?" I said, sitting back on my knees.

She came back in without the sweater. Her hat was gone, and her hair was mussed up, as if something had thrashed around in it. "I hope you're not still refusing to write a Christmas newsletter," she said, going into the kitchen and coming out again with two plates of cheesecake. "Come sit down and eat your dessert," she said.

I did, still watching her warily.

"Making up things!" she said. "What an idea! Aunt Margaret wrote me just the other day to tell me how much she loves hearing from you girls and how interesting your newsletters always are." She cleared the table. "You can stay for a while, can't you? I hate waiting here alone for news about Dakota."

"No, I've got to go," I said, and stood up. "I've got to . . ."

I've got to . . . what? I thought, feeling suddenly overwhelmed. Fly to Spokane? And then, as soon as Dakota was okay, fly back and run wildly around town turning up thermostats until I fell over from exhaustion? And then what? It was when people fell asleep in the movies that the aliens took them over. And there was no way I could stay awake until every parasite was exposed to the heat, even if they didn't catch me and turn me into one of them. Even if I didn't turn my ankle.

The phone rang.

"Tell them I'm not here," I said.

"Who?" Mom asked, picking it up. "Oh, dear, I hope it's not Mitch with bad news. Hello?" Pause. "It's Sueann," she said, putting her hand over the receiver, and listened for a long interval. "She broke up with her boyfriend."

"With David?" I said. "Give me the phone."

"I thought you said you weren't here," she said, handing the phone over.

"Sueann?" I said. "Why did you break up with David?"

"Because he's so deadly dull," she said. "He's always calling me and sending me flowers and being nice. He even wants to get married. And tonight at dinner, I just thought, 'Why am I dating him?' and we broke up."

Mom went over and turned on the TV. "In local news," the CNN guy said, "special-interest groups banded together to donate fifteen thousand dollars to City Hall's Christmas display."

"Where were you having dinner?" I asked Sueann. "At McDonald's?"

"No, at this pizza place, which is another thing. All he ever wants is to go to dinner or the movies. We never do anything *interesting.*"

"Did you go to a movie tonight?" She might have been in the multiplex at the mall.

"No. I *told* you, I broke up with him."

This made no sense. I hadn't hit any pizza places.

"Weather is next," the guy on CNN said.

"Mom, can you turn that down?" I said. "Sueann, this is important. Tell me what you're wearing."

"Jeans and my blue top and my zodiac necklace. What does that have to do with my breaking up with David?"

"Are you wearing a hat?"

"In our forecast just ahead," the CNN guy said, "great weather for all you people trying to get your Christmas shopping d—"

Mom turned the TV down.

"Mom, turn it back up," I said, motioning wildly.

"No, I'm not wearing a hat," Sueann said. "What does that have to do with whether I broke up with David or not?"

The weather map behind the CNN guy was covered with 62, 65, 70, 68. *"Mom,"* I said.

She fumbled with the remote.

"You won't *believe* what he did the other day," Sueann said, outraged. "Gave me an engagement ring! Can you imag—"

"—unseasonably warm temperatures and *lots* of sunshine," the weather guy blared out. "Continuing right through Christmas."

"I mean, what was I thinking?" Sueann said.

"Shh," I said. "I'm trying to listen to the weather."

"It's supposed to be nice all next week," Mom said.

It was nice all the next week. Allison called to tell me Dakota was back home. "The doctors don't know what it was, some kind of bug or something, but whatever it was, it's completely gone. She's back taking ice-skating and tap-dancing lessons, and next week I'm signing both girls up for Junior Band."

"You did the right thing," Gary said grudgingly. "Marcie told me her knee was really hurting. When she was still talking to me, that is."

"The reconciliation's off, huh?"

"Yeah," he said, "but I haven't given up. The way she acted proves to me that her love for me is still there, if I can only reach it."

All it proved to me was that it took an invasion from outer space to make her seem even marginally human, but I didn't say so.

"I've talked her into going into marriage counseling with me," he said. "You were right not to trust me, either. That's the mistake they always make in those body-snatcher movies, trusting people."

Well, yes and no. If I'd trusted Jim Bridgeman, I wouldn't have had to do all those thermostats alone.

"You were the one who turned the heat up at the pizza place where Sueann and her fiancé were having dinner," I said after Jim told me he'd figured out what the aliens' weakness was after seeing me turn up the thermostat on fifth. "You were the one who'd checked out *Attack of the Soul Killers.*"

"I tried to talk to you," he said. "I don't blame you for not trusting me. I should have taken my hat off, but I didn't want you to see my bald spot."

"You can't go by appearances," I said.

🌲

By December fifteenth, hat sales were down, the mall was jammed with ill-tempered shoppers, at City Hall an animal-rights group was protesting Santa Claus's wearing fur, and Gary's wife had skipped their first marriage-counseling session and then blamed it on him.

It's now four days till Christmas, and things are completely back to normal. Nobody at work's wearing a hat except Jim, Solveig's naming her baby Durango, Hunziger's suing management for firing him, antidepressant sales are up, and my mother called just now to tell me Sueann has a new boyfriend who's a terrorist, and to ask me if I'd sent out my Christmas newsletters yet. And had I met anyone lately at work.

"Yes," I said. "I'm bringing him to Christmas dinner."

Yesterday Betty Holland filed a sexual harassment suit against Nathan Steinberg for kissing her under the mistletoe, and I was nearly run over on my way home from work. But the world has been made safe from cankers, leaf wilt, and galls.

And it makes an interesting Christmas Newsletter.

Whether it's true or not.

Wishing you and yours a very Merry Christmas and a Happy New Year,

Nan Johnson

Epiphany

"But pray ye that your flight be not in the winter,
neither on the sabbath day."
—Matthew 24:20

A little after three, it began to snow. It had looked like it was going to all the way through Pennsylvania, and had even spit a few flakes just before Youngstown, Ohio, but now it was snowing in earnest, thick flakes that were already covering the stiff dead grass on the median and getting thicker as he drove west.

And this is what you get for setting out in the middle of January, he thought, *without checking the Weather Channel first.* He hadn't checked anything. He had taken off his robe, packed a bag, gotten into his car, and taken off. Like a man fleeing a crime.

The congregation will think I've absconded with the money in the collection plate, he thought. *Or worse.* Hadn't there been a minister in the paper last month who'd run off to the Bahamas with the building fund and a blonde? They'll say, "I *thought* he acted strange in church this morning."

But they wouldn't know yet that he was gone. The Sunday night Mariners' Meeting had been canceled, the elders' meeting wasn't till next week, and the interchurch ecumenical meeting wasn't till Thursday.

He was supposed to play chess with B.T. on Wednesday, but he could call him and move it. He would have to call when B.T. was at work and

leave him a message on his voice mail. He couldn't risk talking to him—
they had been friends too many years. B.T. would instantly know something was up. And he would be the last person to understand.

*I'll call his voice mail and move our chess game to Thursday night after
the ecumenical meeting,* Mel thought. *That will give me till Thursday.*

He was kidding himself. The church secretary, Mrs. Bilderbeck, would
miss him Monday morning when he didn't show up in the church office.

I'll call her and tell her I've got the flu, he thought. No, she would insist
on bringing him over chicken soup and zinc lozenges. *I'll tell her I've
been called out of town for a few days on personal business.*

She will immediately think the worst, he thought. *She'll think I have
cancer, or that I'm looking at another church. And anything they con-
clude, even embezzlement, will be easier for them to accept than the
truth.*

The snow was starting to stick on the highway, and the windshield
was beginning to fog up. Mel turned on the defroster. A truck passed
him, throwing up snow. It was full of gold-and-white Ferris wheel baskets. He had been seeing trucks like it all afternoon, carrying black Octo-
pus cars and concession stands and lengths of roller-coaster track. He
wondered what a carnival was doing in Ohio in the middle of January.
And in this weather.

Maybe they were lost. *Or maybe they suddenly had a vision telling
them to head west,* he thought grimly. *Maybe they suddenly had a nervous breakdown in the middle of church. In the middle of their sermon.*

He had scared the choir half to death. They had been sitting there,
midway through the sermon, thinking they had plenty of time before
they had to find the recessional hymn, when he'd stopped cold, his hand
still raised, in the middle of a sentence.

There had been silence for a full minute before the organist thought
to play the intro, and then a frantic scramble for their bulletins and their
hymnals, a frantic flipping of pages. They had straggled unevenly to
their feet all the way through the first verse, singing and looking at him
like he was crazy.

And were they right? Had he really had a vision or was it some kind
of midlife crisis? Or psychotic episode?

He was a Presbyterian, not a Pentecostal. He did not have visions. The
only time he had experienced anything remotely like this was when he

was nineteen, and that hadn't been a vision. It had been a call to the
ministry, and it had only sent him to seminary, not haring off to who
knows where.

And this wasn't a vision, either. He hadn't seen a burning bush or an
angel. He hadn't seen anything. He had simply had an overwhelming
conviction that what he was saying was true.

He wished he still had it, that he wasn't beginning to doubt it now
that he was three hundred miles from home and in the middle of a
snowstorm, that he wasn't beginning to think it had been some kind of
self-induced hysteria, born out of his own wishful thinking and the fact
that it was January.

He hated January. The church always looked cheerless and abandoned, with all the Christmas decorations taken down, the sanctuary
dim and chilly in the gray winter light, Epiphany over and nothing to
look forward to but Lent and taxes. And Good Friday. Attendance and
the collection down, half the congregation out with the flu and the other
half away on a winter cruise, those who were there looking abandoned,
too, and like they wished they had somewhere to go.

That was why he had decided against his sermon on Christian duty
and pulled an old one out of the files, a sermon on Jesus's promise that
He would return. To get that abandoned look off their faces.

"This is the hardest time," he had said, "when Christmas is over, and
the bills have all come due, and it seems like winter is never going to end
and summer is never going to come. But Christ tells us that we 'know
not when the master of the house cometh, at even, or at midnight, or at
the cock-crowing, or in the morning,' and when he comes, we must be
ready for him. He may come tomorrow or next year or a thousand years
from now. He may already be here, right now. At this moment . . ."

And as he said it, he had had an overwhelming feeling that it was
true, that He had already come, and he must go find Him.

But now he wondered if it was just the desire to be somewhere else,
too, somewhere besides the cold, poinsettia-less sanctuary.

If so, you came the wrong way, he thought. It was freezing, and the
windshield was starting to fog up. Mel kicked the defroster all the way
up to high and swiped at the windshield with his gloved hand.

The snow was coming down much harder, and the wind was picking
up. Mel switched on the radio to hear a weather report.

"... and in the last days, the Book of Revelation tells us," a voice said, "'there will be hail and fire mingled with blood.'"

He hoped that wasn't the weather report. He hit the scan button on the radio and listened as it cycled through the stations:... "latest on the scandal involving the President and"... the voice of Randy Travis, singing "Forever and Ever, Amen"... "hog futures at"... "and the disciples said, 'Lord, show us a sign....'"

A sign, that was what he needed, Mel thought, peering at the road. A sign that he was not crazy.

A semi roared past in a blinding blast of snow and exhaust. He leaned forward, trying to see the lines on the pavement, and another truck went by, full of orange-and-yellow bumper cars. Bumper cars. How appropriate. They were all going to be driving bumper cars if this snow kept up, Mel thought, watching the truck pull into the lane ahead of him. It fishtailed wildly as it did, and Mel put his foot on the brake, felt it skid, and lifted his foot off.

Well, he had asked for a sign, he thought, carefully slowing down, and this one couldn't be clearer if it was written in fiery letters: Go home! This was a crazy idea! You're going to be killed, and then what will the congregation think? Go home!

Which was easier said than done. He could scarcely see the road, let alone any exit signs, and the windshield was starting to ice up. He swiped at the window again.

He didn't dare pull over and stop—those semis would never see him— but he was going to have to. The defroster wasn't having any effect on the ice on the windshield, and neither were the windshield wipers.

He rolled down the window and leaned out, trying to grab the wiper and slap it against the windshield to shake the ice off. Snow stabbed his face, stinging it.

"All right, all right," he shouted into the wind. "I get the message!"

He rolled the window back up, shivering, and swiped at the inside of the windshield again. The only kind of sign he wanted now was an exit sign, but he couldn't see the side of the road.

If I'm on *the road,* he thought, trying to spot the shoulder, a telltale outline, but the whole world had disappeared into a featureless whiteness. And what would keep him from driving right off the road and into a ditch?

He leaned forward tensely, trying to spot something, anything, and thought he saw, far ahead, a light.

A yellow light, too high up for a taillight—a reflector on a motorcycle, maybe. That was impossible, there was no way a motorcycle could be out in this. One of those lights on the top corners of a semi.

If that was what it was, he couldn't see the other one, but the light was moving steadily in front of him, and he followed it, trying to keep pace.

The windshield wipers were icing up again. He rolled down the window, and in the process lost sight of the light. *And the road,* he thought frightenedly. No, there was the light, still high up, but closer, and it wasn't a light, it was a whole cluster of them, round yellow bulbs in the shape of an arrow.

The arrow on top of a police car, he thought, telling you to change lanes. There must be some kind of accident up ahead. He strained forward, trying to make out flashing blue ambulance lights.

But the yellow arrow moved steadily ahead, and as he got closer, he saw that the arrow was pointed down at an angle. And that it was slowing. Mel slowed, too, focusing his whole attention on the road and on pumping his brakes to keep the car from skidding.

When he looked up again, the arrow had slowed nearly to a stop, and he could see it clearly. It was part of a lighted sign on the back of a truck. "Shooting Star" it said in a flowing script, and next to the arrow in neon pink, "Tickets."

The truck came to a complete stop, its turn light blinking, and then started up again, and in its headlights he caught a glimpse of snow-spattered red. A stop sign.

And this was an exit. He had followed the truck off the highway onto an exit without even knowing it.

And now he was hopefully following it into a town, he thought, clicking on his right-turn signal and turning after the truck, but in the moment he had hesitated, he had lost it. And the blowing snow was worse here than on the highway.

There was the yellow arrow again. No, what he was seeing was a Burger King crown. He pulled in, scraping the snow-covered curb, and saw that he was wrong again. It was a motel sign. "King's Rest," with a crown of sulfur-yellow bulbs.

He parked the car and got out, slipping in the snow, and started for the office, which had, thank goodness, a "Vacancy" sign in the same neon pink as the "Tickets" sign.

A little blue Honda pulled up beside him and a short, plump woman got out of it, winding a bright purple muffler around her head. "Thank goodness you knew where you were going," she said, pulling on a pair of turquoise mittens. "I couldn't see a thing except your taillights." She reached back into the Honda for a vivid green canvas bag. "Anybody who'd be on the roads in weather like this would have to be crazy, wouldn't they?"

And if the blizzard hadn't been sign enough, here was proof positive. "Yes," he said, although she had already gone inside the motel office, "they would."

He would check in, wait a few hours till the storm let up, and then start back. With luck he would be back home before Mrs. Bilderbeck got to the office tomorrow morning.

He went inside the office, where a balding man was handing the plump woman a room key and talking to someone on the phone.

"Another one," he said when Mel opened the door. "Yeah." He hung up the phone and pushed a registration form and a pen at Mel.

"Which way'd *you* come from?" he asked. "East," Mel said.

The man shook his balding head. "You got here in the nick of time," he said to both of them. "They just closed all the roads east of here."

> *"And thus I saw the horses in the vision,*
> *and them that sat upon them."*
> —Revelation 9:17

*

In the morning, Mel called Mrs. Bilderbeck. "I won't be in today. I've been called out of town."

"Out of town?" Mrs. Bilderbeck said, interested.

"Yes. On personal business. I'll be gone most of the week."

"Oh, dear," she said, and Mel suddenly hoped that there was an emergency at the church, that Gus Uhank had had another stroke or Lottie Millar's mother had died, so that he would have to go back.

"I told Juan you'd be in," Mrs. Bilderbeck said. "He's putting the sanctuary Christmas decorations away, and he wanted to know if you want to save the star for next year. And the pilot light went out again. The church was *freezing* when I got here this morning."

"Was Juan able to get it relit?"

"Yes, but I think someone should look at it. What if it goes out on a Saturday night?"

"Call Jake Adams at A-1 Heating," he said. Jake was a deacon.

"A-1 Heating," she said slowly, as if she were writing it down. "What about the star? Are we going to use it again next year?"

Is there going to be *a next year?* Mel thought. "Whatever you think," he said.

"And what about the ecumenical meeting?" she asked. "Will you be back in time for that?"

"Yes," he said, afraid if he said "no," she would ask more questions.

"Is there a number where I can reach you?"

"No. I'll check in tomorrow." He hung up quickly, and then sat there on the bed, trying to decide whether to call B.T. or not. He hadn't done anything major in the fifteen years they'd been friends without telling him, but Mel knew what he'd say. They'd met on the ecumenical committee, when the Unitarian chairman had decided that, to be truly ecumenical, they needed a resident atheist and Darwinian biologist. And, Mel suspected, an African American.

It was the only good thing that had ever come out of the ecumenical committee. He and B.T. had started by complaining about the idiocies of the ecumenical committee, which seemed bent on proving that denominations couldn't get along, progressed to playing chess and then to discussing religion and politics and disagreeing on both, and ended by becoming close friends.

I have to call him, Mel thought, *it's a betrayal of our friendship not to.*

And tell him what? That he'd had a holy vision? That the Book of Revelation was coming literally true? It sounded crazy to Mel, let alone to B.T., who was a scientist, who didn't believe in the First Coming, let alone the Second. But if it *was* true, how could he not call him?

He dialed B.T.'s area code and then put down the receiver and went to check out.

The roads east were still closed. "You shouldn't have any trouble heading west, though," the balding man said, handing Mel his credit card receipt. "The snow's supposed to let up by noon."

Mel hoped so. The interstate was snow-packed and unbelievably slick, and when Mel positioned himself behind a sand truck, a rock struck his windshield and made a ding.

At least there was hardly any traffic. There were only a few semis, and a navy blue pickup with a bumper sticker that said "In case of the Rapture, this car will be unoccupied." There was no sign of the blue Honda or of the carnival. They had seen the light and were still at the King's Rest, sitting in the restaurant, drinking coffee. Or headed south for the winter.

He passed a snow-obscured sign that read "For Weather Info Tune to AM 1410."

He did. ". . . and in the last days Christ Himself will appear," an evangelist, possibly the one from yesterday, or a different one—they all had the same accent, the same intonation—said. "The Book of Revelation tells us He will appear riding a white horse and leading a mighty army of the righteous against the Antichrist in that last great battle of Armageddon. And the unbelievers—the fornicators and the baby-murderers—will be flung into the bottomless pit."

The ultimate "Wait till your father gets home" threat, Mel thought.

"And how do I know these things are coming?" the radio said. "I'll *tell* you how. The Lord came to me in a dream, and He said, 'These shall be the signs of my coming. There will be wars and rumors of wars.' Iraq, my friends, that's what he's talking about. The sun's face will be covered, and the godless will prosper. Look around you. Who do you see prospering? Abortion doctors and homosexuals and godless atheists. But when Christ comes, they will be punished. He told me so. The Lord spoke to me, just like he spoke to Moses, just like he spoke to Isaiah . . ."

He switched off the radio, but it didn't do any good. Because this was what had been bothering him ever since he started out. How did he know his vision wasn't just like some radio evangelist's?

Because his is born out of hatred, bigotry, and revenge, Mel thought. *God no more spoke to him than did the man in the moon.*

And how do you know He spoke to you? Because it felt *real? The voices telling the bomber to destroy the abortion clinic felt real, too. Emotion isn't proof. Signs aren't evidence.* "Do you have any outside confirmation?" he could hear B.T. saying skeptically.

The sun came out, and the glare off the white road, the white fields, was worse than the snow had been. He almost didn't see the truck off to the side. Its emergency flashers weren't on, and at first he thought it had just slid off the road, but as he went past, he saw it was one of the carnival trucks with its hood up and steam coming out. A young man in a denim jacket was standing next to it, hooking his thumb for a ride.

I should stop, Mel thought, but he was already past, and picking up hitchhikers was dangerous. He had found that out when he'd preached a sermon on the Good Samaritan last year. "Let us not be like the Levite or the Pharisee who passes by the stranded motorist, the injured victim," he had told his congregation. "Let us be like the Samaritan, who stopped and helped."

It had seemed like a perfectly harmless sermon topic, and he had been totally unprepared for the uproar that ensued. "I cannot believe you told people to pick up hitchhikers!" Dan Crosby had raged. "If one of my daughters ends up raped, I'm holding you responsible."

"What were you thinking of?" Mrs. Bilderbeck had said, hanging up after fending off Mabel Jenkins. "On CNN last week there was a story about somebody who stopped to help a couple who was out of gas, and they cut off his head."

He had had to issue a retraction the next Sunday, saying that women had no business helping anyone (which had made Mamie Rollet mad, for feminist reasons) and that the best thing for everyone else to do was to alert the state patrol on their cell phones and let them take care of it, unless they knew the person, although somehow he couldn't imagine the Good Samaritan with a cell phone.

There was a median crossing up ahead, but it was marked with a sign that read "Authorized Vehicles Only." *And if I get my head cut off,* he thought, *the congregation will have no sympathy at all.*

But it was threatening to snow again, and the green interstate sign up ahead said "Wayside 28." And the carnival had been his Good Samaritan last night.

"'Inasmuch as ye have done it unto one of the least of these, you have done it unto me,'" he murmured, and turned into the median crossing and onto the eastbound side of the highway, and started back.

The truck was still there, though he couldn't see the driver. *Good,* he thought, looking for a place to cross. Some other Samaritan picked him up. But when he pulled up behind the truck, the man got out of the truck's cab and started over to the car, his hands jammed into his denim jacket. Mel began to feel sorry he'd stopped. The man had a ragged scar across his forehead, and his hair was lank and greasy.

He slouched over to the side of the car, and Mel saw that he was much younger than he'd looked at first. *He's just a kid,* Mel thought.

Yeah, well, so was Billy the Kid, he reminded himself. *And Andrew Cunanan.*

Mel leaned across and pulled down the passenger window. "What's the trouble?"

The kid leaned down to talk to him. "Died," he said, and grinned.

"Do you need a lift into town?" he asked, and the kid immediately opened the car door, keeping his right hand in his jacket pocket. *Where the gun is,* Mel thought.

The kid slid in and shut the door, still using only one hand. *When they find me robbed and murdered, they'll be convinced I was involved in some kind of drug deal,* Mel thought. He started the car.

"Man, it was cold out there," the kid said, taking his right hand out of his pocket and rubbing his hands together. "I been waiting forever."

Mel kicked the heater over to high, and the kid leaned forward and held his hands in front of the vent. There was a peace sign tattooed on the back of one of them and a fierce-looking lion on the other. Both looked like they'd been done by hand.

The kid rubbed his hands together, wincing, and Mel took another look. His hands were red with cold and between the tattoo lines there were ugly white splotches. The kid started rubbing them again.

"Don't—" Mel said, putting out his hand unthinkingly to stop him. "That looks like frostbite. Don't rub it. You're supposed to . . ." he said, and then couldn't remember. Put them in warm water? Wrap them up? "They're supposed to warm up slowly," he said finally.

"You mean like by warming 'em up in front of a heater?" the kid said, holding his hands in front of the vent again. He put up his hand and touched the ding in the windshield. "That's gonna spread," he said.

His hand looked even worse now that it was warming up. The sickly white splotches stood out starkly against the rest of his skin.

Mel took off his gloves, switching hands on the steering wheel and using his teeth to get the second one off. "Here," he said, handing them to the kid. "These are insulated."

The kid looked at him for a minute and then put them on.

"You should get your hands looked at," Mel said. "I can take you to the emergency room when we get to town."

"I'll be okay," the kid said. "You get used to being cold, working a carny."

"What's a carnival doing here in the middle of winter, anyway?" Mel asked.

"Best time," the kid said. "Catches 'em by surprise. What're you doin' out here?"

He wondered what the kid would say if he told him. "I'm a minister," he said instead.

"A preacher, huh?" he said. "You believe in the Second Coming?"

"The Second Coming?" Mel gasped, caught off guard.

"Yeah, we had a preacher come to the carny the other day telling us Jesus was coming back and was gonna punish everybody for hanging him on the cross, knock down the mountains, burn the whole planet up. You believe all that's gonna happen?"

"No," Mel said. "I don't think Jesus is coming back to punish anybody."

"The preacher said it was all right there in the Bible."

"There are lots of things in the Bible. They don't always turn out to mean what you thought they did."

The kid nodded sagely. "Like the Siamese twins."

"Siamese twins?" Mel said, unable to remember any Siamese twins in the Bible.

"Yeah, like this one carny up in Fargo. It had a big sign saying 'See the Siamese Twins,' and everybody pays a buck, thinking they're gonna see two people hooked together. And when they get there it's a cage with two Siamese kittens in it. Like that."

"Not exactly," Mel said. "The prophecies aren't a scam to cheat people, they're—"

"What about Roswell? The alien autopsy and all that. You think that's a scam, too?"

Well, there was some outside confirmation for you. Mel was in a class with scam artists and UFO nuts.

"After what happened the first time, I don't know if I'd wanta come back or not," the kid said, and it took Mel a minute to realize he was talking about Christ. "If I did, I'd wear some kind of disguise or something."

Like the last time, Mel thought, *when He came disguised as a baby.*

The kid was still preoccupied with the ding. "There's stuff you could do to keep it from spreading for a little while," he said, "but it's still gonna spread. There ain't nothing that can stop it." He pointed out the window at a sign. "Wayside, exit 1 mile."

Mel pulled off and into a Total station, apparently all there was to Wayside. The kid opened the door and started to take off the gloves.

"Keep them," Mel said. "Do you want me to wait till you find out if they've got a tow truck?"

The kid shook his head. "I'll call Pete." He reached into the pocket of the denim jacket and handed Mel three orange cardboard tickets. They were marked "Admit One Free."

"It's a ticket to the show," the kid said. "We got a triple Ferris wheel, three wheels one inside the other. And a great roller coaster. The Comet."

Mel splayed the tickets apart. "There are three tickets here."

"Bring your friends," the kid said, slapped the car door, and ambled off toward the gas station.

Bring your friends.

Mel got back on the highway. It was getting dark. He hoped the next exit wasn't as far, or as uninhabited, as this one.

Bring your friends. *I should have told B.T.,* he thought, *even though he would have said, Don't go, you're crazy, let me recommend a good psychiatrist.*

"I still should have told him," he said out loud, and was as certain of it as he had been of what he should do in that moment in the church. And now he had cut himself off from B.T. not only by hundreds of miles of closed highways and "icy and snow-packed conditions," but by his deception, his failure to tell him.

The next exit didn't even have a gas station, and the one after that nothing but a Dairy Queen. It was nearly eight by the time he got to Zion Center and a Holiday Inn.

He walked straight in, not even stopping to get his luggage out of the trunk, and across the lobby toward the phones.

"Hello!" The short, plump woman he'd seen the night before waylaid him. "Here we are again, orphans of the storm. Weren't the roads awful?" she said cheerfully. "I almost went off in the ditch twice. My little Honda doesn't have four-wheel drive, and—"

"Excuse me," Mel interrupted her. "I have a phone call I *have* to make."

"You can't," she said, still cheerfully. "The lines are down."

"Down?"

"Because of the storm. I tried to call my sister just now, and the clerk told me the phone's been out all day. I don't know what she's going to think when she doesn't hear from me. I promised *faithfully* that I'd call her every night and tell her where I was and that I'd gotten there safely."

He couldn't call B.T. Or get to him. "Excuse me," he said, and started back across the lobby to the registration desk.

"Has the interstate going east opened up yet?" he asked the girl behind the counter.

She shook her head. "It's still closed between Malcolm and Iowa City. Ground blizzards," she said. "Will you be checking in, sir? How many are there in your party?"

"Two," a voice said.

Mel turned. And there, leaning against the end of the registration desk, was B.T.

> *"And there appeared another wonder in heaven,*
> *and behold a great red dragon."*
> —Revelation 12:3

*

For a moment he couldn't speak for the joy, the relief he felt. He clutched the checkout counter, vaguely aware that the girl behind the counter was saying something.

"What are you doing here?" he said finally.

B.T. smiled his slow checkmate smile. "Aren't I the one who should be asking that?"

And now that he was here, he would have to tell him. Mel felt the relief turn into resentment. "I thought the roads were closed," he said.

"I didn't come that way," B.T. said.

"And how would you like to pay for that, sir?" the clerk said, and Mel knew she had asked him before.

"Credit card," he said, fumbling for his wallet.

"License number?" the clerk asked.

"I flew to Omaha and rented a car," B.T. said.

Mel handed her his MasterCard. "TY 804."

"State?"

"Pennsylvania." He looked at B.T. "How did you find me?"

"'License number?'" B.T. said, mimicking the clerk. "'Will you be putting this on your credit card, sir?' If you've got a computer, it's the easiest
thing in the world to find someone these days, especially if they're using
that." He gestured at the MasterCard the clerk was handing back to Mel.

She handed him a folder. "Your room number is written inside, sir.
It's not on the key for security purposes," the clerk said, as if his room
number weren't in the computer, too. B.T. probably already knew it.

"You still haven't answered my question," B.T. said. "What are you
doing here?"

"I have to go get my suitcase," Mel said, and walked past him and out
to the parking lot and his car. He opened the trunk.

B.T. reached past him and picked up Mel's suitcase, as if taking it into
custody.

"How did you know I was missing?" Mel asked, but he already knew
the answer to that. "Mrs. Bilderbeck sent you."

B.T. nodded. "She said she was worried about you, that you'd called
and something was seriously wrong. She said she knew because you
hadn't tried to get out of the ecumenical meeting on Thursday. She said
you always tried to get out of it."

They say it's the little mistakes that trip criminals up, Mel thought.

"She said she thought you were sick and were going to see a special-
ist," B.T. said, his black face gray with worry. "Out of town, so nobody in
the congregation would find out about it. A brain tumor, she said." He
shifted the suitcase to his other hand. "Do you have a brain tumor?"

A brain tumor. That would be a nice, convenient explanation. When
Ivor Sorenson had had a brain tumor, he had stood up during the offer-
tory, convinced there was an ostrich sitting in the pew next to him.

"Are you sick?" B.T. said.

"No."

"But it is something serious."

"It's freezing out here," Mel said. "Let's discuss this inside."

B.T. didn't move. "Whatever it is, no matter how bad it is, you can tell
me."

"All right. Fine. 'For ye know neither the day nor the hour wherein the

Son of Man cometh.' Matthew 25:13," Mel said. "I had a revelation. About the Second Coming. I think He's here already, that the Second Coming's already happened."

Whatever B.T. had imagined—terminal illness or embezzlement or some other, worse crime—it obviously wasn't as bad as this. His face went even grayer. "The Second Coming," he said. "Of Christ?"

"Yes," Mel said. He told him what had happened during the sermon Sunday. "I scared the choir half out of their wits," he said.

B.T. nodded. "Mrs. Bilderbeck told me. She said you stopped in the middle of a sentence and just stood there, staring into space with your hand up to your forehead. That's why she thought you had a brain tumor. How long did this . . . vision last?"

"It wasn't a vision," Mel said. "It was a revelation, a conviction . . . an epiphany."

"An epiphany," B.T. said in a flat, expressionless voice. "And it told you He was here? In Zion Center?"

"No," Mel said. "I don't know where He is."

"You don't know where He is," B.T. repeated. "You just got in your car and started driving?"

"West," Mel said. "I knew He was somewhere west."

"Somewhere west," B.T. said softly. He rubbed his hand over his mouth.

"Why don't you say it?" Mel said. He slammed the trunk shut. "You think I'm crazy."

"I think we're both crazy," he said, "standing out here in the snow, fighting. Have you had supper?"

"No," Mel said.

"Neither have I," B.T. said. He took Mel's arm. "Let's go get some dinner."

"And a dose of antidepressants? A nice straitjacket?"

"I was thinking steak," B.T. said, and tried to smile. "Isn't that what they eat here in Iowa?"

"Corn," Mel said.

> *"And when I looked, behold . . . the appearance of the wheels*
> *was as the colour of a beryl stone and . . . as if a*
> *wheel had been in the midst of a wheel."*
> —Ezekiel 10:9–10

*

Neither corn nor steak was on the menu, which had the Holiday Inn star on the front, and they were out of nearly everything else. "Because of the interstate being closed," the waitress said. "We've got chicken teriyaki and beef chow mein."

They ordered the chow mein and coffee, and the waitress left. Mel braced himself for more questions, but B.T. only asked, "How were the roads today?" and told him about the problems he'd had getting a flight and a rental car. "Chicago O'Hare was shut down because of a winter storm," he said, "and Denver *and* Kansas City. I had to fly into Albuquerque and then up to Omaha."

"I'm sorry you had to go to all that trouble," Mel said.

"I was worried about you."

The waitress arrived with their chow mein, which came with mashed potatoes and gravy and green beans.

"Interesting," B.T. said, poking at the gravy. He made a halfhearted attempt at the chow mein, and then pushed the plate away.

"There's something I don't understand," he said. "The Second Coming is when Christ returns, right? I thought He was supposed to appear in the clouds in a blaze of glory, complete with trumpets and angel choirs."

Mel nodded.

"Then how can He already be here without anybody knowing?"

"I don't know," Mel said. "I don't understand any of this any more than you do. I just know He's here."

"But you don't know where."

"No. I thought when I got out here there would be a sign."

"A sign," B.T. said.

"Yes," Mel said, getting angry all over again. "You know. A burning bush, a pillar of fire, a star. A sign."

He must have been shouting. The waitress came scurrying over with the check. "Are you through with this?" she said, looking at the plates of half-eaten food.

"Yes," Mel said. "We're through."

"You can pay at the register," the waitress said, and scurried away with their plates.

"Look," B.T. said, "the brain's a very complicated thing. An alteration in brain chemistry—are you on any medications? Sometimes medications can cause people to hear voices or—"

Mel picked up the check and stood, reaching for his wallet. "It wasn't a voice."

He put down money for a tip and went over to the cash register.

"You said it was a strong feeling," B.T. said after Mel had paid. "Sometimes endorphins can—nothing like this has ever happened to you before, has it?"

Mel walked out into the lobby. "Yes," he said, and turned to face B.T. "It happened once before."

"When?" B.T. said, his face gray again.

"When I was nineteen. I was in college, studying pre-law. I went to church with a girlfriend, and the minister gave a hellfire-and-brimstone sermon on the evils of dancing and associating with anyone who did. He said Jesus said it was wrong to associate with nonbelievers, that they would corrupt and contaminate you. Jesus, who spent all His time with lowlifes—tax collectors and prostitutes and lepers! And all of a sudden I had this overwhelming feeling . . . this—"

"Epiphany," B.T. said.

"That I had to do something, that I had to fight him and all the other ministers like him. I stood up and walked out in the middle of the sermon," Mel said, remembering, "and went home and applied to seminary."

B.T. rubbed his hand across his mouth. "And the epiphany you had yesterday was the same as that one?"

"Yes."

"Reverend Abrams?" a woman's voice said.

Mel turned. The short, plump woman who'd been on the phone and at the motel the night before was hurrying toward them, lugging her bright green tote bag.

"Who's that?" B.T. said.

Mel shook his head, wondering how she knew his name.

She came up to them. "Oh, Reverend Abrams," she said breathlessly, "I wanted to thank you—I'm Cassie Hunter, by the way." She stuck out a plump, beringed hand.

"How do you do?" Mel said, shaking it. "This is Dr. Bernard Thomas, and I'm Mel Abrams."

She nodded. "I heard the desk clerk say your name. I didn't thank you the other night for saving my life."

"Saving your life?" B.T. said, looking at Mel.

"There was this awful whiteout," Cassie said. "You couldn't see the road at all, and if it hadn't been for the taillights on Reverend Abrams's car, I'd have ended up in a ditch."

Mel shook his head. "You shouldn't thank me. You should thank the driver of the carnival truck *I* was following. He saved both of us."

"I *saw* those carnival trucks," Cassie said. "I wondered what a carnival was doing in Iowa in the middle of winter." She laughed, a bright, chirpy laugh. "Of course, you're probably wondering what a retired English teacher is doing in Iowa in the middle of winter. Of course, for that matter, what are *you* doing in Iowa in the middle of winter?"

"We're on our way to a religious meeting," B.T. said before Mel could answer.

"Really? I've been visiting famous writers' birthplaces," she said. "Everyone back home thinks I'm *crazy,* but except for the last few days, the weather's been *fine.* Oh, and I wanted to tell you, I just talked to the clerk, and she thinks the phones will be working again by tomorrow morning, so you should be able to make your call."

She rummaged in her voluminous tote bag and came up with a room key folder. "Well, anyway, I just wanted to thank you. It was nice meeting you," she said to B.T., and bustled off across the lobby toward the coffee shop.

"Who were you trying to call?" B.T. asked.

"You," Mel said bitterly. "I realized I owed it to you to tell you, even if you did think I was crazy."

B.T. didn't say anything.

"That *is* what you think, isn't it?" Mel said. "Why don't you just say it? You think I'm crazy."

"All right. I think you're crazy," B.T. said, and then continued angrily, "Well, what do you expect me to say? You take off in the middle of a blizzard, you don't tell anyone where you're going, because you saw the Second Coming in a *vision*?"

"It wasn't—"

"Oh, right. It wasn't a vision. You had an epiphany. So did the woman in *The Globe* last week who saw the Virgin Mary on her refrigerator. So did the Heaven's Gate people. Are you telling me *they're* not crazy?"

"No," Mel said, and started down the hall to his room.

"For fifteen years you've raved about faith healers and cults and preachers who claim they've got a direct line to God being frauds," B.T. said, following him, "and now you suddenly believe in it?"

He kept walking. "No."

"But you're telling me I'm supposed to believe in *your* revelation because it's different, because this is the real thing."

"I'm not telling you anything," Mel said, turning to face him. "You're the one who came out here and demanded to know what I was doing. I told you. You got what you came for. Now you can go back and tell Mrs. Bilderbeck I don't have a brain tumor, it's a chemical imbalance."

"And what do you intend to do? Drive west until you fall off the Santa Monica pier?"

"I intend to find Him," Mel said.

B.T. opened his mouth as if to say something and then shut it and stormed off down the hall.

Mel stood there, watching him till a door slammed, far down the hall.

Bring your friends, Mel thought. *Bring your friends.*

> *"For now we see through a glass darkly,*
> *but then face to face."*
> —I Corinthians 13:12

*

"I intend to find Him," Mel had said, and was glad B.T. hadn't shouted back "How?" because he had no idea.

He had not had a sign, which meant that the answer must be somewhere else. Mel sat down on the bed, opened the drawer of the bedside table, and got out the Gideon Bible.

He propped the pillows up against the headboard and leaned back against them and opened the Bible to the Book of Revelation.

The radio evangelists made it sound like the story of the Second Coming was a single narrative, but it was actually a hodgepodge of isolated scriptures—Matthew 24 and sections of Isaiah and Daniel, verses out of Second Thessalonians and John and Joel, stray ravings from Revelation and Jeremiah, all thrown together by the evangelists as if the authors were writing at the same time. As if they were even writing about the same thing.

And the references were full of contradictions. A trumpet would sound, and Christ would come in the clouds of heaven with power and great glory. Or on a white horse, leading an army of a hundred and forty-four thousand. Or like a thief in the night. There would be earthquakes and pestilences and a star falling out of heaven. Or a dragon would come up out of the sea, or four great beasts, with the heads of a lion and a bear and a leopard and eagles' wings. Or darkness would cover the earth.

But in all the assorted prophecies there were no locations mentioned. Joel talked about a desolate wilderness and Jeremiah about a wasteland, but not about where they were. Luke said the faithful would come "from the east, and from the west, and from the north" to the kingdom of God, but neglected to say where it was located.

The only place mentioned by name in all the prophecies was Armageddon. But Armageddon (or Har-Magedon or Ar Himdah) was a word that appeared only once in the Scriptures and whose meaning was not known, a word that might be Hebrew or Greek or something else altogether, that might mean "level" or "valley plain" or "place of desire."

Mel remembered from seminary that some scholars thought it referred to the plain in front of Mount Megiddo, the site of a battle between Israel and Sisera the Canaanite. But there was no Mount Megiddo on ancient or modern maps. It could be anywhere.

He put on his shoes and his coat and went out to the parking lot to get his road atlas out of the car.

B.T. was leaning against the trunk.

"How long have you been out here?" Mel asked, but the answer was obvious. B.T.'s dark face was pinched with cold, and his hands were jammed into his pockets like the carnival kid's had been.

"I've been thinking," he said, his voice shivering with the cold. "I don't have to be back until Thursday, and I can fly out of Denver just as easily as out of Omaha. If we drive as far as Denver together, it'll give us more time—"

"For you to talk me out of this," Mel said, and then was sorry when he saw the expression on B.T.'s face.

"For us to talk," B.T. said. "For me to figure this—epiphany—out."

"All right," Mel said. "As far as Denver." He opened the car door. "You can come inside now. I'm not going anywhere till morning." He leaned inside the car and got the atlas. "It's a good thing I came out for this. You didn't actually intend to stand out here all night, did you?"

B.T. nodded, his teeth chattering. "You're not the only one who's crazy."

> *"By hearing ye shall hear, and shall not understand,*
> *and seeing ye shall see and shall not perceive."*
> —Matthew 13:14

*

There wasn't a Hertz rental car agency in Zion Center. "The nearest one's in Redfield," B.T. said unhappily.

"I'll meet you there," Mel said.

"Will you?" B.T. said. "You won't take off on your own?"

"No," Mel said.

"What if you see a sign?"

"If I see a burning bush, I'll pull off on the side and let you know," Mel said dryly. "We can caravan if you want."

"Fine," B.T. said. "I'll follow you."

"I don't know where the rental place is."

"I'll pull ahead of you once we get to Redfield," B.T. said, and got into his rental car. "It's the second exit. What are the roads supposed to be like?"

"Icy. Snow-packed. But the weather report said clear."

Mel got into his car. The kid from the carnival had been right. The ding had started to spread, raying out in three long cracks and one short one.

He led the way over to the interstate, being careful to signal lane changes and not to get too far ahead, so B.T. wouldn't think he was trying to escape.

The carnival must have stayed the night in Zion Center, too. He passed a truck carrying the Tilt-A-Whirl and one full of stacked, slanted mirrors for, Mel assumed, the Hall of Mirrors. A Blazer roared past him with the bumper sticker "When the Rapture comes, I'm outta here!"

As soon as Mel was on the interstate, he turned on the radio. ". . . and snow-packed. Partly cloudy becoming clear by midmorning. Interstate 80 between Victor and Davenport is closed, also U.S. 35 and State Highway 218. Partly cloudy skies, clearing by midmorning. The following schools are closed: Edgewater, Bennett, Olathe, Oskaloosa, Vinton, Shellsburg. . . ."

Mel twisted the knob.

". . . but the Second Coming is not something we believers have to be afraid of," the evangelist, this one with a Texas accent, said, "for the Book of Revelation tells us that Christ will protect us from the final tribulation, and when He comes to power we will dwell with Him in His Holy City, which shines with jewels and precious stones, and we will drink from living fountains of water. The lion shall lie down with the lamb, and there . . . be . . . more—"

The evangelist sputtered into static and then out of range, which was just as well because Mel was heading into fog and needed to give his whole attention to his driving.

The fog got worse, descending like a smothering blanket. Mel turned on his lights. They didn't help at all, but Mel hoped B.T. would be able to see his taillights the way Cassie had. He couldn't see anything beyond a few yards in front of him. And if he had wanted a sign of his mental state, this was certainly appropriate.

"God has told us His will in no uncertain terms," the radio evangelist thundered, coming suddenly back into range. "There can't be any question about it."

But he had dozens of questions. There had been no Megiddo on the map of Nebraska last night. Or of Kansas or Colorado or New Mexico, and nothing in all the prophecies about location except a reference to the New Jerusalem, and there was no New Jerusalem on the map either.

"And how do I know the Second Coming is at hand?" the evangelist roared, suddenly back in range. "Because the Bible *tells* us so. It tells us *how* He is coming and when!"

And that wasn't true, either. "Ye know neither the day nor the hour wherein the Son of man cometh," Matthew had written, and Luke, "The Son of man cometh at an hour when ye think not," and even Revelation, "I will come on thee as a thief, and thou shalt not know what hour I will come." It was the only thing they were all agreed on.

"The signs are *all* around us," the evangelist shouted. "They're as plain as the nose on your face! Air pollution, liberals outlawing school prayer, wickedness! Why, anybody'd have to be *blind* not to recognize them! Open your eyes and see!"

"All I see is fog," Mel said, turning on the defrost and wiping his sleeve across the windshield, but it wasn't the windshield. It was the world, which had vanished completely in the whiteness.

He nearly missed the turnoff to Redfield. Luckily, the fog was less dense in town, and they were able to find not only the rental car place, but the local Tastee Freez. Mel went over to get some lunch to take with them while B.T. checked the car in.

It was full of farmers, all talking about the weather. "Damned meterologists," one of them, red-faced and wearing a John Deere cap and earmuffs, grumbled. "Said it was supposed to be clear."

"It is clear," another one in a down vest said. "He just didn't say *where*. You get up above that fog, say thirty thousand feet, and it's clear as a bell."

"Number six," the woman behind the counter called.

Mel went up to the counter and paid. There was a fluorescent green poster for the carnival taped up on the wall beside the counter. "Come have the time of your life!" it read. "Thrills, chills, excitement!"

Chills is right, Mel thought, thinking of how cold being up in a Ferris wheel in this fog would be.

It was an old sign. "Littletown, Dec. 24," it read. "Ft. Dodge, Dec. 28. Cairo, Dec. 30."

B.T. was already in the car when Mel got back with their hamburgers and coffee. He handed him the sack and got back on the highway.

That was a mistake. The fog was so thick he couldn't even take a hand off the wheel to hold the hamburger B.T. offered him. "I'll eat it later," he said, leaning forward and squinting as if that would make things clearer. "You go ahead and eat, and we'll switch places in a couple of exits."

But there were no exits, or Mel couldn't see them in the fog, and after twenty miles of it, he had B.T. hand him his coffee, now stone cold, and took a couple of sips.

"I've been looking at the Second Coming scientifically," B.T. said. "'A great mountain burning with fire was cast into the sea and the third part of the sea became blood.'"

Mel glanced over. B.T. was reading from a black leather Bible. "Where'd you get that?" he asked.

"It was in the hotel room," B.T. said.

"You *stole* a Gideon Bible?" Mel said.

"They put them there for people who need them. And I'd say we qualify. 'There was a great earthquake, and the sun became black as sack-cloth of hair and the moon became as blood. And the stars of heaven fell into the earth. And every mountain and island were moved out of their places.'

"All these things are supposed to happen along with the Second Coming," B.T. said. "Earthquakes, wars and rumors of wars, pestilence, locusts." He leafed through the flimsy pages. "'And there arose a smoke out of the pit, as the smoke of a great furnace, and the sun and the air were darkened. And there came out of the smoke locusts upon the earth.'"

He shut the Bible. "All right, earthquakes happen all the time, and there have been wars and rumors of wars for the last ten thousand years, and I guess this—'and the stars shall fall from the sky'—could refer to meteors. But there's no sign of any of these other things. No locusts, no bottomless pit opening up, no 'third part of trees and grass were burnt up and a third part of the creatures which were in the sea died.'"

"Nuclear war," Mel said.

"What?"

"According to the evangelists, that's supposed to refer to nuclear war," Mel said. "And before that, to the Communist threat. Or fluoridation of water. Or anything else they disapprove of."

"Well, whatever it stands for, no bottomless pit has opened up lately or we would have seen it on CNN. And volcanoes don't cause locust swarms. Mel," he said seriously, "let's say your experience was a real epiphany. Couldn't you have misinterpreted what it meant?"

And for a split second, Mel almost had it. The key to where He was and what was going to happen. The key to all of it.

"Couldn't it have been about something else?" B.T. said. "Something besides the Second Coming?"

No, Mel thought, trying to hang on to the insight, *it* was *the Second Coming, but*—it was gone. Whatever it was, he'd lost it.

He stared blindly ahead at the fog, trying to remember what had triggered it. B.T. had said, "Couldn't you have misunderstood what it meant?" No, that wasn't right. "Couldn't you—"

"What is it?" B.T. was pointing through the windshield. "What is that? Up ahead?"

"I don't see anything," Mel said, straining ahead. He couldn't see anything but fog. "What was it?"

"I don't know. I just saw a glimpse of lights."

"Are you sure?" Mel said. There was nothing there but whiteness.

"There it is again," B.T. said, pointing. "Didn't you see it? Yellow flashing lights. There must be an accident. You'd better slow down."

Mel was already barely creeping along, but he slowed further, still unable to see anything. "Was it on our side of the highway?"

"Yes . . . I don't know," B.T. said, leaning forward. "I don't see it now. But I'm sure it was there."

Mel crawled forward, squinting into the whiteness. "Could it have been a truck? The carnival truck had a yellow arrow," he said, and saw the lights.

And they were definitely not a sign for a carnival ride. They filled the road just ahead, flashing yellow and red and blue, all out of synch with each other. Police cars or fire trucks or ambulances. Definitely an accident. He pumped the brakes, hoping whoever was behind him could see his taillights, and slowed to a stop.

A patrolman appeared out of the fog, holding up his hand in the sign for "stop." He was wearing a yellow poncho and a clear plastic cover over his brown hat.

Mel rolled his window down, and the patrolman leaned in to talk to them. "Road up ahead's closed. You need to get off at this exit."

"Exit?" Mel said, looking to the right. He could just make out a green outline in the fog.

"It's right there, up about a hundred yards," the patrolman said, pointing into nothingness. "We'll come tell you when it's open again."

"Are you closing it because of the weather?" B.T. asked.

The patrolman shook his head. "Accident," he said. "Big mess. It'll be a while." He motioned them off to the right.

Mel felt his way to the exit and off the highway. At least it had a truck stop instead of just a gas station. He and B.T. parked and went into the restaurant.

It was jammed. Every booth, every seat at the counter was full. Mel and B.T. sat down at the last unoccupied table, and it immediately became clear why it had been unoccupied. The draft when the door opened made B.T., who had just taken his coat off, put it back on and then zip it up.

Mel had expected everyone to be angry about the delay, but the waitresses and customers all seemed to be in a holiday mood. Truckers leaned across the backs of the booths to talk to each other, laughing, and the waitresses, carrying pots of coffee, were smiling. One of them had, inexplicably, a plastic Kewpie doll stuck in her beehive hairdo.

The door opened again, sending an Arctic blast across their table, and a paramedic came in and went up to the counter to talk to the waitress. "...accident..." Mel heard him say, shaking his head, "...carnival truck..."

Mel went over. "Excuse me," he said. "I heard you say something about a carnival truck. Is that what had the accident?"

"Disaster is more like it," the paramedic said, shaking his head. "Took a turn too sharp and lost his whole load. And don't ask me what a carnival's doing up here in the middle of winter."

"Was the driver hurt?" Mel asked anxiously.

"Hurt? Hell, no. Not a scratch. But that road's going to be closed the rest of the day." He pulled a bamboo Chinese finger trap out of his pocket and handed it to Mel. "Truck was carrying all the prizes and stuff for the midway. The whole road's covered in stuffed animals and baseballs. And you can't even see to clean 'em up."

Mel went back to the table and told B.T. what had happened.

"We could go south and pick up Highway 33," B.T. said, consulting the road atlas.

"No, you can't," the waitress, appearing with two pots of coffee, said. "It's closed. Fog. So's 15 north." She poured coffee into their cups. "You're not going anywhere."

The draft hit them again, and the waitress glanced over at the door. "Hey! Don't just stand there—shut the door!"

Mel looked toward the door. Cassie was standing there, wearing a bulky orange sweater that made her look even rounder, and scanning the restaurant for an empty booth. She was carrying a red dinosaur under one arm and her bright green tote bag over the other.

"Cassie!" Mel called to her, and she smiled and came over.

"Put your dinosaur down and join us," B.T. said.

"It's not a dinosaur," she said, setting it on the table. "It's a dragon. See?" she said, pointing to two pieces of red felt on its back. "Wings."

"Where'd you get it?" Mel said.

"The driver of the truck that spilled them gave it to me," she said. "I'd better call my sister before she hears about this on the news," she said, looking around the restaurant. "Do you think the phones are working?"

B.T. pointed at a sign that said "Phones," and she left.

She was back instantly. "There's a line," she said, and sat down. The waitress came by again with coffee and menus, and they ordered pie, and then Cassie went to check the phones again.

"There's still a line," she said, coming back. "My sister will have a fit when she hears about this. She already thinks I'm crazy. And out there in that fog today I thought so, too. I wish my grandmother had never looked up verses in the Bible."

"The Bible?" Mel said.

She waved her hand dismissively. "It's a long story."

"We seem to have plenty of time," B.T. said.

"Well," she said, settling herself. "I'm an English teacher—*was* an English teacher—and the school board offered this early-retirement bonus that was too good to turn down, so I retired in June, but I didn't know what I wanted to do. I'd always wanted to travel, but I hate traveling alone, and I didn't know where I wanted to go. So I got on the sub list—our district has a terrible time getting subs, and there's been all this flu."

It is *going to be a long story,* Mel thought. He picked up the finger trap and idly stuck his finger into one end. B.T. leaned back in his chair.

"Well, anyway, I was subbing for Carla Sewell, who teaches sophomore lit, *Julius Caesar,* and I couldn't remember the speech about our fate being in the stars, dear Brutus."

Mel stuck a forefinger into the other side of the finger trap.

"So I was looking it up, but I read the page number wrong, so when I looked it up, it wasn't *Julius Caesar,* it was *Twelfth Night.*"

Mel stretched the finger trap experimentally. It tightened on his fingers.

"'Westward ho!' it said," Cassie said, "and sitting there, reading it, I had this epiphany."

"Epiphany?" Mel said, yanking his fingers apart.

"Epiphany?" B.T. said.

"I'm sorry," Cassie said. "I keep thinking I'm still an English teacher. 'Epiphany' is a literary term for a revelation, a sudden understanding, like in James Joyce's *The Dubliners.* The word comes from—"

"The story of the wise men," Mel said.

"Yes," she said delightedly, and Mel half expected her to announce that he had gotten an A. "'Epiphany' is the word for their arrival at the manger."

And there it was again. The feeling that he knew where Christ was. The wise men's arrival at the manger. James Joyce.

"When I read the words 'Westward ho!'" Cassie was saying, "I thought, that means me. I have to go west. Something important is going to happen." She looked from one to the other. "You probably think I'm crazy, doing something because of a line in *Bartlett's Quotations*. But whenever my grandmother had an important decision to make, she used to close her eyes and open her Bible and point at a Scripture, and when she opened her eyes, whatever the Scripture said to do, she'd do it. And, after all, *Bartlett's* is the Bible of English teachers. So I tried it. I closed the book and my eyes and picked a quotation at random, and it said, 'Come, my friends, 'tis not too late to seek a newer world.'"

"Tennyson," Mel said.

She nodded. "So here I am."

"And has something important happened?" B.T. asked.

"Not yet," she said, sounding completely unconcerned. "But it's going to happen soon—I'm sure of it. And in the meantime, I'm seeing all these wonderful sights. I went to Gene Stratton-Porter's cabin in Geneva, and the house where Mark Twain grew up in Hannibal, Missouri, and Sherwood Anderson's museum."

She looked at Mel. "Struggling against it doesn't work," she said, pushing her index fingers together, and Mel realized he was struggling vainly to free his fingers from the finger trap. "You have to push them together."

There was a blast of icy air and a patrolman wearing three pink plastic leis around his neck and carrying a spotted plush leopard came in.

"Road's open," he said, and there was a general scramble for coats. "It's still real foggy out there," he said, raising his voice, "so don't get carried away."

Mel freed himself from the finger trap and helped Cassie into her coat while B.T. paid the bill. "Do you want to follow us?" he asked.

"No," she said, "I'm going to try to call my sister again, and if she's heard about this accident, it'll take forever. You go on."

B.T. came back from paying, and they went out to the car, which had acquired a thin, rock-hard coating of ice. Mel, chipping at the windshield with the scraper, started a new offshoot in the rapidly spreading crack.

They got back on the interstate. The fog was thicker than ever. Mel peered through it, looking at objects dimly visible at the sides of the road. The debris from the accident—baseballs and plastic leis and Coke bottles. Stuffed animals and Kewpie dolls littered the median, looking in the fog like the casualties of some great battle.

"I suppose you consider this the sign you were looking for," B.T. said.

"What?" Mel said.

"Cassie's so-called epiphany. You can read anything you want into random quotations," B.T. said. "You realize that, don't you? It's like reading your horoscope. Or a fortune cookie."

"The Devil can quote Scripture to his own ends," Mel murmured.

"Exactly," B.T. said, opening the Gideon Bible and closing his eyes. "Look," he said "Psalm 115, verse 5. 'Eyes have they, but they see not.' Obviously a reference to the fog."

He flipped to another page and stabbed his finger at it. "'Thou shalt not eat any abominable thing.' Oh, dear, we shouldn't have ordered that pie. You can make them mean anything. And you heard her, she'd retired, she liked to travel, she was obviously looking for an excuse to go somewhere. And her epiphany only said something important was going to happen. It didn't say a word about the Second Coming."

"It told her to go west," Mel said, trying to remember exactly what she had said. She had been looking for a speech from *Julius Caesar* and had stumbled on *Twelfth Night* instead. Twelfth night. Epiphany.

"How many times is the word 'west' mentioned in *Bartlett's Quotations*?" B.T. said. "A hundred? 'Oh, young Lochinvar is come out of the west'? 'Go west, young man'? 'One flew east, one flew west, one flew over the cuckoo's nest'?" He shut the Bible. "I'm sorry," he said. "It's just—" He turned and looked out his window at nothing. "It looks like it might be breaking up."

It wasn't. The fog thinned a little, swirling away from the car in little eddies, and then descended again, more smothering than ever.

"Suppose you do find Him? What do you do then?" B.T. said. "Bow down and worship Him? Give Him frankincense and myrrh?"

"Help Him," Mel said.

"Help Him what? Separate the sheep from the goats? Fight the battle of Armageddon?"

"I don't know," Mel said. "Maybe."

"You really think there's going to be a battle between good and evil?"

"There's always a battle between good and evil," Mel said. "Look at the first time He came. He hadn't been on earth a week before Herod's men were out looking for Him. They murdered every baby and two-year-old in Bethlehem, trying to kill Him."

And thirty-three years later they succeeded, Mel thought. *Only killing couldn't stop Him. Nothing could stop Him.*

Who had said that? The kid from the carnival, talking about the windshield. "Nothing can stop it. There's stuff you could do to keep it from spreading for a while, but it's still going to spread. There ain't nothing that can stop it."

He felt a flicker of the feeling again. Something about the kid from the carnival. What had he been talking about before that? Siamese twins. And Roswell. No. Something else.

He tried to think what Cassie had said at the truck stop. Something about the wise men arriving at the manger. And not struggling. "You have to push them together," she had said.

It stayed tantalizingly out of reach, as elusive as a road sign glimpsed in the fog.

B.T. reached forward and flicked on the radio. "Foggy tonight, and colder," it said. "In the teens for eastern Nebraska, down in the . . ." It faded to static. B.T. twisted the knob.

"And do you know what will happen to us when Jesus comes?" an evangelist shouted, "The Book of Revelation tells us we will be tormented with fire and brimstone, unless we repent *now,* before it's too late!"

"A little fire and brimstone would be welcome right about now," B.T. said, reaching forward to turn the heater up to high.

"There's a blanket in the backseat," Mel said, and B.T. reached back and wrapped himself up in it.

"We will be scorched with fire," the radio said, "and the smoke of our torment will rise up forever and ever."

B.T. leaned his head against the doorjamb. "Just so it's warm," he murmured, and closed his eyes.

"But that's not all that will happen to us if we do not repent," the evangelist said, "if we do not take Jesus as our personal Savior. The Book of Revelation tells us in Chapter 14 that we will be cast into the winepress of God's wrath and be *trodden* in it till our blood covers the ground for a thousand *miles*! And don't fool yourselves, that day is coming *soon*! The signs are all around us! Wait till your father gets home."

Mel switched it off, but it was too late. The evangelist had hit it, the problem Mel had been trying to avoid since that moment in the sanctuary.

I don't believe it, he had thought when he'd heard the minister talking about Jesus forbidding believers to associate with outcasts. And he had thought it again when he heard the radio evangelist that first day talking about Christ coming to get revenge.

"I don't believe it," he thought, and when B.T. stirred in his corner, he realized he had spoken aloud.

"I don't believe it," he murmured. God had so loved the world, He had sent His only begotten Son to live among men, to be a helpless baby and a little boy and a young man, had sent Him to be cold and confused, angry and overjoyed. "To share our common lot," the Nicene Creed said. To undergo and understand and forgive. "Father, forgive them," He had said, with nails driven through His hands, and when they had arrested Him, He had made the disciples put away their weapons. He had healed the soldier's ear Peter had cut off.

He would never, *never* come back in a blaze of wrath and revenge, slaughtering enemies, tormenting unbelievers, wreaking fire and pestilence and famine on them. Never.

And how can I believe in a revelation about the Second Coming, Mel thought, *when I don't believe in the Second Coming?*

But the revelation wasn't about the Second Coming, he thought. He hadn't seen earthquakes or Armageddon or Christ coming in a blaze of clouds and glory. *He's already here,* Mel had thought, *now,* and had set out to find Him, to look for a sign.

But there aren't any, he thought, and saw one off in the mist. "Prairie Home 5. Denver 468."

Denver. They would be there tomorrow night. And B.T. would want him to fly home with him.

Unless I figure out the key, Mel thought. *Unless I'm given a sign. Or unless the roads are closed.*

> "And, lo, the star, which they saw in the east,
> went before them."
> —Matthew 2:9

*

"They should be open," the woman at the Wayfarer Motel said. The Holiday Inn and the Super 8 and the Innkeeper had all been full up, and the Wayfarer had only one room left. "There's supposed to be fog in the morning, and then it's supposed to be nice all the way till Sunday."

"What about the roads east?" B.T. asked.

"No problem," she said.

The Wayfarer didn't have a coffee shop. They ate supper at the Village Inn on the other end of town. As they were leaving, they ran into Cassie in the parking lot.

"Oh, good," she said. "I was afraid I wouldn't have a chance to say goodbye."

"Goodbye?" Mel said.

"I'm heading south tomorrow to Red Cloud. When I consulted *Bartlett's,* it said, 'Winter lies too long in country towns.'"

"Oh?" Mel said, wondering what this had to do with going south.

"Willa Cather," Cassie said. "*My Ántonia.* I didn't understand it, either, so I tried the Gideon Bible in my hotel, it's so nice of them to leave them there, and it was Exodus 13:21, 'And the Lord went before them by day in a pillar of a cloud, to lead them the way; and by night in a pillar of fire.'"

She smiled expectantly at them. "Pillar of fire. Red Cloud. Willa Cather's museum is in Red Cloud."

They said goodbye to her and went back to the motel. B.T. sat down on his bed and took his laptop out of his suitcase. "I've got some email I've got to answer," he said.

And send? Mel wondered. "Dear Mrs. Bilderbeck, we'll be in Denver tomorrow. Am hoping to persuade Mel to come home with me. Have straitjacket ready."

Mel sat down in the room's only chair with the Rand McNally and looked at the map of Nebraska, searching for a town named Megiddo or New Jerusalem. There was Red Cloud, down near the southern border of Nebraska. Pillar of fire. Why couldn't he have had a nice straightforward sign like that? A pillar of smoke by day and a pillar of fire by night. Or a star.

But Moses had wandered around in the wilderness for forty years following said pillar. And the star hadn't led the wise men to Bethlehem. It had led them straight into King Herod's arms. They hadn't had a clue where the newborn Christ was. "Where is He that is born king of the Jews?" they'd asked Herod.

"Where is He?" Mel murmured, and B.T. glanced up from his laptop and then back down at it again, typing steadily.

Mel turned to the map of Colorado. Beulah. Bonanza. Firstview.

"Even if your—epiphany—was real," B.T. had asked him this afternoon, "couldn't you have misinterpreted what it means?"

Well, if he had, he wouldn't have been the first one. The Bible was full of people who had misinterpreted prophecies. "Dogs have compassed me; the assembly of the wicked have enclosed me," the Scriptures said, "they pierced my hands and my feet." But nobody saw the Crucifixion coming. Or the Resurrection.

His own disciples didn't recognize Him. Easter Sunday they walked all the way to Emmaus with Him without figuring out who He was, and even when He told them, Thomas refused to believe Him and demanded to see the scars of the nails in His hands.

They had never recognized Him. Isaiah had plainly predicted a virgin who would bring forth a child "out of the root of Jesse," a child who would redeem Israel. But nobody had thought that meant a baby in a stable.

They had thought he was talking about a warrior, a king who would raise an army and drive the hated foreigners out of their country, a hero on a white horse who would vanquish their enemies and set them free. And He had, but not in the way they expected.

Nobody had expected Him to be a poor itinerant preacher from an obscure family, with no college degree and no military training, a nobody. Even the wise men had expected Him to be royalty. "Where is the *king* whose star we have seen in the east?" they had asked Herod.

And Herod had promptly sent soldiers out to search for a usurper, a threat to his throne.

They had been looking for the wrong thing. *And maybe B.T.'s right, maybe I am, too, and that's the answer. The Second Coming isn't going to be battles and earthquakes and falling stars, and Revelation means something else, like the prophecies of the Messiah.*

Or maybe it wasn't the Second Coming, and Christ was here only in a symbolic sense, in the poor, the hungry, in those in need of help. "As ye have done this unto the least of these—"

"Maybe the Second Coming really is here," B.T. said from the bed. "Look at this."

He turned the laptop around so Mel could see the screen. "Watch, therefore," it read, "for ye know neither the day nor the hour wherein the Son of man cometh."

"It's a website," B.T. said. "www.watchman."

"It probably belongs to one of the radio evangelists," Mel said.

"I don't think so," B.T. said. He hit a key, and a new screen came up. It was full of entries.

"Meteor, 12-23, 4 mi. NNW Raton."

"Examined area. 12-28. No sign."

"Weather Channel 11-2, 9:15 A.M. PST. Reference to unusual cloud formations."

"Latitude and longitude? Need location."

"8.6 mi. WNW Prescott AZ 11-4."

"Denver Post 914P8C2—Headline: 'Unusually high lightning activity strikes Carson National Forest.' MT2427."

"What do you think that stands for?" B.T. said, pointing at the string of letters and numbers.

"Matthew 24, verse 27," Mel said. "'For the lightning cometh out of the west and shineth even unto the east, so shall also the coming of the Son of man be.'"

B.T. nodded and scrolled the screen down.

"Triple lightning strike. 7-11, Platteville CO. Nov. 28. Two injured."

"Lightning storm, Dec. 4, Truth or Consequences."

"What about that one?" B.T. said, pointing at "Truth or Consequences."

"It's a town in southern New Mexico," Mel said.

"Oh." B.T. scrolled the screen down some more.

"Falling star, 12-30, 2 mi. W of U.S. State Hwy 191, west of Bozeman, mile marker 161."

"Coma patient recovery, Yale—New Haven Hosp. Connection?"

"Negative. Too far east."

"Possible sighting Nevada."

"Need location."

Need location. "'Go search diligently for the young child,'" Mel murmured, "'and when ye have found him, bring me word again, that I may come and worship him.'"

"What?" B.T. said.

"It's what Herod said when the wise men told him about the star." He stared at the screen:

"L.A. Times Jan 2 P5C1. Fish die-off. RV89?"

"Possible sighting. Old Faithful, Yellowstone Nat'l Pk, Jan. 2."

And over and over again:

"Need location."

"Need location."

"Need location."

"They obviously think the Second Coming's happened," B.T. said, staring at the screen.

"Or aliens have landed at Roswell," Mel said. He pointed to the convenience store entry. "Or Elvis is back."

"Maybe," B.T. said, staring at the screen.

Mel went back to looking at the maps. Barren Rock. Deadwood. Last Chance.

Need location, he thought. Maybe he and Cassie and whoever had written "Too far east" on the website had all misinterpreted the message, and it was not "west" but "West."

He turned to the gazetteer in the back. West. Westwood Hills, Kansas. Westville, Oklahoma. West Hollywood, California. Westview. Westgate. Westmont. There was a Westwood Hills in Kansas. Colorado had a Westcliffe, a Western Hills, and a Westminster. Neither Arizona nor New Mexico had any Wests. Nevada didn't either. Nebraska had a West Point.

West Point. Maybe it wasn't even in the west. Maybe it was West Orange, New Jersey, or West Palm Beach. Or West Berlin.

He shut the atlas and looked over at B.T. He had dozed off, his face tired and worried-looking even in sleep. His laptop was on his chest, and the Gideon Bible he had stolen from the Holiday Inn lay beside him.

Mel shut the laptop off and quietly closed it. B.T. didn't move. Mel picked up the Bible.

The answer had to be in the Scriptures. He opened the Bible to Matthew. "Then if any man shall say unto you, Lo, here is Christ, or there; believe it not."

He read on. Disasters and devastation and tribulation, as the prophets had spoken.

The prophets. He found Isaiah. "Hear ye indeed but understand not; and see ye indeed but perceive not."

He shut the Bible. *All right,* he thought, standing it on its spine on his hand. *Let's have a sign here. I'm running out of time.*

He opened his eyes. His finger was on I Samuel 23, verse 14. "And Saul sought him every day, but God delivered him not into his hand."

> *"For all these things must come to pass,*
> *but the end is not yet."*
> —Matthew 24:6

*

All the roads were open, and, from Grand Island, clear and dry, and the fog had lifted a little.

"With roads like this, we ought to be in Denver by tonight," B.T. said.

Yes, Mel thought, finishing what B.T. had said. *If you fly back with me, we could be there in time for the ecumenical meeting.* Nobody'd ever have to know he'd been gone, except Mrs. Bilderbeck, and he could tell her he'd been offered a job by another church, but had decided not to take it, which was true.

"It just didn't work out," he would tell Mrs. Bilderbeck, and she would be so overjoyed that he wasn't leaving, she wouldn't even ask for details.

And he could go back to doing sermons and giving the choir plenty of warning, storing the star, and keeping the pilot light going, as if nothing had happened.

"Exit 312," a green interstate sign up ahead said. "Hastings 18. Red Cloud 57."

He wondered if Cassie was already at Willa Cather's house, convinced she had been led there by *Bartlett's Quotations.*

Cassie had no trouble finding signs—she saw them everywhere. *And maybe they are everywhere, and I'm just not seeing them. Maybe Hastings is a sign, and the truck full of mirrors, and those stuffed toys all over the road. Maybe that Chinese finger trap I got stuck in yesterday was—*

"Look," B.T. said. "Wasn't that Cassie's car?"

"Where?" Mel said, craning his neck around.

"In that ditch back there."

This time Mel didn't wait for an "Authorized Vehicles Only" crossing. He plunged into the snowy median and back along the other side of the highway, still unable to see anything.

"There," B.T. said, pointing, and he turned onto the median.

He had crossed both lanes and was onto the shoulder before he saw the Honda, halfway down a steep ditch and tilted at an awkward angle. He couldn't see anyone in the driver's seat.

B.T. was out of the car before Mel got the car stopped and plunging down the snowy bank, with Mel behind him. B.T. wrenched the car door open.

Cassie's green tote bag was on the floor of the passenger seat. B.T. peered into the backseat. "She's not here," he said unnecessarily.

"Cassie!" Mel called. He ran around the front of the car, though she couldn't have been thrown out. The door would have been open if she'd been thrown out. "Cassie!"

"Here," a faint voice said, and Mel looked down the slope. Cassie lay at the bottom in tall dry weeds.

"She's down here," he said, and half walked, half slid down the ravine.

She was lying on her back with her leg bent under her. "I think it's broken," she said to Mel.

"Go flag a semi down," Mel said to B.T., who'd appeared above them. "Have them call an ambulance."

B.T. disappeared, and Mel turned back to Cassie. "How long have you been here?" he asked her, pulling off his overcoat and tucking it around her.

"I don't know," she said, shivering. "There was a patch of ice. I didn't think anybody'd see the car, so I got out to climb up to the road, and that's when I slipped. My leg's broken, isn't it?"

At that angle, it had to be. "I think it probably is," Mel said.

She turned her face away in the dry weeds. "My sister was right."

Mel took off his jacket, rolled it up, and put it under her head. "We'll have an ambulance here for you in no time."

"She told me I was crazy," Cassie said, still not looking at Mel, "and this proves it, doesn't it? And she didn't even know about the epiphany." She turned and looked at Mel. "Only it wasn't an epiphany. Just low estrogen levels."

"Conserve your strength," he said, and looked anxiously up the slope.

Cassie grabbed at his hand. "I lied to you. I wasn't offered early retirement. I asked for it. I was so sure 'Westward ho!' meant something. I sold my house and took out all my savings."

Her hand was red with cold. Mel wished he had taken his gloves back when the kid from the carnival offered them. He took her icy hand between his own and held it tightly.

"I was so *sure*," she said.

"Mel," B.T. called from above them. "I've had four semis go by without stopping. I think it's the color." He pointed to his black face. "You need to come up and try."

"I'll be right there," Mel called back up to him. "I'll be right back," he said to Cassie.

"No," she said, clutching his hand. "Don't you see? It didn't mean anything. It was nothing but menopause, like my sister said. She tried to tell me, but I wouldn't listen."

"Cassie," Mel said, gently releasing her hand, "we need to get you out of here and into town to a hospital. You can tell me all about it then."

"There's nothing to tell," she said, and let go of his hand.

"Come on, there's another truck coming," B.T. called down, and Mel started up the slope. "No, never mind," B.T. said. "The cavalry's here," he said, and, amazingly, he laughed.

There was a screech of hydraulic brakes. Mel scrambled up the rest of the way. A truck was stopping. It was one of the carnival's, loaded with merry-go-round horses, white and black and palomino, with red-and-gold saddles and jeweled bridles. B.T. was already running toward the cab, asking, "Do you have a CB?"

"Yeah," the driver said, and came around the back of the truck. It was the kid Mel had picked up, still wearing the gloves he had given him.

"We need an ambulance," Mel said. "There's a lady hurt here."

"Sure thing," the kid said, and disappeared back around the truck.

Mel skidded back down the slope to Cassie. "He's calling an ambulance," he said to her.

She nodded uninterestedly.

"They're on their way," the kid called down from above them. He went over to the Honda, B.T. following, and stuck his head under the back of it. He walked all around it, squatting next to the far wheels, and then disappeared back up the slope again.

"He says his truck doesn't have a tow rope," B.T. said, coming back to report, "and he doesn't think he could get the car out anyway, so he's calling a tow truck."

Mel nodded. "I saw a sign that said the next town was only ten miles. They'll have you in out of the cold before you know it."

She didn't answer. Mel wondered if perhaps she was going into shock. "Cassie," he said, taking her hands again and rubbing them in spite of what he'd told the kid about frostbite. "We were so surprised to see your car," he said, just to be saying something, to get her to talk. "We thought you were going down to Red Cloud. What made you change your mind?"

"*Bartlett's,*" she said bitterly. "When I was putting my tote bag in the car, it fell out onto the parking lot, and when I picked it up, the first thing I read was from William Blake. 'Turn away no more,' it said. I thought it meant I shouldn't turn south to Red Cloud, that I should keep going west. Can you imagine anybody being that stupid?"

Yes, Mel thought.

The ambulance pulled up, sirens and yellow lights blazing, and two paramedics leaped out with a stretcher, skidded down the slope to where Cassie was, and began maneuvering her expertly onto it.

Mel went over to B.T. "You go in with her in the ambulance," he said, "and I'll wait here for the tow truck."

"Are you sure?" B.T. said. "I can wait here."

"No," Mel said. "I'll follow the tow truck to the garage and find out what I can about her car. Then I'll meet you at the hospital. What time's the earliest flight home from Denver tomorrow?"

"Flight?" B.T. said. "No. I'm not going home without you."

"You won't have to," Mel said. "What time's the earliest flight?"

"I don't understand—"

"Or we can drive back. If we take turns driving we can be back in time for the ecumenical meeting."

"But—" B.T. said bewilderedly.

"I wanted a sign. Well, I got it," he said, waving his arm at Cassie, at her car. "I don't have to be hit over the head to get the message. I'm out here in the middle of nowhere in the middle of winter on a fool's errand."

"What about the epiphany?"

"It was a hallucination, a seizure, a temporary hormonal imbalance."

"And what about your call to the ministry?" B.T. said. "Was that a hallucination, too? What about Cassie?"

"The Devil can quote Scripture, remember?" Mel said bitterly. "And *Bartlett's Quotations.*"

"Can you give us a hand here?" one of the paramedics called. They had Cassie on the stretcher and were ready to carry it up the slope.

"Coming," Mel said, and started toward them.

B.T. took his arm. "What about the others who are looking for Him? The watchman website?"

"UFO nuts," Mel said, and went over to the stretcher. "It doesn't mean anything."

Cassie lay under a gray blanket, her head turned to the side, the way it had been when Mel found her.

"Are you all right?" B.T., taking hold of the other side of the stretcher, asked.

"No," she said, and a tear wobbled down her plump cheek. "I'm sorry I put you to all this trouble."

The kid from the carnival took hold of the front of the stretcher. "Things aren't always as bad as they look," he said, patting the blanket. "I saw a guy fall off the top of the Ferris wheel once, and he wasn't even hurt."

Cassie shook her head. "It was a mistake. I shouldn't have come."

"Don't say that," B.T. said. "You got to see Mark Twain's house. And Gene Stratton-Porter's."

She turned her face away. "What good are they? I'm not even an English teacher anymore."

Things might not have been as bad as they looked for the guy who fell off the Ferris wheel, but they were even worse than they looked

when it came to the snowy slope and getting Cassie up it. By the time
they got her into the ambulance, her face was as gray as the blanket and
twisted with pain. The paramedics began hooking her up to a blood
pressure cuff and an IV.

"I'll meet you at the hospital," Mel said. "You can call Mrs. Bilderbeck
and tell her we're coming."

"What if the roads are closed?" B.T. said.

"You heard the clerk last night. Clear both directions." He looked at
B.T. "I thought this was what you wanted, for me to come to my senses,
to admit I was crazy."

B.T. looked unhappy. "Animals don't always leave tracks," he said. "I
learned that five years ago banding deer for a Lyme disease project.
Sometimes they leave all sorts of sign, other times they're invisible."

The paramedics were shutting the doors. "Wait," B.T. said. "I'm going
with her."

He clambered up into the back of the ambulance. "Do you know the
only way you can tell for sure the deer are there?"

Mel shook his head.

"By the wolves," B.T. said.

> *"Therefore the Lord himself shall give you a sign."*
> —Isaiah 7:14

✳

It took nearly an hour for the tow truck to get there. Mel waited in his
car with the heater running for a while, and then got out and went over
to stare at Cassie's Honda.

Wolves, B.T. had said. Predators. "'For wheresoever the carcass is,'" he
quoted, "'there will the eagles be gathered together.' MT2428."

"The Devil can quote Scripture," he said aloud, and got back into the
car.

The crack in the windshield had split again, splaying out in two new
directions from the center. A definite sign.

You've had dozens of signs, he thought. *Blizzards, road closures, icy
and snow-packed conditions. You just chose to ignore them.*

"Why, anybody'd have to be *blind* not to recognize them," the radio
evangelist had said, and that was what he had been, willfully blind, pre-

tending the yellow arrow, the roads closing behind him, were signs he was going in the right direction, that Cassie's "Westward ho!" was outside confirmation.

"It didn't mean anything," he said.

It was getting dark by the time the tow truck finally got there, and pitch-black by the time they got Cassie's Honda pulled up the slope.

And that was a sign, too, Mel thought, following the tow truck. Like the fog and the carnival truck jackknifed across the highway and the "No Vacancy" signs on the motels. All of them flashing the same message: It was a mistake. Give up. Go home.

The tow truck had gotten far ahead of him. He stepped on the gas, but a very slow pickup pulled in front of him, and an even slower recreation vehicle was blocking the right lane. By the time he got to the gas station, the mechanic was already sliding out from under the Honda and shaking his head.

"Snapped an axle and did in the transmission," he said, wiping his hands on a greasy rag. "Cost at least fifteen hundred to fix it, and I doubt if it's worth half that." He patted the hood sympathetically. "I'm afraid it's the end of the road."

The end of the road. *All right, all right,* Mel thought, *I get the message.*

"So what do you want to do?" the mechanic asked.

Give up, Mel thought. *Come to my senses. Go home.* "It's not my car," he said. "I'll have to ask the owner. She's in the hospital right now."

"She hurt bad?"

Mel remembered her lying there in the weeds, saying, "It didn't mean anything."

"No," he lied.

"Tell her I can do an estimate on a new axle and a new transmission if she wants," the mechanic said reluctantly, "but if I was her I'd take the insurance and start over."

"I'll tell her," Mel said. He opened the trunk and took out her suitcase, and then went around to the passenger side to get her green bag out of the backseat.

There was a bright yellow flyer rolled up and jammed in the door handle. Mel unrolled it. It was a flyer from the carnival. *The kid must have stuck it there,* Mel thought, smiling in spite of himself.

There was a drawing of a trumpet at the top, with "Come one, come all!" issuing from the mouth of it.

Underneath that, there was a drawing of the triple Ferris wheel, and scattered in boxes across the page, "Marvel at the Living Fountains," "Ride the Sea Dragon!," "Popcorn, Snow Cones, Cotton Candy!," "See a Lion and a Lamb in a Single Cage!"

Mel stared at the flyer.

"Tell her if she wants to sell it for parts," the mechanic said, "I can give her four hundred."

A lion and a lamb. Wheels within wheels. "For the Lamb shall lead them unto living fountains of waters."

"What's that you're reading?" the mechanic said, coming around the car.

A midway with stuffed animals for prizes—bears and lions and red dragons—and a ride called the Shooting Star, a hall of mirrors. "For now we see in a glass darkly but then we shall see face to face."

The mechanic peered over his shoulder. "Oh, an ad for that crazy carnival," he said. "Yeah, I got a sign for it in the window."

A sign. "For behold, I give you a sign." And the sign was just what it said, a sign. Like the Siamese twins. Like the peace sign on the back of the kid's hand. "For unto us a son is given, and his name shall be called Wonderful, Counsellor, the Prince of Peace." On the kid's scarred hand.

"If she wants an estimate, tell her it'll take some time," the mechanic said, but Mel wasn't listening. He was gazing blindly at the flyer. "Peer into the Bottomless Pit!" it said. "Ride the Merry-Go-Round!"

"'And thus I saw the horses in the vision,'" Mel murmured, "'and them that sat upon them.'" He started to laugh.

The mechanic frowned at him. "It ain't funny," he said. "This car's a real mess. So what do you think she'll want to do?"

"Go to a carnival," Mel said, and ran to get in his car.

*"And there shall be no night there;
and they need no candle, neither light of the sun."*
—Revelation 22:5

*

The hospital was a three-story brick building. Mel parked in front of the emergency entrance and went in.

"May I help you?" the admitting nurse asked.

"Yes," he said, "I'm looking for—" and then stopped. Behind the desk was a sign for the carnival with dates at the bottom. "Crown Point, Dec. 14" it read. "Gresham, Jan. 13. Empyrean, Jan. 15."

"May I help you, sir?" the nurse said again, and Mel turned to ask her where Empyrean was, but she wasn't talking to him. She was asking two men in navy blue suits.

"Yes," the taller one said, "we're starting a hospital outreach, ministering to people who are in the hospital far from home. Do you have any patients here from out of town?"

The nurse looked doubtful. "I'm afraid we're not allowed to give out information about patients."

"Of course, I understand," the man said, opening his Bible. "We don't want to violate anyone's privacy. We'd just like to be able to say a few words of comfort, like the Good Samaritan."

"I'm not supposed to . . ." the nurse said.

"We understand," the shorter man said. "Will *you* join us in a moment of prayer? Precious Lord, we seek—"

The door opened, and as they all turned to look at a boy with a bleeding forehead, Mel slipped down the hall and up the stairs.

Where would they have taken her? he wondered, peering into rooms with open doors. Did a hospital this small even have separate wards, or were all the patients jumbled together?

She wasn't on the first floor. He hurried up the stairs to the second, keeping an eye out for the men in the navy blue suits. They didn't know her name yet, but they would soon. Even if they couldn't get it out of the admitting nurse, Cassie would have given them her health insurance card. It would all be in the computer. *Where* would they have taken her? *X-ray,* he thought.

"Can you tell me how to get to X-ray?" he asked a middle-aged woman in a pink uniform.

"Third floor," she said, and pointed toward the elevator.

Mel thanked her, and as soon as she was out of sight, he took the stairs two at a time.

Cassie wasn't in X-ray. Mel started to look for a technician to ask and then saw B.T. down at the end of the hall.

"Good news," B.T. said as he hurried up to him. "It's not broken. She's got a sprained knee."

"Where is she?" Mel asked, taking B.T.'s arm.

"In 308," B.T. said, and Mel propelled him into the room and shut the door behind them.

Cassie, in a white hospital gown, was lying in the far bed, her head turned away from them as it had been in the frozen weeds. She looked pale and listless.

"She called her sister," B.T. said, looking anxiously at her. "She's on her way down from Minnesota to get her."

"She told me I was lucky I hadn't gotten into worse trouble than a sprained knee," Cassie said, turning to look at Mel. "How's my car?"

"A dead loss," Mel said, stepping up to the head of the bed. "But it doesn't matter. We—"

"You're right," she said, and turned her head on the pillow. "It doesn't matter. I've come to my senses. I'm going home." She smiled wanly at Mel. "I'm just sorry you had to go to all this trouble for me, but at least it won't be for much longer. My sister should be here tomorrow night, and the hospital is keeping me overnight for observation, so you two don't have to stay. You can go to your religious meeting."

"We lied to you," Mel said. "We're not on our way to a religious meeting," and realized they were. "You aren't the only one who had an epiphany."

"I'm not?" she said, and pushed herself partway up against the pillows.

"No. I got a message to go west, too," Mel said. "You were right. Something important *is* going to happen, and we want you to come with us."

B.T. cut in, "You know where He is?"

"I know where He's going to be," Mel said. "B.T., I want you to go get the road atlas and look up a town called Empyrean and see where it is."

"I know where it is," Cassie said, and sat up all the way. "It's in Dante."

They both looked at her, and she said, half apologetically, "I'm an English teacher, remember? It's the highest circle of Paradise. The Holy City of God."

"I doubt if that's going to be in Rand McNally," B.T. said.

"It doesn't matter," Mel said. "We'll be able to find it by the lights. But we've got to get her out of here first. Cassie, do you think you can walk if we help you?"

"Yes." She flung the covers off and began edging her bandaged knee toward the side of the bed. "My clothes are in the closet there."

Mel helped her hobble to the closet.

"I'll go check her out," B.T. said, and went out.

Cassie pulled her dress off the hanger and began unzipping it. Mel turned his back and went over to the door to look out. There was no sign of the two men.

"Can you help me get my boots on?" Cassie said, hobbling over to the chair. "My knee's feeling a lot better," she said, lowering herself into the chair. "It hardly hurts at all." Mel knelt and eased her feet into her fur-edged boots.

B.T. came in. "There are two men down at the admissions desk," he said, out of breath, "trying to find out what room she's in."

"Who are they?" Cassie asked.

"Herod's men," Mel said. "It'll have to be the fire escape. Can you manage that?"

She nodded. Mel helped her to her feet and went and got her coat. He and B.T. helped her into it, and each took an arm and helped her to the door, opening it cautiously and looking both ways down the hall, and then over to the fire escape.

"I should call my sister," Cassie said, "and tell her I've changed my mind."

"We'll stop at a gas station," B.T. said, opening the door fully and looking both ways again. "Okay," he said, and they went down the hall, through the emergency exit door, and onto the fire escape.

"You go bring the car around," B.T. said, and Mel clattered down the metal mesh steps and ducked across the parking lot to the car.

The emergency room door opened and two men stood in its light for a moment, talking to someone.

Mel jammed the key into the ignition, switched it on, and pulled the car around to the side of the hospital, where B.T. and Cassie were working their way down the last steps.

"Come on," B.T. said, grabbing Cassie under the arm, "hurry," and hustled her across to the car.

A siren blared. "Hurry," Mel said, yanking the door open and pushing her into the backseat, slamming the door shut. B.T. ran around to the other side.

The siren came abruptly closer and then cut off, and Mel, reaching for the door handle, looked back toward the entrance. An ambulance pulled in, red and yellow lights flashing, and the two men in the door reached forward and took a stretcher off the back.

And this is crazy, Mel thought. *Nobody's after us.* But they would be, as soon as the nurse saw Cassie was missing, and if not then, as soon as Cassie's sister got there. "I saw two men push a woman into a car and then go peeling out of here," one of the interns unloading that stretcher would say. "It looked like they were kidnapping her." And how would they explain to the police that they were looking for the City of God?

"This is insane," Mel started to say, reaching for the door handle.

There was a flyer wedged in it. Mel unrolled it and read it by the parking lot's vapor light. "Hurry, hurry, hurry! Step right up to the Greatest Show on Earth!" it read in letters of gold. "Wonders, Marvels, Mysteries Revealed!"

Mel got into the car and handed the flyer to B.T. "Ready?" he asked.

"Let's go," Cassie said, and leaned forward to point at the front door. Two men in navy blue suits were running down the front steps.

"Keep down," Mel said, and peeled out of the parking lot. He turned south, drove a block, turned onto a side street, pulled up to the curb, switched off the lights, and waited, watching in his rearview mirror until a navy blue car roared past them going south.

He started the car and drove two blocks without lights on, and then circled back to the highway and headed north. Five miles out of town, he turned east on a gravel road, drove till it ended, turned south, and then east again, and north onto a dirt road. There was no one behind them.

"Okay," he said, and B.T. and Cassie sat up.

"Where are we?" Cassie asked.

"I have no idea," Mel said. He turned east again and then south on the first paved road he came to. "Where are we going?" B.T. asked.

"I don't know that, either. But I know what we're looking for." He waited till a beat-up pickup truck full of kids passed them and then pulled over to the side of the road and switched on the dome light.

"Where's your laptop?" he asked B.T.

"Right here," B.T. said, opening it up and switching it on.

"All right," Mel said, holding the flyer up to the light. "They were in Omaha on January fourth, Palmyra on the ninth, and Beatrice on the tenth." He concentrated, trying to remember the dates on the sign in the hospital.

"Beatrice," Cassie murmured. "That's in Dante, too."

"The carnival was in Crown Point on December fourteenth," Mel went on, still trying to remember the dates, "and Gresham on January thirteenth."

"The carnival?" B.T. said. "We're looking for a carnival?"

"Yes," Mel said. "Cassie, have you got your *Bartlett's Quotations*?"

"Yes," she said, and began rummaging in the emerald green tote bag.

"I saw them between Pittsburgh and Youngstown on Sunday," Mel said to B.T., who had started typing, "and in Wayside, Iowa, on Monday."

"And the truck spill was at Seward," B.T. said, tapping keys.

"What have you got, Cassie?" Mel said, looking in the rearview mirror.

She had her finger on an open page. "It's Christina Rossetti," she said. "'Will the day's journey take the whole long day? From morn to night, my friend.'"

"They're skipping all over the map," B.T. said, turning the laptop so Mel could see the screen. It was a maze of connecting lines.

"Can you tell what general direction they're headed?" Mel asked.

"Yes," B.T. said. "West."

"West," Mel repeated. Of course. He started the car again and turned west on the first road they came to.

There were no cars at all, and only a few scattered lights, a farm and a grain elevator, and a radio tower. Mel drove steadily west across the flat, snowy landscape, looking for the distant glittering lights of the carnival.

The sky turned navy blue and then gray, and they stopped to get gas and call Cassie's sister.

"Use my calling card," B.T. said, handing it to Cassie. "They're not looking for me yet. How much cash do we have?"

Cassie had sixty and another two hundred in traveler's checks. Mel had a hundred sixty-eight. "What did you do?" B.T. asked. "Rob the collection plate?"

Mel called Mrs. Bilderbeck. "I won't be back in time for the services on Sunday," he told her. "Call Reverend Davidson and ask if he'll fill in. And tell the ecumenical meeting to read John 3:16–18 for a devotion."

"Are you sure you're all right?" Mrs. Bilderbeck asked. "There were some men here looking for you yesterday."

Mel gripped the receiver. "What did you tell them?"

"I didn't like the looks of them, so I told them you were at a ministerial alliance meeting in Boston."

"You're wonderful," Mel said, and started to hang up.

"Oh, wait, what about the furnace?" Mrs. Bilderbeck said. "What if the pilot light goes out again?"

"It won't," Mel said. "Nothing can put it out."

He hung up and handed the phone and the calling card to Cassie. She called her sister, who had a car phone, and told her not to come, that she was fine, her knee hadn't been sprained after all, just twisted.

"And I think it must have been," she said to Mel, walking back to the car. "See? I'm not limping at all."

B.T. had bought juice and doughnuts and a large bag of potato chips. They ate them while Mel drove, going south across the interstate and down to Highway 34.

The sun came up and glittered off metal silos and onto the star-shaped crack in the windshield. Mel squinted against its brilliance. They drove slowly through McCook and Sharon Springs and Maranatha, looking for flyers on telephone poles and in store windows, calling out the towns and dates to B.T., who added them to the ones on his laptop.

Trucks passed them, none of them carrying Tilt-A-Whirls or concession stands, and Cassie consulted *Bartlett's* again. "A cold coming we had of it," it said. "Just the worst time of the year."

"T. S. Eliot," Cassie said wonderingly. "'Journey of the Magi.'"

They stopped for gas again, and B.T. drove while Mel napped. It began to get dark. B.T. and Mel changed places, and Cassie got in front, moving stiffly.

"Is your knee hurting again?" Mel asked.

"No," Cassie said. "It doesn't hurt at all. I've just been sitting in the car too long," she said. "At least it's not camels. Can you *imagine* what that must have been like?"

Yes, Mel thought, *I can. I'll bet everyone thought they were crazy. Including them.*

It got very dark. They continued west, through Glorieta and Gilead and Beulah Center, searching for multicolored lights glimmering in a cold field, a spinning Ferris wheel and the smell of cotton candy, listening for the screams of the roller coaster and the music of a merry-go-round.

And the star went before them.

Just Like the Ones We Used to Know

The snow started at 12:01 A.M. Eastern Standard Time just outside of Branford, Connecticut. Noah and Terry Blake, on their way home from a party at the Whittiers' at which Miranda Whittier had said, "I guess you could call this our Christmas Eve *Eve* party!" at least fifty times, noticed a few stray flakes as they turned onto Canoe Brook Road, and by the time they reached home, the snow was coming down hard.

"Oh, good," Tess said, leaning forward to peer through the windshield, "I've been hoping we'd have a white Christmas this year."

At 1:37 A.M. Central Standard Time, Billy Grogan, filling in for KYZT's late-night radio request show out of Duluth, said, "This just in from the National Weather Service. Snow advisory for the Great Lakes region tonight and tomorrow morning. Two to four inches expected," and then went back to discussing the callers' least favorite Christmas songs.

"I'll tell you the one I hate," a caller from Wauwatosa said. "'White Christmas.' I musta heard that thing five hundred times this month."

"Actually," Billy said, "according to the *St. Cloud Evening News,* Bing Crosby's version of 'White Christmas' will be played 2,150 times during the month of December, and other artists' renditions of it will be played an additional 1,890 times."

The caller snorted. "One time's too many for me. Who the heck wants a white Christmas anyway? I sure don't."

"Well, unfortunately, it looks like you're going to get one," Billy said. "And, in that spirit, here's Destiny's Child, singing 'White Christmas.'"

At 1:45 A.M., a number of geese in the city park in Bowling Green, Kentucky, woke up to a low, overcast sky and flew, flapping and honking loudly, over the city center, as if they had suddenly decided to fly farther south for the winter. The noise woke Maureen Reynolds, who couldn't get back to sleep. She turned on KYOU, which was playing "Holly Jolly Oldies," including "Rockin' Around the Christmas Tree" and Brenda Lee's rendition of "White Christmas."

At 3:15 A.M. Mountain Standard Time, Paula Devereaux arrived at DIA for the red-eye flight to Springfield, Illinois. It was beginning to snow, and as she waited in line at the express check-in (she was carrying on her maid-of-honor dress and the bag with her shoes and slip and makeup—the last time she'd been in a wedding, her luggage had gotten lost and caused a major crisis) and in line at security and in line at the gate and in line to be de-iced, she began to hope they might not be able to take off, but no such luck.

Of course not, Paula thought, looking out the window at the snow swirling around the wing, *because Stacey wants me at her wedding.*

"I want a Christmas Eve wedding," Stacey'd told Paula after she'd informed her she was going to be her maid of honor, "all candlelight and evergreens. And I want snow falling outside the windows."

"What if the weather doesn't cooperate?" Paula'd asked.

"It will," Stacey'd said. And here it was, snowing. She wondered if it was snowing in Springfield, too. *Of course it is,* she thought. *Whatever Stacey wants, Stacey gets,* Paula thought. *Even Jim.*

Don't think about that, she told herself. *Don't think about anything. Just concentrate on getting through the wedding. With luck, Jim won't*

even be there except for the ceremony, and you won't have to spend any
time with him at all.

She picked up the in-flight magazine and tried to read, and then
plugged in her headphones and listened to Channel 4, "Seasonal Favorites." The first song was "White Christmas" by the Statler Brothers.

🎄

At 3:38 A.M., it began to snow in Bowling Green, Kentucky. The geese
circling the city flew back to the park, landed, and hunkered down to sit
it out on their island in the lake. Snow began to collect on their backs,
but they didn't care, protected as they were by down and a thick layer of
subcutaneous fat designed to keep them warm even in subzero temperatures.

🦌

At 3:39 A.M., Luke Lafferty woke up, convinced he'd forgotten to set the
goose his mother had talked him into having for Christmas Eve dinner
out to thaw. He went and checked. He *had* set it out. On his way back to
bed, he looked out the window and saw it was snowing, which didn't
worry him. The news had said isolated snow showers for Wichita, ending by mid-morning, and none of his relatives lived more than an hour
and a half away, except Aunt Lulla, and if she couldn't make it, it wouldn't
exactly put a crimp in the conversation. His mom and Aunt Madge
talked so much it was hard for anybody else to get a word in edgewise,
especially Aunt Lulla. "She was always the shy one," Luke's mother said,
and it was true; Luke couldn't remember her saying anything other than
"Please pass the potatoes" at their family get-togethers.

What did worry him was the goose. He should never have let his
mother talk him into having one. It was bad enough her having talked
him into having the family dinner at his place. He had no idea how to
cook a goose.

"What if something goes wrong?" he'd protested. "Butterball doesn't
have a goose hotline."

"You won't need a hotline," his mother had said. "It's just like cooking
a turkey, and it's not as if you had to cook it. I'll be there in time to put it

in the oven and everything. All you have to do is set it out to thaw. Do you have a roasting pan?"

"Yes," Luke had said, but lying there, he couldn't remember if he did. When he got up at 4:14 A.M. to check—he did—it was still snowing.

🌲

At 4:16 Mountain Standard Time, Slade Henry, filling in on WRYT's late-night talk show out of Boise, said, "For all you folks who wanted a white Christmas, it looks like you're going to get your wish. Three to six inches forecast for western Idaho." He played several bars of Johnny Cash's "White Christmas," and then went back to discussing JFK's assassination with a caller who was convinced Clinton was somehow involved.

"Little Rock isn't all that far from Dallas, you know," the caller said. "You could drive it in four and a half hours."

Actually, you couldn't, because I-30 was icing up badly, due to freezing rain which had started just after midnight and then turned to snow. The treacherous driving conditions did not slow Monty Luffer down, as he had a Ford Explorer. Shortly after five, he reached to change stations on the radio so he didn't have to listen to "those damn Backstreet Boys" singing "White Christmas," and slid out of control just west of Texarkana. He crossed the median, causing the semi in the left-hand eastbound lane to jam on his brakes and jackknife, resulting in a thirty-seven-car pileup that closed the road for the rest of the night and all the next day.

🦌

At 5:21 A.M. Pacific Standard Time, four-year-old Miguel Gutierrez jumped on his mother, shouting, "Is it Christmas yet?"

"Not on Mommy's stomach, honey," Pilar murmured and rolled over.

Miguel crawled over her and repeated his question directly into her ear. "*Is it Christmas yet?*"

"No," she said groggily. "Tomorrow's Christmas. Go watch cartoons for a few minutes, okay, and then Mommy'll get up," and pulled the pillow over her head.

Miguel was back again immediately. *He can't find the remote,* she thought wearily, but that couldn't be it, because he jabbed her in the ribs with it. "What's the matter, honey?" she said.

"Santa isn't gonna come," he said tearfully, which brought her fully awake.

He thinks Santa won't be able to find him, she thought. *This is all Joe's fault.* According to the original custody agreement, she had Miguel for Christmas and Joe had him for New Year's, but he'd gotten the judge to change it so they split Christmas Eve and Christmas Day, and then, after she'd told Miguel, Joe had announced he needed to switch.

When Pilar had said no, he'd threatened to take her back to court, so she'd agreed, after which he'd informed her that "Christmas Day" meant her delivering Miguel on Christmas Eve so he could wake up and open his presents at Joe's.

"He can open your presents to him before you come," he'd said, knowing full well Miguel still believed in Santa Claus. So after supper she was delivering both Miguel *and* his presents to Joe's in Escondido, where she would not get to see Miguel open them.

"I can't go to Daddy's," Miguel had said when she'd explained the arrangements, "Santa's gonna bring my presents *here*."

"No, he won't," she'd said. "I sent Santa a letter and told him you'd be at your daddy's on Christmas Eve, and he's going to take your presents there."

"You sent it to the North Pole?" he'd demanded.

"To the North Pole. I took it to the post office this morning," and he'd seemed contented with that answer. Till now.

"Santa's going to come," she said, cuddling him to her. "He's coming to Daddy's, remember?"

"No, he's not," Miguel sniffled.

Damn Joe. I shouldn't have given in, she thought, but every time they went back to court, Joe and his snake of a lawyer managed to wangle new concessions out of the judge, even though until the divorce was final, Joe had never paid any attention to Miguel at all. And she just couldn't afford any more court costs right now.

"Are you worried about Daddy living in Escondido?" she asked Miguel. "Because Santa's magic. He can travel all over California in one night. He can travel all over the *world* in one night."

Miguel, snuggled against her, shook his head violently. "No, he can't!"
"Why not?"

"Because it isn't *snowing*! I want it to snow. Santa can't come in his
sleigh if it doesn't."

🎄

Paula's flight landed in Springfield at 7:48 A.M. Central Standard Time,
twenty minutes late. Jim met her at the airport. "Stacey's having her hair
done," he said. "I was afraid I wouldn't get here in time. It was a good
thing your flight was a few minutes late."

"There was snow in Denver," Paula said, trying not to look at him. He
was as cute as ever, with the same knee-weakening smile.

"It just started to snow here," he said.

How does she do it? Paula thought. You had to admire Stacey. Whatever she wanted, she got. *I wouldn't have had to mess with carrying this
stuff on,* Paula thought, handing Jim the hanging bag with her dress in
it. *There's no way my luggage would have gotten lost. Stacey wanted it
here.*

"The roads are already starting to get slick," Jim was saying. "I hope
my parents get here okay. They're driving down from Chicago."

They will, Paula thought. *Stacey wants them to.*

Jim got Paula's bags off the carousel and then said, "Hang on, I promised Stacey I'd tell her as soon as you got here." He flipped open his cell
phone and put it to his ear. "Stacey? She's here. Yeah, I will. Okay, I'll
pick them up on our way. Yeah. Okay."

He flipped the phone shut. "She wants us to pick up the evergreen
garlands on our way," he said, "and then I have to come back and get
Kindra and David. We need to check on their flights before we leave."

He led the way upstairs to ticketing so they could check the arrival
board. Outside the terminal windows snow was falling, large, perfect,
lacy flakes.

"Kindra's on the 2:19 from Houston," Jim said, scanning the board,
"and David's on the 11:40 from Newark. Oh, good, they're both on time."

Of course they are, Paula thought, looking at the board. The snow in
Denver must be getting worse. All the Denver flights had "delayed" next
to them, and so did a bunch of others: Cheyenne and Portland and Rich-

mond. As she watched, Boston and then Chicago changed from "on time" to "delayed" and Rapid City went from "delayed" to "canceled." She looked at Kindra's and David's flights again. They were still on time.

⚜

Ski areas in Aspen, Lake Placid, Squaw Valley, Stowe, Lake Tahoe, and Jackson Hole woke to several inches of fresh powder. The snow was greeted with relief by the people who had paid ninety dollars for their lift tickets, with irritation by the ski resort owners, who didn't see why it couldn't have come two weeks earlier when people were making their Christmas reservations, and with whoops of delight by snowboarders Kent Slakken and Bodine Cromps. They promptly set out from Breckenridge without maps, matches, helmets, avalanche beacons, avalanche probes, or telling anyone where they were going, for an off-limits backcountry area with "totally extreme slopes."

🌲

At 7:05, Miguel came in and jumped on Pilar again, this time on her bladder, shouting, "It's snowing! Now Santa can come! Now Santa can come!"

"Snowing?" she said blearily. In L.A.? "Snowing? Where?"

"On TV. Can I make myself some cereal?"

"No," she said, remembering the last time. She reached for her robe. "You go watch TV some more and Mommy'll make pancakes."

When she brought the pancakes and syrup in, Miguel was sitting, absorbed, in front of the TV, watching a man in a green parka standing in the snow in front of an ambulance with flashing lights, saying, "— third weather-related fatality in Dodge City so far this morning—"

"Let's find some cartoons to watch," Pilar said, clicking the remote.

"—outside Knoxville, Tennessee, where snow and icy conditions have caused a multicar accident—"

She clicked the remote again.

"—to Columbia, South Carolina, where a surprise snowstorm has shut off power to—"

Click.

"—problem seems to be a low-pressure area covering Canada and the northern two thirds of the United States, bringing snow to the entire Midwest and Mid-Atlantic States and—"

Click.

"—snowing here in Bozeman—"

"I told you it was snowing," Miguel said happily, eating his pancakes, "just like I wanted it to. After breakfast can we make a snowman?"

"Honey, it isn't snowing here in California," Pilar said. "That's the national weather, it's not here. That reporter's in Montana, not California."

Miguel grabbed the remote and clicked to a reporter standing in the snow in front of a giant redwood tree. "The snow started about four this morning here in Monterey, California. As you can see," she said, indicating her raincoat and umbrella, "it caught everybody by surprise."

"*She's* in California," Miguel said.

"She's in northern California," Pilar said, "which gets a lot colder than it does here in L.A. L.A.'s too warm for it to snow."

"No, it's not," Miguel said, and pointed out the window, where big white flakes were drifting down onto the palm trees across the street.

***

At 9:40 Central Standard Time the cell phone Nathan Andrews thought he'd turned off rang in the middle of a grant money meeting which was already going badly. Scheduling the meeting in Omaha on the day before Christmas had seemed like a good idea at the time—businessmen had hardly any appointments that day and the spirit of the season was supposed to make them more willing to open their pocketbooks—but instead they were merely distracted, anxious to do their last-minute Mercedes-Benz shopping or get the Christmas office party started or whatever it was businessmen did, and worried about the snow that had started during rush hour this morning.

Plus, they were morons. "So you're saying you want a grant to study global warming, but then you talk about wanting to measure snow levels," one of them had said. "What does snow have to do with global warming?"

Nathan had tried to explain *again* how warming could lead to increased amounts of moisture in the atmosphere and thus increased precipitation in the form of rain and snow, and how that increased snowfall could lead to increased albedo and surface cooling.

"If it's getting cooler, it's not getting warmer," another one of the businessmen had said. "It can't be both."

"As a matter of fact, it can," he'd said, and launched into his explanation of how polar melting could lead to an increase in freshwater in the North Atlantic, which would float on top of the Gulf Stream, preventing its warm water from sinking and cooling, and effectively shutting the current down. "Europe would freeze," he'd said.

"Well, then, global warming would be a good thing, wouldn't it?" yet another one had said. "Heat the place up."

He had patiently tried to explain how the world would grow both hotter and colder, with widespread droughts, flooding, and a sharp increase in severe weather. "And these changes may happen extremely quickly," he'd said. "Rather than temperatures gradually increasing and sea levels rising, there may be a sudden, unexpected event—a discontinuity. It may take the form of an abrupt, catastrophic temperature increase or a superhurricane or other form of megastorm, occurring without any warning. That's why this project is so critical. By setting up a comprehensive climate database, we'll be able to create more accurate computer models, from which we'll be able to—"

"Computer models!" one of them had snorted. "They're wrong more often than they're right!"

"Because they don't include enough factors," Nathan said. "Climate is an incredibly complicated system, with literally thousands of factors interacting in intricate ways—weather patterns, clouds, precipitation, ocean currents, man-made activities, crops. Thus far, computer models have only been able to chart a handful of factors. This project will chart over two hundred of them and will enable the models to be exponentially more accurate. We'll be able to predict a discontinuity before it happens—"

It was at that point that his cell phone rang. It was his graduate assistant Chin Sung, from the lab. "Where *are* you?" Chin demanded.

"In a grant meeting," Nathan whispered. "Can I call you back in a few minutes?"

"Not if you still want the Nobel Prize," Chin said. "You know that harebrained theory of yours about global warming producing a sudden discontinuity? Well, I think you'd better get over here. Today may be the day you turn out to be right."

"Why?" Nathan asked, gripping the phone excitedly. "What's happened? Have the Gulf Stream temp readings dropped?"

"No, it's not the currents. It's what's happening here."

"Which is what?"

Instead of answering, Chin asked, "Is it snowing where you are?"

Nathan looked out the conference room window. "Yes."

"I thought so. It's snowing here, too."

"And that's what you called me about?" Nathan whispered. "Because it's snowing in Nebraska in December? In case you haven't looked at a calendar lately, winter started three days ago. It's *supposed* to be snowing."

"You don't understand," Chin said. "It isn't just snowing in Nebraska. It's snowing everywhere."

"What do you mean, everywhere?"

"I mean everywhere. Seattle, Salt Lake City, Minneapolis, Providence, Chattanooga. All over Canada and the U.S. as far south as"—there was a pause and the sound of computer keys clicking—"Abilene and Shreveport and Savannah. No, wait, Tallahassee's reporting light snow. As far south as Tallahassee."

The jet stream must have dipped radically south. "Where's the center of the low pressure system?"

"That's just it," Chin said. "There doesn't seem to be one."

"I'll be right there," Nathan said.

A mile from the highway, snowboarders Kent Slakken and Bodine Cromps, unable to see the road in heavily falling snow, drove their car into a ditch. "Shit," Bodine said, and attempted to get out of it by revving the engine and then flooring it, a technique which only succeeded in digging them in to the point where they couldn't open either car door.

It took Jim and Paula nearly two hours to pick up the evergreen garlands and get out to the church. The lacy flakes fell steadily faster and thicker, and it was so slick Jim had to crawl the last few miles. "I hope this doesn't get any worse," he said worriedly, "or people are going to have a hard time getting out here."

But Stacey wasn't worried at all. "Isn't it beautiful? I wanted it to snow for my wedding more than anything," she said, meeting them at the door of the church. "Come here, Paula, you've got to see how the snow looks through the sanctuary windows. It's going to be perfect."

Jim left immediately to go pick up Kindra and David, which Paula was grateful for. Being that close to him in the car had made her start entertaining the ridiculous hopes about him she'd had when they first met. And they were ridiculous. One look at Stacey had shown her that.

The bride-to-be looked beautiful even in a sweater and jeans, her makeup exquisite, her blond hair upswept into glittery snowflake-sprinkled curls. Every time Paula had had her hair done to be in a wedding, she had come out looking like someone in a bad 1950s movie. *How does she do it?* Paula wondered. *You watch, the snow will stop, and start up again just in time for the ceremony.*

But it didn't. It continued to come down steadily, and when the minister arrived for the rehearsal, she said, "I don't know. It took me half an hour to get out of my driveway. You may want to think about canceling."

"Don't be silly. We can't cancel. It's a Christmas Eve wedding," Stacey said, and made Paula start tying the evergreen garlands to the pews with white satin ribbon.

🌲

It was sprinkling in Santa Fe when Bev Carey arrived at her hotel, and by the time she'd checked in and ventured out into the Plaza, it had turned into an icy, driving rain that went right through the light coat and thin gloves she'd brought with her. She had planned to spend the morning shopping, but the shops had signs on them saying "Closed Christmas Eve and Christmas Day," and the sidewalk in front of the Governor's Palace, where, according to her guidebook, Zunis and Navajos sat to sell authentic silver-and-turquoise jewelry, was deserted.

But at least it's not snowing, she told herself, trudging, shivering, back to the hotel. And the shop windows were decorated with *ristras* and lights in the shape of chili peppers, and the Christmas tree in the hotel lobby was decorated with kachina dolls.

Her friend Janice had already called and left a message with the hotel clerk. *And if I don't call her back, she'll be convinced I've taken a bottle of sleeping pills,* Bev thought, going up to her room. On the way to the airport, Janice had asked anxiously, "You haven't been having suicidal thoughts, have you?" and when her friend Louise had found out what Bev was planning, she'd said, "I saw this piece on *Dateline* the other night about suicides at Christmas, and how people who've lost a spouse are especially vulnerable. You wouldn't do anything like that, would you?"

They none of them understood that she was doing this to save her life, not end it, that it was Christmas at home, with its lighted trees and evergreen wreaths and candles, that would kill her. And its snow.

"I know you miss Howard," Janice had said, "and that with Christmas coming, you're feeling sad."

Sad? She felt flayed, battered, beaten. Every memory, every thought of her husband, every use of the past tense, even—"Howard liked . . . ," "Howard knew . . . ," "Howard was . . . "—was like a deadly blow. The grief-counseling books all talked about "the pain of losing a loved one," but she had had no idea the pain could be this bad. It was like being stabbed over and over, and her only hope had been to get away. She hadn't "decided to go to Santa Fe for Christmas." She had run there like a victim fleeing a murderer.

She took off her drenched coat and gloves and called Janice. "You promised you'd call as soon as you got there," Janice said reproachfully. "Are you all right?"

"I'm fine," Bev said. "I was out walking around the Plaza." She didn't say anything about its raining. She didn't want Janice saying I told you so. "It's beautiful here."

"I should have come with you," Janice said. "It's snowing like crazy here. Ten inches so far. I suppose you're sitting on a patio drinking a margarita right now."

"Sangria," Bev lied. "I'm going sightseeing this afternoon. The houses here are all pink and tan adobe with bright blue and red and yellow doors, and right now the whole town's decorated with *luminarias*. You should see them."

"I wish I could," Janice sighed. "All I can see is snow. I have no idea how I'm going to get to the store. Oh, well, at least we'll have a white Christmas. It's so sad Howard can't be here to see this. He always loved white Christmases, didn't he?"

Howard, consulting the *Farmer's Almanac,* reading the weather forecast out loud to her, calling her over to the picture window to watch the snow beginning to fall, saying, "Looks like we're going to get a white Christmas this year," as if it were a present under the tree, putting his arm around her—

"Yes," Bev managed to say through the sudden, searing stab of pain. "He did."

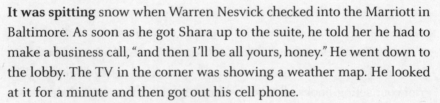

It was spitting snow when Warren Nesvick checked into the Marriott in Baltimore. As soon as he got Shara up to the suite, he told her he had to make a business call, "and then I'll be all yours, honey." He went down to the lobby. The TV in the corner was showing a weather map. He looked at it for a minute and then got out his cell phone.

"Where *are* you?" his wife Marjean said when she answered.

"In St. Louis," he said. "Our flight got rerouted here because of snow at O'Hare. What's the weather like there?"

"It's snowing," she said. "When do you think you'll be able to get a flight out?"

"I don't know. Everything's booked because of it being Christmas Eve. I'm waiting to see if I can get on standby. I'll call you as soon as I know something," and hung up before she could ask him which flight.

It took Nathan an hour and a half to drive the fifteen miles to the lab, during which he considered the likelihood that this was really a discontinuity and not just a major snowstorm. Global warming proponents (and opponents) confused the two all the time. Every hurricane, tornado, heat wave, or dry spell was attributed to global warming, even though nearly all of them fell well within the range of normal weather patterns.

And there had been big December snowstorms before. The blizzard of 1888, for instance, and the Christmas Eve storm of 2002. And Chin was probably wrong about there being no center to the low pressure system. The likely explanation was that there was more than one system involved—one centered in the Great Lakes and another just east of the Rockies, colliding with warm, moist air from the Gulf Coast to create unusually widespread snow.

And it *was* widespread. The car radio was reporting snow all across the Midwest and the entire East Coast—Topeka, Tulsa, Peoria, northern Virginia, Hartford, Montpelier, Reno, Spokane. No, Reno and Spokane were west of the Rockies. There must be a third system, coming down from the Northwest. But it was still hardly a discontinuity.

The lab parking lot hadn't been plowed. He left the car on the street and struggled through the already knee-deep snow to the door, remembering when he was halfway across the expanse that Nebraska was famous for pioneers who got lost going out to the barn in a blizzard and whose frozen bodies weren't found till the following spring.

He reached the door, opened it, and stood there a moment blowing on his frozen hands and looking at the TV Chin had stuck on a cart in the corner of the lab. On it, a pretty reporter in a parka and a Mickey Mouse hat was standing in heavy snow in front of what seemed to be a giant snowman. "The snow has really caused problems here at Disney World," she said over the sound of a marching band playing "White Christmas." "Their annual Christmas Eve Parade has—"

"Well, it's about time," Chin said, coming in from the fax room with a handful of printouts. "What took you so long?"

Nathan ignored that. "Have you got the IPOC data?" he asked.

Chin nodded. He sat down at his terminal and started typing. The upper left-hand screen lit up with columns of numbers.

"Let me see the National Weather Service map," Nathan said, unzipping his coat and sitting down at the main console.

Chin called up a U.S. map nearly half covered with blue, from western Oregon and Nevada east all the way to the Atlantic and up through New England and south to the Oklahoma panhandle, northern Mississippi, Alabama, and most of Georgia.

"Good Lord, that's even bigger than Marina in '92," Nathan said. "Have you got a satellite photo?"

Chin nodded and called it up. "And this is a real-time composite of all the data coming in, including weather stations, towns, and spotters reporting in. The white's snow," he added unnecessarily.

The white covered even more territory than the blue on the NWS map, with jagged fingers stretching down into Arizona and Louisiana and west into Oregon and California. Surrounding them were wide uneven pink bands. "Is the pink rain?" Nathan asked.

"Sleet," Chin said. "So what do you think? It's a discontinuity, isn't it?"

"I don't know," Nathan said, calling up the barometric readings and starting through them.

"What else could it be? It's snowing in Orlando. And San Diego."

"It's snowed in both of those places before," Nathan said. "It's even snowed in Death Valley. The only place in the U.S. where it's never snowed is the Florida Keys. And Hawaii, of course. Everything on this map right now is within the range of normal weather events. You don't have to start worrying till it starts snowing in the Florida Keys."

"What about other places?" Chin asked, looking at the center right-hand screen.

"What do you mean, other places?"

"I mean, it isn't just snowing in the U.S. I'm getting reports from Cancún. And Jerusalem."

At **11:30 Pilar** gave up trying to explain that there wasn't enough snow to make a snowman and took Miguel outside, bundled up in a sweatshirt, a sweater, and his warm jacket, with a pair of Pilar's tube socks for mittens. He lasted about five minutes.

When they came back in, Pilar settled him at the kitchen table with crayons and paper so he could draw a picture of a snowman and went into the living room to check the weather forecast. It was really snowing hard out there, and she was getting a little worried about taking Miguel down to Escondido. Angelenos didn't know how to drive in snow, and Pilar's tires weren't that good.

"—snowing here in Hollywood," said a reporter standing in front of the nearly invisible Hollywood sign, "and this isn't soap flakes, folks, it's the real thing."

She switched channels. "—snowing in Santa Monica," a reporter standing on the beach was saying, "but that isn't stopping the surfers. . . ."

Click. "—*por primera vez en cincuenta años en Marina del Rey*—"

Click. "—snowing here in L.A. for the first time in nearly fifty years. We're here on the set of *xXx Two* with Vin Diesel. What do you think of the snow, Vin?"

Pilar gave up and went back in the kitchen, where Miguel announced he was ready to go outside again. She talked him into listening to Alvin and the Chipmunks instead. "Okay," he said, and she left him warbling "White Christmas" along with Alvin and went in to check the weather again. The Santa Monica reporter briefly mentioned the roads were wet before moving on to interview a psychic who claimed to have predicted the snowstorm, and on a Spanish-language channel she caught a glimpse of the 405 moving along at its usual congested pace.

The roads must not be too bad, she thought, *or they'd all be talking about it,* but she still wondered if she hadn't better take Miguel down to Escondido early. She hated to give up her day with him, but his safety was the important thing, and the snow wasn't letting up at all.

When Miguel came into the living room and asked when they could go outside, she said, "After we pack your suitcase, okay? Do you want to take your Pokémon jammies or your Spidermans?" and began gathering up his things.

🌲

By noon Eastern Standard Time, it was snowing in every state in the lower forty-eight. Elko, Nevada, had over two feet of snow, Cincinnati was reporting thirty-eight inches at the airport, and it was spitting snow in Miami.

On talk radio, JFK's assassination had given way to the topic of the snow. "You mark my words, the terrorists are behind this," a caller from Terre Haute said. "They want to destroy our economy, and what better way to do it than by keeping us from doing our last-minute Christmas shopping? To say nothing of what this snow's going to do to my relationship with my wife. How am I supposed to go buy her something in this weather? I tell you, this has got Al Qaeda's name written all over it."

During lunch, Warren Nesvick told Shara he needed to go try his
business call again. "The guy I was trying to get in touch with wasn't in
the office before. Because of the snow," he said, and went out to the lobby
to call Marjean again. On the TV in the corner, there were shots of snow-
covered runways and jammed ticket counters. A blond reporter in a
tight red sweater was saying, "Here in Cincinnati, the snow just keeps on
falling. The airport's still open, but officials indicate it may have to close.
Snow is building up on the runways—"

He called Marjean. "I'm in Cincinnati," he told her. "I managed to get
a flight at the last minute. There's a three-hour layover till my connecting flight, but at least I've got a seat."

"But isn't it snowing in Cincinnati?" she asked. "I was just watching
the TV and . . ."

"It's supposed to let up here in an hour or so. I'm really sorry about
this, honey. You know I'd be there for Christmas Eve if I could."

"I know," she said, sounding disappointed. "It's okay, Warren. You
can't control the weather."

The television was on in the hotel lobby when Bev came down to lunch.
". . . snowing in Albuquerque," she heard the announcer say, "Raton,
Santa Rosa, and Wagon Mound."

But not in Santa Fe, she told herself firmly, going into the dining
room. "It hardly ever snows there," the travel agent had said, "New Mexico's a desert. And when it does snow, it never sticks."

"There's already four inches in Española," a plump waitress in a ruffled blouse and full red skirt was saying to the busboy. "I'm worried
about getting home."

"I'd rather it didn't snow for Christmas," Bev had teased Howard last
year, "all those people trying to get home."

"Heresy, woman, heresy! What would Currier and Ives think to hear
you talk that way?" he'd said, clutching his chest.

Like she was clutching hers now. The plump waitress was looking at
her worriedly. "Are you all right, *señora*?"

"Yes," Bev said. "One for lunch, please."

The waitress led her to a table, still looking concerned, and handed her a menu, and she clung to it like a life raft, concentrating fiercely on the unfamiliar terms, the exotic ingredients: blue corn tortillas, quesadillas, chipotle—

"Can I get you something to drink?" the waitress asked.

"Yes," Bev said brightly, looking at the waitress's name tag. "I'd like some sangria, Carmelita."

Carmelita nodded and left, and Bev looked around the room, thinking, *I'll drink my sangria and watch the other diners, eavesdrop on their conversations,* but she was the only person in the broad tiled room. It faced the patio, and through the glass doors the rain, sleet now, drove sharply against the terra-cotta pots of cactus outside, the stacked tables and chairs, the collapsed umbrellas.

She had envisioned herself having lunch out on the patio, sitting in the sun under one of those umbrellas, looking out at the desert and listening to a mariachi band. The music coming over the loudspeakers was Christmas carols. As she listened, "Let It Snow" came to an end and the Supremes began to sing "White Christmas."

"What would cloud-seeding be listed under?" Howard had asked her one year when there was still no snow by the twenty-second, coming into the dining room, where she was wrapping presents, with the phone book.

"You are *not* hiring a cloud seeder," she had replied, laughing.

"Would it be under 'clouds' or 'rainmaker'?" he'd asked mock-seriously. "Or 'seeds'?" And when it had finally snowed on the twenty-fourth, he had acted like he was personally responsible.

I can't stand this, Bev thought, looking frantically around the dining room for Carmelita and her sangria. *How do other people do it?* She knew lots of widows, and they all seemed fine. When people mentioned their husbands, when they talked about them in the past tense, they were able to stand there, to smile back, to talk about them. Doreen Matthews had even said, "Now that Bill's gone, I can finally have all pink ornaments on the Christmas tree. I've always wanted to have a pink tree, but he wouldn't hear of it."

"Here's your sangria," Carmelita said, still looking concerned. "Would you like some tortilla chips and salsa?"

"Yes, thank you," Bev said brightly. "And I think I'll have the chicken enchiladas."

Carmelita nodded and disappeared again. Bev took a gulp of her sangria and got her guidebook out of her bag. She would have a nice lunch
and then go sightseeing. She opened the guidebook to Area Attractions.
"Pueblo de San Ildefonso." No, that would involve a lot of walking around
outside, and it was still sleeting outside the window.

"Petroglyphs National Monument." No, that was in Albuquerque,
where it was snowing. "El Santuario de Chimayo. 28 mi. north of Santa
Fe on Hwy. 76. Historic weaving center, shops, chapel dubbed 'American
Lourdes.' The dirt in the anteroom beside the altar is reputed to have
healing powers when rubbed on the afflicted part of the body."

But I hurt all over, she thought.

"Other attractions include five nineteenth-century reredoses, a carv-
ing of El Santo Niño de Atocha, a carved wooden altarpiece. (See also
Lágrima, p. 98.)"

She turned the page to ninety-eight. "Chapel of Our Lady of Perpetual
Sorrow, Lágrima, 28 mi. SE of Santa Fe on Hwy 41. Sixteenth-century
adobe mission church. In 1968 the statue of the Virgin Mary in the tran-
sept was reported to shed healing tears."

Healing tears, holy dirt, and wasn't there supposed to be a miraculous
staircase right here in town? Yes, there it was. The Loretto Chapel. "Open
10–5 Apr–Oct, closed Nov–Mar."

It would have to be Chimayo. She got out the road map the car rental
place had given her, and when Carmelita came with the chips and salsa,
she said, "I'm thinking of driving up to Chimayo. What's the best route?"

"Today?" Carmelita said, dismayed. "That's not a good idea. The road's
pretty curvy, and we just got a call from Taos that it's really snowing
hard up there."

"How about one of the pueblos, then?"

She shook her head. "You have to take dirt roads to get there, and it's
getting really icy. You're better off doing something here in town.
There's a Christmas Eve mass at the cathedral at midnight," she added
helpfully.

But I need something to do this afternoon, Bev thought, bending over
the guidebook again. Indian Research Center—open weekends only. El
Rancho de las Golondrinas—closed Nov-Mar. Santa Fe Historical
Museum—closed Dec 24–Jan 1.

The Georgia O'Keeffe Museum—open daily.

Perfect, Bev thought, reading the entry: "Houses world's largest permanent collection of O'Keeffe's work. A major American artist, O'Keeffe lived in the Santa Fe area for many years. When she first arrived in 1929, she was physically and psychologically ill, but the dry, hot New Mexico climate healed and inspired her, and she painted much of her finest work here."

Perfect. Sun-baked paintings of cow skulls and giant tropical flowers and desert buttes. "Open daily. 10 A.M.–6 P.M. 217 Johnson St."

She looked up the address on her map. Only three blocks off the Plaza, within easy walking distance even in this weather. Perfect. When Carmelita brought her enchiladas, she attacked them eagerly.

"Did you find somewhere to go in town?" Carmelita asked curiously.

"Yes, the Georgia O'Keeffe Museum."

"Oh," Carmelita said, and vanished again. She was back almost immediately. "I'm sorry, *señora,* but they're closed."

"Closed? It said in the guidebook the museum's open daily."

"It's because of the snow."

"Snow?" Bev said, and looked past her to the patio, where the sleet had turned to a heavy, slashing snow.

🌲

At 1:20, Jim called from the airport to tell them Kindra's and David's planes had both been delayed, and a few minutes later the bakery delivered the wedding cake. "No, no," Stacey said, "that's supposed to go to the country club. That's where the reception is."

"We tried," the driver said. "We couldn't get through. We can either leave it here or take it back to the bakery, take your pick. If we can *get* back to the bakery. Which I doubt."

"Leave it here," Stacey said. "Jim can take it over when he gets here."

"But you just heard him," Paula said. "If the truck can't get through, Jim won't be able to—" The phone rang.

It was the florist, calling to say they weren't going to be able to deliver the flowers. "But you have to," Stacey said. "The wedding's at five. Tell them they have to, Paula," and handed the phone to her.

"Isn't there any way you can get here?" Paula asked.

"Not unless there's a miracle," the florist said. "Our truck's in a ditch out at Pawnee, and there's no telling how long it'll take a tow truck to get there. It's a skating rink out there."

"Jim will have to go pick up the flowers when he gets back with Kindra and David," Stacey said blithely when Paula told her the bad news. "He can do it on his way to the country club. Is the string quartet here yet?"

"No, and I'm not sure they'll be able to get here. The florist said the roads are really icy," Paula said, and the viola player walked in.

"I told you," Stacey said happily, "it'll all work out. Did I tell you, they're going to play Boccherini's Minuet No.8 for the wedding march?" and went to get the candles for the altar stands.

Paula went over to the viola player, a lanky young guy. He was brushing snow off his viola case. "Where's the rest of the quartet?"

"They're not here yet?" he said, surprised. "I had a lesson to give in town and told 'em I'd catch up with them." He sat down to take off his snow-crusted boots. "And then my car ended up in a snowbank, and I had to walk the last mile and a half." He grinned up at her, panting. "It's times like these I wish I played the piccolo. Although," he said, looking her up and down, "there are compensations. Please tell me you're not the bride."

"I'm not the bride," she said. *Even though I wish I was.*

"Great!" he said, and grinned at her again. "What are you doing after the wedding?"

"I'm not sure there's going to be one. Do you think the other musicians got stuck on the way here, too?"

He shook his head. "I would have seen them." He pulled out a cell phone and punched buttons. "Shep? Yeah, where are you?" There was a pause. "That's what I was afraid of. What about Leif?" Another pause. "Well, if you find him, call me back." He flipped the phone shut. "Bad news. The violins were in a fender bender and are waiting for the cops. They don't know where the cello is. How do you feel about a viola solo of Minuet No.8?"

Paula went to inform Stacey. "The police can bring them out," Stacey said blithely, and handed Paula the white candles for the altar stands. "The candlelight on the snow's going to be just beautiful."

At 1:48 P.M. Eastern Standard Time, snow flurries were reported at Sunset Point in the Florida Keys.

"I get to officially freak out now, right?" Chin asked Nathan. "Jeez, it really *is* the discontinuity you said would happen!"

"We don't know that yet," Nathan said, looking at the National Weather Service map, which was now entirely blue, except for a small spot near Fargo and another one in north-central Texas which Nathan thought was Waco and Chin was convinced was the President's ranch in Crawford.

"What do you mean, we don't know that yet? It's snowing in Barcelona. It's snowing in Moscow."

"It's supposed to be snowing in Moscow. Remember Napoleon? It's not unusual for it to be snowing in over two thirds of these places reporting in: Oslo, Katmandu, Buffalo—"

"Well, it's sure as hell unusual for it to be snowing in Beirut," Chin said, pointing to the snow reports coming in, "and Honolulu. I don't care what you say, I'm freaking out."

"You can't," Nathan said, superimposing an isobaric grid over the map. "I need you to feed me the temp readings."

Chin started over to his terminal and then came back. "What do *you* think?" he asked seriously. "Do you think it's a discontinuity?"

There was nothing else it could be. Winter storms were frequently very large—the February 1994 European storm had been huge, and the one in December 2002 had covered over a third of the U.S.—but there'd never been one that covered the entire continental United States. *And Mexico and Manitoba and Belize,* he thought, watching the snowfall reports coming in.

In addition, snow was falling in six locations where it had never fallen before, and in twenty-eight, like Yuma, Arizona, where it had snowed only once or twice in the last hundred years. New Orleans had a foot of snow, for God's sake. And it was snowing in Guatemala.

And it wasn't behaving like any storm he'd ever seen. According to the charts, snow had started simultaneously in Springfield, Illinois; Hoodoo, Tennessee; Park City, Utah; and Branford, Connecticut, and spread in a completely random pattern. There was no center to the storm, no leading edge, no front.

And no letup. No station had reported the snow stopping, or even diminishing, and new stations were reporting in all the time. At this rate, it would be snowing everywhere by—he made a rapid calculation—5 o'clock.

"Well?" Chin said. "Is it?" He looked really frightened.

And him freaking out is the last thing I need with all this data to feed in, Nathan thought. "We don't have enough data to make a determination yet," he said.

"But you think it might be," Chin persisted. "Don't you? You think all the signs are there?"

Yes, Nathan thought. "Definitely not," he said. "Look at the TV."

"What about it?"

"There's one sign that's not present." He gestured at the screen. "No logo."

"No what?"

"No logo. Nothing qualifies as a full-fledged crisis until the cable news channels give it a logo of its own, preferably with a colon. You know, *O.J.: Trial of the Century* or *Sniper at Large* or *Attack: Iraq.*" He pointed at Dan Rather standing in thickly falling snow in front of the White House. "Look, it says *Breaking News,* but there's no logo. So it can't be a discontinuity. So feed me those temps. And then go see if you can scare up a couple more TVs. I want to get a look at exactly what's going on out there. Maybe that'll give us some kind of clue."

Chin nodded, looking reassured, and went to get the temp readings. They were all over the place, too, from eighteen below in Saskatoon to thirty-one above in Fort Lauderdale. Nathan ran them against average temps for mid-December and then highs and lows for the twenty-fourth, looking for patterns, anomalies.

Chin wheeled in a big-screen TV on an AV cart, along with Professor Adler's portable, and plugged them in. "What do you want these on?" he asked.

"CNN, the Weather Channel, Fox—" Nathan began.

"Oh, no," Chin said.

"What? What is it?"

"Look," Chin said, and pointed to Professor Adler's portable. Wolf Blitzer was standing in the snow in front of the Empire State Building. At the lower right-hand corner was the CNN symbol. And in the upper left-hand corner: *Storm of the Century.*

As soon as Pilar had Miguel's things packed, she checked on the TV again.

"—resulting in terrible road conditions," the reporter was saying. "Police are reporting accidents at the intersection of Sepulveda and Figueroa, the intersection of San Pedro and Whittier, the intersection of Hollywood and Vine," while accident alerts crawled across the bottom of the screen. "We're getting reports of a problem on the Santa Monica Freeway just past the Culver City exit and . . . this just in: The northbound lanes of the 110 are closed due to a five-car accident. Travelers are advised to take alternate routes."

The phone rang. Miguel ran into the kitchen to answer it. "Hi, Daddy, it's snowing," he shouted into the receiver. "We're going outside and make a snowman," and then said, "Okay," and handed it to Pilar.

"Go watch cartoons and let Mommy talk to Daddy," she said, and handed him the remote. "Hello, Joe."

"I want you to bring Miguel down now," her ex-husband said without preamble, "before the snow gets bad."

"It's already bad," Pilar said, standing in the door of the kitchen watching Miguel flip through the channels:

"—really slick out here—"

"—advised to stay home. If you don't have to go someplace, folks, don't."

"—treacherous conditions—"

"I'm not sure taking him out in this is a good idea," Pilar said. "The TV's saying the roads are really slick, and—"

"And I'm saying bring him down here now," Joe said nastily. "I know what you're doing. You think you can use a little snow as an excuse to keep my son away from me on Christmas."

"I am not," she protested. "I'm just thinking about Miguel's safety. I don't have snow tires—"

"Like hell you're thinking about the kid! You're thinking this is a way to do me out of my rights. Well, we'll see what my lawyer has to say about that. I'm calling him *and* the judge and telling them what you're up to, and that I'm sick of this crap, I want full custody. And then I'm coming up there myself to get him. Have him ready when I get there!" he shouted and hung up the phone.

At 2:22 P.M., Luke's mother called on her cell phone to say she was going to be late and to go ahead and start the goose. "The roads are terrible, and people do *not* know how to drive. This red Subaru ahead of me just *swerved* into my lane and—"

"Mom, Mom," Luke cut in, "the goose. What do you mean, start the goose? What do I have to do?"

"Just put it in the oven. Shorty and Madge should be there soon, and she can take over. All you have to do is get it started. Take the bag of giblets out first. Put an aluminum foil tent over it."

"An aluminum foil what?"

"Tent. Fold a piece of foil in half and lay it over the goose. It keeps it from browning too fast."

"How big a piece?"

"Big enough to cover the goose. And don't tuck in the edges."

"Of the oven?"

"Of the tent. You're making this much harder than it is. You wouldn't *believe* how many cars there are off the road, and every one of them's an SUV. It serves them right. They think just because they've got four-wheel drive, they can go ninety miles an hour in a *blizzard*—"

"Mom, Mom, what about stuffing? Don't I have to stuff the goose?"

"No. Nobody does stuffing inside the bird anymore. Salmonella. Just put the goose in the roasting pan and stick it in the oven. At 350 degrees."

I can do that, Luke thought, and did. Ten minutes later he realized he'd forgotten to put the aluminum foil tent on. It took him three tries to get a piece the right size, and his mother hadn't said whether the shiny or the dull side should be facing out, but when he checked the goose twenty minutes later, it seemed to be doing okay. It smelled good, and there were already juices forming in the pan.

After Pilar hung up with Joe, she sat at the kitchen table a long time, trying to think which was worse, letting Joe take Miguel out into this snowstorm or having Miguel witness the fight that would ensue if she tried to stop him. "Please, please . . ." she murmured, without even knowing what she was praying for.

Miguel came into the kitchen and climbed into her lap. She wiped hastily at her eyes. "Guess what, honey?" she said brightly. "Daddy's going to come get you in a little bit. You need to go pick out which toys you want to take."

"Hunh-unh," Miguel said, shaking his head.

"I know you wanted to make a snowman," she said, "but guess what? It's snowing in Escondido, too. You can make a snowman with Daddy."

"Hunh-*unh,*" he said, climbing down off her lap and tugging on her hand. He led her into the living room.

"What, honey?" she said, and he pointed at the TV. On it, the Santa Monica reporter was saying, "—the following road closures: I-5 from Chula Vista to Santa Ana, I-15 from San Diego to Barstow, Highway 78 from Oceanside to Escondido—"

Thank you, she murmured silently, *thank you.* Miguel ran out to the kitchen and came back with a piece of construction paper and a red crayon. "Here," he said, thrusting them at Pilar. "You have to write Santa. So he'll know to bring my presents here and not Daddy's."

⁂

By ordering sopapillas and then Mexican coffee, Bev managed to make lunch last till nearly 2 o'clock. When Carmelita brought the coffee, she looked anxiously out at the snow piling up on the patio and then back at Bev, so Bev asked for her check and signed it so Carmelita could leave, and then went back up to her room for her coat and gloves.

Even if the shops were closed, she could window-shop, she told herself, she could look at the Navajo rugs and Santa Clara pots and Indian jewelry displayed in the shops, but the snowstorm was getting worse. The *luminarias* that lined the walls were heaped with snow, the paper bags that held the candles sagging wetly under its weight.

They'll never get them lit, Bev thought, turning into the Plaza.

By the time she had walked down one side of it, the snow had become a blizzard, it was coming down so hard you couldn't see across the Plaza, and there was a cutting wind. She gave up and went back to the hotel.

In the lobby, the staff, including the front desk clerk and Carmelita in her coat and boots, was gathered in front of the TV looking at a weather map of New Mexico. "... currently snowing in most of New Mexico," the announcer was saying, "including Gallup, Carlsbad, Ruidoso, and Roswell. Travel advisories out for central, western, and southern New Mexico, including Lordsburg, Las Cruces, and Truth or Consequences. It looks like a white Christmas for most of New Mexico, folks."

"You have two messages," the front desk clerk said when he saw her. They were both from Janice, and she phoned again while Bev was taking her coat off.

"I just saw on TV that it's snowing in Santa Fe, and you said you were going sightseeing," Janice said. "I just wondered if you were okay."

"I'm here at the hotel," Bev said. "I'm not going anywhere."

"Good," Janice said, relieved. "Are you watching TV? The weathermen are saying this isn't an ordinary storm. It's some kind of extreme megastorm. We've got three feet here. The power's out all over town, and the airport just closed. I hope you're able to get home. Oops, the lights just flickered. I'd better go hunt up some candles before the lights go off," she said, and hung up.

Bev turned on the TV. The local channel was listing closings—"The First United Methodist Church Christmas pageant has been canceled and there will be no *Posadas* tonight at Our Lady of Guadalupe. Canyon Day Care Center will close at 3 P.M. . . ."

She clicked the remote. CNBC was discussing earlier Christmas Eve snowstorms, and on CNN, Daryn Kagan was standing in the middle of Fifth Avenue in a snowdrift. "This is usually the busiest shopping day of the year," she said, "but as you can see—"

She clicked the remote, looking for a movie to watch. *Howard would have loved this,* she thought involuntarily. *He would have been in his element.*

She clicked quickly through the other channels, trying to find a movie to watch, but they were all discussing the weather. "It looks like the whole country's going to get a white Christmas this year," Anderson Cooper was saying, "whether they want it or not."

You'd think there'd be a Christmas movie on, Bev thought grimly, flipping through the channels again. *It's Christmas Eve.* Christmas in Connecticut *or* Holiday Inn. *Or* White Christmas.

Howard had insisted on watching it every time he came across it with the remote, even if it was nearly over. "Why are you watching that?" she'd ask, coming in to find him watching the next-to-the-last scene. "We own the video."

"Shh," he'd say. "It's just getting to the good part," and he'd lean forward to watch Bing Crosby push open the barn doors to reveal fake-looking snow falling on the equally fake-looking set.

When he came into the kitchen afterward, she'd say sarcastically, "How'd it end this time? Did Bing and Rosemary Clooney get back together? Did they save the General's inn and all live happily ever after?"

But Howard would refuse to be baited. "They got a white Christmas," he'd say happily, and go off to look out the windows at the clouds.

Except for news about the storm, there was nothing at all on except an infomercial selling a set of Ginsu knives. *How appropriate,* she thought, and sat back on the bed to watch it.

🎄

At 2:08, the weight of the new loose snow triggered a huge avalanche in the "awesome slopes" area near Breckenridge, knocking down huge numbers of Ponderosa pines and burying everything in its path, but not Kent and Bodine, who were still in their Honda, trying to keep warm and survive on a box of Tic-Tacs and an old doughnut they found in the glove compartment.

🦌

By 2:30, Madge and Shorty still weren't there, so Luke checked the goose. It seemed to be cooking okay, but there was an awful lot of juice in the pan. When he checked it again half an hour later, there was over an inch of the stuff.

That couldn't be right. The last time he'd gotten stuck with having the Christmas Eve dinner, the turkey had only produced a few tablespoons of juice. He remembered his mom pouring them off to make the gravy.

He tried his mom. Her cell phone said, "Caller unavailable," which meant her batteries had run down, or she'd turned it off. He tried Aunt Madge. No answer.

He dug the plastic and net wrapping the goose had come in out of the trash, flattened it out, and read the instructions: "Roast uncovered at 350° for twenty-five minutes per pound."

Uncovered. That must be the problem, the aluminum foil tent. It wasn't allowing the extra juice to evaporate. He opened the oven and removed it. When he checked the goose again fifteen minutes later, it was sitting in two inches of grease, and even though, according to the wrapping, it still had three hours to go, the goose was getting brown and crispy on top.

At 2:51 P.M., Joe Gutierrez slammed out of his house and started up to get Miguel. He'd been trying ever since he hung up on Pilar to get his goddamned lawyer on the phone, but he wasn't answering.

The streets were a real mess, and when Joe got to the I-15 entrance ramp, there was a barricade across it. He roared back down the street to take Highway 78, but it was blocked, too. He stormed back home and called Pilar's lawyer, but he didn't answer, either. He then called the judge, using the unlisted cell phone number he'd seen on his lawyer's PalmPilot.

The judge, who had been stuck waiting for AAA in a Starbucks at the Bakersfield exit, listening to Harry Connick, Jr., destroy "White Christmas" for the last three hours, was not particularly sympathetic, especially when Joe started swearing at him.

Words were exchanged, and the judge made a note to himself to have Joe declared in contempt of court. Then he called AAA to see what was taking so long, and when the operator told him he was nineteenth in line, and it would be at least another four hours, he decided to revisit the entire custody agreement.

By 3 o'clock, all the networks and cable news channels had logos. ABC had *Winter Wonderland,* NBC had *Super Storm,* and Fox News had *Winter Wallop.* CBS and MSNBC had both gone with *White Christmas,* flanked by a photo of Bing Crosby (MSNBC's wearing the Santa Claus hat from the movie).

The Weather Channel's logo was a changing world map that was now two thirds white, and snow was being reported in Karachi, Seoul, the Solomon Islands, and Bethlehem, where Christmas Eve services (usually canceled due to Israeli–Palestinian violence) had been canceled due to the weather.

At 3:15 P.M., Jim called Paula from the airport to report that Kindra's and David's flights had both been delayed indefinitely. "And the USAir guy says they're shutting down the airport in Houston. Dallas International's already closed, and so are JFK and O'Hare. How's Stacey?"

Incorrigible, Paula thought. "Fine," she said. "Do you want to talk to her?"

"No. Listen, tell her I'm still hoping, but it doesn't look good."

Paula told her, but it didn't have any effect. "Go get your dress on," Stacey ordered her, "so the minister can run through the service with you, and then you can show Kindra and David where to stand when they get here."

Paula went and put on her bridesmaid dress, wishing it wasn't sleeveless, and they went through the rehearsal with the viola player, who had changed into his tux to get out of his snow-damp clothes, acting as best man. As soon as they were done, Paula went into the vestry to get a sweater out of her suitcase. The minister came in and shut the door. "I've been trying to talk to Stacey," she said. "You're going to *have* to cancel the wedding. The roads are getting really dangerous, and I just heard on the radio they've closed the interstate."

"I know," Paula said.

"Well, she doesn't. She's convinced everything's going to work out."

And it might, Paula thought. *After all, this is Stacey.*

The viola player poked his head in the door. "Good news," he said.

"The string quartet's here?" the minister said.

"Jim's here?" Paula said.

"No, but Shep and Leif found the cello player. He's got frostbite, but otherwise he's okay. They're taking him to the hospital." He gestured toward the sanctuary. "Do you want to tell the Queen of Denial, or shall I?"

"I will," Paula said, and went back into the sanctuary. "Stacey—"

"Your dress looks beautiful!" Stacey cried, and dragged her over to the windows. "Look how it goes with the snow!"

When the doorbell rang at a quarter to four, Luke thought, *Finally! Mom!* and literally ran to answer the door. It was Aunt Lulla. He looked hopefully past her, but there was no one else pulling into the driveway or coming up the street. "You don't know anything about cooking a goose, do you?" he asked.

She looked at him a long, silent moment and then handed him the plate of olives she'd brought and took off her hat, scarf, gloves, plastic boots, and old-lady coat. "Your mother and Madge were always the domestic ones," she said. "I was the theatrical one," and while he was digesting that odd piece of information, "Why did you ask? Is your goose cooked?"

"Yes," he said, and led her into the kitchen and showed her the goose, which was now swimming in a sea of fat.

"Good God!" Aunt Lulla said. "Where did all that grease come from?"

"I don't know," he said.

"Well, the first thing to do is pour some of it off before the poor thing drowns."

"I already did," Luke said. He took the lid off the saucepan he'd poured the drippings into earlier.

"Well, you need to pour off some more," she said practically, "and you'll need a larger pan. Or maybe we should just pour it down the sink and get rid of the evidence."

"It's for the gravy," he said, rummaging in the cupboard under the sink for the big pot his mother had given him to cook spaghetti in.

"Oh, of course," she said, and then thoughtfully, "I *do* know how to make gravy. Alec Guinness taught me."

Luke stuck his head out of the cupboard. "Alec Guinness taught you to make *gravy*?"

"It's not really all that difficult," she said, opening the oven door and looking speculatively at the goose. "You wouldn't happen to have any wine on hand, would you?"

"Yes." He emerged with the pot. "Why? Will wine counteract the grease?"

"I have no idea," she said, "but one of the things I learned when I was playing off-Broadway was that when you're facing a flop or an opening night curtain, it helps to be a little sloshed."

"You played off-Broadway?" Luke said. "Mom never told me you were an actress."

"I wasn't," she said, opening cupboard doors. She pulled out two wineglasses. "You should have seen my reviews."

❦

By 4:00 P.M., all the networks and cable news channels had changed their logos to reflect the worsening situation. ABC had *MegaBlizzard*, NBC had *MacroBlizzard*, and CNN had *Perfect Storm*, with a graphic of a boat being swamped by a gigantic wave. CBS and MSNBC had both gone with *Ice Age*, CBS's with a question mark, MSNBC's with an exclamation point and a drawing of the Abominable Snowman. And Fox, ever the responsible news network, was proclaiming *End of the World!*

"*Now* can I freak out?" Chin asked.

"No," Nathan said, feeding in snowfall rates. "In the first place, it's Fox. In the second place, a discontinuity does not necessarily mean the end of the wo—"

The lights flickered. They both stopped and stared at the overhead fluorescents. They flickered again.

"Backup!" Nathan shouted, and they both dived for their terminals, shoved in zip drives, and began frantically typing, looking anxiously up at the lights now and then.

Chin popped the zip disk out of the hard drive. "You were saying that a discontinuity isn't necessarily the end of the world?"

"Yes, but losing this data would be. From now on we back up every fifteen minutes."

The lights flickered again, went out for an endless ten seconds, and came back on again to Anderson Cooper saying, "—Huntsville, Alabama, where thousands are without power. I'm here at Byrd Middle School, which is serving as a temporary shelter." He stuck the microphone under the nose of a woman holding a candle. "When did the power go off?" he asked.

"About noon," she said. "The lights flickered a couple of times before that, but both times the lights came back on, and I thought we were okay, and then I went to fix lunch, and they went off, like that—" She snapped her fingers, "without any warning."

"We back up every five minutes," Nathan said, and to Chin, who was pulling on his parka, "Where are you going?"

"Out to my car to get a flashlight."

He came back in ten minutes later, caked in snow, his ears and cheeks bright red. "It's four feet deep out there. Tell me again why I shouldn't freak out," he said, handing the flashlight to Nathan.

"Because I don't think this is a discontinuity," Nathan said. "I think it's just a snowstorm."

"Just a snowstorm?" Chin said, pointing at the TVs, where red-eared, red-cheeked reporters were standing in front of, respectively, a phalanx of snowplows on the Boardwalk in Atlantic City, a derailed train in Casper, and a collapsed Walmart in Biloxi, "—from the weight of a record fifty-eight inches of snow," Brit Hume was saying. "Luckily, there were no injuries here. In Cincinnati, however—"

"*Fifty-eight* inches," Chin said. "In *Mississippi*. What if it keeps on snowing and snowing forever till the whole world—?"

"It can't," Nathan said. "There isn't enough moisture in the atmosphere, and no low pressure system over the Gulf to keep pumping moisture up across the lower United States. There's no low pressure system at all, and no ridge of high pressure to push against it, no colliding air masses, nothing. Look at this. It started in four different places hundreds of miles from each other, in different latitudes, different altitudes, none of them along a ridge of high pressure. This storm isn't following any of the rules."

"But doesn't that prove it's a discontinuity?" Chin asked nervously. "Isn't that one of the signs, that it's completely different from what came before?"

"The *climate* would be completely different, the *weather* would be completely different, not the laws of physics." He pointed to the world map on the mid-right-hand screen. "If this were a discontinuity, you'd see a change in ocean current temps, a shift in the jet stream, changes in wind patterns. There's none of that. The jet stream hasn't moved, the rate of melting in the Antarctic is unchanged, the Gulf Stream's still there. El Niño's still there. *Venice* is still there."

"Yeah, but it's snowing on the Grand Canal," Chin said. "So what's causing the megastorm?"

"That's just it. It's not a megastorm. If it were, there'd be accompanying ice storms, hurricane-force winds, microbursts, tornadoes, none of which has shown up on the data. As near as I can tell, all it's doing is snowing." He shook his head. "No, something else is going on."

"What?"

"I have no idea." He stared glumly at the screens. "Weather's a remarkably complex system. Hundreds, thousands of factors we haven't figured in could be having an effect: cloud dynamics, localized temperature variations, pollution, solar activity. Or it could be something we haven't even considered: the effects of de-icers on highway albedo, beach erosion, the migratory patterns of geese. Or the effect on electromagnetic fields of playing 'White Christmas' hundreds of times on the radio this week."

"Four thousand nine hundred and thirty-three," Chin said.

"What?"

"That's how many times Bing Crosby's 'White Christmas' is played the two weeks before Christmas, with an additional nine thousand and sixty-two times by other artists. Including Otis Redding, U2, Peggy Lee, the Three Tenors, and the Flaming Lips. I read it on the Internet."

"Nine thousand and sixty-two," Nathan said. "That's certainly enough to affect something, all right."

"I know what you mean," Chin said. "Have you heard Eminem's new rap version?"

By 4:15 P.M., the spaghetti pot was two thirds full of goose grease, Luke's mother and Madge and Shorty still weren't there, and the goose was nearly done. Luke and Lulla had decided after their third glass of wine apiece to make the gravy.

"And put the tent back on," Lulla said, sifting flour into a bowl. "One of the things I learned when I was playing the West End is that uncovered is not necessarily better." She added a cup of water. "Particularly when you're doing Shakespeare."

She shook in some salt and pepper. "I remember a particularly ill-conceived nude *Macbeth* I did with Larry Olivier." She thrust her hand out dramatically. "'Is this a dagger which I see before me?' should *not* be a laugh line. Richard taught me how to do this," she said, stirring the mixture briskly with a fork. "It gets the lumps out."

"Richard? Richard *Burton*?"

"Yes. Adorable man. Of course he drank like a fish when he was depressed—this was after Liz left him for the second time—but it never seemed to affect his performance in bed *or* in the kitchen. Not like Peter."

"Peter? Peter Ustinov?"

"O'Toole. Here we go." Lulla poured the flour mixture into the hot drippings. It disappeared. "It takes a moment to thicken up," she said hopefully, but after several minutes of combined staring into the pot, it was no thicker.

"I think we need more flour," she said, "and a larger bowl. A much larger bowl. And another glass of wine."

Luke fetched them, and after a good deal of stirring, she added the mixture to the drippings, which immediately began to thicken up. "Oh, good," she said, stirring. "As John Gielgud used to say, 'If at first you don't succeed . . . ' Oh, dear."

"What did he say that for— Oh, dear," Luke said, peering into the pot where the drippings had abruptly thickened into a solid, globular mass.

"That's not what gravy's supposed to look like," Aunt Lulla said.

"No," Luke said. "We seem to have made a lard ball."

They both looked at it awhile.

"I don't suppose we could pass it off as a very large dumpling," Aunt Lulla suggested.

"No," Luke said, trying to chop at it with the fork.

"And I don't suppose it'll go down the garbage disposal. Could we stick sesame seeds on it and hang it on a tree and pretend it was a suet ball for the birds?"

"Not unless we want PETA and the Humane Society after us. Besides, wouldn't that be cannibalism?"

"You're right," Aunt Lulla said. "But we've got to do something with it before your mother gets here. I suppose Yucca Mountain's too far away," she said thoughtfully. "You wouldn't have any acid on hand, would you?"

🌲

At 4:23 P.M., Slim Rushmore, on KFLG out of Flagstaff, Arizona, made a valiant effort to change the subject on his talk radio show to school vouchers, usually a surefire issue, but his callers weren't having any of it. "This snow is a clear sign the Apocalypse is near," a woman from Colorado Springs informed him. "In the Book of Daniel, it says that God will send snow 'to purge and to make them white, even to the time of the end,' and the Book of Psalms promises us 'snow and vapours, stormy wind fulfilling his word,' and in the Book of Isaiah . . ."

After the fourth Scripture (from Job: "For God saith to the snow, Be thou on the earth") Slim cut her off and took a call from Dwayne in Poplar Bluffs.

"You know what started all this, don't you?" Dwayne said belligerently. "When the commies put fluoride in the water back in the fifties."

🐎

At 4:25 P.M., the country club called the church to say they were closing, none of the food and only two of the staff could get there, and anybody who was still trying to have a wedding in this weather was crazy. "I'll tell her," Paula said, and went to find Stacey.

"She's in putting on her wedding dress," the viola player said.

Paula moaned.

"Yeah, I know," he said. "I tried to explain to her that the rest of the quartet was *not* coming, but I didn't get anywhere." He looked at her quizzically. "I'm not getting anywhere with you either, am I?" he asked, and Jim walked in.

He was covered in snow. "The car got stuck," he said.

"Where are Kindra and David?"

"They closed Houston," he said, pulling Paula aside, "and Newark. And I just talked to Stacey's mom. She's stuck in Lavoy. They just closed the highway. There's no way she can get here. What are we going to do?"

"You have to tell her the wedding has to be called off," Paula said. "You don't have any other option. And you have to do it now, before the guests try to come to the church."

"You obviously haven't been out there lately," he said. "Trust me, nobody's going to come out in that."

"Then you obviously have to cancel."

"I know," he said worriedly. "It's just . . . she'll be so disappointed."

"Disappointed" is not the word that springs to mind, Paula thought, and realized she had no idea how Stacey would react. She'd never seen her not get her way. *I wonder what she'll do,* she thought curiously, and started back into the vestry to change out of her maid-of-honor dress.

"Wait," Jim said, grabbing her hand. "You have to help me tell her."

This is asking way too much, Paula thought. *I want you to marry me, not her.* "I—" she said.

"I can't do this without you," he said. "Please?"

She extricated her hand. "Okay," she said, and they went into the changing room, where Stacey was in her wedding dress, looking at herself in the mirror.

"Stacey, we have to talk," Jim said, after a glance at Paula. "I just heard from your mother. She's not going to be able to get here. She's stuck at a truck stop outside Lavoy."

"She can't be," Stacey said to her reflection. "She's bringing my veil." She turned to smile at Paula. "It was my great-grandmother's. It's lace, with this snowflake pattern."

"Kindra and David can't get here, either," Jim said. He glanced at Paula and then plunged ahead. "We're going to have to reschedule the wedding."

"Reschedule?" Stacey said as if she'd never heard the word before. *Which she probably hasn't,* Paula thought. "We can't reschedule. A Christmas Eve wedding has to be on Christmas Eve."

"I know, honey, but—"

"Nobody's going to be able to get here," Paula said. "They've closed the roads."

The minister came in. "The governor's declared a snow emergency and a ban on unnecessary travel. You've decided to cancel?" she said hopefully.

"*Cancel?*" Stacey said, adjusting her train. "What are you talking about? Everything will be fine."

And for one mad moment, Paula could almost see Stacey pulling it off, the weather magically clearing, the rest of the string quartet showing up, the flowers and Kindra and David and the veil all arriving in the next thirty-five minutes. She looked over at the windows. The snow, reflected softly in the candlelight, was coming down harder than ever.

"We don't have any other choice than to reschedule," Jim said. "Your mother can't get here, your bridesmaids and my best man can't get here—"

"Tell them to take a different flight," Stacey said.

Paula tried. "Stacey, I don't think you realize, this is a major snowstorm. Airports all over the country are closed—"

"Including here," the viola player said, poking his head in. "It was just on the news."

"Well, then, go get them," Stacey said, adjusting the drape of her skirt.

Paula'd lost the thread of this conversation. "Who?"

"Kindra and David." She adjusted the neckline of her gown.

"To *Houston?*" Jim said, looking helplessly at Paula.

"Listen, Stacey," Paula said, taking her firmly by the shoulders, "I know how much you wanted a Christmas Eve wedding, but it's just not going to work. The roads are impassable. Your flowers are in a ditch, your mother's trapped at a truck stop—"

"The cello player's in the hospital with frostbite," the viola player put in.

Paula nodded. "And you don't want anyone else to end up there. You have to face facts. You can't have a Christmas Eve wedding."

"You could reschedule for Valentine's Day," the minister said brightly. "Valentine weddings are very nice. I've got two weddings that day, but I could move one up. It could still be in the evening," but Paula could tell Stacey had stopped listening at "You can't have—"

"*You* did this," Stacey snapped at Paula. "You've always been jealous of me, and now you're taking it out on me by ruining my wedding."

"Nobody's ruining anything, Stacey," Jim said, stepping between them. "It's a snowstorm."

"Oh, so I suppose it's *my* fault!" Stacey said. "Just because I wanted a winter wedding with snow—"

"It's nobody's fault," Jim said sternly. "Listen, I don't want to wait, either, and we don't have to. We can get married right here, right now."

"Yeah," the viola player said. "You've got a minister." He grinned at Paula. "You've got two witnesses."

"He's right," Jim said. "We've got everything we need right here. You're here, *I'm* here, and that's all that really matters, isn't it, not some fancy wedding?" He took her hands in his. "Will you marry me?"

And what woman could resist an offer like that? Paula thought. *Oh, well, you knew when you got on the plane that he was going to marry her.*

"Marry you," Stacey repeated blankly, and the minister hurried out, saying, "I'll get my book. And my robe."

"Marry you?" Stacey said. *"Marry you?"* She wrenched free of his grasp. "Why on earth would I marry a *loser* who won't even do one simple thing for me? I *want* Kindra and David here. I *want* my flowers. I *want* my veil. What is the *point* of *marrying* you if I can't have what I want?"

"I thought you wanted me," Jim said dangerously.

"You?" Stacey said in a tone that made both Paula and the viola player wince. "I *wanted* to walk down the aisle at twilight on Christmas Eve"— she waved her arm in the direction of the windows—"with candlelight reflecting off the windowpanes and snow falling outside." She turned, snatching up her train, and looked at him. "Will I *marry* you? Are you *kidding*?"

There was a short silence. Jim turned and looked seriously at Paula. "How about you?" he said.

🎄

At six o'clock on the dot, Madge and Shorty, Uncle Don, Cousin Denny, and Luke's mom all arrived. "You poor darling," she whispered to Luke, handing him the green bean casserole and the sweet potatoes, "stuck all afternoon with Aunt Lulla. Did she talk your ear off?"

"No," he said. "We made a snowman. Why didn't you tell me Aunt Lulla had been an actress?"

"An *actress*?" she said, handing him the cranberry sauce. "Is that what she told you? Don't tip it, it'll spill. Did you have any trouble with the goose?" She opened the oven and looked at it, sitting in its pan, brown and crispy and done to a turn. "They tend to be a little juicy."

"Not a bit," he said, looking past her out the window at the snowman in the backyard. The snow he and Aunt Lulla had packed around and on top of it was melting. He'd have to sneak out during dinner and pack more snow on.

"Here," his mom said, handing him the mashed potatoes. "Heat these up in the microwave while I make the gravy."

"It's made," he said, lifting the lid off the saucepan to show her the gently bubbling gravy. It had taken them four tries, but as Aunt Lulla had pointed out, they had more than enough drippings to experiment with, and, as she had also pointed out, three lardballs made a more realistic snowman.

"The top one's too big," Luke had said, scooping up snow to cover it with.

"I may have gotten a little carried away with the flour," Aunt Lulla had admitted. "On the other hand, it looks exactly like Orson." She stuck two olives in for eyes. "And so appropriate. He always was a fathead."

"The gravy smells delicious," Luke's mother said, looking surprised. "*You* didn't make it, did you?"

"No. Aunt Lulla."

"Well, I think you're a saint for putting up with her and her wild tales all afternoon," she said, ladling the gravy into a bowl and handing it to Luke.

"You mean she made all that stuff up?" Luke said.

"Do you have a gravy boat?" his mother asked, opening cupboards.

"No," he said. "Aunt Lulla wasn't really an actress?"

"*No.*" She took a bowl out of the cupboard. "Do you have a ladle?"

"No."

She got a dipper out of the silverware drawer. "Lulla was never in a single play," she said, ladling the gravy into a bowl and handing it to Luke, "where she hadn't gotten the part by sleeping with somebody. Lionel Barrymore, Ralph Richardson, Kenneth Branagh . . ." She opened the oven to look at the goose. ". . . and that's not even counting Alfred."

"Alfred *Lunt*?" Luke asked.

"Hitchcock. I think this is just about done."

"But I thought you said she was the shy one."

"She was. That's why she went out for drama in high school, to overcome her shyness. Do you have a platter?"

At 6:35 P.M., a member of the Breckenridge ski patrol, out looking for four missing cross-country skiers, spotted a taillight (the only part of Kent and Bodine's Honda not covered by snow). He had a collapsible shovel with him, and a GPS, a satellite phone, a walkie-talkie, Mylar blankets, insta-heat packs, energy bars, a thermos of hot cocoa, and a stern lecture on winter safety, which he delivered after he had dug Kent and Bodine out and which they really resented. "Who did that fascist geek think he was, shaking his finger at us like that?" Bodine asked Kent after several tequila slammers at the Laughing Moose.

"Yeah," Kent said eloquently, and they settled down to the serious business of how to take advantage of the fresh powder that had fallen while they were in their car.

"You know what'd be totally extreme?" Bodine said. "Snowboarding at night!"

Shara was quite a girl. Warren didn't have a chance to call Marjean again until after seven. When Shara went in the bathroom, he took the opportunity to dial home. "Where *are* you?" Marjean said, practically crying. "I've been worried sick! Are you all right?"

"I'm still in Cincinnati at the airport," he said, "and it looks like I'll be here all night. They just closed the airport."

"Closed the airport . . ." she echoed.

"I *know*," he said, his voice full of regret. "I'd really counted on being home with you for Christmas Eve, but what can you do? It's snowing like crazy here. No flights out till tomorrow afternoon at the earliest. I'm in line at the airline counter right now, rebooking, and then I'm going to try to find a place to stay, but I don't know if I'll have much luck." He paused to give her a chance to commiserate. "They're supposed to put us up for the night, but I wouldn't be surprised if I end up sleeping on the floor."

"At the airport," she said, "in Cincinnati."

"Yeah." He laughed. "Great place to spend Christmas Eve, huh?" He paused to give her a chance to commiserate, but all she said was, "You didn't make it home last year, either."

"Honey, you know I'd get there if I could," he said. "I tried to rent a car and drive home, but the snow's so bad they're not even sure they can get a shuttle out here to take us to a hotel. I don't know how much snow they've had here—"

"Forty-six inches," she said.

Good, he thought. From her voice he'd been worried it might not be snowing in Cincinnati after all. "And it's still coming down hard. Oh, they just called my name. I'd better go."

"You do that," she said.

"All right. I love you, honey," he said, "I'll be home as soon as I can," and hung up the phone.

"You're married," Shara said, standing in the door of the bathroom. "You sonuvabitch."

Paula didn't say yes to Jim's proposal after all. She'd intended to, but before she could, the viola player had cut in. "Hey, wait a minute!" he'd said. "I saw her first!"

"You did not," Jim said.

"Well, no, not technically," he admitted, "but when I did see her, I had the good sense to flirt with her, not get engaged to Vampira like you did."

"It wasn't Jim's fault," Paula said. "Stacey always gets what she wants."

"Not this time," he said. "And not me."

"Only because she doesn't want you," Paula said. "If she did—"

"Wanna bet? You underestimate us musicians. And yourself. At least give me a chance to make my pitch before you commit to this guy. You can't get married tonight anyway."

"Why not?" Jim asked.

"Because you need two witnesses, and I have no intention of helping *you,*" he pointed at Jim, "get the woman *I* want. I doubt if Stacey's in the mood to be a witness, either," he said as Stacey stormed back in the sanctuary, with the minister in pursuit. Stacey had on her wedding dress, a parka, and boots.

"You can't go out in this," the minister was saying. "It's too danger-ous!"

"I have no intention of staying here with him," Stacey said, shooting Jim a venomous glance. "I want to go home *now*." She flung the door open on the thickly falling snow. "And I want it to stop *snowing*!"

At that exact moment, a snowplow's flashing yellow lights appeared through the snow, and Stacey ran out. Paula and Jim went over to the door and watched Stacey wave it down and get in. The plow continued on its way.

"Oh, good, now we'll be able to get out," the minister said, and went to get her car keys.

"You didn't answer my question, Paula," Jim said, standing very close.

The plow turned and came back. As it passed, it plowed a huge mass of snow across the end of the driveway.

"I mean it," Jim murmured. "How about it?"

"Look what I found," the viola player said, appearing at Paula's elbow. He handed her a piece of wedding cake.

"You can't eat that. It's—" Jim said.

"—not bad," the viola player said. "I prefer chocolate, though. What kind of cake shall we have at our wedding, Paula?"

"Oh, look," the minister said, coming back in with her car keys and looking out the window. "It's stopped snowing."

🌲

"**It's stopped snowing**," Chin said.

"It has?" Nathan looked up from his keyboard. "Here?"

"No. In Oceanside, Oregon. And in Springfield, Illinois."

Nathan found them on the map. Two thousand miles apart. He checked their barometer readings, temperatures, snowfall amounts. No similarity. Springfield had thirty-two inches, Oceanside an inch and a half. And in every single town around them, it was still snowing hard. In Tillamook, six miles away, it was coming down at the rate of five inches an hour.

But ten minutes later, Chin reported the snow stopping in Gillette, Wyoming; Roulette, Massachusetts; and Saginaw, Michigan, and within half an hour the number of stations reporting in was over thirty, though they seemed just as randomly scattered all over the map as the storm's beginning had been.

"Maybe it has to do with their names," Chin said.

"Their names?" Nathan said.

"Yeah. Look at this. It's stopped in Joker, West Virginia; Bluff, Utah; and Blackjack, Georgia."

At 7:22 P.M., the snow began to taper off in Wendover, Utah. Neither the Lucky Lady Casino nor the Big Nugget had any windows, so the event went unnoticed until Barbara Gomez, playing the quarter slots, ran out of money at 9:05 P.M. and had to go out to her car to get the emergency twenty she kept taped under the dashboard. By this time, the snow had nearly stopped. Barbara told the change girl, who said, "Oh, good. I was worried about driving to Battle Mountain tomorrow. Were the plows out?"

Barbara said she didn't know and asked for four rolls of nickels, which she promptly lost playing video poker.

By 7:30 P.M. CNBC had replaced its logo with *Digging Out,* and ABC had retreated to Bing and *White Christmas,* though CNN still had side-by-side experts discussing the possibility of a new ice age, and on Fox News, Geraldo Rivera was intoning, "In his classic poem 'Fire and Ice,' Robert Frost speculated that the world might end in ice. Today we are seeing the coming true of that dire prediction—"

The rest had obviously gotten the word, though, and CBS and the WB had both gone back to their regular programming. The movie *White Christmas* was on AMC.

"Whatever this was, it's stopping," Nathan said, watching "I-80 now open from Lincoln to Ogalallah," scroll across the bottom of NBC's screen.

"Well, whatever you do, don't tell those corporate guys," Chin said, and, as if on cue, one of the businessmen Nathan had met with that morning called.

"I just wanted you to know we've voted to approve your grant," he said.

"Really? Thank you," Nathan said, trying to ignore Chin, who was mouthing, "Are they giving us the money?"

"Yes," he mouthed back.

Chin scribbled down something and shoved it in front of Nathan. "Get it in writing," it said.

"We all agreed this discontinuity thing is worth studying," the businessman said, then, shakily, "They've been talking on TV about the end of the world. You don't think this discontinuity thing is that bad, do you?"

"No," Nathan said, "in fact—"

"Ix-nay, ix-nay," Chin mouthed, wildly crossing his arms.

Nathan glared at him. "—we're not even sure yet if it is a discontinuity. It doesn't—"

"Well, we're not taking any chances," the businessman said. "What's your fax number? I want to send you that confirmation before the power goes out over here. We want you to get started working on this thing as soon as you can."

Nathan gave him the number. "There's really no need—" he said.

Chin jabbed his finger violently at the logo *False Alarm* on the screen of Adler's TV.

"Consider it a Christmas present," the businessman said, and the fax machine began to whir. "There *is* going to be a Christmas, isn't there?"

Chin yanked the fax out of the machine with a whoop.

"Definitely," Nathan said. "Merry Christmas," but the businessman had already hung up.

Chin was still looking at the fax.

"How much did you ask them for?"

"Fifty thousand," Nathan said.

Chin slapped the grant approval down in front of him. "And a merry Christmas to you, too," he said.

At 7:40 P.M., after watching infomercials for NordicTrack, a combination egg poacher and waffle iron, and the revolutionary new DuckBed,

Bev put on her thin coat and her still-damp gloves and went downstairs. There had to be a restaurant open somewhere in Santa Fe. She would find one and have a margarita and a beef chimichanga, sitting in a room decorated with sombreros or piñatas, with striped curtains pulled across the windows to shut the snow out.

And if they were all closed, she would come back and order from room service. Or starve. But she was *not* going to ask at the desk and have them phone ahead and tell her El Charito had closed early because of the weather; she was not going to let them cut off all avenues of escape, like Carmelita. She walked determinedly past the registration desk toward the double doors.

"Mrs. Carey!" the clerk called to her, and when she kept walking, he hurried around the desk and across the lobby to her. "I have a message for you from Carmelita. She wanted me to tell you midnight mass at the cathedral has been canceled," he said. "The bishop was worried about people driving home on the icy roads. But Carmelita said to tell you they're having mass at eight o'clock, if you'd like to come to that. The cathedral's right up the street at the end of the Plaza. If you go out the north door," he pointed, "it's only two blocks. It's a very pretty service, with the *luminarias* and all."

And it's somewhere to go, Bev thought, letting him lead her to the north door. *It's something to do.* "Tell Carmelita thank you for me," she said at the door. "And *Feliz Navidad.*"

"Merry Christmas." He opened the door. "You go down this street, turn left, and it's right there," he said, and ducked back inside, out of the snow.

It was inches deep on the sidewalk, and snowing hard as she hurried along the narrow street, head down. By morning it would look just like back home. *It's not fair,* she thought. She turned the corner and looked up at the sound of an organ.

The cathedral stood at the head of the Plaza, its windows glowing like flames, and she had been wrong about the *luminarias* being ruined— they stood in rows leading up the walk, up the steps to the wide doors, lining the adobe walls and the roofs and the towers, burning steadily in the descending snow.

It fell silently, in great, spangled flakes, glittering in the light of the streetlamps, covering the wooden-posted porches, the pots of cactus, the pink adobe buildings. The sky above the cathedral was pink, too, and the whole scene had an unreal quality, like a movie set.

"Oh, Howard," Bev said, as if she had just opened a present, and then flinched away from the thought of him, waiting for the thrust of the knife, but it didn't come. She felt only regret that he couldn't be here to see this, and amusement that the sequined snowflakes sifting down on her hair, on her coat sleeve, looked just like the fake snow at the end of *White Christmas.* And, arching over it all, like the pink sky, she felt affection—for the snow, for the moment, for Howard.

"You did this," she said, and started to cry.

The tears didn't trickle down her cheeks, they poured out, drenching her face, her coat, melting the snowflakes instantly where they fell. *Healing tears,* she thought, and realized suddenly that when she had asked Howard how the movie ended, he hadn't said, "They lived happily ever after." He had said, "They got a white Christmas."

"Oh, Howard."

The bells for the service began to ring. *I need to stop crying and go in,* she thought, fumbling for a tissue, but she couldn't. The tears kept coming, as if someone had opened a spigot.

A black-shawled woman carrying a prayer book put her hand on Bev's shoulder and said, "Are you all right, *señora*?"

"Yes," Bev said, "I'll be fine," and something in her voice must have reassured the woman because she patted Bev's arm and went on into the cathedral.

The bells stopped ringing and the organ began again, but Bev continued to stand there until long after the mass had started, looking up at the falling snow.

"I don't know how you did this, Howard," she said, "but I know you're responsible."

At 8 P.M., after anxiously checking the news to make sure the roads were still closed, Pilar put Miguel to bed. "Now go to sleep," she said, kissing him good night. "Santa's coming soon."

"Hunh-unh," he said, looking like he was going to cry. "It's snowing too hard."

He's worried about the roads being closed, she thought. "Santa doesn't need roads," she said. "Remember, he has a magic sleigh that flies through the air even if it's snowing."

"Hunh-*unh*," he said, getting out of bed to get his Rudolph book. He showed her the illustration of the whirling blizzard and Santa shaking his head, and then stood up on his bed, pulled back the curtain, and pointed through the window. She had to admit it did look just like the picture.

"But he had Rudolph to show the way," she said. "See?" and turned the page, but he continued to look skeptical until she had read the book all the way through twice.

At 10:15 P.M. Warren Nesvick went down to the hotel's bar. He had tried to explain to Shara that Marjean was his five-year-old niece, but she had gotten completely unreasonable. "So I'm a canceled flight out of Cincinnati, am I?" she'd shouted. "Well, I'm canceling you, you bastard!" and slammed out, leaving him high and dry. On Christmas Eve, for Christ's sake.

He'd spent the next hour and a half on the phone. He'd called some women he knew from previous trips, but none of them had answered. He'd then tried to call Marjean to tell her the snow was letting up and United thought they could get him on standby early tomorrow morning and to try to patch things up—she'd seemed kind of upset—but she hadn't answered, either. She'd probably gone to bed.

He'd hung up and gone down to the bar. There wasn't a soul in the place except the bartender. "How come the place is so dead?" Warren asked him.

"Where the hell have you been?" the bartender said, and turned on the TV above the bar.

"... most widespread snowstorm in recorded history," Dan Abrams was saying. "Although there are signs of the snow beginning to let up here in Baltimore, in other parts of the country they weren't so lucky. We take you now to Cincinnati, where emergency crews are still digging victims out of the rubble."

It cut to a reporter standing in front of a sign that read "Cincinnati

International Airport." "A record forty-six inches of snow caused the roof of the main terminal to collapse this afternoon. Over two hundred passengers were injured, and forty are still missing."

🎄

The goose was a huge hit, crispy and tender and done to a turn, and everyone raved about the gravy. "Luke made it," Aunt Lulla said, but Madge and his mom were talking about people not knowing how to drive in snow and didn't hear her.

It stopped snowing midway through dessert, and Luke began to worry about the snowman but didn't have a chance to duck out and check on it till nearly eleven, when everyone was putting on their coats.

It had melted (sort of), leaving a round greasy smear in the snow. "Getting rid of the evidence?" Aunt Lulla asked, coming up behind him in her old-lady coat, scarf, gloves, and plastic boots. She poked at the smear with the toe of her boot. "I hope it doesn't kill the grass."

"I hope it doesn't affect the environment," Luke said.

Luke's mother appeared in the back door. "What are you two doing out there in the dark?" she called to them. "Come in. We're trying to decide who's going to have the dinner next Christmas. Madge and Shorty think it's Uncle Don's turn, but—"

"I'll have it," Luke said, and winked at Lulla.

"Oh," his mother said, surprised, and went back inside to tell Madge and Shorty and the others.

"But not goose," Luke said to Lulla. "Something easy. And nonfat."

"Ian had a wonderful recipe for duck á l'orange Alsacienne, as I remember," Lulla mused.

"Ian McKellen?"

"No, of course not, Ian Holm. Ian McKellen's a terrible cook," she said. "Or—I've got an idea. How about Japanese blowfish?"

🦌

By 11:15 P.M. Eastern Standard Time, the snow had stopped in New England, the Middle East, the Texas panhandle, most of Canada, and Nooseneck, Rhode Island.

"The storm of the century definitely seems to be winding down," Wolf Blitzer was saying in front of CNN's new logo: *The Sun'll Come Out Tomorrow,* "leaving in its wake a white Christmas for nearly every-one—"

"Hey," Chin said, handing Nathan the latest batch of temp readings. "I just thought of what it was."

"What what was?"

"The factor. You said there were thousands of factors contributing to global warming, and that any one of them, even something really small, could have been what caused this."

He hadn't really said that, but never mind. "And you've figured out what this critical factor is?"

"Yeah," Chin said. "A white Christmas."

"A white Christmas," Nathan repeated.

"Yeah! You know how everybody wants it to snow for Christmas, lit-tle kids especially, but lots of adults, too. They have this Currier-and-Ives thing of what Christmas should look like, and the songs reinforce it: 'White Christmas' and 'Winter Wonderland' and that one that goes, 'The weather outside is frightful,' I never can remember the name—"

"'Let It Snow,'" Nathan said.

"Exactly," Chin said. "Well, suppose all those people and all those little kids wished for a merry Christmas at the same time—"

"They *wished* this snowstorm into being?" Nathan said.

"*No.* They *thought* about it, and their—I don't know, their brain chem-icals or synapses or something—created some kind of electrochemical field or something, and that's the factor."

"That everybody was dreaming of a white Christmas."

"Yeah. It's a possibility, right?"

"Maybe," Nathan said. Maybe there was some critical factor that had caused this. Not wishing for a white Christmas, of course, but something seemingly unconnected to weather patterns, like tiny variations in the earth's orbit. Or the migratory patterns of geese.

Or an assortment of factors working in combination. And maybe the storm was an isolated incident, an aberration caused by a confluence of these unidentified factors, and would never happen again.

Or maybe his discontinuity theory was wrong. A discontinuity was by definition an abrupt, unexpected event. But that didn't mean there might not be advance indicators, like the warning flickers of electric lights before the power goes off for good. In which case—

"What are you doing?" Chin said, coming in from scraping his windshield. "Aren't you going home?"

"Not yet. I want to run a couple more extrapolation sets. It's still snowing in L.A."

Chin looked immediately alarmed. "You don't think it's going to start snowing everywhere again, do you?"

"No," Nathan said. Not yet.

At 11:43 P.M., after singing several karaoke numbers at the Laughing Moose, including "White Christmas," and telling the bartender they were going on "a moonlight ride down this totally killer chute," Kent Slakken and Bodine Cromps set out with their snowboards for an off-limits, high-avalanche-danger area near Vail and were never heard from again.

At 11:52 P.M., Miguel jumped on his sound-asleep mother, shouting, "It's Christmas! It's Christmas!"

It can't be morning yet, Pilar thought groggily, fumbling to look at the clock. "Miguel, honey, it's still nighttime. If you're not in bed when Santa comes, he won't leave you any presents," she said, hustling him back to bed. She tucked him in. "Now go to sleep. Santa and Rudolph will be here soon."

"Hunh-unh," he said, and stood up on his bed. He pulled the curtain back. "He doesn't need Rudolph. The snow stopped, just like I wanted, and now Santa can come all by himself." He pointed out the window. Only a few isolated flakes were still sifting down.

Oh, no, Pilar thought. After she was sure he was asleep, she crept out to the living room and turned on the TV very low, hoping against hope.

"—roads will remain closed until noon tomorrow," an exhausted-looking reporter said, "to allow time for the snow plows to clear them:

I-15, State Highway 56, I-15 from Chula Vista to Murrieta Hot Springs, Highway 78 from Vista to Escondido—"

Thank you, she murmured silently. *Thank you.*

🌲

At 11:59 P.M. Pacific Standard Time, Sam "Hoot'n'Holler" Farley's voice gave out completely. The only person who'd been able to make it to the station, he'd been broadcasting continuously on KTTS, "Seattle's talk 24/7," since 5:36 A.M. when he'd come in to do the morning show, even though he had a bad cold. He'd gotten steadily hoarser all day, and during the 9:00 P.M. newsbreak, he'd had a bad coughing fit.

"The National Weather Service reports that that big snowstorm's finally letting up," he croaked, "and we'll have nice weather tomorrow. Oh, this just in from NORAD, for all you kids who're up way too late. Santa's sleigh's just been sighted on radar over Vancouver and is headed this way."

He then attempted to say, "In local news, the snow—" but nothing came out.

He tried again. Nothing.

After the third try, he gave up, whispered, "That's all, folks," into the mike, and put on a tape of Louis Armstrong singing "White Christmas."

A Final Word on the Subject

As Jo March said in *Little Women,* Christmas wouldn't be Christmas without any presents. The giving and getting of gifts is inextricably bound up with the holiday and the Christmas story—from the Magis' gold, frankincense, and myrrh to the partridge in the pear tree, from the turkey "bigger than a boy" that the formerly stingy Scrooge sends the Cratchits to the small bottle of cologne the still-stingy Amy buys for Marmee so she'll have enough money to buy some drawing pencils, from heart's desires like Ralphie's "Red Ryder repeating carbine with a compass mounted in the stock" to more symbolic gifts, like Amahl's crutch—and the ham the Herdmans brought the Holy Family.

So it seems fitting to end this book by giving you readers some sort of gift. This is easier said than done. I can't get you a BB gun. You'd shoot your eye out. And I don't know what size you wear or whether you're lactose intolerant or allergic to wool, whether you have long hair or have sold it to buy a watch fob or the money for a train ticket for Marmee. I don't know anything about you, really, except that you like reading Christmas stories.

When I was a kid, one of my chief joys was finding a wonderful new book or author, especially if the place I found it was in the pages of a book. When the March girls read *The Pickwick Papers* and played *Pilgrim's Progress*, it was as if Jo was personally recommending those books to me. I discovered Jerome K. Jerome's *Three Men in a Boat* in the pages of Robert A. Heinlein's *Have Space Suit—Will Travel*—Kip's dad wasn't listening to him because he was intent on reading it—and I discovered

Tennyson's "The Lady of Shalott" in the pages of L. M. Montgomery's *Anne of Green Gables* because Anne nearly drowned while acting it out. And when I went to find them, I discovered other books, other authors.

I've mentioned some of my favorite books and movies in the stories in this collection—*A Little Princess* by Frances Hodgson Burnett in "Adaptation," *Miracle on 34th Street* in "Miracle," E. M. Forster's *A Room with a View* in "deck.halls@boughs/holly," all my favorite (and non-favorite) Christmas songs in "All Seated on the Ground," but there are lots of Christmas stories and movies I didn't mention, stories and movies I love and that my family reads out loud and watches together every Christmas.

So it seems an appropriate Christmas present to introduce you to them, the way Anne Shirley introduced me to "The Highwayman" and Kip Russell introduced me to *The Tempest*.

So here they are for you, a list of movies and TV shows and stories you might enjoy!

Merry Christmas!

—Connie Willis

An Advent Calendar of Great Christmas Movies to Watch (in No Particular Order)

Our family starts watching Christmas movies the day after Thanksgiving, and over the years we've added so many of them to our list that we're not done by the twenty-fifth and have to keep going straight through to Epiphany.

Which is kind of a miracle since we don't watch just any old thing (like say, for instance, the sappy movies on the Hallmark Channel or anything with bad Santas or Alvin and the Chipmunks in it). And the list of Christmas movies we loathe is nearly as long as the ones we love. Beginning with *Jingle All the Way*.

So this list isn't complete, but it's enough to get you to Christmas, and I'm sure you have your own to add.

1. *Miracle on 34th Street*: The best Christmas movie ever made. (See Introduction.) I am of course talking about the original, with Natalie Wood and Edmund Gwenn. In black and white. Don't even *think* about either of the wretched remakes.

2. *Love, Actually*: Tied for first, and possibly the best Christmas movie ever made because it shows us all sides of the holiday—and all sides of the love that underpins it. It's by turns funny, sad, ironic, ridiculous (Mother: "*First* lobster? There was more than one lobster present at the birth of the baby Jesus?" Daughter: "Duh."), romantic, wincingly painful, and uplifting. And the open-

ing scene at Heathrow contains a Christmas message we could all use right now.

3. *A Christmas Story*: A close second, this Jean Shepherd story of a boy who desperately wants a BB gun ("You'll shoot your eye out, kid!") for Christmas is that rarest of things—nostalgic without a trace of sentimentality. It has a number of hilarious scenes—the tongue stuck to the flagpole, the Bumpus dogs and the turkey, the trip to see the department-store Santa. Pick your favorite. Mine is the Major Award, no, wait, the Ovaltine magic decoder ring, no, wait. . . . But it's not just a series of comic set pieces. More than any other holiday movie, *A Christmas Story* captures just how badly you want things when you're a kid and how central Christmas is to the kid's year.

4. *The Sure Thing*: I almost didn't go see this movie. The preview (and the title) made it look like a beery teen sex movie. But then I noticed that certain scenes looked an awful lot like *It Happened One Night* and decided to take a chance. Now, every year we watch this great road picture about Alison, who's going to visit her boyfriend for Christmas, and Gib, who's trying to get to California for "a sure thing" and who, in classic romantic-comedy fashion, happens to hitch a ride in the same car with Alison.

5. *The Miracle of Morgan's Creek*: Most movies made during World War II were about brave soldiers and the girls who waited faithfully for them on the home front. Preston Sturges instead decided to tell the story of a girl who goes to an Army dance and ends up getting married (maybe) and pregnant (definitely), and of her 4-F boyfriend, Norval, who tries to help her out of her predicament. But everything they attempt only makes things worse till nothing short of a miracle can save them, and you can't even imagine a miracle that would do any good.

6. *The Shop Around the Corner*: This Ernst Lubitsch–directed film about the people who work in a little shop in Depression-era Austria is a classic in every sense of the word. Not only does it star

Jimmy Stewart and Margaret Sullavan as pen pals who don't know the other's identity, but it's full of wonderful supporting characters, from Frank Morgan as the cranky boss to the long-suffering Pirovitch and the incorrigible Pepi. And it has Vienna at Christmastime.

(NOTE: You can also watch the remake, *You've Got Mail,* with Tom Hanks and Meg Ryan, which I like a lot, but the original is better.)

7. *A Christmas Carol: The Movies*. There are a jillion versions of this, starring everybody from Alastair Sim to Captain Picard to Bill Murray. My two favorites are the Muppets' and Mr. Magoo's. Not only are they the most literarily faithful (okay, okay, the Muppet one has two Marleys, but it also has Charles Dickens as a character—and Rizzo the Rat), but they're the most fun. And they have wonderful scores. The Muppets' songs were written by Paul Williams. Mr. Magoo's were done by the Broadway team of Jule Styne and Bob Merrill, and include the wonderful "When You're Alone in the World."

8. *The Santa Clause*: I fully expected to hate this movie about a divorced father who accidentally kills Santa Claus and then finds himself legally required to take over for him. It had all the things I despise about modern Christmas movies—big-budget production values, over-elaborate special effects, flatulent-reindeer jokes. And Tim Allen, who I loathed. Until I saw him in *Galaxy Quest,* where he totally won me over with his smart-mouthed, self-centered portrayal of Captain Jason Nesmith.

He won me over in *The Santa Clause,* too, and so did the whole movie, with its smart-aleck dialogue and its clever twists on an old story, from a second-in-command at the North Pole named Bernard to the Oscar Meyer Weiner pennywhistle. And a team of elf commandos with some unusual weapons: "Tinsel. Not just for decoration."

9. *The Homecoming*: This TV movie about a West Virginia family coping with the Depression and waiting for their father to come home (if he *is* coming) was the pilot for the TV series *The Waltons*. But unlike the series, it doesn't pull any punches about how hard the Depression was—or what it did to families. And to Christmas.

10. *Christmas in Connecticut*: This 1945 movie about a Martha Stewart–type magazine writer who can't actually cook and a sailor whose ship was torpedoed and who spent eighteen days on a raft dreaming of food not only has Barbara Stanwyck, but Sydney Greenstreet, Dennis Morgan, and "Cuddles" Sakall as her Uncle Felix, who's worth watching this movie for all by himself, especially the scene at the smorgasbord where Barbara's agreed to marry a man she doesn't love and he's telling her why she's made a good decision, as Felix, under the guise of filling a plate for her, tells her (and us) exactly how *he* feels about the situation: "Bologna . . . horseradish . . . nuts."

11. *Amahl and the Night Visitors*: This one-act opera by Gian Carlo Menotti about the wise men stopping at a poor widow's on their way to Bethlehem was originally produced for television. It's out on video, but, even better, it's often performed at Christmas by churches, colleges, and community theater groups, and I definitely recommend seeing it live. The story is haunting, the music is heartbreaking, and every production adds something to the simple story of the crippled shepherd boy, his embittered mother, and their distinguished visitors.

12. *While You Were Sleeping*: This sweet and romantic comedy with Sandra Bullock and Bill Pullman is about the loony complications that can result from being all alone at Christmastime and wishing you were part of a family.

13. *3 Godfathers*: A Christmas story in the last place you'd ever expect to find one—a John Ford Western starring John Wayne— *3 Godfathers* tells the story of three bank robbers who find a pioneer woman about to give birth in a godforsaken place. This is the perfect movie to watch when you've overdosed on mistletoe and Santas and snow, and it may introduce you to John Ford's West-

erns and convince you to go on to *Stagecoach, Fort Apache,* and *The Searchers.*

14. *Off Season*: Set at a rundown motel in Florida, *Off Season* doesn't look at all like a Christmas movie, and at first it doesn't feel like one, but this story of a little boy who thinks the old man living at their rundown Florida hotel is really Santa Claus is great. Santa's actually a con man wanted in several states—or is he? Either way, he's Hume Cronyn, who's terrific.

15. *Home Alone*: However you feel about John Hughes, and yes, he *is* capable of exactly the kind of schmaltz I've railed against, or about Three Stooges humor (in this case, two stooges, both of them incredibly dumb), this is a great movie about our complicated relationships with our families. And the song "Somewhere in My Memory" (which I think should be a Christmas classic) and the scene in the church are worth the price of admission all by themselves.

16. *Meet John Doe*: Frank Capra's other Christmas movie—you know the one I mean—is a lot more famous than this one (and shown approximately 987 times a day through the entire month of December), but this one, which stars Gary Cooper as a down-and-out hobo and Barbara Stanwyck as an enterprising reporter, is *really* interesting, especially in these days of religious cults, hungry-for-power politicians, a rampant press, and even more rampant cynicism.

17. *Elf*: Having seen only the annoying Will Ferrell, I had to be talked into going to see this movie, but now it's one of our favorites, mostly because of the aforesaid Mr. Ferrell, who plays the role of Buddy the Elf absolutely straight, without a hint of irony or "Isn't this ridiculous?" Zooey Deschanel is wonderful, and the movie's full of great lines, from "The yellow ones don't stop" to "I passed through the seven levels of the candy cane forest, through the sea of swirly-twirly gumdrops, and then I walked through the Lincoln Tunnel." And Gimbel's finally gets its chance to compete with Macy's!

18. *Bachelor Mother*: No Christmas is complete without Ginger Rogers, who here is a department store employee who spots a baby being left on an orphanage doorstep and tries to rescue it. But in this world no good deed goes unpunished, so she finds herself labeled the mother, and the harder she tries to straighten out the mess, the worse it gets. The movie also stars Charles Coburn, who has my favorite line in any movie ever—"I don't care who the baby's father is. *I'm* the grandfather!" and David Niven, whose life was saved during World War II by this movie. During the Battle of the Bulge, he was working for British Intelligence when he was stopped by an armed American sentry. "Who won the World Series?" the sentry asked, posing a question that German spies couldn't answer. "I have no idea," Niven replied, "but I *did* star with Ginger Rogers in *Bachelor Mother*." It did the trick. The sentry let him through.

19. *About a Boy*: Hugh Grant stars as a man who's stuck in perpetual adolescence (thanks to his father, who wrote a Christmas song that allows him to live off the royalties)—until he meets a boy with a suicidal mother. The script is by Nick Hornby, whom I adore. 'Nuff said?

20. *Meet Me in St. Louis*: Except for the ending, this isn't really a Christmas movie—we sometimes watch it in October instead because of its wonderful Halloween scene—but it has one of the all-time-great Christmas songs in it—"Have Yourself a Merry Little Christmas"—and its theme of a Christmas marked by partings and sadness is one that makes the movie truly memorable.

21. *The Lemon Drop Kid*: Not only is this based on a Damon Runyon story (see comments on Runyon under "Dancing Dan's Christmas"), but it has Bob Hope. And the song "Silver Bells."

22. *Spotlight*: This Oscar-winning picture about the team of *Boston Globe* reporters who exposed a far-reaching scandal in the Catholic Church isn't technically a Christmas movie, though it takes place during the holidays, and its subject matter is heavier than that of the other films on this list. But its theme—truth and justice fighting against seemingly overwhelming odds—is entirely appropriate for the season. And more timely than ever.

23. *Little Women*: This isn't a Christmas movie, either, but it starts out at Christmas, and the book has one of the great Christmas-story first lines ever, the aforementioned "'Christmas won't be Christmas without any presents,' grumbled Jo, lying on the rug." Plus, I watched it every Christmas when I was a kid. There are three versions to choose from. The one I grew up on was the June Allyson one (with Elizabeth Taylor perfectly cast as snotty Amy). The Katharine Hepburn version is generally acknowledged to be the best, but my personal favorite is the new one with Winona Ryder and Kirsten Dunst. Or you could watch them all.

24. And finally, *White Christmas*: I know, I know, it's a complete cliché. And by rights, it should have been a disaster. In the first place, it was a sequel (to *Holiday Inn*, which isn't nearly as good), and was written solely to capitalize on the success of the song "White Christmas." In the second place, it didn't have a real score, just a bunch of random Irving Berlin songs pulled from hither and yon, and its story of "Hey, kids, let's put on a show," is the most overused plot in the book. Plus, Fred Astaire bailed, and then his replacement, Donald O'Connor, got sick. But somehow it managed to pull it all together to become a great movie, with bits like Bing Crosby and Danny Kaye doing "Sisters" in drag and the general sending his replacement off on a wild-goose chase, which get better every year. Plus, there's Mary Wickes and the whole running gag of Danny's injured arm. And the faces of the young boys, far from home and waiting to be called into battle, listening to a song from home. Inspired.

And a Score of Christmas Stories and Poems to Read After You've Gone to Bed

Good things to read at Christmas are trickier to find than good movies. Everything out there right now seems to be either treacly, annoyingly inspirational, or about someone attempting to overcome drug addiction, prostitution, and/or abusive parents. But here are twenty that manage to avoid being pious, goopily sentimental, and/or suicidally depressing.

1. **The Original Christmas Story (Matthew Chapter 1:18–25, 2:1–18, Luke Chapter 1:5–80, 2:1–52):** It's got everything you could ask for in a story: adventure, excitement, love, betrayals, good guys, bad guys, narrow escapes, mysterious strangers, and a thrilling chase scene. And the promise of a great sequel.

2. *A Christmas Carol* **by Charles Dickens**: The perfect Christmas story, which proves beyond a shadow of a doubt that the only way to begin a Christmas story is with the line, "Marley was dead: to begin with." And just because you know it all by heart—Scrooge and Tiny Tim and the Ghost of Christmas Past, "I forged these chains in life," and the bed-curtains and the turkey and "God bless us, every one!"—is no reason not to read it again.

3. **"The Tree That Didn't Get Trimmed" by Christopher Morley**: Obviously inspired by Hans Christian Andersen's sickeningly sen-

timental "The Fir Tree," this story of a tree that doesn't get bought by anyone and instead gets thrown away not only avoids all the sins of its antecedent, but ends by telling a touching parable of those ultimate Christmas themes, suffering and redemption.

4. "Christmas Trees" by Robert Frost: Robert Frost is one of my favorite poets. His poems are the essence of New England—taciturn and down-to-earth—and unique. Take, for example, that other poem of his that people associate with Christmas, "Stopping by Woods on a Snowy Evening." Or this one, about a man with a hill full of fir trees—and the man from the city who wants to buy them.

5. *The Best Christmas Pageant Ever* by Barbara Robinson: This modest children's story of a church Nativity pageant invaded by the horrible Herdman kids, who steal and swear and smoke cigars (even the girls), accomplishes the nearly impossible—the creation of a new classic—and makes the reader look at the story of Mary and Joseph and the baby "wrapped in wadded-up clothes" as the Herdmans do, with new eyes.

6. "Santaland Diaries" by David Sedaris: I first heard this on NPR, and I was riveted. I'd never heard a take on Christmas so wry, so cynical, and so dead-on. David Sedaris has gone on to write lots of pieces about Christmas, but this diary of his days as an elf in the toy department at Macy's remains my favorite.

7. "The Santa Claus Compromise" by Thomas Disch: This parable of a future in which six-year-olds have finally gotten their political rights and are intent on doing investigative journalism to expose Santa Claus's true identity could have been written in today's group-rights-activism climate. The fact that it was written back in 1974, when satire was still possible, makes it chilling as well as funny.

8. "Journey of the Magi" by T. S. Eliot: The Bible doesn't tell us anything about what the wise men's journey to Bethlehem was like, or how much it must have cost them emotionally to make it.

Or what happened to them afterward, when it was time to go back home.

9. "Dancing Dan's Christmas" by Damon Runyon: When the dust settles on the twentieth century, it's my belief that Damon Runyon will finally be recognized as one of our greatest writers and will be fully appreciated for his clever plots, his unerring ear for language, and his cast of guys, dolls, gangsters, bookies, chorus girls, crapshooters, Salvation Army soul-savers, high rollers, low-lifes, louts, and lovable losers. I chose "Dancing Dan's Christmas," a story involving a mean mobster, a Santa Claus suit, a diamond vanity case, and a few too many Tom and Jerrys, to include here, but it was a tough call. "Palm Beach Santa Claus" and "The Three Wise Guys" were both a close second.

10. "The Star" by Arthur C. Clarke: One of the classics of science fiction by one of the masters in the field, this tells a troubling story about the star that guided the wise men to Bethlehem.

11. "The Gift of the Magi" by O. Henry: O. Henry is another under-appreciated author, as witness the fact that dozens of stories, screenplays, and sitcoms have copied the plot of this story. But none of them have ever managed to copy the charm or the style of the original, a simple little tale of a watch fob and a set of tortoise-shell combs.

12. *The Memorial Hall Murder* by Jane Langton: For all you mystery fans, Christmas offers an abundance of Christmas stories and detectives, from Sherlock Holmes ("The Adventure of the Blue Carbuncle") to Hercule Poirot (*Murder for Christmas*), but you may not have met Detective Homer Kelly or read this mystery about a murder that occurs while a college choir's rehearsing the "Messiah." And it doesn't get any more Christmassy than Handel and choirs. Or murder.

13. "Rumpole and the Spirit of Christmas" by John Mortimer: If you've encountered the irascible Old Bailey hack, Horace Rumpole, on PBS's *Mystery,* he seems like the last person to have any Christmas spirit, and he is. Which is why this story works so well. Leave it to John Mortimer to teach us a new meaning of "the Christmas spirit."

14. "The Chimes" by Charles Dickens: *A Christmas Carol* is only one of a score of holiday stories Dickens wrote. A few years ago I decided to read them all, and when I read "The Chimes," I got a huge shock, as will you. I won't give it away, but let's just say the plot of a certain *very* famous Christmas movie bears a suspicious resemblance to this Dickens story about a man who wishes he'd never been born.

15. *Wishin' and Hopin': A Christmas Story* **by Wally Lamb**: Set in the era of LBJ, *Dragnet,* and the Beatles, this story, about a fifth-grade boy who has a famous cousin (whom no one in the family has actually ever met) and who's been cast as the little drummer boy in the Catholic school Christmas pageant but who's more interested in girls, has pretty much everything you could want: nuns, rosaries, impure thoughts, angels with light-up halos, suicide Cokes, dodgeball, Dondi—and Annette Funicello.

16. *The Tailor of Gloucester* **by Beatrix Potter**: When Beatrix Potter (of *Peter Rabbit* fame) was staying with relatives in the west of England, she heard a story of a tailor who'd fallen ill before he could finish sewing a coat he was making for the mayor and found it miraculously completed when he returned to work, and spun it into a Christmas tale about a bad cat, some beleaguered mice, and a twist of cherry-colored thread. The illustrations are some of Potter's loveliest, and the story's charming.

17. "Christmas Eve: Nearing Midnight in New York" by Langston Hughes: One of my favorite poets, Langston Hughes has written Christmas-themed poems in several moods and modes, from the traditional "Shepherd's Song at Christmas" to the slashingly bitter "Merry Christmas," and you should read them all. But I like this one, with its city images and tentative "almosts," the best.

18. "Another Christmas Carol" by P. G. Wodehouse: There's no way to describe a P. G. Wodehouse story, so I won't even try. I'll just say that this is the only Christmas story I know of that involves the bubonic plague and tofu, and that, if you've never read him, there could be no better Christmas gift than discovering P. G. Wodehouse.

19. "Down Pens" by Saki (H. H. Munro): I love all Saki stories, but I'm especially fond of this take on the task of writing Christmas thank-yous, since my research on the subject for my novel *Crosstalk* (which consisted mostly of reading advice columns) proved conclusively that human beings think more about thank-you notes than anything else. Including sex.

20. "For the Time Being: A Christmas Oratorio" by W. H. Auden: Part play, part poem, all masterpiece, this long work is what you should read in January, when you're taking down the Christmas decorations (and your sense of good will toward men) and putting them away for another year—and then facing the bleak post-Bethlehem world we all find ourselves living in.

Plus a Half-Dozen TV Shows You May Not Have Seen That Haven't Succumbed to "Very-Special-Christmas-Episode" Syndrome

One of the blessings of our so-called information age is that all these episodes are available to watch on YouTube or Netflix or Hulu. Or, in the case of *Dr. Who,* on BBC America or Syfy. Enjoy!

1. *Frasier,* **Season 3, Episode 9, "Frasier Grinch":** Even though Frasier's son really wanted an Outlaw Laser Robo-Geek, Frasier bought him an educational toy—which didn't arrive. So he and Niles have to try to find a present for him at the mall on Christmas Eve. Classic slapstick, brilliant title cards (as usual), and the ending had me in tears.

2. *Murphy Brown,* **Season 3, Episode 11, "Jingle Hell, Jingle Hell, Jingle . . .":** Murphy talked everyone in the office into making a charitable donation instead of exchanging gifts, and then broke the bargain by buying presents (just little ones), sending everyone scrambling for last-minute gifts in the only store open on Christmas Eve—the drugstore. Which has a large (and very breakable) collection of gnomes.

3. *Big Bang Theory,* **Season 2, Episode 11, "The Bath Item Gift Hypothesis":** All of this series' Christmas episodes are good and

well worth watching, but none of them can top this one, in which Sheldon approaches the custom of giving gifts in his usual hyper-rational, unemotional way, calculating the precise exchange rate for small, medium, and large baskets of bath oil, soap, and scented candles—and gets a lesson in higher mathematics (and Christmas) from Penny, of all people.

4. *The Muppet Christmas Special with John Denver*: This was the first of the Muppet Christmas specials, and it's the best. Highlights include "When the River Meets the Sea," an altercation with Miss Piggy over the words "figgy pudding," a truly awful rendition of "The Twelve Days of Christmas," and a lively rendition of "Little Saint Nick."

5. *Doctor Who,* **The Christmas Specials**: All the *Doctor Who* Christmas specials—"The Husbands of River Song," "Last Christmas," "The Time of the Doctor," "The Snowmen," "The End of Time," "The Day of the Doctor"—are terrific. My favorite is probably "Tooth and Claw," having, as it does, Queen Victoria, a werewolf, Scotland, the birth of Torchwood, and the Koh-i-Noor diamond, but don't make me choose. You should watch them all.

6. *The Twilight Zone,* **"Five Characters in Search of an Exit"**: *The Twilight Zone* did a number of memorable Christmas stories. The most famous is "The Night of the Meek," with Art Carney as a drunken department-store Santa, but "Five Characters in Search of an Exit" is more quintessentially *Twilight Zone*–ish, with its five mismatched people—a hobo, a bagpiper, a ballet dancer, a clown, and an Army major—trapped in a strange place with no idea what's going on and no way out. And Rod Serling (who was born on Christmas) intoning, "Tonight's odd cast of players on the odd stage known as—the Twilight Zone."

PHOTO: © G. MARK LEWIS

CONNIE WILLIS is a member of the Science Fiction Hall of Fame and a Grand Master of the Science Fiction and Fantasy Writers of America. She has received seven Nebula awards and eleven Hugo Awards for her fiction. *Blackout* and *All Clear*—a novel in two parts—and *Doomsday Book* won both. Her other works include *Crosstalk, Passage, To Say Nothing of the Dog, Lincoln's Dreams, Bellwether, Remake, Uncharted Territory, The Best of Connie Willis, Impossible Things,* and *Fire Watch.* Willis lives with her family in Colorado and adores Christmas in all of its many merry and sometimes ridiculous manifestations.

conniewillis.net

About the Type

This book was set in Celeste, a typeface that its designer, Chris Burke (b. 1967), classifies as a modern humanistic typeface. Celeste was influenced by Bodoni and Waldman, but the strokeweight contrast is less pronounced. The serifs tend toward the triangular, and the italics harmonize well with the roman in tone and width. It is a robust and readable text face that is less stark and modular than many of the modern fonts, and has many of the friendlier old-face features.